MILITARY HISTORY

OF

ULYSSES S. GRANT,

FROM APRIL, 1861, TO APRIL, 1865.

BY

ADAM BADEAU,

BREVET BRIGADIER-GENERAL UNITED STATES ARMY,
LATE MILITARY SECRETARY AND AIDE-DE-CAMP
TO THE GENERAL-IN-CHIEF.

Pulchrum est benefacere reipublicæ.—SALLUST.

VOLUME III.

NEW YORK:
D. APPLETON AND COMPANY,
1, 3, AND 5 BOND STREET.
1881.

CONTENTS OF VOLUME III.

CHAPTER XXV.

CHAPTER XXVI.

CONTENTS.

CHAPTER XXVIII.

reach the parapet—Formidable character of work—Fighting on the parapet—Capture of Fort Fisher—Losses—Arrival of Stanton —Seizure of blockade runners—Conduct of troops—Gallantry of defence— Harmony of Porter and Terry—General observations—Results . 282

CHAPTER XXXI.

CHAPTER XXXII.

Vlll CONTENTS.

CHAPTER XXXIII.

CHAPTER XXXIV.

THEATRE OF WAR.

VIRGINIA.

SHERIDAN'S OPERATIONS IN VALLEY OF VIRGINIA.
OPERATIONS BETWEEN ATLANTA AND NASHVILLE.
BATTLE OF CEDAR CREEK.
BATTLE OF NASHVILLE.
SHERMAN'S MARCHES THROUGH GEORGIA AND THE CAROLINAS.
OPERATIONS AGAINST FORT FISHER.
BATTLE OF FIVE FORKS.
APPOMATTOX CAMPAIGN.

The campaigns of the last year of the war were so various, and the operations so complicated, that reference to the same maps is required for different periods. The illustrations have therefore been placed at the end of the volumes, with the exception of the maps of the Theatre of War, of Virginia, and of the Operations around Richmond and Petersburg, which will be found in pockets attached to the covers.

CHAPTEE XXV.

General view of situation after fall of Atlanta—Defences of Richmond and Petersburg—

National entrenchments—Depression of public spirit at the North—Political situation—Approach of Presidential election—Difficulties in drafting troops—Anxiety about Washington—Grant's strategy covers the capital—Early reinforced by Anderson—Sheridan's manoeuvres in the Valley—Relations between Grant and Sheridan—Anderson recalled to Richmond—Grant's visit to Sheridan—Confidence of both commanders— Battle of Winchester—Blunder of Early—Sheridan's plan—Sheridan's attack—Original success of rebels—Sheridan restores the day—Torbert's cavalry charge—Victory of national forces—Retreat of Early, " whirling through Winchester "—Pursuit by Sheridan—Battle of Fisher's Hill-Second defeat of Early—Further retreat of rebels—Effect of success at the North—Grant's orders to Sheridan—Early abandons the Valley—Censures of Lee—Disappointment in Richmond.

ATLANTA had fallen, the Weldon road was carried, and Early's exit from the Yalley had been barred, but the end was not yet. A long and tedious prospect still stretched out before the national commander. Hood's army was not destroyed, the rebels were in force in Sheridan's front, and Lee had not abandoned Kichmond. Grant looked the situation full in the face, and lost no time in adapting his plans to the actual emergencies. On the 8th of September, Sherman had entered Atlanta in person, and on the 10th, he was instructed: "As. soon as your men are sufficiently rested, and preparations

can be made, it is desirable that another campaign should be commenced. We want to keep the enemy constantly pressed till the close of the war." To Sheridan Grant said: "If this war is to last another year, we want the Shenandoah Valley to remain a barren waste ;" and to Meade : " I do not want to give up the Weldon road, if it can be avoided, until we get Richmond. That may be months yet." Accordingly he ordered a railroad to be built, to bring supplies from City Point to the national front at Petersburg, and the entire line of entrenchments to be strengthened from the James river on the right to "Warren's left beyond the Weldon road.

The system of field-works which at this time encircled both Richmood and Petersburg, and covered the surrounding country, was complicated in the extreme, and in some respects unprecedented in war. Both cities were embraced in what may be termed besieging operations; both were the object of incessant menace and attack for nearly a year; both were defended with vigor, skill, and gallantry; yet neither was completely invested, nor was either regularly approached by parallels, and only one important sortie was ever made against the assailants' works by the beleaguered garrison. The siege of Richmond was conducted at a distance of twenty miles by an army which retrenched itself, while owing to the intervening rivers, and forests, and swamps, as well as to the complexity of the manoeuvres—the extensions and retractions, the advances and withdrawals, on the right and left—the hostile works stretched out hundreds of miles.

On the north side of the James, Richmond was

defended by a triple line of fortifications. First of all, at an average distance of a mile and a half from the centre of the city, a series of detached field-works was constructed, so placed as to command the principal avenues of approach. These works were twelve in number, five of them complete redoubts, and all arranged for either siege or field artillery, while some were provided with magazines. They had been built by slave labor in the first year of the war, every proprietor in the neighborhood having been compelled to furnish from one-sixth to one-third of his entire slave force for their erection.

Exterior to these was a continuous line completely encircling the town, at a distance of three miles. It consisted of epaulements, arranged generally for field artillery, sometimes in embrasure, sometimes in barbette, and connected by rifle-trench. These works were not extended to the southern bank until after Butler's attack on Drury's Bluff in May, 1864, when the rebels, fearing another advance from the same direction, completed the line. It was never attacked except by reconnoitring forces in 1864 and 1865.

The third line, starting from the river above the town, and crossing the country at a general distance of six miles from Richmond, reached to the bluffs overlooking the valley of the Chickahominy, the crests of which it followed for a while, and then took an easterly course, striking the James again, at the strong entrenched position on Chapin's Farm, opposite Drury's Bluff. This was the line occupied by the rebel armies during the last year of the war, and attained a high stage of development. . It consisted of a series of strong forts, with ditches and

palisadoed gorges, connected by infantry parapet. The batteries of course were the vital points, commanding the entire line; the ditches here were deep, and several rows of abatis and chevaux de frise were planted in close musket-range along the front. Outside the connecting parapet, shallower ditches were dug and obstacles placed, and a line of loaded shells was laid at intervals among the entanglements, at the points confronted by national troops. Splinter and bomb shelters were erected, and to increase the amount of fire, high mounds were built behind the breastworks, which served as bomb-proof shelters underneath, while the top was arranged for infantry fire. Listening galleries were dug to prevent successful mining operations; dams were constructed to flood the ground where streams ran towards the rebel lines, and every appliance of the defensive art was called in play to render the fortifications impregnable.

On the opposite side of the James, the main rebel line started from Drury's Bluff, and then ran south to the Hewlett House, on the high commanding ground that overlooks Dutch Gap; here the rivet-in its windings intervened again, and the peninsula of Bermuda Hundred was crossed, the line still running almost due south, till it struck the Appo-mattox, north-east of Petersburg. From this point the works extended south-westerly to the Weldon road, when they turned to the north, and completed the circuit of the town. In front of Butler, on Bermuda Hundred, the rebel line was extremely strong, and like that north of the James, was intended to be held with a comparatively small

force, until in an emergency reinforcements could arrive ; but south and east of Petersburg, Lee kept his main army, and here he relied for defence on men rather than works, though here also the fortifications were elaborate and formidable.

"When the national forces crossed the James, in June, and Smith advanced against Petersburg, although Beauregard came up in time to save the town, the defences on the south and east were captured. Breastworks were thrown up in the night, in rear of the former position, and these were held until Lee's army arrived; but the original works were never regained. For about a mile and a half the new rebel line followed a ridge a quarter of a mile outside the town, and was made exceedingly strong. At intervals of two or three hundred yards, or more, according to the nature of the ground, were batteries, thrown forward as salients, and traced originally either as bastions, demi-bastions, or lunettes. These were united by a line of parapet running from the flank of one to that of the next ; ditches were dug along the entire front, and two and sometimes three rows of chevaux de frise and other obstructions were laid. The batteries in time became elaborate forts, the profile was strengthened, they gave each other good flanking fire, and the approach was everywhere commanded. They were generally armed with Napoleon guns and small columbiads, many of the latter taken from arsenals of the United States at the beginning of the war, by men who wore the uniform of the government they betrayed ; others came from the Kich-mond foundries.

Behind this main line was still another parapet 83

with occasional detached works, or keeps, sometimes redoubts, to which the troops might retire in the event of the principal line being carried; while in front of all were the rifle-pits for the pickets, these also connected by a parapet affording good cover, and forming in fact a field fortification in all but relief; they were even furnished at many points with rude but effective obstructions in the shape of slashed timber, which made a sort of abatis or fraise. These obstructions, however, were sometimes carried away for fuel by the troops on either side, under the tacit understanding so often witnessed between advanced forces in the field.

Besides the works in front of Petersburg, there were two more lines between that city and Richmond, upon which the rebel army might fall back, if those south of the Appomattox should be forced ; but the position at Petersburg was the important one, as any line nearer Richmond would not enable Lee to keep open his communications by the South-side railroad. The whole series of works around Petersburg thus became a part of the defences of Richmond; and, confronted from the middle of June by the entire army of the Potomac and a part of Butler's force, it acquired that character which the presence of a large body of defenders alone made practicable. Forts with very strong relief; a connecting parapet assuming the profile of regular field works, and protected in front by two and even three rows of entanglements ; the whole line well flanked, and its approaches everywhere swept by artillery— these constituted a position, which, when held by only one rank of good troops with breech-loading

weapons—it is the universal testimony of modern war, can hardly be carried by direct assault.

In September, 1864, the national entrenchments extended no further north of the James than the tete de pont at Deep Bottom ; on the south bank the lines ran parallel with the rebel works across Bermuda Hundred, from the James to the Appomattox river. Beyond the Appomattox, starting at a point opposite the rebel left, they followed the defences of Petersburg, and until they struck the Jerusalem plank road, ran extremely close to the enemy's works, approaching at times within a few hundred yards. At the Jerusalem road they diverged to the left, and the distance between the entrenchments widened to more than two miles. On the 1st of September, the national left rested on the Weldon railroad, Warren's skirmishers reaching to the Vaughan and Squirrel level roads; but before long the main works extended to these roads; then running south about a mile and a half, they turned to the east and completely encircled the national camps, striking the Blackwater river, in the rear of Meade's right wing. There were also strong entrenched works at City Point, to protect the base of the army, and batteries were established at intervals on the James, from Chapin's Bluff to Fort Monroe. Each army was thus completely surrounded by its own entrenchments, and one fortified camp was in reality besieged by another.

The national lines, like those of the rebels, consisted of infantry parapet connecting a series of more important works, by which the intermediate entrenchment was enfiladed. These larger works varied very much in magnitude and tracing, but were

generally redoubts, built with a view to containing garrisons strong enough to hold their own, in case the connecting parapet was abandoned and the infantry force withdrawn. In this they differed from the rebel batteries south of the Appomattox, which with few exceptions were open to the rear, and could not be held if the line was broken at any one point. The entrenchments on both sides were built of the red loamy clay found in the eastern parts of Maryland and Virginia, a soil peculiarly adapted for earthworks, as it is easily dug, and stands well when formed into slopes. The parapets were several feet thick and ten or twelve feet high ; the faces were carefully traversed, and some of the guns had shields for protection against rifle-shots, made of three thicknesses of plank nailed together, and fitted over the breech in front of the sight, a slit being cut in the shield, in which the gun was laid.

The revetments were almost always of logs, laid horizontally, and parallel with the crest of the parapet. The chevaux de frise were constructed of square logs, with holes through which the spikes were passed, after which the lengths were lashed together. Covered ways, starting from tunnels under the parapet, gave access to the line of rifle-pits, which was sometimes only twenty-five or thirty yards outside. Immediately in front of Petersburg, where the hostile pickets were very close, and the rifle-firing was continuous day and night, the men laid large logs of wood along the top of the parapet or rifle-pits, and out of the under side a small hole was cut, through which they were able to keep up a sharp fire without being often hit.

One of the principal features of the works was the extensive use made of bomb-proofs. Owing to the great length of the lines, the same troops were often kept in the trenches for weeks, and it was necessary to give them ample protection from the weather as well as from the hostile bombardment. The bomb-proofs were long trenches cut in the ground just behind the parapets and parallel with them; the sides of these trenches were lined with rough wooden slabs, the roof was supported by uprights bearing plates, on which the cross-pieces were laid; and over these, earth was heaped to the depth required. The cross-pieces were laid close, not only for strength, but to prevent the earth from crumbling and falling through. Fireplaces and chimneys were also constructed. According to the shape of the ground, and the site, the bomb-proofs were either sunken, half sunken, or elevated; if the last, the top was sometimes used as a cavalier. In one or two places the very parapet of the main line was converted into a bomb-proof.

The general character of the fortifications was thus the same in both commands, the only important point of difference being that the batteries on the national side were absolute redoubts, while those of the enemy, south of the James, were for the most part open at the rear—a singular oversight. In all other respects the works of either army resembled those to which they were opposed. The lines of each, when seen from the advanced positions of the enemy, showed a parapet of strong profile, supported at intervals by batteries having a flanking fire to the right and left, while in front was a ditch with several rows of abatis. For months the two armies

thus confronted each other on the banks of the Appomattox, like mailed champions armed to the teeth, while Richmond, the prize of the struggle, waited apart, till her fate should be decided. * f J

The people of the North entirely failed to appreciate the importance of the seizure of the "Weldon road. The disaster of Burnside had left an impression that could not easily be effaced, and all the subsequent manoeuvres on the right and left were, to the multitude, unintelligible. It was only perceived that Hancock had twice been moved to the north bank of the James, and twice withdrawn. Not only was the fact unnoticed that by these fnanceuvres the extension on the left had been made practicable; but that extension itself was looked upon as of no especial consequence. Hancock's check at Beam's station more than balanced, in the public mind, all the advantages of Warren's advance. In the same way Sheridan

The map of the battle of Five Forks shows the fortifications around Petersburg, and that of the Appomattox campaign those around Richmond.

f On the 31st of October, 1864, there were one hundred and fifty-three pieces in position on the national lines, of which twenty were field artillery ; and at the fall of Richmond, in April, 1865, one hundred and seventy-five guns were captured, of which forty-one were either 6 or 12 pounders. This does not include the artillery found in the city, nor that taken in the field.

| In my account of the works around Richmond and Petersburg, I have made free use of papers by Major-General Wright, Chief of Engineers, United States Army, and Lieutenant-Colonel Michie, also of the Engineers, published in the "Report on the Defences of Washington," by Major-General Barnard, of the same corps ; as well as of a paper on the " Fortifications of Petersburg," by Lieutenant Feath-erstonaugh, of the Royal (British) Engineers. I am also indebted

for valuable assistance to Major-General Humphreys, late Chief of Engineers, United States Army.

ULYSSES S. GRANT.

as yet appeared to have accomplished nothing in the Valley; in fact he had retired, and Early had followed him; so that on the Potomac also, the prospect was gloomy. Even Sherman's success, gratifying as it was, seemed isolated; the country had no idea that it had been facilitated by the very movements at the East which were deemed so unfortunate ; and although the campaign in Georgia had been ordered by Grant, and formed an essential part of his schemes, its immediate result, so far as he was concerned, was to lessen his hold on the country, and make many declare that the right man for commander-in-chief was the general who had captured Atlanta, not the one who still lay outside of Richmond.

Until the fall of Atlanta, indeed, the gloom at the North was overshadowing. ,The most hopeful had become weary, the most determined were depressed and disappointed. It was forgotten that Grant had warned the country he might have to fight "all summer" on one line; it was not known that he had ordered a siege train when he started from Culpeper, and had arranged for the crossing of the James while he was still north of the Rapidan. Soldiers indeed saw the immense advantages that had been gained, the definite progress made towards the end;"" but soldiers alone. The New York Tribune, the great loyal newspaper

* During the month of July, 1864, I was sent to the North, and had several interviews with the old commander of the army, Lieutenant-General Scott. He expressed the greatest admiration for Grant's achievements, and complete confidence that his operatic would result in entire success. I was especially charged by h to congratulate General Grant upon the manoeuvres and tacti of the Wilderness campaign, and on the strategy which employed

of the North, openly advocated concession; the Secretary of the Treasury resigned his place in the cabinet; gold was sold in the market at a premium of 290 per cent. ; and during Early's raid Halleck reported to Grant that "not a man responded to the President's call for militia,* from New York, Pennsylvania, or the North."

This dissatisfaction was steadily fostered by those who preferred disunion to war. No one can appreciate the difficulties of the national commanders at this critical period who fails to remember the malignant detraction they suffered at home; the persistent efforts to blacken their reputations, to misrepresent their movements, to belittle their successes, and magnify their losses—in order to depress the spirit of the North. A continuous battle was thus carried on at the rear while the soldiers were righting at the front; and the enemies of the nation at home did it nearly as much harm as Lee. They stimulated the South in its resistance, they invited foreign sympathizers to active interference, and did their best to hinder recruiting, to withhold supplies, to damage the financial credit of the country, and to discourage the armies in the field.

The near approach of the Presidential elections reminded this party that it had still another all the armies constantly against the enemy. This was immediately after Early's movement against Washington, and the veteran appeared delighted that his younger successor had not allowed himself to be distracted from his original design, but despite the apparent danger at the North, remained firm in his position before Petersburg.

* The militia, it may be necessary to say, were state troops, summoned for a particular emergency, and entirely distinct from the Volunteers, who were enlisted for definite periods.

chance ; and, when Lincoln was renominated by the Kepublicans, General McClellan became the candidate of the Democrats, who openly declared the war for the Union a failure, and demanded an immediate cessation of hostilities.* The success of the Peace party indeed would secure all that the rebels were fighting for; a fact very well understood by the Eichmond government and its generals. It was worth while to hold out a little longer in the field while their allies in the Northern states went to the polls. The elections would occur on the 8th of November, and until that date every military movement had an immediate political effect. If the rebels could bv some transient success still further discourage the weak-hearted at the North; if by protracted resistance they could even temporarily exhaust the endurance of those who-had persisted so long— they would exert an influence directly favorable to McClellan. t With this view they redoubled their efforts, and with this view the Democrats continued theirs, while a chorus of foreign aristo-

* See resolutions passed by Democratic Nominating Convention, September 1, 1864.

f " We have already referred to the great consideration which attached to the Presidential contest in the North which was now to take place; we have stated that it gave a new hope for the South in 1864; and we have indicated that the political campaign of this year was, in the minds of the Confederate leaders, scarcely less important than the military. Indeed, the two were indissolubly connected; and the calculation in Richmond was, that if military matters could even be held in a negative condition, the Democratic party in the North would have the opportunity of appealing to the popular impatience of the war, and bringing it to a close on terms acceptable to the great mass of the Southern people."— Pollard's "Lost Cause"pp. 556 and 557.

crats assisted to proclaim the downfall of the republic which they naturally hated and feared.

Grant, however, appreciated the situation as» fully as his opponents. On the 16th of August, he wrote : "I have no doubt the enemy are exceedingly anxious to hold out until the Presidential election. They have many hopes from its effects. They hope a counter-revolution. They hope the election of a Peace candidate." Accordingly, he renewed his preparations for a vigorous and, if necessary, protracted series of campaigns. But the enlistment of the Volunteers had been for three years only, and the term of many of the men was now expiring. It was necessary to provide at once for this emergency. On the 18th of July, Grant telegraphed to the President, direct: " There ought to be an immediate call for, say, three hundred thousand men, to be put in the field in the shortest possible time. . . The enemy have their last man in the field. Every depletion of their army is an irreparable loss. Desertions from it now rapid. With the prospect of large additions to our force their desertions would increase. The greater number of men we have, the shorter and less sanguinary will be the war." These representations were heartily seconded by Halleck, and had their proper effect. A call for five hundred thousand troops was issued by the President.*

The response, however, was slow, and if volun-

The call was for five hundred thousand men, but from this number were deducted those already raised, under previous calls, in excess of demand; so that in reality only about three hundred thousand were summoned at this time. See Report of Provost-Marshal General Fry.

teering flagged, the draft must be resorted to. But, when the conscription was ordered, a year before, the enemies of the government had broken out into absolute riot and resistance, burning the houses of prominent citizens, murdering defenceless negroes, and shooting down national officers on duty and in their uniform, in the greatest city of the North. A renewal of these scenes was now threatened,* and, naturally enough, was dreaded by the government. Grant, however, remained urgent, and on the 13th of September, he wrote to Stanton : " We ought to have the whole number of men called for by the President, in the shortest possible time. Prompt action in filling up our armies will have more effect upon the enemy than a victory. They profess to believe, and make their men believe, there is such a party in favor of recognizing Southern independence that the draft cannot be enforced. Let them be undeceived. Deserters come into our lines daily, who tell us that the men are nearly universally tired of the war, and that desertions would be much more frequent, but that they believe peace will be negotiated after the fall elections. The enforcement of the draft and prompt filling up of our armies will save the shedding of blood to an immense extent."

* "The people in many parts of the North and West now talk openly and boldly of resisting the draft, and it is believed that the leaders of the Peace branch of the Democratic party are doing all in their power to bring about this result. The evidence of this has increased very much within the last few days. It is probably thought that such a thing will have its effect upon the next election by showing the inability of the present administration to carry on the war with an armed opposition in the loyal states."— HallecJc to Grant, August, 1864.

The draft was enforced, and no difficulty or disturbance occurred. Those inclined to positive resistance were, after all, few in number; and, as usual, the men who talked the loudest were laggard in action. But above all, at this crisis, the victory of Atlanta revived the drooping spirits of the nation and gave stamina to the government; and coming, as it did, the very day after McClellan's nomination, was a disastrous blow to the Democrats. Volunteering at once revived, and troops again began pouring into the armies.

Meanwhile, the country and even the government still believed that Washington was in danger. It has, however, already been seen that from the outset all of Grant's orders and plans had contemplated the complete protection of the capital. The route from the Rapidan had been selected with this view, and the expedition of Sigel was especially intended to close the avenue which the Shenandoah Valley would otherwise offer to the enemy. The movements of the Wilderness campaign, the constant retreat of Lee and the advance of Grant after every battle, had accomplished this purpose and effectually covered Washington; and up to the time of the crossing of the James there had been no apprehension in any quarter of an invasion of the North. Nor was the movement against Petersburg at all in contravention of the original design; for Hunter's campaign in the Shenandoah and Sheridan's co-operative march towards Charlottes ville were conceived with the express object of destroying the rebel communications north of Richmond, and rendering it impossible for Lee to throw any large force in the direction of the Potomac.

Hunter, it is true, had moved on Lexington instead of towards Charlottesville, and Sheridan, thus left unsupported, was obliged to return to Grant; while afterwards, when repelled from Lynchburg, Hunter retreated entirely away from the Valley, leaving the route to "Washington absolutely open to the enemy. Nevertheless, the invasion of Early had failed, for the very reason which Grant had foreseen. Lee had been so crippled by his losses in the Wilderness that he could not detach a force large enough to endanger Washington without risking his position at Richmond; and when Early reached the capital he found troops assembled there sufficient to repel him. But had Grant moved his army in May by way of the James instead of from Culpeper, the rebels would doubtless at that time have threatened Washington far more seriously than in July. The very danger which was now averted was a justification of the strategy which had prevented its occurrence at a time when relief might have been more difficult to secure.

At this juncture, however, Lee could have had but little hope of capturing Washington, though he doubtless believed that Grant might be compelled to weaken himself in front of Richmond, and perhaps to raise the siege.""" Indeed, had the national general allowed himself to be influenced by the excited apprehensions of civilians and even soldiers at the rear, he would have abandoned all the advantages acquired by months

* McCabe's " Life and Campaigns of General Lee;" a work containing more trustworthy information from rebel sources than anv other I have seen.

of fighting, and moved the army of the Potomac back to the fortifications of the capital. But he had his hand at the throat of the rebellion, and meant not to let go his grasp. Having perceived the vital military point, he had the courage to remain there, despite advice, and entreaties, and almost commands. Thus Lee's plan of obliging him to give up Richmond for the sake of Washington entirely failed. It was a skilful move on the military chess-board, and with some antagonists might have succeeded, but Grant had no more idea of abandoning the goal at which he was aiming because of such a distraction as Early's campaign, than he had of re-crossing the Rapidan after the battle of the Wilderness.

It had now, however, become essential to defeat the movement of Early. Disaster in the Valley would lay open to the rebels the states of Maryland and Pennsylvania for long distances before another army could be interposed to check them; while the Baltimore and Ohio railroad, as well as the Chesapeake and Ohio canal, alike indispensable to the national armies, were alike obstructed by the enemy. The moral effect of all this on the North at this political crisis was most damaging. Grant was therefore extremely anxious that whenever a blow was struck by Sheridan it should be decisive. But to secure this, caution was necessary as well as energy; and although full of confidence in his young lieutenant, the general-in-chief remembered that Sheridan had never yet handled a large command without an immediate superior: he accordingly directed him closely and constantly. Sheridan in his turn continually asked for orders and advice.

He was a born soldier, and joined to his theoretical knowledge a clear conception of the character and requirements of the campaign, while his pugnacity and determination made him a formidable antagonist; but he knew how much depended on success at this juncture ; he knew also the importance of co-operation with the armies on the James ; and though self-reliant, he was thoroughly subordinate. Thus, the relations of the two generals which at first were cordial, soon became intimate, and a military friendship sprang up between them, which in time ripened into a personal one, as close and as unselfish on both sides, as that already existing between Grant and Sherman.

The rebel government was not long in learning that a new commander had superseded the crowd of generals who previously moved up and down the Valleys of the Potomac and the Shenan-doah without concert and without success. They learned also that Sheridan was to be reinforced, and Lee at once determined to resist him. It has already been seen that Anderson was sent with Kershaw's division and FitzLee's cavalry to the neighborhood of Culpeper, to co-operate with Early. Anderson's orders were to cross the Potomac east of the Blue Eidge, while Early entered Maryland higher up the stream, and the two commanders, acting in concert, were to make a second movement against Washington. * This plan, how-

This statement of Lee's orders to Early and Anderson is taken from McCabe, who gives it still more minutely. Early, however, says not a word to indicate that he was expected a second time to cross the Potomac, for if he admitted this, he would have to admit that he was foiled.

ever, had been frustrated by Sheridan's prompt advance into the Valley, and Grant's operations north of the James.

Sheridan had moved from Halltown on the 10th of August, and Early at once fell back as far as Strasburg, to which point he was followed by the national army, both forces arriving at Cedar creek on the 12th. On the 13th, Early retired a few miles further, to Fisher's Hill. Anderson meanwhile had arrived at Culpeper, where he received a despatch from Early, calling for reinforcements. He at once set out with his whole command, and crossing the Blue Ridge at

Chester's Gap, arrived on the 15th, at Front Royal, about ten miles east of Strasburg. The road between was held by Sheridan ; but Masanutten mountain also intervened, and concealed the presence of Anderson. FitzLee therefore rode across the mountain in person to communicate with Early, and preparations were made for a combined attack on Sheridan. A plan of battle was actually arranged. But Sheridan had been already warned: for Grant's opportune despatch of the 12th had arrived, announcing the addition to the enemy's force ; t and on the 17th, when the two rebel columns advanced, the national

* " The intention, so far as I can learn, was to send a column direct from Culpeper to the Potomac, and Early to advance at the same time from Martinsburg. This was frustrated by Early being compelled to fall back, and your operations on the north side of the James."— Sheridan to Grant, August, 20.

See Yol. IT., pp. 507 and 510. "The receipt of this despatch was very important to me, as I possibly would have remained in uncertainty as to the character of the force coming in on my flank and rear, until it attacked the cavalry." Sheridan's Official Report.

troops had retired. Sheridan fell back as far as Berryville, and the enemy's forces were united at Winchester, only five miles off.

At this time, if ever, the rebels should have pressed Sheridan across the Potomac, or crossing the river themselves, have either compelled him to follow, or forced Grant to despatch still further reinforcements from the James. The strength of Early and Anderson combined was at least equal to that of Sheridan, and if they were to accomplish anything at all by the campaign, now was their opportunity. Once more, however, Lee's plans entirely failed. There was some question of rank between the commanders, but this was waived by Anderson, and all the responsibility fell upon Early, who, though a stubborn fighter, and not without fine conceptions, lacked entirely the genius to execute either his own ideas, or those of others, in an emergency. As a corps commander immediately under the eye of a superior, he sometimes displayed ability, but an independent command was beyond his powers.'"'

But if he did no more, Early was to secure the harvests of the Valley. This was one great object of the campaign, and after Early's return from Maryland, his supplies were obtained principally from the lower Valley and the counties west of it. The wheat for nearly all his bread was thrashed and ground by details from his command, while the horses and mules were sustained almost entirely by grazing. But all this was now to end. Grant

* This was McCabe's opinion, as well as the general one at the South; but Early himself entertained a very different one.—See his Memoir, passim. had directed Sheridan: "Do all the damage to railroads and crops you can. Carry off stock of all descriptions, and negroes, to prevent further planting;" and the orders were carried out to the letter. On the 20th of August, Sheridan reported : " I have destroyed everything that was eatable south of Winchester, and they will have to haul supplies from well up to Staunton." His orders were to seize all mules, horses, and cattle that might be useful, and destroy all wheat and hay. " No houses will be burned, and officers in charge of this delicate but necessary duty must inform the people that the object is to make the Valley untenable for the raiding parties of the rebel army." The destruction was not wanton, nor was the suffering inflicted by way of revenge ; Grant was simply determined to prevent another invasion of the loyal states, and to render it impossible for another rebel army to subsist in the Valley. The inhabitants suffered, whether their resources were annihilated by rebel or national soldiers.

And now occurred a series of manoeuvres demanding caution and skill in both commanders. Early's object was to remain as far down the Valley as possible, in order to maintain a threatening attitude towards Maryland and Pennsylvania, and prevent the use of the

Baltimore and Ohio railroad and the Chesapeake and Ohio canal, as well as to detain as many troops as possible from Grant. Sheridan, on the other hand, was watching his opportunity, and whenever Lee recalled any force from the Valley, he meant to fall upon Early and destroy him. The two armies lay in such a position—the enemy on the west bank of the Opequan, covering Winchester,

ULYSSES S. GRANT.

and the national forces between that place and Berryville,—that either could bring on an engagement at any moment; but Early was not anxious for battle at all, although reinforced ;* while an advance of Sheridan, in the event of reverse, exposed the national capital. The rebels, therefore, remained as close to the Potomac as they dared,' and Sheridan waited until circumstances should give him an opportunity to pounce upon the enemy. Meanwhile, the young commander every day reported to his superior on the James, and every day the general-in-chief replied with words of caution or encouragement. At this time every important movement made by Sheridan was either ordered or approved by Grant. " I have taken up a position/' said Sheridan, "near Berryville, which will enable me to get in their rear, if they should get strong enough to push north." Again, on the 20th of August, he telegraphed : " Troops passing from Culpeper into the Valley. I have taken the defensive till their strength is more fully developed . . If they cross the Potomac, they will expose their rear, and I will pitch into them." To this Grant replied from Petersburg : " Warren's corps is now entrenched across the Weldon road ; I shall endeavor to stay there, and employ the enemy so actively that he cannot detach further," On the 20th, Sheridan reported : " I can now calculate on bringing into action about twenty-two thousand or twenty-three thousand infantry, and about eight thousand cavalry."!

* This is Early's own statement, although, according to McCabe and Pollard, he had been ordered to cross the Potomac.

t See Appendix for remarks on the subject of Sheridan's numbers in this campaign.

On the 21st, Early and Anderson advanced, and on the 22nd, Sheridan fell back as far as Halltown. " My position," he said, " in front of Charlestown at best was a bad one, and so much being dependent on this army, I withdrew . . . and took up a new line in front of Halltown." The rebels pressed forward, and on the 25th, seized Shepardstown, on the Potomac, twelve miles above Halltown; upon which Sheridan telegraphed: " I will not give up this place, and hope to be able to strike the enemy divided." On the 26th, however, the rebels fell back from his front, and returned to their former position. Early had crossed the Potomac once, and notwithstanding his orders, had no desire to try the chances again. This day Grant said to Sheridan : " I now think it likely that all troops will be ordered back from the Valley, except what they think the minimum necessary to detain you. . . Yielding up the "Weldon road seems to be a blow the enemy cannot stand. . . Watch closely, and if you find this theory correct, push with all vigor. Give the enemy no rest, and if it is possible to follow to the Virginia Central road—follow that far." On the 26th of August, Lee made his last attempt, at Ream's station, to regain possession of the Weldon road. Unsuccessful there, and finding his plans frustrated in the Valley, he at once, as Grant had foreseen, directed the return of Anderson. On the 28th, Grant telegraphed to Sheridan : " If you are so situated as to feel the enemy strongly without compromising the safety of your position, I think it advisable to do so. I do not know positively that any troops have yet returned from the Valley, but think you will find the enemy in your immediate front weaker than you are."'

Meanwhile, there were rumors that a part of Early's force had been sent west of the Alleghanies, and Grant meant to lose no opportunity. On the 29th, he ordered Sheridan : "If it is ascertained certainly that Breckenridge has been detached to go into Western Virginia, attack the remaining forces vigorously with every man you have; and if successful in routing them, follow up your success with the Sixth and Nineteenth corps, and send Crook to meet Breckenridge." But Sheridan replied on the same day : " There is not one word of truth in the report of Breckenridge being in West Virginia;" and then, with his usual spirit, he added : "I believe no troops have yet left the Valley, but I believe they will, and that it will be their last campaign in the Shenandoah. They came to invade, and have failed. They must leave, or cross the Potomac." The next day he said : "If Early has detached troops for Eichmond, I will attack him vigorously." It was with words like these that the chief and the subaltern inspired each other : they were evidently made of similar stuff.

At last, on the 3rd of September, Anderson started for Eichmond; but towards night he blundered upon Sheridan's lines, and was vigorously attacked, and driven back towards the Opequan after dark. For a while he was in imminent danger, and the next day Early came up to his support. The rebels, however, had no idea of attacking Sheridan, and the whole command executed a rapid retreat to the west bank of the Opequan ; but had Sheridan been aware

of Anderson's intention, he would doubtless have facilitated, rather than interrupted, his march. As it was, he waited now to be certain that troops had started for Richmond. Indeed, for a fortnight this was the whole policy of Grant; but of course the country could not be apprised of the plan, and failing to understand the delay, became impatient again.

On the 8th, thegeneral-in-chief said to Sheridan: " If you want to attack Early, you might reinforce largely from Washington. Whilst you are close in front of the enemy, there is no necessity for a large force there. This is not intended to urge an attack, because I believe you will allow no chance to escape which promises success." Bub Anderson still remained in the Valley, and Sheridan telegraphed : " Early's infantry force and mine number about the same. I have not deemed it best to attack him, but have watched closely to press him hard, so soon as he commences to detach troops for Richmond. This was the tenor of your despatch to me after I took up the defensive." To this Grant replied, on the 9th : "I would not have you make an attack with the advantage against you, but would prefer the course you seem to be pursuing; that is, press closely upon the enemy, and when he moves, follow him up, being ready at all times to pounce upon him, if he detaches any considerable force."

Meanwhile, the enemies at home were making the most of the delay and proclaiming Sheridan to be another failure. Not only the loyal people, but the government, were anxious; the continuous threat of invasion was intolerable, and the use of the rail-

road and canal had become indispensable. Still, Grant hesitated about allowing the initiative to be taken. The condition of affairs throughout the country required great prudence, and defeat in the Valley could be ill afforded. He was unwilling to telegraph the order for an attack without knowing the personal feeling of Sheridan as to the result. He indeed always took into consideration the temper and mood of his generals, and often in actual battle went to the front, not only to observe for himself the condition of the field, but to discover the spirit and inclination of commanders. In the same way he left City Point on the 15th of September, to visit the Valley, and decide, after conference with his lieutenant, what order should be made. He travelled direct to Charlestown, not stopping at Washington on the way.

That night, Sheridan learned that Anderson was moving through Winchester, on his way to Front Royal. He felt then that the time for battle had come, and had almost made up his mind to fight at Newtown, in the rear of Winchester, giving up his own line, and throwing himself on that of the enemy. He was, however, a little timid about this movement, until the arrival of Grant ;* but then he pointed out so distinctly how each army lay, what he could do the moment he was authorized, and expressed such confidence of success, that the general-in-chief declared the only instructions She-

" I was a little timid about this movement until the arrival of General Grant."— Sheridan's Official Report. Sheridan was never timid afterwards. He learned to confide in himself, and to know his own genius. Grant knew it too, and was never anxious about Sheridan again.

ridan needed were to advance. This was on Friday, and the supply trains were waiting at Harper's Ferry for forage. Grant asked if the teams could be brought up in time for an attack on the following Tuesday; and Sheridan replied that he could be ready before daylight on Monday. Grant gave him the orders, and felt so confident of the result, that he left the front, and went to New Jersey, to put his children at school.*

On the 17th of September, Early, with inexcusable folly, still further divided his command. Though weakened already by the loss of Anderson, he marched with two divisions of infantry and a large force of cavalry, to Martinsburg, twenty-two miles away, to do what damage he could to the railroad, leaving the remainder of his force in front of "Winchester. Sheridan at once detected the blunder of his antagonist, and instead of moving to Newtown, as he had intended, determined to attack the enemy in detail, fighting first the two divisions left near Winchester, and then the two that had been moved to Martinsburg. Accordingly, on the afternoon of the 18th, his whole army marched from Berryville towards the Opequan. But at Martinsburg Early learned that Grant had been with Sheridan, and anticipating some movement of importance, he at once

* " You may recollect that, when I visited Sheridan at Charles-town, I had a plan of battle with me to give him. But I found him so thoroughly ready to move, so confident of success when he did move, and his plan so thoroughly matured, that I did not let him know this, and gave him. no order whatever except the authority to move. ... I was so pleased that I left, and got as far as possible from the field before the attack, lest the papers might attribute to me what was due to him."— General Grant to Author, June, 1878.

ULYSSES S. GRANT.

set out to return. At daylight on the 19th, there was one rebel division immediately in front of Sheridan, and another only five miles to the north, while two, still nearer, were marching rapidly up on the road from Martinsburg. Sheridan was promptly informed of these dispositions of the enemy, and understood that he now must fight the entire command of Early.

His plan was to attack the rebels with the Sixth and Nineteenth corps, holding Crook's division in reserve, to be used as a turning column when the crisis of the battle occurred. His cavalry he placed on the right and left of the infantry. The approach to Winchester by the Berryville road is through a difficult gorge, and it was nine o'clock before an advance in line could be effected. The attack was then made in handsome style, without cover; but by this time Early's two divisions from Martinsburg had come upon the ground, and the rebels were not only able to hold their own, but made a countercharge, and the national centre was forced back for a while. Sheridan, however, threw forward Upton's brigade and struck the attacking column in flank, when the rebels in turn were driven back, and the national line was re-established.

The enemy's principal strength was opposite Sheridan's right, where the Martinsburg road comes in, and Crook was now directed to find the left of the rebel line, strike it in flank or rear, and break it up, while Sheridan made a left half wheel of the main line of battle to support him. Crook

* "At Martinsburg . . I learned that Grant was with Sheridan that day, and I expected an early move."— Early'% Memoir, page 84.

advanced with spirit, forcing the enemy rapidly from his position, and at the same moment Torbert's cavalry came sweeping up the Martinsburg road, overlapping Early's left, and driving the rebel cavalry before them in a confused mass, through the broken infantry. Sheridan now rode .rapidly along the line of the Sixth and Nineteenth corps, to order their advance, and at the same time directed Wilson to push to the left with a division of cavalry, and gain the roads leading south from Winchester. Then returning to the right, where the battle was still raging, he ordered Torbert to charge with the remainder of the cavalry. Torbert advanced simultaneously with the infantry. The country was entirely open, and the movement could be distinctly seen by the enemy. Unable to resist any longer, crowded on both flanks, and fearful of being surrounded, the rebels everywhere broke, and as Sheridan said in his famous despatch, he " sent them whirling through Winchester." Night alone saved Early from, complete destruction. He lost, by his own account, forty-five hundred men, of whom twenty-five hundred were prisoners. Two general officers were killed, several others wounded, and five guns and nine battle-flags were captured. The engagement lasted from early morning until five in the afternoon. After that time it became a rout. Sheridan's loss was forty-five hundred men; five hundred killed, three thousand five hundred wounded, and five hundred missing.*"" It was of this battle that Grant declared in his

* The exact figures reported are 558 killed, 3,759 wounded, and 618 missing; but this return includes a part of the loss at Fisher's Hill, three days afterwards. At least half of the wounded

official report: " The result was such that I have never since deemed it necessary to visit General Sheridan before giving him orders."

Early fell back in the night as far as Newtown, and next day to Fisher's Hill, four miles south of Strasburg ; and at daylight on the 20th, Sheridan moved rapidly up the Valley in pursuit. Fisher's Hill is immediately south of a little stream called Tumbling river, and at this point the rebels had erected breastworks reaching across the Valley, here only three and a half miles wide. So secure indeed did Early now consider himself that his ammunition boxes were taken from the caissons and placed behind the breastworks. On the returned to the ranks, so that the actual loss to Sheridan's command did not exceed 3,000.

Early, in his Memoir, pronounces this battle a series of blunders on the part of Sheridan, who, " instead of being promoted, ought to have been cashiered," for his " incapacity;" while his own generalship was supreme. " A splendid victory had been gained." " The enemy's attacking columns were thrown into great confusion and driven from the field." "It was a grand sight to see this immense body hurled back in utter disorder before my two divisions;" and so on : nothing but gallant charges and wonderful repulses by the rebels, all, strangely enough, resulting in " great confusion, for which there was no remedy;" and " nothing was left for us but to retire through Winchester." They retired "whirling." It would, indeed, have been better for Early if Sheridan had been " cashiered" before the battle.

Early asserts, page 87, that he took into this action 7,000 muskets and 2,000 cavalry only; and at the close, declares " the main part of my force and all my trains had been saved." his official report to Lee, written at the time, he gives his loss in infantry and artillery alone at 3,611; that of the cavalry is not reported, but he admits a loss of 348 in killed and wounded this and the succeeding battle, and adds "but many wer

evening of the 20th, Sheridan went into position on the heights of Strasburg, and at once determined to use Crook as a turning column again, and strike the enemy in left and rear, while the remainder of the army made a left half wheel in his support. This manoeuvre, however, demanded secrecy, and the rebels had a signal station in the mountains, from which every movement of national troops by day could be observed. Crook was therefore concealed in the forest on the 21st, while the main national line moved up in front of the rebel position. At the same time Torbert, with the greater part of the cavalry, was sent up the Luray valley on the left, and ordered to cross the mountains, and intercept the enemy at Newmarket, twenty miles in Early's rear.

Before daylight on the 22nd, Crook marched to Little North mountain, the western boundary of the Valley, and massed his troops in the heavy woods along its face. The Sixth and Nineteenth corps were then moved up opposite the rebel centre, while Ricketts's division with Averill's cavalry ostentatiously advanced towards Early's left. The enemy's attention was thus attracted, and when a general firing had begun, Crook suddenly burst from the woods on the hillside, striking the rebels in flank and rear, doubling up their line, and sweeping down behind the breastworks. Sheridan's main line at once took up the movement, first Bicketts swinging in and joining Crook, and then the recaptured ;" so that his loss at Winchester, by his own showing, was 4,500—half of what in the Memoir he declares to have been his entire command. Either he had many more men than he declares, or the " main part of his force " was not saved.

mainder of the Sixth and Nineteenth corps; the works were everywhere carried, and the rout of the enemy was complete. Many of the rebels threw down their arms, abandoning their artillery. Sixteen guns and eleven hundred prisoners fell into the national hands, and Early reported two hundred and forty killed and wounded in the infantry and artillery. Sheridan lost less than a thousand men.' 5 ' 7 It was dark before the battle ended, but the rebels continued their flight through Woodstock, and as far as Narrow Passage, a gorge in the Blue Ridge. Sheridan pursued them during the night, only halting at Woodstock, to rest his men and issue rations.

On the 23rd, he drove the enemy to Mount Jackson, and found the country and small towns filled with their wounded; on the 24th, he followed Early to a point six miles beyond Newmarket, but without being able to bring on an engagement. The rebels moved fast, and Torbert had not arrived with the cavalry in time to check them. He had been detained at a gorge in the mountains,

* Sheridan's return shows 85 killed, 677 wounded, and 9 missing, but this does not include the losses in Crook's command or the cavalry. Early wrote to Lee on October 9th: " The loss in the infantry and artillery was 30 killed, 210 wounded, and 995 missing ; total, 1,235. I have been able to get no report of the loss in the cavalry, but it was slight." If this is true, the demoralization of the rebels must have been extreme: for an army of the size of Early's to yield after a loss of only 240 killed and wounded is disgraceful beyond anything in the war. Beaten commanders, however, are often willing to sacrifice the reputation of their troops in order to save their own; and in this instance it is possible that Early's soldiers made a more gallant defence than their general describes.

where a small rebel force was able for a while to hold his two divisions. Had he succeeded in reaching Newmarket in time to intercept the broken and flying fragments of Early's command, the whole rebel army must have been destroyed. On the 25th, Early abandoned the main Valley road to his victor, and fell back by Port Republic to Brown's Gap, one of the south-eastern exits from the Blue Ridge. The national infantry advanced as far as Harrisonburg, and the cavalry was sent to Port Republic, Staunton, and Waynesboro', to burn bridges, drive off cattle, and destroy all property that might be serviceable to the rebel army. The Valley of Virginia w r as in the possession of Sheridan.

These important successes electrified the country, revived the courage of the weak-hearted, amazed the government, and of course delighted Grant. The authorities at Washington, although they highly appreciated Sheridan's executive ability, had been somewhat unwilling to entrust him with an independent command. Halleck in particular had declared that he was too inexperienced, and had urged this view upon Grant. But these victories established Sheridan in the confidence of the President and the Secretary of War, who were afterwards always ready to allow him full discretion in the management of all the troops under his command.* As for his soldiers, they declared, referring to the Democratic desire for compro-

* " Sheridan is entitled to all the credit of fyis great victory; it established him in the confidence of the President and the Secretary of War, as a commander to be trusted with the fullest discretion in the management of all the troops under him.

nrise, that Sheridan was the bearer of Peace propositions to Jefferson Davis from the North.

Grant had returned to City Point on the 19th of September, and on the 20th, at two P.M., he telegraphed to Sheridan: "I have just received the news of your great victory, and ordered each of the armies here to fire a salute of one hundred guns in honor of it. . . If practicable, push your success and make all you can of it." He was anxious that the full effect of the victory should be reaped at the West as well as the East, and inquired of Halleck: " Has the news of General Sheridan's battle been sent to General Sherman ? If not, please telegraph him." Neither did he forget that his forces on the Shenandoah were co-operating with those on the Potomac and the James. On the 21st, he said to Butler: "Further news from Sheridan is better than the first we had. In pursuing the enemy up the Valley, they may be induced to detach from here. Put every one on the look-out for any movement of the enemy. Should any force be detached, we must either manage to bring them back, or gain an advantage here." To Halleck he explained : "When Sheridan commenced his movement, I thought it possible, though not probable, that Early might turn north, or send his cavalry north; and in that case, wanted troops in Washington, so that a force might be thrown suddenly into Hagerstown, to head them off. I think now it will be safe to send all new organizations here."

Before that, while they highly appreciated him as a commander to execute, they felt a little nervous about giving him too much discretion."— General Grant to Author, June, 1878.

Sheridan himself Grant left at first entirely to his own resources, to reap the harvest of his own victory. After each battle he congratulated him and his army, but gave no detailed orders. On the 23rd, he said: " I have just received the news of your second great victory, and ordered a hundred guns in honor of it. Keep on, and your good work will cause the fall of Richmond." On the 24th, however, Sheridan reported: " I am now eighty miles from Martinsburg, and find it exceedingly difficult to supply this army. The engagements of "Winchester and Fisher's Hill broke up my original plan of pushing up the Valley with a certain amount of supplies, and then returning. There is not sufficient in the Valley to live off the country." To this Grant replied: " If you can possibly subsist your army at the front for a few days more, do it, and make a great effort to destroy the roads about Charlottesville, and the canal, wherever your cavalry can reach it." Sheridan accordingly pushed on to the head of the Valley, and from Harrisonburg, a hundred and four miles from Harper's Ferry, he telegraphed : " The destruction of forage from here to Staunton will be a terrible blow to them. All the grain and forage in the vicinity of Staunton was retained for the use of Early's army. All in the upper part of the Valley was shipped to Richmond, for the use of Lee's army. The country from here to Staunton was abundantly supplied with forage and grain." On the 26th, Grant telegraphed to Sherman: " I have evidence that Sheridan's victory has created the greatest consternation and alarm for the safety of the city."

In fact, everything showed the moral effect of these successes on the enemy. Sheridan not only found hundreds of rebel wounded scattered in the houses as he advanced, and wagons and caissons burned or abandoned by Early in his flight; but he captured many unhurt soldiers, hiding in the forests or making their way to their homes. The rebel commander himself described his condition very graphically to Lee : " My troops are very much shattered, the men very much exhausted, and many of them without shoes. . . I shall do the best I can, and hope I may be able to check the enemy, but I cannot but be apprehensive of the result." " In the affair at Fisher's Hill the cavalry gave way, but it was flanked. This would have been remedied, if the troops had remained steady; but a panic seized them at the idea of being flanked, and without being defeated, they broke, many of them fleeing shamefully. The artillery was not captured by the enemy, but abandoned by the infantry."* Lee fully appreciated the disasters of his subordinate. " I very much regret," he said, "the reverses that have occurred in the Valley. . . You must do all in your power to invigorate your army. . . It will require the greatest watchfulness, the greatest promptness, and the most untiring energy on your part to arrest the progress of the enemy in their present tide of success." These orders were themselves an implied rebuke, but more direct censure was not spared. Lee added words which coming

* The language in the text quoted from Early will not be found in his Memoir ; a fact which shows how necessary it is for commanders to have access to their own records when they attempt to compile a history of their campaigns. 85

from him were significant : " As far as I can judge at this distance, you have operated more with divisions than with your concentrated strength. Circumstances may have rendered it necessary, but such a course is to be avoided, if possible." The Richmond mob also expressed its views, and painted on the fresh artillery ordered to the Valley : " For General Sheridan, care of General Early."

CHAPTEE XXVI.

Grant's original plan at the West to move to the sea—Plan turned over to Sherman when Grant became general-in-chief—Co-operation of Banks and Canby prevented by Red river disaster—Sherman first proposes destruction of railroad to the rear—Unity of instinct between Grant and Sherman-Sherman reverts to original plan—Grant first suggests movement to Savannah, instead of Mobile—Sherman promptly accepts suggestion— Development of views of the two commanders—Hood moves to rear and threatens Sherman's communications—Sherman obliged to follow—Grant makes a movement before Richmond to prevent Lee reinforcing Hood —Sherman still anxious for his onward march—Sherman first suggests leaving Hood in his rear—Hood attacks Chattanooga railroad and Sherman again compelled to follow—Grant meanwhile arranges for Sherman's march to the sea—Attack and defence of Allatoona—Repulse of rebels— Sherman again suggests moving to Savannah, leaving Thomas to contend with Hood—Grant at first prefers Sherman to destroy Hood before moving to sea—Sherman repeats suggestion—Grant sanctions movement, if line of Tennessee can be held—Mutual confidence of Sherman and Graiit —Superior responsibility of Grant—Daring of Sherman's conception—Comparison of Sherman's plan with that of Grant behind Vicksburg— Difference between Grant's original plan and modifications of Sherman— Originality of Sherman—Movement of Grant on the James in support of Sherman and Sheridan—Orders to Butler and Meade—Grant has small expectation of capturing Richmond at this time—Hopes to gain advantage before Petersburg—Complicated responsibilities of general-in-chief—Movement of Butler from Deep Bottom — Capture of Fort Harrison — Ord wounded—National advance interrupted—Grant enters captured work— Assault by Birney repelled—No further advantage gained north of James —Correspondence of Grant with President in regard to Sheridan—Sheridan's operations facilitated by movement on James—Meade moves out to left—Warren captures work on Peeble's farm—Ninth corps at first forced back, but afterwards rallies—Warren holds his position—Three rebel assaults on Fort Harrison—Butler retains his prize—Rebels with-

draw within their lines—Advantage gained by Grant on both flanks— Balancing character of operations Consternation in Richmond—Anxiety of Lee.

IN the midst of Sheridan's brilliant successes in the Valley, the general-in-chief was obliged to turn his attention to the new situation in Georgia; for as soon as Atlanta was won, it became necessary to determine what use should be made of Sherman's victorious army. Grant's original plan, while he still commanded in person at the West, had been to acquire Atlanta, and then, retaining possession of that important place, to fight his way to the sea, thus dividing the Confederacy again, as had already been done when the Mississippi was opened the year before. Mobile was the point he desired to strike, and a co-operative movement, under Sherman or McPherson, was designed, to secure that place as a new base for his army, when it arrived. On the 15th of January, two months before Grant became general-in-chief, he said to Halleck: "I look upon the next line for me to secure to be that from Chattanooga to Mobile, Montgomery and Atlanta being the important intermediate points . . . Mobile would be a second base." A copy of this letter was sent to Sherman, and on the 19th of January, the scheme was also unfolded to Thomas.

When the command at the West was transferred to Sherman, that general was instructed to carry out this programme, and Banks was directed to concentrate his entire strength against Mobile, so as to open up a base for Sherman as he emerged from his southern campaign. The Red river disaster, however, prevented the co-operation of Banks, and after Canby took command at the South-West,' he also was for a long time unable to act offensively. Still, the original idea was kept steadily in mind by both Grant and Sherman. On the 29th of May, Sherman telegraphed from Dallas : " Johnston has in my front every man he can scrape, and Mobile must now be at our mercy, if General Canby and General Banks could send to Pascagoula ten thousand men;" and on the 30th, he proposed that A. J. Smith's division should be reinforced and sent " to act against Mobile, in concert with Admiral Farragut, according to the original plan." To this Grant replied, on the 3rd of June : " If there are any surplus troops West, they could be advantageously used against Mobile, as suggested in Sherman's despatch;" and on the 5th, he added, from Cold Harbor : " The object of sending troops to Mobile now would be, not so much to assist Sherman against Johnston, as to secure for him a base of supplies, after his work is done."

But it was found necessary to transfer A. J. Smith to West Tennessee and the Nineteenth corps to Virginia. Canby was therefore unable to send any force whatever to act against Mobile until late in July, and then only two thousand men under Gordon Granger, to co-operate with the fleet. Farragut, however, with splendid daring, steamed his vessels past the forts at the entrance to Mobile bay, and during the month of August all the defences of the harbor were either evacuated or surrendered. By the 23rd, the fleet had complete possession of the bay, but the city itself remained in the hands of the rebels. On the 13th of August, rumors of these

events reached Sherman, at that time contemplating his final circuit around Atlanta, and he telegraphed at once : " If there be any possibility of Admiral Farragut and the land forces under Gordon Granger taking Mobile, and further, of pushing up to Montgomery, my best plan would be to wait awhile, as now, and operate into the heart of Georgia from there."

This was just at the time when Hood's cavalry under Wheeler had been sent to cut the railroad between Atlanta and Chattanooga, and on the 13th of August, Sherman learned that Wheeler was threatening Dalton. " Before cutting loose, as proposed," he continued, " I would like to know the chance of my getting the use of the Alabama river. could easily break up the railroad back to Chattanooga, and shift my army down to West Point and Columbus, a country rich in corn, and make my fall campaign from there." Large ideas were evidently floating in his brain, but as yet without form and void. The same day he said: " If ever I should be cut off from my base, look out for me about St. Mark's, Florida, or Savannah, Georgia." This was the first mention in the correspondence of either Grant or Sherman, of the destruction of the railroad to the rear, or of the possibility of a campaign in Georgia, like that behind Vicksburg, entirely without a base. Doubtless, the idea was presented to Sherman by the menace to his communications offered by Wheeler's cavalry, as well as by his memory of the strategy which had been so successful in Mississippi, the year before.

On the 18th, Grant replied: "I never would advise going backward, even if your roads are cut so

ULYSSES S. GRANT.

as to prevent receiving supplies from the North. If it comes to the worst, move South, as you suggest" The unity of instinct between the two soldiers was as remarkable as ever. There can be no doubt that if Grant had never directed Sherman to open a line to the sea, that general would himself have conceived the idea ; and if Grant had been on the spot instead of Sherman, events would beyond all question have suggested to him most of the modifications of the plan which occurred to his subordinate. As it was, the thought had passed between them, and was for weeks developing before it took actual and definite form ; affected, in the first place, by the idiosyncrasies of each, and afterwards, as the thoughts and plans of all great soldiers are, by the varying circumstances of war; and in this instance, especially liable to change, when so many campaigns were combined and involved, and so many and distant armies were cooperating.

On the 17th of August, Sherman reverted to the primitive idea : " We must have the Alabama river . . . but of course I must trust to Admiral Farragut and General Canby." To Canby he said on the same day : " If possible, the Alabama river should be possessed by us in connection with my movements. I could easily open communication with Montgomery." On the 4th of September, after Atlanta had fallen, he proposed that he and Canby should each be reinforced by fifty thousand men; that Canby should move to Montgomery, and he himself towards the same point, and, then forming a junction, they should open the line to the Gulf of Mexico. On the 10th, he said to Canby: " We must

have the Alabama river now. . . . My line is so long now that it is impossible to protect it against cavalry raids ; but if we can get Montgomery, and Columbus, Georgia, as bases, in connection with Atlanta, we have Georgia and Alabama at our feet. ... I will be ready to sally forth in October, but ought to have some assurances that, in case of necessity, I can swing into Appalachicola or Montgomery." This of course was to carry out the original strategy of Grant.

The general-in-chief, however, had by this time different views. The rebels west of the Mississippi, relieved of all fear of attack from Canby, had begun themselves to threaten offensive operations. Ten thousand men under Price were marching through Arkansas to invade Missouri, while Kirby Smith had set out to cross the Mississippi and co-operate with the troops opposed to Sherman. These dispositions not only made it necessary to send A. J. Smith to the support of Rosecrans, who commanded in Missouri, but compelled Canby to abandon any idea of reinforcing Granger before Mobile. On the 29th of August, Grant said to Halleck : " I agree with you it would be hazardous and productive of no special good to send Gordon Granger past Mobile towards Atlanta. . . . The movement Sherman is now making, result as it may, cannot be influenced by anything that can be done at Mobile, in obedience to orders from here ;" and on the 10th of September, after Atlanta had actually fallen, and while Sherman was still writing: " We must have the Alabama river," Grant telegraphed to him : " Now that we have all of Mobile that is valuable, I do not know but it will be the best

move for Major-General Canbys troops to act upon Savannah, while you move on Augusta. I would like to hear from you, however, in this matter."

Augusta, on the Savannah river, is a hundred and fifty miles from its mouth, and a hundred and seventy-five miles east of Atlanta; Montgomery, on the Alabama, is a hundred and fifty miles southwest of Atlanta, and two hundred from Mobile. Grant's idea now was for Canby to take Savannah, at the mouth of the river of that name, and then move up to Augusta with supplies; while Sherman, moving south-east instead of south-west, would approach the Atlantic coast instead of the Gulf of Mexico : he would thus sever the only remaining line between Hood and Lee, and be better able, in case of need, to co-operate with Grant. There was still another possible route for Sherman, running almost directly south, to Columbus, Georgia, from which point communication could be opened by the Chat-tahoochee and Appalachicola rivers, with the Gulf of Mexico.

Sherman replied to Grant's telegram the same night, promptly conforming his own views to the new conception of his chief: " Our roads are broken back near Nashville, and Wheeler is not yet disposed of. ... I do not think we can afford to operate further, dependent on the railroad; it takes so many men to guard it, and then it is nightly broken by the enemy's cavalry that swarms around us. . . . If I could be sure of finding provisions and ammunition at Augusta, or Columbus, Georgia, I can march to Milledgeville, and compel Hood to give up Augusta or Macon, and then turn on the other. The country will afford forage and many supplies, but

not enough, in any one place, to admit of a delay. . . . If you can manage to take the Savannah river as high up as Augusta, or the Chattahoochee as far up as Columbus, 1 can sweep the whole state of Georgia; otherwise, I should risk our whole army "by going too far from Atlanta" Both generals were thus in favor of Sherman's cutting loose from Atlanta, but neither as yet dreamed of his setting out except to find another base already opened; and while Grant was considering especially the goal of the journey, Sherman's mind reverted rather to the start; for if the march occurred, Grant must provide supplies when it was over, while Sherman would be endangered, if his communications were cut before it began.

Sherman was now dependent for all his supplies for a hundred thousand men upon a single line of railroad, running from Nashville to Atlanta, a distance of two hundred and ninety miles, all the way through an enemy's country, where every foot must be protected by troops, whose numbers of course were deducted from his offensive force. Wheeler's cavalry raid had accomplished no remarkable results, but nevertheless made it plain that Sherman's communications with the North were constantly liable to interruption; and rumors were now afloat that Forrest was on his way to the same theatre, with the avowed purpose of compelling the national army to fall back from its conquest. On the 12th of September, Sherman said to Halleck : " There is a large abundance of forage in Alabama and Georgia, and independent columns might operate by a circuit from one army to another, and destroy the enemy's cavalry. . . . Our [rail] road is repaired and bring-

ing forward supplies, but I doubt its capacity to do much more than feed our trains and artillery horses." Then, with his usual subordination, he remarked: " As soon as General Grant determines for me the next move on the chess-board, I will estimate the number I will want."

Meanwhile, the general-in-chief was carefully considering this next move, and on the 12th of September, he sent Colonel Horace Porter, of his staff, to make known his views to Sherman and brino- back

o

a reply. He was accustomed to inform the officers of his personal staff very thoroughly of his plans, and often sent them to represent him at the headquarters of his more important generals, with whom he thus communicated more fully and exactly than was possible by other means. Colonel Porter was the bearer of a letter in which, after explaining the situation in Virginia, and announcing a proposed operation against Wilmington, Grant proceeded to develop the suggestion he had already made by telegraph, of a movement towards the Atlantic. " What you are to do with the forces at your command I do not exactly see. The difficulties of supplying your army, except when you are constantly moving beyond where you are, I plainly see. If it had not been for Price's movement, Canby could have sent twelve thousand men to Mobile. From your command on the Mississippi an equal number could have been taken. With this force, my idea would have been to divide them, sending one half to Mobile and the other to Savannah. You could then move as proposed in your telegram, so as to threaten Macon and Augusta equally. Whichever was abandoned by the enemy you could take,

and open up a new base of supplies. My object now in sending a staff-officer to you is not so much to suggest operations for you, as to get your .views, and to have plans matured by the time everything can be got ready."

To invite the views of Sherman on the campaigns and plans of the future was to set fire to an imagination crowded with thick-coming fancies, and to open the flood-gates of an eloquence which never lacked language to embody all that his genius conceived. His reply covered the whole ground : touched upon the strategy of Grant in front of Richmond ; discussed the capture of Wilmington and the topography of its waters; considered the value of Mobile and the possibility of Southern independence ; proposed reinforcements for Meade and campaigns for Canby; glanced at the side-movements of Price and Rosecrans ; treated of Hood's army and the Appalachicola river; but nevertheless narrowed itself down to a definite answer to Grant's inquiry and a positive plan for his own army, which did not differ materially from that suggested by the general-in-chief.

In regard to Mobile, he partly adopted the new view of Grant. " Now that Mobile is shut out to the commerce of our enemy, it calls for no further effort on our part, unless the capture of the city can be followed by the occupation of the Alabama river and the railroad to Columbus, when that place would be a magnificent auxiliary to my further progress into Georgia." But Savannah, he said, " once in our possession, and the river open to us, I would not hesitate to cross the state of Georgia with sixty thousand men, hauling some stores and de-

pending on the country for the balance. Where a million of people find subsistence, my army won't starve. ... I will therefore give it as my opinion that your army and Canby's should be reinforced to the maximum; that after you get Wilmington, you should strike for Savannah and its river ; that General Canby should hold the Mississippi river, and send a force to take Columbus, Georgia, either by the way of the Alabama or Appalachicola river; that I should keep Hood employed and put my army in fine order for a march on Augusta, Columbia, and Charleston, and start as soon as Wilmington is sealed to commerce, and the city of Savannah is in our possession." Again, in the same letter, he said : " If you will secure Wilmington and the city of Savannah from your centre, and let General Canby have command over the Mississippi river and country west of it, I will send a force to the Alabama and Appalachicola . . . and if you will fix a day to be in Savannah, I will insure our possession of Macon and a point on the river below Augusta." This was not different from what Grant had first suggested in his telegram of the 10th of September.

But at this moment the whole situation changed as suddenly as the scenery in a theatre. Sherman's letter was dated September 20th, and on the 21st, Hood moved his army from

Lovejoy's, where he had remained since the capture of Atlanta, to Palmetto station, on the West Point railroad, twenty-four miles soiith-west of the national position. From this place, on the 22nd, he announced to Bragg : " I shall, unless Sherman moves south, so soon as I can collect supplies, cross the Chatta-

hoochee river, and form line of battle near Powder Springs. This will prevent him from using the Dalton railroad, and force him to drive me off, or move south, when I shall fall upon his rear." It is strange to note how the very movement which Grant and Sherman were discussing, had been considered nearly as soon by the rebel general. He even appeared to desire the national advance, and purposely left the way open for Sherman into Central Georgia. Anticipating the probabilities of the campaign, Hood continued: " Would it not be well to move a part of the important machinery at Macon to the east of the Oconee, and do the same at Augusta to the east side of the Savannah ?" As Grant declared in his official report, the rebels " exhibited the weakness of supposing that an army which had been beaten and decimated in a vain attempt at the defensive could successfully undertake the offensive -against the force that had so often defeated it."

Sherman promptly reported the new manoeuvre of the enemy: "Hood is falling back from Lovejoy's. but I will not follow him now. I will watch him, as I do not see what he designs by this movement." He had not long to wait. The rebel President had come from Richmond to the camp of Hood, and all along the road, with extraordinary fatuity, proclaimed the new campaign. At Columbia, in South Carolina, at Macon, and at Palmetto station, he publicly announced that Atlanta was to be recovered ; that Forrest was already on the national roads in Middle Tennessee; that Sherman would meet the fate of Napoleon in the retreat from Moscow ; and, finally, addressing the army, he turned to a division of Tennessee troops, and exclaimed: " Be of good cheer, for in a short while your faces will be turned homeward, and your feet pressing Tennessee soil." This imprudent disclosure o.f the rebel plans was published in the Southern newspapers, and Sherman was of course forewarned. The speech at Macon was made on the 23rd of September, and on the 27th, Sherman telegraphed it to Washington.

Even on the 24th, however, Sherman had said : " I have no doubt Hood has resolved to throw himself on our flanks to prevent our accumulating stores, etc. here, trusting to our not advancing into Georgia." He accordingly ordered a division at once to Home, to protect the railroad. On the 25th, he said : " Hood seems to be moving as it were to the Alabama line, leaving open to me the road to Macon, as also to Augusta. If I was sure that Savannah would be in our possession, I would be tempted to make for Milledgeville and Augusta, but I must secure what I have." Forrest, however, was now rapidly advancing towards the railroad between Nashville and Chattanooga, two hundred miles in Sherman's rear, and Grant, with his usual pugnacity, preferred to fight the enemy before the march should be made. He replied to Sherman's telegram : " It will be better to drive Forrest from Middle Tennessee as a first step, and then do anything else that you may feel your force sufficient for. When a movement is made on any part of the sea-coast, I will advise you." The same day Sherman asked for reinforcements, saying: " In Middle Tennessee we are weak. ... I have already sent one division to Chattanooga and another to Kome. . . .

If I send back much more, I will not be able to threaten Georgia much."

In fact, every preparation was now rapidly making to resist the double attack which it was evident was about to be attempted on Sherman's extended communications. He himself called reinforcements from Kentucky, and concentrated at Nashville every man he could spare from the rear, while Grant directed all recruits and new troops to be sent to the same place, to receive their orders from Sherman. " It is evident," he said, " from the tone of the Richmond press, and all other sources, that the enemy intend making a desperate effort to drive you from where you are." " I shall give them another shake here before the end of the week." To Halleck, on the 28th of September, he telegraphed : " Everything indicates that the enemy are going to make a last and spasmodic effort to regain what they have lost, and especially against Sherman. Troops should be got to Sherman as rapidly as the lines of communication will carry them. If there are no troops in the Western states, then send them there from further East." On the same day, Sherman announced : " Forrest has got into Middle Tennessee, and will, I feel certain, get on my main road to-night or to-morrow; but I will guard well from this back to Chattanooga, and trust to troops coming up from Kentucky to hold Nashville and forward to Chattanooga." On the 28th, he sent Thomas in person back to Chattanooga, to supervise operations in Middle Tennessee.

It would indeed have been a sad ending to Sherman's brilliant campaign, to have lost his army in the heart of Georgia, for want of supplies, or to have been forced to make his way back to the Tennessee, discomfited and repelled. Armies larger than his and as successful at the start, had met such a fate before, in history; some in this very war; and on such a result the rebel President and his new general evidently counted ; such they promised their soldiers and people should be the end of the new campaign.

But although obliged for a while to retrace his steps and defend what he had won, Sherman was still looking to his onward march. The crisis so imminent in his rear only made him more eager to advance. On the 28th of September, he said : "1 want Appalachicola arsenal taken, also Savannah, and if the enemy does succeed in breaking up my roads, I can fight my way across to one or the other place; but I think better to hold on to Atlanta and strengthen to my rear, and am therefore glad you have ordered troops to Nashville." The emergency itself inspired him with bolder and still bolder conceptions ; his genius flashed like lightning through the darkness, and amid dangers that would have daunted many a brave soldier, he began to see his way across the Confederacy. At the same time, these tremendous demands upon Grant, these imperative calls that the chief should at once protect Nashville, three hundred miles in the rear, and take Appalachicola and Savannah, a thousand miles away, in front, show the absolute faith of Sherman that Grant both could and would supervise all. He had said himself six months before : " I tell you, this made us act with confidence. I knew ... if I got in a tight place, you would help me out, if alive."

On the 29th of September, Hood crossed the Chattahoochee, and on this day Grant made, as he 86 had promised, another movement in front of Richmond, partly in order to distract the rebels from too exclusive attention to Sherman, and partly to favor the operations of Sheridan in the Valley.On the 1st of October, Sherman reported the advance of Hood, and added : " If he tries to get on my road this side of the Etowa, I shall attack him; but if he goes on to Selma and Talladega [due west], why would it not do for me to leave Tennessee to the forces which Thomas has, and the reserves soon to come to Nashville, and for me to destroy Atlanta, and then march across Georgia to Savannah or Charleston, breaking roads and doing irreparable damage ?" This at last was the full-born thought. This was the idea which was afterwards embodied in the memorable march. This was to give up not only Atlanta, but the line in the rear to Chattanooga; to set out into an enemy's country, ignorant whether Hood would follow or not, and to push into the interior without supplies, until the sea should be reached. It was not to Augusta, but to Savannah, that Sherman now proposed to move, and it might be necessary at the end of the march, to fight before an exit could be made and supplies obtained.

But the rebels at once attacked the national railroad south of the Etowa, and Sherman was obliged to follow with his army. His whole attention for a while was concentrated upon the rear, and the new suggestion remained for a week or more unanswered. During this time, however,

Grant was considering Sherman's future and arranging to facilitate his operations, though without his knowledge. Sherman's telegram was dated October 1st, and on the 4th, the general-in-chief wrote to Halleck : " When this cam- paign was commenced nothing else was in contemplation but that Sherman, after capturing Atlanta, should connect with Canby at Mobile. Drawing the Nineteenth corps from Canby, however, and the movements of Kirby Smith demanding the presence of all of Canby's surplus forces in another direction, has made it impossible to carry out the plan as early as was contemplated. Any considerable force to co-operate with Sherman on the sea-coast must not be sent from here. The question is whether, under such circumstances, Augusta and Savannah would not be a better line than Selma, Montgomery, and Mobile. I think Savannah might be taken by surprise with one corps from here, and such other troops as Foster could spare from the Department of the South. This is my view, but before giving positive orders, I want to make a visit to Washington and consult on the subject. All Canby can do with his present force is to make demonstrations on Mobile, or up the Appalachicola towards Columbus."

Then came the reasons that recommended the movement: " Either line would cut off the supplies from the rich districts of Georgia, Alabama, and Mississippi equally well. Whichever way Sherman moves, he will undoubtedly encounter Hood's army, and in crossing to the sea-coast, will sever the connection between Lee's army and his district of country." Indeed, if Grant had not supposed that Hood would still be Sherman's objective point, he. certainly would neither have suggested nor commended the movement. But he went on to, say: " I wrote to Sherman on this subject, sending my letter by a staff officer. He is ready to attempt (and feels

confident of his ability to succeed) to make his way either to the Savannah river, or any of the navigable streams emptying into the Atlantic or Gulf, if he is only certain of finding a base for him when he arrives." On the 6th of October, the general-in-chief went to Washington, to ascertain definitely upon what reinforcements he could rely, and to shape his plans accordingly.

Meanwhile, as we have seen, when Hood had once crossed the Chattahoochee, Sherman was obliged, however reluctantly, to follow; but still, as corps after corps was sent north in pursuit, his despatches were full of suggestions of counter-moves ; he was looking back constantly to the fields that he preferred. " Keep your folks ready," he said to Schofield, "to send baggage into Atlanta, and to start on short notice." " If we make a counter-move, I will go out myself with a large force, and take such a route as will supply us, and at the same time make Hood recall the whole or part of his army." Thomas had now arrived in Chattanooga, and on the 30th of September, Sherman said to him : "There is no doubt some of Hood's infantry is across the Chattahoochee, but I don't think his whole army is across. If he moves his whole force to Blue Mountain, you watch him from the direction of Stevenson, and I will do the same from Rome, and as soon as all things are ready, I will take advantage of his opening to me all of Georgia."

Blue Mountain was at this time the terminus of the Selma and Talladega railroad, about sixty miles south-west of Rome ; and as Hood had now abandoned the Macon and "West Point roads, this was the nearest point at which he could connect with the few remaining railroads in the South. West. He must either move towards Blue Mountain, or to the Tennessee river, or attack Sherman's communications. He chose the last-named course, and at the same time Forrest captured Athens and moved up into the interior of Tennessee, threatening the line between Thomas and Nashville. On the 3rd of October, Hood reached Lost Mountain, which made it certain that he would attempt to strike the railroad in the neighborhood of Marietta, in Sherman's rear. Sherman at once ordered the Twentieth corps to hold Atlanta, and moved himself with the remainder of his army, upon Marietta.

He crossed the Chattahoochee on the 3rd and 4th of October, and learned that heavy masses of artillery, infantry, and cavalry had been seen from Kenesaw mountain, marching north.

Allatoona, where more than a million of rations were stored, was evidently their objective point. It was held by only a small brigade. Sherman signalled from mountain-top to mountain-top, over the heads of the enemy, a message for Corse, who was at Rome with a division of infantry, to hasten to the succor of Allatoona, and himself reached Kenesaw early on the morning of the 5th. But the rebels had already struck the railroad, and the whole line at his feet for fifteen miles was marked by the fires of the burning road. He could discern the smoke of the battle of Allatoona, and hear the faint reverberation of the cannon, eighteen miles away.

He at once ordered the Twenty-third corps to march due west, burning houses or piles of brush as it advanced, to mark the head of the column.

His hope was to interpose this corps between Hood and the detachment of five thousand rebels now attacking Allatoona. The remainder of the national army was directed straight upon Allatoona itself. The signal officer on Kenesaw mountain reported that since daylight he had failed to obtain any answer to his messages to Allatoona; but while Sherman was with him. he caught a glimpse of the tell-tale flag through an embrasure, and made out the letters C. K. S. E. H. E. R, and translated the message: " Corse is here." This was the first assurance Sherman had that Corse had received his orders, and that the place was adequately garrisoned.

He watched with painful suspense the indications of the battle, impatient enough at what seemed the slow approach of the relieving column, whose advance was marked by burning houses, according to orders; but about two o'clock the smoke about Allatoona grew less and less, and at four ceased altogether; and later the signal flag announced that the attack had been repulsed, but Corse was wounded. The next day Sherman's aide-de-camp received a despatch, not intended for history, but worthy to be preserved : " I am short a cheek-bone and an ear, but able to whip all hell yet."

The fight had been severe, but French, in command of the rebel detachment, was definitely repelled before the arrival - of the Twenty-third corps. He doubtless knew r of its approach, for he was in full retreat on the Dallas road before the head of the national column appeared. The rebels, however, had struck the railroad a heavy blow; the estimate for repairs called for thirty-five thousand new ties, and six miles of iron. But ten thousand men were distributed to repair the road, and in about seven days all was right again.*

Nevertheless, all this had delayed Sherman, and engrossed his attention. Between the 1st and the 9th of October he sent no despatch to the general-in-chief or to Washington, but on the last named day he renewed his recommendations to Grant. " It will be a physical impossibility to protect the roads, now that Hood, Forrest, Wheeler, and the whole batch of devils are turned loose without home or habitation. I think Hood's movements indicate a diversion to the end of the Selma and Talladega railroad, at Blue Mountain, about sixty miles southwest -of Rome, from which he will threaten Kingston, Bridgeport, and Decatur, Alabama. I propose that we break up the railroad from Chattanooga, and strike out with wagons for Milledgeville, Millen, and Savannah. Until we can repopulate Georgia it is useless to occupy it; but the utter destruction of its roads, houses, and people will cripple their military resources. By attempting to hold the roads we will lose one thousand men monthly, and will gain no result. I can make the march and make Georgia howl. ..."

On the 10th, he learned that Hood had crossed the Coosa river, between Eome and the railroad.

* At this time a national officer at the outposts overheard a group of rebel soldiers conversing. "Well," said one, "the Yankees must retreat now, for Wheeler has blown up the tunnel at Dalton, and they can get no more rations by the railroad." "Oh, hell!" replied another, "don't you know that Sherman carries a duplicate tunnel along 1 "

He was compelled again to follow, but on the way he telegraphed to Grant: " Hood is now crossing the Coosa, twelve miles below Home—bound west. If he passes over to the Mobile and Ohio road, had I not better execute the plan of my letter sent by Colonel Porter, and leave General Thomas with the troops now in Tennessee, to defend the state ? He will have an ample force when the reinforcements ordered reach Nashville."

Grant, however, with his usual desire to make armies his objective points, at first was unwilling for Sherman to turn his back on the enemy. A movement to the sea, it is true, had all along entered into his plans, and we have seen that as soon as Sherman took possession of Atlanta, the general-in-chief proposed that he should march towards the Savannah; but Grant then supposed that Hood would be in front, and that Sherman would be obliged to fight him. Hood, however, had now entirely changed the situation. By attacking Sherman's communications he had compelled that commander to retrace his steps nearly to Chattanooga ; and if Sherman turned off now to the southeast, he would leave Tennessee open to Hood, with nothing to withstand him but the forces that could be got together under Thomas. Grant always preferred to fight his enemy; Sherman, perhaps, liked better to win by manoeuvring. Grant, as we have constantly seen, believed that only the destruction of the rebel armies could end the war, and the proposition of Sherman to plunge into the interior, leaving Hood's army still undestroyed, at first did not strike him favorably.

He replied on the llth, at eleven A.M. : "Your despatch of October 10th received. Does it not look as if Hood was going to attempt the invasion of Middle Tennessee, using the Mobile and Ohio and the Memphis and Charleston roads to supply his base on the Tennessee river about Florence or Decatur ? If he does this, he ought to be met, and prevented from getting north of the Tennessee river. If you were to cut loose, I do not believe you would meet Hoods army, but would be bushwhacked by all the old men, little boys, and such railroad guards as are still left at home. Hood would probably strike for Nashville, thinking that by going north, he could inflict greater damage upon us than we could upon the rebels by going south. If there is any way of getting at Hoods army, I should prefer that; but I must trust to your judgment. I find I shall not be able to send a force from here to act with you on Savannah. Your movements therefore will be independent of mine ; at least until the fall of Richmond takes place. I am afraid Thomas, with such lines of road as he has to protect, could not prevent Hood from going north. With Wilson turned loose with all your cavalry, you will find the rebels put much more on the defensive than heretofore."*

Sherman, with his usual ardor, had not waited for Grant's reply, but on the llth, he sent the following despatch, dated the same hour with Grant's— eleven A.M. " Hood moved his army from Palmetto station, across by Dallas and Cedartown, and is now on the Coosa river, south of Rome. He threw one corps on my road at Ackworth, and I was

Wilson had been sent from Sheridan's army a few days bo-fore, to take command of Sherman's cavalry.forced to follow. I hold Atlanta with the Twentieth corps, and have strong detachments along my line. This reduces my active force to a comparatively small army. We cannot remain here on the defensive. With the twenty-five thousand men and the bold cavalry he has, he can constantly break my roads. I would infinitely prefer to make a wreck of the road and of the country from Chattanooga to Atlanta, including the latter city, send back all my wounded and worthless, and with my effective army, move through Georgia, smashing things, to the sea. Hood may turn into Tennessee and Kentucky, but I believe he will be forced to follow me. Instead of my being on the defensive, I would be on the offensive ; instead of guessing at what he means to do, he would have to guess at my plans. The difference in war is full twenty-five per cent. I can make Savannah, Charleston, or the mouth of the Chattahoochee. Answer quick, as I know we shall not have the telegraph long."

Grant answered the same night at 11.30 P.M. : " Your despatch of to-day received. If you are satisfied the trip to the sea-coast can be made, holding the line of the Tennessee firmly, you may make it, destroying all the railroad south of Dalton or Chattanooga, as you think best."

The only question on which they had for a few hours differed was whether it was not better to fight Hood before the march was made. Sherman declared that Hood would follow him; Grant was certain that the rebel army would go north. Sherman first suggested the destruction of the railroad, but to this Grant never objected, although it left the national army at the start a hundred and

fifty miles from any communications. But the more important point was whether Hood should be first destroyed. This Grant would undoubtedly have preferred. It was his nature to attack directly, and not evade, far less move away from, an enemy. But he had almost unbounded faith in Sherman's genius, and as has been often seen, he always took into consideration the temper of his subordinates. He believed also that confidence was one of the first requisites of success, and when he found his great lieutenant so impetuous in his eagerness, he gave the word. Yet he himself would probably never have made the march, leaving Hood in the rear. In the Yicksburg campaign, it is true, he moved away from Pember-ton, but it was to attack Johnston; and when he set out from the Mississippi, he fully intended to turn and crush Pemberton, as soon as Johnston was destroyed. Had he been in Sherman's place now, he would have been quite as determined to make the march, but not until Hood was annihilated.

He felt, however, that he was able to supervise all; to provide troops for Thomas sufficient to withstand Hood, and supplies to meet Sherman when he emerged; and his confidence in Sherman's generalship determined him to permit the move. "Such an army," he said to Stanton on the 13th, "and with such a commander, is hard to corner or to capture." This confidence was reciprocal. If Sherman could not have reposed absolutely on Grant, if he had not felt certain that the chief would provide supplies to meet him, wherever, on the Atlantic or the Gulf of Mexico, he should

strike the coast; if he had not been equally sure that Grant would protect the forces and the country that were left behind—he would no more have attempted the march than Grant would have allowed it, without his own belief in Sherman's ability to make it successful. It needed the two to conceive and perform their double parts in this act of the drama; neither was complete without the other.

It must, however, be remembered that Grant's responsibility continued far beyond Sherman's. Neither the general-in-chief nor the government^ nor, it must be said, Sherman himself, nor his own subordinates, by this time felt overweening anxiety about any of Sherman's great movements. He had shown too unmistakably that he possessed the qualities of a great commander. In this especial instance, Grant had no fear of absolute disaster to Sherman, and doubted not that he would find or fight his way to the sea-coast. It was not on account of Sherman, who was to set out with sixty thousand men, and no organized army to oppose him, that the anxiety was entertained. It was because Hood was left behind to contend with Thomas; and if Thomas was defeated, the states of Tennessee and Kentucky were opened to the enemy, and possibly the country beyond the Ohio. Here was the responsibility; here was the danger. Sherman would start on his novel, and romantic, and dashing campaign; with dangers in front and, possibly, behind; into an unknown region, where for a month he would be lost to the outer world. Hood might follow him, but Sherman had already defeated and depleted Hood ; and both Grant and Sherman knew that no other important

ULYSSES S. GRANT.

force could be collected in the entire South to oppose Sherman, so long as Lee was held at Richmond. But Thomas's troops were scattered from the Missouri to the Alleghanies. Sherman could no longer direct him ; would no longer be responsible for him ; and up to this time Thomas had never commanded an independent army; while great defeat on the Tennessee would balance all that the national forces had achieved in every other theatre of war. It was this that made Grant pause; it was this that alarmed the government, which opposed the movement from the beginning. It was this that made Thomas himself declare that he did not wish to be left behind to command the forces in defence of Tennessee.'"" It was this that made the great and supreme responsibility which the general-in-chief alone could and did assume.Sherman's proposed attempt was like, and also unlike, Grant's Vicksburg campaign. It was like, because it was abandoning one base, and seeking another ; plunging into an enemy's country, and relying on a hostile region for resources. It was unlike, because Sherman did not expect an enemy in his front, while Grant penetrated between two hostile forces; and because Sherman was uncertain where he should strike, while Grant intended from the beginning to reach the Walnut Hills. It was undoubtedly suggested by Grant's success behind Vicksburg; for Sherman had this one indisputable quality of greatness,—he could be convinced : and

" There is one thing, however, I don't wish—to be in command of the defence of Tennessee, unless you and the authorities in Washington deem it absolutely necessary."—Tliomas to Sherman, October 18.

although, originally, he had not favored the Vicks-burg campaign, yet when the result had demonstrated its practicability, he was willing to push its principles to the utmost. He contemplated now marching much further than Grant, when he left Grand Gulf; he proposed in some respects a grander movement. He did it, however, with the full concurrence of his chief, and aware that every preparation would await him on the coast; while Grant's campaign was countermanded, although too late, by Halleck, and he had to provide his own supplies. Grant moved with thirty-five thousand -men, Sherman, with sixty thousand : Grant's force was therefore easier to subsist, but less formidable in case it met an enemy. The campaigns were, in fact, two great and heretofore unparalleled movements in war, with points of striking likeness and dissimilarity.

As to the original idea of the march, the germ was undoubtedly Grant's; but Sherman's march was a far different one from that which Grant had contemplated. The general-in-chief, as has been shown, meant at the start to open a line from Chattanooga to Mobile; but he did not at the start propose to abandon the railroads, and he never meant, or would have proposed, to leave an enemy in his rear. Sherman did conceive his peculiar march, destroying Atlanta as Cortez burnt his ships, and abandoning the railroad as Grant did the Mississippi at Vicksburg; but Grant had conceived ano ther march much earlier. Grant first proposed that Sherman should move to Savannah whenever Canby was ready to meet him ; but—and this is the greatest and most audacious part of Sher- man's conception, and this is all his own he was willing to move to the sea, after he knew that Grant could send no forces to meet him. He destroyed his communications for a hundred and fifty miles to the rear, and he had none for three hundred miles in front, and this distance he had to march, uncertain whether at the close he should find friend or foe. All this was Sherman's own suggestion. There can be no depreciating the daring or the originality of the idea.

Whether an enemy followed him or not, whether he should meet one on the way, or at the end — of all this he was in ignorance. If Grant was able to care for the region that was left behind, so much the better; but if disaster came in the rear, what then ? while if by any chance, evil happened at the East, Lee might detach, or Davis assemble, an army between him and the sea. Grant had indeed contemplated opening a line to the coast; and if he had arrived at Atlanta, and found it impossible to hold his communications with Chattanooga, he would undoubtedly have desired to cut loose from both those points; but it still remains that it was Sherman who proposed this severance to Grant. The march to the sea—in ignorance of what the rebels might do in his rear, or what enemy might be found in his front, and without knowing where he should be able to strike the coast—all this was indisputably, and absolutely, and exclusively, the idea of Sherman.

While these great strategic schemes at the West were maturing, Grant had been planning another operation north of the James, in support of the movements of Sherman and Sheridan, and announced his intentions to both commanders in advance. On the 26th of September, he said to Sherman : " I will give them another shake here before the end of the week;" and the next day he sent word to Sheridan : " No troops have passed through Richmond to reinforce Early. . . I shall make a break here on the 29th." Like all his undertakings, however, this one was designed to be more than co-operative. Grant's idea of a demonstration always was that it might be converted into an absolute success ; and he made his preparations and issued his orders so that the movement he now contemplated should be susceptible of being carried, if necessary, to the inside of .Richmond.

The operation resembled in many respects his previous manoeuvres on the James. Butler was directed to hold Bermuda Hundred with artillery and some new regiments which had just arrived, so that the entire Tenth arid Eighteenth corps might be available. The troops were to cross the river by night and be ready on the morning of the 29th, to start from Deep Bottom and the Aiken House, and assault the enemy's lines. " The object of the movement," said Grant, "is to surprise and capture Richmond, if possible. This cannot be done if time is given to the enemy to move forces to the north side of the river. . . Should the outer line be broken, the troops will push for Richmond with all promptness. . . It is known that the enemy has entrenched positions back of the river, between Deep Bottom and Richmond, such as Chapin's Farm, which are garrisoned. If these can be captured in passing, they should be held." Then, with his usual determination, he added : " Should you succeed in getting to Rich-

ULYSSES S. GRANT.

mond, the interposition of the whole [rebel] army between you and your supports need cause you no alarm."*

But although thus inciting Butler, and anxious to take advantage of any success which that commander might attain, the general-in -chief at this time hardly hoped for the capture of Richmond, and carefully prepared for the alternative. The pith of Butler's instructions was in the words : " If the enemy resists you by sufficient force to prevent your advance, it is confidently expected that General Meade can gain a decisive advantage at his end of the line. The prize sought is either Bichmond, or Petersburg, or a position which will secure the fall of the latter." With Meade Grant was still more explicit: " Although the troops will be instructed to push directly for Richmond, if successful in breaking through the outer line of rebel works, it is hardly expected that so much can be accomplished. . . . Have the army of the Potomac under arms at four o'clock, A.M., on the 29th, ready to move in any direction. . . Should the enemy draw off such a force as to justify in moving either for the Southside road or Petersburg, I want you to do it without instructions, and in your own way. One thing, however, I would say : if the [rail] road is reached, or a position commanding it, it should be held at all hazards."

" Should you succeed in getting to Richmond, the interposition of the whole army between you and your supports need cause you no alarm. With the army under General Meade, supplies would be cut off from the enemy in the event of so unexpected a move, and communication be opened with you, either by-the south side or from the White House, before the supplies you would find in the city would be exhausted. Grant to Butler, September 27. 87

Meade was also directed to make a movement of troops towards the left, the day before Butler advanced, so as to give the appearance of massing in that direction. " The Tenth corps, moving to Bermuda Hundred to-night, will be missed from its position in the morning ; and if the enemy can be deceived into thinking they have gone around to the left, it will aid us."

At this juncture, Grant's cares and responsibilities were crowding upon him from every quarter, as closely as at any period during the war. While arranging the details of Butler's movement, withdrawing troops from the forts on the James, and directing pontoons to be towed out of sight of the enemy—he was obliged to discuss the condition of Canby on the Mississippi river, and the needs of commanders in East Tennessee ; to order reinforcements to Sherman, and to consult the Secretary of War about affairs in Missouri and the North-West; at the same time he forwarded the latest news from Sheridan, and wrote an elaborate letter to the government on the subject of the elections in the camps.*

Before dawn on the 29th of September, Butler moved from Deep Bottom ; the Eighteenth corps, under Ord, marched by the Varina road, nearest the river ; and the Tenth, under Birney, by the Newmarket road; while Kautz, with the cavalry, took the Darbytown road, on the right of the army. All these routes run direct to Richmond, only ten miles north of Deep Bottom. The attack by Ord on the left had been ordered for half-past three ; it was

* For this very interesting letter see page 167.not made until several hours later, but was then completely successful. Fort Harrison, the strongest rebel work north of the James, was carried, with fifteen guns, and a long line of entrenchments below Chapin's Farm. Several hundred prisoners also fell into Butler's hands. Ord, however, who commanded the assaulting column, was wounded in the leg and obliged to leave the field, and this circumstance prevented any further advantage being taken of the success at the moment, when time was all-important. Birney also had advanced on the right, and carried the entrenchments on the Newmarket road, scattering the enemy in every direction ; but he too halted when he should have pushed on with vigor.

Grant was at Deep Bottom in person at an early hour, and though anxious to remain at a point where he could communicate promptly with Meade, he rode out at this crisis to Butler's front, visiting first Birney's lines, and then the fort captured by the Eighteenth corps. This was a large enclosed work, projecting from the rebel line, but still commanded by other important batteries. Dismounting, in order to cross the ditch, Grant walked into the redoubt. The ground was covered with blood and shells, and here and there a dying rebel looked up vacantly at his captors; while from a work not many hundred yards away the enemy was throwing shells directly inside the parapet. Grant stepped upon the banquette and got a nearer view of the defences of Kichmond than he had at any time before been able to obtain. The whole line could be seen through the smoke, in reverse, for miles; and on the left, the spires of the rebel capital. He determined at once to push forward both wings of Butler's army, and seated himself on the ground, with his back to the parapet, to write the order. While he wrote, a shell burst immediately over his head, and instinctively every one around him stooped, to avoid the fragments. Grant did not look up, his hand was unshaken, and he went on writing his order as calmly as if he had been in camp.

The despatch was to Birney, and in these words : " General Ord has carried very strong works and some fifteen pieces of artillery, and his corps is now ready to advance in conjunction with you. . . . Push forward on the road I left you on." Having thus directed the immediate advance of Butler's entire command, the general-in-chief returned to Deep Bottom at noon, to communicate with Meade, from whom he had not heard since early morning. He announced the capture of Fort Harrison to Meade, and informed him that rebel reinforcements were arriving from Petersburg. " If this continues," he said, " it may be well for you to attack the enemy." Meanwhile, Kautz, with the cavalry, had advanced on the Darbytown road to a point within six miles of Richmond, and a division of Butler's infantry was ordered to his support.

But word soon came in that a gallant assault by Birney had been repulsed with heavy loss, and the whole advance was checked. The impetus of the first success was already lost, and everything in this movement depended upon celerity and surprise. The Eighteenth corps, on the left, however, had reached a point north of one of the rebel bridges on the James, so that Lee was now able to send troops from Petersburg to Butler's rear. Instructions had been given early in the day to destroy this bridge with artillery, but the national gunners were unable to reach it, and at mid-day Grant directed Butler: " If your troops do not reach Richmond this afternoon, my opinion is that it will be unsafe to spend the night north of the enemy's lower bridge. I think it advisable to select a line now to which the troops can be brought back to-night, if they do not reach Richmond." This was accordingly done, and a position taken up, extending from the river at Cox's ferry, to the Darby town road, where Kautz had pushed on to the line of redoubts nearest Richmond.

Thus the success of the day was limited to the capture of Fort Harrison in the morning, and a later advance on the right, by which no especial result was attained. The advantage gained by Ord had not been properly pushed at the instant; the enemy was warned and prepared for the second assault; and although the captured work was important, a rebel line of great strength still intervened between the national forces and Richmond.

Grant, however, as has been seen, had hardly hoped for better fortune north of the James, and meanwhile was waiting for developments at the other end of his line. At 3.50 P.M., he said to Butler : " I send you a despatch just received from General Meade. It would seem probable the enemy have sent but one division from Petersburg. It would be well under such circumstances to hold all the ground we can to-night, and feel out to the right in the morning."

During the day, the President sent an anxious

despatch about Sheridan, who had reached the head of the Valley and could no longer communicate with Washington. To this Grant replied: " I am taking steps to prevent Lee sending reinforcements to Early, by attacking him here." At four o'clock, he telegraphed again : " I did not expect to carry Richmond, but was in hopes of causing the enemy so to weaken the garrison of Petersburg as to be able to carry that place. The great object, however, is to prevent the enemy sending reinforcements to Early : " and still later : " Operations to-day prevented getting Richmond papers,* and consequently hearing of Sheridan. . . I am satisfied no troops have gone from here against him, and they cannot in the next two days. By that time he will be through, and on his way to a position where he can defend and supply himself."

In the meantime the rebels were evidently moving large bodies of troops from Petersburg to the Richmond front; and half an hour before midnight Grant said to Meade : " . . You need not move out at daylight, but be prepared to start, say at eight o'clock, if you find the enemy still further reduced, or if ordered. . . When you do move out, I think it will be advisable to manoeuvre to get a good position from which to attack, and then, if the enemy is routed, follow him into Petersburg, or where circumstances seem to direct. I do not think it advisable to try to extend our line to the South-side road, unless a very considerable part of the

* Information in regard to national movements was frequently-obtained from the rebel newspapers, and was especially valuable when commanders like Sherman and Sheridan were separated from their base or communications. enemy is drawn across the James, and then only when we are able to withdraw Butler's force rapidly and send it to you." Butler also was informed : " If the enemy have detached largely, Meade may be able to carry Petersburg. If so, I can send him two corps, using railroads and steamers for the infantry. On account of this attack I want to remain here through the day. I will go to Deep Bottom, now-ever, to meet you, leaving here at five A.M."

Before daylight, accordingly, Grant went up the river to Deep Bottom, and finding everything quiet in that quarter, at eight o'clock he returned to City Point, and sent orders to Meade to move out and see if an advantage could be gained. " General Butler's forces will remain where they are for the present, ready to advance, if found practicable. . . It seems to me the enemy must be weak enough at one or the other place to let us in." Meade, accordingly, with four divisions of infantry under Warren and Parke, advanced towards Poplar Spring church and Peeble's farm, about two miles west of the Weldon road, while Gregg's division of cavalry moved still further to the left and rear. Hancock was left in command of the trenches in front of Petersburg.

Warren, who held Meade's right in this movement, soon came upon the enemy entrenched at Peeble's farm; he made a vigorous attack, and carried two redoubts with a line of rifle-pits, capturing one gun and a hundred prisoners. Grant promptly announced the success to Butler, and cautioned him: " Be well on your guard, to act defensively. If the enemy are forced from. Petersburg, they may push to oppose you." To Meade he said : " If the enemy can be broken and started, follow him up closely. I can't help believing that the enemy are prepared to leave Petersburg, if forced a little." Later in the afternoon, Parke, moving on Warren's left, towards the Boydtown road, was fiercely attacked, and forced back with heavy loss ; but Warren sent a division promptly to his support, and the Ninth corps rallied. For a time the fighting was severe, but the rebels were finally repulsed, losing heavily in their turn. The position carried in the morning was held, and Warren entrenched himself, and extended his right to the Weldon road.

Butler also was assaulted, at Fort Harrison, three times during the afternoon. The loss of this work troubled the rebels greatly, for it commanded the shortest road to Richmond. Four divisions were hurried to the spot, Lee was present in person, and the troops were told the fort must be re-taken at every hazard. Their efforts were desperate, but each assault was repulsed, and Butler retained possession of his prize. The rebel loss was estimated at nearly one thousand killed and wounded,† and Butler reported the capture of more than two hundred prisoners. His own losses were insignificant. Thus, at each end of his line Lee made energetic efforts to regain what he had lost, and at each he was foiled.

Nevertheless, the rebels had made a good fight, and it was difficult to know at what point they were

As usual, Lee reported his first success, but failed to state that he was finally repulsed, and that the national troops retained possession of one of his forts.

Rebel War Clerk's Diary, Vol. II., page 297.

most vulnerable. At 9.40 P.M. on the 30th, Meade was instructed : "You need not advance to-morrow, unless in your judgment an advantage can be gained, but hold on to what you have, and be ready to advance. We must be greatly superior to the enemy in numbers on one flank or the other, and by working around at each end, we will find where the enemy's weak point is." To Butler Grant described the operations on the left, and said: " This would look as if no heavy force had been sent north of the James. I think it will be advisable for you to reconnoitre up the Darby town road, and if there appears to be any chance for an advance, make it." No further movement of importance, however, occurred on either front. The enemy modified his defensive line north of the James, and Grant strengthened Fort Harrison and turned its guns against those who had constructed it, while Butler pushed out his cavalry as far as the fortifications on the Charles City road; but neither army attempted another assault. On the 1st of October, Warren and Gregg were each attacked on the extreme left, but each repulsed the enemy; on the 2nd, Meade advanced his whole force and discovered the rebels, withdrawn to their main line, and refusing battle outside of fortifications. The necessary works were then laid out, and the national line was extended from the Weldon road to the position gained at Peeble's farm. This was a little more than a mile from the Boydtown road, and not more than two miles from the Southside railroad.

In these operations there were about sixty-six thousand men engaged on a side. Butler lost on the

29th and 30th of September, three hundred and ninety-four men killed, fifteen hundred and fifty-four wounded, and three hundred and twenty-four missing. Meade's losses, from September 30th to October 2nd, were one hundred and fifty-one killed, five hundred and ten wounded, and thirteen hundred and forty-eight missing. As usual, there is no record of the rebel loss.

The balancing character of the operations had now become extremely delicate. Ground had been gained by Grant at each extremity; the right and left wings were both advanced under the very eye of Lee; north of the river, the rebel line was actually broken, and a position had been seized full of danger to Richmond; while on the left, the enemy seemed almost out-flanked at last. Nevertheless, with his admirable defences and the immense advantage of interior lines, Lee was still able to hold the national columns off, until reinforcements could be thrown from one side to the other of the James. Holding the chord of the circle, he could transfer troops in a few hours, while Grant, on the arc, required a day to move his men from Petersburg to the Richmond front, or from Fort Harrison to Peeble's farm. The superiority in numbers possessed by one was more than equalized by the position the other enjoyed.

Grant, however, was steadily .acquiring ground which must in the end enable him to drive the rebels out of both Richmond and Petersburg. Lee could not possibly stretch his line much further, and the greatest consternation prevailed in Richmond at these double assaults. Refugees and- prisoners reported that the evacuation of the city was con-

templated, lest the lines of supply, or even of retreat, should be intercepted. The local reserves were in Butler's front, even to the police and the clerks of the government. The publication of the newspapers was suspended, for the printers were called out to defend the city. Offices and shops were closed ; the church bells sounded the alarm for hours; and when the capture of Fort Harrison became known, the excitement was greater than ever before. Guards were sent into the streets to impress every able-bodied man they met, and even members of the government did not escape arrest. Every white male in Richmond between the ages of seventeen and fifty-five was ordered under arms.

But it was not only the inhabitants of Richmond who were alarmed. On the 4th of October, Lee himself wrote to his government in desponding terms. " I beg leave to inquire whether there is any prospect of my obtaining any increase to this army. If not, it will be very difficult for us to maintain ourselves. The enemy's numerical superiority enables him to hold the lines with an adequate force, and extend on each flank with numbers so much greater than ours that we can only meet his corps increased by recent recruits, with a division reduced by long and arduous service.* We cannot fight to advantage with such

* The disparity in numbers was by no means so great as Lee declared. The returns of each array for the month of September show Grant's fighting force, in the armies of the Potomac and the James, to have been 76,000, and Lee's 50,000. There were besides 6,000 rebel troops in the Department of Richmond, and several thousand local reserves in the city, all of whom were sent to the front at this crisis. The national divisions had been reduced by odds, and there is the gravest reason to apprehend the result of every encounter. . . It is certain that the need of men was never greater. . . The men at home on various pretexts must be brought out and put in the army at once, unless we would see the enemy reap the great moral and material advantages of a successful issue of this most costly campaign. . . If we can get our entire arms-bearing population in Virginia and North Carolina, and relieve all detailed men with negroes, we may be able, with the blessing of God, to keep the enemy in check till the beginning of winter. If we fail to do this, the result may be calamitous."There have been critics who pronounced Grant's method of extending north and south of the James simultaneously a blunder; but Lee, it appears, was of a different mind. the same "long and arduous service" as Lee's, and Grant's " recent recruits " had not been numerous. The above statement of the national force includes the garrisons of the various forts on the James, as well as all details. There were not more than 66,000 men engaged in the two movements of Butler and Meade, including those in the trenches.

ULYSSES S. GRANT.

CHAPTER XXVII.
Grant directs Sheridan to move upon Charlottesville—Sheridan recommends reduction of his command—Lee reinforces Early—Sheridan moves down the Valley—Early follows—Cavalry battle at Tom's Brook—Rout of the rebels—Sheridan moves to Cedar Creek—Sheridan summoned to Washington—Wright left in command—Early determines to attack Sheridan's army—Topography—Battle of Cedar Creek—Movement of Early, in night of October 18th—Assault on left of national army—Wright driven back in confusion seven miles—Sheridan arrives at Winchester on 18th— Rides towards Cedar Creek on 19th—Turns the tide of fugitives—" Face the other way"—Re-forms the line—Last attack of Early repulsed— Sheridan attacks in his

turn—Rout of the rebels—Magnitude of rebel disaster—End of campaign in Shenandoah Valley—Sheridan's military achievements and character—Faults of Early—End of Early's career-Grant's policy of destroying resources of the Valley—Justified by necessity, by results, and by course pursued by rebels—Grant moves against Lee's communications—Instructions to Meade and Butler—Geography of country —Army of Potomac crosses Hatcher's run—Warren fails to connect with Hancock—Grant at Burgess's mill—Enemy's line found to extend further than expected—Grant suspends operation—Returns to City Point, supposing connection made between Warren and Hancock—Enemy comes into gap between Fifth and Second corps—Gallant behavior of Egan—Repulse of rebels—Butler moves against fortified works, contrary to orders— Repulse of Butler—Criticism of entire movement—General remarks on Grant's operations before Petersburg.

WHILE these events were passing in Georgia and on the James, Sheridan had advanced as far as Staunton and Waynesboro', south of which points no rebel force at this time existed in the Valley. Until the 1st of October, he was occupied in carrying out Grant's commands for the destruction of crops and mills, and on that day he reported: "The rebels have given up the Valley, excepting Waynesboro', which has been occupied by them since our cavalry was there." The general-in-chief was now extremely anxious that Sheridan should strike the railroads east of the mountains, by which important supplies were still conveyed to Richmond. As early as the 26th of September, he said : " If you can possibly subsist your army at the front for a few days more, do it, and make a great effort to destroy the roads about Charlottes-ville, east of the Blue Ridge." Sheridan, however, was opposed to this movement, and replied at once : " The difficulty 'of transporting this army through the mountain passes on to the railroad at Char-lottesville is such that I regard it as impracticable with my present means of transportation. ... I think that the best policy will be to let the burning of the crops of the Valley be the end of this campaign, and let some of this army go somewhere else."

It is not every general who, after a successful campaign, recommends his own command to be reduced and his troops distributed; but Sheridan always cared more for his cause than for his own interest or importance. He was now very much in earnest, and wrote the same day to Halleck: "I strongly recommend General Grant to terminate this campaign by the destruction of the crops in the Valley and the means of planting, and the transfer of the Sixth and Nineteenth corps to his army at Richmond. . . There is now no objective point but Lynchburg, and it cannot be invested on the

line of this valley, and the investing army supplied. . . With Crook's force the Valley can be held." To this Grant replied on the 3rd of October; " You can take up such position in the Valley as you think can and ought to be held, and send all the force not required for this immediately here." This, it has been seen, was always his policy. He disliked to overrule the judgment of a distant subordinate ; if he distrusted a general, he preferred to remove him; but in Sheridan he now placed almost implicit confidence.

He still, however, omitted no precaution which, as general-in-chief, it was his duty to employ, and carefully considered the supplies and communications of his lieutenant in the Valley. On the 27th of September, he said to Halleck : " I think the railroad towards Sheridan should be put in order as far as protection can be furnished for it. . . I would like Sheridan to decide which road should be opened ;" and on the same day he ordered : " Now that Sheridan has pushed so far up the Valley, General Augur should send, if it is possible, a force of cavalry and infantry out by Culpeper, with scouts, as far as they can go, to watch if any troops move north on the east side of the Blue Ridge, to get in upon Sheridan's rear."

At the same time, he was watching the effect which events in the Valley might have on the devices and movements of Lee. On the 1st of October, he said to Butler :. "The strong works about Chapin's Farm should be held or levelled. Sheridan, for want of supplies, if there should be no other reason, will be forced to fall back. The enemy may take advantage of such an occurrence to bring the rem-

nants of Early's force here, relying upon his ability to get it back to the Valley before Sheridan could fit up and return. In such case he would fall upon either flank as now exposed, and inflict great damage." Again, on the 3rd, he said : " A despatch is just received from Sheridan up to the 1st instant. The enemy have entirely left his front and gone to Charlottesville or Gordonsville.* He cannot reach them there, so that we may now confidently expect the return here of at least Kershaw's division and Rosser's cavalry-. It will require very close watching to prevent being surprised by the reinforcement." Thus, Early's manoeuvres furnished a reason for levelling or holding the forts on the James; so completely was the campaign in the Valley a part of the operations against Bichmond.

But Lee could not yet make up his mind to Abandon the important region beyond the Blue Ridge. Early had not absolutely crossed the mountains, but only fled to their western base, and after his defeats at Winchester and Fisher's Hill, Kershaw and Fitz-Lee were ordered to return to him. Kershaw had already reached Culpeper on his way to Richmond, but on the receipt of these orders, he re-crossed the Blue Ridge at Swift's Gap, and came up with the beaten army on the 25th of September, at Brown's Gap, where Lomax and Fitz-Lee had arrived the day before. Rosser's brigade

* " Early was driven out of the Valley, and only saved himself by getting through Brown's Gap in the night, and has probably taken position at Charlottesville, and will probably fortify, holding Waynesboro' and Rockfish Gap." Sheridan to Halleck, Oct. 1. This information afterwards proved incorrect, but it was the foundation for the despatch quoted in the text.

of cavalry had also been sent from Lee's army, and reported to Early on the 5th of October; troops were ordered from Breckenridge, at this time in South-West Virginia; while all the reserves in the Valley were embodied and placed under Early's command. Altogether these reinforcements amounted to more than ten thousand men,* and Early, now finding himself stronger than he had been at Winchester, determined to attack the national forces in position at Harrisonburg.

But on the 6th of October, Sheridan began his retrograde movement, stretching the cavalry across the Valley from the Blue Ridge to the eastern

* " The arrival of Kershaw will add greatly to your strength. . . All the r<»serves in the Valley have been ordered to you. Breck-enridge will join you, or co-operate, as circumstances will permit, with all his force. Rosser left this morning for Burksville . . where he will shape his force as you direct."— Lee to JEarly, Sept. 27. Early also admits the arrival of Fitz-Lee and Lomax's cavalry. He states in his Memoir that Rosser's brigade did not exceed 600 mounted men for duty, and that Kershaw's division numbered 2,700 ' \'7d he gives no estimate of Fitz-Lee or Lomax's strength, and says not a word of Breckenridge or the reserves; but declares that " these reinforcements about made up my losses at Winchester and Fisher's Hill."

The returns, however, tell a different tale. The latest from these commands, prior to Sept. 27, were as follows :—

July 10 Fitz-Lee 1,706 effective.
Aug. 31 Kershaw 3,445 ,,
Sept. 10 Lomax 3,568 ,,

Breckenridge succeeded late in September to the command in South-West Virginia, and on the 13th of that month, Echols, his predecessor, reported 3,904 effective men. I can find no return of Rosser's force, n6r of the reserves ; but Grant telegraphed to Halleck, Sept. 30: "Rosser's brigade of cavalry has gone to Early. The brigade numbered 1,400 men."

It has already been shown that the rebels never include the 88

slope of the Alleghanies, with directions to burn all forage and drive off all stock, as they moved to the rear. This was in compliance with Grant's orders to " leave nothing for the subsistence of an army on any ground abandoned to the enemy." " The most positive orders were given, however, not to burn dwellings." Early followed at a respectful distance, but on the 8th, his cavalry under Rosser, came up with Sheridan near Woodstock, and harassed Ouster's division as far as Tom's Brook, three or four miles south of Fisher's Hill. That night Torbert, in command of the national horse, was ordered to engage the rebel cavalry at daybreak, and notified

reserves ill any statement of their strength, although these were always put into battle, and fought as well as any. Early speaks, page 97 of his Memoir, of two companies of reserves, coming from different points, one with two pieces of artillery, and covering Kockfish Gap against Sheridan's cavalry; it is difficult to see why such troops should not be included in an estimate of his force.

In the same way, in computing Lee's numbers, the rebels and their friends never reckon the troops, 5,000 to 7,000, in the city of Richmond, nor the local reserves, who were put into the trenches in every battle. Yet from these two sources alone Lee had always an addition to his fighting force of 10,000 soldiers. The endeavors of the rebels since the war to belittle the strength of their armies are as ingenious as their strategy was in the field, but hardly so creditable.

On the 6th of October, an order was published by the rebel government, revoking all details from the army of persons between the ages of sixteen and forty-five. "If this be rigidly enforced, it will add many thousands to the army. It is said there are 8,000 details in the military bureaux of this state."— Rebel War Clerk's Diary. " From General Early's army we learn that the detailed men and reserves are joining in great numbers, and the general asJcs 1,000 muskets."October l.—Ibid., Yol. II., p. 310.

that the infantry would halt until after the defeat of the enemy. At an early hour on the 9th, the heads of the opposing columns came in contact, and after a short but severe engagement, the rebels were completely routed, losing eleven guns, together with caissons, battery forges, head-quarters' wagons, and everything else that was carried on wheels. Three hundred and thirty prisoners were captured. Sheridan's casualties did not exceed sixty. He reported the battle in his usual vigorous style : " The enemy, after being charged by our gallant cavalry, were broken, and ran; they were followed by our men on the jump twenty-six miles, through Mount Jackson, and across the North Fork of the Shenandoah. I deemed it best to make this delay of one day here to settle this new cavalry general." The eleven pieces of artillery taken this day made thirty-six cannon captured in the Yalley since the 19th of September. Some of it was new and had never been used before. It had evidently just arrived from Richmond, as the rebels said, " for General Sheridan, care of General Early."

The unlucky commander reported his new defeat in an agony of shame. " God knows I have done all in my power to avert the disasters which have befallen this command, but the fact is that the enemy's cavalry is so much superior to ours both in numbers and equipment, and the country is so favorable to the operations of cavalry, that it is impossible for ours to compete with his." Lomax's " command is and has been demoralized all the time. It would be better if they could all be put into the infantry, but if that were tried, I am afraid they would all run off. . . Sheridan has laid waste nearly

all of Rockingham and Stienandoah, and I shall have to rely on Augusta for my supplies, and they are not abundant here. Sheridan's purpose under Grant's orders has been to render the

Valley untenable by our troops, by destroying the supplies. . . What shall I do if he sends reinforcements to Grant, or remains in the lower Valley V

On the 10th of October, the national army resumed its march, the main body crossing to the north side of Cedar Creek, while the Sixth corps moved as far as Front Royal, on its way to rejoin Meade ; but after his third defeat, Early did not venture further down the Valley until the 12th. On that day he heard that Sheridan was preparing to send part of his troops to the army of the Potomac, and accordingly the rebel command was advanced as far as Fisher's Hill. In consequence of this movement, however, the Sixth corps was at once recalled, to await the development of Early's new intention.

Grant meanwhile, though deferring to the opinion of Sheridan, so far as to direct the return of the Sixth corps to Meade, had not abandoned his views in regard to the necessity of breaking up the railroads east of the Blue Ridge. On the 11th of October, he said to Halleck: " After sending the Sixth corps and one division of cavalry here, I think Sheridan should keep up as advanced a position as possible towards the Virginia Central road, and be prepared to advance on to that road at Gordonsville and Charlottesville at any time the enemy weakens himself sufficiently to admit of it. The cutting of that road and of the canal would

be of vast importance to us." This despatch he directed should be sent to Sheridan ; but Halleck added to the order and otherwise modified it in transmission. " Lieutenant-General Grant wishes a position taken far enough south to serve as a base for further operations upon Gordonsville and Char-lottesville. It must be strongly fortified and provisioned. Some point in the vicinity of Manassas Gap would seem best suited for all purposes. Colonel Alexander, of the engineers, will be sent to consult with you." Grant had said nothing about fortifying, or provisioning, or about Manassas Gap, or consulting with engineers. He left all these details entirely to Sheridan, in whose independent judgment Halleck even yet appeared to have but little confidence.

Sheridan still objected to the plan as it was proposed to him; and on the 14th, Grant telegraphed : " What I want is for you to threaten the Virginia Central railroad and canal in the manner your judgment tells you is best, holding yourself ready to advance, if the enemy draw off their forces. If you make the enemy hold a force equal to your own for the protection of those thoroughfares, it will accomplish nearly as much as their destruction. If you cannot do this, then the next best thing to do is to send here all the force you can. I deem a good cavalry force necessary for your offensive, as well as defensive operations. You need not therefore send here more than one division of cavalry." On the 13th of October, Sheridan was summoned to Washington by the Secretary of War, who telegraphed direct : " If you can come here, a consultation on several points is extremely desirable.

I propose to visit General Grant, and would like to see you first."

On the evening of the 15th, accordingly, Sheridan set out for the capital. There seemed no prospect of an immediate movement of the enemy, and the entire cavalry force accompanied him as far as Front Royal; for, like a good soldier, he intended to push Torbert through Chester Gap as far as Charlottesville, in accordance with Grant's views, although he disagreed with them. On the night of the 16th, he arrived at Front Royal, but there received a despatch from Wright, who had been left at Cedar Creek, in command of the army. A message to Early had been intercepted; it was in these words : " Be ready to move as soon as my forces join you, and we will crush Sheridan. — LONGSTREET." This information was contrary to any possessed by either Grant or Sheridan. Longstreet was believed to be at Richmond, and no rebel force existed either in or near the Valley, except that which Early himself commanded. The despatch had been taken from a rebel signal station, and was probably incorrectly rendered; but it served to warn Sheridan, who at once abandoned the cavalry raid, and ordered Torbert to return to Wright at Cedar Creek.

This was on Sunday, the 16th of October. Wright had announced : " If the enemy should be strongly reinforced in cavalry, he might, by turning our right, give us a. great deal of trouble. I shall hold on here until the enemy's movements are developed, and shall only fear an attack on my right, which I shall make every preparation for guarding against and re-

sisting." To this Sheridan replied from Front Royal: " The cavalry is all ordered back to you; make your position strong. If Longstreet's despatch is true, he is under the impression that we have largely detached. . . Close in on General Powell, who will be at this point. If the enemy should make an advance, I know you will defeat him. Look well to your ground, and be well prepared." He then went on to Washington. Grant meanwhile had been notified of the intercepted despatch, and telegraphed at once to Halleck : " Sheridan should follow and break up Longstreet's force, if he can, and either employ all the force the enemy now have in the Valley, or send his surplus forces here."

Early was indeed preparing for a supreme effort to crush Sheridan. It is impossible not to admire the determination and the spirit of the commander who, after the succession of disasters which had broken his army, could so soon attempt an offensive movement against a victorious enemy. But whatever his faults, Early was morally as well as physically brave. He had now, however, been heavily reinforced; his army was as large as before the battle of Winchester, while Sheridan's command had not been increased. Early knew besides that great dissatisfaction existed both in the army and out of it, because of his reverses; the Governor of Virginia had peremptorily urged that he should be relieved, and although Lee had generously supported his subordinate, he had nevertheless written in the strongest terms to stimulate the unfortunate commander. "Every one should exert all his energies and strength to

meet the emergency. One victory will put all things right. You must do all in your power to invigorate your army. Manoeuvre so, if you can, as to keep the enemy in check till you can strike him with all your strength. . . You must use the resources you have so as to gain success. The enemy must be defeated, and I rely upon you to do it." Spurred on thus by every motive, personal and military, by ambition, hope, revenge, and desperation, as well as by unflinching loyalty to his cause, Early made one more effort to overthrow his redoubtable antagonist. He had, besides, the very practical incentive of utter lack of supplies. " I was now," he says, " compelled to move back for want of provisions and forage, or attack the enemy in his position with the hope of driving him from it, and I determined to attack."

Cedar Creek empties into the North Fork of the Shenandoah river about two miles east of Stras-burg. At this point the creek runs nearly south and the river east, but in both streams there are many windings. The national army lay entrenched on the eastern bank of the creek and north of the Fork, with its left about a mile from the junction,— an exceedingly strong position. The rebels were encamped at Fisher's Hill, five miles away. On the night of the 16th of October, Early sent Rosser with two brigades of cavalry, and one of infantry mounted behind the horsemen, to make a reconnois-sance of the national right. The position, however, was found well guarded, for it was here that Wright apprehended an attack; * and Early accordingly

* See page 90.

turned Ms attention to the opposite flank, where Sheridan had directed Wright to close in on Powell. But Powell was at the junction of the South Fork with the Shenandoah river, seven miles at least from the left of the national command. Early had a signal station on Masanutten mountain from which he ascertained exactly the situation of the national camps. The cavalry was on the right, Crook had the left, while the Sixth and Nineteenth corps, under Getty and Emory, lay between. To turn the left of "Wright's command the rebels must first cross the North Fork near Fisher's Hill, then move by a rugged pathway between the base of the mountain and the stream, and finally re-cross the river at a ford below the mouth of Cedar Creek. The road at the foot of the mountain was impracticable for artillery ; but Torbert's cavalry was massed on the opposite flank, and Rosser's reconnoissance had attracted attention to that quarter, so that it was closely picketed. Early, therefore, determined to attack the national left.

Accordingly, on the night of the 18th of October, he sent three divisions of infantry across the North Fork and around the mountain, under command of Gordon, one of the ablest of the rebel generals; while with Kershaw and Wharton he himself marched direct through Strasburg. The plan was for Gordon to move around in the national rear, Kershaw ta attack the left flank, and Wharton to advance in front with the artillery, which would open on Wright as soon as he turned upon Gordon and Kershaw. Rosser was sent to the national right, to occupy the cavalry, and Lomax (who had been pushed down the Luray Valley) was ordered to pass by Front Royal, cross the Shenandoah river, and seize the road to Winchester, in the rear of the national army. It was one of the best concerted schemes of the war.

Soon after dark the rebels moved silently from Strasburg and Fisher's Hill. Favored by night and a heavy fog, Gordon crossed the river, crept unobserved under the guns of Crook, re-crossed the North Fork at Bowman's ford, and before daybreak had struck the rear of Wright's command. Kershaw's attack on the national left was simultaneous, and the outposts were driven in, the camps invaded, the position was turned. This was followed by a direct attack along the entire front, and the whole national left was driven back in confusion. Eighteen pieces of cannon were captured, and nearly a thousand prisoners; a very large part of the infantry not preserving even a company organization. The Sixth corps on the right, however, had not been surprised ; the firing on the left gave it warning, and there was time for Getty * to form and move out of camp to a ridge west of the main road, where considerable resistance was offered. But the rebel artillery was now brought up and opened fire, and Getty fell back to the north of Middletown, where he again made a stand. Custer and Merritt were at this time transferred to the left of the line, to protect the road to Winchester, which Lomax had not seized; and a general retreat was ordered. The condition of the troops was still deplorable, and the whole army fell back to a point six or seven miles in rear of its first position in the morning.

* Ricketts commanded the Sixth corps at daybreak, but was wounded early in the battle, when Getty took his place.

Sheridan had arrived at Washington on the 17th, and at noon the next day he set out to return. On the 18th, he slept at Winchester, twenty miles from his command. At an early hour on the 19th, an officer on picket reported artillery firing, but a reconnoissance had been ordered for that morning, and no attention was paid to the news. At nine o'clock Sheridan rode out of Winchester, still unconscious of the danger of his army. But the sounds of heavy battle soon became unmistakable ; and half a mile from the town the head of the fugitives came in sight, trains and men, with appalling rapidity. He immediately gave directions to halt and park the trains, and ordered the brigade at Winchester to stretch across the country and stop all stragglers. Then, with an escort of twenty men, he pushed to the front, leaving his staff to do what they could to stem the torrent of fugitives. His presence had an electrical effect. He rode hot haste, like a courier, swinging his hat, and shouting as he passed : " Face the other way, boys ! we are going back. Face the other way !" and hundreds of the men turned at once and followed him with cheers.

It was ten o'clock when he reached the front, where he found Merritt and Ouster's cavalry under Torbert, and Getty's division of the Sixth corps opposing the enemy. He at once determined to fight on Getty's line, transferring Custer to the right again, and bringing up the remaining divisions of the Sixth corps, which were two miles to the right and rear. The Nineteenth corps, still further to the right and rear, was also ordered up in line. At first he sent staff officers to hasten these troops,

but soon, convinced that another attack was imminent, he went back in person to urge them on. And now the magnetic influence of the man told in a wonderful way upon the scattered soldiers. He was in full major-general's uniform, mounted on a magnificent black horse, man and beast covered with dust and foam ; and rising in his stirrups, waving his hat and his sword by turns, he called out again and again: " If I had been here, this never would have happened. We are going back. Face the other way, boys ! Face the other way ! " The fugitives recognized their general, stopped at once, and took up the cry : " Face the other way!" It passed rapidly along from one to another, swelling and rolling, like a wave of the sea; the men returned in crowds, falling into ranks as they came, and the discomfited mob was converted again into a line of soldiers. With that wonderful instinct which comes upon men in battle, they knew that they were being led to victory.

Wright now returned to his corps, Getty to his division, and Sheridan was in command. A compact line of battle was formed, and a breastwork of rails and logs thrown up, just in time. Sheridan could see the rebel columns moving to the attack, but his army was prepared. The assault fell principally on the Nineteenth corps, which had lost eleven guns earlier in the day, but now repulsed the enemy handsomely. This was about one o'clock.

The rebels had made their last effort, and exhausted themselves. Gordon, Kershaw, and Eosser all reported that they were unable to advance. The national cavalry threatened their left, and where they expected a broken and disordered mass in front,

they found a steady line of infantry. Early's men, too, had suffered the demoralization which often follows victory. Their success had been so absolute, and happening after so many defeats, was so intoxicating, that the troops became uncontrollable. The destitute soldiers stopped in the captured camps for plunder, even the officers participating, and Early did not deem it prudent to attempt a further advance. He determined to hold the ground he had gained, and endeavor to secure the captured guns and other property.

But Sheridan had different views. The strength of the Sixth and Nineteenth corps was still rapidly augmenting, as the men returned who had gone to the rear early in the day. Even those who had reached Newtown, ten miles away, came back to fight, and such is the strange inconsistency of human nature, many of those who fled panting and panic-stricken in the morning had covered themselves with the glory of heroes long before night. At about three P.M., the national army advanced; a left half wheel of the whole line was made, a division of cavalry turning each flank of the enemy, Ouster on the right. The attack was brilliantly made, but the enemy was protected by rail breastworks, and at some points by stone fences, and the resistance was determined. The rebel line of battle also overlapped the right of Sheridan's, and for a time threatened disaster ; but a turning movement of Early was checked by a counter-charge, led by Sheridan himself, upon the re-entering angle formed by the enemy, and the flanking party was cut off. Gordon's division, on Early's left, first broke, then Kershaw, and finally Eamseur. An attempt was

MILITARY HISTORY OF

made to rally them, and with the help of artillery, the national advance was checked for a while; but Sheridan soon pushed on, and the rebel left again gave way. Upon this the panic spread, when Early gave a general order to retreat, and the whole command fell back in the greatest confusion.

At this stage of the battle Ouster was ordered to charge with his entire division. Simultaneously with his charge, a combined movement of the whole line drove the enemy to the creek, where, owing to the difficulties of crossing, the retreat became a rout. The rebel officers found it impossible to rally their troops; the men would not listen to entreaties, threats, or appeals of any sort. A terror of the national cavalry had seized them, and there was no holding them back. The captured guns had already been carried across Cedar Creek, and Early had also succeeded in passing his own artillery; but Custer now found a ford west of the road, and Devin, with a brigade of Merritt's cavalry, another to the east; each made the crossing just after dark, and dashing across the creek, they got among the wagons and artillery; then, passing through Early's men to the southern side of Strasburg, they tore up the bridge over the North Fork, and thus succeeded in capturing the greatest part of the guns and a number of ordnance and medical wagons and ambulances. The rebel soldiers were scattered on both sides of the road, and the rout was as thorough and disgraceful as ever happened to an army. From Cedar Creek to Fisher's Hill the road was literally blocked with wagons, caissons, ambulances, and artillery.

After the utter failure of all attempts to rally his men, Early went in person to Fisher's Hill, in the hope of forming them in the trenches ; but when that position was reached, the only organized body left was the column of national prisoners taken in the morning, and the provost guard ; and Early declared that it was the appearance of these prisoners, moving in a body, which alone arrested the progress of Sheridan's cavalry; for it was too dark to discover what they really were. About two thousand rebels made their way to the mountains, and for ten miles the line of retreat was covered with small arms and other debris thrown away by the flying enemy. Night alone preserved the fragments of the force from absolute annihilation. Early himself escaped under cover of darkness to Newmarket, twenty miles from Cedar Creek, where once before, on a similar occasion, his army had come together, by the numerous roads converging there. From this point, on the 20th, he announced to Lee : " The enemy is not pursuing, and I will rest here and organize my troops."

Sheridan took possession of Strasburg after the battle; and in the morning he proceeded to Fisher's Hill. He had retaken all the guns lost by Wright, and captured twenty-four pieces of artillery besides. Sixteen hundred prisoners were brought in, and three hundred wagons. Early reported eighteen hundred and sixty killed and wounded. His reinforced command was now in a worse condition than that which had been beaten at Winchester and Fisher's Hill.The unfortunate commander made no attempt at the time to conceal the extent of his disaster. It would, he knew, have been in vain. One cannot but pity the general obliged to pen such sentences as these : " The victory already gained was lost by the subsequent bad conduct of the troops. . . It is mortifying to me, General, to have to make these explanations of my reverses; they were due to no want of effort on my part, though it may be that I have not the capacity or judgment to prevent them . . I know that I shall have to endure censure from those who do not understand my position and my difficulties, but I am still willing to make renewed efforts." Then, conscious of what was inevitable, he suggested his own dismissal. "If you think, however, that the interests of the service would be promoted by a change of commanders, I beg you will have no hesitation in making the change. The interests of the service are far beyond any personal consideration; and if they require it, I

* The details of the rebel disaster, given in the text, are taken from Early's letters to Lee at the time, the contents of which he appears to have forgotten, for in his Memoir he denies the completeness of the defeat, and says it was the case of a " glorious victory given up by his own troops after they had won it," " from the fact that the men undertook to judge for themselves

when it was proper to retire," which, it may be said, beaten troops very generally do. He also scouts the idea that his army was "wrecked" or "fled in dismay before its pursuers." I have therefore inserted his letters to Lee, in full, in the Appendix, to correct his memory.

One of his later statements, however, is disproved by other documents, doubtless also inaccessible to him when he wrote. He declares in the Memoir that he went into the battle of Cedar Creek with 8,500 muskets, and he admits a loss of 3,000 men, besides stragglers; yet on the 31st of October, twelve days after the battle, he reported officially to Richmond, 10,577 effective infantry, having received no reinforcements in the meantime.am willing to surrender my command into other hands."

This battle ended the campaign in the Shenan-doah valley. The rebels made no further attempt to invade the North, and the various detachments of Sheridan's army marched whithersoever they wished, for the whole country between the Potomac and the James was practically in the national hands. The instructions of Grant, faithfully carried out, to denude the Valley of forage and provisions rendered it impossible for the enemy to subsist a large force west of the Blue Ridge; Kershaw's division was therefore returned to Lee, and Cosby's cavalry to Breckenridge ; and not long afterwards an entire rebel corps was transferred to Richmond, leaving with Early only one division of infantry and the cavalry. He was never again entrusted with a command large enough to occasion any anxiety to his opponents. As it now became unnecessary to retain any considerable national force in the Valley, the Sixth corps was restored to the army of the Potomac, and shortly afterwards two other divisions of infantry were withdrawn from the Shenandoah.*

* In all the important battles of Sheridan's campaign Colonel Rutherford B. Hayes, afterwards nineteenth President of the United States, Lad borne an honorable part. Entering the service early in 1861, as major of the 23rd Ohio Volunteers, he was ordered at once to West Virginia, and remained there till the summer of 1862, when his command was transferred to the Potomac, and participated in the battle of South Mountain. In this action Hayes was severely wounded in the arm. He was immediately commended for conspicuous gallantry, and in December of the same year received the colonelcy of his regiment, which had returned to West Virginia. He served under Crook,- in the movement against the Tennessee railroad in the spring of 1864, and led a brigade with marked success in the battle of Cloyd's

Sheridan had assumed command at Halltown, on the 7th of August, and his last great victory in the Valley was achieved on the 19th of October; so that in less than eleven weeks he had accomplished all that he had been put in his place to

Mountain. Afterwards, still in Crook's command, he joined Hunter's army in the march against Lynchburg, was present at the operations in front of that place, and covered the retreat in the difficult and dangerous passage of the Alleghanies.

He was next ordered to the mouth of the Shenandoah Valley, and took part in several engagements between Early and Sheridan's troops, prior to the battle of Winchester. In that important encounter, he had the right of Crook's command, and it was therefore his troops which, in conjunction with the cavalry, executed the turning manoeuvre that decided the fate of the day. Here he displayed higher qualities than personal gallantry. At one point in the advance, his command came upon a deep slough, fifty yards wide, and stretching across the whole front of his brigade. Beyond was a rebel battery. If the brigade endeavored to move around the obstruction, it would be exposed to a severe enfilading fire ; while if discomfited, the line of advance would be broken in a vital part. Hayes, with the instinct of a soldier, at once gave the word " Forward," and spurred his horse into the swamp. Horse and rider plunged at first nearly out of sight, but Hayes struggled on till the beast sank hopelessly into the mire. Then dismounting, he waded to the further bank, climbed to the top, and beckoned with his cap to the men to follow. In the attempt to obey many were shot or drowned, but a sufficient number crossed the ditch to form a nucleus for the brigade ; and Hayes still leading, they climbed the bank and charged the battery. The enemy fled in great disorder, and Hayes re-formed his men and resumed the advance. The passage of the slough was at the crisis of the fight, and the rebels broke on every side in confusion.

At Fisher's Hill he led a division in the turning movement assigned to Crook's command. Clambering up the steep sides of North Mountain, which was covered with an almost impenetrable entanglement of trees and underbrush, the division gained, un-perceived, a position in rear of the enemy's line, and then charged with so much fury that the rebels hardly attempted to resist, but

ULYSSES S. GRANT.

perform. He had utterly routed the rebels in three pitched battles, besides one cavalry engagement in which Torbert commanded; had captured sixty guns in the open field, in addition to the twenty-fled in utter rout and dismay. Hayes was at the head of his column throughout this brilliant charge.

A month later, at Cedar Creek he was again engaged. His command was in reserve, and therefore did not share in the disaster of the main line at daybreak; but when the broken regiments at the front were swept hurriedly to the rear, Hayes's division flew to arms, and changing front, advanced in the direction from which the enemy was coming. Successful resistance, however, was impossible. He had not fifteen hundred effective men, and two divisions of the rebels were pouring through the woods to close around him in flank and rear. There was no alternative but retreat or capture. He withdrew, nevertheless, with steadiness, and maintained his organization unbroken throughout the battle, leading his men back from hill-top to hill-top in face of the enemy. While riding at full speed, his horse was shot under him ; he was flung violently out of the saddle, and his foot and ankle were badly wrenched by the fall. Stunned and bruised, he lay for a moment, exposed to a storm of bullets, but soon recovering, sprang to his feet, and limped to his command.

" For gallant and meritorious service in the battles of Winchester, Fisher's Hill, and Cedar Creek," Colonel Hayes was promoted to the rank of Brigadier-General of Volunteers; he was brevetted Major-General for " gallant and distinguished services during the campaign of 1864, in West Virginia, and particularly in the battles of Fisher's Hill and Cedar Creek." He had commanded a brigade for more than two years, and at the time of these promotions was in command of the Kanawha division. In the course of his service in the army, he was four times wounded, and had four horses shot under him.

That he was of the stuff of which soldiers should be made was shown when he was nominated for Congress in 1864. His political friends then wrote for him to return to Ohio and make the canvass. But Hayes replied : " Any officer fit for duty who at this crisis would abandon his post to electioneer for a seat in Congress, ought to be scalped."

four retaken from the enemy at Cedar Creek ;* the names of thirteen thousand prisoners were inscribed in his provost-marshal's books, and among his records were receipts for forty-nine captured battle flags, forwarded to the Secretary of War. His losses in the four battles were one thousand two hundred and ninety killed, seven thousand five hundred and eighty wounded, and two thousand five hundred and fourteen missing; total, eleven thousand three hundred and eighty-four. There can be no doubt that the killed and wounded in the four times beaten army were at least equal to those of the victorious force, or about nine thousand men.t As Sheridan captured thirteen thousand more, Early's actual loss must have been twenty-two thousand.

* Sixty guns were captured in these four engagements alone, but between the 1st of September and the 1st of January, Sheridan took 101 pieces of artillery from the enemy.

f During the entire period of Sheridan's command in the Valley his losses were 1,938 killed, 11,893 wounded, 3,121 missing; total, 16,952. Supposing Early's killed and wounded, for the same time, equal to those of his conqueror, the rebels lost under that commander, after August 7th, 13,800 men, besides prisoners and stragglers. Of the wounded on both sides, probably half returned to the ranks.

J Sheridan captured more men in the Valley than Early says were in his army. To account for this singular circumstance, Early is obliged to declare: " A number of prisoners fell into the enemy's hands, who did not belong to my command, [to whom did they belong ?] such as cavalry men on details to get fresh horses, soldiers on leave of absence, conscripts on special details, citizens not in the service [that is to say, guerillas], men employed in getting supplies for the Department, and stragglers and deserters from other commands." Every one of these men was put into the ranks, if near a rebel army on the day of a battle, and every one captured was a loss to Early's fighting force. No such deductions were ever made by him in calculating the national numbers.

This calculation takes no account of stragglers, skulkers, and deserters, who, the rebel general himself declares, were numerous, and who, all the showing is, abounded in every part of the Confederacy at this period of the war, when so many were disheartened and despairing. If this was the case elsewhere, it must have been particularly so in an army demoralized to the extent which Early describes,* and which had so lost confidence in its leader, that Lee, on this account, was compelled to relieve him from command.

This seems a proper place to point out one of the many devices resorted to by the rebels to minimize the statement of their own numbers. Early, and, among others, Colonel Taylor, of Lee's staff, in his " Four Years with General Lee," habitually speak of the numbers of " muskets" available, when summing up the rebel strength at any particular time. They thus avoid computing the officers (one at least for every twenty men), as well as the cavalry and the artillery; but when the national force is stated, it is never reduced to muskets; officers, cavalry, artillerymen, details, reserves, and all are counted, and the aggregate is compared with the number of " muskets" said to be engaged on the rebel side. I have striven to avoid a similar unfairness, and in this history the same rule is always applied to both armies. The statement of numbers is that of the effective force, taken from the official returns on record in the War Department. If no such returns exist, or if there seems cause to modify them, the authority or reason for a different statement is given.

" A good many are missing as stragglers, and a number of those reported missing in the infantry were not captured, but are stragglers and skulkers." Early to Lee, Oct. 9, 1864, after Winchester."Very many of the missing in the infantry took to the mountains; a number of them have since come in, and others are still out." Idem, after Fisher's Hill.

" I am sorry to say many men threw away their arms."Idem.Early had indeed been singularly unsuccessful both in strategy and tactics, but it may be doubted whether another general would have met with better fortune. Sheridan had shown himself abundant in resource, instantaneous in acting on his resolves, remorseless in following up a victory ; and while himself sleepless in vigilance, prompt to detect every blunder of his enemy. But beyond these traits, which doubtless contributed in a great degree to his success, he had displayed a rare and fine intellectual ability. In each of his three great battles he conceived and executed movements remarkable as illustrations of the military art. A left half wheel of the main line, in combination with a flank turning movement, was a favorite manoeuvre, employed both at Winchester and Fisher's Hill; it is one that requires the clearest judgment, an unerring eye, an instinctive perception of the situation, and a certainty of design which, united, go far to constitute genius for war. He also exhibited consummate skill in combining great cavalry movements with the evolutions of the entire army in actual battle. Certainly, by no commander on either side during the war was the cavalry arm employed with more signal success at opportune moments in great engagements, and especially in a way in which infantry could not have been used at all. At Winchester, it was this combination of massed cavalry with infantry at a critical juncture which decided the day, and the approach of Torbert's force that sent the rebels "whirling through Winchester;" while at Cedar Creek, the charge of Ouster's division converted the rebel defeat into a disastrous rout. These movements, not planned in advance, but inspired by the circum-

ULYSSES S. GRANT.

stances of actual battle, and executed at the instant when they were of the utmost consequence, evince that innate quality of a great commander which can neither be taught nor acquired; while the charge that Sheridan led in person at Cedar Creek, cuttino-off a large flanking party, as well as his whole conduct in this battle—the magnetic power he exercised over the fugitives, and the manner in which he was able to induce a beaten army to return and rout its victors—all constitute one of the most remarkable instances of personal influence in military history. -As Grant telegraphed to the government: " Turning what bid fair to be disaster into glorious victory stamps Sheridan what I have always thought him, one of the ablest of generals."

His antagonist, however, had not been altogether incompetent. Early was skilful, if over cautious, in his operations at the mouth of the Valley, and although he accomplished no more positive results, he nevertheless prevented Sheridan for some weeks from achieving anything of importance. He finally blundered, in dispatching two divisions to Martinsburg, in the presence of a wary opponent. They were brought rapidly back, it is true, when the danger became manifest; but the mistake undoubted^ contributed to his disaster at Winchester. Early, however, was always quick to return upon Sheridan's steps, when that commander made a retrograde movement; he was rarely deficient in vigor, and the plan of the battle of Cedar Creek was full of design as well as boldness ; but, judging from results, he must have lacked clearness of judgment and quickness of resource in the turmoil of battle : if he met disaster, it was irremediable;

and he was utterly unable to control his troops in an emergency. Again and again he tells of his ineffectual efforts to restrain or rally his broken forces; he might as well have spoken to the wind. Neither officers nor men responded. He was out of accord with his army.

This was the judgment of his superiors; and after one more defeat, of no great consequence, the command of the rebel force in the Valley was transferred to Echols. " I have reluctantly arrived at the conclusion/'said Lee, "that you cannot command the united and willing co-operation which is so essential to success. Your reverses in the Valley, of which the public and the army judge chiefly by results, have, I fear, impaired your influence both with the people and the soldiers, and would add greatly to the difficulties which will, under any circumstances, attend our operations in South-West Virginia. . . I therefore felt constrained to endeavor to find a commander who would be more likely to develop the strength and resources of the country, and inspire the soldiers with confidence." Thus the military career of Early ended in a disgrace inflicted, not by his enemies, but by his friends. To the brave old soldier the blows of Sheridan were probably no harder to bear than the censures of Lee.

The rebels and their apologists have never ceased to complain of the policy, inaugurated by Grant, and carried out to its full extent by Sheridan, of destroying the resources of the Valley. During the first years of the rebellion an opposite course had been pursued. The war was strictly confined to the armies in the field, and the national soldiers

were often employed in guarding rebel property and restoring slaves to rebel masters; while the national granaries were opened to supply the famishing families of men in arms against their government. It was hoped by such leniency to induce the prodigals to return. But the hope was vain, and the leniency misplaced ; the rebels accepted every proffered aid or alms, and remained as obdurate as ever.* The obstinacy, even the heroism they displayed made harsher measures indispensable, and in the end contributed to their completer conquest. Since the population, as well as the armies, of the South was united in rebellion, the population, as well as the armies, must undergo whatever was necessary for its subjection. A change thus came over the spirit of the North, and Grant embodied and represented this change. He saw that it was necessary to deprive the South of its resources as well as of its armies, for both were part of its military power. It was he who introduced and enforced the rule that all property useful to the enemy, adding to their strength, or assisting them to carry on the war, should be destroyed. This rule, laid down by him, was applied with equal rigor by Sherman at the West,t and Sheridan at the East; it was applauded

* " We have tried three years of conciliation and kindness without any reciprocation; on the contrary, those thus treated have acted as spies and guerillas in our rear and within our lines."— Halleck to Sherman, September 28, 1864.

f " When the rich planters of the Oconee and Savannah see their fences and corn and hogs vanish before their eyes, they will have something more than a mean opinion of the Yanks. Even now our poor mules laugh at the fine corn-fields, and our soldiers riot on chesnuts, sweet potatoes, pigs, chickens, etc. The poor people come to me and beg us for their lives, but my customary

by officers and soldiers everywhere in the field, endorsed by the government, and in the end approved by all who wished for the success of the national cause.

It was justified alike by its necessity, by its results, and by the course of the rebels themselves. Its necessity at the East had been proven by the frequent incursions and raids of the enemy into and through the Shenandoah. In the earlier years of the war this region teemed with provisions and forage from one end to the other, and Stonewall Jackson was in part indebted to its abundant supplies for his easy triumphs.* In 1864, Lee informed the rebel government that one object of the movement against Washington was to secure the crops of the Valley; while Early boasted that his army had been self-sustaining throughout the entire campaign, and had sent large quantities of beef cattle to Lee besides. His soldiers ground as well as harvested the grain, so that the destruction of the mills became a military measure of the first necessity. " It is desirable," said Grant, " that nothing should be left to invite the enemy to return. . ." The people should be informed that so long as an army can subsist among them, recurrences of these raids must be expected, and we are determined to stop them, at all hazards." It was nevertheless no act of vengeance, or even of retaliation, that he proposed. He repeatedly directed that dwellings should not be

answer is: ' Your friends have broken our railroads which supplied us bountifully, and you cannot suppose our soldiers will suffer when there is abundance within reach.'"— Slwrman to Halleck, October 19, 3864.

* Early's Memoir, page 118.

ULYSSES S. GRANT.

burned/"" and if the inhabitants could convey their stock and provisions north of the

Potomac he offered no objection ;t but "so long as the'war lasts," he said, "they must be prevented from raising another crop."

Sheridan obeyed his orders to the letter. On the 1st of October, he wrote, from Harrisonburg: " What we have destroyed and can destroy in this Valley is worth millions of dollars to the rebel government;" on the 7th, he said, from Woodstock : " In moving back to this point, the whole country, from the Blue Eidge to the North Mountain, has been made untenable for a rebel army;" and still later : " I will continue the destruction of wheat, forage, etc., down to Fisher's Hill. When this is completed, the Valley, from Winchester up to

* " It is not desirable that buildings should be destroyed; they should rather be protected."— Grant to Hunter, August 5.

"I have thought on your despatch relative to an arrangement between General Lee and myself for the suppression of incendiarism by the respective armies. Experience has taught us that agreements with rebels are binding upon us, but are not observed by them longer than suits their convenience. On the whole, I think that the best that can be done is to publish a prohibitory order against burning private property, except where it is a military necessity, or in retaliation for like acts by the enemy. Where burning is done in retaliation, it must be done by order of a department or army commander, and the order for such burning to set forth the particular act it is in retaliation for."— Grant to Lincoln, August 17, 1864.

f " Do you not think it advisable to notify all citizens living east of the Blue Ridge to move north of the Potomac all their stock, grain, and provisions of every description 1 There is no doubt about the necessity of clearing out that country, so that it will not support Mosby's gang, and the question is whether it is not better that the people should save what they can."— Grant to Sheridan, November 9.

Staunton, ninety-two miles, will have little in it for man or beast." Early also is a witness to the success of the policy. On the 9th of October, he complained bitterly to Lee : " Sheridan has laid waste nearly all of Buckingham and Shenandoah, and I shall have to rely on Augusta for my supplies, and they are not abundant there. Sheridan's purpose under Grant's orders has been to render the Valley untenable by our troops, by destroying the supplies." That purpose was effected. After the battle of Cedar Creek, no rebel army could subsist in the region : " I found it impossible," said Early, "to sustain the horses of my cavalry and artillery where they were, and forage could not be obtained from elsewhere. I was therefore compelled to send Fitz-Lee's two brigades to General Lee, and Lomax's cavalry was brought from across the Blue Ridge, where the country was exhausted of forage, and sent west. . . Rosser's brigade had to be temporarily disbanded, and the men allowed to go to their homes. . . Most of the guns which were without horses were sent to Lynch-burg by railroad. This was a deplorable state of things, but it could not be avoided, as the horses of the cavalry and artillery would have perished, had they been kept in the Valley. Two small brigades of Wharton's division and Nelson's battalion, with the few pieces of artillery which had been retained, were left as my whole available force."*

This was the origin of the complaint, and the cause of the outcry. The enemy felt that the
* Early's Memoir, pp. 121 and 122.

measure was a military success ; that it not only compelled the present abandonment of the Valley, but destroyed all hope of return. The supplies were not only annihilated, but could not be renewed during the war. Washington could never again be threatened from the Shenandoah; and Lynchburg, now become of immense importance to Lee, must remain exposed.

The rebels indeed so thoroughly appreciated Grant's policy that they themselves acted on the same principle. They not only habitually lived upon the country, everywhere, but they also destroyed what they could not consume, whenever it might be of advantage to the national armies. They stripped their own families of provisions, leaving them as the national troops advanced, to be fed by those troops, or to starve; and in many parts of the country, not a mill was left to grind grain for the inhabitants, lest the national commanders might find means to supply their soldiers. Halleck justly remarked, at the time : " We certainly are not required to treat the so-called non-combatant rebels better than they themselves treat each other."* But it was always so. Wherever the enemy was in possession, loyal citizens were persecuted, expatriated, imprisoned, hung; their property was seized, or confiscated ; but if a national commander used the property of men in arms against their government, the rebels raised a cry of shame, and pronounced the outrage unprecedented. Early burnt the undefended town of Chambersburg, but was shocked at the conflagration of mills ; and Lee, who recommended a partisan warfare, refused to recognize

   * Halleck to Sherman, September 28.

negro soldiers as prisoners of war. But with all their soldierly qualities, there was a touch of un-manliness about the Southerners. Unrelenting and vindictive, they were as ready as women to repine when the fortune of war went against them, and never admitted that the same measure should be meted to them which they unsparingly applied to their foes whenever they had the chance.

   It is no new thing, however, for the conquered to criticize their conquerors; and, naturally enough, the severest censors of Grant were those who suffered most by his success. They could hardly be expected to admire the strategy or approve the policy which consummated their own punishment. In the same way, when the Greeks received the Roman yoke, they decried the civilization of their victors; and the Romans, in their turn, severely disapproved the proceedings of those whom, two thousand years ago, they called " Northern barbarians." But, as Sherman told the inhabitants of Atlanta, when he expelled them from their homes: " War is cruelty, and you cannot refine it." It w r as the men who brought these evils on themselves who were responsible for all the terrible results of their crime. The national commanders were no more answerable, than the weapons they employed, for the destruction and ruin which the rebellion entailed.

   Late in October Grant determined to attack the communications of Lee. The left of Meade's entrenched line was at this time only two miles east of the Boydton plank road, which approaches Petersburg midway between the Southside and the Weldon railways. The rebels were known to have

ULYSSES S. GRANT.

begun the construction of a line of defences to cover this route, along which, since the seizure of the Weldon road, they were obliged to wagon all their supplies from the Atlantic coast ; and before these defences should be completed, Grant designed to move to the left, and not only seize the Boydton road, but, if possible, the Southside road itself, the last of the great avenues connecting Richmond with the outside Confederacy. Six months before, at Culpeper, he had pointed out to his staff the South-side road as the line he intended to secure. " When once my troops are there," he said, "Lee must surrender, or leave Richmond."

   Accordingly, on the 24th of October, he instructed Meade : " Make your preparations to march out at an early hour on the 27th, to gain possession of the Southside railroad, and to hold it, and fortify back to your present left." Butler at the same time was to make a demonstration north of the James, to attract the enemy's attention to that quarter. " General Meade," said Grant, " will move from our left, with the design of seizing and holding the Southside railroad. To facilitate this movement, or rather to prevent reinforcements going from the north side of the James river to Petersburg, I wish you to demonstrate against the enemy in your front. . . I do not want any attack made by you against entrenched and defended positions, but feel out to the right beyond the front, and if you can, turn it. . . Let it be distinctly understood by corps commanders that there is to be no attack made against defended entrenched positions."

In this operation Meade was to take out forty

thousand men,* leaving the remainder of the army of the Potomac to hold the entrenched lines. The movement was to be in three columns. The Ninth corps had the right, immediately west of its former position, the Second corps was on the left with Gregg's cavalry, while the Fifth corps was to move between the other two, on a line part of which had to be opened as the troops advanced. The geography of the country was perplexing in the extreme. Not only was the region covered with a dense forest and an undergrowth as impenetrable as in the Wilderness, but Hatcher's run, a tortuous and difficult stream, must be crossed and re-crossed several times. This creek flows east as far as the Boydton road, crossing it under a bridge at Burgess's mill, but shortly afterwards makes a bend, and then runs almost due south for several miles. It lay directly in the path of the national army, covering every approach to the Boydton road.

Parke, who was to start out nearest the enemy, had been instructed not to assault, if he found the rebels entrenched and their works well manned, but to confront them and be prepared to advance promptly, whenever, by the movement of the other two corps, the enemy was compelled to give way.f

* This was the number reported to Grant by Meade as available for the operation.

t It has been asserted that the plan of this movement included a vigorous attack by Parke upon the right of the rebel entrenched line ; but no such attack was contemplated by Grant. His words to Meade were almost those in the text: " Parke, who starts out nearest to the enemy, should be instructed that if he finds the enemy entrenched and their works well manned, he is not to attack, but confront him and be prepared to advance promptly

Warren, moving on the left of Parke, was to cross Hatcher's run, below the bend, and then support the Ninth corps; but if Parke failed to break the enemy's line, Warren was ordered to re-cross the run above the bend, and open the bridge at Burgess's mill. Hancock was to move on the left of Warren, crossing Hatcher's run below the bend, and proceed to the Boydton road; then turning north, he was to re-cross the run west of the bridge, and strike the Southside road. Gregg's division was on the left of Hancock and under his command.. The whole project was based on the belief that the enemy's works extended only to the crossing of Hatcher's run by the Boydton road,

when he finds that by the movement of the other two columns to the right and rear of them, they begin to give way." Meade's order to Parke, however, contained these words: " It is probable that the enemy's line of entrenchments is incomplete at that point, and the commanding general expects by a secret and sudden movement to surprise them and carry their half-formed works." This did not express Grant's view, and when the order was submitted to him, he said to Meade : " The only point in which I could suggest a change is in regard to Parke. If he finds the enemy's fortifications in good defensible condition, I think he should only confront them until the movement of the other two corps had its effect." To this Meade replied : " The orders for to-morrow intend that Parke should act in the manner you suggest; that is to say, he will not attack if he finds the enemy in such position and force as render it injudicious to do so; but as the movement is to be made at daylight, or just before, he will have to make a partial attack to ascertain the exact condition of affairs, unless he waits until after daylight; and if he does, I am quite sure he will have no chance."

The difficulty Meade found in expressing Grant's idea, may be thought to illustrate the unadvisability of any intervention between the general-in-chief and the corps commanders. 90

and that they were incomplete, and weakly manned. *

The troops broke camp on the 26th, and at an early hour on the 27th, all three corps were in motion. But instead of the rebel line being unfinished and altogether north of Hatcher's run, it was found to extend east of the stream and below the bend, nearly to Armstrong's mill, a distance of at least two miles : it was also quite completed and thoroughly fortified, with slashing and abatis. The consequence was that Parke made no attempt to assault. Warren, however, after cutting a road through the woods, soon struck the rebel skirmishers and drove them into a line of breastworks strongly held. In developing this position he lost a hundred men. The morning was dark and rainy, the roads were unknown and obstructed ; out of about eleven thousand men in the Fifth corps nearly four thousand had never fired a musket, and two thousand were ignorant of the manual of arms.t At half-past nine Warren was notified by Meade that Parke would probably be unable to force the enemy's line, and that it was important for him to connect with the Second corps.

Hancock had moved long before daylight, crossing the run below Armstrong's mill, at a point where the water was waist-deep and trees had been felled to impede the ford ; he carried some slight works

* " This project was based upon information which led to the belief that the enemy's line only extended to the crossing of Hatcher's run by the Boydton plank road, and that it was not completed thus far and was weakly manned."— Meade's Report of the Operation, October 28.

•f Warren's Report.

on the western bank, and then moved rapidly on towards the Boydton road. With the cavalry on his left, he had advanced as far as the bridge at Burgess's mill, and was making his preparations to force a passage, when he was halted by Meade until connection could be opened with the Fifth corps.

Warren, meanwhile, was still groping his way in the woods, feeling out to the left for the end of the enemy's line. At half-past ten Grant and Meade were both at his head-quarters, and he was directed to send a division across Hatcher's run below the bend, place its right on the run, and then move up, supporting Hancock. Warren accordingly sent Crawford's division across the run, and started himself to direct the movement, for he never evaded duty or danger. The head of Crawford's column crossed at 11.45 A.M., and formed line of battle, with its right resting on the creek. But the denseness of the woods and the crookedness of the run caused great delay, as well as breaks in the line and frequent changes of direction. There could be no guide to the movement but sound, and at one o'clock, the troops on the eastern bank were ordered to open fire, to show the position of the enemy's line. Crawford also lost time, by mistaking a branch of the stream for the creek itself, and he found great difficulty in crossing the branch, on account of the fallen timber cut by the enemy. His line of march had by this time led him into a very different position from that which he was expected to assume ; the forest was of great extent; the men were losing themselves in all directions; and whole regiments, unable to find the remainder of the division, went astray. In

this emergency, Warren ordered Crawford to halt, while he went back in person to consult with Meade.

After giving the orders for Crawford's advance, Grant and Meade had ridden on to Hancock's front, where the rebels were now disputing the passage of the bridge, at Burgess's mill. It was at this time reported that the connection with Crawford had been made, but Crawford was in reality three-fourths of a mile from Hancock's right. The rebels had a battery north of the run, directly in front of the Second corps, and another about eight hundred yards from Hancock's left. Unless they were driven from the opposite bank, the national line could not be advanced sufficiently to make the desired movement, nor to form a connection with the entrenched works in front of Petersburg. Grant rode out into an open field, to get a nearer view of the position, his own staff-officers and those of Meade, with a crowd of orderlies, following. The number of horsemen made a conspicuous mark for the rebel batteries, and the group was shelled; one or two men were struck, and one was killed.

Officers of Meade and Hancock now came up to report the situation at the bridge; several of Grant's own aides-de-camp were sent to reconnoitre ; and Hancock, who had been at the extreme front, also explained what he had seen. But the reports were conflicting, and it seemed as if no eyes but his own could ascertain exactly what Grant wanted to know. Calling to Colonel Babcock, of his staff, he bade the others remain where they were, and galloped down the road to within a few yards of the bridge, exposed not only to the enemy's

ULYSSES S. GRANT.

sharpshooters, but to the cross fire of two rebel batteries. The telegraph wires had been cut, and the feet of his horse became entangled. Bab-cock was obliged to dismount and free them, while the officers at the rear looked on in suspense, and thought how many campaigns depended on the life that now w r as endangered. But the chief and his aide-de-camp rode on, till Grant could .clearly discern the rebel line, the condition of the country, the course of the stream, and the nature of the banks.

The rebels were evidently in force north of the creek, with strong defences. Their entrenched line extended far beyond the point at which it had been supposed to turn to the north, and when the national army advanced, Lee had simply moved out and occupied the works already prepared. The contemplated movement was thus impracticable. The rebel position could perhaps be carried, but only with extreme difficulty and loss of life; a loss which the advantage to be gained would not compensate ; while in the event of repulse, disaster might be grave, stretched out as the army wa,s, with its flanks six miles apart, and the creek dividing Warren's corps. Any serious rebuff or loss was especially to be deprecated at this crisis; the Presidential election was only ten days off, and the enemies of the nation at the North were certain to exaggerate every mishap. Success at the polls was just now even more important than a victory in the field, and it would i have been most unwise to risk greatly on this occasion.

Accordingly, when Grant returned from the bridge, he gave orders to suspend the movement.

Hancock was directed to hold his position till the following morning, and then withdraw by the same road along which he had advanced. This was at four o'clock, and Grant and Meade rode back to Armstrong's mill, supposing the connection between Hancock and Crawford to have been made. They took at first a wood road leading directly towards the creek and the right of the Second corps; but soon discovering the mistake, retraced their steps, and Grant proceeded to City Point, to communicate with Butler. Had they kept on, before long they must have been inside the rebel lines.

During these operations on the left, Butler had taken out twenty thousand men north of the James, where Longstreet was now in command. The plan, we have seen, was for Butler to make a demonstration, but not to attack fortified works, the main operation being the attempt to reach the South-side road. Butler moved to the right as far as the Williamsburg road, but found the enemy everywhere in his front, stretching out as fast as he did, and falling back within entrenched works whenever the national forces advanced. During the afternoon he telegraphed that the rebels had extended four miles. " Shall I make a trial/' he asked, " on this outstretched line ? " But the general-in-chief replied from City Point: " Your despatch of 3.30 is only just received—too late to direct an attack. Hold on where you are for the present."

Believing that the operations of the day were over, Grant now telegraphed to the Secretary of War: "I have just returned from the crossing of the Boydton plank road with Hatcher's creek. Our line now extends from its former left to Armstrong's mill, thence by the south bank of Hatcher's creek to the point above named. No attack was made during the day further than to drive pickets and the cavalry inside the main works. Our casualties have been light, probably less than two hundred, killed, wounded, and missing. The same is probably true with the enemy. . . On our right General Butler extended well around towards the Yorktown road, without finding a point unguarded. I shall keep our troops out where they are until towards noon to-morrow, in hope of inviting an attack."

The battle, however, was far from ended, on either flank. Weitzel, who had the right of Butler's command, had not been able to find the rebel left, but his troops became engaged with the enemy, and contrary to Grant's orders and intentions, an assault was made on a fortified work. It was repulsed with loss, but the rebels made no attempt to follow up their advantage, and Butler withdrew and awaited further orders ; when these arrived, they were simply to maintain the position which had been acquired. In this affair, Butler lost eleven hundred men, of whom four hundred were prisoners.

Meanwhile, the connection between Hancock and Warren had not been made, and between four and five o'clock the rebels came into the gap in heavy force, and struck the right and rear of the Second corps. Hancock heard the firing, but supposed it to proceed from Crawford's column; he nevertheless ordered a brigade into the woods to reconnoitre ; but before a report could be made, the continuous firing left no doubt of a rebel advance. The small national force on the right of the road was soon driven back, but Hancock

promptly ordered the division at the bridge to face to the rear and attack the enemy. This force was under Egan, than whom no soldier was better fitted for his task. With the instinct of a commander, he had already changed front, and was in motion against the enemy before Hancock's order arrived. The rebels had also attacked the left and front of the Second corps as well as Gregg's cavalry, but they did not comprehend the position, and had not known of the gap between Hancock and Crawford. Their main attack was intended to be made at the bridge and against Hancock's left, but finding the difficulty of carrying the bridge, they crossed the stream below, and thus struck the right of the Second corps, in the air.

Egan's prompt action, however, took them in flank, and sweeping down with resistless force, he hurled them back in confusion, capturing nine hundred prisoners and several stands of colors. The fight was altogether outside of works, and for a time was severe, but the repulse of the rebels was complete. The victory was due in great measure to the personal exertions of Hancock and Egan, their skill, decision, and gallantry, but every effort of the commanders was more than seconded by their soldiers. Meanwhile, Gregg, on the left, though vigorously attacked by Hampton's cavalry, had also been able to hold his own.

Meade was at Armstrong's mill when he heard of this engagement, and he at once directed Warren to send a division to support the Second corps. Crawford, it was thought, would not be able to reach the field in time, and Ayres, who was at Armstrong's mill, began his march at once; but

night came on before he could cross the run. He therefore advanced no further. The assault on Hancock, however, had been so completely broken that the rebels were unable to re-form. If Crawford could have attacked them at this crisis, the destruction of the whole assaulting force must have been inevitable. As it was, several hundred rebels strayed within his lines and were captured. One party of six had even seized a national officer, but finding themselves inside of Warren's lines, they gave themselves up to their prisoner.

Meade now authorized Hancock to use his discretion, and either retire, or hold the ground from which he had repelled the enemy, offering him the assistance of two divisions of Warren. Hancock, however, was eight miles from the national entrenchments ; in case of disaster, he had but one line of retreat, and that difficult and interrupted by the run ; his ammunition at the front was nearly exhausted, and a fresh supply could only be brought up over the same heavy and crowded road. He therefore deemed it advisable to withdraw. This decision was approved by Meade, and was in conformity with the orders and intentions of Grant when he left the field. Hancock began moving at ten P.M., and Warren at one o'clock ; and by noon of the 28th, the whole army was back in its former camps.*

At midnight Grant said to Meade: "Your despatch, with those from Hancock, just received.

* It is stated by rebel writers that during the night of the 27th, Lee massed 15,000 infantry and all of Hampton's cavalry opposite Hancock, with a view of crushing the Second corps in the morning; but in the morning the corps was gone.

Now that the enemy have taken to attacking, I regret the necessity of withdrawing, but see the cogency of your reasoning. If ammunition coul'd have been taken up on pack animals, it might have enabled us after all to have gained the end w~e started for. The enemy attacking rather indicates that he has been touched in a weak point. Do not change, however, the directions that have been given." To Stanton, he telegraphed on the 28th : " The attack on General Hancock, now that a report is received, proves to be a decided success. He repulsed the enemy and remained in position, holding possession of the field until midnight, when he commenced withdrawing. Orders had been given for the withdrawal of the Second corps before the attack was made.* We lost no prisoners except the usual stragglers who are always picked up."t

The national loss in this operation was one hundred and forty-three killed, six hundred and fifty-three wounded, four hundred and eighty-eight missing : total, twelve hundred and eighty-four." J The enemy

* " Lieutenant-General Grant and General Meade left the field, giving me verbal orders to hold my position until the following morning, when I was to fall back by the same road I had come."— Hancock's Official Report.

Lee reported the capture of four hundred prisoners. Hancock, however, distinctly declared that he lost no prisoners in battle; but in withdrawing, he was obliged from lack of ambulances to place some of his wounded in the neighboring houses, leaving them under the care of his own surgeons. These—wounded, surgeons, and all—were doubtless included in Lee's report.

All my statements of national losses are from returns in the Adjutant-General's office at Washington. The estimates made by commanders the day after a battle were sometimes larger; but these included the very slightly wounded and the stragglers, all

lost in prisoners alone more than that number. His killed and wounded, Lee, as usual, failed to report.*

This whole movement, it has been shown, was based on the belief that Lee's entrenchments extended only to the crossing of Hatcher's run by the Boydton road. But when, instead of this, they were found to stretch several miles to the south, covering the lower crossings of the run, and defended by slashing and abatis, while the stream itself was impeded by fallen timber and other obstructions,—the extension was seen to be impracticable, and the operation was converted into a reconnoissance in force.

It was the only movement of the army of the Potomac, after the explosion of Burnside's mine, which did not result in a positive and tangible success. The rebel works, however, had been constructed in advance, and were only occupied when the national army moved. Covered as they were by cavalry,

of whom shortly returned to the ranks. I have desired to give the absolute loss ; and have applied the same rule to both armies. None other is possible with the rebels, as their records have been to so great an extent destroyed ; indeed, when the disclosure would have been inconvenient, no return at all was made. No cause in history ever had more ingenious or more unscrupulous adherents in camp or civil life, than the Slaveholders' great rebellion.

* On the 27th, Lee sent the following despatch, which was withheld from print, and has not found its way into any rebel history : " General Hill reports that the enemy crossed Rowanty creek below Burgess's mill, and forced back the cavalry. In the afternoon General Heth attacked and at first drove them, but found them in too strong force. Afterwards the enemy attacked and were repulsed. They still hold the plank road at Burgess's mill. Heth took colors and some prisoners." The despatch given by McCabe and other rebel writers is not on file at Washington.

and by the forest, the extent and direction of the lines could not have been discovered except by just such a movement as had now been made ; while the difficulties of the country could not have been avoided, even if foreseen. Meade has been censured for halting Hancock at Burgess's mill, but the result proved the wisdom of his course. Had Hancock crossed the bridge, he must have encountered the same force which afterwards attacked him, and the rebels would have had him at a disadvantage when he debouched, with the river in his rear, and entirely disconnected with the remainder of the army. Even if the enemy had not been ready to resist him, an advance, before connection with Warren was made, would have been foolhardy in the extreme. Grant entirely approved of the action of Meade, but he seriously complained of the delay of Crawford's division. No blame was imputed to Crawford, but there seemed reason to regret the order of Warren suspending his advance. Had that order not been given, Crawford would have been exactly in position to complete the destruction of the rebel attacking column. The indecision of Warren was all his own, and makes it probable that his frequent hesitations were owing to a quality which must always have prevented his becoming a great commander.

The success of Hancock, however, more than compensated for all misadventures, and once again made it evident that, when the national troops were attacked, even at a disadvantage and without cover, they were more than a match for the best soldiers of Lee. The movement cost the rebels far more than it did Grant; and it gave him the idea upon

ULYSSES S. GRANT.

which he acted in his final campaign. "This reconnaissance," he said to Stanton, " which I had intended for more, points out to me what is to be done."

Grant's general operations before Petersburg were essentially distinct in character from the great turning movements in the Wilderness campaign. They were not, as they have sometimes been called, " swinging movements to the left, pivoting on the right," but simple extensions of the line of countervallation. For the advance upon Eichmond and Petersburg had in reality become a siege. City Point was a base of supplies, not a pivotal point; and if, in the extending movements, the assailing force was weaker than that at the base, it was because disaster at the latter place would have been serious, while a temporary check given to any extension to the left was a comparatively unimportant incident of the siege. These extensions indeed had so little of the character of flank movements, in the ordinary military sense of the term, that, usually, the troops had only to halt and face to the right, to be in proper line of battle in front of the enemy. Even the battle at the Weldon road was not conducted on a different principle from the others, except that when it was seen how promptly the enemy sent troops to check the extension, there was a more concentrated movement made by Grant.

But although his operations had thus taken the character of a siege, Grant could not adopt the method of regular approaches without violating one of the most obvious principles of the art of war. All the books lay down the rule that the besiegers-should number at least five or six times as many as

the besieged; but Grant was obliged to conduct his operations with a force only one-third greater than the garrison.""" Regular approaches were out of the question. Besides this, Grant's fundamental purpose was the destruction of Lee's army, not the capture of Petersburg or Richmond. The rebels took shelter behind their works, and therefore Grant besieged the works; but if the troops could be destroyed or captured, he was indifferent about the possession of either town. This made it far better for him to fight at the Weldon road or Peeble's farm, than at any point on the entrenched lines close to Petersburg. While he was running parallels, Lee might defy, or escape him; but by extending the investment, Grant forced the rebels to defend their lines of supply. In fact, he compelled Lee to become in some sort the attacking party, for the rebel general could not permit these extensions to go on without an effort to prevent them ; and whenever he ventured out with a division or a corps, he was invariably repelled with loss.

But although after the first assaults in June, Grant constantly meant to complete his line to the Southside road, not all the separate extensions were designed in advance. The commander who adheres

* It has been said that saps might have been rim from the position held by Burnside at the time of the mine explosion, and that in a month the rebel line could have been stormed. But the point opposite Burnside was the very strongest position held by the enemy in front of Petersburg. Burnside was in a valley, while the rebels occupied a hill, the national mines running into the side of the hill at least thirty or forty feet, under the rebel batteries. Parallels here were impossible.

ULYSSES S. GRANT.

inflexibly to a preconcerted plan must be assured exactly of what his antagonist will do. Grant's method of warfare, however, has been already seen. Instead of adhering rigidly to a preconceived scheme, and

being thrown all aback when any detail failed,

he was always ready to change his plans according to the circumstances of the hour, so that while nothing was accidental, much that was done was the offspring of the moment. Thus several operations intended to accomplish other results were converted into extensions to the left, and when Hancock or Butler made an unsuccessful advance north of the James, Grant promptly seized the opportunity to continue the general movement towards the Southside road.

It has sometimes been said that the national army should have marched around Richmond and thus avoided entrenched lines altogether; but in the fourth year of the war Lee's army was able to entrench itself strongly on any line in a single night. Grant found this out on the 16th of June. He knew that there were surer and speedier results to be obtained by working around Lee's roads, and at the same time supplying himself from his own water base, than by abandoning his communications and hazarding battles on Lee's selected position west of Richmond, where the enemy was certain to be found as strongly entrenched as ever. The rebels, too, could take many risks; their condition was so desperate, that no disaster could make it much worse ; but there w r ere strong political reasons at this time why the army of the Potomac should not lose its connection with a secure base, and run the risk of any great disaster in the field,

to which in pitched battle every general is liable— especially as Grant felt assured that he could accomplish his purpose by other means and with less loss of life, even if it took a little longer. The same strategy, even the same daring, appropriate enough in a subordinate commander in a distant theatre, would have been unseasonable and inexpedient in the general-in-chief, at the head of the principal army of the nation, and at a critical moment in the history of the state, when every check was magnified by disloyal opponents into irremediable disaster, and a serious defeat in the field might entail political ruin to the cause for which all his battles were fought. For, with all his willingness to take risks in certain contingencies, with all his preference for aggressive operations, Grant was no rash or inconsiderate commander. He was able to adapt his strategy to the slow processes of a siege as well as to those imminent crises of battle when fortune hangs upon the decision of a single moment. At times audacious in design or incessant in attack, at others he was cautious, and deliberate, and restrained ; and none knew better than he when to remain immovable under negative or apparently unfavorable circumstances. At present he believed the proper course in front of Petersburg t 0 foe—to steadily extend the investment towards the Southside road, while annoying and exhausting the enemy by menaces and attacks at various points, preventing the possibility of Lee's detaching in support of either Hood or Early, and himself waiting patiently till the moment should come to strike a blow like those he had dealt earlier in the war.

To many this task would have been more unacceptable because, while the chief was lying comparatively inactive in front of Eichmond, the subordinates were fighting important battles and winning brilliant victories elsewhere. Sherman had captured Atlanta, and Sheridan had overrun the Valley, while Thomas was entrusted with a command where the mightiest issues were at stake ; and the interest of the country was transferred from the commander of them all to the great soldiers so rapidly rising into reputations which might eclipse his own. But such considerations not only never influenced Grant, they never seemed to occur to him. He went on soberly and steadily with his work, careless whether it brought him into prominence or left him in the shade; and as glad of any success of the national cause when won by another, as if it had been his own.

Nevertheless, when events over the whole theatre of war were ripe; when Sherman should have reached a base, and the rebel army at the West be destroyed or rendered harmless; when the Presidential election should be over, while Washington remained secure against attacks from the Shenandoah—then, if the extension had not yet reached Lee's last line of supply, Grant intended to force the hand of Lee. He was like a chess-player, looking forward to a daring, but if successful, a finishing move, and clearing the board in advance of the pieces of his adversary which might obstruct his plan. When he telegraphed to Stanton: " This reconnoissance, which I had meant for more, points out to me what is to be done/' he meant, if Lee's lines did not break in the extensiuu. which the rebels also were compelled to make,—to swing the army of the Potomac entirely to the left, cutting loose from his base, and leaving only sufficient troops at City Point and in front of Petersburg to take care of themselves. He made known this intention to some of his staff, as they rode back to camp after the battle of Hatcher's run.

CHAPTER XXVIII.

Grant at City Point—Simplicity of camp life—Traits of President Lincoln— Personal character of Grant—Wife and children at City Point—Military family—Preparations for Sherman's march—Sherman falls back from Atlanta—Pursuit of Hood—Escape of Hood— Reinforcement of Thomas— Anxiety of government—Orders for Sherman's march delayed— Orders renewed—Harmony of Grant and Sherman—Supreme responsibility of Grant —Hood moves to Tennessee river—Sherman's misgivings—Presidential election—Political position of Grant—Views in regard to soldiers' vote—Efforts of enemy at the North—Re-election of Lincoln—Sherman starts for the sea —Change of military situation—Preparations of Grant to meet Hood— Geography of Tennessee—Character of Thomas—Relations of Sherman and Thomas—Difference of character between Grant and Thomas—Grant and Sherman direct concentration in Tennessee—Thomas delays to concentrate —Hood crosses the Tennessee— Forrest moves into West Tennessee—Forces of Thomas—Danger of Thomas—Reinforcement of Thomas by Grant—Situation on the Tennessee—Grant visits the North—Reception in New York and Philadelphia—Recommends dismissal of useless generals—Character of Stanton—Relations of Stanton and Grant.

AT City Point Grant lived a life of great simplicity. After his arrival there in June, his head-quarters' camp was pitched on a bluff, overlooking the junction of the Appomattox and the James ; but when it became certain that the winter must be passed at this spot, tents were exchanged for log huts, in which fires could be built. Grant's cabin was divided by a partition of boards, so that it might, be said to possess two rooms, but in no other

respect did it differ from that of the humblest subordinate on his staff. There was a flooring of plank, a deal table for maps and writing materials, a wooden chair or two, and, in the inner division, a camp bed and an iron washstand : this was the provision made for the general of the armies. During the day the hut was little occupied, except when writing was to be done by one of the staff; for Grant wrote few letters himself, only the despatches to the government and orders for the commanders of armies. Once or twice a week he went to Meade or Butler's front, and sometimes visited the hospitals or fortifications at City Point; but the roads were in miserable condition, the horses sank up to their bellies in mud, and there was little pleasure in any exercise.

Most of the time was spent around a huge wood fire kept up in the centre of the encampment, immediately in front of Grant's own hut. Here a number of rough seats were placed, and two or three officers were almost always to be found. The weather was cold, but wrapped in the overcoat of a private soldier, Grant liked to form one of the group around this fire. The telegraph was close at hand, and despatches were brought him instantly : to this point came messages from Meade, and Butler, and Sherman, and Sheridan, and Thomas, and Canby, and Stanton, and Halleck, and the President; and after reading them, the general-in-chief usually stepped at once into his hut and wrote his reply; he then rejoined the circle around the fire, and often told the contents of the message he had received, as well as of that he sent. On such occasions he rarely consulted any one. Sometimes, of

course, it was necessary to inform himself before replying; if an inquiry was made about troops, or he needed to know something from the quartermaster or the commissary of subsistence, the proper officer was sent for; but when the despatch simply required a decision, Grant made the decision, and announced it after the reply was gone.

One great occupation was the study of the rebel newspapers, which often brought the earliest news from distant commands. They were exchanged for our own on the picket line, almost daily, and the Richmond papers were brought in as regularly as if they had been subscribed for. Prisoners of consequence, or who had important news, were also conveyed to the head-quarters; while of course the highest officers of the army were constant visitors, Meade and Butler most frequent of all. Admiral Porter, who commanded the squadron on the James, often consulted Grant; important personages from Washington, foreign ministers, senators, members of the government, officers of foreign armies, were sometimes guests; and the President himself spent several weeks during the winter at the head-quarters, sleeping on a steamer below the bluffs, while his days were passed familiarly with Grant and his officers.

He liked, when Grant was away for an hour or a day, to sit in the adjutant-general's hut, where despatches came in, and he could receive information promptly. With his long legs twisted and coiled as if he hardly knew what to do with them, he leaned his chair backwards, and talked, apparently with the greatest freedom, even' with junior officers ; yet he never said anything except

exactly what lie meant to say. This daily intercourse for weeks left a profound impression on those who were fortunate enough to share it. The intellectual calibre of the man was most apparent, and most imposing. All through the rough exterior of conversation, the abundant jokes, the plain, homespun talk,—as plain as his face, but as full of power and meaning,—there was evidence enough that Lincoln was a great man. Grant often said at this time that he thought him by far the greatest man who had occupied the Presidential chair since Washington. And in those qualities not purely intellectual, and yet far from devoid of intellectuality, which make men great in times of revolution and civil war, Lincoln was incontestably superior to any of his predecessors, perhaps even to the first.

His task, indeed, was far more difficult than Washington's. He ruled thirty millions of people ; Washington was at the head of only three millions : he had a war to carry on with a part of his own nation; Washington's was with outsiders: his armies numbered half a million soldiers; Washington's, thirty or forty thousand. His enemies were ten times as numerous in the field as those with whom Washington contended. He had the great problem of emancipation to solve, which was not presented to Washington. He had a violent, numerous, dangerous party in his rear, constantly watching to thwart and defeat him ; and though Washington knew something of this difficulty, the opposition to him was insignificant compared with that offered to Lincoln. America in Washington's time was an isolated and inconsiderable colony; the world cared little by comparison for the result of the

struggle in which she was engaged, and whatever sympathy was aroused, was in her behalf; whereas, in Lincoln's day, England and France took the keenest interest in the success of the South, and stood ready and anxious to avail themselves of any favorable opportunity to interfere.

Under these circumstances, the caution mingled with determination with which the President acted, the skill with which he avoided many embarrassments and overcame many obstacles; the tact with which he dealt with the rebels; the foresight he often displayed, of events ; the knowledge of human nature; the patience with men and circumstances; the instinctive sympathy with popular feeling, which impelled him to withstand all advice and entreaties to take important steps before the proper time, and yet to accomplish his purpose promptly when the nation was ready to second him ; the abnegation of self; the charity for personal and public enemies, the tender-heartedness towards offenders; and the steadiness with which he pursued the objects of the war and of the nation—all combined to make him one of the most striking characters in American history.

There was a simplicity and a straightforwardness about him that resembled the same traits in Grant; and when, as necessarily happened in their positions, their minds came in direct and naked contact, they appreciated each other better than clever and ambitious men of the world could appreciate either.

During the day Grant received his letters and dictated the replies, and saw the various officers who came to him for orders or counsel, while" those who formed his military family were busied about

their vaidous duties. The secretaries and adjutants generally remained in camp, while the engineers were sent sometimes to Butler's lines, sometimes to Meade's. The other aides-de-camp were dispatched to more distant parts of the command; often one was with Sherman, another with Sheridan, and a third with Canby; and during actual movements in front of Petersburg and Richmond, Grant always had a representative with that army with which he himself was unable to be present.

The chief and his personal staff always messed together, and their plain table was shared by all the illustrious visitors whom duty, or curiosity, or interest, brought to the head-quarters of the army. A rude log cabin formed the dining-room, and a long deal table received the fare, never garnished with wine or spirits of any kind; coffee and tea at breakfast and supper, with water for the mid-day dinner, were the only drinks offered at these simple, soldiers' meals.

When night came, all the officers on duty at the head-quarters were accustomed to gather round the great camp fire, and the circle often numbered twenty or even thirty soldiers. . Grant always joined it, with his cigar, and from six or seven o'clock till midnight, conversation was the sole amusement. The military situation in every quarter of the country was of course the absorbing theme; the latest news from Sheridan or Sherman, the condition of affairs inside of Richmond, the strength of the rebel armies, the exhaustion of the South; the information extracted from recent prisoners, or spies, or from the rebel newspapers.

From this the transition was easy to earlier

events of the war, and Grant was always ready to relate what he had seen, to tell of his campaigns, to describe the character of his comrades and subordinates. Before the war he had met most of the men who were now prominent, rebels as well as national officers; either in the old army, or at West Point as cadets ; and the knowledge of their character he thus obtained was extremely useful to him at this time. He often said of those opposed to him: "I know exactly what that general will do ;" " I am glad such an one is in my front;" " I would rather fight this one, than another." So also with those who were now his subordinates; what he had learned of them in garrison, on the Canada frontier, or at the West, before the Indians, or crossing the isthmus of Panama, in cholera time,— all was of use now. No man was better able to predict what an individual would do in an emergency, if he had known or seen much of him before. The most ordinary circumstance to him betrayed character ; and as we sat around our fire at City Point, he told stories by the hour of adventures in the Mexican war, or rides on the prairies, or intercourse with Californian miners, which threw a flood of light on the immense events in which the same actors were now engaged. And yet he never seemed to observe, and thus unconsciously deceived many who fancied they were deceiving him.

Of course, all listened eagerly and deferentially to what he had to say, but all took part in the conversation : a simple captain could tell his story without interruption from the general-in-chief—save when he asked for a light for his cigar. P'olitics at home were often discussed, and unless strangers

or foreigners were present, with great freedom. Gossip about men whom most of us had known came in, and tales of West Point life were common. But though familiar, the talk was by no means vulgar; no coarse language was ever used in the presence of the general-in-chief, the most modest man in conversation in the army. A profane word never passed his lips, and if by some rare chance a story a little broad was told before him, he blushed like a girl. Yet he was entirely free from cant, and never rebuked in others the faults which he himself scrupulously avoided.

Grant indeed rarely showed vexation at occurrences, great or small, which must have tried him hard. Sometimes, in great emergencies, his lips became set and his mouth rigid, his expression stern; but even then his eye rarely flashed, and his voice betrayed no emotion. His tones grew calmer and more distinct; his mind seemed to kindle, his intellectual vision quickened; the windows of his soul were opened, and he looked out, through and beyond whatever was obscure; but all this only those who knew him long and intimately, and watched him closely, could discern. To others he was as impassive as ever. I remember only twice during the war to have seen in him what might be called a shadow of excitement: once, when he was indignant at a great wrong put upon a friend; and once, in the field, when we passed a teamster who was ill-using a horse, he shook his clenched hand at the man, and threatened him with arrest for cruelty.

As the night wore on, one and another of the frequenters of the camp fire dropped away, and by midnight, the circle was winnowed to three or four, of whom Grant was always one. The only symptom of anxiety he displayed under the tremendous cares imposed upon him was wakefulness. He never wanted to go to his camp bed. His immediate aides-de-camp discovered this, and as he was willing to sit under the cold clear sky and stars till three and four o'clock, wearing them all out, they at last agreed among themselves to wait up with him in turn. He never knew of this, but we often bargained with each other for an hour or two of rest. Many of these nights can I remember, during that long winter at City Point, when every one was asleep but the commander of the armies and his single officer. If the weather was inclement, we bore it as long as we could outside, and then sought shelter in his cabin. How confidential and intimate his conversation could at such times become, only those thrown closely with him knew. His recollections of the past, the stories of his great battles and campaigns, the personal incidents of Vicksburg, and Donalson, and Chattanooga, and Shiloh; the details of his earlier career; his belief in the ultimate success of our cause; his prediction of events—all were clearly told in terse and often eloquent language; with every now and then a pregnant utterance that showed his appreciation of individual character or close sympathy with men in masses, the native strength of his intellect, or the keen penetration of his judgment.

It was then I learned to know him best and like him most; then I understood that he was really of the Homeric type ; the sort of man that many in our modern artificial civilization fail to recognize. Because he was not great in the way they thought

he ought to be, they pronounced him not great at all. Because he was quiet, simple, unadroit, undemonstrative of power or feeling, absolutely plain in speech and manner and action, they supposed him stolid and dull. But the traits which affect nations and parties, if not dilettanti and doctrinaires ; the directness of purpose and speech, the absolute honesty of intention, the simplicity of behavior, the utter unselfishness, rising at times into heroic proportions ; the freedom from vanity ; the courage which was never daunted, the determination which was never disturbed, the steadiness of nerve that bore him up amid carnage and apparent disaster ; and above all, the supreme self-control that preserved him always calm and unruffled, without elation in victory or despondency in adverse fortune —these were superadded to a clearness and soundness of judgment almost unrivalled, and a power of lucid and exact expression so absolute that when he was in earnest, a child could not mistake his meaning ; a broadness of intellect that comprehended a continent, a fertility of resource in emergencies, displayed in a hundred battles, and a grand power of administration that carried on the campaigns in Georgia and on the sea-coast, in West and East Virginia, and beyond the Mississippi—all at the same time without confusion, and made each tend to the success of every other. Mingled with these was a tender-heartedness that could not bear the sight of unnecessary pain; a clemency for the vanquished never surpassed, and which indeed transcended not only the expectation of the enemy, but the wishes of many of his own friends; a regard for the feelings of others that spared them mortification, sometimes

at the risk of his own fame; a carelessness of triumph, which led him to leave his conquests before he had contemplated them ; a delicacy in conferring benefits, which heightened the obligation he sought to lessen; and finally a devotion to duty so pure that he was unconscious that it was remarkable. Some of these traits were revealed in the shock of battle, some on the tedious march, some in the general intercourse of the camp, but not a few became apparent—all unknown to him who displayed them—during the long night-watches of the siege of Petersburg.

Even when Grant had thrown himself on his bed, one of his staff remained on duty outside his tent, till morning. We had learned of plots to capture prominent officers ;* on a dark night some tiny craft from Richmond might elude the vigilance of the fleet, and a spy or a traitor might be found willing to risk his own life for the chance of taking Grant's. A national ordnance boat had once been exploded beneath the bluff on which the head-quarters were established; t one man was killed and an officer wounded ; so it was arranged that one of the personal staff in turn should watch till daybreak, while the chief was sleeping. His first knowledge of this was gained long after the war.

But at times the military family received an

* Generals Crook and Kelley had thus been abducted from Cumberland, Maryland, by rebel raiders.

t A rebel emissary entered the national lines in disguise, with a torpedo arranged with clockwork, to explode at a given hour. This he deposited on a loaded ordnance boat at the City Point wharf, doubtless hoping to cause the destruction of every one at Grant's head-quarters.

accession. The wife of the commander-in-chief had often spent a few weeks with him in camp or siege, or when he was quartered in a captured town. At Memphis, Vicksburg, Chattanooga, Nashville, she had joined him, and now again in front of Petersburg. His children too visited him, the eldest only fourteen years of age at this time, the youngest seven; and the man who directed the destinies of armies, and was unalterable in his decisions when he believed them right; who ordered the devastation of the Valley of Virginia, and went unshrinking through the Wilderness campaign, was as bland and playful with his wife and children as the humblest soldier in the ranks before he went to war. All the simplicity and gentleness of his nature came out in this companionship. He had been married sixteen years, and still seemed to find his greatest solace in the domestic relations; while, like a true woman, the wife was interested in whatever concerned him; anxious to relieve him from petty cares, proud of his success, but never trenching beyond her proper sphere ; exercising all her woman's influence to soothe and support, never to vex, or annoy, or disturb.

It was curious to watch—not her, for her tact would not have allowed her to make the mistake, but others around him, who thought they had influence. They had influence, undoubtedly, in little things ; in details, in their own province, or department. Grant was not unwilling to let others arrange for him, and decide for him many unimportant matters; and even many matters of consequence, in which he trusted their judgment or knowledge. He would not dictate to a quartermaster the minutiae of his duty ; he rarely told a secre-

tary what language to employ in writing a letter; but when the moment arrived at which he deemed it necessary to decide for himself, no advice, or clever pleading, or adroit management, could avail to shake him. In a great matter he was absolutely immovable, and sometimes equally so in some apparently trivial one, if he considered that the time had come to make his will obeyed. Then, the people who fancied they were so dexterous, or all-powerful, or indispensable, discovered their mistake; and, though Grant often sought to soothe their chagrin or cover their defeat, he did not swerve from his purpose, when once it was determined.

He was, however, always most averse to giving pain; and it may be that harsh critics will censure him as too long-suffering. He certainly sometimes bore with subordinates who were obstinate, or self-seeking, or unskilful, to a point to which many of his friends could not follow him. Several of the generals whom at various times he displaced, contended that their fault had been condoned, because it was not promptly punished. They had been retained after a defeat, or a blunder, or a culpable negligence, and therefore Grant should not subsequently have condemned them. And there is a certain force in the pleading. He did endure conduct which perhaps he should have put an end to sooner; he continued men in command, who, if not failures, were not successful, and, as chief of the armies, it may have been his strict duty to displace them earlier. But this leniency did not proceed from sheer good-nature or soft-heartedness. He was always sanguine; he hoped that these men would reform their faults or redeem their failures; that they would learn and

improve; he was willing to give them another chance. But when, after a succession of mistakes and misdoings, of faults and forgivenesses, the existence of the original erring trait was made evident in some little circumstance, the blow came sudden and sharp. He seemed to arrive all at once at the conclusion that there could be no cure, and action then followed decision instantaneously.

I have said that he was calm, and unimpas-sioned; undemonstrative; but he was not unfeeling. He took the liveliest interest in the fortunes of his friends, in the success of his subordinates. He enjoyed the triumphs of Sherman and Sheridan, and of all national commanders, as keenly as if they had been his own. He also felt to the full the weight of the responsibility that lay upon his shoulders. Of this he rarely spoke, but the sleepless nights he passed were evidence of it, as well as the current of his talk, always, unless diverted by some eddy of the moment, borne along with his thought on the war. His calm was as far as possible from stolidity. It came from a complete apprehension of his subject, a certainty that he had done his best, and that if the decision were to be made again, his judgment would not be different; from a hopefulness at all times and under all circumstances ; and from that faith in ultimate success which never deserted him, and, as Sherman once said, could be likened to nothing else but the faith a Christian has in the Saviour. I remember hearing him tell a foreign officer he felt as sure of capturing Richmond as he did of dying.

This faith inspired those around him ; this confidence he had, of ultimately winning, was contagious.

No man could be long downcast when near him. It was pleasant to receive this influence. One felt more a man when with him, and liked him for it. This with the thoughtful anxiety never to wound another' the watchful care and persistent advancement of the interests of his friends, the steadfast regard, never expressed in words to the individual, but discovered in acts, and sometimes—though rarely—in tones or

glances that he never meant should betray him

these, combined with the fact that he represented the nation, that his success was bound up with that of the country, that he was the incarnation of the cause for which all were fighting— produced a devotion in those who served under and near him, which rivalled that inspired by any of the great commanders in history.

During this period the general-in-chief was making every preparation to support and facilitate Sherman s march. At 11.30 P.M. on the llth of October, he had first authorized the movement. " If you are satisfied the trip to the sea-coast can be made, holding the line of the Tennessee river firmly, you may make it, destroying all the railroads south of Dalton or Chattanooga, as you think best." On the next day, at one P.M., he renewed his permission, and gave Sherman instructions for his conduct on the road. "On reflection," he said, " I think better of your proposition. It will be much better to go south than to be forced to go north. You will no doubt clear the country where you go, of railroad tracks and supplies. I would also move every wagon, horse, mule, and hoof of stock, as well as the negroes. As far as arms can be supplied, either from surplus or by

capture, I would put them in the hands of negro 92

men. Give them such organization as you can. They will be of some use."

On the 13th, at 3.30 P.M., he announced his decision to the government. " On mature reflection, I believe Sherman's proposition is the best that can be adopted. With the long line of railroad in rear of Atlanta, Sherman cannot maintain his position. If he cuts loose, destroying the road from Chattanooga forward, he leaves a wide and destitute country to pass, before reaching territory now held by us. Thomas could retain force enough to meet Hood's army, if it took the other and more likely course." Then, with his usual enthusiasm whenever Sherman was concerned, he added : " Such an army as Sherman has, and with such a commander, is hard to corner or to capture."

Grant indeed was already very much in earnest, and on the same day, October 13th, he issued full and detailed instructions to Halleck to provide supplies for Sherman on his arrival at the coast. " Vessels should be got ready loaded with grain, ordnance-stores, and provisions;—say two hundred thousand rations of grain and fifty thousand rations of provision, and one hundred rounds of ammunition for that number of infantry. . . Soon after it is known that Sherman has started south, these vessels should sail, and rendezvous at Ossabaw Sound. I take it, the first supplies will have to be received by way of that river." In the same despatch he gave directions for the co-operation of Canby and Foster, and added : " Information should be got to Sherman of all preparations made to meet him on the sea-coast. "'*

* General Sherman was evidently unacquainted with the contents of these despatches when he wrote in his Memoirs,

But while the general-in-chief was thus diligently arranging for Sherman's arrival at the Atlantic, Sherman himself had been drawn back by Hood nearly to the Tennessee. After the repulse of the rebels from Allatoona, he reached that place in person on the 9th of October, still in doubt as to the intentions of the enemy. On the 10th, Hood appeared at Home, and Sherman ordered his whole army to march to Kingston in pursuit; he arrived there himself on the llth, but Hood had already decamped. Marching with rapidity along the Chattooga Valley, the rebels appeared before Eesaca on the 12th, and Hood himself demanded the surrender of the post. " No prisoners will be taken," he said, "if the place is carried by assault." But the commander replied : " If you want it, come and take it;" an, invitation which Hood, admonished by his losses before Allatoona, was not inclined to accept. The demand was a mere piece of bluster, and he continued his march north, doing all the damage possible to the railway.

Sherman at first had intended to move into the Chattooga Valley, in the rebel rear, but fearing, in that event, that Hood might cross to the east of the railroad, he marched towards Hesaca instead, and on the 14th, made his dispositions to entrap the enemy at Snake Creek Gap. Hood, however,

Vol. II., page 166, that November 2nd " was the first time that General Grant assented to the march to the sea." The telegrams to Halleck and Stanton he probably never saw, and those to himself, of the llth and 12th of October, appear not to have reached him. The wires were cut between his army and the North at this time. See page 153.

was too quick for him, and escaped through the gap before the national troops could reach the further end. Sherman now hoped to catch up with the rebels at Lafayette and cut off their retreat at that place, but by the time his forces were in position, Hood had again escaped and moved in a southwesterly direction, to the neighborhood of Gadsden. He was encumbered with few .trains and marched with great celerity; evidently anxious to avoid a battle. It*is one of the most difficult feats in war for a pursuing army to overtake its enemy. The stimulus of danger seems always a sharper goad than the hope of victory.

Sherman followed as far as Gaylesville, in the rich valley of the Chattooga, and there on the 19th, he determined to pause. The rebels had altogether failed to make him let go his hold of Atlanta, but had demonstrated their ability at all times to endanger the national communications. They had captured, though they could not hold, Big Shanty, Ackworth, Tilton, and Dalton, and destroyed thirty miles of railroad ; and although Atlanta was not regained, Hood was actually at this moment threatening the invasion of Tennessee, while Forrest had crossed the Tennessee river, captured Athens, and cut the Nashville and Chattanooga railroad.

These movements of the enemy disturbed, but did not change, the plans of the national commanders. On the 10th of October, Sherman said to Thomas, now at Nashville : " Hood has crossed the Coosa. . . If he turns to Chattanooga, I will follow ; but if he shoots off towards Tuscumbia, I will act according to my information of your

ULYSSES S. GRANT.

strength." Sherman, however, was very much in hope that Hood would actually invade Tennessee. On the 16th, he said to Schofield : " I want the first positive fact that Hood contemplates an invasion of Tennessee. Invite him to do so. Send him a free pass in." On the 17th: "We must follow Hood till he is beyond reach of mischief, and then resume the offensive." The same day he said to Thomas : " Hood won't dare go into Tennessee. I hope he will." Again : " If Hood wants to go into Tennessee, west of Huntsville, let him go, and then we can all turn on him, and he cannot escape. . . I will follow him to Gadsden, and then want my whole army united for the grand move into Georgia."

On the 14th of October, when Sherman was at Besaca, Grant telegraphed to Washington : " It looks to me now that Hood has put himself into a position where his army must be to a great extent destroyed. Sherman has Home, and the rich district of country around it, and is in a better condition to live independent of supplies on hand, than Hood. I think now we may look for favorable news from that quarter." The time, however, had not yet come for the destruction of Hood's army. Sherman was at this moment cut off from all communication with the North, and on the 14th, Grant telegraphed to Stanton : " The best that can be done with despatches for Sherman is to send them to Thomas, to be forwarded as soon as communications are opened." Among the despatches thus delayed was Grant's permission of October llth, for Sherman to make his march; so that Grant was actually preparing and arranging for Sherman's campaign,

before Sherman knew that he would be allowed to start. *

On the 17th, Grant said to Sherman: "The moment I know you have started south, stores will be shipped to Hilton Head, where there are transports ready to take them to Savannah. In case you go south, I would not propose holding anything south of Chattanooga, certainly not south of Dalton. Destroy in such case all military stores at Atla,nta." On the 21st, he said to Halleck : " The stores intended for Sherman might now be started for Hilton Head."

But the general-in-chief was at this time even more anxious for the reinforcement of Thomas than for the supply of Sherman, and was ordering all his armies the better to secure this end. As early as the 12th of October, the day after he had authorized Sherman's movement, he said to Halleck : " Thomas should be prepared to concentrate a force on Hood, when he presents himself on the Tennessee river." He then proceeded to direct how this force should be accumulated. Thomas himself was to sacrifice all lesser interests to the paramount one : " It would be advisable for General Thomas to abandon all the railroad from Columbia to Decatur, thence to Stevenson. This will give him much additional force." At the same time Grant planned the transfer of A. J. Smith and Mower's commands from Missouri to Tennessee : " If Crook goes to

* " It was at Ship's Gap that a courier brought me the cipher message from General Halleck which instructed me that the authorities at Washington were willing I should undertake to march across Georgia."— Sherman's Memoirs, Vol. II., page 156. Sherman was at Ship's Gap on the 16th and 17th of October.

Missouri, he will drive Price out of the country in time to send A. J. Smith and Mower to Tennessee, before Hood can get far, even if Sherman's movements do not turn him, as I think they will. Canby's forces also will be relieved for operations, wherever they are needed."

But the troops from Missouri were slow in coming, and on the 26th of October, Grant said to Halleck : " An order, with an officer to see it enforced, should go to Missouri, to send from there all the troops not actually after Price and guards for public stores, to General Thomas, telegraphing Thomas to know at what points he wants them." The next day he repeated the order: " Now that Price is on the retreat, with no probability of his bringing up again, Eosecrans should forward all the troops he can to Thomas. This ought to be done without delay. He has six or eight thousand troops around St. Louis, and within a few hours from it, that can start at once."

On the 29th, becoming still more anxious, he sent his chief of staff, General Rawlins, as bearer of special orders to Rosecrans. In his instructions to Bawlins he said : ". . Now that Price is retreating from Missouri, it is believed that the whole force sent to that state from other departments can be spared at once. . . If it is found that the enemy under Hood or Beauregard have actually attempted an invasion of Tennessee, or those under Forrest are approaching the Ohio river, you will send them directly to Major-General Thomas, to confront and frustrate such a movement. . . General Sherman will be instructed that no force,, except that already south of the Tennessee and such as General Canby

can send, will be used between the Tennessee river and the Atlantic and the Gulf of Mexico. If he goes south, he must take care of himself, without the support of a pursuing column." Then, as if with a premonition of what was about to occur, and to answer objection in advance, he continued : "I am satisfied, on full and mature reflection, that Sherman's idea of striking across for the sea-coast is the best way to rid Tennessee and Kentucky of the threatened danger, and to make the war felt. I do not believe that General Sherman can maintain his communications with Atlanta with his whole force. He can break such an extent of roads that the enemy will be effectually cut in two for several months, by which time Augusta and Savannah can be occupied."

Hawlins, however, was intensely opposed to the proposed march of Sherman, and had combated it with every argument at his disposal. Grant, as a rule, allowed his staff to present their views on military matters freely, and some of them were accustomed to do so with great ability; but when once his decisions were made, they received them as final, and did whatever was in their power to make them succeed. But in this instance, the anxiety of Rawlins led him to an act of downright insubordination. He started for the West, bearing the orders above quoted, and stopped a day at Washington, on the way. Here he saw the President and the Secretary of War, and expressed so forcibly his apprehensions as to the result of allowing Sherman to move south and leave Thomas to contend with Hood, that he actually induced the government to send a despatch to Grant, desiring him to recon-

sider his decision."' 5 " They were the more ready for this, as both the President and the Secretary had been steadily hostile to the movement from the beginning. Halleck also had presented to Grant an elaborate letter recommending an entirely different campaign.! Thus, although the administration would not take the responsibility of countermanding Grant's order, or absolutely overruling his judgment, they did strongly urge him to reconsider both at this late day.

Grant was always properly subordinate, and thought himself obliged to defer to this intimation from his superiors. The despatch from Stanton arrived on the 1st of November, and at six P.M. on the same day, Grant telegraphed to Sherman : "Do you not think it advisable, now that Hood has gone so far north, to entirely settle him before starting on your proposed campaign ? With Hood's army destroyed, you can go where you please with impunity. I believed, and still believe, that if you had started south whilst Hood was in the neighborhood of you, he would have been forced to go after you. Now that he is so far away, he might look upon the chase as useless, and go in one direction whilst you are looking in the other. If you can see the chance for destroying Hood's army, attend to that first, and make your other move secondary."

Sherman himself was struck with the same idea. Indeed, the whole enterprise was of such magnitude, the issues at stake were so tremendous, that all concerned might well ponder before the final step

* Grant never knew the origin of this despatch until after the death of Rawlins.

f See Appendix for this letter.

was taken. Sherman replied to Grant at 12.30 P.M. on the 2nd : " Your despatch is received. If I could hope to overhaul Hood, I would turn against him with my whole force; then he would retreat to the south-west, drawing me as a decoy from Georgia, which is his chief object. If he ventures north of the Tennessee, I may turn in that direction, and endeavor to get between him and his line of retreat; but, thus far, he has not gone above the Tennessee. Thomas will have a force strong enough to prevent his reaching any country in which we have an interest, and he has orders, if Hood turns to follow me, to push for Selma. No single army can catch him, and I am convinced the best results will follow from our defeating Jeff. Davis's cherished plan of making me leave Georgia by manoeuvring. Thus far I have confined my efforts to thwart his plans, and have reduced my baggage so that I can pick up and start in any direction; but I would regard pursuit of Hood as useless. Still, if he attempts to invade Middle Tennessee, I will hold Decatur, and be prepared to move in that direction; but unless I let go Atlanta, my force will not be equal to his." The policy was daring, the strategy complex, and Grant and Sherman, both under pressure from their superiors, both, for a moment, hesitated.

Only for a moment, however. On the morning of the 2nd, Grant received a despatch from Sherman, dated nine A.M. of the day before—nine hours earlier than Grant's own countermanding or delaying the movement. In this despatch Sherman reported Hood's entire strength at less than forty thousand men, exclusive of Forrest's cavalry, while Thomas, he said, had at least forty-five thousand or fifty

thousand soldiers, besides the force that was promised from Kosecrans.* This statement of the relative strength of the two armies at once reassured and decided Grant. At 11.30 A.M. on the 2nd, having yet no response to his own message of the night before, he telegraphed again to Sherman: "' Your despatch of nine A.M. yesterday is just received. I despatched you the same date, advising

* " As you foresaw, and as Jeff. Davis threatened, the enemy is now in the full tide of execution of his grand plan to destroy my communications and defeat this army. His infantry, about 30,000, with Wheeler and Koddy's cavalry, from 7,000 to 10,000, are now in the neighborhood of Tuscumbia and Florence, and the water being low, are able to cross at will. Forrest seems to be scattered from Eastport to Jackson, Paris, and the lower Tennessee, and General Thomas reports the capture by him of a gunboat and five transports. General Thomas has near Athens and Pulaski, Stanley's corps, about 15,000 strong, and Schofield's corps, 10,000, en route by rail; and has at least 20,000 to 25,000 men, with new regiments and conscripts arriving all the time, also. General Rosecrans promises the two divisions of Smith and Mower belonging to me, but I doubt if they can reach Tennessee in less than ten days. If I were to let go Atlanta and North Georgia, and make for Hood, he would, as he did here, retreat to the south-west, leaving his militia, now assembling at Macon and Griffin, to occupy our conquests, and the work of last summer would be lost. I have retained about 50,000 good troops, and have sent back full 25,000, and have instructed General Thomas to hold defensively Nashville, Chattanooga, and Decatur, all strongly fortified and provisioned for a long siege. I will destroy all the railroads of Georgia, and do as much substantial damage as is possible, reaching the sea-coast near one of the points indicated, trusting that Thomas with his present troops, and the influx of new troops promised,

will be able in a few days to assume the offensive.

" Hood's cavalry may do a good deal of damage, and I have sent Wilson back with all dismounted cavalry, retaining only about 4,500. This is the best I can do, and shall therefore, when I get to Atlanta the necessary stores, move south as soon as possible."— /Sherman to Grant, Rome, Georgia, November 1, 9 A.M.

that Hood's army, now that it had worked so far north, ought to be looked upon more as the object. With the force, however, you have left General Thomas, he must be able to take care of Hood and destroy him. I'really do not see that you can withdraw from where you are, without giving up all that we have gained in territory. say then, go on, as you propose."

Sherman was equally prompt in re-asserting his original confidence. At six P.M. on the 2nd, too soon to have heard again from Grant, he telegraphed : "If I turn back, the whole effect of my campaign will be lost. By my movement I have thrown Beauregard to the west, and Thomas will have ample time and sufficient troops to hold him, until reinforcements reach him from Missouri, and recruits. We have now ample supplies at Chattanooga and Atlanta to stand a month's interruption to our communications, and I don't believe the Confederate army can reach our line save by cavalry raids, and Wilson will have cavalry enough to checkmate that. I am clearly of opinion that the best results will follow me in my contemplated move through Georgia."

The two soldiers were in singular harmony. Each, for a moment, thought it might be better to follow Hood, but before either had received the second despatch of the other, each came to the same conclusion, favoring the bolder course. Their separate judgments gave but one response, like instruments of music struck in a single chord. Their despatches crossed each other on the way; Grant directing Sherman: " Go on, as you propose;" while Sherman, ignorant that the revocation origi-

ULYSSES S. GRANT.

nated at Washington, was urging Grant for permission to start. At 9.30 P.M. of the 2nd, however, Grant's second telegram arrived, and Sherman answered at once : " Despatch of 11.30 A.M. received. I will go on and complete my arrangements, and in a few days notify you of the day of my departure. . . I think J eff. Davis will change his tune, when he finds rne advancing in the heart of Georgia, instead of retreating, and I think it will have an immediate effect on your operations at Richmond."

All telegrams between Grant and his subordinates at the West necessarily passed through Washington, where copies were taken off for the War Department, so that this entire correspondence was seen by the government, as it occurred. It was the only reply made by Grant to the despatch of Stanton, but no more was said in any quarter in opposition to Sherman's march.

Thus, upon the general-in-chief alone the responsibility for the movement rented. Neither his civil superiors, nor his military subordinates, could relieve him from this burden. In case of failure, the country would censure him, not the President nor the Secretary of War, who had deferred to his judgment and invested him with absolute command. If Thomas should be destroyed and the North invaded, if Sherman should be intercepted, and suffer the fate of the French in the Moscow campaign, it was Grant who would be held to account, not the men who obeyed his orders and executed his decisions.Indeed, from the moment when he accepted the modifications w T hich Sherman proposed, the plan be came Grant's own. It was he who was responsible for its success or failure; it was he who authorized it; it was he who must provide supplies for one army and reinforcements for the other; who must direct the movements all over the continent, of Canby and Foster and Rosecrans, as well as of Meade and Butler and Sheridan, so that all should contribute to the safety of the imperilled armies; it was he whose downfall was certain, if either campaign proved disastrous; it was he who, seated in his hut at City Point, balanced the armies, and put his troops first into one scale and then into the other, according as emergency required; it was he to whom the nation turned in its agony, knowing that it had committed its destinies into his hands, trusting him as men trust the master of a ship in a storm, as they trust an unknown power when they themselves are helpless—trying hard to hope, but full of anxiety and alarm.

And at no moment during the war was the crisis more tremendous, the responsibility more appalling. Success in both of the great operations now ordered would go far to terminate the rebellion, but failure in either appeared irreparable: the defeat of Thomas would open the entire region north of the Ohio to invasion, while the destruction of the splendid and gallant army of Sherman would shock and dishearten the country beyond measure. And there seemed imminent danger of each catastrophe. Hood was threatening and bold, and Thomas had not yet collected his forces ; while the bare idea of an army plunging, as Sherman was about to do, into the interior of a hostile country, without base, or communications, or supplies,

affected not only the imagination, but the judgment of the gravest and steadiest minds. It was these considerations which the general-in-chief had to contemplate, and these cares he had to sustain.

Hood, meanwhile, had remained at Gadsden only one day, to issue supplies, and on the 21st of October, he took up his line of march for the Tennessee. On the 26th, he arrived at Tuscumbia, on that river, a hundred miles west of Gadsden. This made it evident that the invasion of Tennessee was actually contemplated, and the same day Sherman detached the Fourth corps, with orders to proceed to Chattanooga and report to Thomas. On the 30th, as the danger became more imminent, the Twenty-third corps, under Schofield, was dispatched with the same destination, and Wilson was sent back to Nashville with all dismounted detachments, and ordered to collect as rapidly as possible all cavalry serving in Tennessee and Kentucky, and report to Thomas for duty. With these forces and the garrisons in Kentucky and Tennessee, it was hoped that Thomas would be able to defend the railroad from Chattanooga to Nashville, and still have an army with which he could cope with Hood, until the reinforcements from Missouri and elsewhere should arrive. On the 1st of November, Sherman telegraphed : " I have retained about fifty thousand good troops, and have sent back about twenty-five thousand, and have instructed General Thomas to hold defensively Nashville, Chattanooga, and Decatur, all strongly fortified, and provisioned for a long siege. I shall destroy all the railroads of Georgia, and do as much substantial damage as possible, trusting that

Thomas, with his present troops and the influx of new troops promised, will be able to assume the offensive."

On the 2nd, Sherman himself was at Kingston, and his four corps, the Fifteenth, Seventeeth, Fourteenth, and Twentieth, with one division of cavalry, were stretched along from Rome to Atlanta. The railroad and telegraph lines had been repaired, the sick and wounded were sent back to Chattanooga, the wagon trains were loaded and ready to start at a day's notice ; the paymasters were paying the troops; and Sherman waited only till the Presidential election was over in order to start. There was now no serious enemy in his front. Hood remained at Tuscumbia and Florence, busy in collecting shoes and clothing for his men, and the necessary ammunition and stores for the invasion of Tennessee; while Beauregard, who had been placed in general command at the West, was at Corinth, superintending the rebel preparations.

On the 6th of November, Sherman wrote at great length to Grant, confiding to him the doubts and anxieties, the plans and imaginings that crowded upon his busy mind. He seems even then to have had occasional misgivings about his strategy, which, however, he quickly brushed away. " The only question in my mind," he said, " is whether I ought not to have dogged Hood far over into Mississippi, trusting to some happy accident to bring him to bay and to battle ; but I then thought that by so doing I would play into his hands, by being drawn or decoyed too far away from our original line of advance. . . I felt compelled, therefore, to do what is usually a mistake in war—divide

my forces—send a part back into Tennessee, retaining the balance here. . . I admit that the first object should be the destruction of that army, and if Beauregard moves his infantry and artillery up into the pocket about Jackson and Paris, / shall feel strongly tempted to move Thomas directly against him, and myself move rapidly by Decatur and Purdy to cut off his retreat. But this would involve the abandonment of Atlanta and a retrograde movement, which would be of very doubtful expediency or success. . . I am more than satisfied that Beau-regard has not the nerve to attack fortifications, or to meet me in open battle, and it would be a great achievement for him to make me abandon Atlanta, by mere threats or manoeuvres."

But by far the most important part of this despatch related to his line of march, for his absolute route was yet necessarily undetermined. No man could say what Hood would do, when the departure of the national army became known ; whether he would persist in the invasion of Tennessee, or retrace his steps in pursuit of Sherman. It could not even be certain that a considerable force might not be collected to oppose the advance to the sea. It was therefore indispensable that Sherman should have alternatives ; if repelled or thwarted in one direction, he must be free to turn in another; if he could not reach the Atlantic coast, he must make for the Gulf of Mexico. Thus, at the very moment of starting, neither he nor Grant knew what point would be the terminus of his march ; and in this last despatch to the general-in-chief, Sherman said : " If I start before I hear further from you, or before further developments turn my

course, you may take it for granted that I have moved vid Griffin to Barnesville; that I break up the road between Columbus and Macon good, and then, if I feign on Columbus, will move vid Macon and Millen to Savannah ; or if I feign on Macon, you may take it for granted I have shot off towards Opelika, Montgomery, and Mobile bay or Pensa-cola."

He concluded : "I will not attempt to send couriers back, but trust to the Richmond papers to keep you well advised. . . I will see that the road is broken completely between the Etowa and the Chattahoochee, and that Atlanta itself is utterly destroyed."

On the 7th, he said: "By the 10th, the election will be over, the troops all paid, and all our surplus property will be back to Chattanooga. On that day or the following, if affairs should remain as now in Tennessee, I propose to begin the movement." Grant replied on the same day, at 10.30 P.M.: "Your despatch of this evening received. I see no present reason for changing your plan ; should any arise, you will see it; or if I do, I will inform you. I think everything here favorable now. Great good fortune attend you. I believe you will be eminently successful, and at worst can only make a march less fruitful of results than hoped for." This was the last despatch from Grant that Sherman received before the wires were cut.

The election for President was now close at hand, and Grant, like most of the earnest men in the army, was profoundly anxious for the reelection of Lincoln. His anxiety, however, had nothing to do with ordinary politics. Sherman's despatches show that he was as decided in this matter as Grant, yet neither was a politician, and if either had political sympathies before the rebellion, it was with those who called themselves Democrats. Grant could not but feel the keenest interest in the success of the party that was pledged to carry on the war, but he earnestly deprecated any obtrusion of the army into civil affairs.

It had been proposed by some of the states to allow the soldiers in the field to vote, and the government invited his views on the subject. He was strongly in favor of the measure, but thought it should be surrounded by checks and safeguards. " The exercise of the right of suffrage by an army in the field," he said, " has generally been considered dangerous to constitutional liberty, as well as subversive to military discipline. But our circumstances are novel and exceptional. A very large proportion of the legal voters of the United States are now either under arms in the field, or in hospitals, or otherwise engaged in the military service of the United States. Most of these men, if not regular soldiers in the strict sense of that term, still less" are they mercenaries, who give their services to the government simply for its pay, having little understanding of political questions, or feeling little or no interest in them. On the contrary, they are American citizens, having still their homes and social and political ties binding them to the states and districts from which they come and to which they expect to return. They have left their homes temporarily, to sustain

the cause of their country in its hour of trial. In performing this sacred duty they should not be deprived of a most precious privilege. They have as much right to demand that their votes shall be counted in the choice of their rulers, as those citizens who remain at home; nay more, for they have sacrificed more for their country."

Nevertheless, he was most anxious to avoid any use of the army for party purposes, or any political excitement within the lines. " I state these reasons in full," he continued, " for the unusual thing of allowing armies in the field to vote, that I may urge on the other hand that nothing more than the fullest exercise of this vote should be allowed; for anything not absolutely necessary to the exercise cannot but be dangerous to the liberties of the country. The officers and soldiers have every means of understanding the questions before the country. The newspapers are freely circulated, and so I believe are the documents prepared by both parties to set forth the merits and claims of their candidates. Beyond this, nothing whatever should be allowed ; no political meetings, no harangues from soldier or citizen, and no canvassing of camps or regiments for votes. I see not why a single individual not belonging to the armies should be admitted into their lines to deliver tickets. In my opinion, the tickets should be furnished by the chief provost-marshal of each army, by them to the provost-marshal or some other officer of each brigade or regiment, who shall, on the day of election, deliver tickets, irrespective of party, to whoever may call for them. If, however, it shall be deemed expedient to admit citizens to deliver tickets, then it

should be most positively prohibited that such citizens should electioneer, harangue, or canvass the regiments in any way. Their business should be, and only be, to distribute, on a certain fixed day, tickets to whoever may call for them. . . As it is intended that all soldiers entitled to vote shall exercise that privilege according to their own convictions of right, unmolested and unrestricted, there will be no objection to each party sending to armies easy of access a number of respectable gentlemen to see that these views are carried out."

It would be difficult to frame regulations better calculated to secure the freest exercise of the suffrage in an army, and at the same time obviate the dangers which are instantly so apparent—the possibility of disturbance, the undue biassing of soldiers by their officers, the employment of troops to control opinion or coerce action in civil affairs.

As the day of the election approached, the anxiety in regard to the result became painful. It was the prosecution of the war that was at issue. This was the last opportunity the Democrats would have for years, of regaining power; but if they succeeded, there was little doubt, either at the North or South, that the rebels would attain their end. The enemy therefore made frantic efforts to influence the public mind. The affair at Hatcher's Run was proclaimed a national defeat, the siege of Richmond was declared hopeless; Hood was certain to cross the Ohio, and Sherman could not possibly escape annihilation. These vaunts of the rebels were repeated by their allies in the loyal states, and every endeavor was made to inculcate the belief that while absolute unanimity prevailed throughout the

South, a majority at the North was in favor of acquiescing in the rebel demands.

But this was not all. The enemies of the nation did not confine their efforts to calumny and invective, to misrepresentation in speech and print, or even to seditious attempts to depreciate the currency and lower the financial credit of the country. There was at this time imminent danger of disturbance and outbreak at more than one point in the North. Many Northern cities were infested with rebel spies and refugees, as well as sympathizers; a positive conspiracy against the government was detected at the West, the ramifications of which extended into several states north of the Ohio ; still another plot was discovered to release the rebel prisoners at Chicago, and burn the town; incendiarism was attempted at New York, and riot and insurrection were openly threatened on the day of the election, in the city where they had already occurred. * The gloom and apprehension which existed were wide-spread and profound, and were fully warranted.

But though depressed and alarmed, the government and its friends were not dismayed. They were determined that in every event the Union should be preserved; they relaxed no effort, they neglected no precaution. The conspiracy at the West was detected in time. Measures were taken to prevent or suppress riot; arson was punished, and troops were sent to the points at the North where insurrection was most apprehended.

On the 19th of October, General Dix, in coni-

* See Appendix for documentary proof of these statements, from the files of the War Department.

ULYSSES S. GRANT.

mand at New York, wrote at length to Grant. "I deem it my duty to call your attention, as general-in-chief of the army, to the want of troops in this city and harbor. . . There is more disaffection and disloyalty, independent of the elements of disturbance always here, than in any other city in the Union. * . I feel that the want of preparation would be very injurious, if known, and it is not easy to conceal it long. . . I feel very uneasy under this state of things." Dix was a moderate man, in no way likely to exaggerate, and these representations had great weight. A reinforcement of several thousand troops was ordered to New York.

But the administration was still not satisfied, and desired Grant to send General Butler to that city until'after the election.* Butler was known to be decided in judgment and prompt in action, and would not flinch in executing any measures he deemed necessary at a critical juncture. His name alone would be a terror to those who plotted against the republic. He was accordingly ordered to report to Dix, and the force in New York was temporarily increased by five thousand men.

The election took place on the 8th of November, and resulted in the success of Lincoln, who received a majority of more than four hundred thousand votes. No election of course was held in the ten Southern states in the possession of the enemy, and

* " I am just in receipt of despatch from the Secretary of War, asking me to send more troops to the city of New York, and, if possible, to let you go there until after election. I wish you would start for Washington immediately, and be guided by orders from there in the matter."— Grant to £utler, Nov. 1.

the vote of Tennessee was not counted, although given for Lincoln; but of the remaining twenty-five states, all but three,—New Jersey, Delaware, and Kentucky,—cast their votes for the Union.

Fourteen states had authorized their soldiers in the field to vote. Those of New York sent their ballots home sealed, to be cast by their friends; the votes of the soldiers from Minnesota and of most of those from Vermont were not received by the canvassers in time to be counted; but the soldiers from the eleven remaining states gave a majority for Lincoln, of eighty-five thousand four hundred and sixty-one ;* a proportion of more than three to one.

The state of Illinois, of which Grant was a citizen, had made no provision to receive the ballots of her soldiers. The general-in-chief was therefore unable to vote.

At eleven A.M. on the 10th of November, before the result was known at the headquarters of the armies, Grant telegraphed to Halleck : " I suppose without my saying anything about it, all the troops in the North will now be hurried to the field, but I wish to urge this as of the utmost importance. Sherman's movement may compel Lee to send troops from Richmond, and if he does, I want to be prepared to annoy him." At 10.30 P.M. on the same day, he telegraphed to Stanton : " Enough now seems to be known to say who is to hold the reins of government for the next four

* Beyond all question, this majority would have been doubled, had all the soldiers been allowed to vote; but the marvel is that any man in arms against the rebellion could have opposed the re-election of Abraham Lincoln.

years. Congratulate the President for me for the double victory. The election having passed off quietly, no bloodshed or riot throughout the land, is a victory worth more to the country than a battle won. Rebeldom and Europe will so construe it." There were no more allusions in Grant's despatches to politics.

McClellan at once resigned his commission in the army, the resignation to date from the 8th of November. Some of Grant's friends urged him to oppose its acceptance, but he refused to interfere."*

Sherman was to move immediately after the election, and on the 11th of November, he sent his last despatch. It was addressed to Halleck as chief of staff, but intended of course for Grant and the government. " I have balanced all the figures well," he said, "and am satisfied that General Thomas has in Tennessee a force sufficient for all probabilities." To Thomas he said, on the same day: " You could safely invite Beauregard across the Tennessee, and prevent his ever returning. I still believe, however, that the public clamor will force him to turn and follow me, in which event you should cross at Decatur and move directly

* On the 26th of December, Grant wrote to Halleck : "I am jusfc in receipt of a letter from General G. B. McClellan, saying that he proposes visiting Europe soon with his family, and that Mrs. McClellan desires to see her father before starting, and requests a leave of absence for Colonel Marcy [Mrs. McClellan's father], that this desire may be gratified. I do not know the special duty Colonel Marcy may be on at this time, and do not therefore wish the leave granted [from here], lest it may interfere with important duties. If not inconsistent with the public service, however, I wish the leave to be granted from' Washington."

towards Selma, as far as you can transport supplies." Thomas replied on the 12th: " I have no fears that Beauregard can do me any harm now, and if he attempts to follow you, I will follow him as far as possible. If he does not follow you, I will then thoroughly organize my troops, and I believe, shall have men enough to ruin him, unless he gets out of my way very rapidly." The wires were cut that night, and no further communication was sent or received by Sherman before his army moved.

As he rode towards Atlanta, the last railroad trains were going to the rear with furious speed ; the engineers waved him adieu, and turning his back on Thomas and Hood, Sherman set out on his march to the sea.

The military situation at once entirely changed. The two armies which had been contending for half a year were now marching in diametrically opposite directions, Sherman south-east and Hood northwest ; while, as soon as Sherman started from Kingston, Grant became anxious not to capture the rebel capital, and not to drive Lee out of Petersburg. On the 13th of

November, he said to Stanton : " I would not, if I could, just now, do anything to force the enemy out of Richmond or Petersburg. It would liberate too much of a force to oppose Sherman with." His whole effort at this juncture was to protect and aid the Western armies ; to make a clear path for Sherman, to intercept reinforcements for Hood, and to concentrate whatever force it was possible to give to Thomas, on whom the brunt of the next fighting was certain to fall.

The rebel government was known to be urging

ULYSSES S. GRANT.

Kirby Smith to find some means of bringing the troops west of the Mississippi to join in the coming campaign. Despatches from Jefferson Davis had been intercepted, giving Smith positive orders; and Canby was now directed, not only to prevent the crossing of the river, but to act against the communications of Hood and Beauregard. Two expeditions were accordingly organized for this purpose, one to start from Vicksburg and the other from Baton Rouge. "As large a force as can be sent," said Grant, " ought to go to Meridian or Selma. . . The road from Jackson should be well broken, arid as much damage as possible done to the Mobile and Ohio." At the same time, Foster, in South Carolina, was directed to send a force to destroy the railroad in Sherman's front, between Savannah and Charleston. " I think it would have a good effect to make the attempt . . even if it should not succeed entirely. If the troops cannot get through, they can keep the enemy off of Sherman awhile."* Supplies had already been ordered from Washington to the neighborhood of Savannah, but clothing for sixty thousand men as well as rations for thirty days, and forage for fifteen thousand horses for the same time, were now collected near Mobile bay, to await the possibility of Sherman's appearance there. At the same time, A. J. Smith had been ordered with ten thousand men, from Missouri to Tennessee. Transports on the Atlantic and in the Gulf of

* These co-operative movements of Canby and Foster suggested themselves to Sherman as well as to Grant, as appears by the records. They were indeed so manifestly appropriate that they would doubtless have occurred to any experienced strategist.

Mexico, steamers on the Missouri and the Mississippi, railways east and west of the Alleghanies— all were busy conveying forces and stores for the same object; the troops of Rosecrans, and Canby, and Foster, were all in motion, and their operations were all planned, to support the operations of Thomas and Sherman.

Grant himself remained at City Point, closely watching every contingency, and holding Lee fast so that he could neither reinforce Hood 'nor intercept Sherman. On the 15th of November, he said : " The movement now being made by the army under General Sherman may cause Lee to detach largely from the force defending Richmond. Should this occur, it will become our duty to follow." Orders were accordingly given to prepare for this emergency. To Meade Grant said : " The army north of the James will be promptly withdrawn and put in the trenches about Petersburg, thus liberating all of your infantry and cavalry and a sufficient amount of artillery. . . Hold yourself in readiness to start in the shortest time with twelve days' rations." To Butler he wrote : " In case it should be necessary for you to withdraw from north of the James, abandon all of your present lines except at Deep Bottom and Dutch Gap. Just occupy what you did prior to the movement which secured our present position." This withdrawal, however, was to be temporary only, and with characteristic forethought, Grant continued : " Open to the rear all enclosed works, so that when we want to retake them, they will not be directed against us."

Tennessee, however, was the theatre where the interest of the war now culminated ; the key-point,

at this juncture, of the strategy which enveloped a continent. Nashville, the capital of the state, is situated on the south bank of the Cumberland river, thirty or forty miles from the

Kentucky line, and midway between the eastern and western boundaries. It is connected with the North by a single railroad, starting from Louisville, on the Ohio, two hundred miles away. Along this road the principal reinforcements and supplies had passed for Sherman and Thomas since the beginning of April. Southward, two lines run from Nashville to the great railway which connects Chattanooga with the Mississippi—the Memphis and Charleston road. One of these lines runs south-east, and strikes the Chattanooga road at Stevenson; the other extends south-westerly, to Decatur. Nashville is thus at the apex of a triangle, and was by far the most important strategic point west of the Alleghanies and north of the Tennessee. On the road to Stevenson, the principal positions are Mur-freesboro', Tullahoma, and Decherd ; on the western line—Franklin, Columbia, Pulaski, and Athens. By either route, Nashville is about one hundred and fifty miles from the Memphis and Charleston road, along which the points of importance are Chattanooga, Stevenson, Huntsville, Decatur, Tuscumbia, and Corinth ; the last-named place being at the junction with the road leading into Mississippi and Alabama, by way of Meridian and Selma. The Tennessee river runs west from Chattanooga, and south of the railroad, nearly to Corinth ; but at Eastport it turns to the north, and passing by Pittsburg landing, Johnsonville, Fort Henry, and Paducah, empties at last into the Ohio. Between

Nashville and the Memphis and Charleston road the only two important streams are the Duck and the Elk, both of which flow into the Tennessee. The Harpeth, north of the Duck, received a military importance during the campaign.

This whole region, lying west of the Alle-ghanies, forms part of the Valley of the Mississippi. The country is undulating or level, and one of the most fertile districts in America. Its grain and grass are famous, and the horses and other live stock raised here are not surpassed in the world. The roads were the finest in the Southern states. Middle Tennessee, however, had been a battle-field since the beginning of the war, and its rich plains were devastated, its barns and farm-houses emptied, its cattle and horses seized, by both armies in turn. The inhabitants, outside of the mountain region, were among the most determined rebels in the land.

Major-General George H. Thomas, to whom was now entrusted the defence of Tennessee, was one of the great historical figures of the war. Older than any of his compeers, one of the few soldiers by education who had never left the regular army, a Virginian by birth, but of unswerving loyalty, he was full of noble qualities. He had none of the excitable imagination and fervid passion of Sherman, none of the dashing genius or the personal magnetism of Sheridan, but possessed not a few traits in common with Grant. His judgment was sound, his patience untiring, his courage never shaken, his endurance inexhaustible. Like his chief, he was always calm and collected, and though ordinarily quiet and even gentle, like him he could be resolute when necessary, and was theo immov-

ULYSSES S. GRANT.

able by friend or foe. Grant, so undemonstrative himself, seemed more attracted in others by the traits or temper that contrasted with his own; but he entertained a profound respect and admiration for Thomas's ability and character, and once said to him : " I have as much confidence in your conducting a battle rightly as I have in any other officer." Had he searched the army through, there was not a soldier whom he would have preferred for a great defensive emergency.

Thomas was so unlike Sherman that there could hardly exist between them an absolute personal sympathy, but there was never military discord; and Sherman had a genuine regard for his elder subordinate. With reason, too, for Thomas had outranked Sherman, until the latter was given command of the Mississippi Valley; but he was as cheerful in his obedience then, and as prompt in his acceptance of the new superior, as if it had been the old general-in-chief, General Scott himself, who had been set above him. At the outset of the war he had sacrificed to his country the friendships of a lifetime, as well as what was called State pride, and there seemed no selfish interests or aspirations for him to conquer or abandon afterwards. His patriotism was not a duty only ; it was a devotion, if not a passion. In this at least he was an enthu-

He was the idol of his men, and the personal friend of his immediate officers. Unassuming in manner, apparently unambitious, he never offended an equal, he never had a rival, he never criticized a superior. Yet he could be harsh, when needful, with an offending subordinate, and was merciless

to the enemy till the battle was over. His knowledge of his art was supreme, his tactical skill unerring, and for what he lacked in quickness or brilliancy, he made up by a concentrated energy which at times was terrible. The fortune of war deprived him of many opportunities for the display of strategical ability; he usually served immediately under some other commander, and had therefore originated no great plan of campaign. It was besides not his nature to take the initiative; but on the defensive, he wa,s absolutely superb. At the crisis of the battle of Chickamauga it was his determination that saved the army of the Cumberland from annihilation; and afterwards, with indomitable vigor, he made every disposition for holding Chattanooga, until Grant arrived and assumed command. " I will hold the town," he telegraphed, " till we starve."

He certainly was sometimes slow when there was need of speed, and though without a trace of timidity in his nature, was yet so far from rash as not to be always ready for aggressive operations when his superiors wished : his preparations were so elaborate that they interfered not only with his celerity, but with his promptness; and both Grant and Sherman more than once thought him too deliberate. Nevertheless, he was in some notable instances so eminently successful that the world will probably give a verdict in his favor which greater soldiers might withhold. But in his best moments it was always a defensive genius that he displayed.

Thomas had been sent to Nashville as early as the 3rd of October. His orders were to organize the troops in Middle Tennessee, and drive Forrest from

the national communications in that region, while Sherman watched the movements of the main rebel army in the neighborhood of Atlanta. He announced his arrival to Grant, and from that time reported the situation daily to the general-in-chieJ, although most of his orders still came from Sher man. Forrest had already captured Athens and a few isolated block-houses which he could not hold, cut both the railroads south of Nashville, and seized some scattered stores. He had no hope of accomplishing more, and before Thomas started from Georgia, the rebel cavalry had set out to return. Every disposition was promptly made to intercept the command, but it was now too late, and on the 5th of October, the raiders escaped into Alabama. During the next two weeks Sherman was following Hood northward, and as the rebel army approached the Tennessee, Thomas disposed his troops so as to reinforce Chattanooga and protect the crossings of the river, thus holding the enemy in front so that Sherman might attack him in rear; but Hood eluded the national columns.

Sherman, meanwhile, had promptly notified Thomas of the new campaign in Georgia. On, the 1st of October, when he first proposed to ignore Hood and turn to the sea, he disclosed the idea to his principal subordinate. Then came the interruption occasioned by the rebel movement to the north; but on the 9th, Sherman reverted to the scheme in which Thomas was to play so important a part. " I want to destroy all the road below Chattanooga, including Atlanta, and make for the sea-coast." "In that event I would order back to Chattanooga everything the other side of King-94

ston." Thomas, however, disliked the project. On the 17th, he said, "I hope you will adopt Grant's idea of turning Wilson loose,* rather than undertake the plan of a march with the whole force through Georgia, to the sea, inasmuch as General Grant cannot co-operate with you, as at first arranged." He was especially averse to being left behind, and telegraphed on the 18th: "I don't wish to be in command of the defences in Tennessee, unless you and the authorities at Washington deem it absolutely necessary."

But on the 19th, Sherman gave him positive orders : " I will send back to Tennessee the Fourth corps, all dismounted cavalry, all sick and wounded men, and all encumbrances. . . I want you to remain in Tennessee, and take command of all my division not actually with me. . . If you can defend the line of the Tennessee in my absence of three months, it is all I ask." Thomas's opposition ceased this day. He forwarded a copy of Sherman's despatch to Grant, and although he had objected not only to the movement, but to his own position in it, he said not a word of this to the general-in-chief, but with true soldierly spirit declared : " I

* When Sherman originally proposed to move to the sea, leaving Hood in his rear, Grant, it will be remembered, at once declared that Hood should be first destroyed. It was then that he said : " With Wilson turned loose with all your cavalry, you will find the rebels put much more on the defensive than hitherto." This is the only mention of Wilson's name in Grant's despatches for weeks, and it is to this doubtless that Thomas refers ; but this despatch was dated 11 A.M. on the 11th of October, and Thomas had forgotten, or perhaps never knew, that at 11.30 P.M. the same night, Grant reconsidered his decision, and authorized the march to the sea.
ULYSSES S. GRANT.

feel confident that I can defend the line of the Tennessee with the force Sherman proposes to leave with me. . . Also, I shall be ready to send Sherman all the cavalry he needs, and still have a good number left."

On the 25th, Sherman sent him further instructions. " I do believe you are the man best qualified to manage the affairs of Tennessee and North Mississippi. . . I can spare you the Fourth corps, and about five thousand men not fit for my purpose, but which will be well enough for garrison duty in Chattanooga, Murfreesboro', and Nashville. "What you need is a few points fortified and stocked with provisions, and a good, movable column of twenty-five thousand men that can strike in any direction." A copy of this despatch was forwarded to the gene-ral-in-chief, who was thus kept fully advised of all preparations and orders.

On the 13th of October, having given his sanction to Sherman's movement, Grant said to Halleck : " I think it will be advisable now for General Thomas to abandon all the railroad from Columbia to De-catur, thence to Stevenson. This will give him much additional force.""" Orders to this effect were given to Thomas the same day, but that officer preferred to guard the Tennessee from Decatur to Eastport. " Forrest's pickets," he said, " are on the

* Sherman had the same idea as Grant. On the 9th of October, after Forrest had escaped from Tennessee, he directed Thomas to replace all the guards on the roads to Chattanooga, but referring to the Decatur road, he said : " I doubt the necessity of repairing the road about Elk river and Athens, and suggest that you wait before giving orders for repairs." On the 10th, he ordered: "Collect all your command at some converging place, say Stevenson. . . . Call on all troops within your reach."

south bank of the river, and if Croxton and Granger were withdrawn, I am satisfied he would push across the river, and operate against our direct line of communication, with no adequate force to successfully oppose him." The military instincts of the two were thus entirely opposed. The chief was willing to take great risks in order to attain a cardinal object ; the subordinate preferred to risk nothing, but to make all sure. One, indeed, often abandoned less important places for the sake of securing the most important of all; the other was unwilling to abandon or expose any position whatever. One provided against danger by compelling the enemy to defend himself; the other by carefully guarding his own w r eak points. There are many occasions in war when the offensive is the only practicable defence, and Grant was always on the look-out for these opportunities; Thomas never accepted them till they were thrust upon him, though then he sometimes turned them to superlative account. At this time, however, Grant said no more about abandoning the Decatur railroad. He never overruled a distant subordinate, unless it was indispensable. But four days afterwards, Forrest re-entered Tennessee, in spite of Croxton and Granger.

On the 25th of October, Hood appeared before Decatur in force, for, contrary to Sherman's expectations, he intended to invade Tennessee. Thomas, however, remained confident. He had been notified that A. J. Smith was to reinforce him with ten thousand troops from Missouri, and when he reported to Grant the approach of Hood, he also announced: " If Rosecrans's troops can reach Eastport early

next week, I shall have no further fears, and will set to work immediately to prepare for an advance, as Sherman has directed, should Beauregard follow him." He was ready, not indeed to assume, but always to sustain, responsibility. He sometimes shrank, but never flinched. This day Sherman said : " General Thomas is well alive to the occasion, and better suited to the emergency than any man I have. He should be strengthened as soon as possible, as the successful defence of Tennessee should not be left to chance."

Hood, however, made only a demonstration before Decatur, and on the 29th, withdrew his force. The same day, the heads of his columns were reported in. the neighborhood of Florence, fifty miles westward, and north of the Tennessee. Sherman telegraphed at once in the most urgent manner: " If necessary, break up all minor points, and get about Columbia as big an army as you can, and go at him. . . If, to make up a force adequate, it be necessary, abandon Huntsville and that line, and the Nashville and Decatur road, except so far as it facilitates an army operating towards Florence." Again, on the same day, he said: " I repeat, should the enemy cross the Tennessee in force, abandon all minor points, and concentrate at some point where you cover the road from Murfreesboro' to Stevenson." These instructions were identical with those that Grant had given two weeks before. But Thomas abandoned nothing. He simply concentrated two divisions of cavalry near Florence, and directed them to prevent a crossing, until the Fourth corps, tinder Stanley, now on its way from Georgia, could

arrive. On the 30th, the Twenty-third corps, under Schofield, was added to Thomas's command.

It was not too soon. On the 31st of October, Thomas reported to Grant that his cavalry had been unable to prevent the crossing of the rebel army. "The Tennessee having fallen so low as to be ford-able at several points, the enemy succeeded yesterday afternoon in crossing . . above . . and below Florence, in spite of Croxton's efforts to prevent them." The problem of Hood's intentions was solved at last. The rebel army was north of the Tennessee. Thomas, however, at once declared: " With Schofield and Stanley, I feel confident I can drive Hood back." This day, the advance of the Fourth corps reached Athens, and Stanley was ordered to concentrate at Pulaski, until Schofield, who was moving from Resaca, by way of Nashville, could arrive. Sherman now repeated his former order: " You must unite all your men into one army, and abandon all minor points, if you expect to defeat Hood. He will not attack posts, but march around them." But Thomas's way of making war was different from Sherman's.

In the meantime, Forrest had moved north from Corinth, and reached Fort Heiman, on the Tennessee, seventy miles from the Ohio; here, he captured a gunboat and two transports with supplies. On the 2nd of November, he appeared before Johnsonville, the western terminus of a short railroad connecting Nashville with the Tennessee. This point was one of Thomas's bases of supplies, and the approach of Forrest created great consternation among the quartermasters.

Gunboats and transports were fired to prevent their falling into

ULYSSES S. GRANT.

the hands of the enemy, and stores to the value of a million and a half of dollars were destroyed. At this juncture Schofield arrived at Nashville with the advance of the Twenty-third corps, and Thomas at once directed the entire corps to move to Johnson-ville, instead of Pulaski. Schofield reached Johnson -ville on the night of the 5th of November, but found that the enemy had already disappeared. Thomas then instructed him to leave a strong force to protect the place, and with the remainder of his corps proceed to Pulaski, as originally ordered. More than a week was lost by this diversion, and the Twenty-third corps was for a while divided; but Hood took no advantage of the opportunity, and Stanley remained unmolested at Pulaski until the 14th of November, when Schofield arrived and was placed in command of all the forces in front of the rebel army.

Thomas had now under Schofield's orders twenty-two thousand infantry and about five thousand two hundred horse.* In spite of the repeated

* " My effective force at this time consisted of the fourth corps, about 12,000 men, under Major-General D. S. Stanley; the Twenty-third corps, about 10,000, under Major-General J. M. Schofield; Hatch's division of cavalry, about 4,000; Croxton's brigade, 2,500; and Capron's brigade, about 1,200. The balance of my command was distributed along the railroad, and posted at Murfreesboro', Stevenson, Bridgeport, Huntsville, Decatur, and Chattanooga, to keep open communications and hold the posts above named, if attacked, until they could be reinforced; as up to this time it was impossible to determine which course Hood would take—advance on Nashville, or turn towards Huntsville." — Thomas's Official Report.

On the 20th of November, Thomas returned 24,264, present equipped for duty, in the Fourth and Twenty-third corps, and 5,543 cavalry. Whether all the cavalry was under Schofield's

orders of Grant and Sherman, he persisted in main-taining garrisons at numerous places which they had directed him to abandon, and his army was numerically smaller than either of them supposed or intended. Granger was at this time at Decatur with five thousand men, Rousseau at Murfreesboro' with five thousand more, and Steedman at Chattanooga with five thousand, though not a company of rebels was under arms within a hundred miles of either position ; for the entire strength of the Confederacy between the Mississippi and the Alleghanies was concentrated in front of Schofield. On the 20th of November, there were reported " present, equipped for duty," in Thomas's command, fifty-nine thousand five hundred men. Of these, twenty-five thousand were scattered in garrisons away from the actual front. Hood's effective force at the same time was thirty thousand six hundred infantry, and, as near as can be ascertained, seven thousand cavalry.*

orders the return does not state. On the 31st of October, Thomas returned 10,624 in the Twenty-third corps, 11,911 in the Fourth corps, and 5,328 cavalry.

Wilson says, in his official report, that on the 23rd of November, when he took command of the cavalry under Schofield, he had in all 4,300 men.

* General Thomas says in his " Official Report:" "My information from all sources confirmed the reported strength of Hood's army to be from 40,000 to 45,000 infantry, and from. 12,000 to 15,000 cavalry." This, however, was a very large over-estimate. Hood's returns show his effective total, on the 6th of November, to have been 30,600, not including Forrest's cavalry. There is no actual return of Forrest's command in existence later than that of July 30, 1864, when he reported his effective total as 5,357. He states, in his report dated Jan. 24, 1865: "On my arrival at Florence [Nov. 17], I was placed in

Until Smith could arrive from Missouri and "Wilson remount his cavalry, Schofield's force was therefore inferior to Hood's ; but when the reinforcements (from all quarters were concentrated, the national numbers would exceed those of the enemy. To effect this concentration was of course of vital importance ; to this consideration all others were secondary. Schofield was accordingly instructed to watch the movements of Hood, and retard his advance as long as possible, without risking a

command of the entire cavalry then with our army of Tennessee, consisting of Brigadier-General Jackson's division and a portion of Debrell's brigade, under command of Colonel Biffle, amounting to about 2,000 men, together with three brigades of my former command, making in all about 5,000 cavalry."

On the 10th of November, General Richard Taylor returned his effective force at 15,024, and on the 20th, 10,422 : in his column of remarks of the latter date appears this note : " Forrest's command transferred to army of Tennessee." This would make Forrest's numbers 4,602, in addition to the 2,000 he says he found in the army of the Tennessee. Even allowing for the depreciation of a beaten commander, his force can hardly have been more than 7,000 strong. Schofield and Wilson, however, both estimated it at 10,000.

The rule I have adopted, in determining the numbers of armies, is to accept the official returns as conclusive, whenever they are in existence j not the reports after a battle or a campaign, when figures on both sides are often only estimates, but the field returns, made by commanders to their military superiors, so far as possible, without reference to any particular engagement. If this rule is applied to both sides, I know of none fairer.

I have made careful examination of the rebel records, and there is nothing in any despatch, report, or return, to show that Hood received the reinforcement of a man, after he left the Tennessee; or that any troops were included in his command, besides those on the above return, and Forrest's cavalry. See Appendix for Returns of Thomas and Hood, during October, November, and December, 1864.

general engagement. Meanwhile, all available troops from every direction were hurried to Thomas. New regiments and recruits poured in on him from the North; convalescents and fur-loughed men, returning to Sherman's army, were detained at Chattanooga ; Pope spared two regiments from the Indian frontier, and Smith was making strenuous efforts to reach Tennessee from the interior of Missouri. But twelve of the new regiments were absorbed in supplying the place in garrison of those whose terms of service had expired; and Smith's arrival was delayed beyond all expectation. The Missouri river was so low that it was thought he could reach the Mississippi sooner by marching than in boats; but after he started, the roads became almost impassable from snow and heavy rains, and several streams were found too high to cross. On the 14th of November, his command was still at St. Louis. Wilson, too, had great difficulty in remounting his cavalry.

Grant made full allowance for all these embarrassments, and after Hood had crossed the Tennessee, he sent no despatch to Thomas for a fortnight, leaving him to work out his own problem, without interference. Thomas, however, knew what was expected of him, and sent frequent telegrams to Washington, assuring the general-in-chief and the government of his own anxiety to undertake aggressive movements. On the 8th of November, he said: " As soon as Smith's troops arrive and General Wilson has the balance of his cavalry mounted, I shall be prepared to commence moving on the enemy ;" on the 9th : " It is my intention to take the offensive, as soon as I can get the troops

from Missouri. You may rest assured, I will do all in my power to destroy Beauregard's army, but I desire to be prepared before making the undertaking." On the 10th, he repeated: " As soon as I can concentrate my forces, I shall assume the offensive."

The rebels, however, knew the significance of this concentration quite as well as the national authorities, and Breckenridge, with about three thousand men, was dispatched from West Virginia, to distract, if possible, some of the troops in Tennessee. He succeeded only too well. On the 13th of November, he attacked a force of fifteen hundred men under General Gillem, stationed near Morris-town, in East Tennessee, driving them back as far as Knoxville, with a national loss of about two hundred, in killed, wounded, and prisoners. Thomas at once gave directions to Stoneman, at Louisville, and to Steedman at Chattanooga, to reinforce Knoxville. On the 16th, he telegraphed: "Ammen reported that he had sent reinforcements to General Gillem." On the 17th: " I heard from Steedman this morning that he was preparing last night to reinforce Knoxville, in accordance with my directions. . . He will be able to send two thousand men. . . Stoneman telegraphs me, from Louisville, that he can concentrate five mounted regiments in three days, to go to the relief of General Ammen." On the 18th, however, the rebels withdrew as rapidly as they had advanced. Nevertheless, Stoneman was ordered to concentrate as large a force as he could in East Tennessee, and either destroy Breckenridge, or drive him into Virginia. Thus, the enemy was able to make important diversions of national

troops at this critical moment, both on the right and left. Schofield had first been sent with an entire corps to Johnsonville, and afterwards ordered to leave a portion of his command in that neighborhood ; while Breckenridge attracted a large force to Knoxville, in East Tennessee, at the moment when every man, at every hazard, should have been concentrated in front of Hood. For, if the principal rebel army of the West was destroyed, not only Johnsonville and Morristown, but both East and West Tennessee, could easily be regained.

On the 12th of November, Sherman severed communication with the forces on the Tennessee, and from this time Thomas received his orders direct from Grant. He was now in command of all the national troops between the Mississippi and the Alleghanies. To him, from this moment, was committed the defence, not only of Tennessee, but of all the territory acquired in the Atlanta, or even in the Chattanooga, campaign. The same army, depleted it is true, but still the same command that had confronted Sherman so long and so valiantly, now stood before Thomas, and threatened all at the West, that, in a year of battle, either Grant or Sherman had gained. After wandering hundreds of miles, Hood had at last found a base, and railroad communication was uninterrupted in his rear, from Corinth to Selma and Mobile. The troops beyond the Mississippi had been ordered to reinforce him, and the only successful leader of rebel cavalry during the later years of the war, had been placed under his command. Not only did Hood outnumber Schofield, but Sherman, with the pick and flower of his army, men, horses, pontoons even,—

whatever he chose to take, all in the best state of preparation, had marched in another direction; and a desperate effort, it was evident, was about to be made to strike at Thomas, whose fragmentary command was still scattered from Missouri to East Tennessee.

The very boldness of Hood's movement was calculated to affect the spirit of his troops. They knew, if defeated, that no other army remained, or could be collected at the West, in defence of their cause. They were to meet their old enemy. The eyes of the South were upon them ; the rebel President himself had journeyed from Richmond to incite them. Sherman had left them an open door ; and they were about to re-claim the soil upon which many of them had been born. Had Hood attacked Thomas before Schofield arrived, the result must have been disastrous to the national cause. But Forrest had not returned from West Tennessee, and the rebel chief had lost some of the ardor which characterized the assaults before Atlanta. If his strategy was still bold, his tactics were certainly tamer. He lingered around Florence when every hour's delay was of incalculable advantage to his adversary, and for twenty days, at this crisis of his fortune, he neither followed Sherman nor assaulted Schofield.

On the 17th of November, as there were no indications of an immediate movement in any quarter of the field, Grant travelled from City Point to Burlington, New Jersey, where his children were at school. He took with him a single aide-de-camp, and a telegraph operator, that he might retain communication with the armies. On the 19th, a rumor caine from Richmond that Early had been recalled from the Valley by Lee, and Grant sent word at once to City Point: " Should such a thing occur, telegraph me, and I will get back as fast as steam can carry me. If it is true that Early is going back, it behooves General Meade to be well on his guard, and Butler to reinforce him at the shortest notice." At the same time he directed Sheridan: "If you are satisfied this is so, send the Sixth corps to City Point without delay. If your cavalry can cut the Virginia Central road, now is the time to do it." No rebel movement, however, was attempted, and Grant proceeded to New York. But although general-in-chief of the armies, he thought it not unbecoming his dignity to say to the Secretary of War: " I start for New York at three P.M. If there is any reason for my not going, please telegraph me ; or if you think I should be at the front, let me know, and I will get there as soon as possible."

He had not visited New York, nor indeed any point east of Washington, since the days when he travelled by stage-coach, a graduate of the Military Academy, twenty-one years of age. His coming now was unannounced, and he went quietly to an hotel; but it was quickly known that the commander of the national armies had arrived, and the most prominent citizens came in crowds to offer him civilities. He declined all invitations, but was glad of the opportunity to express his views about the war. His visitors were amazed at first when he spoke of his anxiety to detain the rebels in Petersburg, arid delay the capture of Richmond; but he soon explained the paradox. Most of them

ULYSSES S. GRANT.

were extremely anxious in regard to Sherman, whose romantic enterprise had affected the public imagination far more than the greater but more ordinary peril of Thomas, in Tennessee. Grant, however, allayed their fears : he showed them how Thomas being set to hold Hood, and Sheridan retained to watch Early, while Meade and Butler held fast to Lee, left no large force to oppose the advance of Sherman; and that Sherman in his turn moved in such a way as to cut off Lee's supplies, the most important of which now came from Georgia, since Sheridan had laid waste the Valley.

When the listeners understood how each army was thus supported by some other force in a different quarter of the military theatre, and each operation tended to the success of another movement hundreds of miles away, their interest was heightened in the great lieutenants who were working out the scheme. And then the chief kindled into magnanimous enthusiasm. He declared that the country could not think higher of Sheridan and Thomas and Schofield than he did, nor than they deserved; that the men themselves could not be gladder at their own success than he. Thomas, he said, was like a rock, when attacked; while if Sherman came safely through his present campaign, he would stand in the estimation of all, where he already stood in his—the greatest general of the age.

They to whom Grant spoke were themselves the leaders and makers of opinion, and in their presence the usually taciturn soldier was roused to fluent utterance. He told them of the waning spirit of the South, and proved it by the desertions' from Lee's army, which, since the elections, had amounted

to hundreds a day ; by the absentees from all the other rebel commands; by the frantic but futile efforts of Davis to enforce his conscription laws. He repeated what he had often said before—that the Confederacy was a hollow shell, which Sherman was about to penetrate ; that old men and boys were pressed into the rebel ranks; that the cradle and the grave had been robbed, to repair the losses in the Wilderness and the Western campaigns. Hitherto, also, the slaves had been detained at home, thus allowing the entire white population of the South to be put into the field; but now there was talk on every hand of arming the blacks. If this were done, there would be absolutely no men left for the ordinary labor of life, and one enormous advantage which the rebels had until now possessed, would be destroyed. Besides, what security could there be that the slaves would fight for slavery ?

To listen to this talk from one who knew so absolutely the truth of what he said, awoke new faith. His hearers began to breathe his spirit, to share his confidence. They saw now the method of his strategy, the significance of his battles. They understood his persistent advance in the Wilderness ; they appreciated his object in detaining Lee in Richmond; and though many went away marvelling at what he said about Thomas, and Schofield, and Sheridan, and most of all Sherman, others left his presence saying to themselves : " At last we have found the man able to end the war."*

* This is no fanciful picture. I accompanied General Grant on this journey, and was present at these interviews, and it was to me that many of his listeners confided the impressions they received.

ULYSSES S. GRANT.

The general-in-chief remained two days in New York, and returned to Washington by way of Philadelphia. In the latter city he went out to walk, but was recognized at once from his portraits, and an enormous crowd collected around him, at first with salutations only, but soon with cheers. He was compelled to retreat, and the Mayor organized an impromptu reception in Independence Hall. So many, however, sought to shake his hand that it was impossible to gratify them all, and he was taken to a carriage by a private way. Still the populace found and followed him, and the carriage windows were broken by those determined not only to see, but to touch, the man who led the national armies.

On the 23rd of November, he arrived in Washington, and spent a day with the President and the Secretary of War. At this time he recommended the muster out of eight major-generals and thirty-three brigadiers, to make room for officers who had won promotion in the field. Many of these, he said, " it might be advisable to notify, so as to give them an opportunity of resigning, if they elect so to do;" but " with regard to all the general officers named in the list, I am satisfied the good of the service will be advanced by their withdrawal." Some of them were his own warm personal friends, and the President reminded him of this. Grant replied that he knew it well, but they were not good generals ; and the names remained.

There was talk between Lincoln and Grant, of a new Secretary of War, and the President promised that he would not appoint another without first allowing the general-in-chief to express his Grant, however, desired no change, and declared that the President could hardly find a more efficient war minister ; certainly none more earnest, or more ready to hold up the hands of the commander of the army. Lincoln was glad to find that he entertained these views, for the attempts to overthrow the Secretary were persistent and numerous.

Stanton indeed had many enemies, among them every rebel and traitor in the land. He, however, was indifferent to the animosity that he provoked, and seemed rather to enjoy the hatred of his adversaries. It was not his custom to propitiate those by whom he was opposed; he seldom sought to mollify their temper or avert their rage. He believed in terrifying those who were half inclined to take sides against him; in crushing out rebellion ; in punishing treason. The time for concession and conciliation, he considered, was past ; the plan of recalling the rebels by kindness or compromise had been tried and failed; every weapon in his hands was now to be employed, every avowed or secret enemy was to be subdued. With these general views Grant was, at this stage of the war, in complete accord, but the measures that Stanton resorted to were sometimes harsher than he approved. The minister, however, had treacherous civilians to deal with at the rear; the soldier only open enemies in the field. Grant would have been perhaps more lenient to those who had no weapons in their hands, but Stanton felt that these were as determined in their hostility as armies, and that it was quite as important to destroy them as Lee.

Overpowering in will, masterful in passion, bending men and means and circumstances to his own

purpose, massive in intellect, sleepless in energy,— Stanton loomed grandly among the most important characters of his time. He was harsh and blunt in speech, abrupt and careless in manner, severe and sometimes cruel in his judgments, vindictive and relentless in his punishments. Yet his friendships were warm, his friends devoted, and in his family he was tenderly loved. For little children he had an especial charm : they were always fond of him. His genius was broad as well as vigorous, his administrative faculty prodigious, his penetration keen ; but his great characteristic was the resistless energy which trampled down obstacles, overcame all opposition, endured no delays, and either infused others with his own ardor or subjected them to his will. It is perhaps easy to be energetic when one is omnipotent; and in time of war, at the head of a war department, with a nation at his back,—a minister—if ever, in a republic, is omnipotent. Still, a weak man would have failed even under these circumstances. He would have found the machine too ponderous, the task too gigantic, the weapons unwieldy. But, whatever his faults, Stanton was not weak. He fired the engine and worked it too. He was at once stoker and engineer. He organized and administered his department with consummate skill as well as power. He accomplished what the nation and the general-in-chief required. He created and maintained the army.

As long as Grant was in supreme command, Stanton was his loyal and efficient ally, and supported him with all the vigor of his intense nature. He sent him every man that he could raise, and

every horse that he could buy, or sometimes seize. He urged the conscriptions, he ransacked the hospitals, he emptied the garrisons. He bought and manufactured and transported supplies of arms and food and clothing; he not only employed the complex and wide-spread machinery of his own department, but he absorbed, and exerted, and directed the whole political influence of the government, for the one purpose of sustaining and reinforcing Grant. He did more than this, and achieved what was doubtless for him a harder task. He subdued his own imperious temper. He refrained absolutely from interference with the strategy in the field. He not only never thwarted, or even opposed any military plan; he never proposed one of his own. He never insisted on retaining any man in prominent place at the front, if Grant positively urged his removal. He never refused to give any man command, if Grant declared it was essential to his schemes. And yet he was by nature greedy of power, and anxious at this very time to retain every atom of control which he did not think it indispensable to yield. But he had convinced himself that in no other way than by strengthening and upholding the general-in-chief • was the rebellion to be overthrown; and for this he, was willing to sacrifice his own instincts, his own will, his own ambition.

Stanton's ambition, however, was not an ordinary one. He liked power and place, as all men do, who attain them. But his great passion was patriotism. It was to secure the salvation and unity of the country that all his efforts were made; not to gratify either personal ambition, or vanity,

or pride. He was absolutely free from selfishness; unspotted in personal purity;

incorruptible and poor, in the midst of unparalleled opportunities. He was cast in Titanic mould, and littlenesses had no place in his nature.

Such a man hated, and if he could, destroyed his enemies; but not from malice. Such a man might be unjust and tyrannical with his subordinates, but not from meanness, or intention. His injustice was an incident, not a purpose, nor an end. It arose either from carelessness of details and individuals, or from an overpowering determination to rule, and to show others that they musi obey. If he sent officers into exile, if he was domineering in manner, harsh in decision, sometimes insulting to those who could not reply; if, above all, he sometimes forgot that he was dealing with those who risked their lives for the cause in which he was engaged—it was from no personal motive, but from the same passionate force that swept everything before it, small as well as great; the same force that enabled him to achieve his great results, to organize the military power of the nation, the tangible material of armies, which he then turned over to Grant. Force, force, force—was the expression and epitome of the man; not mere brute force, but mental force, employing brute force; force in controlling the wills of others, force in mastering matter, force in breaking the neck of circumstances. Such a man behind Grant was invaluable. He forged the weapons which the other used; and in the old mythology, Vulcan was divine as well as Mars.

CHAPTER XXIX.

Hood m6ves north from the Tennessee—Thomas directs Schofield to fall back — Schofield evacuates Columbia—Hood crosses Duck river—Affair at Spring Hill—Schofield extricates his army—Battle of Franklin—Repulse of Hood—Thomas directs Schofield to retreat to Nashville—Grant disapproves this strategy—Anxiety of government—Correspondence between Grant and Thomas—Difference of views between the two commanders— First news from Sherman—Proposed movement against mouth of Cape Fear river—Orders to Butler and Weitzel—Orders to Sheridan—Movement of Meade against Hicksford—Situation at Nashville— Thomas delays to fight—Grant gives peremptory orders—Excuses of Thomas—Grant's general supervision of armies—Butler starts in person for Fort Fisher, contrary to Grant's expectation— Further delay of Thomas—Correspondence between Grant and the government—Grant orders Thomas to be relieved— Suspends the order—Starts for Nashville—Receives news of Thomas's success—Goes no further than Washington—Topography around Nashville—Dispositions of Hood and Thomas—Thomas's plan of battle—Fighting on loth of December —Success of national movements—Battle of 16th —Rout of Hood—Pursuit of rebel army—Hood crosses Tennessee — Congratulations of Grant and the government—Further urging of Thomas— Thomas defends his course—News of Sherman's arrival at the coast— Thomas prepares to go into winter quarters—Grant makes different dispositions—Results of campaign against Nashville—Criticism of Hood— Behavior of national troops—Criticism of Thomas— Justification of Grant's judgment—Temperament of Thomas—Friendly relations between Grant and Thomas—In war, nothing which is successful, is wrong.

THOMAS'S plans and operations were now all dependent on the course that Hood might take when the designs of Sherman could no longer be concealed; and the forces at Florence were anxiously watched to ascertain whether the national army was to advance

into Alabama, or remain for awhile on the defensive in Tennessee. Grant's first order to Thomas after Sherman moved was typical of his character and of what was to follow. On the 13th of November, Thomas telegraphed: " Wilson reports to-night that the cavalry arms and equipments applied for some weeks since have not yet reached Louisville. Their non-arrival will delay us in preparing for the field." But it was still possible that Hood might re-cross the Tennessee, in pursuit of Sherman. In that event, not a moment must be lost; and Grant telegraphed at once : "If Hood commences falling back, it will not do to wait for the full equipment of your cavalry, to follow. He should, in that case, be pressed with such force as you can bring to bear." Thomas replied the same night: " Your telegram of this A.M. just received. Am watching Hood closely, and should he move after Sherman, I will follow with what force I can raise at hand."

Hood, however, had no idea of following Sherman. The campaign into Middle Tennessee was his own design,"* and the dispositions of the national commanders appeared not in the least to disturb his plans. On the 16th of November, Sherman marched out of Atlanta, and the same day Beauregard telegraphed the news to Richmond : " Sherman is about to move with three corps from Atlanta to Augusta, or Macon, thence probably to Charleston or Savannah, where a junction may be formed with enemy's fleet." On the 19th, he announced again : " Enemy are turning their columns on shortest road

" The plan of campaign into Middle Tennessee was correct, as originally designed by General Hood."-— Beauregards Endorsement on Hood's Report, January 9,1865.

to Macon, and scouts . . report Fourteenth corps crossed Chattahoochee to join Sherman, giving him four corps. This information has been communicated to General Hood. It is left optional with him to divide, and reinforce Cobb [in Central Georgia], or take the offensive immediately, to relieve him." Hood chose the latter course, and Grant declared : This " seemed to me to be leading to his certain doom. . . Had I had the power to command both armies, I should not have changed the orders under which he seemed to be acting."

On the 21st of November, the rebel columns were in motion from the Tennessee, marching by the roads west of Pulaski, near which point Schofield was encamped. Hood evidently hoped to interpose his army between the national forces and Nashville; but Thomas divined his purpose, and at once directed Schofield to fall back from Pulaski, and concentrate in the viciuity of Columbia, so as to reach that place before the enemy. " Hood's force," he said to Grant, " is so much larger than my present available force, either in infantry or cavalry, that I shall have to act on the defensive."* His only resource, he declared, was to " retire

* " . . General Stanley's corps being only 12,000 effective, and General Schofield's 10,000 effective. As yet General Wilson can raise only about 3,000 effective cavalry. Grierson's division [of cavalry] is still in Missouri, arid the balance of the cavalry belonging to the array of the Cumberland, not having yet received their horses and equipments, at Louisville. I have a force of about 4,000 men at Decatur and on the Memphis and Charleston railroad, which might be made available, if Decatur and that road were abandoned, but as General Sherman is very anxious to have Decatur held if possible, I have kept the force there up to this time. I will, however, if you approve, withdraw and add it to my

slowly, delaying the enemy's progress as much as possible, to gain time for reinforcements to arrive, and concentrate." The portion of the Twenty-third corps which had been left at John-sonville was now brought rapidly up to Scho-field ; and as all possibility of Hood's forces following Sherman was at an end, the garrisons along the Memphis and Chattanooga railroad were called in; but according to Thomas's invariable policy of guarding every possible point, these troops, instead of being sent to Schofield, were moved to Stevenson and Murfreesboro', still further away from the enemy. On the night of the 23rd, Schofield evacuated Pulaski, and on the 24th, he reported himself in position at Columbia. This town is on the south bank of the Duck river, which here runs from west to east, and is at the crossing of the direct road to Nashville, distant only sixty miles. About half way between Columbia and Nashville, is Franklin.

On the 24th of November, Grant returned to City Point from the North, and at four P.M. that day, he telegraphed to Thomas : " Do not let Forrest get off without punishment/' Thomas replied at length, detailing his difficulties, but concluded : " The moment I can get my cavalry, I will march against Hood. If Forrest can be found, he will be punished."* On the 25th, Grant telegraphed to

main force at Columbia, and shall then be, on the arrival of General A. J. Smith with his force, as strong in infantry as the enemy; but his cavalry will greatly outnumber mine, until I can get General Wilson's force back from Louisville."— Thomas to Hal-leck, November 21.

* " Yours of 4 P.M. yesterday just received. Hood l s entire army is in front of Columbia, and so greatly outnumbers mine that I am compelled to act on the defensive. None of General Smith's

Halleck : " I think it advisable to send orders to Missouri that all the troops coming from there should receive their directions from General Thomas, and not listen to conflicting orders." These instructions were promptly carried out, and Thomas was made absolute master of all the troops within his territorial command.

corps have arrived yet, although embarked on Tuesday last. The transportation of Hatch and Grierson's cavalry was ordered by Washburne, I am told, to be turned in at Memphis, which has crippled the only cavalry I have at this time. All of my cavalry were dismounted to furnish horses to Kilpatrick's division, which went with General Sherman. My dismounted cavalry is now detained in Louisville, awaiting arms and horses. Horses arrive slowly ; arms have been detained somewhere en route for more than a month. General Grierson has been delayed by conflicting orders in Kansas, and from Memphis. It is impossible to say when he will reach here.

" Since being placed in charge of affairs on Tennessee, T have lost nearly 15,000 men, discharged by expiration of service, and permitted to go North : my gain probably 12,000 perfectly raw troops; therefore as the enemy so greatly outnumbers me in both infantry and cavalry, I am compelled for the present to act on the defensive. The moment I can get my cavalry, I will march against Hood. If Forrest can be found, he will be punished."— Thomas to Grant, November 25.

When Thomas says in this despatch " all my cavalry was dismounted," etc., he must be understood as meaning all the cavalry of the original army of the Cumberland, for on this date he had a cavalry force equipped for duty, of 5,500 men. See his return of November 20.

Wilson distinctly states in his report: " All the serviceable horses of McCook's and Garrard's divisions and Colonel Garrard's brigade were turned over to the Third [Kilpatrick's] division, and every effort was made to put it upon a thoroughly efficient footing ; while the dismounted men of the First and Second divisions were ordered by rail to Louisville, Kentucky, for removal and equipment." These were the only troops dismounted for Sherman.

On the 27th, he announced the approach of detachments from Missouri. "As soon as Smith's troops arrive," he said, " and are adjusted, I shall be ready to take the field and assume the offensive." The same day Grant telegraphed to him : " Savannah papers just received state that Forrest is expected in rear of Sherman, and that Brecken-ridge is already on the way to Georgia from East Tennessee. If this proves true, it will give you a chance to take the offensive against Hood, and to cut the railroads up into Virginia with a small cavalry force." There were few events in war which to Grant did not seem to offer " a chance to take the offensive." Thomas, however, replied: " We can as yet discover no signs of the withdrawal of Forrest from Tennessee; he is closely watched, and our movement will commence against Hood as soon as possible, whether Forrest leaves Tennessee or not." Thomas was very well aware of the peculiarities of his chief, and the knowledge of them doubtless stimulated his anxiety; but nothing could goad him into action until he felt certain that every preparation was made, and every contingency cared for.During the 24th and 25th, the enemy skirmished with Schofield's troops in front of Columbia, but showed only dismounted cavalry; and on the 26th and 27th, the rebel infantry came up, and pressed the national lines strongly, still without assaulting. These movements betrayed an undoubted intention to cross the river above or below the town, and during the night of the 27th,.Scho-field evacuated Columbia, and withdrew to the northern bank. He had at first strong hopes of

being able to hold the line of Duck river until reinforcements could arrive. Two divisions of infantry were posted to hold all the crossings in the neighborhood of Columbia, Stanley was placed in reserve on the Franklin road, to keep open communication in that direction, and the cavalry, under Wilson, covered the crossings on the left or east of the command. But on the 28th, the rebel cavalry succeeded in pressing Wilson back, and effected a crossing at Hewey's Mills, five miles above Columbia, and by daybreak on the 29th, Hood's infantry was following in force. From Hewey's Mills a road leads direct to Spring Hill, fifteen miles in rear of the national army, and on the Franklin road. If the rebels could reach Spring Hill in advance of Schofield, they would be able either to cut off his retreat, or strike him in flank as he moved.

Schofield at once sent Stanley with two divisions of infantry to occupy Spring Hill and cover the trains, directing Cox to hold the crossings at Columbia, while the remainder of the infantry was faced towards Hewey's Mills, where the rebel arnry was crossing. Wilson was cut off, and no communication could be had with the cavalry. Stanley reached Spring Hill just in time to drive off a body of rebel cavalry, and save the trains; and about four o'clock Hood came upon the ground in force. Stewart and Cheatham's corps were with him, and one division of S. D. Lee; the remainder of the rebel infantry was left at Columbia, the only point where artillery could pass the river. Cheat-ham had the advance, and the attack on Stanley was made at once. The engagement was serious

and lasted until after dark, but Stanley held his own, and repulsed the enemy repeatedly, with heavy loss. At about three P.M. Schofield became convinced that Hood would make no attack at Columbia, but was pushing his principal columns direct upon Spring Hill. He thereupon gave orders for the withdrawal of Cox's force at dark, and pushed on himself with Ruger's troops to open communication with Stanley. The head of the main column followed close behind. Schofield struck the enemy's cavalry at dark, about three miles south of Spring Hill, brushing them away without difficulty, and reaching Spring Hill at seven. Here he found Stanley still in possession, but the rebel army bivouacking within eight hundred yards of the road. Posting one brigade to hold the road, he pushed on with Kuger's division to Thompson's station, three miles beyond. At this point the camp fires of the rebel cavalry were still burning, but the enemy had disappeared, and the cross-roads were secured without difficulty. The withdrawal of the force at Columbia was now safely effected, and Spring Hill was passed without molestation in the night, the troops moving within gun-shot of the enemy. Before daylight, the entire national column had passed, and at an early hour on the 30th, Schofield's command was in position at Franklin.*

* Hood attributed his lack of success entirely to Cheathana's remissness. " Major-General Cheatham was ordered at once to attack the enemy vigorously and get possession of this pike [the Franklin road] ; yet although these orders were frequently and earnestly repeated, he made but a partial and feeble attack, failing to reach the point indicated. Darkness soon came on,.and to our mortification the enemy continued moving along this road, almost in ear-shot, in hurry and confusion nearly the entire night.

Thus one of the most difficult and dangerous operations in war was executed with equal success and skill; the army was extricated from a situation of imminent peril, in the face of greatly superior numbers, and the opportunity for which Hood had labored so long was snatched from his grasp. It was one of the most brilliant exploits of the war, and one of the most important, as well, for had Schofield been defeated at Columbia, the entire North-West might have been endangered. Chicago and Cincinnati were defended at Spring Hill.

Immediately upon the evacuation of Columbia, Thomas ordered the abandonment of Tullahoma, on the Chattanooga railroad; Nashville was placed in a state of defence, additional works were constructed, and the fortifications were manned by a garrison composed of army clerks and railroad employes. A detachment of six thousand men,"* belonging to Sherman's column, left behind at Chattanooga, was recalled, and a brigade of colored troops, from the same point, was ordered

Thus was lost the opportunity for striking the enemy for which we labored so long, the best which the campaign has offered, and one of the best afforded us during the war. Major-General Cheatham has frankly confessed the error of which he was guilty, and attaches much blame to himself."— Hood to Beauregard, December 11.

No reason, however, is given by Hood for the failure to attack the column of Schofield after dark.

* " This P.M. I gave the orders to General Steedman, who was at Go wan with 6,000 men [between Chattanooga and Tullahoma], to embark on the railroad cars and come to Nashville immediately, and I presume he will be here by to-morrow morning."— Thomas to Hal-leck, November 30.

In his official report, dated January 20, 1865, Thomas puts this force at 5,000 ; perhaps the colored brigade made up the 6,000.

to Nashville. At an early hour on the 30th, the advance of A. J. Smith's command arrived, at last. Thomas's combined infantry force was now more than equal to that of the enemy.

But Franklin was twenty-five miles from Nashville, and Hood had not yet abandoned the hope of striking Schofield before he could be reinforced. The rebel army followed close on the national rearguard. Schofield, nevertheless, at first hoped to cross the Harpeth, at Franklin, before Hood's columns could come up in sufficient force to attack him. The river at this point runs from east to west, and leaving two brigades to retard the rebel advance, Schofield moved one division to the north bank, to cover the flanks, should the enemy attempt to cross above or below the town. His principal forces, however, remained on the southern side, with both flanks resting on the river. But Hood brought up and deployed two corps with astonishing rapidity, and moved at once to the attack. The national outposts, imprudently brave, held their ground too long, and hence were compelled to fall back at a run. In passing over the parapet, they carried with them the troops of the main line for a short space, arid thus permitted several hundred of the enemy to follow; but the reserves on the right and left instantly sprang forward, and after a furious battle, regained the parapet, and captured every rebel who had passed. The enemy afterwards assaulted persistently and continuously with his whole force, from half-past three until dark; and afterwards made numerous intermittent attacks until nearly ten o'clock ; but w r as steadily repulsed at every point on the line, which was two miles long.

Wilson, meanwhile, had been driven back by Forrest, and crossed the Harpeth river above Franklin, leaving the national left and rear entirely open to the rebel cavalry. On the 30th, Schofield ordered him to send a division forward again, and hold Forrest in check till the troops and trains could all reach Franklin. This task was committed to Hatch, who performed it with great success, and then re-crossed the river and connected with the infantry. A short time before the principal assault, Forrest forced a crossing above Franklin, and seriously threatened the trains, which were accumulating on the northern bank, and moving towards Nashville. Wilson, however, drove him back to the southern side, and the immediate left and rear were again, for a time, secure.

In the battle of Franklin, Schofield had not more than twenty-two thousand infantry and four thousand three hundred cavalry engaged. * Hood's force was at least thirty thousand infantry and seven thousand cavalry. Schofield lost one hundred and eighty-nine killed, one thousand and thirty-three wounded, and eleven hundred and four missing ; total, two thousand three hundred and twenty-six. The rebel loss was seventeen hundred and fifty killed, three thousand eight hundred wounded, and seven hundred and two prisoners; total, six thousand two hundred and fifty-two.f Six general

* " The Fifth division contained at this time but 2,500 men, Croxton's brigade about 1,000, and Capron's 800—in all, about 4,300 men."— Wilson's Report.

•f " At the time of the battle the enemy's loss was known to be severe, and was estimated at 5,000 ; the exact figures were only obtained, however, on the reoccupation of Franklin by our forces, after the battles of December 15 and 16, at Brent wood Hills, near

officers of the enemy were wounded, five killed, and one was captured. The unusual disparity in the losses was of course occasioned by the fact that; the rebels assaulted breastworks, while the national troops, except at a single point, remained entirely under cover. Half of Schofield's loss occurred in the two brigades which remained in front of the line after their proper duty as outposts was accomplished, and in the hand-to-hand encounter which ensued over the portion of the parapet which was temporarily lost by the precipitate retreat of this force. Nevertheless, Hood admitted that the stand made on the hills occasioned him a delay of several hours.

This victory was of enormous consequence to the national cause. It not only saved Schofield's army and at the same time greatly weakened Hood, but it was a fatal blow to all the expectations of the enemy, and created a depression in the rank and file from which they never recovered. But, notwithstanding the repulse he had inflicted, Schofield very well knew that Hood was still his superior in numbers, and would doubtless promptly attempt to avail himself of that superiority before it was gone. The national flank and rear were insecure, and communication with Nashville was threatened. Schofield considered that to remain at Franklin was to hazard the loss of his army, by

Nashville, and are given as follows : Buried upon the field, 1,750; disabled and placed in hospital at Franklin, 3,800; which, with the 702 prisoners already reported, make an aggregate loss in Hood's army, of 6,252."— Thomas's Official Report.

The later rebel estimates do not place their loss at less than 5,000 or 6,000.giving the rebels another chance to cut him off from his reinforcements. After consulting with his corps and division commanders, and receiving the approval of Thomas, he determined to retire at once to Nashville. * Accordingly, at midnight of the 30th of November, the army was withdrawn from the trenches, and crossed the river without loss. Hood brought his artillery forward in the night, so as to open on Schofield in the morning, but in the morning the national forces had disappeared. During the 1st of December they assumed position in front of Nashville.

At 11.30 P.M. on the 30th of November, Thomas announced the result of the battle to Grant, and the arrival of A. J. Smith's last division at Nashville. " 1 am in hopes now," he said, "to be able to manage Hood, notwithstanding the great superiority in numbers of his cavalry." Schofield had not yet withdrawn from Franklin, and Grant understood from this despatch that Thomas meant to move at once with his reinforcements upon the defeated enemy, and complete the success which had been already achieved. But the next day, at nine P.M., Thomas reported different plans : " After Schofield's fight yesterday, feeling convinced that the enemy far outnumbered him both in infantry

* Thomas had ordered Schofield to fall back, to Nashville, before the battle of Franklin

was fought.

"General Wilson has telegraphed me very fully the movements of the enemy yesterday and this morning. He believes Forrest is aiming to strike this place, while the infantry will move against you, and attempt to get in on your flank. If you discover such to be his intention, you had better cross the Harpeth at Franklin, and then retire along the Franklin pike to this place."— Thomas to Schqfield, Nashville, Nov. 29, 11 P.M.

and cavalry, I determined to retire to the fortifications around Nashville, until General Wilson can get his cavalry equipped; he has now but about one-fourth the number of the enemy, and consequently is no match for him. I have two ironclads here with several gunboats, and Commander Fitch assures me Hood can neither cross Cumberland river, nor blockade it. I therefore think it best to wait here until Wilson equips all his cavalry. If Hood attacks me here, he will be more seriously damaged than yesterday. If he remains until Wilson gets equipments, I can whip him, and will move against him at once. I have Murfreesboro' strongly held, and therefore feel easy in regard to its safety. Chattanooga, Bridgeport, Stevenson, and Elk river bridge have also been strongly garrisoned."

This determination of Thomas to remain on the defensive, after a victory, was in direct opposition to both the judgment and instincts of Grant. He preferred to take advantage of Schofield's success, and to press the enemy at once with the reinforced army, before the influence of defeat was gone. At eleven A.M. on the morning of the 2nd, he telegraphed : "If Hood is permitted to remain quietly about Nashville, you will lose all the road back to Chattanooga, and possibly have to abandon the line of the Tennessee. Should he attack you, it is all well; but if he does not, you should attack him before he fortifies. Arm, and put in the trenches, your quartermaster's employes, citizens, etc."

The government shared very fully this anxiety of the general-in-chief, and an hour after sending his own despatch to Thomas, Grant received one from the Secretary of War: « The President feels solicitous

about the disposition of Thomas to lay in fortifications for an indefinite period, ' until Wilson gets equipments.' This looks like the McClellan and Rosecrans strategy of do nothing, and let the enemy raid the country. The President wishes you to consider the matter." To this Grant replied: " Immediately on receipt of Thomas's despatch, I sent him a despatch which no doubt you read, as it passed through the office." He was not satisfied with this, however, and at 1.30 P.M. on the same day, forwarded a second message to Thomas : " With your citizen employes armed, you can move out of Nashville with all your army, and force the enemy to retire, or fight upon ground of your own choosing. After the repulse of Hood at Franklin, it looks to me that, instead of falling back to Nashville, we should have taken the offensive against the enemy, where he was. At this distance, however, I may err as to the best method of dealing with the enemy. You will now suffer incalculable injury upon your railroads, if Hood is not speedily disposed of. Put forth, therefore, every possible exertion to attain this end. Should you get him to retreating, give him no peace."

Then, as the equipment of the cavalry was the great reason assigned by Thomas for delay, he telegraphed at 7.30 P.M. the same night to Stanton: " Do you not think it advisable to authorize Wilson to press horses and mares in Kentucky, to mount his cavalry, giving owners receipts, so they can get their pay ? It looks as if Forrest will flank around Thomas, until Thomas is equal to him in cavalry." At ten P.M., he said to Halleck : " Is it not possible now to send reinforce-

ments to Thomas from Hooper's department ? If there are new troops organized, state militia, or anything that can go, now is the time to annihilate Hood's army. Governor Bramlette [of Kentucky] might put from five to ten thousand horsemen into the field to serve only to the end of the campaign." At ten P.M. this night, Thomas replied to his chief: "Your two telegrams of eleven A.M. and 1.30 P.M. received. At the time that Hood was whipped at Franklin, I had a,t this place but about five thousand men of Smith's command, which added to the force under Schofield, would not have given me more than twenty-five thousand; besides, Schofield felt convinced that he could not hold the enemy at Franklin until the five thousand could reach him. As General Wilson's cavalry force also made only about one-fourth that of Forrest's, I thought best to withdraw troops back to Nashville, and wait the arrival of the remainder of Smith's force, and also of a force of about five thousand, commanded by Steed-man, which I had ordered up from Chattanooga. The division of General Smith arrived yesterday morning [December 1], and Steedman's troops arrived last night. / now have infantry enough to assume the offensive, if I had more cavalry ; and will take the field anyhow, as soon as McCook's division of cavalry reaches here, which I hope will be in three or four days. We can neither get reinforcements nor equipments at this great distance from the North very easily, and it must be remembered that my command was made up of two of the weakest corps of General Sherman's army and all the dismounted cavalry except one brigade; and the task of reorganizing and equipping has met with

many delays which have enabled Hood to take advantage of my crippled condition. I earnestly hope, however, that in a few days more I shall be able to give him a fight."

Grant was unconvinced by this reasoning, for he believed that Hood's obstacles and disadvantages were equal to those of Thomas, and that one gained as much as the other, by delay. For a day or two, however, he refrained from further urging his subordinate, but on the 3rd, he said to Sherman, with whom he was attempting to communicate : " Thomas has got back into the defences of Nashville, with Hood close upon him. Decatur has been abandoned, and so have all the roads, except the main one leading to Chattanooga. Part of the falling back was undoubtedly necessary, and all of it may have been. It did not look so, however, to me. In my opinion Thomas far outnumbers Hood in infantry. In cavalry Hood has the advantage in morale and numbers. I hope yet Hood will be badly crippled, if not destroyed."

Grant was entirely right in his estimate of the relative numbers of the opposing armies. Sherman had left sufficient men behind for every emergency, and it was only Thomas's policy of scattering his forces and defending every assailable point, which had left so small an army for Schofield at Pulaski and Franklin, and made the first falling back inevitable. Steedman might have been recalled on the day that Hood advanced from the Tennessee, and even Stoneman would have been better occupied resisting the principal rebel army at the West, than in following Breckenridge's three thousand men with double their number in East Tennessee. Thomas

ULYSSES S. GRANT.

219

also very greatly over-estimated Hood's force, both in infantry and cavalry; but after Hood was defeated with a loss of six thousand men at Franklin, and Thomas was reinforced by ten thousand men under Smith, and five thousand under Steedman, as well as the black brigade from Chattanooga, while additions were daily making to Wilson's command, there could be no question of the national preponderance. On the 2nd of December, Thomas's infantry in front of Nashville, numbered forty thousand,* while Hood was reduced to twenty-three thousand; yet Thomas remained behind his fortifications and Hood enjoyed all the moral and substantial results of a victory. The national army was besieged by a force at least one-third smaller than its own; every railroad but one was abandoned to the enemy, and there was no telegraph line out of Nashville except to the North. These were not the fruits which should have followed a victory; and either Grant, Sherman, or Sheridan would undoubtedly have moved upon the enemy, disordered by defeat arid weakened by loss, before he had time to recover. Doubtless there were difficulties. Thomas com-

* The field returns of Thomas's command for November 30,
1864, show present for duty, equipped: —
INFANTRY.
Fourth corps Twenty-third corps Smith Steedman
Officers.
724 494 483 199
Enlisted Men.
15,378 10,033
8,284 6,757
1,900 40,452 Hood's return for December 10 was—-Effective total, 23,053.
There is nothing to show that any force was included in Hood's army, outside of this return, except Forrest's cavalry.

plained that liis cavalry was inefficient, and it was certainly inferior in numbers to that of the enemy; but both Grant and Sherman considered that Thomas needed a smaller body of horse than he himself was persuaded he required. Wilson, his cavalry commander, was a young man with very large ideas of what he wanted; full of energy and spirit, but lacking in judgment and headstrong in opinion. He desired a large and admirably equipped command of cavalry. There can be no doubt that such a command was eminently desirable, but it was not indispensable. It was far from being necessary to risk the security of Tennessee, or the upsetting of all Grant's plans at the South and East as well as the West, in order to raise or equip another thousand or two of horse. A cavalry officer might be excused for magnifying the importance of his command, or insisting on the necessity of his accoutrements ; the latter at least was within his province ; though Wilson himself was the very man to have moved, ready or not, at the word of command. But the general of a great army should have risen to a height from which all the contingencies of the campaign and all the circumstances of the field would have assumed their proper proportions. Thomas's own campaign was, after all, but one of many, and it was necessary for the general success that it should be fought at a certain time. Canby's operations in the rear of Hood were intended to be co-operative with Thomas's advance; and Sherman and Meade and Butler and Sheridan were all included in the scheme, in which the army in Tennessee bore only a part. Thus the delay of Thomas might defeat operations a thousand miles away.

Besides this, Grant contemplated possibilities that were perhaps not so apparent to his subordinate. In all military matters, his imagination was not only vivid, but what may be called dramatic, as well. He knew what he himself would do in Hood's position, and often said at the time that so long as Hood was free, the whole West was in danger. Had he commanded the rebel army, he would have ignored Nashville altogether, and allowing Thomas to reinforce and refit his cavalry at leisure, would have moved to the North, when Thomas would have had nothing to do, but to follow. It was not only Nashville that Grant was considering, but Louisville, and the country beyond the Ohio. At no period of the war did those who approached him closest perceive so many signs of anxiety as now. He feared the undoing of all that had been achieved at so much cost at the West; he feared another race between the armies, for the Ohio ; the necessity for raising fresh levies; the arousing of disaffection in Indiana;—issues compared with which the remount of Thomas's cavalry, or even the fate of Nashville, was insignificant.

What added to his solicitude at this crisis was the personal respect and regard he entertained for Thomas. The kindly nature of the man had won upon Grant; and still more the splendid services he had rendered the country; the firm loyalty Thomas had displayed at the beginning of the war; the genuine truthfulness, the sturdy honesty, the steadfast patriotism, that were part of his character. Grant was thoroughly assured that Thomas intended well; that it was a feeling of duty "which held him back; that the subordinate's love for the

country and devotion to the cause were no less than his own. It pained him to differ with the soldier with whom he had shared so many campaigns ; he was unwilling to show distrust in the efficiency of one who had been so efficient; to over-rule the general who was the object of so much deserved attachment from individuals and armies.

And yet he had no doubt that Thomas's judgment was wrong; that the arming of even five thousand cavalry was of far less importance than the immediate destruction of Hood; that the danger which existed so long as Hood was unde-stroyed was infinitely more important than all the good which ten thousand fresh cavalrymen could accomplish; and above all, that the army on the Cumberland was fully able, at this moment, to destroy its opponent. And so there came, amid all the other anxieties that crowded on the general-in-chief, this new and unexpected care created by Thomas's determination to delay.

Meanwhile, the first news from Sherman was received, through the rebel newspapers. Immense supplies in kind, intended for Hood and Lee, had been piled along the roads, all of which Sherman had seized, or the enemy was obliged to destroy, to prevent their falling into his hands. The consternation on his line of march was universal. Spies and scouts, prisoners and refugees, soon confirmed the story. There were even indications of a disposition to submit, such as had hitherto not been permitted to appear. Four newspapers on one day called for another leader. " The people," they declared, " will follow. They are tired of this madness, and if it

does not cease, nothing but ruin is before them." Every effort, nevertheless, was made by the rebel rulers to withstand the advance of Sherman. Bragg and Beauregard were summoned, the one from the East, the other from the West; for unless the rebels meant to yield everything, they must defend Augusta and Savannah. But there was no organization, and little to organize. Breckenridge was reported to have been ordered from West Virginia, and Early from the Valley ; but these rumors were soon ascertained to be false ; Wilmington, however, was certainly stripped of its garrison, and the governors of five states were called upon for the reserves. Information also came from various sources that an attempt would be made to throw troops into Savannah. Ossabaw Sound, in that vicinity, was the point where it was expected Sherman would appear. Here supplies were waiting for him, and hither Grant sent a messenger with orders, to greet him on his arrival. The inland fortifications were believed to be weak, but the obstructions in the Savannah river prevented any aid to Sherman by the fleet, until he actually struck the coast.

As yet, however, it was far from certain that Sherman would not turn to the Gulf of Mexico, and maps and newspapers were carefully studied by Grant, to divine his course. Meanwhile, the cooperative movement of Canby was delayed, as we have seen. Until Thomas assumed the offensive against Hood, Canby was obliged to hold Vicks-burg and Memphis so that they could not be seriously threatened, and his own expedition into the interior was thus postponed. At last, came Tumors of the capture of Millen by Sherman, and, on the

same day, the news of Schofield's victory at Franklin ; and Grant again proclaimed at the camp fire his admiration for Sherman, while all remembered how constantly he had insisted that Schofield was a fine soldier, and needed nothing but opportunity to prove it. Grant, indeed, had kept him in place against determined opposition from various quarters; and now, if only the success at Franklin was followed up, so that Canby could move into Mississippi, the danger at the West was past.

But while thus zealously watching the varied interests and changing circumstances in Georgia and Tennessee, as well as at Richmond and in the Valley, Grant had also planned to take advantage of Sherman's march by a new movement on the Atlantic coast. Wilmington, near the mouth of the Cape Fear river, in North Carolina, was the only important seaport now open to the enemy. At this point the rebels still received supplies of arms and clothing from abroad, and hence they sent out in return cotton and other products, by British blockade-runners. The Bermuda isles are close at hand, and if they once arrived at Nassau, the British flag protected-rebel goods as well as the vessels of rebel sympathizers. During the entire war, indeed, whole branches of British industry had thriven on this contraband commerce, at the expense of the Union. Batteries of cannon were cast at Manchester for the rebel army, and ships were built in Liverpool and Glasgow yards, especially to run the national blockade; and by these means the existence of the rebellion was undoubtedly prolonged. At first, Mobile, and Charleston, and other ports had shared this traffic; but during the last year, the blockade

had become so efficient that Wilmington was the only entrance left by sea for any considerable amount of supplies. Strenuous efforts had of course been made to seal this harbor, but hitherto with only partial success. The nature of the outlet of Cape Fear river is such that without possession of the land at a point near the mouth, it is impossible to entirely close the port. To secure the possession of this point required the co-operation of a military force; and during the summer of 1864, Grant agreed to furnish a sufficient number of troops for the purpose.

A formidable fleet was accordingly assembled, the command of which was entrusted to Admiral Porter, with whom Grant had served with complete co-operation and success in his Mississippi campaigns. It was originally intended that the expedition should set out in October; but through the imprudence of officers both of the army and the navy, and afterwards of the public press, the exact object of the enterprise became known; and the enemy thus warned, prepared to resist it. This caused a postponement of the expedition; but towards the end of November, the project was revived ; and six thousand five hundred men were promised from the army of the James. Grant selected Major-General Weitzel to command the force, and sent him down the coast, to reconnoitre the ground, and procure all the information possible in regard to the character and strength of the forts at the mouth of Cape Fear river. Butler of course was fully informed of the enterprise committed to his subordinate, and had frequent conferences with Grant on the subject.

In the meantime, as we have seen, Sherman had proceeded so far into Georgia that the rebels, in order to raise a force against him, had nearly abandoned Wilmington, as well as Fort Fisher, at the mouth of the Cape Fear river. On the 30th of November, Grant notified Butler that Bragg, who had been in command at Wilmington, had set out for Georgia, taking with him most of the forces in North Carolina. "It is therefore important," he said, " that Weitzel should get off during his absence ; and if successful in making a landing, he may, by a bold dash, succeed in capturing Wilmington. Make all the arrangements for his departure, so that the navy will not be detained one moment by the army." In conjunction with Weitzel's movement, Butler had been ordered to send a force of from three thousand to four thousand men, under General Palmer, to cut the Weldon railroad south of the Roanoke river, and Grant now asked : " Did you order Palmer to make the proposed move yesterday ? It is important he should do so without dej.ay." In answer to this, Butler visited Grant in person at City Point, and received further instructions for Weitzel to move as soon as the fleet was ready. The same day Grant said to Admiral Porter: " Southern papers show that Bragg, with a large part of his force, has gone to Georgia. If we can get off during his absence, we will stand a fair chance, not only to carry Fort Fisher, but to take Wilmington. The troops will be ready to start the moment you are ready."

In connection with this expedition, an experiment had been suggested by Butler, from which that commander hoped important results. His idea was to blow up a vessel loaded with gunpowder, in the neighborhood of Fort Fisher, with the expectation that the fort would be injured, if not destroyed, by the explosion. Grant had little faith in the scheme, and the opinions of the engineers were adverse ; but the naval authorities, including Admiral Porter himself, favored an attempt. On the 3rd of December, Grant wrote to Sherman : " Bragg has gone from Wilmington. I am trying to take advantage of his absence to get possession of that place. Owing to some preparations Admiral Porter and General Butler are making to blow up Fort Fisher, and which, while I hope for the best, I do not believe a particle in, there is a delay in getting the expedition off. I hope they will be ready to start by the 7th, and that Bragg will not have started back by that time." On the 4th, he said to Butler : " I feel great anxiety to see the Wilmington expedition off, both on account of the present fine weather, which we can expect no great continuance of, and because Sherman may now be expected to strike the sea-coast at any day, leaving Bragg free to return. I think it advisable for you to notify Admiral Porter, and get off without delay, with or without your powder-boat."

On the 3rd, as has been stated, the general-in-chief wrote to Sherman, sending his despatch to the blockading squadron, to be forwarded as soon as the army was heard from on the coast. " Since you left Atlanta," he said, " no very great progress has been made here. The enemy has been closely watched, though, and prevented from detaching against you. I think not one man has gone from here, except some twelve or fifteen hundred cavalry."

He then went on to state a general idea of his plans for Sherman's future action, but without giving minute directions. " With your veteran army, I hope to get control of the only two through routes from East to West, possessed by the enemy before the fall of Atlanta. This condition will be filled by holding Savannah and Augusta, or by holding any other port to the east of Savannah and Branchville. If Wilmington falls, a force from there will co-operate with you?

All this while, he remained as anxious as ever to utilize his various forces in every field. On the 28th of November, he had said to Sheridan : "My impression- now is that you can spare the Sixth corps with impunity: I do not want to make the order for it imperative, but unless you are satisfied that it is necessary for the defence of the Valley, I should like to get it here as early as possible." On the 3rd of December, he announced to Meade : " The Sixth corps will probably begin to arrive here to-night, or in the morning. As soon as it does get here, I want you to move with the Second, and about two divisions of the Fifth corps, down the Weldon road, destroying it as far to the south as possible." Later on the same day, he continued : " I think there should be a force of twenty thousand, and then all the reserves that can possibly be spared from the lines should be held ready to go after the enemy, if he follows." This movement would be simultaneous with that of Palmer in North Carolina, and both were intended, not only to distress Lee still further for his supplies, but to prevent reinforcements being sent to

Wilmington, when Weitzel's expedition should start.

It was at this time reported that Lee's cavalry had been sent to Georgia, to aid in the resistance against Sherman, and on the 30th of November, Grant said to Meade : " Try to ascertain how much force Hampton has taken from here with him. He has gone himself, beyond doubt." Then with his usual policy, he continued : " If the enemy has reduced his cavalry much, we must endeavor to make a raid upon the Danville road. Bragg has taken most of the troops from Wilmington to Georgia, which will aid an expedition I have ordered to cut the Weldon road south of the Roanoke." At the same time, as Hampton had been sent to Georgia, and Lee's infantry would be occupied in watching Meade's movement southward, Grant reverted to his constant idea of destroying the connection between Richmond and the Shenan-doah Valley. On the 4th of December, he telegraphed to Sheridan : " Do you think it possible now to send cavalry through to the Virginia Central road ? It is highly desirable this should be done, if it is possible."

On the 5th, he gave Meade instructions to move down the Weldon road as far south as Hicksford ; and on the 6th, he said to Butler: " A movement will be commenced on the left to-morrow morning. Make immediate preparations so that your forces can be used north of the river, if the enemy withdraw ; or south, if they should be required. . . During to-morrow night, withdraw to the left of your line at Bermuda Hundred the troops you propose to' send south [under Weitzel], unless otherwise directed." 97

Thus, while bringing troops from the Shenandoah, and suggesting new operations to Sheridan; while planning a movement for the army of the Potomac, which might necessitate drawing largely from that of the James; Grant at the same time availed himself of the absence of Bragg, occasioned by Sherman, to initiate an attack on Wilmington ; and directed the co-operation of Palmer with the expeditions of both Weitzel and Meade ; he also sent orders to Sherman to guide him on his arrival at the coast, and he made Canby's movements depend on those of the army in Tennessee. He once declared that his first object, on assuming command of all the armies, was to use the greatest number of troops possible against the enemy ; and his second, to hammer continuously against the armed force of the rebels, until by mere attrition, if in no other way, there should be nothing left for them but submission to the laws of the land. His first object had certainly been achieved; all the troops possible w r ere constantly in use against the enemy : and as for the second,—although there was a good deal besides hammering in the elaborate strategy of 1864, the attrition undoubtedly went on.

In the meantime, the situation at Nashville was becoming daily more humiliating and dangerous. Although Thomas telegraphed on the 3rd of December : " Have succeeded in concentrating a force of infantry about equal to that of the enemy," he remained entirely on the defensive, and the rebels entrenched themselves on a line only two miles from the city : the national fortifications extended from the Cumberland river on the right to the river again on the left, and all outside was held by Hood.

" No telegraph communication south," said the operator there, on the 3rd, to his fellow at Grant's head-quarters ; "No telegraph communication south, from Nashville, of course, but we can communicate with Chattanooga vid Cumberland Gap and Knox-ville. Nothing heard from Forrest, but General Wilson is looking after him, and no apprehension is felt." And this was the mortifying sequence to the great campaigns of Grant and Sherman for Chattanooga and Atlanta. The national troops were held in Nashville, and communication with Chattanooga was by the North. Comfort was even taken by the besieged that no apprehension was felt in regard to Forrest; although even this comfort the general of the Western army did not share; for he telegraphed, on this day, to Halleck : " As soon as I can get the remaining brigade of General McCook's division of cavalry here, I will move against the enemy, although my cavalry force will not be more than half that of the enemy. I have labored under many disadvantages since assuming direction of affairs here ; not the least of which was reorganizing, remounting, and equipping of a cavalry force sufficient to contend with Forrest." On the same day, he reported: "The enemy made no demonstration to-day except to advance his pickets on Nolensville, Franklin, and Hillsboro' pikes. I have a good entrenched line on the hills around Nashville, and hope to be able to report ten thousand cavalry mounted and equipped, in less than a week, when I shall feel able to march against Hood."

Forrest, meanwhile, was operating on the blockhouse and telegraph lines, between Nashville' and Murfreesboro', and on the 3rd and 4th of December,

he captured three stockades, as well as a train of cars on the Chattanooga railroad, and reported two hundred and sixty prisoners. So secure, indeed, did Hood now feel, that, on the 4th, he ordered Forrest to move with two divisions of cavalry, nearly his entire force/* and a division of infantry, against Murfreeshoro', thirty miles away. Forrest started on the morning of the 5th, and Thomas's cavalry force was then far superior to that which remained with Hood.

On the 4th, the enemy extended his lines and threw up new works ; at the nearest point the rebel skirmishers were now only four hundred yards from Thomas's main works. Citizens and negroes were impressed to complete the entrenchments. That night Thomas reported that the enemy had planted a battery on the river, and captured two steamboats, but the naval force drove the battery away, and recaptured the steamers. " I have heard," he said, " from Tullahoma, ~by Knoxville, today. The railroad is uninjured that far, and no signs of the enemy in that neighborhood. I have heard nothing in direction of Murfreesboro', and therefore infer enemy has made no move in that direction yet, but is now turning his attention to crossing the river below. Any such attempt I am prepared to meet."

* "The enemy still holding Murfreesboro' with some 6,000 troops, Major-General Forrest, with the larger portion of the cavalry and Bates's division of infantry, was sent there to see if it was practicable to take the place."— Hood to fieauregard, January 9, 1865.

" On the morning of the 4th I received orders to move with Buford's and Jackson's divisions to Murfreesboro'."— Forrest's Report, January 24, 1865.

Grant had anticipated this danger, and was now intensely anxious in regard to the situation. On the 5th, he telegraphed : " Is there not danger of Forrest moving down the Cumberland to where he can cross it ? It seems to me, whilst you should be getting up your cavalry as rapidly as possible to look after Forrest, Hood should be attacked where he is. Time strengthens him in all probability as much as it does you" In this surmise he was entirely right, for Hood, at this very juncture, reported to his superiors : " Our line is strongly entrenched, and all the available positions upon our flanks and in rear of them are now being fortified with strong self-supporting detached works, so that they may be easily defended, should the enemy move out upon us. The enemy," he continued, " still have some six thousand troops strongly entrenched at Murfreesboro'. This force is entirely isolated, and I now have the largest part of the cavalry under Forrest, with two brigades of infantry in observation of these forces, and to prevent their foraging in the country. Should this force attempt to leave Murfreesboro', or should the enemy attempt to reinforce it, I hope to be able to defeat them."

On the night of the 5th, Thomas telegraphed : " If I can perfect my arrangements, I shall move against the advanced portion of the enemy on the 7th;" but on the 6th, he suspended the movement again. At eight P.M. that night, he telegraphed to Grant: "Your telegram of 6.30 P.M., December 5, just received. As soon as I can get up a respectable force of cavalry, I will march against Hood. General Wilson has parties now out pressing horses,

and I hope to have some six or eight thousand cavalry mounted in three or four days from this time. General Wilson has just left me, having received instructions to hurry the cavalry remount as rapidly as possible. I do not think it prudent to attack Hood with less than six thousand cavalry to cover my flanks, because he has under Forrest at least twelve thousand. I have no doubt Forrest will attempt to cross the river, but I am in hopes the gunboats will be able to prevent him."

Before receiving this despatch, Grant had finally given a peremptory order. At four P.M. on the 6th, he telegraphed: " Attack Hood at once, and wait no longer for a remount of your cavalry. There is great danger of delay resulting in a campaign back to the Ohio river." Thomas replied, at nine P.M., the same night: " Your telegram of four P.M. this day just received. I will make the necessary dispositions and attack at once, agreeably to your orders, though I believe it will be hazardous, with the small force of cavalry now at my service."

That night news came from Van Duzer, the operator at Nashville : " Scouts report large force twenty miles down river, towards Harpeth shoals, and say rebels propose to cross Cumberland river there, soon as it can be forded and river is too low for gunboats, which will be soon, unless rain falls." It looked, indeed, as if Hood's boasts were about to be realized. Not only was the national army enclosed in the capital of Tennessee, but if the rebels once crossed the river, it would be cut off entirely from the North. Nevertheless, Thomas did not attack.

Hood at this time reported : " Middle Tennessee, although much injured by the enemy, will furnish

abundance of commissary stores. . . The cars can now run from here to Pulaski. . . We have sufficient rolling stock captured from the enemy to answer our purposes. I will endeavor to put this road in order from Pulaski to Decatur, as soon as possible. As yet 1 have not had time to adopt any general system of conscription, but hope soon to do so, and to bring into the army all men liable to military duty."

There were delays at the East, as well as the West; and on the 5th, Grant said to Meade : " We will not wait for Getty's division. How soon can you move troops ? I have been waiting to get off [Weitzel's] troops down the coast, but as Palmer has already moved from Newbern, will wait no longer." " Palmer probably started from Newbern yesterday, with a force of from three to four thousand men, to cut the same [Weldon] road south of the Roanoke."

On the 6th, he gave Butler detailed orders for Weitzel's operations. " The first object of the expedition under General Weitzel is to close to the enemy the port of Wilmington. There are reasonable grounds to hope for success, if advantage can be taken of the absence of the greater part of the enemy's forces now looking after Sherman in Georgia. . . The object of the expedition will be gained by effecting a landing on the main land between Cape Fear river and the Atlantic, north of the north entrance to the river. Should such landing be effected while the enemy still hold Fort Fisher and the batteries guarding the entrance to the river, then the troops should entrench themselves, and by co-operating with the navy, effect the reduction and capture of those places."

That night General Butler embarked his troops at Bermuda Hundred. He proceeded himself to City Point, and then for the first time Grant learned his intention to accompany the expedition. The general-in-chief had not designed nor desired to entrust the command of these forces to Butler ; for, as repeatedly shown, although he was entirely satisfied with that officer's zeal and general ability, he was convinced that he lacked some quality essential in a commander in the field : whether the military coup d'ceil, or the judgment of a general, or the faculty of handling troops in the presence of the enemy, Grant did not pronounce; but he felt certain that the peculiar talent of a successful soldier was not possessed by the commander of the army of the James.

He therefore had directed him to place Weit-zel in command of the expedition; and had in fact committed to Butler movements in support of those of Meade, which he intended should detain him at Bermuda Hundred. Nevertheless, he did not now forbid Butler to accompany Weitzel. It was difficult thus to affront a commander of so high rank, unless it was intended to relieve him entirely from command; and this Grant was not prepared to do, without consulting the government, which he knew would dislike, and perhaps forbid, the step. He fancied, besides, that Butler's object might be to witness the explosion of the powder-boat, in which he took great interest, rather than to direct the expedition itself; thus no disapproval of his purpose was indicated. Tt is certain, however, that it would have been better if Grant had frankly and peremptorily ordered Butler back to the army of the

James, to superintend the movements there. His dislike to wound the feelings of another should doubtless, at this crisis, have been sacrificed. Those who have never been placed in situations of great delicacy and responsibility, or who cannot realize the various considerations, military, political, and personal, which affect the decisions of men in power —will doubtless here find cause to censure Grant.

This day the general-in-chief sent further and more definite orders to Sherman, to guide him on his arrival at the coast. " Establish a base on the sea-coast. Fortify, and leave all your artillery and cavalry, and enough infantry to protect them, and at the same time so threaten the interior that the militia of the South will have to be left at home. With the balance of your command come here by water, with all dispatch. Select yourself the officer to leave in command; but you, I want, in person. Unless you see objections to this plan which I cannot see, use every vessel going to you, for purposes of transportation." In the same letter, he informed Sherman: "Hood has Thomas close in Nashville. I have said all I could to force him to attack, without giving the positive order, until to-day. To-day, however, I could stand it no longer, and gave the order, without any reserve. I think the battle will take place to-morrow."

On this day Grant's hands and time were full indeed. He sent orders to Thomas to attack Hood, " without any reserve " ; he gave directions to Sherman to move his army by sea to Richmond; he wrote detailed instructions to Butler for Weitzel's expedition, and minute orders to Meade for the movement southward against the Weldon road.

On the 7th, he telegraphed to Butler, now at Fort Monroe: " Let General Weitzel get off as soon as possible. "We don't want the navy to wait an hour." At ten P.M., he reported to the government: " General Warren, with a force of twelve thousand infantry, six batteries, and four thousand cavalry, started this morning, with the view of cutting the Weldon railroad as far south as Hicksford. Butler, at the same time, is holding a threatening attitude north of the James, to keep the enemy from detaching there. To-night he has moved six thousand five hundred infantry and two batteries across James river, to be embarked at Bermuda Hundred, to cooperate with the navy in the capture of the mouth of Cape Fear river. Palmer has also moved, or is supposed to have moved, up the Roanoke, to surprise Rainbow, a place the enemy are fortifying, and to strike the Weldon road south of Weldon."

It was not a single hammer, however ponderous, that was at work; but a great and complicated mechanism, with springs, and levers, and pulleys, and wheels; and the simultaneous blows that fell at numerous and distant points were all directed and controlled by the mind of the master-workman.

On the same day, taking every contingency into consideration, Grant said to Meade : "If the enemy send off two divisions after Warren, what is there to prevent completing the investment of Petersburg with your reserve ?"

The country meanwhile had become uneasy, and the government was even more anxious than Grant, in regard to Thomas. On the 7th of December, at 10.20 A.M., Stanton telegraphed: "Thomas seems unwilling to attack because it is hazardous,

as if all war was anything but hazardous. If he waits for Wilson to get ready, Gabriel will be blowing his last horn." Grant replied at 1.30 P.M.: "You probably saw my order to Thomas to attack. If he does not do so promptly, I would recommend suspending him by Schofield, leaving Thomas subordinate." Only those who were with him at the time, and in his confidence, could know the pain it gave to Grant to write these words. He was fond of Thomas, personally. He remembered his worth, his services, his patriotism, as well as the devotion of the Western army to its chief. He knew also the extreme risk in changing commanders at such a crisis. As Lincoln said, with homely force, on another occasion, it was like " swopping horses while crossing a stream." But he felt that unless an advance was promptly made in Tennessee, the peril to the entire West was instant and inevitable; and if Thomas refused any longer to obey, there was no option but to put a general in his place who would carry out his orders; and painful though the necessity was, Grant gave the word.

Nothing, however, was done by the government, and nothing was heard from Thomas till nine o'clock on the night of the 7th, when he telegraphed to Halleck : " Captain Fitch, United States navy, started down the river yesterday with a convoy of transports, but was unable to get them down ; the enemy having planted three batteries on a bend of the river, between this and Clarks-ville. Captain Fitch was unable to silence all three of the batteries yesterday, and will return again to-morrow morning, with the assistance of the [gunboat] Cincinnati, now at Clarksville; and

I am in hopes he will be able to clear them out." Thus another avenue of communication with Thomas was cut off. The Cumberland river was closed.

Hosecrans, who had commanded in Missouri, was at this juncture relieved by Dodge, at Grant's request, and on the 8th, the general-in-chief telegraphed to Halleck : " Please direct General Dodge to send all the troops he can spare, to General Thomas. With such order, he can be relied on to send all that can properly go. They had probably better be sent to Louisville, for I fear either Hood or Breckenridge will go to the Ohio river. I will submit whether it is not advisable to call on Ohio, Indiana, and Illinois, for sixty thousand men for thirty days. If Thomas has not struck yet, he ought to be ordered to hand over his command to Schofield." Yet even now, he had a good word to say for his inert subordinate. " There is no better man to repel an attack than Thomas, but I fear he is too cautious to take the initiative." Halleck replied to this at nine P.M. " If you wish General Thomas relieved, give the order. No one here will, I think, interfere. The responsibility, however, will be yours, as no one here, so far as I am informed, wishes General Thomas removed." To this Grant answered at ten o'clock: "Your despatch of nine P.M. just received. I want General Thomas reminded of the importance of immediate action. I sent him a despatch this evening, which will probably urge him on. I would not say relieve him, until I hear further from him."

The despatch Grant had sent to Thomas was in these words : " 8.30 P.M. It looks to me evident the enemy are trying to cross the Cumberland, and are

scattered. Why not attack at once ? By all means avoid the contingency of a foot race, to see which, you or Hood, can beat to the Ohio. If you think necessary, call on governors of states to send a force into Louisville, to meet the enemy, if he should cross the river. You clearly never should cross, except in rear of the enemy. Now is one of the finest opportunities ever presented of destroying one of the three armies of the enemy. If destroyed, he never can replace it. Use the means at your command, and you can do this, and cause a rejoicing from one end of the land to the other." He left nothing undone to stimulate, and encourage, and rouse, the powerful but dogged nature, which needed sometimes a goad, but when once incited into action, was as irresistible as it before had been immovable. On the 9th, at 10.30 A.M., in obedience to Grant's orders, Halleck telegraphed to Thomas: " Lieutenant-General Grant expresses much dissatisfaction at your delay in attacking the enemy. If you wait till General Wilson mounts all his cavalry, you will wait till doom's day, for the waste equals the supply. Moreover, you will be in the same condition that Rosecrans was last year—with so many animals that you cannot feed them. Reports already come in of a scarcity of forage." Thomas replied, at two P.M. : " Your despatch, of 10.30 A.M. this date, is received. I regret that General Grant should feel dissatisfaction at my delay in attacking the enemy. I feel conscious that I have done everything in my power to prepare, and that the troops could not have been gotten ready before this. And if he should order me to be relieved, I will submit without a murmur.

A terrible storm of freezing rain has come on since daylight, which will render an attack impossible, till it breaks."

Meanwhile, at eight P.M. of the 8th, Van Duzer, the telegraph operator at Nashville/* reported : " No change in position since last report. Enemy sfcill in force in front, as was found out by reconnoissance, and large artillery force on south bank of the Cumberland, between here and shoals. One of our gunboats came to grief in the exchange of iron at Bell's Ferry. Rebel General Ewell holds same bank, below Harpeth's to Fort Donelson, but don't fight gunboats." At 9.30 P.M. the same night, Thomas himself reported : " With every exertion on the part of General Wilson, he will not be able to get his force of cavalry in condition to move before Sunday [December 11th]."

But Grant had directed Thomas to move without regard to Wilson, and on the receipt of these despatches, he telegraphed, on the 9th, to Halleck: "Despatch of eight P.M. last evening, from Nashville, shows the enemy scattered for more than seventy miles down the river, and no attack yet made by Thomas. Please telegraph orders relieving him at once, and placing Schofield in command. Thomas should be ordered to turn over all orders and despatches received since the battle of Franklin, to Schofield."

Before, however, this direction could be obeyed,

* The operators at the different head-quarters were in the habit of sending telegrams to each other, which sometimes conveyed important information, in addition to that communicated by the commanding officers.

Thomas himself telegraphed to Grant, in reply to the despatch of the general-in-chief of the night before : " December 9, one P.M. Your despatch of 8.30 P.M. of the 8th is just received. I had nearly completed my preparations to attack the enemy to-morrow morning, but a terrible storm of freezing rain has come on to-day, which will make it impossible for our men to fight at any advantage. I am therefore compelled to wait for the storm to break, and make the attack immediately after. Admiral Lee is patrolling the river above and below the city, and I believe will be able to prevent the enemy from crossing. There is no doubt but that Hood's forces are considerably scattered along .the river with the view of attempting to cross, but it has been impossible for me to organize and equip troops for an attack at an earlier moment. General Halleck informs me you are much dissatisfied with my delay in attacking. I can only say I have done all in my power to prepare, and if you shall deem it necessary to relieve me, I shall submit without a murmur." It is impossible not to admire the spirit that prompted these words, however much one may regret the peculiarities that made them necessary. Thomas was aware that his delay was greatly in opposition to the views of his chief and to the wishes of the government; he was aware that to neither did the delay seem necessary : he was conscious that it was a positive disobedience of orders, and might be visited, according to military rule, with that severest of punishments to a soldier, removal from command in the presence of the enemy. Yet he could not bring himself 'to act contrary to his own judgment and instincts, and deliberately suggested to his superiors the fate, which he declares he should submit to without a murmur. There is a determination and unselfishness combined in all this amounting to magnanimity. But the high-mindedness was not all on one side. Halleck read the message as it passed through Washington, and telegraphed to Grant at four P.M., on the 9th : " Orders relieving General Thomas had been made out, when his telegram of this P.M. was received. If you still wish these orders telegraphed to Nashville, they will be forwarded." Grant replied at 5.30 P.M.: " General Thomas has been urged in every possible way to attack the enemy, even to giving the positive order. He did say he thought he should be able to attack on the 7th, but he did not do so, nor has he given a reason for not doing it. I am very unwilling to do injustice to an officer who has done as much good service as General Thomas, however, and will therefore suspend the order until it is seen whether he will do anything." To Thomas himself, at 7.30 P.M., he said : " Your despatch of one P.M. received. I have as much confidence in your conducting a battle rightly as I have in any other officer. But it has seemed to me that you have been slow, and I have had no explanation of affairs to convince me otherwise. Receiving your despatch of two P.M. from General Halleck before I did the one to me, 1 telegraphed to suspend the order relieving you until we should hear further. I hope most sincerely that there will be no necessity of repeating the order, and that the facts will show that you have been right all the time." It would be difficult for a superior to show greater consideration for a sub-

ordinate, when they differed in judgment at a momentous crisis, than to hope, and to state the hope, that the man who persisted in disobeying might prove to have been right all the time.

Thomas replied at 11.30 P.M.,* the same night: "Your despatch of 7.30 P.M. is just received. I can only say in further extenuation why I have not attacked Hood, that I could not concentrate my troops and get their transportation in order in shorter time than it has been done ; and am satisfied I have made every effort that was possible to complete the task." Still he did not attack.

At 9.30 P.M. he telegraphed to Halleck: " There is no perceptible change in the appearance of the enemy's line to-day. Have heard from Cumberland, between Harpeth and Clarksville. There are no indications of any preparation on the part of the enemy to cross. The storm continues."

On the 10th, no despatches passed between Thomas and either Grant or the government; but on that day the general-in-chief directed Halleck: " I think it probably will be better to bring Winslow's cavalry to Thomas, until Hood is driven out. So much seems to be awaiting the raising of a cavalry force, that everything should be done to supply this want." Hearing nothing whatever from Thomas, at four P.M., on the llth, Grant telegraphed him once more: "If you delay attacking longer, the mortifying spectacle will be witnessed of a rebel army moving for the Ohio river, and you will be forced to act, accepting such weather as you find. Let there be no further

* This despatch has sometimes been published with the date of December 7th, but that given in the text is evidently correct. 98

delay. Hood cannot even stand a drawn battle, so far from his supplies of ordnance stores. If he retreats and you follow, he must lose the material, and much of his army. I am in hopes of receiving a despatch from you to-day, announcing that you have moved. Delay no longer, for weather, or reinforcements/'

Butler had not yet started for the Cape Fear river; and to him also on this day Grant was obliged to say: " Richmond papers of the 1 Oth show that on the 7th, Sherman was east of the Ogeechee, and within twenty-five miles of Savannah, having marched eighteen miles the day before. If you do not get off immediately, you will lose the chance of surprise and weak garrison."

Good news, however, came in from Warren. He had completely destroyed the railroad, from the Nottoway river to Hicksford, meeting with only trifling opposition. The weather had been bad, and marching and working were difficult; but he was now on his return to Meade. Upon the receipt of this news, Grant telegraphed to Sheridan: " The inhabitants of Richmond are supplied exclusively over the roads north of James river. If it is possible to destroy the Virginia Central road, it will go far towards starving out the garrison of Richmond. The Weldon road has been largely used until now, notwithstanding it has been cut to Stony creek. It is now gone to Hicksford, and I think can be of no further use. If the enemy are known to have retired to Staunton, you will either be able to make a dash on his communications, north of the James, or spare a part of your force."

On the llth, at 9.30 P.M., Thomas telegraphed to Halleck : " The position of the enemy appears the same to-day as yesterday. Weather continues very cold, and the hills are covered with ice. As soon as we have a thaw, I will attack Hood." In the same despatch he reported that a force of between two and three thousand rebels had crossed the Cumberland river, and were supposed to be moving northward, towards Bowling Green. Thomas had sent two brigades of cavalry after them. A rebel attack had also been made on Murfreesboro', but repelled. Thus Hood had become bold enough to throw large detachments of infantry and cavalry both to the north and south of Nashville, and in spite of the storms and ice that held Thomas fast, the rebel troops were in constant motion.

At 10.30 P.M. this night, Thomas replied to Grant's order for an immediate attack : " Your despatch of four P.M. this day is just received. Will obey the order as promptly as possible, however much I may regret it, as the attack will have to be made under every disadvantage. The whole country is covered with a perfect sheet of ice and sleet, and it is with difficulty the troops are able to move about on level ground. It was my intention to attack Hood as soon as the ice melted, and would have done so yesterday, had it not been for the storm." He nevertheless did not obey, but on the 12th, at 10.30 P.M., he still continued: " I have the troops ready to make an attack on the enemy, as soon as the sleet which now covers the ground has melted sufficiently to enable men to march; as the whole country is

now covered with a sheet of ice so hard and slippery, it is utterly impossible for troops to ascend steeps, or even move over level ground in anything like order. It has taken the entire day to place my cavalry in position, and it has only finally been accomplished, with imminent risk and many serious accidents, resulting from the number of horses falling with their riders on the roads. Under these circumstances, I believe an attack at this time would only result in an useless sacrifice of life." On the 13th, again: "There is no change in the weather, and as soon as there is, I shall move against the enemy, as everything is ready and prepared to assume the offensive."

On the 14th, at 12.30 P.M., Halleck telegraphed, without Grant's knowledge, but doubtless by the order of the President or the Secretary of War: "It has been seriously apprehended that while Hood, with a part of his forces, held you in check near Nashville, he would have time to co-operate against other important points left only partially protected. Hence, Lieutenant-General Grant was anxious that you should attack the rebel forces in your front, and expresses great dissatisfaction that his order had not been carried out. Moreover, so long as Hood occupies a threatening position in Tennessee, General Canby is obliged to keep large forces on the Mississippi river, to protect its navigation, and to hold Memphis, Yicksburg, etc., although General Grant had directed a part of these forces to co-operate with Sherman. Every day's delay on your part, therefore, seriously interferes with General Grant's plans." To this Thomas replied at eiolit P.M. : " Your telegram of 12.30 P.M, to-day

received. The ice having melted away to-day, the enemy will be attacked to-morrow morning. Much as I regret the apparent delay in attacking the enemy, it could not have been done before with any reasonable prospect of success."

But before these two despatches were exchanged, Grant had given up all hope of inducing Thomas to move. Major-General Logan was at this time visiting the head-quarters of the army, and as Grant knew him to be a good fighter, an order was made out for him to proceed to Nashville. He was informed that he was to take command of the army of the Cumberland, provided that on his arrival, Thomas had still made no advance; but Grant intended to proceed himself to the West, and assume control in person of all the operations there. He started from City Point, for this purpose, on the night of the 14th of December; but on arriving at Washington, on the 15th, was met by the news that Thomas had attacked Hood and driven him on the Franklin road, a distance of nearly eight miles.

Nashville lies in one of the numerous bends of the Cumberland river, surrounded by steep and rugged hills, eminently suited for the operations of a siege. Thomas's entrenchments were on the southern side, extending across the bend, and along the crest of one of these ridges. Hood's lines were immediately opposite, on another range, somewhat lower than the national position, but otherwise equally well-situated. A combination of roads from the south centres within the town, converging, like the sticks of an open fan. The principal ones, beginning on the national right, are the Charlotte,

Hardin, Hillsboro', Granny White, Franklin, No-lensville, and Murfreesboro' roads. Besides these, the three railroads to Johnsonville, Decatur, and Chattanooga, all meet at Nashville, but all were controlled by the rebels. The Cumberland river was also closed above and below the town, and Thomas's only avenue of communication was towards the north.

To the south, the hills are higher and steeper, as you advance, and at Brentwood, ten miles from Nashville, they become precipitous, and are only penetrated by narrow gaps, through which the Franklin and Granny White roads are carried. In case of a rebel disaster, these two roads would become of immense importance, for they would constitute Hood's only possible line of retreat; and even they soon unite, the Granny White entering the Franklin road, south of the Brentwood Hills. Hood drew abundance of food and forage from the country, but all of his ordnance came by the Decatur railroad, which was open from the rebel rear to Pulaski; at the latter point there was an interval unrepaired, but from Cherokee the road was unbroken, to the interior of Mississippi and Alabama.

On the 14th of December, Forrest was still in the neighborhood of Murfreesboro', with two divisions of cavalry, and two brigades of infantry. The remainder of Hood's command lay in front of Nashville, the right wing under Cheatham, the left under Stewart, while S. D. Lee had the centre, across the Franklin road; the flanks extended to the river on either side, and a little west of the centre a salient projected to a point within six

hundred yards of the national line: this work was admirably situated on a prominence known as Montgomery Hill, commanding the Granny White road. On the national side, Thomas had placed Steedman on the extreme left; Wood, with the Fourth corps, was at the centre, in front of Montgomery Hill; and A. J. Smith had the right. Schofield was held in reserve, ready to support the left of Wood, and the cavalry, which had hitherto guarded the flanks, was now massed on the right of Smith. The interior works were manned by quartermasters' employes, so that all the enlisted troops of the command could be put into action. Thomas's infantry was now fifty-five thousand strong ; Hood's, about twenty-two thousand. The national cavalry in front of Nashville numbered twelve thousand men; the rebel, seventeen hundred.*

* On the 10th of December Thomas returned present equipped
for duty :

INFANTRY.
Officers. Enlisted Men.
Fourth corps 646 13,526
Twenty-third corps 488 9,719
A. J. Smith 561 9,990
District of Tennessee 637 15,884
District of Etowa 209 7,541
In his entire command... 70,272

Hood's effective present, as already shown, was 23,053, including the infantry force at Murfreesboro'.

Wilson states in his official report, that after the battle of Franklin he spent ten days remounting and equipping, and then he had, exclusive of two brigades of the First division, sent towards Bowling Green, nearly 9,000 mounted men; besides these, there were two brigades of 1,500 dismounted men each.

There is no return of Forrest's force other than that already given; but whatever its strength, it was all at Murfreesboro', with the exception of Chalmer's command. There is hardly another instance in war of a general with a force so large as Thomas commanded, allowing himself to be beleaguered so long by an army of less than half his numbers.

Hood seems to have had no designs, after once reaching Nashville. His despatches and reports give no inkling of any settled purpose, except that he hoped to recruit his army by conscriptions in Kentucky and Tennessee, "in time for a spring campaign." He suggested also that the Trans-Mississippi troops should be sent to him, but he gave no order to Forrest to cross the Cumberland river, and he made no preparation himself for such a move. The boldness that inspired the conception of his campaign entirely disappeared in the execution. It is possible that the failures at Spring Hill and Franklin had convinced the rebel commander that his army was unfit or unprepared for aggressive operations ; and he was perhaps deceived by Thomas's inertness, and fancied that he should be allowed to remain before Nashville until reinforcements could be found and forwarded to him. He certainly flattered himself that he could resist assault. On the 11th of December, he wrote to his superiors: " I think the position of this army is now such as to force the enemy to take the initiative." In this, at least, he was not deceived.

On the afternoon of the 14th of December, Thomas called a meeting of his corps commanders, and discussed with them his plan of battle. Steed-man, on the left, was ordered to make a demonstration east of the Nolensville road, while to Smith, on the right, was entrusted a vigorous assault against the enemy's left, from the direction of the Hardin

ULYSSES S. GRANT.

road. Wood, at the centre, was to support Smith's left, on the Hillsboro' road, and operate against the rebel advanced position on Montgomery Hill. Wilson was ordered to send one division of cavalry by the Charlotte road, to protect the right rear of the army, and with the remainder of his force, support the movement of Smith, while Schofield was still held somewhat in reserve, but instructed to cooperate with Wood, at the centre of the line. The plan was simple, but well designed; a heavy demonstration on the left, and under cover of this, a grand turning movement and assault from the right, supported by the centre and reserve. As in all of Thomas's operations, every commander had his work laid out, and every contingency was cared for in advance. He left nothing to chance. In the event of bad weather, the attack was to be still longer deferred.

On the morning of the 15th, however, the weather was favorable, and the troops were in motion at an early hour. The formations were partially concealed from the enemy by the broken nature of the ground, as well as by a dense fog, which hung close to the earth till noon. Under this double cover, Smith and Wilson advanced along the Charlotte and Hardin roads, Smith moving in echelon, so as to facilitate the turning movement, and Wilson on his right. As soon as these troops had taken position, Steedman was ordered to make his demonstration on the extreme left. He succeeded, with some difficulty and loss, in drawing the enemy's attention to that portion of the field ; and when this was apparent, Smith and Wilson began the grand movement of the day,

wheeling to the right, sweeping around the left flank of Hood's position, and crossing the Hardin and Hillsboro' roads. The cavalry was dismounted, and first struck the enemy, driving him rapidly back, and capturing a redoubt with four guns, which were quickly turned upon the rebel line. McArthur's division, of Smith's command, participated in this assault, vying with the cavalry. A second redoubt, stronger than the first, was next assailed, and carried; four more guns and three hundred prisoners were captured, the cavalry and infantry reaching the position simultaneously, and both laying claim to the artillery and the prisoners.

Smith, however, had not taken ground as far to the right as had been expected, and Thomas now ordered Schofield to move from his position, in reserve, to the right of Smith, and thus enable the cavalry to operate more freely towards the enemy's rear. The movement was rapidly accomplished, and Schofield's troops participated in all the subsequent operations on this flank

Meanwhile, as soon as Smith had struck the rebel left, Wood, at the centre, assaulted Montgomery Hill, and carried the entire rebel line in his front, capturing several pieces of artillery, and five hundred prisoners. The enemy was thus driven completely out of his original line of works, and forced back to a second range of hills, still holding, however, his line of retreat by the Franklin and Granny White roads.

At nightfall, Thomas readjusted his line, which now ran parallel to and east of the Hillsboro' road; Schofield was on the national right, Smith at the centre, and Wood on the left; while the cavalry remained

on the right of Schofield, and Steedman a little in advance of the position he held in the morning. The total result of the day's operations was the capture of sixteen guns and twelve hundred prisoners, and the forcing hack of the enemy's line. The casualties on both sides were extremely light. Thomas's entire command bivouacked in line of battle, on the ground occupied at dark, and prepared to renew the attack in the morning. During the night the enemy's line was shortened, and his left thrown back. As the principal national attack was evidently directed against Hood's left, Cheat-ham's corps was passed from the right to the left of the rebel army, leaving Lee on the new right, who had previously held the centre; while Stewart, who had before been on Hood's left, now became the centre of the line.

At six o'clock on the morning of the 16th, Wood pressed back the rebel skirmishers across the Franklin road ; and swinging lightly to the right, advanced due south from Nashville, driving the enemy before him, till he came to a new work constructed during the night. This was about five miles south of the city, on Overton Hill, east of the Franklin road. Steedman at the same time moved out by the Nolensville road, securing Wood's left flank, while Smith established connection on the right of the Fourth corps, and completed the new line of battle. Schofield remained in the position taken the day before, facing east, and looking to the enemy's left flank; while Wilson's dismounted cavalry was again formed on the right of Schofield's command. By noon, the cavalry had succeeded in gaining the enemy's rear, and stretched across the

Granny White road, one of Hood's two outlets to Franklin.

As soon as these dispositions were complete, and Thomas had visited in person the different commands, he directed the movement against the rebel left to be continued. The entire national line now approached within six hundred yards of the enemy at all points. The rebel centre was weak, but Hood was strong both on the right at Overton Hill, and at the left on the heights bordering the Granny White road. Still, Thomas had hopes of gaining Hood's rear, and cutting off his retreat to Franklin. At about three P.M., two brigades of Wood's command, and one of colored troops from Steed man's force, were ordered to assault the position at Overton Hill. The ground on which the columns were formed was open, and exposed to the view of the enemy, and the assault was met by a tremendous fire of canister and musketry. The men, nevertheless, moved steadily up the hill till near the crest, when the rebel reserves arose, and poured into the advancing column a withering fire. The troops first wavered, then halted, and at last fell back, leaving their dead and wounded in the abatis, black and white indiscriminately mingled. Wood, however, re-formed his troops in the position they had occupied before the assault.

About this time, McArthur, in command of one of Smith's divisions, sent word that he could carry the hill on his right, by assault. Thomas was with Smith when the message arrived, and it was referred to him for decision. He, with his usual caution, directed Smith to delay the movement till Schofield could be heard from, on the right. McArthur, however, receiving no reply, and fearing if he longer

delayed, that the enemy would strengthen his works —advanced without orders."' The troops pressed on with splendid ardor, sweeping up the hill, through mud and thickets, and over stone walls and earthworks. " Powder and lead," said the rebels, " could not resist such a charge." Prisoners were taken by the regiment, and artillery, by batteries.

Immediately, Smith and Schofield moved their entire commands, and carried everything before them. A panic seized the rebel left; the line was broken irreparably in a dozen places ; literally, all the artillery and thousands of prisoners were captured. Wilson's cavalry, still dismounted, had advanced simultaneously with Schofield and Smith; and striking the rebels in rear, they now gained firm possession of the Granny White road, and completely cut off that line of retreat from the enemy. At the same time Wood and Steedman's troops, hearing the shouts of victory from the right, rushed impetuously forward, renewed the assault on Overton Hill, and though meeting still a heavy fire, their onset was irresistible. The rebel troops, hopelessly broken, fled in confusion on the Franklin road, and all efforts to re-form them were fruitless. The Fourth corps followed in close pursuit for several miles, till darkness intervened to save the fugitives.

* " About 3 o'clock P.M. General McArthur sent word that he could carry the hill on his riglit by assault. Major-General Thomas being present, the matter was referred to him, and I was requested to delay the movement until he could hear from General Schofield, to whom he had sent. General McArthur not receiving any reply, and fearing if the attack should be longer delayed, the enemy would use the night to strengthen his works, directed the first brigade to storm the hill."— A. J. Smith's Report, January 10, 1865.

Meanwhile, Wilson had hastily mounted two divisions of his command, and directed them to move along the Granny White road, so as to reach Franklin in advance of the flying enemy. But the croops had pushed on so far, dismounted, that time was necessarily lost before the horses could be brought up. The column then pushed on, but had not proceeded more than a mile when the advance came upon the rebel cavalry posted across the road, behind barricades. The command was again dismounted, and a battle ensued after dark. The rebels were scattered in all directions, but the delay was of inestimable value to the routed army. It saved Hood from annihilation, for Wilson proceeded no further, but went into bivouac, while the rebels continued their flight on the Franklin road. A victorious army seldom equals a routed one, in speed.

At Brentwood, about four miles from his line of battle on the morning of the 16th, Hood was first able to collect some of his scattered troops, and S. D. Lee took command of the rear-guard, camping for the night in the neighborhood of the Brentwood Hills, which were filled with fugitives, unable to escape by the roads. The enemy had abandoned all his dead and wounded on the field. Four thousand four hundred and sixty-two prisoners were taken during the two days' battle, and fifty-three pieces of cannon. When the rebel guns were placed in position on the night of the 15th, the horses had been sent to the rear, and the giving way of the lines was so sudden that it was impossible to remove the artillery. The killed and wounded were not numerous on either side ; for after the first break in front of Smith,

there was no severe fighting. It was no longer a battle, but a rout.

At daylight on the 17th, the pursuit was resumed. The Fourth corps pushed on by the direct Franklin road, and the cavalry moved by the Granny White, to its intersection with the Franklin turnpike, and then took the advance. Wilson now sent one division, under Johnson, to the right, on the Hillsboro' road, with directions to cross the Harpeth river and move rapidly to Franklin, in advance of the enemy. In the meantime, the main cavalry column came up with Hood's rear-guard, four miles north of Franklin, and pressed with great boldness and activity, repeatedly charging the infantry with the sabre, and several times quite penetrating the lines. The rebels now fell back across the Harpeth, and Johnson's division coming up on the southern side, compelled them to retire altogether from the river banks; the cavalry then took possession of Franklin, capturing two thousand wounded. On the night of the 17th, the rebels encamped at Spring Hill, and on the 18th, Hood continued his retreat across the Duck river, to Columbia.

On leaving the field on the 16th, the rebel general had dispatched an officer to notify Forrest of the disaster, arid directed him to rejoin the army with as little delay as possible, and protect the rear; but Forrest was detained by swollen streams, and unable to overtake the infantry until the night of the 18th, at Columbia. Even after his defeat, Hood at first had hoped to remain in Tennessee, on the line of the Duck river, but at Columbia he became convinced that the condition of his army made it

necessary to re-cross the Tennessee river without delay.*

But just here the pursuit was interrupted for three days. On the 18th, the national cavalry arrived at Rutherford's creek, three miles north of Columbia; but the rains were falling heavily, and the stream was swollen ; the bridges were destroyed, and the pontoons had been sent by mistake on the Murfreesboro' road. The whole country was inundated, and the roads were almost impassable ; nevertheless, the army crossed the Harpeth, and Wood's corps closed up with the cavalry. It was not, however, till the 20th, that a floating bridge could be constructed out of the wreck of the old railroad bridge. Hatch's division of cavalry at once crossed Rutherford creek, but found on reaching Duck river that the enemy had already passed all his infantry, and removed his pontoon train. Duck river was a torrent, and another bridge must be laid. The pontoons had now arrived, but the weather had changed from dismal rain to bitter cold, and the colored troops employed in laying the bridges were half frozen as they worked in the stream. This occasioned further delay.

It was not till the 22nd that Wilson and Wood were ordered forward, the infantry moving by the main road, and the cavalry on either flank, in the fields. Smith and Schofield marched more leisurely behind. Forrest was now in command of the rebel rear-guard, composed of what was left of his cavalry, and five brigades of infantry, altogether about five thousand men. The inclemency of the weather was at this time the cause of great suffering in both

* Hood's Report.

armies. In both armies also there was lack of food, for the supply trains were impeded by the wretched condition of the roads. The horses had to be pushed up to their knees and often to their bellies through . slush and mud ; while the men marched slowly, with sleet and snow beating on their heads and shoulders, and sometimes waded waist-deep in the ice-cold streams. The flying troops, besides, were often shoeless. The rebel army of Tennessee had become a disheartened and disorganized rabble of half-armed and half-clad men; the principal part of Hood's ordnance had already been abandoned, and at Pulaski, where the roads became altogether impracticable for wheels, a further quantity of ammunition was destroyed. The country was strewn with abandoned wagons, limbers, blankets, and small-arms, from Nashville to the Tennessee river. Nevertheless, the rebel rear-guard was undaunted and firm, and did its work to the last. It frequently delayed the advance of the national cavalry, and never allowed Wilson again to strike the main command. Twice, in narrow gorges, Forrest made a stand, where a few hundred men were able to obstruct a division, and under cover of this resistance, the fugitive army moved off. He was once even able to capture a gun from his pursuers, which was not regained. From Pulaski, Hood moved by the most direct roads to Bainbridge, on the Tennessee river. Wood's corps kept well closed up with the cavalry, but Smith followed no further than Pulaski, and Schofield remained at Columbia. On the 27th of December, the whole rebel army, including the rearguard, crossed the Tennessee river, and on the 28th, Thomas directed further pursuit to cease. On that day, the advanced guard of the cavalry reached the Tennessee, just in time to see the rebel pontoons swing to the other side.*

The news of the first day's battle at Nashville reached Grant as he stepped from the steamer at Washington, and he telegraphed at once to Thomas: "11.30 P.M. : I was just on my way to Nashville, but receiving a despatch from Van Duzer, detailing your splendid success of to-day, I shall go no further. Push the enemy now, and give him no rest till he is entirely destroyed. Your army will cheerfully suffer many privations to break up Hood's army and render it unfit for future operations. Do not stop for trains or supplies, but take them from the country, as the enemy has done. Much is now expected." Half an hour later, Thomas himself reported: " Attacked enemy's left this morning. Drove it from the river very nearly to Franklin Pike. Distance, about eight miles." To this Grant replied at midnight: " Your despatch of this evening just received. I congratulate you and the army under your command for to-day's operations, and feel a conviction that to-morrow will add more fruits to your victory." Lincoln and Stanton also sent messages of congratulation and encouragement. The President declared : " You have made a magnificent beginning. A grand consummation is within your reach." He added : " Do not let it slip."

No further news from Tennessee arrived till the 17th, when a long despatch from Thomas was

* My authorities for this account of the battle of Nashville, are almost exclusively the reports of Thomas and Hood, and those of their subordinate commanders. There are no important discrepancies between the statements of rebel and national officers.

received, dated : " Six miles from Nashville," and giving full details of the victory. This day the good news came in fast, for despatches were also brought from Sherman. He had reached the coast, carried Fort McAllister, opened Ossabaw Sound, communicated with the fleet, and invested Savannah. On the 18th, Grant congratulated both his generals.

To Sherman he wrote : " I have just received . . and read, I need not tell you with how much gratification, your letter to General Halleck. I congratulate you and the brave officers and men under your command, on the successful termination of your most brilliant campaign. I never had a doubt of the result. When apprehensions for your safety were expressed by the President, I assured him that with the army you had, and you in command of it, there was no danger but that you would strike bottom, on salt water, some place ; that I would not feel the same confidence and security—in fact, would not have entrusted the expedition to any other living commander."

Then reverting to the Tennessee campaign, he continued : " It has been hard work to get Thomas to attack Hood. I gave him the most peremptory order, and had started to go there myself before he got off. He has done magnificently, however, since he started."

The same day came a second despatch from Sherman, dated December 12, in which he said: "1 am . . somewhat astonished at the attitude of things in Tennessee. I purposely delayed at Kingston, until General Thomas assured me he was all ready ; and rny last despatch from him of the 12th November was full of confidence; in this he promised me that he would ' ruin Hood/ if he dared to advance ironi Florence urging me to go

ahead and give myself no concern about Hood's army in Tennessee. Why he did not turn on Hood at Franklin, after checking him and discomfiting him, surpasses my understanding. Indeed, I do not approve of his evacuating Decatur, but think he should have assumed the offensive against Hood from Pulaski, in the direction of Waynesboro'. I know full well that General Thomas is slow in mind and in action, but he is judicious and brave, and the troops have great confidence in him. I still hope that he may outmanoeuvre Hood."

Meanwhile, Logan had arrived at Louisville, on his way to Nashville, and receiving the news of the victory, he telegraphed at once to Grant: " Just arrived. . . People here jubilant over Thomas's success. Confidence seems to be restored. I will remain here to hear from you. All things going right, it would seem best that I return soon to join my command with Sherman." Grant replied : " The news from Thomas is in the highest sense gratifying. You need not go further."

On the 18th, the general-in-chief said to Thomas : " The armies operating against Bichmond have fired two hundred guns in honor of your great victory. . . In all your operations we hear nothing of Forrest. Great precautions should be taken to prevent him crossing the Cumberland or Tennessee rivers below Eastport. After Hood is driven as far as possible to follow him, you want to reoccupy Decatur and all other abandoned points." Thomas replied the same day : " I have already given orders to have Decatur occupied, and also to throw a strong column on south side, of Tennessee river, for the purpose of capturing Hood's depot there, if possible, and gain-

ing possession of his pontoon bridge." This column was Steedman's, % which was sent on the 18th, by way of Murfreesboro', and thence by rail to the Tennessee. Thomas had also requested Admiral Lee, in command of the gunboat fleet at the West, to proceed up the Tennessee to Florence and East-port, and prevent the laying of pontoons there, or destroy the bridge, if one should have been already laid. At the same time he reported the attack on Murfreesboro', which had been made before the battle of Nashville, and in which Forrest had been repelled.

On the 19th, the Secretary of War proposed to confer on Thomas the vacant major-generalcy in the regular army, and the general-in-chief replied : " I think Thomas has won the major-generalcy, but I would wait a few days before giving it, to see the extent of damage done/' This day Thomas declared : " If the expedition against Florence be successful, I am confident we shall be able to capture the greater part of Hood's army." " I feel the utmost confidence we shall be able to overtake him, before he can reach and cross the Tennessee."

But on the 21st, came news of the delay in crossing Duck river, and Halleck now sent a despatch to Thomas without instructions from Grant, but doubtless by order of either the President or the Secretary of War, urging the importance of hot pursuit of "Hood's army. "Every possible sacrifice should be made, and your men for a few days will submit to any hardships and privations to accomplish the great result. . . A most vigorous pursuit on your part is, therefore, of vital importance. . . No sacrifice must be spared to obtain so important a result."

Thomas was evidently hurt by the persistent goading, and replied to Halleck at length, and with spirit: "Your despatch of 12 A.M. this day is received. General Hood is being pursued as rapidly and as vigorously as it is possible for one army to pursue another. We cannot control the elements, and you must remember that, to resist Hood's advance into Tennessee, I had to reorganize and almost thoroughly equip the force under my command. I fought the battles of the 15th and 16th insts. with the troops but partially equipped, and, notwithstanding the inclemency of the weather and the partial equipment, have been enabled to drive the enemy beyond Duck river, crossing two streams with my troops, and driving the enemy from position to position, without the aid of pontoons, and with but little transportation to bring up supplies of provisions and ammunition. I am doing all in my power to crush Hood's army, and if it be possible, will destroy it. But pursuing an enemy through an exhausted country, over mud roads completely sogged with heavy rains, is no child's play, and cannot be accomplished as quickly as thought of. I hope, in urging me to push the enemy, the Department remembers that General Sherman took with him the complete organization of the Military Division of the Mississippi, well supplied in every respect, as regards ammunition, supplies, and transportation, leaving me only two corps, partially stripped of their transportation, to accommodate the force taken with him, to oppose the advance into Tennessee of that army which had resisted the advance of the army of the

Military Division of the Mississippi on Atlanta, from the commencement of the campaign till its close, and which is now in addition aided by Forrest's cavalry. Although my progress may appear slow, I feel assured Hood's army can be driven from Tennessee, and eventually driven to the wall by the force under my command. But too much must not be expected of troops which have to be reorganized, especially when they have the task of destroying a force, in a winter's campaign, which was able to make an obstinate resistance to twice its numbers, in spring and summer. In conclusion, I can safely state that this army is willing to submit to any sacrifice to oust Hood's army, or to strike any other blow w r hich may contribute to the destruction of the rebellion."

The defence w r as eloquent, but on one or two points hardly fair. Sherman left Thomas much more than two corps, as has been repeatedly shown; and Thomas had been, since the 3rd of October, in command of all the district north of the Tennessee. His head-quarters were established at the greatest depot west of the Alleghanies, where thousands of quartermasters' employes were at his disposal to provide transportation, and every facility was afforded for supplying and equipping his troops. Few armies during the war were better furnished than that which fought so successfully at Nashville. It was to ensure this readiness that Thomas had so persistently retreated and delayed; and during the few days before the battle, he had himself repeatedly assured the general-in-chief that he was entirely ready for offensive operations, and waited only for favorable weather. The completeness of his success demqp strates that he was ready. As to the willing-ness of both Thomas and his army to make every sacrifice and every effort, that had been displayed on many fields, but never more conspicuously than in this campaign. Nothing was at fault but the disposition for elaborate preparation which, at all times, and under all circumstances, was so marked a feature of Thomas's character.

Grant had not stinted his acknowledgments of the brilliant success which had already been attained, but he was most anxious to secure the greatest possible result, and when this dispatch was received, he telegraphed at once to Thomas: "You have the congratulations of the public for the energy with which you are pushing Hood. I hope you will succeed in reaching his pontoon bridge at Tuscumbia, before he gets there. Should you do so, it looks to me that Hood is cut off. If you succeed in destroying Hood's army, there will be but one army left to the so-called

Confederacy, capable of doing us any harm. I will take care of this, and try to draw the sting from it, so that in the spring we shall have easy sailing. You have now a big opportunity, which I know you are availing yourself of. Let us push and do all we can, before the enemy can derive benefit, either from the raising of negro troops on the plantations, or the concentration of white troops now in the field."

On the 23rd, he said to Stanton : " I think it would be appropriate now to confer on General Thomas the vacant major-generalcy in the regular army. He seems to be pushing Hood with energy, and I doubt not he will completely destroy that army." The appointment was made the next day.

On the 24th, Thomas replied to Grant: " Your telegram of 22nd is just received. I am now, and shall continue to push Hood as rapidly as the state of the weather and roads will permit. I am really very hopeful that either General Steedman or Admiral Lee will reach the Tennessee in time to destroy Hood's pontoon bridge, in which event I shall certainly be able to capture or destroy almost the entire army now with Hood."

Steedman, however, had not proceeded further than Decatur, when he learned that the rebels had re-crossed the Tennessee. Admiral Lee also reached and held Florence, but owing to the falling of the water, his gunboats could ascend no higher; and Hood made his crossing at Bainbridge, eight miles above Florence, with Lee and the national fleet on the right, Steedman on the left, and Wilson and Wood in his rear. So liable are the best combinations in war to be intercepted and marred. As if to complete the mockery of events, the rebel pontoon train was captured, after the enemy had crossed. A cavalry force of six hundred men, from Steedman's command, overtook and destroyed it, on the 31st of December, at a distance of two hundred miles from Nashville. This was the last blow of the campaign.

Thomas now directed A. J. Smith to take position at Eastport; Wood was to concentrate his troops at Huntsville and Athens, in Alabama; Schofield was ordered back to Dal ton, on the Chattanooga railroad, and Wilson to send one division of cavalry to Eastport, and concentrate the remainder at Huntsville. The different commands were to go into winter quarters, and "recuperate, for

the spring campaign." These dispositions, however, were not approved by the general-in-chief, and Thomas was promptly notified that it was not intended his army should go into winter quarters.

Hood had moved from the Tennessee on the 21st of November, at the head of a compact and veteran army, reinforced by the finest body of cavalry in the rebel service ; boasting that he was about to redeem Kentucky and Tennessee, and threatening to carry the war into the North. When he re-crossed the same river thirty-six days later, half of his force had been absolutely destroyed ; and the remainder, defeated, disorganized, shattered beyond recovery, was flying in dismay before its conquerors. Thomas had captured, in the same period, thirteen thousand one hundred and eighty-nine prisoners, and seventy-two pieces of serviceable artillery; two thousand deserters had also given themselves up, and taken the oath of allegiance to the government; and when Hood reached Northern Mississippi, a large proportion of his troops were furloughed, and went to their homes. In January he was superseded by General Richard Taylor, and what was left of the rebel army of Tennessee was shortly afterwards transferred to the Atlantic coast, to oppose the advance of Sherman. In all the region between the Mississippi river and Virginia, there was then no formidable organized force to oppose the national armies. Thomas's entire loss, during the campaign, did not exceed ten thousand men, in killed, wounded, and missing; and half of the wounded were speedily able to return to the ranks.

The expedition into Tennessee was conceived by

Hood, but approved by Jefferson Davis and Beau-regard. The design avowedly was, either to force Sherman to fall back from Atlanta to Chattanooga, or, failing in this, to crush the force that was left behind, and at least secure Nashville and large reinforcements and supplies. Even more than this, however, was generally expected, and the invasion of Kentucky and of the country beyond the Ohio was confidently anticipated by the greater part of the rebel army.

Hood's first blunder undoubtedly consisted in remaining three weeks on the Tennessee, and allowing Thomas time to collect his scattered commands. After this, he was six days marching to Columbia, and at Spring Hill his campaign really failed; for here he had the opportunity he sought, of striking Schofield, in motion and in flank, and greatly his inferior in numbers. But from whatever cause, Hood was unable to inflict the blow; and Schofield marched by unhurt, within gun-shot of the rebel army, which bivouacked when it could, and should, have destroyed him. The battle of Franklin, however, was splendidly fought by the rebels; they seemed determined to atone for the fault of the day and the night before. But Schofield was able to hold his own. His position Avas admirable, his men behaved like heroes; and though the rebels were equally gallant, they Avere repelled. Hood lost six thousand men in a feAv hours. This Avas the deathblow of his army. His men never fought so well again.

Beauregard censured Hood for his course at the beginning of the campaign, and still more severely for his conduct after the repulse at Franklin. " It

is clear to my mind/' he said, " that after the great loss of life at Franklin, the army was no longer in a condition to make a successful attack on Nashville, a strongly fortified city, defended by an army nearly as strong as our own, and which was being reinforced constantly by river and railroad."* This, it has been seen, was the opinion of both Grant and Sherman; and Schofield wrote, on the 27th of December: " By uniting my troops to Stanley's, we were able to hold Hood in check at Columbia . . and Franklin, until General Thomas could concentrate at Nashville, and also to give Hood his death-blow at Franklin. Subsequent operations have shown how little fight was then left in his army, and have taken that little out of it. 5>

After this, Hood seemed to lose all his skill, and even the boldness, which had previously characterized him, disappeared. He acted as if he had a premonition that his troops would fail him. Doubtless their lack of spirit was apparent to him, and affected him without his knowledge; for commanders receive the impulses of their troops at least as often as they impart their own. At Nashville, the rebels certainly felt that they were outnumbered, and that their chance was gone; and on the night of the 15th of December, Hood made his preparations for retreat, although the issue was yet undecided, t The behavior of the troops on the next day is described in caustic terms, not only by Hood himself, but by his corps commanders, in their official reports. After the first break in the line, a panic ensued, and it was

* Beauregard's Endorsement on Hood's Report, January 9, 1865.

f Reports of Hood's corps commanders.

impossible to rally the army. These panics, which seized upon veteran troops in the Valley of the Shenandoah and in Tennessee, almost at the same epoch of the war, were doubtless the result of the conviction, gradually pressing itself home to soldiers and civilians at the South, that their cause was hopeless. The all-embracing strategy of Grant, his remorseless energy, his ceaseless attacks, dispirited and unmanned the bravest of his foes. The rank and file of Hood's command had heard that Sherman was penetrating Georgia, while Lee was held at Richmond ; they knew of Early's disasters, and jfelt that even their own success could only delay the inevitable end. When troops are imbued with feelings like these, a slight reverse is easily converted into irremediable ruin.

The condition of the rebel army, however, detracts in no degree from the skill of Thomas or the gallantry of his soldiers at Nashville. After that sturdy commander finally made up his mind to fight, his dispositions were admirable, and he was ably seconded by his generals. Every movement originally planned was carried out, and the battle proceeded by regular steps to its intended consummation. The only material change in the plan consisted in the removal of Schofield from his place in reserve and in rear of Wood, to the point, on the right of Smith, where his presence was more important: and this use of the reserve, though not absolutely designed in advance, was all the more creditable to Thomas, for it showed him able to develop his schemes and adapt them to new and unforeseen emergencies. But though there was development, there was no interruption of his plan. Even the resistance at

Overton Hill was anticipated and overcome ; it postponed, but did not avert the end, nor did it occasion the slightest change in the instructions to any commander.

The national troops, throughout both days, behaved with splendid steadiness. The rebel works were built on difficult heights, covered with timber, hard to climb, and bristling with artillery; and, notwithstanding Thomas's preponderance in numbers, had the defenders fought with their usual spirit, they must have inflicted terrible loss. But Hood, as well as his men, was cowed. He attempted no counter-move in any direction, and Thomas worked out his schemes as completely and as successfully as if the enemy, too, had been under his orders. It was like one of those lessons in chess, where all is laid down in advance, and each player knows exactly what his antagonist will do. On the night of the 15th, the rebels perceived their situation perfectly; they knew that they were enveloped ; that they had but one line of retreat, which Thomas was reaching out to grasp. Yet they were unable to extricate themselves from the web which the national commander was weaving. * They were forced to do exactly what Thomas expected and designed.

The victory was as. complete as in any battle of the war, and was followed by pursuit, which, for twenty-four hours, was as vigorous as could be desired. Afterwards, the obstacles were provoking, and, for a time, insurmountable. They, indeed, prevented any further important result being reaped from the victory. Hood was driven

* Reports of Hood's corps commanders.

from Tennessee; but he made up his rnind to this at Columbia, where he arrived on the 18th, and after that day, no important captures of guns or prisoners occurred, and no fighting on a scale worthy of record. All the harm was done on the battle-field, or before the rebels reached Columbia. Afterwards, though the national cavalry followed hard, they were never able to recover what was lost, or to bring Hood's main army again to a stand. The elements,—the rain, the snow, the icy streams—did more injury to the enemy than Wilson's pursuing column.

Thomas's strategy in the earlier part of the campaign has already been fully described. It was simply to fall back until he could concentrate his forces, and consider himself strong enough to attack or resist the enemy. It has also been shown that this was contrary to the expectations or wishes of either Grant or Sherman, neither of whom considered the falling back necessary. At any time after the 12th of November, Thomas could have called in his detachments from Chattanooga, Murfreesboro', and Decatur, leaving the guards at his railroad block-houses, and thus have made up an army of veterans sufficient to have defeated Hood at Pu-laski, at Columbia, or Franklin. He, however, preferred to wait at Nashville. This was with no far-seeing intention of decoying Hood, of which there is not an intimation in his dispatches, nor a suggestion in his report; but solely from his inveterate disposition to cover every line and hold every point. In consequence, he had not the army in front of Hood which Grant expected and Sherman had arranged.

" I did not turn my back on Thomas," wrote General Sherman, " until he himself assured me that he had in hand troops enough to prevent Hood from endangering the national interests in my rear." * " I have no fear," said Thomas to Sherman, on the 12th of November, " that Beauregard can do us any harm now, and if he attempts to follow you, I will follow him as far as possible." In fact, when Sherman and Thomas first discussed the campaign, and calculated the relative forces, Thomas asked for the Fourth corps only, and Sherman added the Twenty-fourth, to make assurance doubly sure; t and when Sherman started for the coast, Thomas had in hand a force superior by ten thousand to Hood's army. Steedman, and Granger, and Rousseau were all nearer to him than to the enemy—the very men who afterwards overwhelmed, by numbers, the rebel command entrenched before Nashville. There was thus no necessity for the falling back, except what Thomas imposed on himself, by not concentrating earlier.

Still, with this strategy, although it would never have been his own, Grant found no positive fault; for it was possible that the delay made Hood weaker and Thomas stronger, and thus increased the preponderance which rendered victory secure. It was when the troops had been concentrated, and the enemy had been beaten, and Thomas still remained in his fortifications in front of a manifestly inferior army, while the country was anxious and operations elsewhere were dependent on those in Tennessee—

* General Sherman to Author, February, 1880. i Ibid.

it was then that Grant became, first, disturbed, and filially, peremptory.

The event showed how true his instincts and perceptions were. The very completeness of the victory was the best proof that he had been right all the time. The national army which so easily conquered its foe, could have accomplished the same result, had it gone into action immediately after Smith and Steedman arrived. Thomas's success was not at all because of the delay, but in spite of it. All that he gained could have been gained two weeks before, for all that delay secured was a somewhat more efficient cavalry ; and Wilson's cavalry was not engaged on either day of the battle, as cavalry. It fought as well as any part of the army, and distinguished itself as greatly; but it fought dismounted, and the horses were, in reality, a weakness, for one man out of four was detained at the rear to hold them. It was of great use as cavalry on the 17th, undoubtedly ; acting with boldness and inflicting serious injury ; and it certainly hastened the flight of the rebel army : but this, too, could have been accomplished a fortnight earlier; for on the 17th, Forrest had not arrived from Murfreesboro', and there was only Chalmer's cavalry to oppose, not two thousand strong. Three days were lost at Duck river, and that time was never made up again. There was nothing in what occurred to justify either the long delay, or the anxiety which the delay had caused. The victory would have been as splendid, and the rout as desperate, had Thomas moved on the day when he was first ordered to advance.

On the other hand, if Hood had displayed the daring which distinguished him in front of Atlanta, or which apparently inspired the conception of this very campaign ; if he had realized the expectations of the South, or the fears of the North; if he had acted as half a score of generals, on either side, had acted on half a score of occasions during the war—Grant's apprehensions might have been terribly justified. Had the rebel commander moved to the Ohio, and compelled Thomas to follow, that officer would never have been forgiven. As it was, the rebels lived upon the country for a fortnight;* they fortified strongly in front of Nashville, and doubled the loss of life that Thomas incurred to oust them; they gave extreme uneasiness to the country and the government, and for a while endangered the success of Grant's plans elsewhere—and all of this might have been saved: the proof of which is that Hood, instead of striking Thomas, remained to receive the blow. The blow, it is true, when it came, was well considered, admirably aimed, perfectly executed, and the result all that had been hoped or desired; but if Grant's other subordinates had taken it upon themselves at critical moments to defy his judgments and disregard his orders, the strategy which gave Thomas the opportunity to strike that blow would have come to naught. No general can count on success when those to whom he entrusts the execution of his plans take it upon themselves to determine that lie is wrong. If Thomas's own lieutenants had acted towards him as he did to

* On the 12th, Forrest destroyed the railroad from Lavergne to Murfreesboro', and on the 13bh, captured a train of 17 cars loaded with 60,000 rations sent from Stevenson, and 200 prisoners.

Grant, the battle of Nashville would have been a rebel triumph.

Grant, however, was the last man to quarrel with victory. He was too much in earnest to care whether it was won in accordance with his own views, or in opposition to them. He sent congratulation after congratulation to Thomas and his soldiers. He recommended him for a major-generalcy in the regular army. He refrained from all censure or reference to his previous course ; and there never was a particle of coolness in their relations afterwards.

Grant, indeed, did not regard the inaction of Thomas as defiant or disrespectful. He attributed it to temperament rather than to judgment. For Thomas was always heavy and slow, though powerful. He would never have acted contrary to orders, in a positive matter. He would not have fought against orders, although he delayed in spite of them. He was nicknamed " Slow Trot" at West Point, and his mates in the army used to say : " Thomas is too slow to move, but too brave to run away." Caution is not always wisdom in war, but his caution and phlegm were combined with vigor, when once aroused. If he had the quality of inertia, he possessed momentum as well. He was like an elephant crossing a bridge, and feeling his way with ponderous feet before every step, but woe to the enemy he met on the opposite side.

Grant knew all this well. The same traits which were exhibited in the Nashville campaign, he had seen evinced at Chattanooga a year before ; the same provoking, obstinate delay before the battle, the same splendid, victorious, irresistible energy after

wards. He believed, indeed, in Thomas more than Thomas did in himself. The subordinate always shrank from responsibility.* He appeared relieved, when Sherman was appointed above him in May, 1864 ; and he was unwilling at first to be left behind in tha very command where he was destined to reap such a harvest of fame. But Grant's confidence in his ability was one reason why he wanted Thomas to fight. He was sure he would win, if once he became engaged.

When the war was over, and the general-in-chief made his formal report of the operations of the year, he at first wrote out an elaborate criticism of Thomas's course; but afterwards determined to refrain from even the appearance of censure of one who had done so well for his country; and instead of dispraise, he declared in so many words, that though his own opinions were unchanged, Thomas's " final defeat of Hood was so complete that it would be accepted as a vindication of that distinguished officer's judgment."

And, indeed, when criticism is spent, the fact remains that Thomas at Nashville did as much to end the rebellion as any one general in any one battle of the war. And in military matters nothing which is successful, is wrong.

After the victory, the revulsion in feeling at the North was marked. The country passed in two days from extreme uneasiness and anxiety to exultation and confidence. The event of the 15th of December dispelled at once all fear of disaster at Nashville, or of the invasion of Kentucky ; while that of the 16th

* " Thomas always shrank from supreme command and consequent responsibility.'*— General Sherman to Author, April, 1879.

ULYSSES S. GRANT.

announced the overthrow of the rebellion itself at the West, and foreshadowed its speedy and utter annihilation all over the land. Thomas naturally, and appropriately, became one of the heroes of his time, and took his place among the great captains whom the war rendered historical.

CHAPTEK XXX.

Sherman moves from Atlanta—Object of Sherman's march—Character of march—Foraging—Alarm of enemy—Rebel movements in Sherman's front—Arrival at Milledgeville—Second stage of march—Movements of cavalry—Increased consternation of rebels—Futile efforts to obstruct Sherman—Arrival at Millen—Policy of Sherman—Turns his columns towards Savannah—Character of country on Savannah river—Arrival in front of Savannah—Situation of city—Capture of Fort McAllister—Sherman communicates with the fleet—Supplies awaiting him at Port Royal— Results of march—Delight of country—Dispatches from Grant—Sherman ordered to embark his army for Richmond—Preparations to obey—Orders revoked—Investment of Savannah—Evacuation—Escape of garrison—Occupation of city—Expedition against Fort Fisher starts—Butler's powder-boat—Lack of co-operation between Butler and Porter—Explosion of powder-boat—Situation of Fort Fisher—Strength of defences—Garrison—Naval bombardment, December 24th—Arrival of Butler—Landing of troops—Reconnoissance—Butler determines against assault—Withdrawal of troops—Protest of Porter—Butler sails for Fort Monroe— Grant's dispatch to President—Butler's disobedience of orders—Unnecessary failure—Porter's dispatches—Chagrin of Grant—Second expedition determined on—Secrecy—Butler relieved from command—Second expedition starts—Terry's instructions—Arrival off Fort Fisher—Landing of troops—Movements of Hoke—Bombardment of January 13th—National line across peninsula—Supineness of Hoke—Reconnoissance—Arrangements for combined assault—Bombardment of January 15th—Cur-tis's advance—Ames's assault — National troops reach the parapet — Formidable character of work—Fighting on the parapet—Capture of Fort Fisher—Losses—Arrival of Stanton—Seizure of blockade runners— Conduct of troops—Gallantry of defence—Harmony of Porter and Terry —General observations—Results.

ON the 12th of November, Sherman's army stood detached, and cut off from all communication with the rear. It was composed of four corps: the Fifteenth and Seventeenth constituted the right wing
under Howard, and the Fourteenth and Twentieth the left wing under Slocum. The aggregate strength was sixty thousand infantry, besides five thousand five hundred cavalry, commanded by Kilpatrick. The artillery had been reduced to sixty guns. Each soldier carried forty rounds of ammunition on his person, and in the wagons were cartridges enough to make up two hundred rounds per man. One million two hundred thousand rations were in the trains, sufficient for twenty days; and there was a good supply of beef-cattle to be driven on the hoof; but forage was taken for only five days. Twenty-five hundred wagons and six hundred ambulances accompanied the command.

All the foundries, machine-shops, and warehouses in Atlanta were now destroyed, and on the morning of November 15th, the march began. Sherman's first object was to place his army in the heart of Georgia, interposing between Macon and Augusta, so as to oblige the rebels to divide their forces and defend not only those two points, but Millen, Charleston, and Savannah. The right wing and the cavalry accordingly moved southeast, towards Jonesboro', while Slocum led off to the east, by way of Decatur and Madison. These were divergent lines, designed not only to threaten Macon and Augusta, but to prevent a concentration upon Milledgeville, which lies between, and was the point that Sherman desired first to strike. Milledgeville is the capital of the state, and distant from Atlanta about a hundred miles. The time allowed for each column to reach it was seven days.

The army habitually moved by four roads as nearly parallel as possible, converging at points that were indicated from time to time in orders. The marches were from ten to fifteen miles a day, though sometimes on the extreme flanks it was necessary to travel as many as twenty miles; but the rate was regulated by the wagons. The troops started at the earliest break of dawn, and went into camp soon after midday. No tents were taken, but a nightly bivouac was made of the abundant pine-boughs, which served for shelter as well as beds; and, after dark, the whole horizon was lurid with the bonfires of railroad-ties, while all night groups of men were busy carrying the heated iron to the nearest trees, and bending it around the trunks; for the destruction of the railroads was one of the most important duties of the army.

The troops were ordered to forage liberally upon the country. The region was rich, and had never before been visited by a hostile force. The recent crop had been excellent, and was just gathered and laid by for winter. Meal, bacon, poultry, and sweet potatoes were abundant, as well as cows, oxen, horses, and mules. The skill and success displayed in collecting forage was one of the notable features of the march. Each brigade commander detailed a company, usually of about fifty men, under officers selected for their boldness and enterprise. These parties were dispatched before daylight, with a knowledge of the intended day's march as well as of the site of camp; they proceeded on foot five or six miles from the route travelled by their brigade, and then visited every farm and plantation within range. They usually procured a wagon or a family carriage, loaded it with bacon, corn-meal, turkeys, chickens, ducks, and anything else that could be

used for food or forage, and would then regain the main road, generally in advance of their train. When this came up, they delivered the supplies thus gathered by the way. These foraging parties, waiting at the roadside for their wagons, often presented an amusing spectacle: mules, horses, cattle even, were packed with old saddles and loaded with hams, live fowl, or bags of grain and flour; while the men themselves were mounted on all sorts of beasts, and surrounded by swarms of negroes. The cattle and horses, of course, were taken from them, but the next day they started out on foot again, to repeat the experience of the day before.

The main columns also gathered much forage and food, and it was the duty of each division and brigade quartermaster to refill his wagons as fast as the contents were issued to the troops. The wagon trains always had the right to the road, but each wagon was required to keep closed up, so as to leave no gaps in the column; and if, for any purpose, a single wagon or a group dropped out of place, it had to wait for the rear. This was always dreaded, for every brigade commander wanted his train up as soon as possible after the men reached camp.*

* " I have seen much skill and industry displayed by these quartermasters on the march, in trying to load their wagons with corn and fodder by the way without losing their place in column. They would, while marching, shift the loads of wagons so as to have six or ten of them empty. Then, riding well ahead, they would secure possession of certain stacks of fodder near the road, or cribs of corn, leave some men in charge, then open fences and a road back for a couple of miles, return to their trains, divert the empty wagons out of column and conduct them rapidly to their forage, load up, and regain their place in column without losing distance. On one occasion I remember to have seen ten or a dozen wagons thus loaded

No requisitions were made as in European armies, for the country was sparsely settled, and the civil authorities were unable to respond. The system adopted was simply indispensable to success; but the troops were supplied with all the essentials of life and health, and the animals of the command were kept well fed. Doubtless, acts of pillage, robbery, and violence occurred, as in every war, but such acts were exceptional and incidental. Sherman's "bummers," as they were called, committed neither murder nor rape; and no houses were burned except by order of a corps commander, and then only when the troops had been molested, the roads destroyed, or bridges burned by the inhabitants.

The day the national army moved, the alarm and confusion of the enemy began. On the 16th of November, Cobb, who was in command in Georgia, sent word to Richmond that Sherman had burned Atlanta, and was marching in the direction of Macon. " We have no force," he said, " to hinder him, and must fall back to Macon, where reinforcements should be sent at once." Beauregard, on the same day, telegraphed from Tuscumbia: " I would advise all available force which can be sent from North and South Carolina be held ready to move

with corn from two or three full cribs, almost without halting. These cribs were built of logs, and roofed. The train guard, by a lever, had raised the whole side of the crib a foot or two. The wagons drove close alongside, and the men in the cribs, lying on their backs, kicked out a wagon load of corn in the time I have taken to describe it."— Sherman's Memoirs, vol. ii.

In all my descriptions of the famous march, I have made free use of General Sherman's reports and dispatches, as well as of his "Memoirs," not scrupling even to avail myself of his eloquent language to enliven and adorn my narrative.

ULYSSES S. GRANT.

to defence of Augusta or crossing of Savannah river;" but he was informed that no troops out of his own department could be sent to him. Bichard Taylor, at Selma, however, was ordered to call on the governors of Alabama and Mississippi for all the state troops they could furnish, and to keep himself in readiness to move at a moment's notice, with all his available force; while Wheeler, with thirteen brigades of cavalry,* was instructed to watch the national movements closely, and attack and harass Sherman at all favorable points.

On the 17th, Cobb announced from Macon: "We are falling back rapidly to this place. We are too weak to resist them, unless reinforced promptly. The prisoners should be removed from this place." The same day Hardee was sent from the sea-coast, and directed to " concentrate detachments from garrisons, convalescents from hospitals, reserves, militia, and volunteers." On the 18th, the governor of Georgia telegraphed to Jefferson Davis: "A heavy force of the enemy is advancing upon Macon, laying waste the country, and burning the towns. We have not sufficient force. I hope you will send us troops as reinforcements, until the emergency is past." On the 19th, Hardee arrived at Macon, but the rebels were now distracted by the division of Sherman's force; on this day, the approach of a strong column of all arms along the line of railroad from Atlanta to Augusta was reported, and Hardee declared: " My opinion, hastily formed from the information before me, is that the enemy will ultimately form junction and march upon Augusta. General Cobb concurs.". Both Cobb and Beauregard, however, greatly underrated Sherman's force, neither estimating it higher than thirty-five thousand. On the 20th, communication was cut between Augusta and Macon, and on the 21st, Fry, the commander at Augusta, reported to the rebel Secretary of War: " The enemy are coming towards this place; I can save most of the powder-works and machinery, if permitted. I can collect about three thousand men. Shall I attempt to move machinery?" This day Hardee ordered all his available force from Macon to Augusta. On the 22nd, Fry reported: "Twentieth and Fourteenth corps, under Slocum, form left of Sherman's army, and is moving from Oconee river. May move either on Augusta or Savannah."

Sherman, however, as we have seen, had no intention of attacking either Macon or Augusta. On the 22nd of November, he rode into Milledgeville, where the Twentieth corps had already arrived; and during that day the entire left wing was united, while Kil-patrick and Howard were at Gordon, twelve miles off. The governor and other officers of the state, including the legislature, had fled from Milledgeville, but the inhabitants remained. The arsenal was destroyed, with such other public buildings as might easily be converted to hostile uses, but no important damage was done to private property. Thus the first stage of the journey was accomplished without serious opposition, except at a single point. On the 22nd, Kilpatrick made a feint on Macon, driving the enemy inside his entrenchments, and then fell back to Griswold, where he was joined by Wolcott's brigade of infantry. The two commands were engaged in covering the right

flank, when the rebels came out of Macon and attacked Wolcott in position, but were handsomely repulsed, and driven back with a loss of six hundred men.* Meanwhile Howard continued his movement along the Savannah railroad, tearing up the rails and destroying the iron. At the Oconee river a slight resistance was offered, but a pontoon bridge was quickly laid, and the right wing crossed.

On the 23rd, the next stage of the march was ordered. Howard was to move by roads south of the Savannah railroad, and the left wing to San-dersville, while the cavalry was directed to make a circuit to the north and march rapidly for Millen, a hundred miles away, and rescue the national prisoners confined there. The rebel cavalry, under Wheeler, had now moved around to Sherman's front, and Hard.ee was in command of about ten thousand irregular infantry, to oppose the national army. There was, however, nothing but skirmishing, except in Kilpatrick's front. A brigade of rebel horse was deployed in front of Sandersville, but was driven in by the skirmish line of the Twen tieth corps. At this place the enemy themselves set fire to stacks of fodder standing in the fields, and Sherman at once made known to the citizens that any attempt to burn food or fodder on his route would ensure a complete devastation of the country. This had the desired effect, and the destruction of food along the road by rebels ceased, The two wings marched on, tearing up the railroads and feeding on the fatness of the land.

Meanwhile, Kilpatrick was moving rapidly to-

* Report of G. W. Smith, the rebel commander.

wards Waynesboro, on the road between Millen and Augusta. Here he skirmished with Wheeler's cavalry, but the national prisoners had been removed from Millen, and Kilpatrick fell back by Sherman's orders as far as Louisville, where he remained two days to rest his horses ; and, as Wheeler seemed disposed to fight, Sherman added an infantry division to Kilpatrick's command, and told him to engage the rebel cavalry. He at once advanced upon Waynesboro, driving Wheeler through the town and across Brier creek, in the direction of Augusta, thus fostering the delusion that the main army was moving upon that point. The spirited movements of the cavalry were at this time of great importance to Sherman, for they relieved both the infantry column and the wagon train from all molestation during the march on Millen. Having effectually covered the left flank, Kilpatrick now turned to the south and followed the movements of the Fourteenth corps for a while. The cavalry thus formed a shifting curtain, concealing the operations of the various columns in turn.

As the national army advanced, the consternation of the rebels increased. On the 22nd of November, the commander at Augusta declared: " I can as yet count on only four thousand for defence here. Am gathering all. People show little spirit." On the 23rd, Hardee reported from Savannah : " I could gain no definite or reliable information respecting the movements of the enemy's infantry. Wheeler attacked the enemy's cavalry at Clinton, Sunday, but gained no advantage. The same day Colonel Cross drove the enemy from Griswold, but, being reinforced, Cross was in his turn driven from the place, Monday."

Bragg was at this juncture ordered to the front. On the 26th, he was at Augusta, and reported that Sherman had interposed between him and Macon, so that he could rely only on the forces east of the national army. These he declared were " feeble in number, wanting in organization and discipline, and very deficient in equipment. No offensive movement," he said, " can be undertaken, and but a temporary defence of our scattered posts. If no more means can be had, our only policy is to make sacrifices and concentrate. The country is being utterly devastated, wherever the enemy moves."

On the 28th, the adjutant-general at Richmond said to the commander at Charleston, now clamoring for help: " You must be as fully aware as the authorities here that there are no reinforcements that can be sent you." On the 29th, Hardee telegraphed from Savannah: " As railroad and telegraphic communication may soon be cut with Charleston, I desire you to know that I have, including the local troops, less than ten thousand men of all arms. General Smith is expected with twenty-five hundred, but has not yet arrived. If railroad communication is cut with Charleston, which is threatened by ten gunboats and barges, of course no reinforcements can be sent from Augusta." On the 30th, Beauregard's command was extended from the Mississippi to the sea-coast, and the governor of North Carolina was informed by Seddon: " There is urgent need for more forces to meet the advance of General Sherman's army. It would be wise as well as patriotic, on the part of North Carolina, to give all assistance possible to defeat or frustrate the designs of Sherman, while remote from her borders."

Amid these futile appeals of governors and generals to each other for help, these efforts to reinforce without reinforcements, this abandonment of posts and removal of prisoners and destruction of machinery, the national army moved steadily .forward. On the 3rd of December, Sherman entered Millen with the Seventeenth corps, and paused one day to communicate with all parts of his command. Howard was now south of the Ogeechee river with the Fifteenth corps, and opposite Scarborough; Slocum was four miles north of Millen with the Twentieth corps; the Fourteenth was ten miles further north, and the cavalry within easy supporting distance. The whole command was in good position and in excellent condition. The troops had subsisted largely on the country, and the wagons were full of forage and provisions. Two-thirds of the distance between Atlanta and the sea had been traversed.

At Millen Sherman heard that Bragg was at Augusta, and that Wade Hampton had been ordered to the same point from Richmond, to organize a cavalry force. The national commander, nevertheless, determined to push on towards Savannah. He had no desire to spend his time in front of fortified cities, or to encumber his wagons with wounded men. His policy was to avoid any contest that might delay him in the establishment of a new base of operations and supplies.» What he aimed at was to destroy the great lines of communication between the rebel armies and the important rebel towns. Macon and Augusta had no strategic value when those lines were annihilated. They were, it is true, filled with munitions of war, but the destruction of these was of far less consequence than the arrival of the army at the coast; while, if isolated by the interruption of the roads, the stores would be as useless to the enemy as if they had fallen into Sherman's hands. Pivoting, therefore, his army on Millen, and swinging it slowly around from its eastern course, Sherman turned his columns southward upon Savannah, marching by the four main roads.

At Ogeechee church, about fifty miles from the sea, he found fresh earthworks, the first since leaving Atlanta; but the rebel commander doubtless perceived that both his flanks could be turned, and prudently retreated without a fight; and the national columns leisurely pursued their march. As they approached the coast, the country became more sandy and barren, and corn and grass were scarce; but the rice-fields on the Savannah and Ogeechee rivers proved a substitute. The weather continued fine, the roads were good, the trains in excellent order, and the men marched easily their fifteen miles a day. No enemy opposed them, and only a faint reverberation on the left or rear told that Kil-patrick was skirmishing at times with "Wheeler's cavalry. A rebel division was falling back in front, as if to show the road to Savannah, and a few pris oners were picked up now and then. But this was all that looked like war.

Once the column turned out of the highway, marching through the fields, for torpedoes had been discovered planted in the road, with friction-matches to explode them when trodden on. There had been no resistance at this point, nothing to give warning of danger, and Sherman immediately ordered a 101

squad of rebel prisoners to be armed with picks and spades, and made to march in close order along the road, and explode their own torpedoes, or discover and dig them up. They begged hard, but he was inexorable, and, stepping gingerly on, they removed ten of the concealed instruments. Only one national soldier was hurt by the rebel torpedoes.

On the 8th of December, the advance reached Pooler's station, eight miles from Savannah. Sherman himself rode forward to reconnoitre, and entered a dense wood of pine, oak, and cypress, where he dismounted, and looking through a railroad opening, discerned a rebel parapet, about eight hundred yards away, encompassed with ditches, canals, and bayous, all filled with water. It was one of the outworks of Savannah. Another siege appeared inevitable.

The city lies on the west bank of the Savannah river, about twenty miles from the sea. The Ogee-chee river is at this point twelve or fifteen miles west of the Savannah, with which it runs generally parallel, emptying into Ossabaw sound. In the Ogeechee are many windings, and, at one of these, on the western bank, the rebels had erected a strong field-work, which they called Fort McAllister. It completely commanded the Ogeechee river and all communication with the sea. The country around Savannah is marshy and difficult, and the rebel lines followed two swampy creeks, one emptying into the Savannah above the city, and the other flowing in an opposite direction and emptying into the Little Ogeechee. These streams were bordered by rice-fields, which were flooded either by the tide or by inland ponds, the gates to which the enemy con-

trolled with heavy artillery. The only approaches to the city were by five narrow causeways, two of which were railroads, and the others the common country roads leading to Augusta, Louisville, and the Ogeechee. These were all obstructed by fallen trees and commanded by artillery.

As an assault could only be made at great disadvantage, Sherman proceeded to invest the city from the north and west. Slocum, on the left, rested on the Savannah, and Howard, on the right, reached to the Little Ogeechee, so that no supplies could reach Savannah by any of its accustomed channels, the river below the town being blockaded by the national fleet. There was still, however, a possible exit for the rebels across the Savannah to the left bank, and thence by the Charleston road. It was to cut this road that Grant, two months before, had ordered an expedition from Foster's command.

It was now of vital importance to open communication with the fleet, supposed to be waiting with supplies in Tybee, Ossabaw, and Wassaw sounds; and, on the 13th of December, Sherman ordered a division of infantry, under Brigadier-General Hazen, to march down the west bank of the Ogeechee, and carry Fort McAllister by storm. The fort was a strong, enclosed work, manned by two companies of artillery and three of infantry, and mounting twenty-five guns. Hazen deployed his division about the place, with both flanks resting on the river, posted his skirmishers judiciously behind the trunks of trees, whence they picked off the rebel artillerists, and then advanced in three lines, above, below, and in rear of the fort. The three parties reached the parapet simultaneously, trampling on a line of tor-

pedoes, which exploded as they passed, blowing many of the men to atoms. The national line moved on over every obstacle, driving the garrison to the bomb-proofs, where a hand-to-hand fight ensued. The rebels only succumbed as each man was individually overpowered; but McAllister was carried. Hazen lost twenty-four men killed, and one hundred and ten wounded. The garrison, of course, fell into his hands.

Meantime the national signal officers, from their stations in the trees and on the mill-tops, had been two days looking eagerly over the rice-fields and the salt marshes, in the direction of Ossabaw, but as yet perceived no indication of the fleet. But, while watching Hazen's preparations for the assault, Sherman himself descried what seemed the smoke-pipe of a steamer, becoming more and more distinct against the horizon, until, almost at the moment of the assault, a vessel was plainly visible below the fort, and the army signals were answered. As soon as the colors were fairly planted on the rebel wall, Sherman proceeded to the fort, and, finding a skiff in the neighborhood, a crew of oarsmen from the army pulled him rapidly down the stream. Night had already set in, but six miles below McAllister he saw a light, and was hailed by a vessel at anchor. It was the advance ship of the squadron, awaiting the approach of the army. The March to the Sea was over.

At 11.30 P. M. on the 13th of December, Sherman went aboard and wrote dispatches to Grant and the government. Later that night he met General Foster, who had come up the Ogeechee to communicate with him, and in Wassaw sound

he found Admiral Dahlgren in command of the blockading squadron. At Port Royal there were abundant stores of bread, provisions, and clothing, as well as siege-guns and ammunition. Foster, he learned, had made several unsuccessful attempts to cut the Charleston railroad; and it was now arranged to forward supplies to the army and heavy ordnance for an assault upon Savannah. On the 15th, Sherman returned to his lines in the rear of the town.

It was just one month since the army had started from Atlanta. On the 12th of November, Sherman severed communication with the North; on the 13th of December, he reopened it with Foster and the fleet. In these thirty-one days he had utterly destroyed two hundred miles of railroad, breaking up every connection between the rebel forces east and west of Georgia.* He had consumed the corn and fodder, as well as the cattle, hogs, sheep, and poultry, in a region sixty miles wide, carried away more than ten thousand horses and mules, and liberated countless numbers of slaves. Many of the stores and provisions were essential to the armies of Hood and Lee. The damage done to the state of Georgia he estimated at one hundred millions of dollars, of which twenty millions inured to the national advantage; the remainder was simple waste and destruction.

Sixty-five thousand men and thirty-five thousand animals had obtained abundant food for forty days, and the troops reached the coast, needing no provisions but bread. They started with five thou-

* "No report from General Hood since the 20th ult."— Beaure-gard to Richmond, December 13.

sand head of cattle, and arrived with ten thousand. The teams were in splendid flesh, and not a wagon was lost on the road. Kilpatrick collected all his remounts, and every officer had three or four led horses, while every regiment was followed by at least fifty negroes and footsore soldiers, riding on horses or mules. Besides this, great numbers of horses were shot, by Sherman's order, because of the disorganizing effect of so many idlers mounted.

In all the march through Georgia the rebels had only once obliged Sherman to use more than a skirmish line. His casualties were one hundred and three killed, four hundred and twenty-eight wounded, two hundred and seventy-eight missing. He had captured thirteen hundred and thirty-eight prisoners. As for the men, whether called on to fight, to march, to wade streams, to make roads, clear away obstructions, build bridges, or tear up railroads, they were always ready. Their spirit was superb.

Sherman himself declared : * " I only regarded the march from Atlanta to Savannah as a ' shift' of base, as the transfer of a strong army, which had no opponent and had finished its then work, from the interior to a point on the sea-coast, from which it could achieve other important results. I considered this march as a means to an end, and not as an essential act of war." But, however easy of actual accomplishment, however unobstructed by opposition, however unmolested by an enemy, the march to the sea will always be regarded as one of the most splendid achievements in military history. The daring of the conception and the originality of

* " Sherman's Memoirs," vol. ii., p. 220.

the design are not lessened because danger disappeared before the skill of the execution or difficulties amid the consternation of the enemy. An abler opponent might have concentrated the garrisons of Augusta, Macon, Charleston, and Savannah, and stayed, at least for a while, the advance of the national army. On the 6th of December, Beaure-gard reported to Jefferson Davis that he had counted upon a force of thirty thousand men to oppose Sherman;* and with this number, the difficulties that could have been interposed before an army advancing without either communications or base, might have been not only formidable, but to some commanders, insuperable; for after the advance had once begun, delay must have been disastrous, and disaster absolute ruin.

But the selection of the lines, the direction of the columns, and the dispositions of the troops so

* " In October last, when passing through Georgia to assume command of the Military Division of the West, I was informed by Governor Brown that he could probably raise, in case of necessity, about 6,000 men, which I suppose might be doubled in a levy en masse. General Cobb informed me at the same tima that at Augusta, Macon, and Columbus, he had about 6,500 local troops, and that he hoped shortly to have collected, at his reserve and convalescent camp near Macon, 2,500 more. Of these 9,000 men, he supposed about one-half, or 5,000, could be made available as movable troops for an emergency.

"To oppose the advance of the enemy from Atlanta, the state of Georgia would thus have probably 17,000 men, to which number must be added the thirteen brigades of Wheeler's cavalry, amounting to about 7,000 men. The troops which could have been collected from Savannah, South Carolina, and North Carolina, before Sherman's forces could reach the Atlantic coast, would have amounted, it was supposed, to 5,000 men. Thus it was a reasonable supposition that about 29,000 or 30,000 men could be collected in time to defend the state of Georgia, and ensure the destruction of Sherman's army."— Beauregard to Dams, December 6, 1864.

confused and deceived the rebel generals that neither concentration nor effective opposition was accomplished. The army marched straight on, as it had been ordered; it was never seriously incommoded or obstructed; its route was unchanged, its progress unimpeded; no plan was foiled, except when the prisoners were removed from Millen; and the sea was reached with the command absolutely in better condition than at the start.

Not only was the injury done to the resources of the enemy all that had been contemplated, but the moral effect upon the rebel population and authorities everywhere was prodigious. The realities of war were brought home for the first time to many who had been instrumental in involving both the North and the South in its calamities; while the march of a national army directly through the Confederacy was a demonstration that the government was irresistible. Sixty thousand men had been transferred to a position from which Grant could either move them at once against Richmond, or attempt whatever other military enterprise he deemed desirable.

The victory at Nashville, occurring almost on the same day on which Sherman reached the sea, made a completeness of success, extending over half a continent, seldom rivalled in war. The justification of Sherman's original boldness and of Grant's comprehensive sagacity was absolute. The whole country rang with applause. Antiquity was searched for a parallel, and the march of Sherman was compared with that of Xenophon. And, indeed, the disappearance of an army for a month from the outside

world, its passage through hostile regions, and final emergence with undiminished numbers and enhanced prestige, constituted a romantic episode that might well dazzle the imagination of indifferent spectators, and threw the nation which that army served into an ecstasy of delight and admiration. Even Thomas's success was for the time less esteemed, and although his operations had been worked out with equal effort, and were by soldiers appreciated at least as highly as the unobstructed movements of Sherman, yet to the popular apprehension the march was the more brilliant achievement of the two, and eclipsed in fame the solid results and arduous labors in Tennessee.

Not only this, but in the moment of its elation the country had no thought for him who had controlled and supervised both Thomas and Sherman; who had not only dictated the movements of each, but, by holding Lee, had rendered the success of either practicable. While every meed was offered, and justly offered, to the great soldiers who had saved Tennessee and traversed Georgia, men saw before Richmond only the general who had been besieging the rebel capital for nearly a year, and had not yet succeeded. It was Sherman and Thomas whose names were in all men's mouths. It was Sherman especially who was the hero of the hour.

On the 16th of December, a steamer passed up the Ogeechee, with dispatches from Grant, dated the 3rd, and mails for the troops who had been for more than a month cut off from all communication with the outer world. "Not liking," said Grant, " to rejoice before the victory is assured, I 'abstain from congratulating you, and those under your com-

mand, until bottom has been struck. I have never had a fear, however, for the result." The dispatch contained no minute instructions. " In this letter," he said, " I do not intend to give you anything like directions for future action, but will state a general idea I have, and will get your views after you have established yourself on the sea-coast."

The next day, however, Grant's letter of December 6th arrived, with definite orders : " I have concluded that the most important operation towards closing out the rebellion will be to close out Lee and his army. You have now destroyed the roads of the South, so that it will probably take them three months without interruption to re-establish a through line from East to West. In that time I think the job here will be effectually completed. My idea now is that you establish a base on the sea-coast, fortify, and leave in it all your artillery and cavalry, and enough infantry to protect them, and at the same time so threaten the interior that the militia of the South will have to be kept at home. With the balance of your command, come here with all dispatch. Select yourself the officer to leave in command, but you I want in person. Unless you see objections to this plan which I cannot see, use every vessel going to you for purposes of transportation."

Sherman at once prepared to carry out these orders, but, as some time would probably be required to collect the necessary shipping, at least a hundred steam or sailing vessels being necessary, he determined to push his operations, with the hope of securing the city of Savannah before he started for the North. Grant's orders arrived on the 15th, and on the 16th, Sherman wrote in reply : " Since the re-

ceipt of yours of the 6th, I have initiated measures looking principally to coming to you with fifty thousand or sixty thousand infantry, and incidentally to capture Savannah, if time will allow." He was very enthusiastic about his new work. " My four corps," he said, " full of experience and full of ardor, coming to you en masse, equal to sixty thousand men, will be a reinforcement that Lee cannot disregard. Indeed, with my present command, I had expected, after reducing Savannah, instantly to march to Columbia, South Carolina, thence to Raleigh, and thence to report to you. But this would consume, it may be, six weeks' time after the fall of Savannah; whereas, by sea, I can probably reach you with my men and arms before the middle of January." The letter concluded: " Our whole army is in fine condition as to health, and the weather is splendid. For that reason alone, I feel a personal dislike to turning northward. ... I shall not delay my execution of your order of the 6th, which will depend alone upon the time it will require to obtain transportation by sea."

Grant, however, had already ascertained that the requisite transportation could not be collected so soon as he had at first supposed. Two months at least would be required for the movement of Sherman's army by sea; and on the very day when Sherman was announcing his readiness to start, the general-in-chief gave him different directions. On the 16th, Halleck wrote to Sherman: "Lieutenant-General Grant informs me that, in his last dispatch sent to you, he suggested the transfer of your infantry to Richmond. He now wishes me to say that you will retain your whole force, at least for the

present, and, with such assistance as may be given you by General Foster and Admiral Dahlgren, operate from such base as you may establish on the coast." On the 18th, Halleck wrote again: " When Savannah falls, then for another wide swath through the centre of the Confederacy. But I will not anticipate. General Grant is expected Jiere this morning, and will probably write you his own views."

As Halleck expected, Grant wrote, on the same day and at length, to Sherman: " I did think the best thing to do was to bring the greater part of your army here, and wipe out Lee. The turn affairs now seem to be taking has shaken me in that opinion. I doubt whether you may not accomplish more towards that result where you are than if brought here, especially as I am informed, since my arrival in this city, that it will take about two months to get you here, with all the other calls there are for ocean transportation.

" I want to get your views about what ought to be done. . . . My own opinion is that Lee is averse to going out of Virginia, and, if the cause of the South is lost, he wants Richmond to be the last place surrendered. If he has such views, it may be well to indulge him until we get everything else into our hands.

" Congratulating you and the army again upon the splendid results of your campaign, the like of which is not read of in past history, I subscribe myself more than ever, if possible, your friend."

On the 16th of December, Sherman made a formal demand for the surrender of Savannah, declaring that he could throw heavy shot into the heart of the town, and that for some days he had

held and controlled every avenue by which the people and garrison could be supplied. Hardee, who was in command, replied that the national lines were, at the nearest point, at least four miles from the heart of Savannah, and that he was in free and constant communication with the exterior. The surrender was refused. Sherman therefore made his preparations to assault. On the 18th, he wrote to Grant: " I should like very much to take Savannah before coming to you; but, as I wrote you before, I will do nothing rash or hasty, and will embark for James river as soon as General Easton, who is gone to Port Royal for that purpose, reports to me that he has an approximate number of vessels for the transportation of the contemplated force. I fear even this will cost more delay than you anticipate, for already the movement of our transports and the gunboats has required more time than I had expected. But I still hope that events will give me time to take Savannah, even if I have to assault with some loss. ... I have a faint belief that you will delay operations long enough to enable me to succeed here."

Sherman had now completely invested the place on the north, west, and south, but there still remained to the enemy on the east the use of the old dike, or plank road, leading into South Carolina from the left bank of the Savannah; and Hardee could easily throw a pontoon bridge across the river to this point. Sherman therefore determined to order Foster to move down upon this road from the direction of Port Royal. On the 19th, he went in person to Port Royal to arrange the movement, leaving directions with Howard and Slocum to make

all possible preparations, but not to assault the city during his absence. His return through the network of channels connecting Tybee and Ossabaw sounds was delayed by high winds and ebb tides, and on the 21st, he was met by a messenger from his own head-quarters, with the news that Savannah had been evacuated the night before. Hardee had crossed the river by a pontoon bridge, and marched off on the Charleston road, carrying with him his garrison of at least ten thousand men and all his light artillery, and blowing up the ironclad vessels and the navy-yard, but leaving one hundred and fifty heavy guns, twenty-five thousand bales of cotton, and all other public property.*

Early on the morning of the 21st, the national skirmishers detected the absence of the enemy, and occupied the lines simultaneously along their whole extent. Savannah, with all its forts, and the valuable harbor and river, was once more in the national hands. Sherman was greatly disappointed that Hardee should have escaped with his garrison, but Grant, when he announced the news to the Secretary of War, declared: " It was a good thing as it stands, and the country may well rejoice at it."

Meanwhile the important operations on the North Carolina coast, so often contemplated, and so long delayed, had at last begun. The Cape Fear river runs due south from Wilmington to the Atlantic, a distance of twenty miles, and is separated from the

* General Sherman says : "My first report was as here stated. The actual result was more than 200 guns and 34,000 bales of cotton. This was the exact inventory of Easton and Barry, but I forget where it can be found."

sea by only a narrow peninsula, not more than a mile across, the extremity of which is known as Federal Point. At the mouth of the Cape Fear and directly south of Federal Point lies Smith's island, on either side of which are the two principal entrances to the river. The southern or outer channel was protected by Fort Caswell, on another island adjoining the mainland; and the northeast entrance, known as New Inlet, was commanded by Fort Fisher, which stretched across Federal Point from the river to the sea. Butler, it will be remembered, had been instructed that the object of the expedition would be gained when a landing was effected on the peninsula, north of the north entrance to the river. " Should such a landing be effected," said Grant, "whilst the enemy still holds Fort Fisher and the batteries guarding the entrance to the river, then the troops should entrench themselves, and, by co-operating with the navy, effect the capture and reduction of those places. These in our hands, the navy could enter the harbor, and the port of Wilmington would be sealed." *

On the 9th of December, Butler's troops were all aboard, off Fort Monroe, but a heavy gale isprang up, and it was impossible to put to sea for several days. The powder boat was still unprepared, and this also contributed to the delay. Grant, we have seen, had learned that Wilmington, as well as the works at the mouth of the river, had been nearly stripped of troops, and he was extremely anxious to take advantage of this circumstance. At ten A. 31. on the 14th, he telegraphed to Butler: " What is the prospect for getting your expedition started ? It is

* See pages 224, 235, et seq.

a pity we were not ten or twelve days earlier. I am confident it would have been successful." Half an hour later Butler replied: " Porter started yesterday. Transport fleet are at Cape Henry. I am just starting." On the 13th and 14th of December, the greatest armada ever assembled in American waters sailed.

On the 15th, Butler arrived off New Inlet, but Porter's fleet ran into Beaufort harbor, seventy miles further north, to take in ammunition, for the ironclads were unable to carry heavy supplies, and obliged to load as near as possible to the point of attack. At Beaufort there was another delay in the preparation of the powder boat, which was now altogether in the hands of the navy.

This vessel, the Louisiana, was a gunboat of two hundred and ninety-five tons burden, disguised as a blockade-runner, with a false and real smoke-pipe. The hold was filled with open barrels of gunpowder, standing on end, over which were placed layers of bags, each containing sixty pounds of powder. Altogether, two hundred and fifty tons of gunpowder were aboard. Fuses were wound through this mass in every direction, clock-work was arranged to ignite the fuses, and when all was ready the vessel was to be run ashore and the fuses fired. The result, it was hoped, would be to blow up Fort Fisher, and perhaps the town of "Wilmington itself.

On the 18th, Porter came out of Beaufort harbor, and was ready to perform his part in the operations, but the troops had now been ten days aboard the transports, and Butler, in his turn, was obliged to send his vessels into Beaufort for coal and water. At the same time another gale arose, during which

it would have been impossible to land the troops, and there was no smooth sea until the 23rd. The interval was spent by Butler in coaling and watering, but Porter remained outside.

There was doubtless at this time a lack of concert, and even of cordial co-operation, between the naval and the military chiefs. Butler was not popular with the other branch of the service, and after the expedition started from Hampton roads, neither commander visited the other. Their written communications were few, and it was the chief of staff of the admiral, or the ranking officer under Butler, through whom the views or wishes of either were made known to the other. Porter thought that his advice was not taken at times when it should have been controlling, and Butler imagined that Porter acted without duly considering or consulting him. Each was besides annoyed at delays which, though most inopportune, were unavoidable, and neither made sufficient allowance for the difficulties of that arm of the service with which he was less familiar. They seemed indeed to be playing at cross purposes. When Butler was supplied with coal, Porter wanted ammunition, and when Porter had all the powder he needed, Butler was out of coal. Even the elements conspired against them, and, when one could ride on the open sea, the other was obliged to stay inside.

On the 23rd, however, the storm had abated, and the admiral, finding the sea smooth enough to land sailors but not soldiers, determined to take advantage of the weather, and attack Fort Fisher and its outworks. The transports with the troops were still at Beaufort, and at five P. M. Porter sent word to Butler that he proposed to explode the powder boat

' 102

that night. Butler at the same time dispatched an officer to notify Porter that on the 24th he would be at the rendezvous, ready to begin the attack; but their messengers apparently crossed each other, and Porter proceeded with his preparations.

At half-past ten on the night of the 23rd, the powder vessel started in towards the bar. She was towed by the gunboat Wilderness, until the embrasures of Fort Fisher could be distinctly seen. The Wilderness then cast off, and the Louisiana proceeded, under steam, to a point within three hundred yards of the beach and about five hundred from the fort. Commander Rhind, the officer in charge, was better able to accomplish his task, as a blockade-runner had gone in before him, and the forts made signals both to the blockade-runner and the Louisiana. The night was perfectly clear, and it was therefore necessary to anchor the Louisiana. The fires were hauled as well as possible, the fuses lighted, and the hulk of the vessel set on fire. Then, taking to their boats, the gallant party made their escape to the Wilderness, lying close at hand. That vessel at once put off, to avoid the effects of the explosion.

At fifty-five minutes past one on the morning of the 24th, the explosion took place. The shock was not severe, and was scarcely felt on the Wilderness, while to the watchers in the fleet about twelve miles off the report seemed no louder than the discharge of a piece of light artillery. It was heard at Wilmington, however, and the commander at that point telegraphed to Fort Fisher to inquire the cause. The reply was: "Enemy's gunboat blown up." ISTo damage of any description was done to the rebel works or forces, and the experiment was an absolute failure.

For five miles north of Federal Point the peninsula is sandy and low, not rising more than fifteen feet above high tide; the interior abounds in freshwater swamps, often wooded and almost impassable, and much of the dry land, except in the immediate vicinity of the fort, is covered with wood or low underbrush. Fort Fisher consisted of two fronts; one, four hundred and eighty yards in length, running nearly across the peninsula; and the other, extending parallel with the beach, a distance of thirteen hundred yards. The land front was intended to resist any attack from the north, and the sea face to prevent a naval force from running through New Inlet, or landing troops on Federal Point. The land front consisted of a curtain with bastions at each extremity, mounting twenty-one guns and three mortars; the parapet was twenty-five feet thick and twenty in height, with traverses reaching back thirty or forty feet. A palisade with a banquette, and loop-holed, ran along this face, at a distance of fifty feet from the fort, from Cape Fear river to the sea, and another between the right of the front and the ocean. The sea face consisted of a series of batteries mounting in all twenty-four guns, and connected by a strong infantry parapet so as to form a continuous line. The same system of heavy, bomb-proofed traverses was employed here as on the other front*

Several miles north of the fort were two small outworks, known as the Flagpond and Half-moon batteries ; these were mere sand-hills, each mounting a single gun.

* Report of Brevet Brigadier-General Comstock, United States Engineers, aide-de-camp to General Grant, attached to the expedition.

On the 16th of December, Fort Fisher was garrisoned by four companies of infantry and one light battery, together numbering six hundred and sixty-seven men, while about eight hundred reserves were at Sugar Loaf, five miles up the peninsula.* The arrival of the double fleet, however, was at once discovered, and reinforcements were promptly forwarded from Richmond. On the 19th, General Whiting, in command at Wilmington, reported: " Information seems reliable of formidable attack here. The troops ordered away cannot return. If not helped, the forts must be turned, and the city goes. The reduced garrisons are not able to hold this ex tended position without support." Lee at once ordered Hoke's division, about six thousand strong, to North Carolina. On the 20th, Bragg, who had returned to Wilmington and resumed command of the district, telegraphed: " The head of the enemy's fleet arrived off this point during the night. Over thirty steamers are now assembling, and more are following." On the 23rd, he reported further: " The fleet, which drew off in the rough weather, is again assembled. Seventy vessels came in sight on the coast. The advance of the troops only reached here to-night." On this day the Governor of North Carolina issued a proclamation, calling on all men in the state, who could stand behind breastworks and fire a musket, to rally to the defence of Wilmington. On the 23rd, one hundred and ten artillery-men, fifty sailors, and two hundred and fifty junior reserves were thrown into the fort. The garrison then numbered one thousand and seventy-seven men.

* Whiting's letter to Butler, February 28, 1865.—" Report on Conduct of the War," 1865, Vol. II.

At daylight on the 24th, the fleet got under way, and stood in, in line of battle. Fifty vessels were under orders, thirty-three for the attack and seventeen smaller ones in reserve. The iron-clads, four in number, first took position three-quarters of a mile north-east of the fort, but only a quarter of a mile from shore. They anchored directly in line with the beach, and not more than a length apart, leaving space only for a gunboat to lie outside and fire between or over them. The nine largest ships were next formed in line of battle, south of the iron-clads, heading parallel with the land, but anchored a mile from the fort. Eight vessels of intermediate size took position outside and between the larger ones, and four small gunboats were stationed in the same way outside the monitors, to keep up a rapid fire while these were loading. The remainder of the force was posted on the left of the main line, to operate against the sea front and the works commanding the inlet, while the monitors and the larger ships were ordered to concentrate their fire upon the heaviest batteries of the enemy on the north. The whole command formed a half moon, with the horns approaching the shore.

At 11.30 A. M. Butler had not arrived, but General Ames, on the steamer Baltic, with about twelve hundred men, had reported to the admiral that he was ready ta co-operate, and Porter signalled to engage the fort. The iron-clads opened battle with deliberate but rapid fire, covering themselves as they anchored, and the bombardment soon became incessant. One hundred and fifteen shells a minute were thrown. Fort Fisher replied at once with all its guns, but those on the north-east face were

silenced almost as soon as the monitors opened their terrific fire, and by the time the last of the large vessels had anchored and got their batteries into play, only one or two of the enemy's guns were able to reply. The shower of shells had driven the gunners to the bomb-proofs.* In one hour and fifteen minutes after the first gun was fired, not a shot came from the fort. Two magazines had been blown up, and the fort set on fire in several places. Such a torrent of missiles was falling and bursting that it was impossible for anything human to stand. As soon as he found the batteries completely silenced, Porter directed his ships to keep up a moderate fire, in the hope of attracting the attention of the transports and bringing them in. At sunset Butler arrived with a portion of his command, but it was now too late for further operations, and the admiral signalled to the fleet to retire and anchor for the night.

The men had been at the guns five hours, but not a sailor in the fleet had been injured by the rebel fire. The bursting of six heavy guns, however, occasioned a loss of ten killed and thirty-four wounded. Several of the ships had been struck, and, the boiler of one being perforated, ten persons were badly scalded; but only one vessel left the line to report damages. On the rebel side one man was mortally wounded, three severely, and nineteen were slightly hurt. Five gun-carriages were disabled, but no guns dismounted, and no

* Whiting says the gunners were in no instance driven from their guns, but he is contradicted by the universal testimony of national and rebel witnesses. Naval officers, prisoners, and even the correspondent of the London (' Times " in Wilmington, all assert that the entire garrison was driven to the bomb-proofs.

very serious damage had been done to the enemy's works.*

On the morning of the 25th, Butler sent Weitzel to Porter to arrange the programme for the day. It was decided that the fleet should attack the fort again, while the troops were to land, and, if possible, assault under cover of the naval fire, as soon as the Half-moon and Flagpond batteries were silenced. At seven o'clock the fleet again took up position within a mile of the fort, not a shot being fired by the enemy, except at the last four vessels as they were moving into line. The naval fire this day was slow, and only intended to occupy the enemy while the troops were landing. At twelve o'clock the batteries above the fort were reported silenced, and a detachment of about twenty-three hundred men of Ames's command was landed at a point two and a half miles north of the fort. The debarkation was effected under cover of the fire of seventeen gunboats, which raked the woods and drove away any force that might have opposed.

Five hundred men under General Curtis were the first to land. He pushed his skirmish-line to within a few yards of Fort Fisher, causing, on the way, the surrender of the garrison of Flagpond battery, already silenced by the naval fire. Weitzel accompanied Curtis, and approached within eight hundred yards of the work. He counted seventeen guns in position bearing up the beach, observed the traverses and stockade, the glacis, ditch, and coun-

* These statements of the rebel losses are taken from Whiting's letter to Butler of February 28th, which I have found to be incorrect in several instances. Incomplete, however, as the authority is, there is no other on the subject to which I can refer.

terscarp, and decided that the work had not been materially injured by the naval fire. Weitzel, too, had been in many unsuccessful assaults, and never in a victorious one. He had a distinct and vivid recollection of this experience, and returned to Butler, and reported that it would be butchery to assault.*

In the mean time the remainder of Ames's division had captured two hundred and eighteen men and ten officers of the reserves from Sugar Loaf. From these- Butler learned the approach of Hoke's advance from the rebel army on the James. About sixteen hundred men had already arrived, and the division itself, six thousand strong, would doubtless soon be in his rear. He therefore determined at once to abandon the enterprise, and ordered the troops to be re-embarked. At this moment not a soldier had been hurt on the national side, except ten men, who were struck by the shells of the fleet.

Curtis was now within fifty yards of the fort, and sent word to Ames that he could take the work, whereupon Ames, not knowing Butler's determination, gave orders for an assault. Curtis at once moved forward, but by the time he reached his position, night had come on, and the fleet had nearly ceased its fire. Some of the rebel troops who had been driven to their bomb-proofs during the day now returned to their guns. At this juncture the orders to re-embark arrived, and no assault was made. Curtis, and the officers with him, declared that the fort could have been carried; that, at the moment when they were recalled, they virtually had possession, having actually approached so close that a rebel

* Weitzel's Report; also Weitzel's Testimony before Committee on Conduct of the War.

flag had been snatched from the parapet and a horse brought away from inside the stockade.* Three hundred rebel prisoners had been captured outside. Inside, the enemy's loss was three killed and thirty-seven wounded. Four gun-carriages had been disabled and three guns.

That night Butler informed the admiral that he and Weitzel were of the opinion that the place could not be carried by assault; having been left substantially uninjured as a defensive work by the naval fire. Seventeen guns, he said, two only of which were dismounted, were bearing up the beach, covering a strip of land, the only practicable route, not more than wide enough for a thousand men in line of battle. Hoke's reinforcements were approaching, and, as only the operations of a siege would reduce the fort, he had caused the troops to re-embark. " I shall therefore sail," he said, " for Hampton Roads as soon as the transport fleet can be got in order."

The admiral, however, was of a different mind, and replied : " I have ordered the largest vessels to proceed off Beaufort, and fill up with ammunition, to be ready for another attack, in case it is decided to proceed with this matter by making other arrangements. We have not commenced firing rapidly

* " General Weitzel advanced his skirmish-line within fifty yards of the fort, while the garrison was kept in their bomb-proofs by the fire of the navy, and so closely that three or four

men of the picket-line ventured upon the parapet and through the sally-port of the work, capturing a horse, which they brought off, killing the orderly, who was the bearer of a dispatch from the chief of artillery of General Whiting to bring a light battery within the fort, and also brought away from the parapet the flag of the fort."— Butler to Porter, December 25.

yet, and could keep any rebels inside from showing their heads, until an assaulting column was within twenty yards of the works. I wish some more of your gallant fellows had followed the officer who took the flag from the parapet, and the brave fellow who brought the horse from the fort. I think they would have found it an easier conquest than is supposed."

Butler, nevertheless, remained unshaken in his determination, and, on the night of the 25th, he embarked all his troops except Curtis's command, when the surf became high, and he sailed away, leaving these ashore. " They were under cover of the gunboats," he said, " and I have no doubt they are all safely off." * On the 27th, he arrived at Fort Monroe, and on the 28th, had an interview with Grant, after which the general-in-chief telegraphed to the President: " The Wilmington expedition has proven a gross and culpable failure. Many of the troops are back here. Delays and free talk of the object of the expedition enabled the enemy to move troops to Wilmington to defeat it. After the expedition started from Fort Monroe, three days of fine weather were squandered, during which the enemy was without a force to protect himself. Who is to blame will, I hope, be known."

This dispatch was written before Grant had heard from Porter, or from Butler's own subordinates. Subsequently, he was inclined to attribute the failure of the expedition to other causes. Neither military nor naval officers were answerable for the weather, and all the readiness imaginable would not have enabled the transports to sail from Hampton

* Butler to Grant, December 27.

roads between the 9th and the 13th of December, or from Beaufort between the 18th and the 23rd. The delay of the fleet on the 16th and 17th was also sufficiently explained. It was not considered safe to take the entire load of powder aboard the Louisiana at Norfolk; the vessel was deep, and the powder might have been wet on the passage; but, as soon as the additional fifty-five tons were put aboard, the admiral joined the transport fleet off Wilmington.

The various preparations for the powder boat had occasioned weeks of delay, but this was unavoidable, if the experiment was to be made at all; and the attempt had the sanction, not only of the naval authorities and the War Department, but of the President himself.* It was indeed a fanciful experiment, more likely to commend itself to an unprofessional mind than to a practical soldier; but, having been allowed, no one engaged in the arrangements necessary for complete success could be censured because those arrangements were complicated and elaborate, and subject to vexatious interruptions. In a military history of Grant, however, it should be remembered that he never believed in the success of the plan, and frequently said and wrote so in advance.

But, whatever the delay, and whatever its cause, these made no difference in the result. The troops and the fleet were at the rendezvous, the work was silenced and the landing effected, before any reinforcements reached the fort. On the morning of the 25th, only sixteen hundred men had arrived at Wilmington. This day General Lee telegraphed to Sed-

* Lincoln said : " We might as well explode the notion with powder as with anything else."

don: " Bragg reports tlie enemy made a landing on sea-beach, three miles north of Fort Fisher, about two P. M. to-day, and were still landing at 5.30 p. M. General KirHand\s the only troops arrived, except four hundred of Hagood's." Whiting also stated in his report: " The garrison remained steadily awaiting a renewal of the assault or bombardment, until Tuesday morning

[December Nth], when they were relieved by the supports of Major-General Hoke, and the embarkation of the enemy." Whatever number arrived before the 27th, they made no attempt to molest Curtis's little band of five hundred men, who remained ashore two days after Butler left, with no support except from the guns of the squadron. On the 25th, therefore, there were thirty-five hundred men opposed to Butler's six thousand five hundred.* The garrison, it is true, were in a work of decided strength; but Butler had the most formidable fleet that was ever assembled to cover and protect his movements.

Doubtless, if he had not at once assaulted and captured the work, the whole of Hoke's division, and perhaps a thousand militia or reserves, altogether seven thousand men, would have been assem-

* According to Whiting, on December 18th, there were 667 men in the garrison, and 800 reserves at Sugar Loaf ; and on the 23rd, 410 reinforcements were thrown into the fort, of whom 250 were reserves. This makes 1,077 inside, and 550 at Sugar Loaf. On the 25th, Bragg reported Kirkland's brigade and 400 of Hagood's men arrived. Hoke's effective strength was returned, December 20th, as 5,893. He had four brigades. My calculation is :

Garrison 1,077
Reserves at Sugar Loaf 550
Kirkland 1,473
Hagood (Lee's dispatch) 400
3,500

bled on the peninsula under Bragg. But this was the very contingency against which Grant had provided. His instructions were clear that, if a landing was effected above Fort Fisher, that in itself was to be considered a success; the object of the expedition would be gained; and, if the fort did not fall immediately upon the landing, the troops were to entrench themselves, and remain and co-operate with the fleet for the reduction of the place. When Butler's orders to Weitzel, before the expedition started, were submitted to Grant, the general-in-chief at once sent word : " The number of entrenching tools, I think, should be increased three or four times."* The position could certainly have been fortified, and, under cover of the fleet, have been easily held against double or treble any force that Bragg could have brought against it. As soon as Grant understood the circumstances, he declared that, in leaving after a landing had been effected, Butler had violated his instructions.

Butler, indeed, maintained that he had not effected a landing; that only a third of his troops were ashore when the sea became so rough that he could land no more. But his subordinates did not bear him out in this assertion; f and, as he was able to get all his force aboard except Curtis's command, he could certainly have put them ashore.

* Grant to Butler, December 6.

t "General Grant said it was his intention, after we had made a landing there, finding it was not possible to assault, that General Butler should entrench there.

"What was there to prevent compliance with such an order ?"

"There was nothing to prevent compliance with it. There would have been difficulties at that season of the year."—WeitzeVs Testimony. Report of Committee on Conduct of the War, 1865, Vol. II, Fort Fisher Expedition, page 79.

The failure to assault, however, was no disobedience of orders. Grant gave no order to any one to assault; that was a matter left to the discretion of the commanding officer. The work was doubtless formidable; the guns were not dismounted, as appeared to some of the naval officers; they were silenced, but not dismounted, and not many were even disabled; and the rebels returned to man their works when the fire from the fleet was discontinued at dark. The thousand men inside would probably have made a good defence, and there was a relieving force of eighteen hundred men at Sugar Loaf, five miles off. But, on the other hand, the naval guns could certainly have kept down the fire of the fort until the assailants reached the parapet; the relieving force made no attempt to molest Curtis's command, only five hundred strong; three hundred rebels had given themselves up outside, without a struggle; and, above all, Curtis and his men believed they could carry the fort. Curtis said at the time he could do it with a brigade. The garrison were in the bomb-proofs, and fifteen hundred men, inspired with the idea that Curtis and his troops entertained, would have been very likely to accomplish their task. In war, as in everything else, it is the men who believe in success who succeed. Far more difficult works than Fort Fisher have been carried by storm, and in the Peninsular wars of Europe well-manned forts with vertical walls fifteen to twenty feet high were repeatedly scaled. A bold and accomplished soldier would doubtless have assaulted and carried Fort Fisher on the 25th of December.

It would, nevertheless, be preposterous to suppose that General Butler was not anxious for vie-

tory, or that his movements were ever intentionally delayed. On the contrary, he was most zealous and energetic, and, in many things, efficient. He simply on this occasion displayed once more the unmilitary features of his character. Not being a professional soldier, he was disinclined to overrule a skilful engineer, the very man whom Grant had selected to command the expedition; and, not going ashore, he did not encounter Curtis, or ascertain his temper or that of his men. He was impressed, naturally enough, by Weitzel's description of the strength of the fort, and he gave too much importance to the fact of approaching reinforcements. But, above all, he had not appreciated the force of Grant's in structions in regard to remaining and entrenching on the peninsula, or else he forgot them altogether at the crisis. Weitzel had never seen them, and knew nothing of them, or he would doubtless have reminded Butler of their peremptory character.*

The lack of co-operation between Porter and Butler was, at this juncture, again apparent, and again

* "The order of General Grant to General Butler, which I saw published in the papers—I never saw the original of the order—stated that, in certain cases, he was to entrench and hold his position, and co-operate with the navy in the reduction of the fort."

"Was there anything done, or omitted to be done, which you would not have done, or omitted, if you had had full command of the expedition ?"

"Yes, sir. If I had had the instructions that General Grant gave to General Butler, I would have done one thing that General Butler did not do—I would have entrenched and remained there. I should certainly have done that, and I have written to General Butler that I was sorry he did not show me that letter of instructions so that I could have advised him about that. There is where General Butler clearly made a mistake. The order seems to be explicit that he should remain there."— WeitzeVs Testimony.

most unfortunate. The admiral was a man not only of brilliant talent, but of extraordinary nerve and force of character, and, though extravagant and inconsiderate in language, written as well as spoken, he understood his profession thoroughly; he was aggressive in his nature, and always favored an attack. He doubtless, in this instance, overrated the results accomplished by the fleet, but that very circumstance would have made his counsels more audacious ; and audacity is sometimes a very desirable quality in a commander. If, instead of writing or sending to Porter, and announcing his withdrawal, Butler, who was the senior in rank, had waived his prerogative, and sought and obtained a personal interview, it is possible that he might have been convinced by the arguments, or incited by the spirit of the sailor into remaining ashore. As it was, he sailed off, leaving Porter to pick up the troops he left behind, and, in his dread of encountering disaster, he incurred, what to a soldier is infinitely worse —the imputation of unnecessary failure.

Grant, of course, was greatly disappointed at the miserable result of an expedition from which so much had been expected, but his chagrin was increased when Curtis and several of his officers reported that the troops had nearly reached the parapet before they were recalled, and that Fort Fisher could have been carried without severe loss. Butler, however, had said nothing about the intention of Porter to prepare for another assault, and Grant at first supposed that, when the military force was withdrawn, the admiral also had abandoned the enterprise. But, on the 29th of December, the Secretary of the Navy received a letter from Porter,

announcing that the fleet had remained off Fort Fisher, and that, under a proper leader, he believed the place could be carried.

The admiral could not be accused of concealing his sentiments. "'My dispatch of yesterday," he said to the government, " will give you an account of the operations, but will scarcely give you an idea of my disappointment at the conduct of the army authorities in not attempting to take possession of the fort. . . . Had the army made a show of surrounding it, it would have been ours; but nothing of the kind was done. The men landed, reconnoitred, and, hearing that the enemy were massing troops somewhere, the orders were given to re-embark. . . . There never was a fort that invited soldiers to walk in and take possession more plainly than Fort Fisher. ... It can be taken at any moment in one hour's time, if the right man is sent with the troops. They should be sent to stay. . . . I trust, sir, you will not think of stopping at this, nor of relaxing your endeavors to obtain the right number and the means of taking the place."

A copy of this letter was forwarded to Grant, together with the substance of various other dispatches and reports, all to the same effect, and on the 30th of December, the Secretary of the Navy telegraphed: " The ships can approach nearer to the enemy's works than was anticipated. Their fire can keep the enemy away from their guns. A landing can easily be effected upon the beach north of Fort Fisher, not only of troops, but all their supplies and artillery. This force can have its supplies protected by gunboats. . . . Admiral Porter will remain off Fort Fisher, continuing a moderate fire to prevent

new works being erected. . . . Under all these circumstances I invite you to such a military co-operation as will ensure the fall of Fort Fisher. . . . This telegram is made at the suggestion of the President."

The general-in-chief did not need to be urged. The same day he sent a message to Porter: " Please hold on wherever you are for a few days, and I will endeavor to be back again, with an increased force, and without the former commander. . . . Your dispatch to the Secretary of the Navy was only received to-day. I took immediate steps to have transports collected, and am assured they will be ready with coal and water by noon of the 2nd of January. There will be no delay in embarking and sending off the troops. ... If they effect a lodgment, they can at least fortify and maintain themselves until reinforcements can be sent. Please answer by bearer, and designate where you will have the fleet congregated."

Every precaution was now taken to secure secrecy. " It is desirable," said Grant, " the enemy should be lulled into all the security possible, in hopes he will send back here, or against Sherman, the reinforcements sent to defend Wilmington." Only two persons in Washington and two officers of Grant's staff were informed of the destination of the expedition. The chief commissary of subsistence was sent to Fort Monroe to victual the transports, but was allowed to suppose that they were intended for Sherman's army; and Grant telegraphed to the Secretary of War: " I will instruct him to say confidentially that he thinks we are either sending for Sherman, or that we are going to reinforce him, in-

clining to the latter opinion." * To Porter he wrote : " The commander of the expedition will probably be Major-General Terry. He will not know of it till he gets out to sea. He will go with sealed orders. It will not be necessary for me to let troops or commanders know even that they are going anywhere, until the steamers intended to carry them reach Fortress Monroe."

On the 31st of December, the Secretary of • the Navy also announced to the admiral: " Lieutenant-General Grant will send immediately a competent force, properly commanded, to co-operate in the capture of the defences on Federal Point. . . . The Department is perfectly satisfied with your efforts thus far."

On the 1st of January, Porter replied to Grant from Beaufort harbor: " I have just received yours of December 30th. I shall be all ready; and thank God we are not to leave here with so easy a victory at hand. , Thank you for so promptly trying to rectify the blunder so lately committed. I knew you would do it. I would like the troops to rendezvous here. They should have provisions to last them on shore, in case we are driven off by gales; but I can cover any number of troops, if it blows ever so hard. . . . We lost one man killed. You may judge what

* I have no doubt that in this Machiavellian attempt to mislead his own subordinate Grant signally failed. He was so utterly unversed in the arts of dissimulation that his efforts in this direction were the subject of great amusement to those who surrounded him. He could repel an effort to extort his views, or to elicit information which he chose to withhold, with a silence which was like a wall between himself and his interrogator; but when he positively attempted to deceive—which he never did except to affect the public enemy— his conscience troubled him so that he generally made an ignominious failure.

a simple business it was. I will work night and day to be ready. . . . Please impress the commander with the importance of consulting with me freely as regards weather and landing."

Butler received no intimation of the renewal of the expedition. Grant simply telegraphed him on the 2nd of January: "Please send Major-General Terry to City Point to see me this morning." " I cannot go myself," he said to the Secretary of War, "so long as Butler would be left in command." Grant was always slow to anger, and it was not till the accumulated testimony of naval and military officers convinced him that the failure was owing solely to Butler's military incapacity that he took decided measures. He often seemed to be worked gradually up to an important point, but, when once this was reached, he never receded.

On the 4th of January, he asked for the removal of Butler; " I am constrained to request the removal of Major-General Butler from the command of the Department of Virginia and North Carolina. I do this with reluctance, but the good of the service requires it. In my absence General Butler necessarily commands, and there is a lack of confidence felt in his military ability, making him an unsafe commander for a large army. His administration of the affairs of his department is also objectionable." Stanton had just left the capital on a visit to Sherman, at Savannah, and this letter at first received no answer; but Grant was now very much in earnest, and on the 6th, he telegraphed direct to the President : " I wrote a letter to the Secretary of War, which was mailed yesterday, asking to have General Butler removed from command. Learning that the

Secretary left Washington yesterday, I telegraph you, asking that prompt action be taken in this matter." The order was made the next day, and on the 7th of January, Butler was relieved. He never received another command. Major-General E. O. C. Ord succeeded him.

Brevet Major-General A. H. Terry was a volunteer officer who had served in the Department of the South from the first year of the war until April, 1864, when he was transferred to Butler's command. He had been engaged in siege operations, bombardments, and assaults, before Forts Pulaski, Sumter, and Wagner, as well as in most of the important actions of the army of the James, gradually rising to the command of the Tenth corps. Grant desired to send against Fort Fisher the same force which he had originally intended for its capture, but under a different commander; and Terry, who was gallant, intelligent, and soldierly, seemed the most appropriate selection.

On the 2nd of January, he received from Grant in person orders to take command of the troops intended for the movement. A small brigade numbering fifteen hundred men had been added to the original force, and the command now consisted- of eight thousand men. Terry, however, was still unaware of his real destination, and supposed that he was to reinforce Sherman. On the 3rd, Grant announced to Stanton: " Here, there is not the slightest suspicion where the troops are going. The orders to officers commanding enjoin secrecy, and designate Savannah and to report to Sherman as their destination." On the 5th, Terry proceeded to Fort Monroe, and Grant accompanied him to issue his final in-

structions. On the way the general-in-chief made known to Terry the point against which he was to operate, and that evening the transports were ordered to put to sea with sealed orders, to be opened off Cape Henry.

Terry's instructions were in these words : " The expedition entrusted to your command has been fitted out to renew the attempt to capture Fort Fisher, North Carolina, and Wilmington ultimately, if the fort falls. ... It is exceedingly desirable that the most complete understanding should exist between yourself and the naval commander. I suggest, therefore, that you consult with Admiral Porter, and get from him the part to be performed by each branch of the public service, so that there may be unity of action. It would be well to have the whole programme laid down in writing. I have served with Admiral Porter, and know that you can rely on his judgment and his nerve to undertake what he proposes. I should, therefore, defer to him as much as is consistent with your own responsibilities.

" The first object to be attained is to get a firm position on the spit of land on which Fort Fisher is built, from which you can operate against that fort. You want to look to the practicability of receiving your supplies, and to defending yourself against superior forces sent against you by any of the avenues left open to the enemy. If such a position can be obtained, the siege of Fort Fisher will not be abandoned until its reduction can be accomplished, or another plan of campaign is ordered from these headquarters. ... In case of failure to effect a landing, bring your command back to Beaufort, and

report to these headquarters for further instructions."

At four o'clock on the morning of the 6th of January, the transports sailed. During the day a severe storm arose, which greatly impeded their movements, but on the 8th, they arrived at the rendezvous, many of them damaged by the gale. This day Terry communicated with Porter, but the weather continued unfavorable, and it was not until the 12th, that the combined force arrived off Federal Point; even then, in accordance with the decision of the admiral, the disembarkation was deferred until the following morning.

At daylight, on the 13th of January, Porter formed his fleet in three lines, and stood in, close to the beach, to cover the landing. One division an chored within six hundred yards of the shore, and the transports followed, taking position as near as possible in a parallel line, two hundred yards outside. The iron-clads moved down within range of the fort, and opened fire; another division was placed so as to protect the troops from any attack from the north by land, and the reserves took charge of the provision vessels. Boats were sent at once to take off the troops, and by three o'clock nearly eight thousand men were safely landed, with nine days' rations and entrenching tools. The point selected was about five miles from the fort, below the neck of Myrtle sound, a long and shallow piece of water, separated from the ocean by a sandspit not more than a hundred yards across.

Since the bombardment on Christmas day, Hoke had remained with his division in the neighborhood of Wilmington, and on the 13th, during the landing,

lie approached the shore, and drew up his troops parallel with Terry's command, to watch, and, if possible, intercept the operation; but the cover afforded by the naval fire prevented the rebels from offering any opposition; and, after the landing was once effected, Myrtle sound intervened between the national force and the enemy, so that any rebel attack or movement around its inner extremity would have to be made under the fire of the whole fleet. Hoke therefore simply established a line facing the sea, and threw out cavalry to his right to observe the national movements.*

Porter this day pursued a somewhat different plan from that he had adopted at the first bombardment. At half-past seven on the 13th, he sent the iron-clads in alone, thus tempting the enemy to engage them that he might ascertain what guns the rebels had, and be able to dismount them; for so much had been said about the guns not being dismounted, although silenced, in the first bombardment, that he determined now to dismount as many as possible. The fort opened on the monitors as they approached, but they quickly took up their old position and returned the rebel fire. The engagement soon became spirited. Traverses began to crumble, and the northeast angle of Fort Fisher looked very dilapidated.

After the troops were all debarked, Porter signalled to the larger vessels also to attack the batteries, one division remaining to cover the landing party. The vessels took their positions handsomely,

* Pollard's "Lost Cause," and " Southern History of the War ; " also, correspondence of the London "Times."—Charleston and Wilmington, 1864-'5.

delivering fire as they fell in, and one after another the enemy's pieces were silenced, until only one heavy gun in the southern angle replied. No damage was inflicted on the fleet. The firing continued until after dark, when the wooden ships dropped out to their anchorage, but the iron-clads maintained their position during the night, now and then firing a shell. The enemy had long ceased to respond, and kept within his bomb-proofs. That night Porter sent a dispatch to the government, reporting the day's proceedings. " The firing of the fleet," he said, " will commence as soon as we get breakfast, and be kept up as long as the ordnance department provides us with shells and guns."

As soon as the first troops were landed, Terry threw out his pickets, and the presence of Hoke's division was ascertained. The first object, of course, was to establish a national line across the peninsula; but the ground was marshy and ill adapted for earthworks, cut up with ponds and salt-water bogs, and the afternoon was consumed in reconnoitring. Terry's men, however, evaded the rebel cavalry, and, threading their way through the swampy undergrowth, by nine o'clock they had reached the river, and at two A. M. a line was selected only two miles from the fort. Tools were brought rapidly up, and entrenching began. All night the work went on, and by eight o'clock on the morning of the 14th, a good breastwork extended from the river to the sea, partially covered with abatis, and already in a defensible condition. The foothold on the peninsula was secure. Early on this day the landing of the artillery was begun, and by sunset all the light guns were ashore. Most of them were placed on the river-side, where, in case of a rebel attack, they would be less exposed to the naval fire.

On the 14th, Hoke shifted his line so as to confront Terry, and Bragg gave him orders to attack the national works; but Hoke made a reconnoissance, and decided that the line was too strong to be carried. In this opinion Bragg concurred.*

This day Porter again attempted to dismount the guns on the face of the work where an assault was to be made. The attack began at one o'clock, and lasted till after dark.

During the morning of the 14th, Curtis's brigade was taken out of line and moved up in reconnoissance towards the fort. By noon his skirmishers had reached a small unfinished outwork in front of the west extremity. This was at once seized and turned into a defensive line, to be held against any attempt from the fort. The reconnoissance showed that the palisading in front of the main work had been seriously injured by the naval fire, and only nine guns could be seen on the land face, where seventeen had been counted on Christmas day. The steady fire of the navy had prevented the enemy from using either musketry or artillery against the reconnoitring party, and it seemed probable that the troops could be brought within two hundred yards of the fort without serious loss. In case of a storm, there might be difficulty in landing supplies or material for a siege on the open and tempestuous beach; and Terry decided not to delay for regular approaches, but to attempt an assault on the following day.

This decision was at once communicated to Porter, and that evening Terry went aboard the ad-

* Pollard's "Lost Cause."

miral's flag-ship to arrange the plan of battle. There was a perfect understanding between the two commanders, and a system of signals was established by which they could communicate, though a mile apart, and in the midst of battle. It was agreed that a heavy bombardment from all the naval vessels should begin at an early hour, and continue up to the moment of assault, and that even then it should not cease, but be diverted from the points of attack to other parts of the work. The assault was to be made at three P. M. ; the army to attack on the western half of the land face nearest the river, and a column of marines and sailors, armed with cutlasses and revolvers, to move against the north-east bastion. The fire of the navy was continued during the night, to exhaust the garrison and prevent them from repairing damages. One vessel was employed at a time, each firing one hour, when it was relieved.

At daylight on the 15th, the monitors and the eleven-inch gunboats again commenced battering the work, and at ten o'clock all the vessels, except a division left to aid in the defence of Terry's northern line, moved into position, each opening a powerful and accurate fire as they got their anchors down. For six hours the mighty fleet, in three divisions, with an armament of nearly six hundred guns, poured torrents of shell and metal missiles on every spot of earth about the fort. The guns in the upper batteries replied as on the day before, and Mound Hill battery, at the southern extremity, kept up an especially galling fire, but no vessel was injured enough to interfere with her efficiency, and the rebels were finally driven from their pieces and into the-bomb-proofs along the entire extent of the parapet. Every

gun was silenced, and the storm fell upon a deserted battlement. While Fort Fisher was thus enveloped in a concentric fire, and the tossing clouds of smoke rolled up incessantly from the sea, Terry was organizing his forces for the assault.

Brigadier - General Payne, with four thousand seven hundred men, had been placed in command on the northern defensive line, three-quarters of a mile in length, and Ames's division was selected for the charge. It was three thousand three hundred strong, and in three brigades, under Curtis, Penny-packer, and Bell. At this time there were in Fort Fisher about twenty-four hundred men. Curtis was already at the outwork which had been gained the day before, and in the trenches close around; and at noon Pennypacker and Bell were moved up within supporting distance. The battle line of the division was now within eight hundred yards of the fort, and crossed the peninsula parallel with Payne's defences, a mile and a half away. The two lines faced, of course, in different directions, and, in the space between, all the manoeuvres of the troops, whether for attack or defence, were made.

At two o'clock the immediate preliminaries of the assault began. A hundred sharpshooters, all volunteers, were thrown forward at a run, to a point not two hundred yards from the fort. They were provided; with shovels, and soon dug pits for shelter in the sand, and began firing at the parapet. This movement could be plainly seen by the garrison, and the parapet was manned at once, the enemy opening fire with musketry and artillery, regardless of the storm of shot and shell which belched from every gun of the navy on the fort. As soon as the sharp-

shooters were in position, Curtis was moved forward by the regiment, in double quick time, and formed line about five hundred yards from the fort, where his men lay down, scooping out shallow trenches with their hands and tin cups, to cover themselves from the fierce and increasing fire of musketry and artillery now pouring from the parapet. When Curtis moved from the outwork, Pennypacker was brought up to it, and Bell was moved into line, two hundred yards in Pennypacker's rear. It was now discovered that good cover could be found for Curtis on the reverse slope of a mound only fifty yards in the rear of the sharpshooters, and his men were again moved forward, one regiment at a time, and again covered themselves in trenches in the sand. Pennypacker followed Curtis, and occupied the ground vacated by him, and Bell was brought up to the outwork.

It had been proposed to blow up and cut down the palisades; bags of powder with fuses attached had been prepared, and a party of volunteer axemen organized; but the fire of the navy had been so effective during the preceding night and morning that it was thought unnecessary to use the powder. The axemen, however, were sent in with the leading brigade, and did good service by making openings in portions of the palisading which the guns of the navy had not been able to reach.

At 3.25 p. M. all the preparations were completed ; the order to move forward was given by Ames; and the concerted signal was made to Porter to change the direction of his fire.

The vessels at once turned their guns • upon the upper batteries ; all the steam whistles were blown,

and troops and sailors darted ahead, vieing with each other in the attempt to reach the parapet; the sailors advancing along the beach, and the troops further to the right, against the palisades. The large guns of the fort were so injured that they could not be used against the national columns, but the garrison, stiff and benumbed with their long imprisonment of fifty hours, came out of the bomb-proofs to resist the charge.

The sailors and marines, two thousand in number, were under the command of Lieutenant-Commander Breese, and had already worked their way, by digging ditches, to a point within two hundred yards of the fort. The plan was for the marines to remain in the ditches, and act as sharpshooters to keep the garrison from the parapet, while the sailors made the assault. But the marines did not go close enough for their work; and, on rushing through the palisades which extended from the bastion to the sea, the head of the column received a murderous fire. The parapet now swarmed with troops who exposed themselves with reckless gallantry. At this juncture, had the marines performed their duty, every rebel on the sea face would have been either killed or wounded. But the marines scarcely fired at all, or with no precision. Nevertheless, the officers and sailors in the lead pressed on, and some even reached the parapet, while many gained the ditch or counterscarp.

But the advance was swept from the walls like chaff, and, in spite of all the efforts made by commanders of companies, the men in the rear, seeing the slaughter in front, and that they were not covered by the marines, began to retreat. In a moment

more the whole force turned and ran. The attack on the sea face was repelled. Two hundred and eighty sailors and marines were killed or wounded.

Meanwhile, at the order to advance, Curtis's brigade at once sprang from the trenches and dashed forward in line. Its left was exposed to a severe enfilading fire, and it obliqued to the right so as to envelop the left of the land front. The ground over which it moved was marshy and difficult; sometimes the men sank waist-deep in the ponds, and not a few of the wounded perished in the mire; but the brigade soon reached the palisades, dashed through them, and rushed to the sally-port. This was a bomb-proof postern, covered by a redan mounting two twelve-pound howitzers; and a line of the enemy extended behind the earthworks from the battery to the river. Two reliefs of rebel gunners with their supports were shot down at this point before the enemy gave way; but finally they could stand no longer, and over dead bodies in blue and grey the charging column entered the fort. The rebel line was broken, and the national soldiers mounted the parapet.

When Curtis moved forward in the assault, Ames directed Pennypacker to advance as far as the rear of the sharpshooters, and brought up Bell to Penny-packer's last position; and, as soon as Curtis got a foothold on the parapet, Pennypacker was sent in to his support. He advanced, overlapping Curtis's right, and drove the enemy from the heavy palisading which extended from the west end of the land front to the river, capturing a number of prisoners. Then, pressing forward to their left, the two brigades together drove the enemy from about one quarter of the land face.

Ames now brought up Bell's brigade, and moved it between the work and the river. On this side there was no regular parapet, but the rebels found abundance of cover in the cavities from which sand had been taken for the construction of the fort, the ruins of barracks and storehouses, and the large magazines, behind which they stubbornly resisted the national advance.

It was not until the work was absolutely entered that its formidable character became fully apparent. The heaviest fortifications extended from the gateway which Curtis had forced to the ocean beach, and thence along the sea front a mile away. Twenty-one guns and three mortars had been mounted on the land face, twenty feet above the ditch. The stockade outside was twenty feet high, and the guns were placed to play over it. Between each pair of guns and its neighbor, or sometimes between two guns, a traverse crossed the embankment, rising twenty feet higher. The distance from the glacis to the top of the traverse was thus forty feet. These traverses were made of sand, twelve feet thick at the top, entirely filling the spaces between the guns, and extending nearly across the parapet. There were seventeen of them between the sallyport and the bastion at the north-east corner. Each traverse covered a bomb-proof, and was a fort in itself. From the north-east bastion an enfilading fire could be obtained in either direction, and the guns along the parapet could be trained to work against the interior of the fort as well as outwards.

And now began such a system of fighting as has seldom been equalled in modern battle. The rebels had fallen back, but it was only to rally. Fort Fisher was not captured because the parapet was reached. Whiting and Lamb brought up their men, encouraging and cheering them to heroic efforts. The huge traverses were used for breastworks, and over their tops the contending parties fired into each other's faces, while Porter with his iron-clads opened from the sea on those still occupied by the enemy. The bomb-proofs now swarmed with rebel soldiers, and between them the infantry was stationed to protect the gunners and obstruct the national assault; but Ames's men charged up the embankment and met the enemy in hand-to-hand encounters at almost every step. They fired into the bomb-proofs, and the rebels came out, like rats from a sinking ship. They charged over the traverses and around the inner ends, and either drove the rebels from their positions or killed or captured them, and carried three, four, five, six of the traverses in an hour.

Meanwhile, at about four o'clock, Hoke, doubtless perceiving the movement against the fort, advanced upon Terry's northern line, apparently with the design of attacking it, and thus relieving the garrison. But, if this was his intention, it was speedily abandoned, and, after slight skirmishing with the national pickets, the rebel command withdrew. Terry now requested Porter to reinforce the troops on the outer line with Breese's sailors and marines. The admiral promptly complied, and Terry was able to bring Abbott's brigade and a regiment of colored troops to the southern front. These troops arrived at dusk, and reported to Ames.

The whole command was now fighting like lions,

104

chasing the rebels from traverse to traverse, while the iroii-clads fired on the bomb-proofs in advance and enfiladed the level strip of land leading to Federal Point, to prevent reinforcements being put ashore from the river. Porter kept up constant communication with Terry, and until six o'clock the fire of the navy continued upon that portion of the work not occupied by national forces; after that time, it w T as directed entirely on the beach to prevent the coming up of rebel reinforcements.

The fighting was continued from traverse to traverse, until, at nine o'clock, the troops had nearly reached the bastion. Bell had been killed and Pen-nypacker wounded, and Curtis now sent back for reinforcements. The advance party was in imminent peril, for the guns from both the bastion and the mound batteries were turned upon them. At this crisis a staff officer brought orders from Terry to stop the fighting and begin entrenching. Curtis was inflamed with the magnificent rage of battle, and fairly roared at this command. " Then we shall lose whatever we have gained. The enemy will drive us from here in the morning." While he spoke, he was struck by a shell, and fell senseless to the earth. The hero of Fort Fisher had fallen, and the fort was not yet carried. Ames, who was near him, sent an officer to Terry to report that Curtis was killed, and that his dying request was that the fighting might go on. It was also Ames's opinion that the battle should proceed. Terry caught the contagion, and determined to continue the assault, even if it became necessary to abandon the line of defence towards Wilmington. Abbott's reinforcements were at once ordered forward, and

as they entered tlie fort the rebels on the bastion gave way, and Fort Fisher was carried. Curtis was not dead, and heard the shouts of victory.

It was ten o'clock at night, and the battle had lasted seven hours. Cheer upon cheer went up from the national soldiers, and the shouts were taken up by the fleet before Terry could signal to Porter the news. In a moment the sky was ablaze with rockets, and the bands struck up the national airs.

But there was something besides rejoicing yet to be done. Abbott's brigade, with a regiment of colored soldiers, was immediately pushed down the point to Battery Buchanan, whither many of the garrison had fled, and here all who had not previously been captured were made prisoners, including Major-General Whiting and Colonel Lamb, the commandant of the fort, both severely wounded.*

During the nights of the 16th and 17th of January, the enemy blew up Fort Caswell, and abandoned, not only that fortification, but the extensive works on Smith's Island, thus placing in the national hands all the works erected to defend the mouth of Cape Fear river. One hundred and sixty-nine guns were captured, nearly all heavy artillery, two thousand stand of small arms, and full supplies of ammunition. One hundred and twelve commissioned officers and nineteen hundred and seventy-one enlisted men were taken prisoner. About seven hundred rebels were either killed or wounded. Terry's loss

* Valuable material for the account of this assault has been obtained from a paper entitled "Capture of Fort Fisher," by First Lieutenant George Simpson, 142d New York Volunteers, and acting aide-de-camp to General Curtis.

was one hundred and ten killed and five hundred and thirty-six wounded.

The battle of Fort Fisher occurred on Sunday, and early on Monday morning Secretary

Stanton, returning from a visit to General Sherman at Savannah, sailed into New Inlet, ignorant of the victory. There was nothing to indicate the result at the fort, and the fleet stood off from shore with the flags at half-mast. But at sunrise the stars and stripes were run up at the outworks, and the great War Minister was made aware of the national triumph. He steamed quickly alongside of the flag-ship, and, soon obtaining the names of those who had distinguished themselves in the fight, promoted and brevetted them on the spot.

A few days after the fall of the fort, two British blockade-runners, ignorant of its fate, ran into the inlet, signalling as usual to the fort. The signals were answered in conformity with the rebel alphabet, a negro wfio had been captured having imparted the secret to a national officer. The blockade-runners anchored off the fort, and their commanders came ashore to deliver their papers, but, instead of handing them to Lamb, were obliged to give them up to Terry. Two valuable cargoes and two of the fastest-sailing vessels in these waters thus fell into the national hands. Several British officers, attracted by motives of curiosity or sympathy with the rebellion, were aboard, and, while they were enjoying themselves in the cabin, the stars and stripes were run up at the mast-head.

The conduct of the national troops in this battle was never excelled in war. The three brigade commanders were all wounded: Curtis, as we have seen,

ULYSSES S. GRANT.

345

rifle in Land, in the front rank of his men; Penny-packer, carrying the standard of a regiment and mounting a traverse in a charge; while Bell was mortally hurt near the palisades. The coolness, judgment, and skill of Ames were pronounced by Terry to be conspicuous, and the reports of all commanders were crowded with the names of officers and men who had distinguished themselves by deeds of peculiar heroism.

The gallantry of the defence was in no way less than that of the assault. The weary garrison, stunned and deafened and depressed by the terrific bombardment, cramped and exhausted by their long confinement in the bomb-proofs, aware that succor was impossible, and almost certain in advance that conquest must be their fate, yet fought on that historic rampart with a stubborn valor that held the assailants off from victory for nine long hours of day and darkness ; rivalling the achievements of all other garrisons in ancient or modern war, and making their enemies proud that they were their countrymen.

The co-operation of the navy had been more than admirable. In all ranks, from the commander to the lowest seaman, there was manifest the desire, not only to do their proper work, but to facilitate by every possible means the operations of the land forces. To Porter and the untiring efforts of his subordinates it was due that men and stores and ammunition were safely and expeditiously landed; to the great accuracy and power of their fire it must be ascribed that Terry had not to confront a formidable artillery in the assault, and that he was able, with but little loss, to push forward the troops to a point nearly as favorable as they would have occu-

pied had the place been systematically approached by siege operations. Even the assault of the sailors and marines, although it failed, contributed to the final success, distracting the attention of the enemy at the moment of the main attack.

It is impossible not to look upon the first expedition against Fort Fisher by the light afforded by the events of the second. The difficulties which Terry surmounted almost excuse the failure of his predecessor. If these extraordinary efforts were necessary to secure the prize, it is not so surprising that a commander was found to turn aside. The fortifications were acknowledged by Porter to rival those of the Malakoff, which he had seen, and the stubbornness of the defence was entirely unexpected, if not unprecedented. The naval fire at the second bombardment was far more accurate than it had been in December, and three-fourths of the heavy guns were actually dismounted before the assault began.

On the other hand, the garrison was twice as large in January as on Christmas day; the rebels had been warned, and doubtless taken every precaution in the interval to strengthen their works. Hoke had arrived, and was on the ground with his whole command before Terry landed. Indeed, the supineness of Bragg and Hoke was as discreditable as the gallantry of the garrison was pre-eminent.

On the second occasion eveiything was done to secure success that foresight could suggest or skill or courage execute. The difficulties of the weather and the season on one of the stormiest coasts in the world were overcome; the disadvantages incident

to all combined operations entirely disappeared; and the dispositions of the admiral and the military chief at the time of the landing, and during the subsequent operations, up to and including the assault, were a marvel of harmonious effort.

The sailor, of course, stood at the head of his profession, and might have been expected to manoeuvre his fleet iu storm and battle so as to ensure victory ; but Terry had hitherto been untried in independent command. He had the fate of his predecessor before his eyes, calculated, perhaps, as much to unnerve as inspire a neophyte ; but his skill in debarking his force in the face of Hoke, his prompt and dexterous selection and fortification of the defensive line under the enemy's eyes, his courage in ordering the assault, and the masterly handling of his men in the actual and complicated attack, were evidence of a rare talent for war, and amply justified the judgment of Grant in selecting him for the command.

Of the general officers engaged in this expedition, Butler, as we have seen, had already been relieved ; Terry was confirmed as major - general of volunteers, and, on Grant's nomination, appointed brigadier-general in the regular army: Ames was promoted to be major-general of volunteers; and Curtis, who had been only brigadier-general by brevet, was made full brigadier-general and brevet major-general of volunteers. Porter, on the death of Admiral Farragut, was promoted to the full command of the navy.

The importance of the victoiy was instantly recognized, by rebels and loyal people alike; its effect was felt at home and abroad. Lee knew its signifi-

cance as thoroughly as Grant, and the rejoicing at the North was not more general or more heartfelt than the despondency it occasioned inside the Confederacy. The gate through which the rebels had obtained their largest and most indispensable supplies was for ever sealed. In little more than a year before the capture of the fort, the ventures of British capitalists and speculators with Wilmington had amounted to sixty-six millions of dollars, and sixty-five millions of dollars in cotton had been exported in return. In the same period three hundred and ninety-seven vessels had run the blockade. All this was at an end. Europe perceived, the inevitable consequences; and the British government, which till now had held out hopes to the rebel emissaries,* after the fall of Fort Fisher sent a communication to Jefferson Davis, through Washington, rebuking the rebels for their stubbornness, f There could be no surer evidence that the cause was desperate.

But the capture of Fort Fisher not only closed the last important inlet of supplies to the enemy from abroad, at a juncture when Grant was cutting off those supplies in every direction at home, and thus formed an important adjunct to his general plan of exhausting as well as destroying the Confederacy ; it had also a strategical consequence, not apparent at the time to outsiders, but which with him was paramount to all other considerations. The circle was now gradually closing around the prey. Sherman had reached Savannah, Thomas was mas-

* See Appendix.

t See Appendix for letter of Earl Russell to Messrs. Mason, Slidell, and Mann.

ter of Tennessee, and Sheridan of the Valley of Virginia, while Grant still held the principal rebel force at Richmond. At this crisis the possession of Cape Fear river opened another base for operations into the interior. It enabled the general-in-chief to look forward to supporting Sherman's future movements, and presented an opportunity to complete the isolation of Lee.

CHAPTER XXXI.

Approach of the end—Consternation of rebels—Desertions from Lee's army —Discord in Richmond—Arming of slaves—Attempts at compromise— Preparations to evacuate Richmond—Renewed efforts of Grant—Sherman to march northward—Relations of Sherman and Grant—Comprehensive strategy of Grant—Schofield transferred to North Carolina— Dissatisfaction with Thomas—Canby ordered to move into Alabama—Schofield to cooperate with Sherman—Stoneman ordered into East Tennessee—Position of Sherman in January— Moves to Pocotaligo—Grover brought from the Shenandoah to Savannah—Strength of Sherman's army— Strength of his enemy—Difficulties and dangers of Sherman's new campaign—Sherman starts—Dispositions of Grant in his support—General control of Grant— Cavalry movement ordered from West Tennessee to support Canby—First news from Sherman— Schofield arrives in North Carolina—Capture of Wilmington—Sheridan ordered to move west of Richmond—Anxiety of President and Secretary of War — Advance of Sherman—Characteristics of Grant—Operations west of Mississippi— Instructions to Canby — Strategical principles of Grant — Delays of Thomas—Situation in Richmond—Distraction and desperation of rebels — Preparations to abandon Richmond — Preposterous suggestions of Breckenridge and Beauregard—Beauregard relieved by Johnston—Desertions from rebel army—Lee's attempt to negotiate with Grant—Correspondence between Lee and Grant, and between Grant and the Government—Subordination of Grant—Lee's overtures repelled—Lee's statement of rebel condition—News from Sheridan—Grant's prescience of Lee's movements—Gradual envelopment of both Lee and Johnston's commands—Dissatisfaction with Canby—First dispatches from Sherman— Further delay of Thomas—Sheridan arrives at White House— Sheridan's Raid—Last defeat of Early—Skilful strategy of Sheridan—Enormous loss inflicted on enemy—Approaching consummation of Grant's plans— Preparations for final blow—Sheridan to co-operate with army of Potomac—Junction of Sherman and Schofield—Sherman's northward march —Difficulties at outset—Advances directly north—Enters Columbia— Conflagration caused by Hampton's orders—Sherman's troops extinguish flames — Fall of Charleston — Sherman pursues Beauregard as far as Winnsboro—Turns eastward—Arrives at Cheraw—Great captures of ordnance—Arrives at Fayetteville—Receives supplies from Wilmington—

ULYSSES S. GRANT.
351

Communicates with Grant—Hardee crosses Sherman's front to join Beau-regard — Sherman starts for Goldsboro—Johnston supersedes Beauregard —Battle of Averysboro— Retreat of rebels—Battle of Bentonsville—Attack by Johnston—Repulse of Slocum—Arrival of Howard—Position of Johnston—Attack by Mower—Opportunity of Sherman—He prefers to wait arrival of Schofield—Retreat of Johnston—Sherman arrives at Goldsboro —Character and results of march through Carolinas—Operations of Schofield prior to joining Sherman— Success of Grant's combinations—Orders to all his generals—Meeting of Lincoln and Sherman at Grant's headquarters—Self-reliance of Grant.

AT last the signs of the approaching end were visible. The mighty edifice which had withstood so many shocks was tottering. When Sherman had reached the sea, and Thomas had annihilated Hood; when the supplies from foreign sympathizers and traders were for ever stopped, and no large organized rebel force remained outside of Virginia, it was impossible to be blind to the inevitable catastrophe. The dismay that had been struck to the heart of the South all along the route through Georgia was renewed and repeated at Nashville, and before men became used to the portentous news from the West, they were startled by the sound of Porter's bombardment on the sea. The rebellion reeled and staggered, like a wounded gladiator, under these repeated blows, and a feeling came over its adherents like that which oppressed the heroes of Homer when they contended against the gods. For it was not one defeat nor one disappointment that overwhelmed them; not the invasion of Georgia, nor the devastation in the Shenandoah, nor the capture of Fort Fisher, nor the repulse on the Cumberland, nor the losses at Richmond, but the aggregation and combination and succession of all of these; the hopelessness of rescue, the certainty that the grasp would not relax, nor the will relent, nor the energy

weaken which had already proven so indefatigable and irresistible; that the mind which had conceived the scheme that wrought them so much ruin, and directed and controlled its intricate and various parts, all tending to a designed and certain consummation, would preside over any future enterprises, and in any further emergencies would direct and control and conceive and execute until the end.

The rebel records that have been preserved all tell the same sad story. Hardee and Early and Bragg and Hood were unanimous. The injuries done to crops and roads and arsenals and machinery by Sherman were reported simultaneously with the breaking up of the rebel army of Tennessee. All through December, dispatches between Beauregard and his government crossed each other, announcing the same disasters; and, while the Richmond authorities were anticipating new demonstrations from Savannah in January, they received the tidings of still another advance, from still another quarter, into North Carolina.

The rank and file, as well as their superiors, understood the significance of this conjunction of calamities, and the panics among the troops of Early and Hood were the indication not of pusillanimity but of despair. Desertions during the winter became numerous among all the rebel forces, from the Mississippi to the Atlantic. A hundred men a day were often received across the lines at Petersburg, and thousands of prisoners were willing to take the oath of allegiance to the government. Lee repeatedly addressed his superiors on the subject, suggesting expedients to counteract or remedy so great an evil. It was even proposed to enlist for-

eigners, and confidently calculated that a considerable force could thus be added to the rebel army; and, finally, the measure which was most antagonistic to the principles on which the rebellion was based was openly advocated. Even-General Lee was in favor of arming the slaves.

This proposition was bitterly opposed, and added another element of discord to those that were rife all through the dissolving Confederacy; for the dissensions which came to a head in Richmond can only be likened to those in Jerusalem before its fall. Jefferson Davis was one of the most unpopular of men among those whom he called his people, and the inhabitants of the capital in which he dwelt were his bitterest enemies. He quarrelled with Beauregard and Bragg and Johnston by turns, and was jealous and overbearing towards Lee. He was denounced in the rebel congress and by the rebel newspapers, and many attributed to him all the disasters of the Confederacy. But he was not alone to blame, and it is probable that another leader of the sinking cause would have incurred the same censures and aroused the same animosities among his followers. The unsuccessful are apt to be acrimonious, and the quarrels of the rebels were no less violent among themselves than with their so-called President.

They vehemently accused each other of treason to the cause, perhaps because each felt that his own fealty was waning; and, if so, it was not strange. The suffering for food, the difficulty of supplying even the army with rations and the horses with fodder, the scarcity of fuel, the depreciation of the currency, the interruption of manufactures, the annihilation of ordinary commerce, the absorption of agri-

culture—all these results of the war were having their natural effect, even in regions where the tread of a hostile army had not been known. The children of wealthy parents in Richmond went shoeless. The greatest ladies wore coarser garments than they had furnished their own servants in other days. In fine houses, black beans were served on silver dishes, and costly wine—all that was left of ancient luxuries—garnished the commonest fare. Every household mourned the loss of a favorite member. Many were deprived of all support and stricken to the earth by the calamities of war. The hospitals were crowded, and not only delicacies but medicines were difficult, and often impossible, to procure for those whose lives depended on their obtaining them.

There was, besides, the constant feeling of uneasiness about the slaves. Wherever the national armies penetrated, slavery was at an end. The field hands deserted their masters by tens of thousands at a time. The house servants, it is true, with the affectionate docility of their race, were generally faithful, and the entire slave population abstained from plunder and worse crimes, incident to a servile revolution, with a unanimity that was one of the most remarkable features of the war. Neither murder nor arson was committed; there was no revengeful or lustful passion displayed by these millions waiting to be freed, who struck no blow against their masters at this crisis in the fate of both. But none the less, the millions believed that they were the great stake of the war; that it was to free them every battle was fought. Their wishes were all for the invaders; and such help as in their simple, ignorant, but earnest way they could afford was never

lacking. They gave important information constantly to national officers; they sheltered and succored and concealed national escaped prisoners and scouts and spies; they welcomed everywhere, with extravagant rejoicings, the advent of the successful national armies.

All this the rebels perfectly knew. They endeavored to conceal the knowledge from the slaves, and from their enemies, and also to restrain the expression of it even among themselves. But there was always this dark shadow of what was possible hanging over them. There was the absolute destruction of slave property inevitable; there was the anxiety what to do with the slaves, and what the slaves might do with themselves. This condition had existed since the beginning of the war, but as the drain upon the troops became greater, and the demand could no longer be supplied, the arming of the blacks began to be discussed, and, in the winter of 1864 and 1865, it was one of the great questions that agitated the public mind throughout the Confederacy. The blacks had been useful soldiers for the Northern armies ; why should they not be made to fight for their masters ? it was asked. Of course, there was the immediate query whether they would fight to keep themselves in slavery; and this opened up a subject into which those who discussed it were afraid to look. Nevertheless, it seemed unavoidable that a black conscription should be attempted. There could be no surer sign of the straits to which the rebels were reduced.

Then there were, all through this winter, many who in spirit were already overcome; who wei*e convinced that it was impossible to hold out much

longer against the North, that aid from abroad was hopeless; and who preferred to yield in time, and thus secure good terms. The bare suggestion of such a course evoked from the sterner spirits the most violent denunciations, and charges of cowardice and treachery were freely bandied. Nevertheless, attempts at compromise were made. Kebel congressmen, for advocating submission, were imprisoned ; prominent men were decried for alleged sympathy with the North, and then attempted to escape from tjie sinking Confederacy. But for all this, the rebel government itself made overtures for peace. They were not such, however, as the national authorities, now conscious that they were rapidly advancing to supreme success, would for a moment consent to listen to. The movements of armies were not even delayed while the rebel commissioners presented their propositions.

Nevertheless, though rancors and heart-burnings were rife, though the councils of the rebellion were divided, though its people suffered and its territory was devastated, though it was deserted in its hour of need by those who had applauded or incited its efforts at the start, neither its leaders nor its soldiers were yet conquered; if depressed, they did not despair. They determined, even at this crisis, to keep up their courage, to gather up their strength, to make still another effort, to try still another scheme. Lee was created general-in-chief, and given supreme command of the rebel armies; Johnston was recalled from the retirement in which he had remained since the Atlanta campaign; the arming of the slaves was sanctioned by the rebel congress; an attempt was made to collect the frag-

ments of Hood's disorganized army and transport them to the East; the evacuation of Richmond was discussed and prepared for; orders were given and arrangements made for the removal of the public archives and stores; and Lee revolved the possibilities of a campaign in South-West Virginia, or in that region where the boundaries of Tennessee and North Carolina are the same.

Grant was thoroughly aware of these various phases of feeling, as well as of the actual circumstances existing within the rebel lines. On the 19th of December, he said to Sherman: "Jefferson Davis is said to be very sick; in fact, deserters report his death. The people had a rumor that he took poison in a fit of despondency over the military situation. I credit no part of this except that Davis is very sick, and do not suppose his reflections on military matters soothe him any." The same day he telegraphed to Stanton: " Rebel congress is now in secret session, and it is believed they are maturing a negro conscription act. These people will all come to us, if they can, but they may be so guarded as to find it diificult to do so."

But the knowledge of the wreck towards which the rebellion was now rapidly tending gave him no disposition to relax his efforts. On the contrary, he said to Stanton: " It is to be hoped that we will have no use for more men than we have now, but the number must be kept up." And as his plans approached their consummation, he renewed his instructions, and varied or developed his combinations to suit the new emergencies, and insure the accomplishment of the purpose at which he had been aiming for a year.

At first, it will be remembered, on the arrival of Sherman's army at the coast, it had been Grant's intention to transport it by sea to Richmond, and in the expediency of this plan Sherman himself concurred ; * but it was speedily found that the delay in providing transportation would be so great that the scheme must be abandoned. "I did think," said Grant, " the best thing to do was to bring the greater part of your army here, and wipe out Lee. The turn affairs now seem to be taking has shaken me in that opinion. ... If you capture the garrison of Savannah, it certainly will compel Lee to detach from Richmond, or give us nearly the entire South." Sherman, however, did not capture the garrison of Savannah, and therefore, as at Atlanta, an important force remained in his front after the technical objective point was gained. This fact also materially modified the plans of the general-in-chief.

Grant's determination now was to move Sherman northward through the Carolinas, assigning him somewhat the same task he had already performed in Georgia, and at the same time bringing him towards the point where the two principal armies of the nation and the rebellion were still opposed. On the 16th of December, Halleck wrote to Sherman, by Grant's order: " Should you have captured Savannah, it is thought that by transferring the water-batteries to the land side that place may be made a good depot and base of operations on Augusta,

Branchville, or Charleston." Branchville is at the junction of the railroad leading north from Savannah with that which crosses from Augusta to Charleston. It was, therefore, the first important

* See page 303.

strategic position in any northern movement of Sherman's army. "As the rebels," continued Halleck, " have probably removed their most valuable property from Augusta, perhaps Branchville would be the most important point at which to strike, in order to sever all connection between Virginia and the South-Western railroad." But, with the usual policy of the general-in-chief towards his important commanders, Halleck was then instructed to say: " General Grant's wishes, however, are that this whole matter of your future actions should be left entirely to your discretion."

Sherman answered promptly on the 24th, and, in response to an invitation from Grant to present his views, he proposed to move on Branchville, ignoring Charleston and Augusta, then occupy Columbia, the capital of South Carolina, and strike for the Charleston and Wilmington railroad, somewhere between the Santee and Cape Fear rivers. "Then," he said, " I would favor an attack on Wilmington, in the belief that Porter and Butler will fail in their present expedition." After Wilmington should have fallen, he proposed to move upon Ealeigh, in North Carolina. He would thus break up the entire railroad system of South and North Carolina, and place himself within a hundred and fifty miles of Grant. " The game then," he said, " would be up with Lee, unless he comes out of Richmond, avoids you, and fights me, in which case I should reckon on your being on his heels."

Grant replied at length on the 27th of December: "Your confidence in being able to march up and join this army pleases me, and I believe it can be done. The effect of such a campaign will be to dis-

organize the South, and prevent the organization of new armies from their broken fragments. Hood is now retreating, with his army broken and demoralized. ... If time is given, the fragments may be collected together, and many of the deserters reassembled. If we can, we should act to prevent this. Your spare army, as it were, moving as proposed, will do it." The possibility of Lee's leaving Richmond in order to attack Sherman was, however, always present to his mind. " This," he said, " is probably the only danger to the easy success of your expedition. In the event you should meet Lee's army, you would be compelled to beat it or find the sea-coast. Of course, I shall not let Lee's army escape if I can help it, and will not let it go without following to the best of my ability."

Accordingly, on the same day he gave explicit orders: " You may make your preparations to start on your northern expedition without delay. Break up the railroads in South and North Carolina, and join the armies operating against Richmond as soon as you can. ... It may not be possible for you to march to the rear of Petersburg, but, failing in this, you could strike either of the sea-coast ports in North Carolina, held by us. . . . From the best information I have, you will find no difficulty in supplying your army until you cross the Roanoke. From there here is but a few days' march, and supplies could be collected south of the river to bring you through. I shall establish communication with you there by steamboat and gunboat. By this means your wants can be partially supplied."

Thus, once again, Grant and Sherman were in complete and peculiar accord. Both had concurred

at first in the opinion that Sherman should move by sea, but, before either could know the second thought of the other, each suggested instead the campaign by land; and, when the decision of Grant was communicated to Sherman, he matured a scheme which was entirely acceptable, in all its details, to the gen-eral-in-chief, while Grant undertook again to provide the co-operation and support indispensable for the success of the design. Had their relations to each other been exactly reversed, the action of neither chief nor subordinate would, in all probability, have been different.

Even on a minor point there was the same curious identity of judgment between them. Sherman, in his dispatch of December 24th, declared: " Charleston is a mere desolated wreck, and it is hardly worth the time it would take to starve it out. Still, I am well aware that historically and politically much importance is attached to the place, and it may be that, apart from its military importance, both you and the administration may prefer I should give it more attention. ... It would be well for you to give me some general idea on the subject." Again, on the 31st, he said: " If you want me to take Charleston, I think I can do it." Grant's answer will be anticipated by those familiar with his history. On the 7th of January, he wrote to the Secretary of War: " Please say to General Sherman I do not regard the capture of Charleston of any military importance. He can pass it by, unless in doing so he leaves a force in his rear which it will be dangerous to leave there."

The remarkable personal relations which united the two soldiers were at this juncture as apparent
as at every other point in their career. On the 31st of January, Sherman said: " I am fully aware of your friendly feeling towards me, and you may always depend on me as your steadfast supporter. Your wish is law and gospel to me, and such is the feeling that pervades my army. I have an idea you will care to see me before I start." He had already written, a few days earlier: " I wish you could run down and see us. It would have a good effect, and show to both armies that they are acting on a common plan."

The brilliant achievements of Sherman, however, had kindled, as was natural, a lively admiration for his genius at the North, and came near creating a party in favor of his further advancement. There were some who loudly proclaimed that it was he who should have been chief, instead of Grant; and it was even proposed to promote him to a lieutenant-gener-alcy, when he would become eligible to command the army. But the knowledge of this fact served only to cement the friendship which it seemed calculated to disturb. The superior had no selfish jealousy, the loyal subordinate no ambition to supplant his friend.

On the 21st of January, Sherman wrote to Grant: " I have been told that Congress meditates a bill to make another lieutenant-general for me. I have written to John Sherman to stop it, if it is designed for me. It would be mischievous, for there are enough rascals who would try to sow differences between us, whereas you and I now are in perfect understanding. I would rather have you in command than anybody else, for you are fair, honest, and have at heart the same purpose that should ani-
mate all. I should emphatically decline any commission calculated to bring us into rivalry; and I ask you to advise all your friends in Congress to this effect, especially Mr. Washburne. I doubt if men in Congress fully realize that you and I are honest in our professions of want of ambition. I know I feel none, and to-day will gladly surrender my position and influence to any other who is better able to wield the power. The flurry attending my recent success will soon blow over, and give place to new developments."

It would be difficult to match this in disinter-restedness, but Grant replied: " I have received your very kind letter, in which you say you would decline, or are opposed to, promotion. No one would be more pleased at your advancement than I; and, if you should be placed in my position, and I put subordinate, it would not change our relations in the least. I would make the same exertions to support you that you have ever done to support me, and I would do all in my power to make our cause win." These were not mere professions on either side. They were pledges made in the view of very possible contingencies. And they would have been fulfilled.

But Sherman's prediction was verified. The excitement which his success had occasioned subsided, and no serious attempt was made to elevate him above the grade of major-general.

Grant's plans at this time assumed a grander and more comprehensive character than at any other epoch of the war. The concentration of his armies went on from the most distant quarters, and cooperative movements were directed on a scale hith-

erto quite unprecedented. When Sherman was ordered to move into the Carolinas and destroy, not only the resources of those states, but all the remaining railroads between the Atlantic and the rebel armies, Thomas was at the same time instructed to send Schofield from West Tennessee, with his entire corps, to the Potomac. This w r as with the intention of transporting Schofield to North Carolina, so that he might move into the interior with supplies, and be ready to meet Sherman on his northward march. On the 7th of January, Grant said to Halleck: " Order General Thomas, if he is assured of the departure south of Hood from Corinth, to send Schofield here with his corps, with as little delay as possible."

Schofield was at Clifton, on the Tennessee, when, on the 14th of January, he received his orders, and the movement was begun on the following day. The troops were sent with their artillery and horses, but without wagons, by steam transports, along the Tennessee and Ohio rivers to Cincinnati, and thence by rail to Washington and Alexandria. It was midwinter, and the weather unusually severe. The movement was delayed by snow and ice and violent storms ; the Baltimore and Ohio railroad had to be especially guarded against guerrillas during the passage ; but the troops moved night and day, through fogs and sleet on the Ohio and snows in the mountains, and on the 31st of January, the whole command had arrived at Washington and Alexandria. Here, however, another unavoidable delay was caused by the freezing of the Potomac, which rendered navigation impossible for several weeks.

Grant early notified Sherman of this co-operation, and announced: "If Wilmington is captured, Scho-

field will go there. If not, lie will be sent to New-bern. In either event, all the surplus force at the two points will move to the interior towards Golds-boro, in co-operation with your movement. . . . All these troops will be subject to your orders as you coine in communication with them."

But this was not all; the torpor of Thomas in the Nashville campaign had determined the general-in-chief to intrust to that commander no more operations in which prompt, aggressive action was necessary. Hood's movements, however, were for a while uncertain; and on the 30th of December, Grant said to Halleck : " I have no idea of keeping idle troops at any place, but before taking troops away from Thomas it will be advisable to see whether Hood's army halts at Corinth. I do not think he will, but think he is much more likely to be thrown in front of Sherman. If so, it will be just where we want them to go. Let Thomas collect all his troops not essential to hold his communications, at Eastport. . . . and be in readiness for their removal where they can be used."

As the plans of the rebels became more apparent, Grant gave orders to break up Thomas's army. On the 14th of January, as we have seen, Scho-field's corps was withdrawn from Tennessee, and on the 18th, the general-in-chief said to Halleck: " I now understand that Beauregard has gone west to gather up what he can save from Hood's army, to bring against Sherman. If this be the case, Selma and Montgomery can be easily reached. I do not believe, though, that General Thomas will ever get there from the north. He is too ponderous in his preparations and equipments to move through a country rapidly enough to live off of it. . . . West of the Mississippi we do not want to do more than defend what we now hold, but I do want Canby to make a winter campaign either from Mobile bay or Florida. . . . What I would order is that Canby be furnished cavalry horses and be directed to prepare to commence a campaign, and that Thomas be telegraphed to say what he could do, and when, and get his choice, looking upon Selma as his objective. Thomas must make a campaign, or spare his surplus troops."

Sherman had requested that Thomas should be ordered to move southward with a large force, but this Grant was unwilling to order; and on the 21st of January, he wrote to Sherman : " Before your last request to have Thomas make a campaign into the heart of Alabama, I had ordered Schofield to Annapolis,* Maryland, with his corps. ... I did not believe Thomas could possibly be got off before spring. His pursuit of Hood indicated a sluggishness that satisfied me he would never do to conduct one of your campaigns. The command of the advance of the pursuit was left to subordinates, whilst Thomas followed far behind. When Hood had crossed the Tennessee, and those in pursuit had reached it, Thomas had not much more than half crossed the state, from which he returned to Nashville to take steamer for Eastport. He is possessed of excellent judgment, great coolness and honesty, but he is not good in a pursuit. He also reported his troops fagged, and that it was necessary to equip up. This report and a determination to give the enemy no rest determined me to use his surplus troops else-

* A later order changed Schofield's destination to Alexandria.

where." Accordingly, on the 26th of January, Grant directed Thomas to forward A. J. Smith's division to Canby, and three thousand cavalry to Vicksburg.

Canby, meanwhile, had received his orders to move from the Gulf of Mexico towards Montgomery and Selma. On the 18th of January, the general-in-chief instructed him to "make an independent campaign, looking to the capture of Mobile first, if the job does not promise to be too long a one, and Montgomery and Selma, and the destruction of all roads, machine-shops, and stores the main object." The two last-named places were the greatest storehouses and factories for railroad engines and ordnance now left to the rebels, west of Augusta and Richmond, and their destruction constituted an object of primal importance, which Grant was far more anxious to accomplish than the capture of Mobile. That town had been closed as a port by the seizure of the forts in August, 1864, and its absolute possession was to him of secondary consequence. It was the essentials only that he ever sought to obtain, and the acquisition of the munitions of war at Selma or Montgomery far outweighed in importance, to his practical mind, the glory of the capture of Mobile.

His orders in regard to Schofield's movement were now minute and constant, and he in reality directed the operation as closely as if he had been chief of staff. On the 24th of January, he said: "As rapidly as it can be sent, in addition to previous calls, I want fifteen miles of railroad iron sent from Norfolk or elsewhere to Beaufort, North Carolina. Men will also be required to lay the track

from Newbern to Kinston." Even the roads over which Sherman must be supplied were to be carried towards the rendezvous, to meet his column on its northward march.

In the latter part of January, the Potomac still being frozen, the general-in-chief proceeded with Schofield, in advance of the troops, to the mouth of the Cape Fear river, to consult with Porter and Terry, and to study the situation on the coast. Schofield was now placed in command of all the forces in North Carolina, and ordered to report to Sherman as soon as the latter came within communication. On the 21st, Grant wrote out his full instructions : " The first point to be attained," he said, " is to secure Wilmington. Goldsboro will then be your objective point, moving either from Wilmington or Newbern, or both, as you deem best. Should you not be able to reach

Goldsboro, you will advance on the line or lines of railway connecting that place with the sea-coast, or as near to it as you can, building the road behind you. The enterprise under you has two objects : the first is to give General Sherman material aid, if needed, in his march north; the second, to open a base of supplies for him on his line of march. As soon, therefore, as you can determine which of the two, Wilmington or Newbern, you can best use for throwing supplies from to the interior, you will commence the accumulation of twenty days' rations and forage for sixty thousand men and twenty thousand animals. You will get of these as many as you can house and protect to such point in the interior as you may be able to occupy."

Thus Schofield was first to establish himself on the coast and capture Wilmington, and then to

carry Sherman's base along with him to some at present unknown point in the interior of the enemy's country, which Sherman might be able to strike after his march. The annals of war may be searched in vain for a parallel to this enterprise. " Communicate with me," said Grant, " by every opportunity, and, should you deem it necessary at any time, send a special boat to Fortress Monroe, from which you can communicate by telegraph."

Both his own experience and that of Sherman had now inspired Grant with a peculiar boldness in design, and, as he had great faith in Schofield's courage and ability, he continued: " The movements of the enemy may justify you, or even make it your imperative duty, to cut loose from your base, and strike for the interior to aid Sherman. In such case you will act on your own judgment, without waiting for instructions. You will report, however, what you propose doing. The details for carrying out these instructions are necessarily left to you." The especial fitness of Grant for supreme command consisted in his ability to select subordinates in whom he could confide, and then, in his willingness to trust and even incite them to act on their own responsibility ; laying down some general or principal aim or objective point, but leaving them to work out their own success in their own way; assisting them with instruments, and means, and co-operation, but never anxious lest they should acquire too much authority or fame. This is indeed the secret of all administrative genius, but never more indispensable or rarer than in war.

There was one injunction, however, that he never omitted, and he now added: " I would urge, if I did

not know that you are already fully alive to the importance of it, prompt action."

Full information of all these arrangements was forwarded to Sherman, so that he might conform his own movements to them, and know where to look for a relieving army in case of disaster, and whither to go in search of supplies.

But Grant was not content with dispositions on the coast in Sherman's favor. On the day on which these instructions were given to Schofield, Thomas was directed to send a cavalry expedition from East Tennessee, under General Stoneman, to penetrate South Carolina, well down towards Columbia, destroying the railroads and military resources of the country, and visiting a portion of the state that could not be reached by Sherman's column. Stoneman was to take three thousand men, and Thomas was also directed to send a small force of infantry to hold the mountain passes in his rear. "As the expedition goes to destroy," said Grant, "and not to fight battles, but to avoid them when practicable against anything like equal forces, or when a great object is to be gained, it should go as light as possible. . . . Let there be no delay in the preparations for the expedition, and keep me advised of its progress."

It was on the 27th of December, that the gen-eral-in-chief definitely instructed Sherman to march with his entire army north by land. At the same time, he directed the formation of an entrenched camp about Pocotaligo or Coosawhatchie, on the railroad between Savannah and Charleston. " This," he said, " will give us a position in the South from which we can threaten the interior without marching over

long narrow causeways, easily defended, as we have heretofore been compelled to do." Sherman replied on the 2nd of January, announcing that he would be ready to start on the 15th, if he could get the necessary supplies in the wagons by that time. "But until these supplies are in hand," he said, " I can do nothing. After they are, I shall be ready to move with great rapidity."

In fulfilment of Grant's directions, Sherman now moved the Fifteenth corps on transports to the neighborhood of Pocotaligo, while his left wing with the cavalry was also thrown forward, working slowly at first to open a road, and then by a rapid movement, to secure Sister's ferry on the Savannah river, and the Augusta railroad as far west as Robertsville. The country around Pocotaligo is all low alluvial land, cut up by salt-water swamps and fresh-water creeks, and easily susceptible of defence by a small force; but the terrible energy the rebels had displayed in the earlier stages of the war was beginning to yield, and the important position of Pocotaligo, interrupting all communication between Charleston and the South, was secured with a loss of only two officers and eight men.

Foster's troops, in the Department of the South, had originally been directed to protect Savannah; but Grant at this time ordered Grover's division from the Shenandoah Valley, where all fighting was at an end, to Savannah, of which it was to form the garrison. Grover took command of the city on the 18th of January, and Foster's troops were placed at Sherman's disposal.

Thus by the middle of January, a lodgment had been effected in South Carolina, and Sherman had

his whole army once more in hand as a moving column. He had no idea of wasting time on either Charleston or Augusta, but he determined to play upon the fears of the rebels, and compel them to retain a force to protect those places, which might otherwise be concentrated in his front, and render the passage of the great rivers that crossed his route more difficult and dangerous. Accordingly he gave out with some ostentation that he was moving upon either Charleston or Augusta.

Early in January the heavy winter rains set in, rendering the roads almost impassable; and the Savannah river became so swollen that it filled its many channels, and overflowed the vast extent of rice-fields on its eastern bank. This flood delayed the departure of the column for quite two weeks; it swept away a pontoon bridge at Savannah, and came near drowning an entire division of the Fifteenth corps, with several heavy trains of wagons, on the way from Savannah to Pocotaligo by the causeways. Sherman had also difficulties to encounter at Sister's ferry, where the Savannah river was three miles wide from the flood, and it became almost impossible to cross on the frail pontoons.

This delay, however, in no way disarranged Grant's plans or interfered with his manifold operations. There were no combinations obstructed by Sherman's inaction, no other armies whose advance could be interrupted or rendered dangerous because he was unable to start. There was no enemy in his own immediate front to become bolder and more defiant because undisturbed, no possibility of a contrary campaign because he remained in camp. His column was at this juncture the central one, and the

movements of all the others were directed to assist and strengthen him. The others waited, it is true, till he was ready to start, but each was acquiring new strength and assuming more desirable positions during the delay; and the rains that impeded Sherman, in reality aided Schofield and Thomas and Canby to perfect their arrangements to co-operate with him.

On the 1st of February, the army designed for the active campaign from Savannah northward was again sixty thousand strong; and, as before, was composed of two wings, the right under Howard and the left under Slocum. Kilpatrick was once more chief of cavalry. Sixty-eight guns accompanied the command. The wagons were twenty-five hundred in number, and carried an ample supply of ammunition for one great battle, forage for a week, and provisions for twenty days. For fresh meat Sherman depended on beeves driven on the hoof, and such cattle, hogs, and poultry as might be gathered on the march. The same general orders were in force as in the previous campaign, of which this indeed was only a continuation. Sherman calculated that he could safely rely on the country for a moderate quantity of supplies, and that if he should by any possibility be cut off from other resources, his army could live for several weeks on the mules and horses of the trains.

The enemy at this time occupied the cities of Charleston and Augusta, with garrisons capable of making a respectable if not successful defence, but utterly unable to meet the veteran columns of Sherman in the open field. Wheeler's cavalry, now greatly reduced, was expected to resist or delay the national progress, and Wade Hampton had been

106

dispatched from Virginia to South Carolina, his native state, with extraordinary powers to raise men, money, and horses.* He was supposed by Sherman to have two small divisions of cavalry in the neighborhood of Columbia. The scattered fragments of Hood's army were also hurrying rapidly across Georgia by way of Augusta, to make junction in the national front; and these, with Hardee, Wheeler, Bragg, and Hampton's troops, would amount to forty thousand men; a formidable force, sufficient, if handled with spirit and energy, to make the passage of rivers like the Santee and Cape Fear a difficult undertaking.

Both Grant and Sherman therefore instructed Foster to watch the inland progress as closely as possible, and provide points of security or refuge along the coast, to which the army could turn in case of disaster. Schofield also was directed by the general-in-chief to make careful and anxious preparations for such a contingency. It was, however, extremely desirable that Sherman should reach Goldsboro at a single stride. The distance was four hundred and twenty-five miles, but the place was of exceeding importance in any ulterior operations. Goldsboro is the first point north of Columbia where any railway running east crosses the great northern and southern line; but here the railroads meet that leave the coast at Wilmington and Newbern. Upon Goldsboro, therefore, Grant had directed the co-operative movement of Schofield, and, as far as it was possible to determine in a campaign of this peculiar character, Goldsboro was to be the objective point of Sherman's column.

* Sherman's " Memoirs."

The great danger was that Lee might not be inclined to sit quietly in Richmond, besieged by Grant, while Sherman, comparatively unopposed, passed through the states of South and North Carolina, cutting off and consuming the supplies on which the army of Northern Virginia relied, and assuming a position from which the two great national armies could be united in co-operation against the rebel capital. If Lee should succeed in escaping from Grant, and, reinforced by Beauregard's command, strike Sherman inland, between Columbia and Raleigh, the danger to the national forces would be extreme. But Grant had said to Sherman on the 18th of January: "From about Richmond I will watch Lee closely, and if he detaches much more, or attempts to evacuate, will pitch in. In the mean time, should you be brought to a halt anywhere, I can send two corps of thirty thousand effective men to your support from the works about Richmond."

This was indeed a very different campaign from the famous march, which, after all, was a march, and not a campaign. Then Sherman moved away from his enemy, and left a subordinate to destroy him; now he was advancing upon one, and possibly against two, rebel armies; for not only the fragments of Hood's command, and the garrison of Savannah, and all the movable forces which had been unable to withstand the advance from Atlanta, were certain to be in his path, but Lee himself with the army of Northern Virginia might combine with these to destroy him. In his former march he had advanced towards the sea, completely across the theatre of war; now he was to strike a point in the interior of the enemy's country, towards which another national army was

moving at right angles with his own, and their junction at a point still in the enemy's hands was indispensable. Sherman himself declared : " Were I to express my measure of the relative importance of the march to the sea, and of that from Savannah northward, I would place the former at one, and the latter at ten, or the maximum." *

On the 29th of January, he wrote to Grant: " You may rest assured that I will keep my troops well in hand, and if I get worsted, will aim^to make the enemy pay so dearly that you will have less to do. ... I must risk Hood, and trust to you. . . . to hold Lee, or be on his heels, if he conies south." This was the last dispatch Grant had from Sherman till the 12th of March.

Amid all these movements of his great subalterns, the general-in-chief himself remained apparently quiescent; but he was not without his reasons for this course. On the 4th of February, he said to Stanton: " I do not want to do anything to force the enemy from Richmond until Schofield carries out his programme. He is to take Wilmington, and then push out to Goldsboro, or as near it as he can go, and build up the road after him. He will then be in a position to assist Sherman if Lee should leave Richmond with any considerable force, and the two together will be strong enough for all the enemy have to put against them. Terry is being reinforced from here with the fragments of divisions which were left behind when he started on his expedition. ... I shall necessarily have to take the odium of apparent inactivity, but if it results, as I expect it will, in the discomfiture of Lee's army, I shall be entirely satisfied."

Sherman's "Memoirs," vol. ii., page 221.

ULYSSES S. GRANT.

377

Thus Grant was busy, directing every portion of his vast command : planning the magnificent combination by which Sherman was sure of support, in case of need, along the march, and when he reached the interior of North Carolina, should find another army of forty thousand men with a secure base on the Atlantic coast, and the supplies which he was certain to require; bringing Schofield in the depth of winter, by steamer and railroad, from the heart of Tennessee to the frozen Potomac, and then dispatching him again on ocean transports to the tempestuous North Carolina coast, where a foothold had just been gained at so much cost; thence again directing him to move rapidly out, capturing Wilmington and building a railroad as he advanced, to be ready to meet the great marcher in the interior: at the same time stripping Thomas of troops, to send east and south, where they could be more effectually employed; adding reinforcements of veterans and recruits to Sherman and Terry ; transferring Grover from the Shenandoah to the Savannah, so as to set Foster free ; dispatching an expedition to favor Sherman from East Tennessee ; inspiring one advance from the north and another from the south, one from the Tennessee and another from the Gulf of Mexico, against the last great arsenals and storehouses left to the rebellion west of the Alleghanies; and himself still firmly holding the largest army of the enemy in his front, and thus alone rendering practicable all his other designs.

But at this juncture he inaugurated still another campaign. Thomas's command was now very much depleted. Stoneman had been ordered to- South Carolina, and Grierson, with three thousand cavalry,

to Vicksburg; A. J. Smith was sent to Canby, and Schofield to the Atlantic coast ; and all the fur-loughed veterans, recruits, and convalescent troops of Sherman's army had been forwarded to Savannah; nevertheless, Grant was anxious to employ offensively whatever force was still left in Tennessee. On the 14th of February, he said to Thomas: "Canby is preparing a movement from Mobile bay against Mobile and the interior of Alabama. His force will consist of about twenty thousand men, besides A. J. Smith's command. The cavalry you have sent to Canby will be debarked at Vicksburg. It, with the available cavalry already in that section, will move from there eastwardly in co-operation. Hood's army has been terribly reduced by the severe punishment you gave it in Tennessee, by desertion consequent upon that defeat, and now by the withdrawal of many of them to oppose Sherman. . . . Canby's movement will attract all the attention of the enemy, and leave an advance from your standpoint easy. I think it advisable, therefore, that you prepare as much of a cavalry force as you can spare, and hold it in readiness to go south. The object will be threefold : first, to attract as much of the enemy's force as possible, to ensure success to Canby; second, to destroy the enemy's line of communications and military resources; third, to destroy or capture their forces brought into the field. Tuscaloosa and Selma would probably be the points to direct the expedition against. This, however, would not be so important as the mere fact of penetrating deep into Alabama."

On the 15th, he telegraphed to Thomas : "It is desirable to start Stoneman without delay." ULYSSES S. GEANT.

Meanwhile, it was becoming important for Scho-field to move, and, on the 8th of February, Grant said to that commander: " The quicker you can bring your troops against Wilmington, the smaller the force you will have to contend against." Sherman preferred that Schofield should start from ISTew-bern, but the general in-chief was anxious to provide against every contingency, and, in the event of disaster to the advancing column, the road from Wilmington, bearing further south, would be preferable. On the 19th, therefore, he instructed Schofield to turn his attention to Wilmington. " You will either capture the place," he said, "or hold considerable of the enemy from Sherman's front."

A dispatch from Sherman had now been received by Admiral Dahlgren, off the coast, and forwarded to the general-in-chief; and on the 19th, Grant communicated the contents to Schofield : " Sherman," he wrote, was "encountering bad roads and much water, and was not certain but those causes would force him to turn upon Charleston. In that case, he would want his supplies sent to Bull's bay. Richmond papers of yesterday, however, announce the capture of Columbia on the 17th. As he was then across the Congaree, it is not likely he will turn back. This success will probably force the evacuation of Charleston. In that case, Gillmore [who had superseded Foster in South Carolina] * will have a disposable force of ten or twelve thousand men, which I have directed him to send to you. Should you find an advance on Wilmington impracticable,

* Foster was relieved solely because of physical incapacity, resulting from an old wound. "We want a man," said Grant, "who is not confined to his quarters."

keep up such a threatening attitude that the enemy will be compelled to retain all the force he now has, and push on the column from Newbern."

On the 9th of February, Schofield's advance arrived at the mouth of the Cape Fear river, and Cox's division of the Twenty-third corps was landed on the peninsula above Fort Fisher. Terry still held a line about two miles north of the fort, as well as Smithville and Fort Caswell, on the opposite side of Cape Fear river; while the squadron covered the flanks on the sea-coast and in the stream. The rebel line in front of Terry reached across the peninsula, and on the western bank the enemy occupied Fort Anderson, about twelve miles below Wilmington, with a line three-fourths of a mile in length, the right resting on a swamp: Hoke was in general command. Schofield pronounced Fort Anderson impregnable to a direct attack, and made his dispositions to turn it. Sending two divisions, under Cox and Ames, to the west bank of the river, and then entrenching two brigades to occupy the enemy, he marched the remainder of the force around the swamp that covered the rebel right, to strike the road to Wilmington, in rear of the fort. The rebels were warned of the movement by their cavalry, and, during the night of the 19th of February, they hastily abandoned their works, falling back behind Town creek, about four miles below the city. Possession was thus secured of the principal defences of Cape Fear river and Wilmington, with ten heavy guns and large quantities of ammunition. During' these operations the fleet had kept up a constant fire from the river, but no gun was dismounted in Fort Anderson.

Ames's division was now returned to Terry, and

on the 20th, Cox again advanced, on the western bank. He succeeded in crossing Town creek by a single flat-boat found in the stream, and, wading the swarnps, he reached the enemy's flank and rear, attacked and routed him at once, capturing two pieces of artillery and three hundred and seventy-five prisoners. During the night he rebuilt the bridge which the rebels had burned, and in the morning pushed on towards Wilmington, meeting with no opposition. Terry, meanwhile, on the eastern shore, had advanced to a point about four miles below the town, where he found the enemy strongly posted, in numbers greater than his own. Nevertheless, he so occupied the rebels in his front that no force could be sent to replace that which Cox had destroyed.

On the 21st, Cox, still advancing, secured a rebel pontoon bridge, and threatened to cross the Cape Fear river above Wilmington, whereupon the rebels at once set fire to their steamers, cotton, and military and naval stores, and abandoned the town. Cox entered Wilmington on the 22nd of February, while Terry pursued the rebels across Northeast river. The total national loss in these operations, from the 11th of February to the capture of Wilmington, was not more than two hundred, in killed and wounded. The enemy lost about as many,* besides eight hundred prisoners. Fifty-one pieces of heavy ordnance and fifteen light guns fell into Schofield's hands.

While these movements were occurring in North Carolina, Grant, in order to prevent any attempt at the evacuation of Richmond, directed still another movement in the rear of the ill-starred capital. Sherman was approaching from the south, Meade

* Schofield's Report.

and Ord were besieging it in front, Stoneman had been ordered to move athwart the country from East Tennessee in the direction of South Carolina, and Sheridan was now instructed to penetrate to the west of Richmond from the Valley of the Shenan-doah. As early as the 8th of February, Grant had said to Sheridan: " I believe there is no enemy now to prevent you from reaching the Virginia Central railroad, and possibly the canal, when the weather will permit you to move." On the 13th, however, he said: " I do not care about your moving until the weather and roads are such as to give assurance of overcoming all obstacles except those interposed by the enemy." Finally, on the 20th, he issued full instructions : " As soon as it is possible to travel, I think you will have no difficulty about reaching Lynchburg with a cavalry force alone. From there you could destroy the railroad and canal in every direction, so as to be of no further use to the rebellion. . . . This additional raid, with one now about starting from East Tennessee, under Stoneman, numbering about four or five thousand cavalry; one from Eastport, Mississippi, ten thousand cavalry; Canby, from Mobile bay, with about eighteen thousand mixed troops—these three latter pushing for Tuscaloosa, Selma, and Montgomery, and Sherman, with a large army eating out the vitals of South Carolina—is all that will be wanted to leave nothing for the rebellion to stand upon. I would advise you to overcome great obstacles to accomplish this. Charleston was evacuated on Tuesday last."

Grant now looked upon the destruction of the principal armies of the enemy as near at hand, and

these simultaneous raids into the Carolinas, Alabama, Mississippi, and Virginia, were intended to break up the railroads of the entire South, so that the transportation of supplies or troops would be an absolute impossibility for another year; while the destruction of food, as well as of arsenals and manufactories of arms, would render the rebellion helpless to recover whenever the blow should be struck which had impended so long.

The government, however, felt some uneasiness about the departure of Sheridan, and what was considered the exposure of the capital. This was intimated to Grant, and on the 26th of February, he telegraphed to Lincoln, explaining his strategy. " Sheridan's movement," he said, " is in the direction of the enemy, and the tendency will be to protect the Baltimore and Ohio railroad, and to prevent any attempt to invade Maryland and Pennsylvania." Even this did not allay the anxiety entertained at Washington, and, on the 2nd of March, Grant was obliged to say to Stanton: " If the returns I have of troops for the Department of Washington are anything like correct, there need not be the slightest apprehension for the safety of the capital. At this time, if Lee could spare any considerable force, it would be for the defence of points now threatened, which are necessary for the very existence of his army." Again, on the same day, he telegraphed to the Secretary of War, " I don't think it possible for Lee to send anything towards Washington, unless it should be a brigade of cavalry."

There is a sort of apprehension, difficult to describe or define, that sometimes seizes upon men not only personally brave, but who undoubtedly

possess great moral courage, under circumstances or in situations when they feel and appreciate their own ignorance. All men lack nerve when they don't know what to do, and know that they don't. In emergencies, certainly, knowledge is power, and the lack of it weakness. This was the secret of Butler's inefficiency, and this was undoubtedly the cause of what now seemed the timidity of the government.

But civilians in high place have at all times been bad counsellors in time of war; and even soldiers of great technical and scientific acquirements often prove themselves lacking in the quality of audacity, so indispensable for success in the field. It is not only the daring that sees and seizes critical moments in battle, and which all admit to be among the first requisites of a commander; there is also quite as necessary a certain faculty, based, it is true, upon knowledge and coolness combined, but the essence of which, after all, is courage. This must not only flash across an emergency, but must be apparent and persistent in anxious moments, when adverse advice is pressed by those entitled to offer it, when contrary judgments are formed by competent critics, when nothing but the convictions of his own mind and the firmness of his own determination, and, still more, the passion of his own nature for advance and aggression against difficulty and absolute danger, can sustain him who is to decide. He must take risks, he must advance sometimes when he seems unprepared, he must leave possibilities in his rear, he must proceed in ignorance of what may occur, not only not knowing what the enemy may do, but not caring, determined to do himself, and so control the enemy's plans and com-

pel his movements. Unless he is able and willing and ready to do all this, unless he does all this in spite of obstacles and opposition, he may be an engineer or a strategist, a tactician or a scientist—he is not a general. No man but a hero is fit to command armies.

Meanwhile Grant had got word, through the rebel newspapers, first of the fall of Branchville, then of Columbia, and then of Charleston, which the rebels could not hold after Sherman had passed. It fell like Jericho, without being attacked, and Gill-more was ordered to occupy it. This last news arrived on the 20th of February, and on the 21st, intelligence came that Fort Anderson was in Scho-field's hands. On the 24th, Grant learned of the capture of Wilmington, and at once recommended Schofield for a brigadier-generalcy in the regular army. He made the reward an incentive, and, when he announced the promotion to Schofield, continued

: " I hope and know you will push out and form a connection with Sherman at the earliest practicable moment. If you reach Goldsboro and have a fair prospect of getting your road finished soon, it may be unnecessary for Sherman to come down to the coast. Make every effort to communicate with Sherman at once. . . . Every effort has been made to get you troops and all else called for through, but the ice has kept everything back very much. . . . If you and Sherman are united, you can keep as far in the interior of North Carolina as you may be able to supply yourselves. With the large force you will have united, Raleigh may not be found too far off."

At this time Schofield was dissatisfied with one of his subordinates, and Grant wrote to him: " Do

not hesitate in making any changes in commanders you think necessary." He always held that a general, like a workman, should choose his tools; and, even if the superior was mistaken, in his judgment, he must be allowed to relieve a subaltern with whom he was dissatisfied. The military service, indeed, does not pretend to spare, or hardly to consider, the feelings of individuals; it is the success of the cause only which it can regard; and soldiers, who constantly risk their lives, must expect sometimes to put even their reputations in jeopardy.

On the 25th, Grant said to Halleck: " It is well enough to occupy Georgetown until Sherman is in communication with the sea-coast. It is barely possible, though not probable, he may require supplies from Georgetown. I expect nothing of the kind, however."

Nothing was more remarkable during these entire operations than the manner in which, while absolutely ignorant of Sherman's actual movements, obtaining his only information for more than a month through rebel sources, Grant still endeavored to support his great lieutenant, and co-operate with the column of whose position he was unaware. Scho-field was now at Wilmington, Gillmore on the South Carolina coast, Stoneman was ordered to come in from Tennessee, and Sheridan had started from the Valley, all aiming to communicate with Sherman, to supply him, to aid him, to combine with him, if events allowed; moving from the most opposite directions into the rebel territory, yet no commander knowing exactly where his forces would strike the marching army he was in search of.

On the 26th of February, the general-in-chief en-

quired of Thomas : " When did Stoneman start on his expedition ? "

Although Grant believed that Sherman would be perfectly safe as soon as he came within supporting distance of Schofield, even if Lee should proceed to North Carolina, this movement of the rebels was what he now most feared, and every effort was made to detect and prevent it. Fifteen thousand men were kept on picket duty on Meade's front, and half the army of the Potomac was constantly prepared for attack. "Our information," says the diary of an officer of the staff, "is that an attack on our centre is probable. Grant says he wishes one might be made, but thinks it would be a cover to hide the movements of Lee southward. . . . The only hope of the enemy now is to fall on Sherman before he can be supported by Schofield." Grant frequently said, at this time, that a daring plan for the enemy would be to gather up his entire force, and rush out through West Virginia into East Tennessee and Kentucky, transferring the seat of war to a territory full of supplies, threatening the states north of the Ohio, and giving a new lease of life to the rebellion, however short. Such an attempt, he said, would surely result in the utter destruction of the army that began it ; but it would have had the strength of desperation, and might have occasioned serious trouble.

At this time the general-in-chief manifested much anxiety about Sherman, more than ever before, and far more than when he was himself engaged in active operations. As the various despatches came in from one army or another, he discussed the- movements of all his commanders, sometimes with the

,3 ••i».

maps before Mm, but oftener without them; for lie had a genius for topography, and having once determined how the ground lay, or where any position was, he never forgot, or found it necessary to refresh his memory. The picture was photographed in his mind indelibly. His supervision at this time was absolute. On one day he wrote with his own hand forty-two dispatches.

Canby now was to come into the game. Grant's instructions to him had hitherto been neither frequent nor detailed. He was outside of telegraphic communication, and most of his command was beyond the Mississippi. After the defeat of Banks on the Red river the year before, Grant had allowed Canby to work his way out of the difficulties he inherited from his predecessor, without much interference ; and when Steele returned to Arkansas and Canby arrived at New Orleans, the Nineteenth corps was withdrawn from the Department of the Gulf, and A. J. Smith brought back within the limits of Sherman's command. In July, Canby sent a few troops to co-operate with Farragut against the defences of Mobile, but this force was too small for any further operations after the seizure of the forts. In August occurred the invasion of Missouri by Price, and A. J. Smith was ordered to report to Rosecrans. Nevertheless, for a while, Price roamed over the state with impunity, doing incalculable mischief, but accomplishing no important interruption to Grant's plans. He was finally brought to battle on the Big Blue river, and defeated with the loss of nearly all his artillery and trains, and a large number of prisoners, and then made a precipitate retreat to northern Arkansas. Grant, however, w^as dis-

satisfied with Rosecrans, and in December that commander was relieved, while Smith reported to Thomas at Nashville.

All these operations were almost independent of Grant. He sent a few orders, and forwarded troops when he could spare them; but it was impossible and undesirable to direct in detail operations so far away, and so disconnected with the great campaigns east of the Mississippi, or indeed with the principal strategic objects of the war. When, however, a positive movement was ordered by Grant from the Gulf of Mexico, in co-operation with his other plans and other armies, he at once assumed different relations with Canby, and gave him directions of that peculiar and personal character which distinguished his instructions to his principal commanders.

General "W. F. Smith was at this time serving, but not with troops, in the Department of the Gulf, and an effort was made to give him command of a corps; but on the 20th of February, Grant wrote: " It will not do for Canby to risk Smith with any military command whatever. The moment Canby should differ with him in judgment as to what is to be done, and he would be obliged to differ or yield to him entirely, he would get no further service out of him, but, on the contrary, he would be a clog. Let Smith continue on the same duty he has been detailed for."

Grant was never willing to try again a subordinate whom he had once definitely relieved. He bore with a man whose characteristics would have been intolerable to some superiors, and put up with even ill-success or insubordination sometimes too Ions;; but if once he determined to free himself from

107

an incompetent, or inefficient, or unmanageable lieutenant, he never relented, nor was willing to be em-barassed by the same cause again. The officers who had failed to satisfy his expectations or demands were often men with strong political or personal influence, and sometimes were able to induce the government to assign them to less important positions than those from which they had been removed; but Grant never consented that those whom he had once dismissed from his plans should be given a place where their action would be of consequence to him again. As has been shown, he always supported his great commanders if they wanted a change in their own subalterns, even to the disregard of rank or seniority; for he regarded harmony between a chief and his subordinates as among the most imperative of military necessities, and made every effort to arrive at this relation with his own lieutenants. If he found it unattainable, for whatever cause—no ability, or experience, or accomplishment, or character, atoned. He refused to employ an instrument with which he had found himself unable to accomplish his designs.

On the 27th of February, he said to Canby: " I am extremely anxious to hear of your forces getting to the interior of Alabama. I send Grierson, an experienced cavalry commander, to take command of your cavalry. . . . Forrest seems to be near Jackson, Mississippi; and if he is, none but the best of our cavalry commanders will get by him. Thomas was directed to start a cavalry force from Eastport, Mississippi, as soon after the 20th of February as possible, to move on Selma, Alabama, which would tend to ward Forrest off. -He promised to start it

by that day, but I know he did not, and I do not know that he has yet started it."

He then proceeded to lay down a few general remarks on strategy, embodying some of the results of his own experience : " It rarely happens that a number of expeditions, starting from various points to act upon a common centre, materially aid each other. They never do, except when each acts with vigor, and either makes rapid marches or keeps confronting the enemy. Whilst one column is engaging anything like an equal force, it is necessarily aiding the other by holding that force. With Grierson I am satisfied you would either find him at the appointed place in time, or you would find him holding the enemy, which would enable the other column to get there." . . .

" I feel a great anxiety," he continued, " to have the enemy entirely broken up at the West. Whilst I believe it will be an easy job, time will enable the enemy to reorganize and collect all their deserters, and get up a formidable force. By giving them no rest, what they now have in their ranks will leave them. It is also important to prevent as far as possible the planting of a crop this year, and to destroy their railroads, machine-shops, etc. It is also important to get all the negro men we can, before the enemy put them into their ranks." These were the identical views entertained by Grant when he assumed command of the armies the year before,* and which he had been urging upon all his commanders since.

He concluded: " Stoneman starts from East Tennessee in a few days to make a raid as far up on

* Vol. ii., chap. I., passim.

the Lynchburg road as lie can. Sheridan started this morning from Winchester, Virginia, to destroy the Virginia Central railroad and James river canal, and to get to Lynchburg if he can. Each starts with cavalry force alone."

Meanwhile, the same peculiarities which had distinguished Thomas in November and December had become apparent in January and February and March. On the 25th of January, Grant said to Halleck: " When Canby is supplied, horses may be sent up the Tennessee, as General Thomas requests, and let him use all exertion to get off during the first favorable weather we may have. It is a great pity that our cavalry should not have taken advantage of Hood's and Forrest's forces being on furlough. They could have fed on the enemy, and where they could have collected their own horses." Yet it was to collect and equip this cavalry that Thomas had delayed so long at Nashville, and, after two weeks' pursuit of the enemy, he was unwilling to send it out again without another season of equipping and delay. Thomas was in some things not unlike Warren in the Eastern army, who was earnest and capable and accomplished, but unequal to the task assigned him; both had difficulties for which they were not always to blame, which impeded and prevented the action that Grant expected of them; but greater soldiers overcame just such "difficulties, and Grant preferred those who did.

Thomas's delay now compelled Grant to change his plans. On the 27th of February, one month after he had first ordered Stoneman's advance, he said to Thomas : " Stonernan being so late in making his start from East Tennessee, and Sherman having

passed out of the state of South Carolina, I think now his course had better be changed. It is not impossible that, in the event of the enemy being driven from Richmond, they may fall back to Lynch-burg with a part of their force, and attempt a raid into East Tennessee. It will be better, therefore, to keep Stoneman between our garrisons in East Tennessee and the enemy. Direct him to repeat the raid of last fall, destroying the railroad as far towards Lynchburg as he can. Sheridan starts to-day from Winchester for Lynchburg. This will vastly favor Stoneman."

Then, with a view to the possibility of a rebel attempt to enter Tennessee from the east, he continued : " Every effort should be made to collect all the surplus forage and provisions of East Tennessee at Knoxville, and to geib there a large amount of stores besides. It is not impossible that we may have to use a force in that section the coming spring. Preparations should be made to meet such a contingency. If it had been possible to have got Stoneman off in time, he would have made a diversion in favor of Sherman, and would have destroyed a large amount of railroad stock cut off and left in North-West South Carolina. It is too late now to do any good except destroy the stock."

And thus the chief informed each general of the movements of "the others with whom he was to cooperate, so that all might act in harmony. The web was complicated, but the threads were held in a single hand. All these various and distant campaigns were directed in their inception and execution according to a single plan. All Grant's instructions were pregnant with the same principles.

Towards eacli quarter of the theatre of war, where there was yet a possibility that a rebel force could be assembled, where rebel lines might still communicate, where rebel stores could be collected, or rebel arms be manufactured, Grant directed a national force, so that at each point the enemy should be obliged to succumb; not only at the central and principal place, but also at the same time at every other spot where the rebellion might by any chance or effort come again to a head. The success that Grant sought he meant should be complete and universal. Every rebel army should be outfought and outgeneralled ; not only overpowered, and crushed, and exhausted, but there should be no loop-hole left, no opportunity of flight or distraction or diversion in any direction. Wherever a rebel force found itself, it must find also an irresistible enemy in its front and rear; every rebel who was not killed must surrender; and that not because he was weary, or disheartened, or chose to yield, but because he must do so or die.

At this time again Grant saw reason to apprehend a movement of Lee before Richmond or Petersburg, either to screen the withdrawal of the rebel army or to distract attention from operations elsewhere. On the 22nd of February, he said to Parke, who was in command of the army of the Potomac for a few days, in the absence of Meade : " As there is a possibility of an attack from the enemy at any time, and especially an attempt to break your centre, extra vigilance should be kept up both by the pickets and the troops on the line. Let commanders understand that no time is to be lost awaiting orders, if an attack is made, in bringing all their resources

to the point of danger. With proper alacrity in this respect, I would have no objection to seeing the enemy get through." On the 25th, he said: " Deserters from the rebel lines north of the James say it is reported among them that Hill's corps has left, or is leaving, to join Beauregard. ... If such a movement is discovered, we must endeavor to break a hole some place."

This expectation of Grant was not without foundation. The rebels were contemplating every contingency, and consulting about every remedy. Their distraction and desperation were now at their height. Lee had been made general-in-chief, and Brecken-ridge secretary of war, in the vain hope that-a change of counsellors or a concentration of authority might avail to stay the approaching catastrophe. On the 19th of February, Lee wrote to the Richmond government : "The accounts received to-day from South and North Carolina are unfavorable. General Beau-regard reports from Charlotte that four corps of the enemy are advancing on that place, tearing up the railroad, and that they will probably reach Charlotte . . . before he can concentrate his troops there. He states General Sherman will doubtless . . . unite with General Schofield at Raleigh or Weldon. General Bragg reports that General Schofield is now preparing to advance from Newbern to Goldsboro. ... He says that little or no assistance can be received from the state N of North Carolina. . . . Sherman seems to be having everything his own way, which is calculated to cause apprehension. General Beauregard does not say what he proposes or what he can do I do not know where his troops are, or on what lines they are moving. . . . General J. E. Johnston

is the only officer whom 1 know who lias the confidence of the army and people, and if he was ordered to report to me I would place him there on duty."

In the same dispatch he said: " It is necessary to bring out all our strength, and, I fear, to unite our armies, as separately they do not seem able to make head against the enemy. Everything should be destroyed that cannot be moved out of the reach of Generals Sherman and Schofield. Provision must be accumulated in Virginia, and every man in all the states must be brought out. I fear it may be necessary to abandon all our cities, and preparations should be made for this contingency"

The most stringent orders were given on the following day to remove or destroy all supplies on the route of Sherman or Schofield, and Brecken-ridge inquired to what point Lee wished to retire, and whither stores should be moved, in the event of the evacuation of Richmond. Lee replied on the 21st: "In the event .of the necessity of abandoning our position on the James river, I shall endeavor to unite the- corps of the army about Burksville (junction of the Southside and Danville railroad), so as to retain communication with the North and South as long as practicable, and also with the West. I should think Lynchburg, or some point west, the most advantageous place to which to remove stores from Richmond." The same day he formally requested that Johnston should be ordered to report to him for duty.

The most extraordinary and extravagant plans were now suggested. The emergency, it was felt, demanded extreme measures, and some of the schemes proposed were the mere frantic imaginings of de-

spair. Others were founded on better judgment, but even they were like the last resource of men who had staked all and lost. On the 21st of February, Breckenridge suggested assembling the handful of infantry still under Early, the one brigade in South-West Virginia, the troops in Western North Carolina, and adding these to "all the available force from other quarters" "to destroy Sherman" "If it was possible," he said to Lee, "to assemble an equal or superior force to meet him, and that force could be wrought into enthusiasm by your personal presence, great results might be achieved; and something of this sort must be done at once, or the situation is lost."

On the same day, Beauregard telegraphed direct to Jefferson Davis, from South Carolina: "Should enemy advance into North Carolina towards Charlotte and Salisbury, as is now almost certain, I earnestly urge a concentration in time of at least twenty-five thousand infantry and artillery at latter point, if possible, to give him battle there and crush him there. Then to concentrate all forces against Grant, and then to march to Washington, to dictate a peace. Hardee and myself can collect about fifteen thousand, exclusive of Cheatham and Stewart [from Hood's army], not likely to reach in time. If Lee and Bragg could furnish twenty thousand more, the fate of the Confederacy would be secure." Beauregard was ill at the time, and it is generous to suppose that his illness had affected his brain. The idea of marching to Washington to dictate a peace at this epoch of the war did not commend itself to the rebel authorities, and the day after this dispatch was received, Johnston superseded Beauregard in

command of the troops opposed to Sherman. The same day, the formal orders were issued by Brecken-ridge to govern the chiefs of bureaux upon the evacuation of Richmond. Lynchburg was the point designated to which stores and material were to be transported, but what was not indispensably requisite might be sent to Danville, or points on the Danville railroad. It was to this region, it will be remembered, that Grant had already directed Sheridan to proceed.

On the 24th of February, Lee called attention to "the alarming number of desertions now occurring in the army. . . . Since the 12th inst.," he said, " they amount in two divisions of Hill's corps . . . to about four hundred. There are a good many from other commands. ... It seems that the men are influenced very much by the representations of their friends at home, who appear to have become very despondent of our success. They think the cause desperate, and write to the soldiers advising them to take care of themselves, assuring them that, if they will return home, the bands of deserters so far outnumber the home guards that they will be in no danger of arrest. . . . These desertions have a very bad effect upon the troops who remain, and give rise to painful apprehensions." On the 25th, he said: " Hundreds of men are deserting nightly, and I cannot keep the army together unless examples are made of such cases." On the 28th, he reported " twelve hundred more. One hundred and seventy-eight in one division are reported to have gone over to the enemy. In addition to the above ... on the night of the 26th, from seventy-five to one hundred deserted. . . . These men generally

went off in bands, taking arms and ammunition, and I regret to say that the greatest number of desertions have occurred among the North Carolina troops, who have fought as gallantly as any soldiers in the army. ... I shall do all in my power to arrest this evil, but I am convinced, as already stated to you, that it proceeds from the discouraging sentiment out of the army, which, unless it can be changed, will bring us to calamity."

One cause of these desertions was the suffering among the troops from lack of food. On the 8th of January, Lee wrote to the rebel government that the entire right wing of his army had been in line for three days and nights, in the most inclement weather of the season. " Under these circumstances," he said, " heightened by assaults and fire of the enemy, some of the men had been without meat for three days, and all were suffering from reduced rations and scant clothing. Colonel Cole, chief commissary, reports that he has not a pound of meat at his disposal. If some change is not made, and the commissary department reorganized, I apprehend dire results. The physical strength of the men, if their courage survives, must fail under this treatment. Our cavalry has to be dispersed for want of forage. Fitz Lee's and Lomax's divisions are scattered because supplies cannot be transported where their services are required. I had to bring Fitz Lee's division sixty miles Sunday night, to get them in position. Taking these facts in connection with the paucity of our numbers, you must not be surprised if calamity befalls us."

At this juncture the rebels made another attempt to avert the blow which they felt was' about to fall. They had already, a month before, dis-

patched the second civil officer of their Confederacy, accompanied by two other of their most prominent men, who had laid before Lincoln himself, and the Secretary of State, propositions for peace, but not for submission;* and, as these had not been accepted, they now bethought themselves of another expedient. It was determined that Lee should approach Grant direct, and endeavor to effect an arrangement through military channels.

On the 2nd of March, therefore, Lee addressed the following letter to Grant: " Lieutenant-General Longstreet has informed me that, in a recent conversation between himself and Major-General Ord, as to the possibility of a satisfactory adjustment of the present unhappy difficulties by means of a military convention, General Ord stated that, if I desired to have an interview with you on the subject, you would not decline, providing I had authority to act. Sincerely desiring to leave nothing untried which may put an end to the calamities of war, I propose to meet you at such convenient time and place as you may designate, with the hope that, upon an interchange of views, it may be found practicable to submit the subjects of controversy between the belligerents to a convention of the kind mentioned. In such event

* " What the insurgent party seemed" chiefly to favor was a postponement of the question of separation upon which the war is waged, and a mutual direction of the efforts of the government, as well as those of the insurgents, to some extrinsic policy or scheme for a season, during which passions might be expected to subside, and all the armies be reduced, and trade and intercourse between the people of both sections be resumed. It was suggested by them that through such postponement we might now have made peace with some not very certain prospect of an ultimate satisfactory adjustment of the political relations between the government and the states, section, or people, now engaged in conflict with it."— Hon. W. H. Seward, Secretary of State, to Hon. Charles Francis Adams, Minister to England.

I am authorized to do whatever the result of the proposed interview may render necessary or advisable. Should you accede to this proposition, I would suggest that, if agreeable to you, we meet at the place selected by Generals Ord and Longstreet for their interview, at eleven A. M., on Monday next."

Grant at once forwarded a copy of this letter to the Secretary of War, with these remarks: " The following communication has just been received from General Lee. General Ord met General Longstreet a few days since, at the request of the latter, to arrange for the exchange of citizen prisoners and prisoners of war improperly captured. He had my authority to do so, and to arrange definitely for such as were confined in his department, arrangements for all others to be submitted for approval. A general conversation ensued on the subject of the war, and has induced the above letter. I have not returned any reply, but promised to do so at twelve M. to-morrow. I respectfully request instructions."

Grant, it will be seen, had taken no step to elicit these overtures, and made no suggestion in regard to the answer he should be instructed to communicate. His dispatch reached Stanton at the Capitol, where the President and his cabinet were assembled on the night of the 3rd of March, awaiting, as is usual, the adjournment of Congress. The document was submitted to Lincoln, who, after pondering a few moments, took up a pen and wrote with his own hand the reply, which he submitted to the Secretaries of State and War. It was then dated, addressed, and signed by Stanton, and telegraphed to Grant. It w^as in these words : " The President directs ' me to say that he wishes you to have no conference with

General Lee unless it be for the capitulation of General Lee's army, or on some minor or purely military matter. He instructs me to say that you are not to decide, discuss, or confer upon any political questions. Such questions the President holds in his own hands, and will submit them to no military conferences or conventions. Meanwhile, you are to press to the utmost your military advantages."

There can be no doubt of the absolute propriety of the decision of the President, nor of the clearness of the language in which it was couched. Grant replied by telegram to the Secretary of War, on the 4th: "Your dispatch of twelve P. M., the 3rd, received. I have written a letter to General Lee, copy of which will be sent you to-morrow. I can assure you that no act of the enemy will prevent me pressing all advantages to the utmost of my ability; neither will I, under any circumstances, exceed my authority, or in any way embarrass the government. It was because I had no right to meet General Lee on the subject proposed by him that I referred the matter for instructions."

His reply to Lee was in these words: " In regard to meeting you on the 6th instant, I would state that I have no authority to accede to your proposition for a conference on the subject proposed. Such authority is vested in the President of the United States alone. General Ord could only have meant that I would not refuse an interview on any subject on which I have a right to act, which, of course, would be such as are purely of a military character, and on the subject of exchanges, which has been intrusted to me."

The result of this attempt was doubtless a woe-
ful disappointment to the rebel authorities. Every door to hope or escape seemed closed. The encircling armies of the nation came nearer day by day, like the walls of that terrible dungeon in the Middle Ages, which approached the prisoner slowly but steadily on every side. The doomed men shut up in Richmond saw their fate in each other's eyes.

On the 5th of March, the day after Grant's letter was received, Jefferson Davis transmitted to the rebel congress a confidential communication from Lee, in regard to " the condition of the country, as connected with defences and supplies." This document was received and considered in secret session, and the awestruck silence of the listeners may be imagined as the appalling message was read from the chief of their armies: " I have received your letter of this date," he said, " requesting my opinion upon the military condition of the country. It must be apparent to every one that it is full of peril, and requires prompt action. My correspondence with the department will show the extreme difficulties under which we have labored the past year to keep this army furnished with necessary supplies. This difficulty is increased, and it seems almost impossible to maintain our present position with the means at the disposal of the government. ... The country within reach of our present position has been exhausted. . . . The only possible relief is in the generous contributions of the people to our necessities, and that is limited by the difficulties of transportation. . . . Unless the men and animals can be subsisted, the army cannot be kept together, and our present lines must be abandoned. Can it be moved to any other position where it can operate to advantage without provisions
to enable it to leave in a body ? ... If the army can be maintained in an efficient condition, I do not regard the abandonment of our present position as necessarily fatal to our success. . . . Everything, in my opinion, has depended and still depends upon the disposition and feeling of the people. Their representatives can best decide how they will bear the difficulties and suffering of their condition, and how they will respond to the demand which the public safety requires."

On the day on which this letter was read, Grant had advices from Sheridan, and telegraphed to Stan-ton : " Last Tuesday Sheridan met Early between Staunton and Charlottesville, and defeated him, capturing nearly his entire command. ... I think there is no doubt Sheridan will at least succeed in destroying the James river canal." On the 12th, he received further intelligence. Sheridan had been extremely successful, but had turned east instead of south, and was now moving to join the army before Kichmond, by the familiar route along the Pamunkey river to White House ; and Grant reported to Stan-ton : " The scouts who brought General Sheridan's dispatch represent having found forage and provisions in great abundance. He also found plenty of horses to remount his men when their horses failed. They say the command is better mounted now than when they left. I shall start supplies and forage for Sheridan to-night. I have also ordered the command that is now on the Potomac to run up to White House and remain there to meet Sheridan." *

* Grant had sent a small force along the west bank of the Potomac to break up a contraband trade existing there. It was these troops that were now ordered to White House to meet Sheridan.

To Sheridan himself he sent a message of encouragement : "Your scouts from Columbia, giving the gratifying intelligence of your success up to that time, have just arrived. ... I congratulate you and the command upon the skill and endurance displayed. ... I send, without delay, one hundred thousand rations and ten days' forage for ten thousand horses. Remain with your command on the Pa-munkey until further orders. I shall not, probably, keep you there many days."

Both Sheridan's movement and that of Stone-man were designed to detain Lee in Richmond, and away from Sherman; and Sheridan undoubtedly prevented the evacuation of the rebel capital, rendering it impossible for Lee to move to Lynchburg at the time proposed. For Grant's object now, as we have seen, was not to obtain possession of the place he had been besieging for a year, but to hem his antagonist in, and postpone as long as possible the national occupation of Richmond. As early as the 3rd of March, he had said to Meade : " For the present, it is letter for us to liold the enemy where he is than to force him south. . . . Sheridan is now on his way to Lynchburg, and Sherman to join Scho-field. After the junction of the two latter is formed, they mil push for Raleigh, North Carolina, and build up the railroad to their rear. To drive the enemy from Richmond now would endanger the success of these two columns. ... It is well to have it understood when and where to attack suddenly, if it should be found at any future time that the enemy are detaching heavily. My notion is that Petersburg will be evacuated simultaneously with any such detaching as would -justify an attack."

108

On the 13th of March, he telegraphed to Stan-ton : " Sheridan is reported to be within five miles of Richmond this morning," and on the 14th, he instructed Meade: " From this time forward keep your command in condition to be moved on the very shortest possible notice, in case the enemy should evacuate, or partially evacuate, Petersburg, taking with you the maximum of supplies your trains are capable of carrying? He evidently meant to follow, and not to return.

On this day also he said to the same commander : " Fitz Lee's cavalry has been ordered on to the Danville road. Private stores, tobacco, cotton, etc., had been turned over to the provost marshal, to be got out of the way, and citizens were ordered to be organized, no doubt to prevent plundering in the city when it is evacuated. The information clearly indicates the intention to fall back to Lynch-burg. Sheridan will be at White House to-day. If there is no falling back for four or five days, I can have the cavalry in the right place." To Sheridan he said, also on the 13th: "Information just received from Richmond indicates that everything was being sent from there to Lynchburg, and that the place would have been cleaned out but for your interruption. I am disposed now to bring your cavalry over here, and to unite it with what we have, and see if the Danville and Southside roads cannot be cut. . . . When you start, I want no halt made until you make the intended raid, unless rest is necessary. In that case, take it before crossing the James." Evidently both Grant and Lee knew the importance to the rebels not only of Lynchburg, but of the Danville road. Both

commanders made their plans with a view to holding the railway and the town.

But, while thus closing and guarding every avenue of escape from the beleaguered capital, and bringing up his forces from north and south and east and west—Sheridan and Sherman and Schofield and Stoneman and Meade—to enmesh and encage and surround at one and the same time both the rebel armies in North Carolina and in Virginia, driving them in to a common centre, as the hunters do their game, Grant was also anxiously supervising the operations he had ordered from the Tennessee and the Mississippi rivers, and from the Gulf of Mexico.

He was becoming dissatisfied with Canby. As early as the 1st of March, he enquired of Halleck: " Was not the order sent for Canby to organize two corps, naming Steele and A. J. Smith as commanders ? I so understood. I am in receipt of a letter saying that Granger and [W. F.] Smith are the commanders. If so, I despair of any good service being done." On the 9th, he said £0 Canby himself : " I am in receipt of a dispatch . . . informing me that you have made requisitions for a construction corps, and material to build seventy miles of railroad. I have directed that none be sent. Thomas's army has been depleted to send a force to you, that they might be where they could act in winter, and at least detain the force the enemy had in the West. If there had been any idea of repairing railroads, it could have been done much better from the north, where we already had the troops. I expected your movements to be co-operative with Sherman's last. This has now entirely failed. I wrote to you long ago, urging you to push promptly

and to live upon the country, and destroy railroads, machine-shops, etc., not to build them. Take Mobile and hold it, and push your forces to the interior, to Montgomery and to Selma. Destroy railroads, rolling stock, and everything useful for carrying on the war, and, when you have done this, take such positions as can be supplied by water. By this means alone you can occupy positions from which the enemy's roads in the interior can be kept broken."

On the 13th, he said to Halleck: " I received a letter from General Canby to-day, of the 1st of March. At that time he said nothing about starting for Mobile. Although I wrote to him he must go in command himself, I have seen nothing from him indicating an intention to do so. In fact, I have seen but little from Canby to show that he intends to do or have anything done."

On the 14th, he telegraphed to Stanton: " I am much dissatisfied with Canby. He has been slow beyond excuse^ [This was always the unpardonable sin in Grant's eyes.] I wrote to him long since that he could not trust Granger in command. After that he nominated him for the command of a corps. I wrote to him that he must command his troops, going into the field in person. On the 1st of March, he is in New Orleans, and does not say a word about leaving there. ... As soon as Sheridan can be spared, I will want him to supersede Canby, and the latter put in command of the Department of the Gulf, unless he does far better in the next few weeks than I now have any reason to hope for." Grant always insisted that obstacles must be overcome. He did not so much blame those who did

not or could not overcome them, but lie wanted some one who could.

Nevertheless, no man knew better how to wait when waiting was inevitable; and he could be patient and forbearing, if there was sufficient reason for the delay of a subordinate. At this very time, the Secretary of War was finding fault with Scho-field, and Grant telegraphed, on the 10th of March, in his defence: " Schofield has been apparently slow in getting started, on account of unprecedented storms and bad weather. There has been but little time when vessels could have run in over the bar, and consequently he was without transportation, and could go no further than men could carry rations to supply them. When he wrote, however, his wagons were arriving, and he was going to start without waiting for full supplies." On the 13th, he said, also to Stanton: " I am in receipt of a letter of the 7th, from General Schofield. At that time Cox was within three miles of Kinston, and repairs on the railroad were going on rapidly. Hoke's division was confronting him. Schofield was going out himself, and expected to push out and take Kinston at once."

On the 14th of March, Grant said to Halleck: " Instruct General Gillmore that if Sherman strikes the sea-coast at any other point than Wilmington before the execution of the transfer of troops, they will join him, wherever he may be."

Of Thomas he enquired on this day : " Has Stone-man started yet on his expedition ? Have you commenced moving troops from Knoxville to Bull's Gap?"

On the 16th of March, Grant heard direct from Sherman, and telegraphed at once to the Secretary

of War: " I am just in receipt of a letter from General Sherman from Fayetteville. He describes his army in fine health and spirits, having met with no serious opposition. Hardee keeps in his front at a respectful distance. At Columbia he destroyed immense arsenals and railroad establishments, and forty-three cannon. At Cheraw he found much machinery and war material, including seventy-five cannon and thirty-six hundred barrels of powder. At Fayetteville, he found twenty pieces of artillery and much other material."

The same day he wrote to Sherman: " I have never felt any uneasiness about your safety, but have felt great anxiety to know just how you were progressing ; I knew, or thought I did, that with the magnificent army with you, you would come out safely some place.

" Ever since you started on the last campaign, and before, I have been attempting to get something done at the West, both to co-operate with you, and to take advantage of the enemy's weakness there to accomplish results favorable to us. Knowing Thomas to be slow beyond excuse, I depleted his army to reinforce Canby so that he might act from Mobile bay in the interior. With all I have said, he had not moved at last advices. Canby was sending a force of about seven thousand men from Vicksburg towards Selma. I ordered Thomas to send Wilson from Eastport towards the same point, and to get him off as soon after the 20th of February as possible. He telegraphed me that he would be off by that date. He is not yet started [March 16], or had not at last advices. I ordered him to send Stoneman from East Tennessee into North-West

South Carolina, to be there about the time you would reach Columbia. He could either have drawn off the enemy's cavalry from you, or would have succeeded in destroying railroads, supplies, and other material which you could not reach. At that time the Richmond papers were full of accounts of your movements, and gave daily accounts of movements in West North Carolina; I supposed all the time it was Stoneman. You may judge my surprise when I afterward learned that Stoneman was still in Louisville, Kentucky, and that the troops in North Carolina were Kirk's forces.

" In order that Stoneman might get off without delay, I told Thomas that three thousand men would be sufficient for him to take. In the meantime I had directed Sheridan to get his cavalry ready, and as soon as the snow in the mountains melted sufficiently, to start for Staunton, and go on and destroy the Virginia Central road and the canal. Time advanced, and he set the 28th of February for starting. I informed Thomas, and directed him to change the course of Stoneman towards Lynchburg, to destroy the road in Virginia as near to that place as possible. Not hearing from Thomas, I telegraphed him about the 12th [March] to know if Stoneman was yet off. He replied that he had not yet started, but that he, Thomas, would start that day for Knoxville to get him off as soon as possible. . . . Sheridan has made his raid with splendid success, so far as heard. I am looking for him at White House."

Thus Stoneman was first ordered to co-operate with Sherman in his march through South Carolina; but Sherman passed through the state before Stoneman started. He was then directed to move into

Virginia to support and co-operate with Sheridan; but Sheridan made his campaign, and arrived at White House, and Stoneman had not yet set out.

On the 19th, Grant said to Thomas: "If Stoneman has not yet got off on his expedition, start him at once with whatever force you can give him. He will not meet with opposition now that can not be overcome by fifteen hundred men. If I am not much mistaken, he will be able to come within fifty miles of Lynchburg."

On the 19th of March, Sheridan arrived at White House with his command. He had started from Winchester on the 27th of February, with ten thousand men, all cavalry. Ouster and Devin were his division generals, and Merritt was chief of cavalry. He took four days' rations in haversacks, and fifteen days' coffee, sugar, and salt in wagons, thirty pounds of forage for each horse, eight ambulances, and his ammunition train. Only two other wagons and a pontoon train for eight boats accompanied the command. His orders were to destroy the Virginia Central railroad and the James river canal, capture Lynchburg, if practicable, and then join Sherman, wherever he might be found, or return to Winchester; but, with regard to joining Sherman, he must be governed by the condition of affairs after leaving Lynchburg. The command was in fine condition, but the weather was bad, for the spring thaws and heavy rains had begun. The snow in the valleys and on the surrounding mountains was fast disappearing, and all the streams were too high to ford.

Sheridan proceeded as rapidly as possible up the Valley, and in two days marched sixty miles.

Guerrillas hovered on his flanks, but did no damage, and no effort was made to molest them. There was some fighting on the third day between Harrison-burg and Mount Crawford, where the enemy attempted to burn a bridge in his front, over the middle fork of the Shenandoah; but two of Sheridan's regiments swam the river above the bridge, and drove the opposing force to Kline's mills, about seven miles from Staunton.

Early, with about three thousand men, was at Staunton, and, as Sheridan approached, the rebel general made a rapid retreat to Waynesboro, whereupon Sheridan entered Staunton. He had now to determine whether to move on Lynchburg, leaving Early in his rear, or to go out and fight him, opening Rockfish Gap, and then pass through the Blue Ridge and destroy the railroads and canal. His instincts were always pugnacious, and he chose the latter course. The rain had been pouring for two days, the roads were bad beyond description, and horses and men could hardly be recognized through the mud that covered them; but Ouster was ordered to take up the pursuit, followed closely by Devin.

Early was found at Waynesboro in a well-chosen position, behind breastworks, with two brigades of infantry and a force of cavalry under Rosser. Ouster, without waiting to make a reconnoissance, and thus allow the enemy to get up his courage by delay, disposed his troops at once for the attack, sending three regiments around the rebel left, which was somewhat exposed, for, instead of resting on the river in the enemy's rear, it was advanced from the stream. Then, in person, with the other two brigades, partly mounted and partly dismounted, he

attacked impetuously, and carried the rebel work, two regiments in columns of fours charging over the breastworks and through the town of Waynesboro, sabring the enemy as they passed, and not stopping till they had crossed the south fork of the Shenan-doah in Early's rear, where they formed with drawn sabres, and held the east bank of the stream. The entire rebel command threw down their arms and surrendered, absolutely cheering at the suddenness with which they had been captured; or else with delight to find themselves prisoners. Early and a few of his officers escaped, hiding in obscure places in the houses of the town, or in the neighboring woods, until dark; but eleven pieces of artillery, two hundred loaded wagons and teams,, seventeen battle flags, and sixteen hundred prisoners were captured, and the crossing of the Blue Ridge was achieved. At any other point this would have been difficult because of the snow. The battle of Waynesboro was fought on the 2nd of March, and before the month was over, Early was relieved from all command, by express direction of Lee.

The prisoners were sent back to Winchester, under guard, and the advance moved to

Charlottes--ville, where the incessant rains had created such a depth of mud that the command was obliged to wait two days for the trains to pass the mountains. This delay compelled Sheridan to abandon the idea of capturing Lynchburg, where the rebels were now prepared. The destruction of the railroad, however, was begun, in the direction of both Gordons ville and Lynchburg. On the 6th of March, one column was sent, under Devin, to destroy every lock on the James river canal for thirty miles, and the other to tear up the railroad to within sixteen miles of Lynchburg. All flour mills, woollen factories, and manufacturing establishments were now demolished, and every bridge was burned between Richmond and Lynchburg.

But Sheridan's eight pontoons would not reach half way across the James, and his scouts reported the enemy concentrating at Lynchburg from the west, while Pickett's infantry and Fitz Lee's cavalry were moving upon the same point from Richmond. The bridges over the James were destroyed, and Sheridan must either return to Winchester or attempt to rejoin Grant. Fortunately, he chose the latter course.

But first he determined to effect a more absolute demolition of the railroads and canal. By hurrying quickly down the canal, and destroying it as far as Goochland, and then moving along the railroad towards Richmond, and tearing that up as close to the city as possible, he felt convinced that he could not only strike a heavy blow at the supplies of the rebel capital and army, but render useless the concentration of troops at Lynchburg. This conception was no sooner formed than acted on, and the entire command moved down the canal. The rain and mud again impeded the advance; the troops were now much worn, and the animals fatigued; but Sheridan replaced his mules with those captured from Early's train; and two thousand negroes who attached themselves to the force rendered effectual aid in the work of destruction. On the 10th of March, he reached Columbia, where he rested a day, and sent a communication to Grant, announcing his success, and requesting that supplies

might be forwarded to White House, on the Pa-munkey river.

He was anxious now about the crossing of the Pamunkey, which the enemy was sure to oppose with a heavy force. His scouts notified him that Pickett and Fitz Lee had returned from Lynchburg, and that Longstreet was preparing to move to prevent the passage of the river; but no advance had yet occurred. Sheridan, however, very well knew that the rebels would be unable to intercept him unless they marched to White House, or in that direction. He, therefore, determined to push boldly towards Richmond, and thus force them to come out and meet him at Ashland. Then he would himself withdraw, cross the North and South Anna rivers, and march rapidly round to White House before the rebels could arrive.

Ouster and Devin accordingly proceeded by different roads towards Ashland, and Longstreet was found only four miles from that place, with Pickett and Johnson's infantry and Fitz Lee's cavalry. The feint had completely succeeded, and Sheridan's course was now entirely clear. One brigade was left to amuse the enemy, while the remainder of the command made haste to cross the North Anna and take up the line of march for White House. Long-street was unable to operate on the Chickahominy, for Grant had given directions to Ord to send out a sufficient force to hold the region along that river. As soon, however, as the rebels discovered their mistake, they moved rapidly towards the Pamunkey, through Hanover court-house, but were unable to cross the river for lack of pontoons. At daylight on the 16th, Sheridan resumed his march, and on the

19th, arrived at "White House, where the bridge had been repaired by orders from Grant, and supplies in abundance awaited his command.

Sheridan's loss during the campaign did not exceed one hundred soldiers, and many of these were the men unable to bear the fatigues of the march. Incessant rain, deep and impassable streams, swamps, mud, and gloom were the impediments offered by nature to his advance. Seventeen pieces of artillery and sixteen hundred prisoners of war were captured. Forty-six canal locks, five aqueducts, forty canal and road bridges, twenty-three railroad bridges, one foundry, one machine • shop, twenty - seven warehouses, forty-one miles of railroad, fourteen mills, and immense quantities of ammunition, gray cloth, saddles, harness, grain, and other supplies were destroyed.

Sheridan's cavalry had annihilated whatever was useful to the enemy between Richmond and Lynch-burg, and, having completed its work in the valley of the Shenandoah, was once more ready to join the army of the Potomac in the struggle which it had shared the year before. Hancock was placed in command of the Middle Military Division, while Sheridan resumed his old command close to Grant, an arrangement welcome to both soldiers, and destined to prove as fortunate for the reputation of the chief as of the subordinate.

The hour had now almost come for Grant himself to strike a blow. The lines were drawn so close that the imprisoned enemy might any day attempt to break the coils, rather than remain to be destroyed, and Grant began to consider what form his- own action should take. On the 16th of March, he said

" Lee has depleted his army but very little recently, and I learn of none going south. The determination seems to be to hold Richmond as long as possible. I have a force sufficient to hold our lines, all that is necessary of them, and move out with plenty to whip his whole army. But the roads are entirely impassable. Until they improve, I shall content myself with watching Lee, and be prepared to pitch into him if he attempts to evacuate the place. I may bring Sheridan over. I think I will, and break up the Danville and Southside railroads. These are the last avenues left to the enemy."

To Sherman on this day he wrote: "When I hear that you and Schofield are together with your back upon the coast, I shall feel that you are entirely safe against anything the enemy can do. Lee may evacuate Richmond, and he cannot get there with force enough to touch you. His army is now demoralized, and deserting very fast, both to us and to their homes. A retrograde movement would cost him thousands of men, even if we did not follow." " My notion," he continued, " is that you should get Raleigh as soon as possible, and hold the railroad from there back. . . . From that point all the North Carolina roads can be made useless to the enemy, without keeping up communication with the rear." "Recruits have come in so rapidly at the West that Thomas has now about as much force as when he attacked Hood. ... I told him to get ready for a campaign towards Lynchburg, if it became necessary. He never can make one there or elsewhere, but the steps taken will prepare for any one else to take his troops and come East, or go towards Rome, whichever may be necessary. I do not believe either will?

On the 17tli of March, he said to Sheridan: "The evening of the 15th, I sent all the cavalry of the army of the James, except necessary pickets, to the Chickahominy, to threaten in that direction, and hold the enemy's cavalry as far as possible. I have ordered them now to move up between the White Oak swamp and the Chickahominy, to attract as much attention as they can, and go as far as they can." This, we have seen, was to cover the national cavalry in its passage between the Pamunkey and the James; for Grant was watching and protecting and supplying Sheridan as closely and carefully and constantly as his great compeers, Sherman and Scho-field, on a different field.

He gave the cavalry little rest, however. On the 19th, the day on which Sheridan arrived at White House, Grant sent him further orders : " Start for this place as soon as you conveniently can; but let me know as early as possible when you will start. I will send cavalry and infantry to the Chickahominy to meet you when you do start. . . . Your problem will be to destroy the Southside and Danville roads, and then either return to this army or go to Sherman, as you deem most practicable." On the 21st, he continued: "I do not want to hurry you, and besides fully appreciate the necessity of having your horses well shod and well rested before starting again on another long march. But there is now such a possibility, if not probability, of Lee and Johnston attempting to unite, that I feel extremely desirous not only of cutting the lines of communication between them, but of having a large and properly commanded cavalry force ready to • act in case such an attempt is made. I think that by Sat-

urday next [March 25th], you liad better start, even if you have to stop here, to finish shoeing up."

This new movement of Sheridan was of extreme importance to the national armies both in Virginia and North Carolina. Lee was at this very time conferring with Johnston in regard to the union of their commands, and all of Johnston's manoeuvres were made with a view to facilitate this result.* Sheridan's movement was intended to prevent it. On the 22nd of March, Grant said to Sherman: " Sheridan will make no halt with the armies operating here, but will be joined by a division of cavalry five thousand five hundred strong, from the army of the Potomac, and will proceed directly to the South-side and Danville roads. His instructions will be to strike the Southside road as near Petersburg as he can, and destroy it so that it can not be repaired for three or four days, and push on to the Danville road as near to the Appomattox as he can get. Then I want him to destroy the road towards Burksville as far as he can, then push on to the Southside road west of Burksville, and destroy it effectually." These, it will be remembered, were the lines and positions to which Lee had announced his intention to retire in the event of the evacuation of Richmond.

" When this movement commences," said Grant, " I shall move out by my left with all the force I can, holding present entrenched lines. I shall start with no distinct view further than holding Lee's forces from following Sheridan. But I shall go along myself, and will take advantage of anything that turns up. If Lee detaches, I will attack, or, if he comes out of his lines, I will endeavor to repulse

* Johnston's " Military Narrative."

him, and follow it up to the best advantage. ... So far, but few troops have been detached from Lee's army. Much machinery has been removed, and material has been sent to Lynchburg, showing a disposition to go there. Points, too, have been fortified on the Danville road. Lee's army is much demoralized, and his men are deserting in great numbers. Probably from returned prisoners and such conscripts as can be picked up, his numbers may be kept up. I estimate his force now at about sixty-five thousand men."

On the 23rd of March, the junction between Sherman and Schofield was formed at Goldsboro.

Sherman had started on his northward march on the 1st of February. On that day his right wing was south of the Salkehatchie river, and his left still struggling in the swamps of the Savannah, at Sister's ferry. As has been shown, he had not the remotest idea of approaching Charleston, but he was able, by seeming preparation, to detain a considerable force of the enemy to contest an advance in that direction, while both his columns were instructed to aim for the South Carolina railroad, west of Branchville. These feints were kept up until he was ready to move.

The Salkehatchie at this time overspread its banks, presenting a formidable obstacle; the enemy also appeared in some force on the opposite side, and cut away all the bridges that spanned the many and deep channels of the swollen stream. But the division generals led their columns through the swamps, the water up to their shoulders, crossed over to the pine land beyond, and then, turning upon the rebels who had opposed the passage, drove them

109

off in utter disorder. All the roads northward had been held for weeks by Wheeler's cavalry, and details of negro laborers had been compelled to fell trees and burn bridges to impede the national march. Sherman's pioneers, however, removed the trees, and the heads of columns rebuilt the bridges before the rear could close up, and the rebels retreated behind the Edisto river at Branchville. Slocum now advanced on the left, and by the 11th of February, the whole command was on the South Carolina railroad, reaching from Midway as far west as Black-ville, with Kilpatrick skirmishing heavily on the left and threatening Augusta. The rebels were now divided; a part, of their force was at Branchville, and part at Aiken and Augusta, while the national army lay between.

Sherman determined to waste no time on Branchville, which the enemy could no longer hold, and turned his columns directly north upon Columbia, where it was supposed the rebels would concentrate. Attempts were made to delay him at the crossings of the rivers ; there were numerous bridge-heads with earth or cotton parapets to carry, and cypress swamps to cross ; but nothing stayed his course. On the 13th, he learned that there was no enemy in Columbia except Hampton's cavalry. Hardee, at Charleston, took it for granted that Sherman was moving upon that place, and the rebels in Augusta supposed that they were Sherman's object; so Charleston and Augusta were protected, while Columbia was abandoned to the care of the cavalry. On the 16th, Sherman had reached the Congaree, opposite the city of Columbia, where the bridge had been burned by the rebels, and he was obliged to wait

ULYSSES S. GRANT.

423

for pontoons. But no force capable of offering resistance was near, and the national columns approached from several directions. Sherman himself was the first to cross the pontoon bridge, and about noon, on the 17th of February, he rode into the capital of South Carolina.

Hampton had ordered all cotton, public and private, to be moved into the streets and fired.* Bales were piled up everywhere, the rope and bagging cut, and the tufts of cotton blown about by the wind, or lodged in the trees and against the houses, presented the appearance of a snow-storm. Some of these piles of cotton were burning in the heart of the town. Sherman, meanwhile, had given orders to destroy the arsenals and public property not needed by his army, as well as railroad stations and machines, but to spare all dwellings, colleges, schools, asylums, and "harmless private property "; and the fires lighted by Hampton were partially subdued by the national soldiers. But before the torch had been put to a single building by Sherman's order, the smouldering fires set by Hampton were rekindled by the wind and communicated to the buildings around. About dark the flames began to spread, and were soon beyond the control of the brigade on duty in the town. An entire division was now brought in, but it was found impossible to check the conflagration, which by midnight had become quite unmanageable. It raged till about four A. M. on the 18th, when the wind subsided, and the flames were got under control.

Sherman was abroad till nearly morning, and Howard, Logan, Wood—his highest generals 1 —were

* Sherman's Report,

laboring all night to save the houses and protect the families of their enemies, thus suddenly deprived of shelter and often of bedding and apparel. Thus, by a calamity, incident indeed to war, but brought about by the mad folly of one of the most reckless of the rebel commanders, who filled a city about to fall into the hands of an enemy with lint, cotton, and tinder, the capital of South Carolina was destroyed. There was a retributive justice in the conflagration, which, though not designed, was felt by the soldiers ; for no man in either rebel or national army but remembered that South Carolina was the state which first seceded from the Union, and that in 1860 the legislature at Columbia did all in its power to precipitate the entire South into a war which many Southerners then deprecated as earnestly as the loyal people of the North *

During the 18th and 19th of February, the destruction of public property was continued. Beau-regard, meanwhile, and the rebel cavalry, had retreated upon Charlotte, in North Carolina, due north from Columbia; and on the 20th and 21st, Sherman followed as far as Winnsboro, sending Kilpatrick to the left, to keep up the delusion that a movement was contemplated in that direction, where Cheat-ham's corps, from Hood's army, was now expected to make a junction with Beauregard. At Winnsboro, however, Sherman turned his principal columns northeastward towards Goldsboro, still two hundred miles away. Heavy rains again impeded his movements,

* There is a story that in one of the battles of the Wilderness a South Carolina regiment, panic-stricken, was flying from the field, when Early, a Virginian, riding up, exclaimed: "God damn you, you got us into this scrape; now help to get us out! "

and much time was necessarily consumed in destroying stores and railroads, and it was not till the 3rd of March that the army arrived at Cheraw. At this point large quantities of guns and ammunition were captured, brought from Charleston under the supposition that here, at least, they would be secure. Hardee had moved due north from Charleston by his only remaining railroad, through Florence, but only reached Cheraw in time to escape with his troops across the Pedee river, just before Sherman arrived. His ordnance and other stores he was obliged to leave behind. The vagrant garrison which had fled from Savannah, and Charleston, and Cheraw, in turn, now set out again on its travels— this time to attempt a junction with Beauregard at Charlotte.

Having secured the passage of the Pedee, however, Sherman had but little uneasiness about the future, for there remained no further great impediment between him and the Cape Fear river, which he felt assured was by this time in the hands of friends. On the 6th of March, he put his army in motion for Fayetteville, on the Cape Fear, north of the boundary line between the Carolinas, and on the direct road to Goldsboro. His course was still north-east, and Kilpatrick was again on the left, to cover the trains. The weather continued unfavorable, and the roads were bad; there was frequent skirmishing with the rebel cavalry ; but on the llth of March, Fayetteville was reached, and Sherman had* traversed the entire extent of South Carolina. On the 12th, he sent a dispatch to Grant, the first since leaving the Savannah.

" We reached this place yesterday," he said, " at

noon, Hardee, as usual, retreating across the Cape Fear, burning the bridges; but our pontoons will be up to-day, and with as little delay as possible I will be after him towards Groldsboro. A tug has just come up from Wilmington, and before I get off from here I hope to get up from Wilmington some shoes and stockings, sugar, coffee, and flour. We are abundantly supplied with all else, having, in a measure, lived off the country. The army is in splendid health, condition, and spirit, although we have had foul weather, and roads that would have stopped travel to almost any other body of men I ever read of.

" Our march was substantially what I designed —straight on Columbia, feigning on Branchville and Augusta. We destroyed, in passing, the railroad from the Edisto nearly up to Aiken; again from Orangeburg to the Congaree; again from Columbia down to Knoxville and the Wateree, and up towards Charlotte as far as the Chester line. ... At Columbia we destroyed immense arsenals and railroad establishments and forty • three cannon; at Cheraw we found also machinery and material of war from Charleston, among which twenty-five guns and thirty-six hundred barrels of gunpowder. Here we find about twenty guns and a magnificent United States arsenal.* ... If I can now add Goldsboro

* " We cannot afford to leave detachments, and I shall therefore destroy this valuable arsenal, for the enemy shall not have its use, and the United States should never again confide such valuable property to a people who have betrayed a trust.

"I could leave here to-morrow, but want to clear my column of the vast crowd of refugees and negroes that encumber me. Some I will send down the river in boats, and the balance I will send to Wilmington by land, under small escort, as soon as we are across Cape Fear river."— Sherman to Grant, March 12.

without too much cost, I will be in a position to aid you materially in the spring campaign. Joe. Johnston may try to interpose between me here and Scho-field above Newbern, but I think he will not try that, but concentrate his scattered armies at Raleigh, and I will go straight at him as soon as I get my men re-clothed and our wagons re-loaded."

On the 15th of March, the command began its march for Goldsboro; the Seventeenth and Fifteenth corps on the right, the Fourteenth and Twentieth on the left, and the cavalry acting in close concert with the left flank. As far as Fay-etteville, Sherman had succeeded in interposing his superior army between the scattered portions of the enemy's command. But he was now aware that the fragments driven from Columbia had been reinforced by Cheatham from the army of the Tennessee, as well as by the garrison of Augusta, and ample time had been given for these to move to his front and flank at Raleigh. Hardee also had crossed the Cape Fear river in advance of Sherman, and was, therefore, able to effect a junction with the other rebel forces. All these troops, indeed all the troops of the enemy in North Carolina, were now under the command of Johnston, who was skilful and wary, and familiar with Sherman's strategy. He would be misled by neither feints nor false reports. Sherman ^estimated the entire rebel force at thirty-seven thousand infantry and eight thousand cavalry; but only Hardee, with ten thousand infantry and one division of cavalry, was in the immediate front. The bulk of the rebel army was supposed to be concentrating on the northwest, at, or in the neighborhood of Raleigh. Sher-

man was determined to give his antagonist as little time for organizing as possible. He felt almost certain that his own left would be attacked, and sent the trains by interior roads, holding eight divisions ready for immediate battle.

On the 15th of March, as he had anticipated, the left, under Slocum, came up with Hardee's force. The rebels, in retreating from Fayetteville, had halted in a narrow swampy neck at Averysboro, between the South and the Cape Fear rivers, and at the junction of the roads to Raleigh and Goldsboro. They evidently hoped to hold Sherman while Johnston concentrated in the rear. It was necessary to dislodge Hardee in order to secure the Goldsboro road, and also to keep up the feint on Ealeigh as long as possible. Sherman proposed to drive Hardee well beyond Averysboro, and then turn to the right, and move by Bentonsville on Goldsboro. Slocum was therefore ordered to press on and carry the rebel position, an attempt rendered difficult by the ground, which at this point was so soft that horses everywhere sank, and even the men could hardly make their way across the common pine barren.

The rebels offered a stubborn resistance, and on the 16th, a brigade was sent to make a wide circuit to the left and catch their line in flank. This movement was entirely successful; the first line of the enemy was swept away; two hundred and seventeen men were captured, and one hundred and eighty killed. Late in the afternoon Slocum's whole command advanced, and drove Hardee within his entrenchments. The night was stormy and the roads were wretched, but in. the morning the enemy was gone. In this action, known as the battle of Averys-

boro, Sherman lost seventy-seven men killed and four hundred and seventy-seven wounded. Hardee reported his loss at five hundred.

From Averysboro both wings turned eastward by different roads, and on the night of the 18th of March, the army was within twenty-seven miles of Goldsboro, and only five from Bentonsville. The columns were now about ten miles apart. Since leaving Fayetteville, Sherman had remained at the left with Slocum's wing, but now, supposing all danger in that direction past, he crossed over to Howard's column, to be near Schofield and Terry, whom he expected to meet at Goldsboro. During the day, however, word was brought him that near Bentonsville Slocum had come upon the entire rebel army.

Johnston, the night before, had marched his whole command, with great rapidity and without unnecessary wheels, intending to overwhelm Sherman's left flank before it could be relieved by its cooperating column. Bragg, Cheatham, Hardee, Hampton, and all the troops the enemy could draw from every quarter were concentrated, and on the morning of the 19th, the head of Slocum's column, as it advanced, at first encountered cavalry, but soon found its progress obstructed by infantry and artillery. The enemy attacked with vigor and gained a temporary advantage, capturing three guns and driving two of the national brigades back upon the main body. But as soon as Slocum perceived that he had the whole of Johnston's army in his front, he deployed two divisions, and, bringing two more rapidly up, arranged them in a defensive line, and hastily threw up barricades. Kilpatrick also came upon the field, and was

massed on the left flank. In this position Slocum received six distinct assaults from the combined forces of Hoke, Hardee, and Cheathain, under the immediate command of Johnston, without giving an inch of ground, and himself doing good execution on the enemy's ranks, especially with artillery.

The moment Sherman was informed of this attack, he sent back orders to act defensively, until he could arrive with reinforcements. He hoped that Slocum would be able to hold Johnston facing west until Howard came up in the rebel rear from the east; and the Fifteenth corps was turned at once toward Bentonsville, while the Seventeenth was ordered to move direct to Slocum's right.

On the morning of the 20th, the Fifteenth corps closed down on Bentonsville, and struck a line of fresh-made parapet. Howard was therefore ordered to proceed with caution until he effected a junction with Schofield. These developments occupied the entire day. Johnston now took up a position in the form of the letter V, the apex reaching the road leading from Averysboro to Goldsboro. Mill creek, with a single bridge, was in his rear, but his flanks were covered by the endless swamps of the region. His lines embraced the village of Bentonsville. Slocum faced one side of the V, and Howard the other ; and Sherman, being uncertain as to Johnston's strength, was disinclined to invite a battle. He had been out from Savannah since the last of January, and his wagons contained but little food. He knew also that Schofield and Terry were approaching Goldsboro from the coast. During the 20th, therefore, he simply held his ground, and started his trains to Kinston for supplies.

ULYSSES S. GRANT.

431

On the 21st, it began to rain, and Sherman remained quiet till noon, when Mower, in Howard's command, broke through the rebel line on their extreme left flank, and pushed with his division straight towards Bentonsville and the bridge across Mill creek—the only line of retreat open to the enemy. But Sherman ordered Mower back to connect with his own corps, and, lest the rebels should concentrate on him, directed a strong skirmish fire to be opened against the entire line of the enemy. Had he followed Mower's lead with the whole right wing, a general battle must have ensued, and the national forces were so vastly superior that success would have been assured. But Sherman preferred to make a junction with Schofield and Terry before engaging Johnston, of whose strength he was ignorant.* During the night the enemy retreated on Smithfield, leaving his pickets to fall into the national hands, with many dead unburied, and the wounded in the hospitals.

The heaviest fighting at Bentonsville was on the 19th, when Johnston struck the head of

Slocum's column, forcing back a division; but as soon as Slocum brought up his troops, he repulsed all attacks, and held his ground, as ordered, to await the arrival of the right wing. The total national loss was one hundred and ninety-one killed, and fourteen hundred

* " I think I made a mistake there, and should rapidly have followed Mower's lead, with the whole of the right wing, which would have brought on a general battle, and it could not have resulted otherwise than successfully to us, by reason of our vastly superior numbers ; but at the moment, for the reasons given, I preferred to make junction with Generals Terry and Schofield, before engaging Johnson's army, the strength of which was utterly unknown."—Sherman's "Memoirs," vol. ii., page 304.

and fifty-five wounded and missing. Johnston states his losses to have been two hundred and twenty-three killed, fourteen hundred and sixty - seven wounded, and six hundred and fifty-three missing; but Sherman captured sixteen hundred and twenty-one prisoners.*

Sherman admits that he committed an error in not overwhelming his enemy. Few soldiers, however, are great enough to accuse themselves of an error, and fewer still but might accuse themselves of greater ones than can ever be laid at Sherman's door.

At daybreak on the 22nd, pursuit was made of the rebels for two miles beyond Mill creek, but it was checked by Sherman's order, and the road being clear, the army moved to Goldsboro, where Schofield had already arrived. On the 25th, the road front Newbern was complete, and the first train of cars came up from the coast. Sherman therefore was able to supply his command.

Thus was concluded one of the longest and most important marches ever made by an organized army in civilized war. The distance from Savannah to Goldsboro is four hundred and twenty-five miles.

* General Johnston declares that his entire force of infantry and artillery in this battle was fourteen thousand one hundred. But the rebel returns of troops under his command at this time are as follows:

Effectives.
Army of Tennessee, March 31st 16,014
Hardie, January 31st 22,654
Bragg, February 10th 11,200
Total 49,868

Making every allowance for detachments, desertions, losses at Averys-boro, in front of Schofield, and elsewhere, he should have had thirty thousand men in front of Sherman. See Appendix to vol. ii., chap, xxiv.

Five large navigable rivers had been crossed—the Edisto, Broad, Catawba, Pedee, and Cape Fear, at either of which a comparatively small force, well handled, might have made the passage difficult, if not impossible. The country generally was in a state of nature, with innumerable swamps, and the roads were masses of mud, nearly every mile of which had to be corduroyed. Columbia, Cheraw, and Fayette-ville—all important depots of supplies, had been captured, the evacuation of Charleston rendered inevitable, all the railroads of South Carolina had been broken up, and a vast amount of food and forage essential to the enemy for the support of his armies had been consumed. The breadth of country traversed averaged forty miles. The journey had been accomplished in mid-winter, in fifty days, the men marching on an average ten miles a day, and resting ten days on the road. When Goldsboro was reached the army was in superb order, and the teams were almost as fresh as when they started from Atlanta.

Schofield, we have seen, was at Goldsboro when Sherman arrived. Immediately after the capture of Wilmington, he had begun his preparations to move to the interior, and repair the railroads, as well as to supply Sherman by the Cape Fear river, at Fayetteville, if this should become necessary. On account of the difficulty in collecting transportation, his advance was made in two columns—one starting from Newbern, and the other from Wilmington. He himself was with the larger force at Newbern, while Terry commanded that which moved from Wilmington. On the 6th of March, both were in motion for Goldsboro. Hoke's command, with a reinforcement from the army of Hood, was in front

of Schofield, and before the national troops had all arrived an attempt was made to prevent their junction. On the 8th, the head of Schofield's column was driven back with a loss of seven hundred prisoners. On the 11th, the attack was renewed, but repelled with severe loss to the enemy, who fell back across the Neuse, destroying the bridge. In this action Schofield's loss was three hundred men. He had no pontoon train, however, and was obliged to wait till the bridge was rebuilt. On the 14th, this was effected, and the enemy at once abandoned Kinston, and moved off to join Johnston's army. Schofield now put a large force of men at work on the reconstruction of the railroad, and brought up supplies. On the 2 0th, he moved from Kinston, and on the 21st of March, took possession of Goldsboro.

Terry, meanwhile, had marched from Wilmington on the 15th; he reached Faison's depot without opposition on the 20th, and on the 22d secured the crossing of the Neuse, and communicated with Sherman.

The result of the various operations of Sherman, Schofield, and Terry was that the whole sea-coast from Savannah to Newbern, with the forts, dockyards, and gunboats, had fallen into the national hands, and one hundred thousand soldiers were now in a position easy of supply, whence they could take an important part in any further operations directed by Grant.

And now, at last, all the great armies were in the positions designated by the general-in-chief. On the 20th of March, Stoneman started in East Tennessee, and the same day Canby moved against Mobile; on the 23rd, the junction between Sherman and Schofield

was effected at Goldsboro; on the 24th, Sheridan set out from White House to rejoin the army of the Potomac after a separation of nearly eight months; and on that day Grant issued his orders to Meade and Ord and the great cavalry leader for a movement against the right of Lee.

He meant to gather up all the threads, and overlooked no quarter, however distant, of the theatre of war. Pope had superseded Rosecrans in Missouri, and on the 21st of March, Arkansas was added to his command. The same day Grant wrote at length, instructing him to begin offensive operations against Price, and drive him across the Red river. "By taking an early start," he said, "going light, Pope will be able at least to throw the enemy beyond the Red river, not to return again." Then, confident that his plans at the East were approaching their consummation, he instructed his subordinate accordingly. "Movements now in progress may end in such results as to enable me to send you forces enough for any campaign you may want to make, even to the overrunning of Texas. If so, and you want them, they will be promptly sent."

On the 24th, he covered all the ground. To Halleck, on this day, he said: " I have no present purpose of making a campaign with the forces in the Middle Department, but want them in the best possible condition for either offensive or defensive operations. If Lee should retreat south, the surplus force under Hancock * could be transferred to another field. If he should go to Lynch burg, they will be required where they are." No contingency was forgotten, no preparation omitted. -

* Hancock had been placed in command of the Middle Department when Sheridan rejoined Grant.

And now Grant waited only for the arrival of Sheridan from the Pamunkey. On the 20th of March, he invited the President to pay him a visit at City Point. Lincoln assented at once, and arrived on the 22nd. On the 25th, Sherman, leaving Schofield in command, also started for City

Point. He had not been summoned, but was naturally anxious to communicate in person with his chief after the long series of important operations in which he had been engaged, as well as to receive orders in regard to his future movements. Grant met him at the steamboat landing, with more than a cordial welcome, and the great brothers in arms went together to pay their respects to the President. Admiral Porter was also present at the interview, and Lincoln listened with the keenest interest to Sherman's graphic story of his march.

There was nothing like a council of war, for Grant never held one in his life. He listened always with proper deference to the views of those of his subordinates who were entitled to offer them, and was never unwilling to receive ideas or information from any source; but his plans were his own, and were invariably announced in the shape of orders. Even when he seemed to adopt the views that were presented to him, those who offered them never knew it at the time, nor did they ever know whether he had conceived them in advance. He never claimed to have originated them, nor did he ever acknowledge an indebtedness. All was left in that obscurity which enveloped so much of his intellectual individuality, and never allowed any one, friend or follower, no matter how intimate, to know his intentions or convictions before they were fully formed.

ULYSSES S. GRANT.

437

In this crisis, lie asked no advice on military matters from the President, who offered none; and he listened to Sherman's eager and restless eloquence, suggestive' and advisory, yet deferential and subordinate, but said nothing in return more definite than he had already written. If there was a man living whose advice in such matters he would have sought, that man was certainly Sherman; and, as he had written and said, if Sherman had been his superior, Grant would have obeyed absolutely; but it was never his nature to seek advice; he sought only information, and without vanity or self-assertion, he came to his own conclusions. He did this always. He did so now.

Meade and Sheridan and Ord were invited to meet Sherman, and on the 28th of March, Grant's little hut was crowded with an illustrious company. On the same day they separated. Sherman returned to his army; the others to their own commands; each thoroughly informed of the part he was to bear in the approaching campaign.

no

CHAPTER XXXII.

Forces before Richmond and Petersburg, March 25, 1865—Grant's dispositions in Virginia and North Carolina—Order for movement in front of Petersburg—Rebel attack on Fort Steadman—Repulse of rebels—Desperate strategy of Lee—Movement of Grant to left, March 29th—Relations of Grant and Sheridan—Characteristics of Grant's strategy—Situation, March 30th—Sheridan ordered to take Five Forks—Lee masses one-third of his army against Grant's left—Warren disposes his forces contrary to orders—Attack on Warren—Repulse of Warren—Dissatisfaction of Grant —Unfortunate peculiarities of Warren—Advance of Humphreys and Warren—Pickett sent against Sheridan—Battle of Dinwiddie—Advance of Pickett—Repulse of rebels on Chamberlain's creek—Pickett pierces Sheridan's centre—Sheridan attacks in return—Sheridan forced back to Dinwiddie—Sheridan holds Dinwiddie—Generalship of Sheridan—Situation, March 31st—Sheridan not dismayed—Grant determines to reinforce Sheridan—Warren ordered to Sheridan's support—Urgency of Grant and Meade—Inexcusable delay of Warren—Chagrin of Grant—Disarrangement of Sheridan's plan—Advance of Sheridan without Warren—Sheridan's new plan of battle—Battle of Five Forks—Dispositions of Sheridan—Further obstructiveness of Warren—Advance of cavalry—Assault by Ayres—Gallantry of

Sheridan—Movements of Mackenzie—Deflection of Crawford—Inefficiency of Warren—Second advance of Ayres—Splendid success of Ayres—Movement of Griffin and Crawford—Simultaneous advance of cavalry—Complete victory of Sheridan—Rout of rebels— Pursuit of rebels—Warren relieved from command—Results of battle— Grant's endorsement of Sheridan—Characteristics of Warren and Sheridan.

ON the 25th of March, 1865, Lee had still seventy thousand effective men in the lines at Richmond and Petersburg, while the armies of the Potomac and the James and Sheridan's cavalry, constituting Grant's immediate command, numbered one hundred and

eleven thousand soldiers.* After the long campaign through the Carolinas, Sherman could not be ready to move again until the 10th of April, but on that day he was to start for the Roanoke river, and thence

* The misstatements of the rebels in regard to the numbers engaged in the final campaign of the war are more flagrant than can readily be believed. Colonel Taylor, adjutant-general of the army of Northern Virginia, in a work entitled " Four Years with General Lee," announces that he has been allowed access to the captured documents in the Rebel Archive office at Washington, and, after "careful examination of the field and monthly returns," he presents what he calls " an authoritative statement of the strength of the army which Lee commanded," extracted from these returns.

Omitting any mention of the sick, the extra-duty men, or those in arrest, Colonel Taylor asserts that on the 28th (he should say 20th) of February, 1865, the date of Lee's last return, the rebel general had exactly 39,879 muskets available. But, in order to make this showing, he excludes from his computation not only the sick, the extra-duty men, and those in arrest, 13,728 in number, but all officers, all artillery, all cavalry, all detached commands, all of Early's force in the Valley, which joined Lee for his last campaign, and all the troops, regular and local, in Richmond. He calculates that, in the attack on Fort Steadman on the 25th of March, Lee lost from 2,500 to 3,000 men, and that during the month of March about 3,000 rebels deserted. Thus, on the 31st of March, says Taylor, Lee had only 33,000 muskets with which to defend his lines. This number he contrasts with an effective total, which he ascribes to Grant, of 162,239. But this total of Grant's includes the sick, the extra-duty men, those in arrest, the officers, the cavalry, the artillery, and the troops in Ord's department at Fort Monroe, Norfolk, and other places a hundred miles from Richmond, as well as the cavalry of Sheridan left in the Middle Military Division.

The actual facts are as follows : Lee reported present for duty on the 20th of February, 1865, 59,094 men, and 73,349 aggregate, in the army of Northern Virginia alone. Ewell, in command of the Department of Richmond, reported, on the same day, 4,391 effective, and 5,084 aggregate present, making 63,485 effective "regular soldiers, and 78,433 aggregate. In addition to the extra-duty men, nearly all of whom the rebels habitually put into battle, there were the local reserves and the crews of the gunboats, who were all at the front in the last engagements, and who took good care to count themselves as soldiers when the time came to be paroled. Lee had not less than 75,000 available fighting men on the 1st of March. He probably lost 2,500 after that time by desertion, and 2,500 or 3,000 in the attack on Fort

either strike the Danville road or join the forces operating against Richmond, as the general-in-chief might determine. Grant's own movement to the left was fixed for the 29th of Maiach, and, unless it was immediately and completely successful, he meant to send Sheridan to destroy the Danville and Southside railroads, and then allow him to move into North Carolina and join Sherman. By this strategy the commands of Lee and Johnston would both be enclosed and driven to a common centre. If they attempted to unite in order to fall upon Sherman, Grant would follow Lee as rapidly as possible; or, if events rendered this course unadvisable, Sherman could be brought to Grant whenever necessary; while Sheridan moved between, destroying the communications of both the rebel armies.

Grant had now spent many days of anxiety lest each morning should bring the news that the enemy had retreated the night before. He was firmly convinced that the crossing of the Roanoke by Sherman would be the signal for Lee to leave; and if Johnston and Lee were combined, a long and tedious and expensive campaign, consuming most of the summer, might become inevitable. His anxiety was well founded; for, during Sherman's delay, the rebel

Steadman ; so that on the 29th'of March he had an army of 70,000 as good soldiers as ever fought.

The field returns of Meade, Prd, and Sheridan for the 30th of March, precisely similar in character to those of Lee, show, in the

Present for duty, equipped.
Army of the Potomac 69,751
Army of the James 27,701
Army of Sheridan 13,695
Total 111,047
See Appendix for the returns of rebel and national commands, complete.

commanders were conferring in order to effect a junction.* Sherman had recommended that Grant should wait for his arrival from North Carolina before taking the initiative, and thus make the result absolutely secure; but the general-in-chief considered that by moving out now and destroying the railroads, he would not only put the armies before Richmond in a better position for pursuit, but retard the concentration of Lee and Johnston, besides compelling the rebels to abandon important material which they might otherwise be able to remove.

He had also another reason for preferring immediate action. The army of the Potomac was in front of its original enemy, with which it had been contending for four weary years, in battles and marches and sieges and campaigns. At last, it had its antagonist down. If assistance was summoned before the final blow, it would be said, and believed by many, that the Eastern troops were unable of themselves to conquer their adversary. But the army of Lee was in reality at the mercy of its old-time foe ; there was no need to call in aid, no need to share the victory. The Western men had laurels enough and to spare. Grant thought of the soldiers he had led for a year, and reserved for them alone the reward they had fairly earned.

On the 24th of March, the orders for the movement were issued. Parke and Wright were at first to be left in the trenches in front of Petersburg, but all of Meade's command except the Ninth corps was under marching orders. Ord, with three divisions from the army of the James, was also to join the moving column, leaving Weitzel in command north

* Johnston's "Military Narrative."

of the river and at Bermuda Hundred. To the force which Sheridan had brought from the Valley, was added the cavalry of the army of the Potomac, under Crook, and eventually about fifteen hundred troopers belonging to Ord. It was then reported to the general-in-chief that Meade could move with sixty thousand effective men, Ord with seventeen thousand, and Sheridan with twelve thousand; in all about ninety thousand soldiers. This was Grant's disposable force.

The object of the operation was announced to the principal commanders in identical language. " On the 29th instant," said Grant, " the armies operating against Richmond will be moved by our left, for the double purpose of turning the enemy out of his present position around Petersburg, and to ensure the success of the cavalry under General Sheridan, ... in its effort to reach and destroy the Southside and Danville roads." * First of all, Ord was to proceed on the night of the 27th, to the left of the army of the Potomac, and relieve the Second corps, now under the command of Humphreys, f On the morning of the 29th, Warren and Humphreys were to move in two columns, taking the roads crossing Hatcher's run nearest the national lines, and both marching at first in a south-westerly direction. At the same time Sheridan, advancing by the Weldon and Jerusalem plank roads far enough south to avoid the infantry, was to pass through Dinwiddie, and then turn to the north and west against the right and rear of the enemy. The Sixth corps would remain in

* See Appendix for this entire order.

t Humphreys had succeeded Hancock in command of the Second corps in November, 1864.

the trenches between Ord and Parke, awaiting the turn of events.

The troops were to start with four days' rations in haversacks and eight days' in wagons, and that Ord might have the same amount of supplies as Meade, he was directed to accumulate rations in advance along the road, and fill up his trains in passing. Sixty rounds of ammunition per man were to be taken in wagons, and as much grain as the trains could carry. The densely wooded character of the country prevented the use of a large artillery force, and not more than six or eight guns were allowed to a division, at the option of army commanders.

The forces of Parke and Wright were to be massed and ready to attack in case the enemy weakened his line in their front, and Weitzel also was instructed to keep vigilant watch, and to break through at any point where it might prove at all practicable. " A success north of the James," said Grant, " should be followed up with great promptness ;" but he added: " An attack will not be feasible, unless it is found that the enemy has detached largely. In that case, it may be regarded as evidence that the enemy are relying upon their local reserves,* principally, for the defence of Richmond."

"By these instructions," continued the general-in-chief, " a large part of the armies operating against Richmond is left behind. The enemy, knowing this, may, as an only chance, strip their lines to the merest skeleton, in the hope of advantage not being taken of it, whilst they hurl everything against the moving column, and return. It cannot be impressed too strongly upon commanders left in the trenches, not

* See note to page 439.

to allow this to occur without taking advantage of it. The very fact of the enemy coming out to attack, if he does so, might be regarded as almost conclusive evidence of such a weakening of his lines. I would have it particularly enjoined upon corps commanders that, in case of an attack from the enemy, those not attacked are not to wait for orders from the commanding officers of the army to which they belong, but that they will move promptly, and notify the commander of their action. I would also enjoin the same action on the part of division commanders when other parts of their corps are engaged. In like manner, I would urge the importance of following up a repulse of the enemy."

Grant was thus persisting in the plan he had adopted in June, when he first perceived that a siege of Petersburg was inevitable. He was still stretching out to the left, to complete the extension of his line and the destruction of the last outward avenue of Lee; but he constantly contemplated the possibility that, in the enemy's effort to extend parallel with the national army, the rebel line would be so depleted as to break, and then he meant to take advantage of the opportunity. He had been nearly a year striving to reach the Southside road, and it was nine months since his first attempt to envelop or penetrate the rebel works at Petersburg; but now he had a premonition of success, and made his dispositions and orders with no view of a return. He declared his intention, in case of necessity or opportunity, to separate entirely from his base, and move around to the right and rear of Lee, and thus for ever terminate all communication between him and Johnston's army.

ULYSSES S. GRANT.

445

On the 25th of March, however, Lee made an attack upon the right of Meade's line, in front of the Ninth corps. The point selected was a fort a little more than half a mile from the Appomattox, where the national works crossed the Prince.George courthouse road, and one of the positions gained in the first assaults on Petersburg. The work was a small one, without bastions, known as Fort Steadman, and the opposing lines were not more than a hundred and fifty yards apart, the pickets only fifty yards. At half-past four on the morning of March 25th, long before dawn, the rebels moved against Parke's line east of Fort Steadman, with Gordon's corps, reinforced by Bushrod Johnson's division.* Taking advantage of Grant's order allowing deserters to bring their arms with them across the lines, they sent forward squads of pretended deserters, who by this ruse gained possession of several of the picket posts. These were closely followed by a strong storming party of picked men, and this again by three heavy columns. Parke's pickets were overwhelmed after one discharge of their pieces; the trench guard, though resisting stoutly, was unable to withstand the rush of numbers, and the main line was broken.

The rebels turned at once to the right and left, and their right-hand column soon gained a small battery, open in the rear, from which they assaulted Fort Steadman. The garrison, consisting of a battalion of heavy artillery, made a vigorous resistance, but being attacked in front, flank, and rear, was overpowered; most of the men were captured, and the guns were turned at once on the national troops on either side. The enemy then pushed gradually

* Parke's Report.

westward, driving the garrisons from several unenclosed batteries. It was still quite dark, and almost impossible to distinguish friend from foe; this, of course, augmented the difficulty of forming the troops to check the progress of the enemy, and rendered the use of artillery from a distance at first altogether impracticable.

But as soon as Parke was made aware of the assault, he brought up his artillery on the hills in rear of the point attacked, and gave orders to re-occupy the captured work. Hartranft, on the left, massed his division- promptly, though one regiment was five miles away; and the rebel skirmishers, who were advancing towards the military railroad that connected Meade's front with City Point, were driven back to the line of works. The column that had turned to the national right was also checked, so that time was gained to bring up reinforcements and form a strong line perpendicular to the entrenchments, which repulsed all further advance of the enemy in that direction. Meanwhile the rebel column, moving westward, had gained temporary possession of several batteries, but the garrisons of these works quickly rallied, and also formed a line perpendicular to the entrenchments, checking any advance towards the national left. At half-past seven, all the open batteries but one had been regained, and a cordon of troops was drawn around Fort Steadman, which forced the rebels back to a point where they were exposed to a concentrated fire from the artillery now opening from the rear. The enemy meanwhile made no attempt to relieve or support the assaulting column.

At 7.45 A. M., Hartranft advanced from the left

with, his whole division to retake the fort. Most of his troops were raw, and for the first time under fire, but they charged with great spirit and resolution, and the work was recaptured with comparatively little loss. The cross-fire of infantry and artillery prevented many of the enemy from even attempting to escape, and nineteen hundred and forty-nine were captured. The whole line was at once re-occupied, and during the following night all damage was repaired. Neither guns nor colors were lost.

This whole battle was fought by Parke, for Meade was at Grant's head-quarters, at City Point, when the first news of the attack was received; the rebels had cut the telegraphic wires, and intelligence came only by courier, so that before Meade could return to the front Fort Steadman had been re-carried. Parke was senior in the trenches, and directed Wright and Warren each to move a division to the

o

threatened point, but the assistance was not required. Parke lost seventy killed, four hundred and twenty-four wounded, and five hundred and twenty-three missing; total, one thousand and seventeen. The enemy was permitted, under a flag of truce, to carry away one hundred and twenty dead and fifteen severely wounded.

When Meade arrived on the field, he promptly ordered Wright and Humphreys to advance and feel the enemy in their respective fronts, west of Parke, but Humphreys had already advanced without orders. Then, pushing forward, the two corps carried the enemy's strongly entrenched picket line in front of their own, and captured eight hundred and thirty-four prisoners. The rebels made several desperate

attempts to retake this line, but without success; it remained in the national hands. The loss in these two corps was fifty-two killed, eight hundred and twenty-four wounded, and two hundred and seven missing ; that of the rebels was probably greater, as they were repelled in several severe assaults.

Ord as well as Meade was at Grant's headquarters, discussing the preparations for the 29th, when the report of the first assault arrived; and Grant at once notified Gibbon, who had been left in command of the army of the James. "This," he said, " may be a signal for leaving. Be ready to take advantage of it." To Meade, after the results of the day were known, he telegraphed: " Your last dispatch reflects great credit on the army for the promptness with which it became the attacking force after repelling an unexpected assault." The next day he recommended that Parke and Humphreys should be announced in orders as commanders of their respective corps, a military compliment they had not yet received ; and that Hartranft should be brevetted major-general for " conspicuous gallantry in driving the enemy from the lodgment made in the national lines."

The object of this movement of Lee was somewhat of a puzzle to Grant, and has never been satisfactorily explained. Lee could hardly have hoped to do any serious damage to Grant's communications with City Point, and he massed too large a force for the assault to make it practicable for him, whether it succeeded or not, to move his army by the right flank from Petersburg.* If it was intended to en-

* It has, indeed, been asserted that Lee designed, under cover of this attack, to evacuate his lines ; but not a shadow of authority for

courage the flagging spirit of the South, the attempt signally failed; the movement was neither felicitous in conception nor successful in execution; and the only result was that several thousand rebels were killed or taken prisoner, and Lee was obliged to ask permission to collect his wounded and bury his dead in the space between what had been his picket line and his main fortifications; while Grant gained ground destined to be of decided advantage before another week had passed.

This was the first and only unprovoked assault made by Lee after the battle of Spottsylvania. In all the varied opportunities of battle or campaign, the rebel general had never once been tempted to expose himself to the chances of attack, unless Grant had first assaulted him. For nearly eleven months he had not invited battle; but now, under the most discouraging circumstances, he moved a column against a strong defensive work, where a single corps was able to repel him without assistance, and no possibility of success was apparent to the most

the statement has been shown. There is no mention of such a purpose in any document that has been preserved ; no evidence in any quarter of any preparation to take advantage of the assault in order to withdraw.

It is a common manoeuvre for some rebel advocate or apologist to assert that such and such was the intention or result of a certain operation, without giving the slightest proof of the correctness of the statement ; and then for all the rest to quote him as authority. If, being a bitter enemy of the national cause or its most successful champions, he represents himself as a Northern writer, he is forthwith claimed by rebels and sympathizing foreigners as an unwilling witness to the truth telling against his own side, whereas his testimony has been carefully manufactured with hostile design.

No statement of national or rebel intentions, or strength, or losses, or of any material fact on either side, should be accepted without positive proof of its correctness ; and it is not sufficient to mention an authority ; the absolute quotation should be verified.

partial critics. It seemed almost as if the great defender was becoming dazed by misfortune, and, finding himself shut in by lines of soldiers that he could not break, was madly dashing against the walls he had no hope of penetrating. The marvelous sagacity, and the still more marvelous patience, for which he had once been known, were beginning to fail.

It may be that he did not dare to lead his troops from Richmond without one effort to break through the cordon which enveloped him. It may be that he had received positive orders from Davis to assault. But even then he should have made the attempt at the other extremity of Meade's line, and in any event have withdrawn .the troops from the north side of the James. But the rebel leaders felt that the fates were against them, and it mattered little what they did—their doom was close at hand. To this condition had the strategy and persistency of Grant reduced his opponents.

This battle made no difference whatever in Grant's plans. The army was to move on the 29th of March, and the orders remained unchanged. On the night of the 27th, Ord left the trenches north of the James, and, by daylight on the 29th, he had reached the position assigned him near Hatcher's run. On the 28th, Grant instructed Sheridan: " The Fifth corps will move by the Vaughan road at three A. M. to-morrow morning. The Second moves at about nine A. M., having but about three miles to march to reach the point designated for it to take on the right of the Fifth corps. . . . Move your cavalry at as early an hour as you can, and without being confined to any particular road or roads. You may go out by the nearest roads in rear of the Fifth

corps, pass by its left, and, passing near to or through Dinwiddie, reach the right and rear of the enemy as soon as you can. It is not the intention to attack the enemy in his entrenched position, but to force him out if possible. Should lie come out and attack us, or get himself where he can be attacked, move in with your entire force in your own way, and with the full reliance that the army will engage or follow, as circumstances will dictate. I shall be on the field, and will probably be able to communicate with you."

Grant read these instructions himself to Sheridan, together with some further passages directing him in certain contingencies to proceed to North Carolina and report to Sherman. As he read, he perceived that the latter part of the order was disagreeable to his listener. Sheridan, however, said nothing, and Grant immediately remarked: "Although I have provided for your joining Sherman, I have no idea that it will be necessary. I mean to end this business here." Sheridan's face brightened at once, and he replied with enthusiasm: u That's

what I like to hear you say. Let us end this busi-

t/ «/

ness here." The two natures struck fire from each other in the contact. It was often so with Grant. He was greatly influenced by what his generals felt able or willing to do. When they were ready, he became inspired; but with sluggish or over-careful subordinates, the best-laid plans were liable to be disconcerted, and circumstance seemed seldom opportune. His own genius was then depressed, if not dormant, and he was like a man whose limbs were numb or lame, and refused to answer to his will. With Sherman or Sheridan he moved like a skilful

rider on a high-bred horse; there was only a single impulse between their will and his own.

On the morning of the 29th, the operations began. The Fifth corps started according to orders at three A. M., and the Second at six. At nine o'clock Grant left City Point by the military railroad. The President accompanied him to the train, and wished him and his officers God-speed. " Goodbye, gentlemen," he said; " God bless you all; and remember, your success is my success." Captain Eobert Lincoln, the son of the President, was of the party, serving on Grant's staff. In less than an hour, they arrived at the front, took horses, and joined the moving column.

Parke and Wright now held the works in front of Petersburg, and Ord's line reached to the crossing of the Vaughan road and Hatcher's run; Humphreys was on the left of Ord, extending north-westerly from Dabney's mill; while Wa-rren had the left of the moving column, and by night had marched to the intersection of the Boydton and Quaker roads, a little south of Burgess's mill. Thus on the night of the 29th, the national line was uninterrupted from the Appomattox to the Boydton road, and the army was formed in the following order: Parke, Wright, Ord, Humphreys, Warren. The Fifth corps had met with a slight resistance on the Quaker road, but had driven the rebels back behind their works, and captured a hundred prisoners. This was the only fighting during the day. Lee, not having attacked in the morning, when the national flank was presented to him, had lost his chance. The head-quarters of Grant this night were on Gravelly run, south of the crossing of the Vaughan road.

At dark Sheridan was at Dinwiddie court-house, where the Boydton, Vaughan, Flatfoot, and Five Forks roads converge. He thus protected the left of the army, but, though communication was unobstructed between him and Grant, the lines of the infantry and cavalry were separated by an interval of five miles.

On the night of the 29th, Grant sent word to Sheridan : " Our line is now unbroken from the Appomattox to Dinwiddie. We are all ready, however, to give up all from the Jerusalem plank road to Hatcher's run, whenever the force can be used advantageously. After getting into line south of Hatcher's run, we pushed forward to find the enemy's position. ... I feel now like ending the matter, if it is possible to do so, before going lack. I do not want you, therefore, to cut loose and go after the enemy's roads at present. In the morning, push around the enemy, if you can, and get on to his right rear. The movements of the enemy's cavalry may, of course, modify your action. We will all act together as one army, until it is seen what can be done with the enemy."

Whoever wishes to learn the secret of Grant's success should study this homely little dispatch to Sheridan; for not a few of the traits by which he was most distinguished are indicated in its lines. His unwillingness to take a retrograde step can be seen in the words: " I feel like ending the matter before we go back ;" his constant aim at concentration in: " We will all act together as one army;" his willingness to sacrifice even important objects for the sake of the paramount one in: " We are ready to give up all from the Jerusalem plank road

to Hatcher's run, whenever the forces can be used advantageously;" his preference for the essential, not the weakest, part of the defence as an objective point, in the order to " push around the enemy and get on his right rear; " and his aggressiveness in the determination to see—not what the enemy will do, but " what can be done with the enemy"

There is also apparent in this letter another peculiarity, which at first might not seem indicative of power, but which, nevertheless, was eminently characteristic of the man. I mean the apparent uncertainty, or rather incompleteness, of plan; the allowance for unexpected contingencies, shown in the general terms in which the orders were conveyed, and in the omission to point out the exact line to be pursued to the end. The object was defined, but the means and the manner were left to be modified or developed by events. Grant, indeed, was always ready to conform to the changing actualities as they occurred. He never tied himself tightly down in advance. He never would say positively how he would act, unless he could know positively the circumstances under which he was expected to act. He was always averse to making decisions or assuming responsibilities until they came and stared him full in the face, and there was no avoiding or blinking them. Then he accepted the responsibilities, and announced his decisions, and always at such moments did his best; for he could always trust to his judgment when the emergency arose. In fact, he waited for the moment, and the instinct which never failed him at the moment, but which he could not himself foresee and never would attempt to foretell. So, at this crisis, one of the most important in

his career, lie simply said to Sheridan: " I feel now like ending the matter. Let us see what can be done with the enemy."

During the night of the 29th, the rain fell in torrents, and before morning it became impossible to move anything on wheels, except as corduroy roads were laid. The country was covered with forests and full of swampy streams; the soil was either clay or sand, and, when these were mixed, the result was a treacherous quicksand. The frosts of winter were just disappearing, and men and animals found little support in the soft and shifting mass. 'The movement of troops was thus rendered nearly impracticable. At this juncture, some of those nearest to Grant strove hard to induce him to order the army to return. Grant listened, but remained of the opinion that his only course, in spite of rain and roads and opposition, was to continue the movement to the end. It was suggested that Johnston might march up from the south and attack the rear of the army. " I wish he would," said Grant; " I would turn around and dispose of him, and then be freer to attack Lee." Meade was not sanguine, and said little; but others strongly urged a retrograde movement. It is easy, however, to advise the most momentous course when a man has not to bear the responsibility which he expects another to assume; and those who are readiest to urge or recommend are often the first to shrink from action or its consequence themselves.

This morning all was gloomy and uncomf ortable. The pouring rain, the struggling beasts that sank to their bellies in the quicksand in front of Grant's head-quarters, the necessary inaction of the army, all

conspired to produce unsatisfactory sensations, until, like a gleam of light, Sheridan, with his cheery manner and never-failing confidence, came riding up from Dinwiddie, to confer with Grant about " ending the matter." The general-in-chief was occupied at the moment in his tent, and Sheridan waited outside at the camp-fire with the staff. He was full of pluck, anxious for his orders, certain that the enemy would be beaten if an attack was made. His splendid talk roused every flagging spirit, and converted every man who dreamed of counselling return. The officers,' who felt the influence of his magnetic manner and stirring words, and knew how apt .Grant was to be affected by the temper of his subordinates, believing that those who expect success are almost certain to succeed; aware, too, how especially he appreciated the soldierly instinct as well as the judgment of Sheridan, urged the cavalry leader to repeat to the chief what he had said to them. Sheridan, however, was modest, and, after all his victories in the Valley, and the reputation they had won for him, was averse to obtruding his opinions on his superior. He thought it a soldier's duty to obey; to carry out the plans of his chief, not to suggest a course for him, at least without invitation. But those who had the right took the great trooper in to Grant, and urged the general to listen to his talk. Grant needed little urging either to listen or to act at this juncture. He saw at once that, with such a subordinate, advance was the safest course. He sympathized with his ardor for battle, and was confirmed in his own aggressive intentions; and Sheridan went back to Dinwiddie with orders to gain possession of Five Forks.

The rebel line at this time extended along the White Oak road to a point about two miles west of Burgess's mill, where it turned abruptly to the north. Four miles west of this point the White Oak road is crossed by that from Dinwiddie as it runs to the Southside railway. Still another road from the south comes in at the junction, and thus the " Five Forks" is formed. It is only two miles from the Southside road, and was, therefore, of vital consequence in all the movements of either army. If Five Forks was gained by Grant, Lee could not remain in Petersburg.

Sheridan pushed out a division from Dinwiddie, but found the enemy in force at the junction, and the condition of the roads still prevented any serious attack by the cavalry. Warren, at the same time, was advanced until his left extended across the Boydton, and in the direction of the White Oak, road. He, too, found the enemy strong in his front, extending westward, but was directed to hold and fortify his new position. Humphreys, meanwhile, drove the rebels behind their main line on Hatcher's run, near Burgess's mill, and Ord, Wright, and Parke made examinations in their fronts to determine the feasibility of assault; for, as the enemy now confronted the national army at every point from Richmond to the Boydton road, Grant concluded that the rebel lines must be weakly held, and could be penetrated, if his estimate of Lee's forces was correct. Wright and Parke reported favorably to an assault, and Grant determined, therefore, to extend his line no further, but to reinforce Sheridan with a corps of infantry, and enable him to turn the rebel flank, while the other corps assaulted the enemy's works in front.

The picket line captured from Lee, after the attack on Fort Steadman, on the 25th, especially favored this design, for it threw the belligerents, at some points, so close to each other that it was but a moment's run between the lines. Preparations were accordingly made for an assault.

To Sheridan he said at the same time: " If your situation is such as to justify the belief that you can turn the enemy's right with the assistance of a corps of infantry entirely detached from the balance of the army, I will so detach the Fifth corps, and place the whole under your command for the operation. Let me know, as early in the morning as you can, your judgment in the matter, and I will make the necessary orders. Orders have been given Ord, Wright, and Parke to be ready to assault at daylight to-morrow morning. They will not make the assault, however, without further directions. ... If the assault is not ordered in the morning, then it can be directed at such time as to come in co-operation with you on the left." Thus Grant with his usual policy was preparing, not only to take advantage of the most favorable opportunity, but to make the opportunity that he desired; to move the cavalry and an entire corps of infantry against the enemy's right, on the South-side road, and when Lee should withdraw troops from Petersburg in order to reinforce the exposed flank, to penetrate the weakened lines in front of Parke, or Wright, or Ord.

The rebel general, however, was alive to the emergency. He, of course, perceived the extension of Grant's left, and understood its significance, as well as the object of the cavalry reconnoissance on the White Oak road. Five Forks was a position

he must hold at every hazard. His embarrassment at this crisis must have been extreme. If he allowed Grant to surround him, escape would be impossible; while if he stretched his line or depleted it further, it could withstand no concentrated assault. Nevertheless, he determined to adhere to the policy he had so often essayed, and, stripping the works before Petersburg, detach a force which might possibly prove sufficient to overwhelm the troops employed in the movement of Sheridan. In the night it was reported to Grant that two more divisions were moving to the rebel right, where Pickett and Bushrod Johnson had already been found in force.

On the morning of the 31st, Sheridan replied to Grant's offer: " My scouts report the enemy busy all night in constructing breastworks at Five Forks, and as far as one mile west of that point. There was great activity on the railroad; trains all going west. If the ground would permit, I could, with the Sixth corps, turn the enemy's right, or break through his lines; but I would not like the Fifth corps to make such an attempt." The Sixth corps, it will be remembered, had served with Sheridan in the Valley, and he knew it well; it shared his spirit, and would follow him whithersoever he led. The Fifth corps he had never at this time commanded.

Grant replied at once: " It will be impossible to give you the Sixth corps for the operation by our left. It is in the centre of our line, between Hatcher's run and the Appomattox river. Besides, Wright thinks he can go through the line where he is, and it is desirable to have troops and a commander there who feel so, to co-operate with you when you get around. I could relieve the Second with the Fifth

A.

<sT ' 'f ""*)f Cte

i 5

•

corps, and give you that." It lias been seen how anxious Grant always was to consult the wishes of his generals in providing them with subordinates. Sheridan evidently did not want the Fifth corps, doubtless because he was aware of the idiosyncracies of its commander; and Grant desired to regard his preference. Events, however, settled the point for them all.

On the morning of the 31st of March, Warren was on the extreme left of the infantry, in the angle between the White Oak and the Boydton roads. On account of the rains and the consequent condition of the ground, it was not intended to make any movement this day; but it was understood that the Second corps would be withdrawn from the line and sent to Sheridan at night. Warren had been notified that the enemy was in force on his left, and that an attack on him was not improbable. On the 30th, Grant said to Meade: " From what General Sheridan reports of the enemy on White Oak road, and the position of his cavalry to-night, I do not think an attack on Warren's left in the morning improbable. I have notified Sheridan of this, and directed him to be prepared to push on to his assistance if he is attacked. Warren, I suppose, will put himself in the best possible position to defend himself, with the notice he has already received; but, in addition to that, I think it will be well to notify him again of the position of Sheridan's cavalry, what he reports the enemy's position on the White Oak road, and the orders he has received."

Meade obeyed these orders, forwarded a copy of Sheridan's dispatch to Warren, and gave him full instructions. He had already directed Warren to cover as much of his front line as possible, putting both Crawford and Griffin in front, with a portion of each in reserve, and keeping Ayres to cover his left flank; * but at 9.55 p. M., he said to Grant: " I sent Warren Sheridan's dispatch, told him to put Ayres on his guard, as he might be attacked at daylight, directed he should move Crawford up at once to his support, if not already there, and move Griffin into supporting distance." Warren, however, in direct violation of his orders, stretched out his three divisions in echelon; placing Ayres on the left, then Crawford, and Griffin in the rear.

On the morning of the 31st, as Grant had anticipated, the Fifth corps was heavily attacked from the north and west. The assault had been prepared, but was precipitated by an advance made by Warren to drive the enemy from the White Oak road, or develop with what force the road was held.f One brigade of Ayres's division, sent forward for this purpose,

* u He [General Meade] is very anxious to have you cover as much of the front line as possible, and his idea was that you would put both Griffin and Crawford in front, keeping a portion of each as a reserve, and keeping Ayres to cover your left flank."— Webb to Warren, March 30, 9.30 A. M.

t "I have just received a'"report from General Ayres that the enemy have their pickets still this side of the White Oak road, so that their communication is continuous along it. I have sent out word to him to try and drive them off, or develop with what force the road is held by them."— Warren to Webb, Meade's Chief of Staff, March 31, 9.40 A. M.

" Your dispatch giving General Ayres's position is received. General Meade directs that, should you determine by your reconnaissance that you can get possession of the White Oak road, you are to do so, notwithstanding the orders to suspend operations."— Webb to Warren, 10.30 A. M.

" On the morning of the 31st, General Warren reported favorably to getting possession of the White Oak road, and was directed to do so."—Grant's Official Report.

was repulsed at half-past ten; and simultaneously a heavy attack of the enemy drove Ayres's whole command back upon Crawford. The rebels followed fast, and all efforts to hold the men in the woods were unavailing; so that both Ayres and Crawford were forced back in confusion upon Griffin. That commander formed his men along a branch of Gravelly run, and Ayres and Crawford retired behind him. Warren promptly notified Humphreys, on his right, of the disaster, and Humphreys sent Miles's division at once to his support. The rebel advance was checked; but the Fifth corps had been driven in a mile.

As soon as the news was brought to Grant, he said to Meade : " If the enemy has been checked in Warren's front, what is to prevent him from pitching in with his whole corps and attacking, before giving him time to entrench or return in good order to his old entrenchments ? I do not understand why Warren permitted his corps to be fought in detail. When Ayres was pushed forward, he should have sent other troops to their support."

The affair was over by noon, and arrangements were at once made to resume the battle. Griffin was ordered to advance, supported by an attack by Humphreys, who was to withdraw from his right all the force he could spare, and assault on the left with Miles. But when these dispositions were reported to Grant, he replied: " Humphreys should not push to the front without a fair chance and full determination to go through." He wanted no more failures. In consequence of this dispatch, Meade determined not to attack in front, but to put all the available troops of the Second corps under Miles,

who was to move forward from the left and attack in flank the troops in front of Warren. This was done, and the eneiny was compelled to fall back. Warren then prepared to push forward his whole force in conjunction with Miles.

Meanwhile, Grant was preparing to support Warren on the other flank, and sent a message to Sheridan: " The enemy have driven Ayres and Crawford's divisions back to near the Boydton road. The whole Fifth corps is now about to attack the enemy in turn. It is desirable that you get up as much of your cavalry as you can, and push towards the White Oak road. ... If the enemy does not go back to his old position, by turning to the right, you may be able to hit the enemy in rear." He followed this up by an order to Ord: " Ayres's division has been driven from near W. Dabney's back to the Boydton road. The Fifth corps is now preparing to take the offensive in turn, aided by the Second corps. Keep the enemy busy in your front, and if a chance presents

itself for attacking, do
so."

At about one o'clock the general-in-chief went out in person to the front to witness the attack, and from there sent another dispatch to Sheridan. "I am now," he said, "at Mrs. Butler's house, on Boydton plank road. My head-quarters will be at Dabney's saw-mill to-night. Warren, and Miles's division of the Second corps are now advancing. I hope your cavalry is up where it can be of assistance. Let me know how matters stand with the cavalry, where they are, what their orders, etc. If it had been possible to have had a division or two of them well up on the right, . . . they could
have fallen on the enemy's rear, as they were pursuing Ayres and Crawford." *

In the midst of this important battle, Grant was looking anxiously for news from North Carolina, and in the same dispatch to Sheridan, he said: " I would like you to get information from the Weldon road. I understand the enemy have some infantry and a brigade of cavalry at Stony creek station; I think it possible, too, that Johnston may be brought up that road to attack us in rear. They will see now that Sherman has halted at Goldsboro, and may think they can leave Raleigh with a small force."

There was a delay of several hours before the Fifth corps was ready, and Meade evidently shared the feeling in regard to Warren that was entertained by Sheridan and Grant, f " You know," he said to Humphreys, " the difficulty of getting two brigades to advance simultaneously. Miles has done handsomely in relieving Warren, and I should be glad to see him take the enemy's line. But if this is dependent on a simultaneous movement, past experience bids me despair." At 2.50 p. M., becoming impatient, Meade sent word by his chief of staff to Warren: " Since Miles is already well forward from your right flank, the general commanding considers that that must be secure. Miles is ordered to take the enemy's works, supported by his own corps. You will see the necessity of moving as soon as possible."

But Warren never seemed to appreciate the tremendous importance, in battle, of time. He elabo-

* Grant was unaware that Sheridan at this time was himself heavily engaged.

t See vol. ii., page 177.

rated, and developed, and prepared, as carefully and cautiously and deliberately in the immediate presence of the enemy as if there was nothing else to do, and, while he was preparing and looking out for his flanks, the moment in which victory was possible usually slipped away. During all the operations of the 30th and 31st of March, he had given great dissatisfaction to Grant. He seemed never to comprehend his instructions until they were repeated and explained, and then he generally disapproved them, and thought they should be modified, or that some one else on either flank should be ordered to do something else before he obeyed. His reports and dispatches were full of suggestions for the movements of other commanders and objections to those he was himself directed to undertake.* He had been

* " You must act independently of Sheridan, and, protecting your flanks, extend to the left as far as possible. If the enemy comes out and turns your left, you must attack him. You will be supported with all the available force to be procured."— Webb to Warren, March 30, 7.50 A. M. "If I extend my line to the left as far as possible, using both Ayres and Crawford, if the enemy turns my left, what will I then have to attack with ? "— Warren to Webb, March 30, 8.30 A. M.

" It will be necessary that Ayres should be put on his guard, and that he should be reinforced without delay, as the enemy may attack him at daylight."— Webb to Warren, March 30, 11 p. M. "I directed the advance of General Ayres to be reinforced at daylight, as it could not be done in the night without a great consumption of time, and loss of rest to the men."— Warren's

Report.

U I have my command all in readiness, but my advance is so far ahead of General Humphreys, and in sight of the enemy across the open ground, that I do not think it advisable to attempt anything more northward until General Humphreys gets into position on my right. My left, on the plank road, cannot be extended with propriety till I can get some idea of General Sheridan's movements, and now rests on Gravelly run, and, if I move, will be in the air. . . I can not move forward, and it does not appear a favorable place in front of Griffin."— Warren to Webb, March 30, 5.50 A. M.

"I do not think it best to advance any further till General Miles gets into position on my right."— Warren to Humphreys, March 30.

expressly ordered to be on the alert for the attack which had driven him in on the 31st, and had been directed to concentrate his force in anticipation of it; but he thought it wiser to spread out his corps, and the consequence was that he was beaten in detail. The general-in-chief was greatly chagrined at this rebuff, especially as he had foreseen the attack and given orders to receive it differently.

Between two and three o'clock, however, Warren made an advance, Miles's division, of the Second corps, supporting him on the right. The troops pushed on, wading a stream waist-deep, and ad-

" Major-General Meade directs you to move up the Quaker road to Gravelly run crossing."— Webb to Warren, March 29, 10.20 A. M. "I think my skirmishers are out on the Quaker road'as far as Gravelly run."— Warren to Webb. "From your last dispatch the major-general commanding would infer that you did not understand the last order."— Webb to Warren, March 29, 12 M. "I did not understand, till Captain Emory came, that I was to move my corps up the Quaker road."— Warren to Webb, March 29.

" The roads and fields are getting too bad for artillery, and I do not believe General Sheridan can operate advantageously. If General Humphreys is able to straighten out his line between my right and the vicinity of the Crow house, he will hold it in pretty strong force ; but the woods are so bad they alone will keep him nearly all day finding out how matters stand." — Warren to Webb, March 30.

"This dispatch placed me in much perplexity. I had already stated that I could not extend further with safety to my remaining in position, yet this dispatch required me to extend further, and yet did not define how far nor for what object. I had no desire but to comply with instructions, but leaving the limit of extension discretionary with me, while being dissatisfied with my use of this discretion, and requiring me to extend further, and not saying how far, was most embarrassing. The fault of these unlimited extensions were," etc., etc. [Then follows a long criticism of the strategy of his superior officers.] — Warren's Report.

" It did seem to me that on General Meade's receiving this dispatch, he should have signified to me whether or not I was to extend my left so as to cross the White Oak road ; if not, how far I should extend it. . . . But General Meade so far differed in judgment with me," etc., etc.— Warren's Report.

vanced a mile before they reached the point that had been lost in the morning. Then Griffin, with portions of Ayres and Crawford's commands, not only regained the original position held by Ayres, but drove the enemy to his breastworks, and secured a lodgment on the White Oak road. Thus Warren atoned for his fault.

Meanwhile, Lee had determined to send Pickett, with two of the best divisions of infantry and all the cavalry of the rebel army, to destroy the command of Sheridan. The rebel force thus accumulated was nearly eighteen thousand strong,* and the attack on Warren was doubtless intended to support the movement, and double up the entire national left. On the afternoon of March 30th, Pickett arrived at Five Forks, and, on the morning of the 31st, he advanced towards Dinwiddie, his principal column moving by the western road, and one division of cavalry on the direct road to the court-house. But Sheridan pushed out at the same time from Dinwiddie, with Merritt and Crook's commands, leaving Custer at the rear to guard the trains and the roads connecting with

* On the 20th of February, Lee reported :

Effective.

Pickett 5,065

Johnson ' 6,936

W. H. F. Lee 4,120

Fitz Hugh Lee 1,921

Total 18,042

In addition to these commands, Rosser's cavalry and a battery of artillery were engaged at Dinwiddie, but of these I can find no return. Pickett states in his report that one of his own brigades, as well as one of Johnson's, was absent on the 31st of March ; but a portion of Heth and Wilcox's troops stood ready to support him, and his own absent brigade returned to him late on the 1st of April. ,On the 20th of February the extra-duty men in Pickett and Johnson's divisions were 1,418 in number.

Meade. Merritt was thrown forward on the principal road to the Forks; and, as he met with some opposition, Sheridan ordered Davies's brigade of Crook's division to join him, while Crook himself, with the remainder of his command, moved to the left to Chamberlain's creek, a little north and west of Dinwiddie, where the enemy was making preparations to cross.

For a hundred yards or more in front of the court-house the ground is .high and clear, and then slopes down to Chamberlain's bed, on the west, the banks of which are thickly wooded. The road that crosses the bed was held by Smith, of Crook's command, on the extreme left of the line, and Gregg took position on the right of Smith. It was here the rebels made their first assault at ten o'clock in the morning. Their cavalry charged across the creek, but were driven back with a loss of five hundred men, and the infantry made no attempt to follow.* The rebels pronounced this one of the severest cavalry fights of the war, but the assault was repelled and the position maintained.

In the meantime Merritt had nearly obtained possession of Five Forks, but, meeting a strong body of infantry, was compelled to retire, and formed a line west of the Five Forks road, with his back to the Boydton plank, and his left connecting with Crook. Gibbes's brigade was held in reserve about a mile north of Dinwiddie. But Pickett, now abandoning the attempt in front of Smith, withdrew his infantry, and succeeded in effecting a crossing at a point nearer the White Oak road. Then, with all

* "Pickett's Men," by Walter Harrison, Adjutant-general of Pick-ett's division.

his infantry and most of his cavalry, striking at Davies's brigade on the left of Merritt, he forced it back after a gallant fight, and penetrated Sheridan's line, isolating Merritt and Davies from the remainder of the command. Sheridan at once ordered this detached force to move to the Boydton road, march down to Dinwiddie, and join the line of battle there. Mounted and dismounted, as the ground permitted, these troops together contested every grove and every knoll, and fell back slowly towards the Boydton road.*

The rebels, deceived by this manoeuvre, which they supposed a rout, followed it up rapidly, making a left wheel, and presenting their own rear to Sheridan's main line north of Dinwiddie. Sheridan instantly perceived his opportunity, and ordered Gibbes and Gregg to advance. Then, as the rebel line w r ent crashing through the woods in pursuit of Merritt, wheeling towards the Boydton road, Gibbes struck them in flank and rear, while Gregg, moving rapidly up from his position on Chamberlain's bed, and taking a wood road, came in on the left of Gibbes, and also in the enemy's rear. This sudden and combined attack compelled the rebels at once to face by the rear rank and abandon the pursuit of Merritt, which, if continued, would have taken in flank and rear the infantry of Warren.

But now the entire rebel command, foot and horse, had turned on the national cavalry covering Dinwiddie; and " here," said Grant, " Sheridan dis-

* For many of the incidents of March 31st and April 1st, such as only an eye-witness could describe, I am indebted to the graphic and often eloquent narrative of Colonel Newhall, entitled "With Sheridan in Lee's Last Campaign, by a Staff Officer." 112

played great generalship." * Instead of retreating with his whole command, to tell the story of superior forces encountered; he deployed the cavalry on foot, leaving only mounted men enough to take charge of the horses. This compelled the enemy also to deploy over a vast extent of woods and broken country, and made the rebel progress slow. Pickett's infantry, however, pushed back Gregg and Gibbes to the court-house, while the rebel cavalry turned on Smith, who had so gallantly maintained the crossing of Chamberlain's creek in the morning. His command again held off the enemy for a while with determined bravery, but the heavy force brought against his flank finally compelled Smith to abandon the position on the creek, and fall back to the main line immediately in front of Dinwiddie. Meanwhile, Sheridan had brought up two brigades of Ouster's division, and these, with Gibbes and Gregg, were now in line; slight breastworks had been thrown up at intervals along this front, and every attempt to force the position was repelled. Pickett, with his entire command, was unable to drive five national brigades of cavalry from the open plain in front of the courthouse. It was after dark when the firing ceased, and the rebels lay on their arms that night not more than a hundred yards from Sheridan's lines. Dinwiddie, however, was held.

Merritt and Davies, with their commands, reached the court-house without opposition by the Boydton road, but too late to participate in the final action of the day.

Thus the rebels had failed to overwhelm the national cavalry. Sheridan had extricated his troops

* Grant's Official Report.

from the complications in which they were involved by the difficult nature of the country and the superior strength of the enemy; he had occupied the attention of a formidable force, which might have caused prodigious annoyance if turned against Warren's disorganized flank; and had retained his hold of the strategic position which threatened the communications of Lee and the objective point indicated by Grant. The promptness and audacity with which, when his line was broken, he conceived and executed a new design, and compelled the pursuing rebels to turn and look to their own defence—not only to reverse their ranks, but to change the direction of their march and the whole character of the battle—constituted one of the most brilliant strokes of military genius displayed during the war; while the determination with which he held out against odds and dangers on every side was worthy of the most famous commanders. Nevertheless, Sheridan had been driven back from the White Oak road a distance of five miles, and he dispatched at once to the general-in-chief that the force in his front was too strong for him.

Lee had certainly shown more than his wonted audacity at this crisis; but it was the desperate daring of the gambler who risks all on his last throw. When he discovered that Grant was again moving to the left, he quickly, in spite of mud and rains and heavy roads, transferred nearly one-third * of his army to the threatened point, and throwing a heavy force

* The forces of Pickett, Anderson, Heth, Wilcox, W. H. F. and Fitz Hugh Lee, and Rosser were all in front of Warren or Sheridan on the 30th of March. These amounted to 27,500 men. See Lee's return of February 20th. But Pickett's Report, published in " Pickett's Men," puts them at 8,000 !

against Warren, sufficient at first to drive him back to the Boydton road, at the same time massed a still larger command in front of Sheridan, and with infantry and cavalry combined, pushed back the entire mounted strength of the national army. On the night of the 31st of March, Sheridan was in actual danger of being cut off and perhaps destroyed. But to do this, Lee had been obliged, not only to weaken his lines in front of Meade, but absolutely to detach Pickett and the cavalry from his army; and Pickett was now in as much danger of being enveloped and destroyed by Grant as Sheridan was by Lee.

But, although pushed back five miles, Sheridan was not dismayed. After the battle he reported to Grant: " The enemy have gained some ground, but we still hold in front of Dinwiddie, and Davies and Devin are coming down the Boydton road to join us. . . . The men behaved splendidly. Our loss in killed and wounded will probably number four hundred and fifty men; very few were lost as prisoners. This force is too strong for us. I will hold out at Dinwiddie court-house until I am compelled to leave." * He asked for no help and made no suggestions, but left it for Grant to determine whether or not he should be reinforced. He was too well acquainted with the temper and character of his chief to suppose for a moment that he would be left unsupported, or that the aggressive movement already dictated would be abandoned.

After sending his dispatch, Sheridan put everything in order for the morrow. Ammunition was

* See Appendix for this dispatch entire.

brought up and distributed, the wagons were parked, the wounded cared for and moved to the rear, the positions of troops assigned; all with a view to advance in the morning.

Grant's head-quarters were now at Dabney's mill, and Meade's were close at hand, at the crossing of the Vaughan road and Hatcher's run, both points about ten miles from Sheridan. Warren was still across the Boydton road, his head-quarters four and a half miles from Meade and five and a half from Dinwiddie. There was communication by military telegraph between Grant and Meade, and between Meade and his corps commanders, but all news from Sheridan came by courier.

During the afternoon, Grant began to be uneasy, and said to Meade : " I think Warren should be instructed to send well down the White Oak road, and also south-west from his left, to watch and see if there is an enemy in either direction. I would much rather have Warren back on the plank road than to be attacked front and rear where he is." To this Meade replied, at half-past five : " Sheridan's firing was heard soon after you left. I have sent word to Warren to push forward a force down the White Oak road to co-operate with Sheridan."

Soon after dark, the news from the battle began to come in. At 6.35 p. M., Meade reported: "A staff officer from General Sheridan was cut off by what is reported two brigades of Pickett's division. . . . The firing has receded towards Dinwiddie courthouse. ... I have directed Warren to send a force down the Boydton plank to try and communicate with Sheridan." Both these orders to Warren-were obeyed. He sent Bartlett's brigade to the left, on the White Oak road, and three regiments by the Boydton road in the direction of Dinwiddie.

At seven o'clock, Grant had further intelligence. Colonel Porter, of his own staff, arrived from the front. He had left before the battle was over, but brought word that Sheridan would contest the ground foot by foot, and could hold the position at Dinwiddie till morning. Sheridan also thought the time had come when the enemy could be forced to fight in the open field, and the national troops should make their blows decisive. Grant at once took an encouraging view of the situation, and expressed the belief that, having the rebels outside of their works, he would now be able to strike a final blow. He waited, however, for further news before taking definite action.

Meanwhile he telegraphed to Meade: " Colonel Porter has returned from Sheridan. He says that Devin has been driven back in considerable confusion south of Boisseau's house. The effort has been to get our cavalry on to the White Oak road west of W. Dabney's house. So far this has failed, and there is no assurance that it will succeed. This will make it necessary for Warren to watch his left all round. The cavalry being where it is will probably make the enemy very careful about coming round much in his rear, but he cannot be too much on his guard." As yet, Grant's anxiety was almost exclusively for Warren.

But, at 7.40 p. M., an aide-de-camp of Sheridan arrived with full reports, and the general-in-chief instantly ordered Meade : " Let Warren draw back at once to his position on the Boydton road, and send a division of infantry to Sheridan's relief. The troops

to Sheridan should start at once, and go down the Boydton road." This was very different from the instructions issued by Meade ten minutes before. The officer who brought the news from Sheridan had missed his way, and stopped at Meade's head-quarters for a guide, and at 7.30 p. M., before the receipt of Grant's directions, Meade sent word to Warren: " Dispatch from General Sheridan says he was forced back to Dinwiddie court-house by a strong force of cavalry, supported by infantry. This leaves your rear and that of the Second corps on the Boydton plank road open, and will require great vigilance on your part. If you have sent the brigade down the Boydton plank, it should not go further than Gravelly ruvij as I don't think it will render any service but to protect your rear."

These orders were indeed in accordance with the tenor of Grant's earlier dispatches before he knew of Sheridan's danger. So long as he had no fears for the cavalry, the general-in-chief simply desired to protect Warren against an intervention of the enemy between his left and Dinwiddie; but the moment he learned that Sheridan was opposed by infantry as well as horse, and had been badly handled by superior numbers, he changed the entire character of his orders. With his invariable instinct in an emergency, he determined to convert the defence into an offensive movement, and ordered an entire division at once to Sheridan. The method of many commanders is first of all to protect themselves, and then to injure the enemy; but Grant's impulse always was to strike first, and he did it so quickly that the blow was sometimes delivered before his judgment was exercised; but it always

told. At such times judgment and instinct with him were identical. Armies, indeed, are like individual men, and the bravest generally wins. Neither skill nor strength is to be despised, but courage counts for more than all.

There was some delay in the transmission of this order, for the telegraphic wires were working badly, but at nine o'clock Meade sent word to Warren: "You will, by direction of the major-general commanding, draw back at once to your position within the Boydton plank road, and send a division down to Dinwiddie court-house, to report to General Sheridan; this division will go down the Boydton plank road. Send Griffin's division." This was received by Warren at 9.17 P. M., and at 9.35 he repeated the order to Griffin.

Grant, however, was not content with a single effort in Sheridan's behalf. At 9.15, he said to Meade: " I wish you would send out some cavalry to Dinwiddie to see if information can be got from Sheridan ;" and at 9.45, he directed Ord to forward the cavalry of the army of the James: " Send Mackenzie at once to Dinwiddie, to the support of Sheridan. He has been attacked by cavalry and infantry, and driven into Dinwiddie. Fighting was still going on, when I last heard from him, which was after dark." At the same hour he telegraphed to Meade: "If you can get orders to Mackenzie to move his cavalry to the support of Sheridan by way of the Vaughan road, do so. I have sent the same directions to General Ord. Please let me know when Griffin gets started. If he pushes promptly, I think there may be a chance for cutting off the infantry the enemy have intrusted so far from home. Urge prompt

movement on Griffin." Still later, he said to Ord: " I want Mackenzie to go through. It may be too late to-morrow morning."

Every one seemed alive to the emergency, and anxious to meet it. Meade sent frequent messages urging Warren, and Warren himself proposed that the Boydton road should be held by Humphreys and the artillery of the Fifth corps. " Then," said he, "let me move down and attack the enemy at Dinwiddie court-house on one side, and Sheridan on the other."' This dispatch was dated 8.40 p. M., before Warren knew of Sheridan's situation, and was not forwarded to Grant; but it shows that Warren had the same idea as his superiors. From Grant down, every man in the army was looking for the moment when the rebels could be attacked outside of their fortifications.

Starting from a point on the White Oak road a mile and a half west of Warren's left on the 31st of March, the Crump road, on which Bartlett was moving, runs directly south about two miles, when it enters the main Five Forks road near the J. Boisseau house. If Warren should move by the Crump road, his route would bring him directly in the rear of Pickett's force as it fronted Dinwiddie. The Fifth corps could then either attack the enemy in rear, or

* "The line along the plank road is very strong. One division, with my artillery, I think, can hold it, if we are not threatened south of Gravelly run. East of the plank road, General Humphreys and my batteries, I think, could hold this securely, and let me move down and attack the enemy at Dinwiddie court-house on one side, and Sheridan on the other. On account of Bartlett's position, they [the enemy] will have to make a considerable detour to reinforce their troops at that point from the north. Unless General Sheridan has been too badly handled, I think we should have a chance for an open-field fight that should be made use of."—Warren to Webb, March 31, 8.40 p. M.

if, alarmed by the national movements, Pickett attempted to withdraw, Warren could strike him in flank and in motion, while Sheridan assaulted from Dinwiddie. This scheme had the advantage that Warren was already in possession of the Crump road, as far as Gravelly run, with Bartlett's brigade.

Accordingly, at 9.45 P..M., Meade enquired of Grant: " Would it not be well for Warren to go down with his whole corps and smash up the force in front of Sheridan ? Humphreys can hold the line to the Boydton plank road, and the refusal along it. Bartlett's brigade is now on the [Crump] road from G. Boisseau running north, where it crosses Gravelly run. Warren could at once move that way and take the force threatening Sheridan in rear, or he could send one division to support Sheridan at Dinwiddie, and move on the enemy's rear with the other two." This was in reality to carry out Grant's plan of the day before of sending a corps to Sheridan; and the general-in-chief instantly replied: " Let Warren move in the way you propose, and urge him not to stop for anything. Let Griffin go on as he was first directed."

At 10.15, therefore, Meade sent explicit and urgent orders to Warren : " Send Griffin promptly, as ordered, by the Boydton plank road, but move the balance of your command by the road Bartlett is on, and strike the enemy in rear, or between him and Dinwiddie. General Sheridan reported his last position as north of Dinwiddie court-house, near Dr. Smith's, the enemy holding the cross-roads at that point. Should the enemy turn on you, your line of retreat will be by J. M. Brooks and R. Boisseau on Boydton plank road. You must be very prompt in this movement, and get the forks of the road at J. M. Brooks before the enemy, so as to open the road to R. Boisseau. The enemy will probably retire towards the Five Forks, that being the direction of their main attack this day. Don't encumber yourself with anything that will impede your progress or prevent your moving in any direction across the country. Let me know when Griffin starts, and when you start. Acknowledge receipt."

But Warren, as usual, was behindhand. He had many difficulties, doubtless, in the way of darkness, unfamiliar country, bad roads, tired and sleepy soldiers, but, above all, in the lack in his own nature of that intense, aggressive energy which overcomes just such difficulties.* He was worried and con-

* "Let us suppose the two divisions that General Grant directed to be moved by J. Boisseau's were expected to reach General Sheridan by midnight. The order which I received was written by General Meade, 10.15 P. M., five minutes after General Grant's to General Sheridan. It reached me 10.50 p. M., thirty-five minutes after being written. Supposing all possible dispatch used, twenty minutes at least would be required for me to make the necessary arrangements ; twenty more would be required to carry my order to the divisions ; twenty more minutes for them to transmit them to the brigades ; and forty minutes at least for the troops to get ready to move ; for it must be remembered that no bugles or drums could be used to sound calls or arouse the men. No general could make plans based on greater rapidity of execution than here allowed, and our experience rarely realized it on the most favorable occasions, while this was one of the least so. Summing up this interval of time, we have two hours to add to the time of General Grant's writing to General Sheridan. I venture to say it took nearly this time for the note itself to reach General Sheridan. Adding these two hours would make it at least twelve o'clock before my two divisions could move. They then had four miles to traverse, taking the White Oak road before reaching the crossing of Gravelly run, which would occupy till two A. M. They had then to strike the rear of the enemy opposed to General Sheridan. . . . To join General Sheridan by midnight, on this route, I finally had to capture or destroy whatever of this force was between me and General Sheridan. Any expec-

fused by the orders lie received; lie proposed modifications, and made changes in them without authority ; he was as cautious as ever, and in the middle of this anxious night, when everything depended on his promptness in reinforcing Sheridan, he actually caused Crawford's division to form and retire in line of battle, so as to meet the enemy should he pursue from his breastworks, as Warren " confidently expected he would." * If Warren had sometimes been as confident that his superiors had energy and ability as he was that these traits were possessed by Lee, he would have oftener contributed to victory. An undue appreciation of the enemy is quite as fatal to success as the opposite fault.

He was directed, as we have seen, to march Griffin by the Boydton road, and the other two divisions by the Crump road. He sent Ay res, instead of Griffin, by the Boydton road, and moved himself with Griffin and Crawford by the other and parallel road.f The first orders for Griffin were sent out by Grant at 7.40 p. M., and those for the combined operation at 10.15; the first were received by Warren at 9.17, and the last named at 10.50 p. M. They were thereafter renewed and reiterated; he was

tations more unreasonable could not have been formed."— '-Warren's Report.

No lines could be written which would better explain the reasons of General Warren's failure than his own. Troops have often moved under just such circumstances as he describes, and with just such expedition as Grant demanded. The Fifth corps so moved, again and again, in this very campaign, but under a different commander.

*"....! remained with Crawford's division, which we formed in line of battle to meet the

enemy, should he pursue us from his breastworks, as I confidently expected he would as soon as he discovered our movements."— Warren's Report.

t Warren's Report.

urged to be prompt and to move at once ; he was told of the immense need of his presence; and he had himself, hours before, suggested the very operation which he had now been ordered to execute. His troops were expected to reach Sheridan by midnight, but Griffin was not ordered to leave his position on the WJiite Oak road till five A. M. on the 1st of April* and Ayres only reported to Sheridan at daylight, f

The bridge on the Boydton road at the crossing of Gravelly run was broken, and at 9.50 p. M., Warren was aware of this fact and announced it to Meade. The stream, however, had been forded the same night by aides-de-camp of both Grant and Sheridan, whose feet were not wet as they sat in their saddles. The infantry would doubtless have had some difficulty in crossing, but war is full of difficulties as well as dangers, and the officer who allows them to deter and overcome him is apt to terminate his career in failure, and never pleases such superiors as Sheridan and Grant.

When Meade heard of this impediment, he wrote, anxiously and imperatively, to Warren: "A dispatch, partially transmitted, is received, indicating the bridge over Gravelly run is destroyed, and time will be required to rebuild it. If this is the case, would not time be gained by sending the troops by the Quaker road ? Time is of the utmost importance. Sheridan cannot maintain himself at Dinwiddie

* " About five A. M. on the morning of April 1st, an order was received through a staff officer to move the First division with all possible despatch via the J. Boisseau house, and report to General Sheridan."— Griffin's Report.

t " As we approached, just after daylight, the enemy decamped."— Ayres's Report.

without reinforcements, and yours are the only ones that can be sent. Use every exertion to get troops to him as soon as possible. If necessary, send troops by both roads, and give up the rear attack. If Sheridan is not reinforced, and compelled to fall back, he will retire by the Vaughan road." This was written by Meade at 11.45 p. M. Warren became anxious after this, but his anxiety determined him to keep the two divisions of Griffin and Crawford where they were till he could learn that Ayres had certainly reinforced Sheridan.* " The men of the two divisions," he said, "were gaining, while waiting this result, a little of that rest they stood so much in need of, on this their fourth night of almost continual deprivation of it, and we had but a short distance to move before reaching the enemy near J. Boisseau's." At five minutes past two A. M. the bridge on the Boydton road was complete, and Ayres advanced; but the other two divisions remained " where they were" till morning, "gaining a little of that rest they so much required."

Grant, however, had done his part, and at 10.05 p. M., he said to Sheridan: " The Fifth corps has been ordered to your support. Two divisions will go by J. Boisseau's and one down the Boydton road. In addition to this I have sent Mackenzie's cavalry, which will reach you by the Vaughan road. All these forces except the cavalry should reach you by twelve M. to-nigh.t. You mil assume command of the whole force sent to operate with you, and use it

* "I therefore determined that it was best to abide the movements already begun, and keep the two divisions, Griffin's and Crawford's, where they were, till I could hear that General Ayres certainly had reinforced General Sheridan."— Warren's Report.

to the best of your ability to destroy the force which your command has fought so gallantly to-day."

At three A. M. on the 1st of April, supposing Warren to be in the position indicated, Sheridan sent him the following orders : " I am holding in front of Dinwiddie court-house, on the road leading to Five Forks, for three-quarters of a mile, with General Ouster's division. The enemy are in his immediate front, lying so as to cover the road just this side of A. Adams' house, which leads out across Chamberlain's bed or run. I understand you have a division at J. Boisseau's; if so, you are in rear of the enemy's line, and almost on his flanks. I will hold on here. Possibly they may attack Ouster at daylight; if so, attack instantly and in full force. Attack at daylight anyhow, and I will make an effort to get the road this side of Adams' house; and if I do, you can capture the whole of them. Any force moving down the road I am holding, or on the White Oak road, will be in the enemy's rear, and in all probability get any force that may escape you by a flank attack. Do not fear my leaving here. If the enemy remains, I shall fight at daylight."

And so, all through this anxious night, the generals were issuing and receiving orders, the officers were marshalling or moving troops, and aides-de-camp and orderlies were riding across dark and muddy roads, threading forests and fording streams. From daylight till daylight again, Grant was sending messages to Lincoln and Sheridan and Meade and Ord; directing first a division and then a corps of infantry, and afterwards another division of cavalry, to the support of his beleaguered subordinate; planning a battle on a field he had never seen; per-
!
sisting in his effort to break through the right of Lee. He had little rest that night in his camp bed at Dabney's saw-mill. His double anxiety was extreme. At no time since the army of the Potomac left the Rapidan had an entire wing of his command been so endangered; at no time had the opportunity for attacking the rebels outside of their works appeared so favorable: and the interminable delays of Warren, lasting from 7.40 p. M. on the 31st of March to long past dawn on the following day—on the White Oak, the Crump, and the Boydton roads; on Gravelly run and in front of Lee—became at last almost unendurable. More than once in that long night Grant thought of relieving him from command. Every plan was confused, every manoeuvre complicated, every object endangered, by his failure to move. The situation which Sheridan described at three A. M. did not exist, solely because Warren had not obeyed his orders; there would be opportunity for the rebels to escape, or there might be danger of the destruction of the cavalry, solely because Warren was not at the appointed place at the appointed time.

At daylight on the 1st of April, hearing as yet nothing from Warren, but strong in the knowledge of reinforcements on the way, Sheridan moved out against the enemy. But Pickett also had learned the approach of the national infantry, and the rebels in Sheridan's front gave way rapidly, moving by the right flank, and crossing Chamberlain's bed.* They

* " The fact being thus developed that the enemy were reinforcing with infantry, and knowing the whole of Sheridan's and Kautz's cavalry were in our front, induced me to fall back at daylight in the morning to the Five Forks. . . . The enemy was, however, pressing upon our rear in force."— PicketVs Report.

were followed fast by Merritt's two divisions, Devin on the right and Ouster on the left, while Crook remained at the rear to hold Dinwiddie and the roads connecting with Meade. The national skirmishers soon overtook the rebel rear guard, and firing began at once in the tangled woods on the right and left, while the main column advanced on the Five Forks road. At the junction with the road leading to the Boydton plank, where Gibbes had attacked the rebels in rear the day before, the head of Ayres's division came in sight, about two and a half miles north of Dinwiddie, having arrived at this point at daylight;* and between seven and eight o'clock a squadron sent out to the right came up with Griffin's command, in front of the J. Boisseau house, on the Crump road. Warren himself was still with Crawford's division, engaged in making a skilful tactical retreat from his old position on the White Oak road, in front of Lee.f

The enemy had thus slipped completely back between the forces of Merritt and Warren, and Sheridan was now obliged to abandon all hope of using the Fifth corps against the- rebel rear, and to form entirely different plans. Any immediate co-

* Sheridan had sent a staff officer to bring Ayres by this route direct from the Boydton plank road.

t "1st of April, early in the morning, while still in camp near the White Oak road, it was announced to me by the major-general commanding [Warren] he was about to move, with his entire command, towards Dinwiddie court-house, to operate in connection with the cavalry, then in the neighborhood of a place called Five Forks. My division was the last to retire. . . . We marched in retreat in a southwest direction until we approached a road leading south to Boisseau's cross-roads, and followed the other two divisions. The enemy did not follow us from his entrenchments upon the withdrawal of our skirmish line, as was expected." — Crawford"s Report. 113

operation of the infantry, however, was still impracticable until Crawford's division arrived. Griffin and Ayres were, therefore, directed to remain in the neighborhood of the Boisseau house, refresh their men, and be ready to move forward when required.

In this emergency, Sheridan devised a new and brilliant scheme. He determined to drive the rebels back to Five Forks with Merritt's column, press them into their works, and make a feint of turning their right flank, and then, while their attention was completely engaged by the cavalry, to quietly move the whole Fifth corps against Pickett's left, and crush the entire rebel command. It was his old manoeuvre, which had been so successful in the Valley ; a feint upon the enemy's front and right, and suddenly a turning movement to overwhelm the left. But in this instance it was more felicitous in its application than ever before; for the success of the Fifth corps would drive westward the rebels who might escape, and isolate them from Lee. It would thus not only secure victory for Sheridan, but, by breaking the right wing of Lee's command, defeat the last manoeuvre of the rebel general, and open a way for Grant to destroy the entire army of Northern Virginia.

Merritt accordingly was directed to press the enemy, and promptly pushed Ouster out by the Scott or western road, and Devin by the main one, to Five Forks. Twice he encountered temporary breastworks, erected since the day before ; but, dismounting part of his men, he charged impetuously and carried both these lines. The fields, however, were all quicksand and the woods all jungle, and

the fighting was severe. The rebels availed themselves of every favorable piece of ground to hold the national column in check, and when Merritt's line was formed and ready to attack, they generally moved off again, their infantry gliding through the woods with ease, while the national troopers labored hard in pursuit, through the thick undergrowth and miry soil. By noon, however, the last of the enemy had retired behind their works along the White Oak road, and Merritt had pressed so close that the rebel skirmishers were called in. They evidently evaded a general battle outside.

In the meantime, Crawford had at last come up with Griffin, and at eleven A. M., Warren reported in person to Sheridan. Mackenzie also had arrived, with the cavalry of Ord's command, and was directed to remain in front of Dinwiddie, and rest his men, until further orders.

Early on this morning Lee directed Pickett to hold Five Forks,* and the rebels had accordingly fortified a line running along the White Oak road for at least two miles, with its left refused at a point about half a mile east of the Forks. They thus covered not only the Forks themselves, but the Ford road, which runs north to the Southside railway, and was the route by which Pickett communicated with Lee. As soon as it was evident that the enemy had retired behind these works, Sheridan ordered Warren to advance on the Five Forks road, in the rear of the cavalry. Then turning to the right, the Fifth corps was to take position obliquely to and a short distance from the

* "Pickett's Men," page 145.

White Oak road, opposite the left flank of the enemy, and about a mile from the Forks. Warren was ordered to place two divisions in the front line, and leave the third in reserve, in rear of the right. The object of this formation was to enable him to strike the enemy with his left division, and then to make a left wheel, and envelop the entire rebel flank with the remainder of his corps.

Having issued these instructions, Sheridan next directed Merritt to demonstrate as though he was attempting to turn the rebel right, and notified him that the Fifth corps would strike the enemy's left. The cavalry was ordered to assault the rebel works as soon as the Fifth corps became engaged, and this would be known by the report of volleys of musketry. He then rode over to the Fifth corps, not yet in position, and coming up slowly. He was exceedingly anxious to attack at once, for the sun was getting low, and he had to fight or go back. " It was no place to entrench ; and it would have been shameful," he said, "to have gone back with no results to compensate for the loss of the brave men who had fallen that day." * But Warren was acting with his usual deliberation. It took him three hours to bring up his troops a distance of less than two miles, f To Sheridan's eager eye he did not seem to exert himself as earnestly as he ought. The ammunition of the cavalry would soon be exhausted;

* Sheridan's Report.

t " At one P. M. an officer brought me an order to bring up the infantry."— Warren's Report.

" About two P. M. I received an order to move."— Griffin's Report.

" I informed him [Sheridan] that they would not all be in position before four p. M." — Warren's Report.

These extracts all refer to the same movement.

the rebels might be reinforced; the sun might go down before the dispositions of Warren were complete, and the impatient, restless commander chafed at the delay.

While Warren was thus elaborately, and, as it seemed to his superior, too slowly, taking position, Sheridan learned that the left of the Second corps of the army of the Potomac had been swung around till it fronted on the Boydton road. This created an opportunity for the enemy to march down from the White Oak road and attack the right or rear of Sheridan's new position. Mackenzie was therefore sent up by the Crump road across Warren's rear, with directions to gain the White Oak road if possible, and attack any enemy he found, at every hazard. He would thus protect the rear of Warren against any intervention of the enemy from that direction. If successful in this, Mackenzie was to march back by the White Oak road and rejoin Sheridan, coming in on the right of the infantry. He executed his orders with skill and courage, attacking a force of the enemy on the White Oak road, and driving it back towards Petersburg. Then countermarching, he rode up to Sheridan, just as the Fifth corps was advancing to the attack. Sheridan directed him to swing around to the right of the infantry, and gain possession of the Ford road at the crossing of

Hatcher's run, and thus cut off the rebel line of retreat towards Lee.

It was five o'clock before the Fifth corps was ready, but at that hour the battle began. The object of the assault was the angle in the rebel fortified line; this was to be destroyed before the troops that held it could be reinforced, while the cavalry

was to keep the main line busy by a vigorous attack, beginning when they heard the fire of the infantry. As soon as the order to advance was given, the Fifth corps marched briskly forward, Ayres on the left, Crawford on the right, and Griffin in reserve. They moved across the miry bottom land that borders Gravelly run, and through an undergrowth of brake to an open plain, Sheridan with his staff riding between the skirmishers and the front line of battle. Ayres was engaged before he reached the White Oak road. He was received with a heavy fire on his left flank, nearest to the enemy, and at once began changing front to the left. His command now entered a piece of woods, and one brigade soon became unsteady, partly from the difficulty of changing front under fire, and partly because Crawford had lost connection on the right, and that flank was in the air.* One or two regiments broke and began to run, and the division was temporarily repelled. Sheridan, however, was on this flank, the critical point, and rode up with his staff to reassure the faltering troops, and the men almost at once came back into line.

Meantime the fire of Ayres's division was heard by Merritt, and the cavalry promptly responded to the signal for their assault. They had the brunt of the battle to bear, for their attack was directly in front, on the main Five Forks road, and the angle

* "The Third brigade, soon after engaging the enemy, finding its right flank in the air (I must confess I experienced anxiety also on this account), portions of it were very unsteady."— Ayres^s Report.

"The connection between the Second division [Ayres's] and my line could not be maintained. . . . Coulter's brigade . . . was brought to fill the gap between me and the Second division."— Crawford's Report.

where Ayres joined the cavalry right was the key of the entire position. If this could be gained, Ayres would completely enfilade the enemy's line on the White Oak road, and render the direct assault comparatively easy; while if the rebels held the Fifth corps in check, they could probably repulse the cavalry with heavy loss, for their works were strong and difficult to approach in front, and, sheltered by these, they could pour out a deadly fire. It was, therefore, vital that the rebel flank should be promptly attacked and broken. The burden of this now fell upon Ayres, for Crawford, on the right, had deflected so far from the line pointed out by Sheridan that he was of no use at all at this juncture. After crossing the White Oak road, he failed to wheel to the left, as ordered, and pushed straight for Hatcher's run, leaving, as we have seen, a gap between himself and Ayres. This deflection was occasioned by Crawford's obliquing his line to avoid the fire of the enemy, instead of pushing directly upon the rebel work. Griffin, who was in reserve on the right, naturally followed Crawford for a while, so that Ayres was left to contend alone with the enemy.

Sheridan was extremely dissatisfied with this condition of affairs, and sent several officers after Warren, who was on the right with Crawford. As Warren did not arrive, he himself remained, encouraging Ayres's men, with words and example. The line was easily steadied, however, for the troops were used to battle, and speedily recovered from the momentary panic; and Sheridan himself took the battle-flag in his hands and plunged into the charge at the head of the command. The flag was shot,

the man who had borne it was killed, and McGoni-gle, of Sheridan's staff, was severely wounded ; but the fiery enthusiasm of the leader, his disregard of danger, his evident belief in victory, were contagious. The bands were ordered to play, and the division burst on the enemy's left like a tornado. The breastwork in front was a hundred yards in length, and screened by a dense undergrowth of pines, but Ayres's troops swept everything before them, overrunning the works at the bayonet-point, breaking the rebel flank past mending, and capturing fifteen hundred prisoners.

At this juncture Sheridan again sent word to Warren that Griffin and Crawford were too far to the right, and directed him- to close them in to the left. Both divisions had by this time advanced a considerable distance north of the White Oak road and beyond the refusal of the enemy's left. In Griffin's front a line of rebel skirmishers extended from the work to Hatcher's run, but Crawford was in reality moving away from battle, and had even crowded Mackenzie to the other side of the run. Griffin, however, had discovered his position before he received his orders, and, changing direction to the left, he moved against the enemy at the double-quick step, coming in on the right of Ayres and capturing fifteen hundred prisoners. Crawford also was finally brought to the Ford road, and then, facing directly south, he took the flying enemy in rear, and captured two guns and a number of prisoners endeavoring to escape from their pursuers on the other side. In the meantime, Mackenzie, finding no force in his front on the further side of Hatcher's run, almost immediately recrossed, and, as the fighting

seemed to be fiercest at the Forks, pushed on in that direction by the Ford road.

Sheridan had been obliged to halt Ayres in his impetuous advance, lest a collision should occur with the cavalry as they charged over the rebel works to effect a junction with the infantry; but when Griffin came up on the right, Ayres again advanced, for the cavalry had now gained the angle and connected with his left inside the rebel breastworks. Devin contested with Ouster the honor of having first gained a foothold, and both divisions had planted their colors on the parapet.

Thus the works in front were carried at several points by Merritt's men, while the Fifth corps doubled up the left; and finally, flanked by Ayres, and assailed in front by Merritt along the White Oak road, the rebels fell back fighting to the Forks. Griffin attacked them before they reached this point, and so absolute was the junction of the national forces that Griffin's men and the cavalry at first fired into each other's lines. Most of Merritt's fighting had been dismounted, but, when his cavalry joined hands with the infantry, he mounted some of his men, who rode into the broken ranks, capturing a battery of artillery, and turning the guns at once upon the enemy. Pickett himself was vainly striving to stem the onset, when a national trooper, astride of a mule, jumped over the works and ordered him to surrender and be damned to him. The rebel commander was almost surrounded before he could gallop away. With him rushed off the remnants of the enemy, the cavalry riding hot haste after them, as fast as they could get up their horses from the rear.

No serious stand was made after the line was broken, and the rebels took to flight in great disorder. Nearly six thousand prisoners fell into Sheridan's hands, and six pieces of artillery, and the fugitives were driven north and westward. Some rushed off by the Ford road, to encounter Crawford and Mackenzie, while those who fled by the White Oak road were followed by Griffin, and afterwards by Merritt's cavalry.

Sheridan, meanwhile, had - been greatly exasperated by the deflection of Crawford at a critical moment of the battle, and by Warren's absence from the key-point; he sent officer after officer to Crawford to direct him to return to the fight, and officer after officer to Warren to say that he wished to see him. In the confusion of the battle and the constant changes of position, Warren could not be found, and Sheridan finally sent him an order relieving him from command. This was received by Warren just before the close of the fight; and as Griffin met the cavalry at Five Forks, Sheridan in person placed him in command of the corps, and ordered him to push down the White Oak road. Griffin kept up the pursuit till after dark, when the command was halted, the cavalry having pushed to the front, out of sight and hearing of the infantry, a distance of at least six miles.

At seven o'clock, the entire rebel force had been either captured or dispersed, and the cavalry was recalled. Griffin was now ordered to countermarch the Fifth corps on the White Oak road, and go into position east of Five Forks, facing Petersburg, for it was feared that Lee might make some attempt to relieve the force that had been detached from his

army. Merritt went into camp west and south of the Forks, and Mackenzie remained on the Ford road at the crossing of Hatcher's run.*

Thus, the daring but desperate manoeuvre of Lee had failed, and, in fact, recoiled on himself. The troops that he had dispatched to crush Sheridan were necessarily separated, as we have seen, from the main rebel line, and although at first they threatened the national cavalry, the prompt action of Grant in forwarding reinforcements gave Sheridan the chance to fall upon this detached force. Sheridan caught eagerly at the opportunity, and, though disappointed and detained at first by Warren's obstructiveness and delays, when he finally found his troops in hand, he planned and fought a battle which, for intelligence in conception and brilliancy of execution and completeness of result, both immediate and far-reaching, has few rivals in any war. The troops, cavalry and infantry, fought as if inspired. They seemed to divine the object of their commander as soldiers seldom can, and to be filled with his energy, and only rivals to each other in gallantry. The generals were as heroic as the men, and the men as intelligent as their officers. The

* No complete return was made of the absolute numbers or losses of the cavalry at the battle of Five Forks. Crook's division, 3,000 strong, was south of Dinwiddie on the 1st of April, and as far from the battle-field as the left of the army of the Potomac. Excluding Crook, the cavalry strength was probably 8,000 ; at Sheridan's headquarters the loss was estimated at 700. General Warren reported his numbers at 12,000, and the losses in the Fifth corps were 634. The former adjutant-general of the army of Northern Virginia estimates the rebel losses at 7,000. See " Four Years with General Lee." See also Appendix for " Official Statement of the Effective Force of the Cavalry under Command of Major-General Sheridan, in the Operations of Dinwiddie Court-House, Va., March 31, 1865, and Five Forks, Va., April, 1865," with remarks.

only fault from beginning to end was the deliberation of Warren in forming his lines and the obliquing of Crawford to avoid the fire under which Ayres also quailed. But both divisions afterwards did as well as men could do, and earned a full share of the laurels of the day.

It was a sad episode of this important victory that a prominent and patriotic national officer should have been relieved on the field. But it seemed inevitable. The eager energy of Sheridan could neither understand nor tolerate the deliberate cautiousness of Warren. The one commander was useless to the other. But to achieve success, generals must have subordinates whom they can inspire. Sheridan was, above everything, a man of genius ; of fiery enthusiasm ; of magnetic influences; exciting and receiving impulses; with a concentrated force that nothing could withstand. In this battle, he rode about with a terrible manner; black in the face with rage; sparing neither reproaches nor threats to incite those who seemed to him dilatory ; shaking his sword and his fist by turns; driving men who had been wounded into the front rank; seizing the colors from the bearer's hands, and plunging mounted into the thickest fire —the very incarnation of battle. Such a man could not endure the careful elaboration with which Warren sought to provide against defeat before he attempted to secure success. Sheridan's way to provide against defeat was to capture victory. If his troops found a fire too hot, they were not to oblique away from it, but to rush up and stop it by seizing the enemy's guns. And, if he was harsh to a man before or in the midst of battle, it was with the same intolerant and irresistible passion with which

lie drove the rebel army. To this passion Warren succumbed as well as the enemy; and it may be that the double downfall was necessary.

At all events, so Sheridan thought and felt. He was aware that critical and instant movements might be precipitated. Lee might even yet turn on him with the bulk of what remained of the rebel army; he was himself isolated still from Grant. He must have a man who shared his spirit and would carry out his orders, and Warren, whatever his merits, was not this man.

Yet there need be no suspicion of Warren's patriotism or gallantry. He was as desirous of success as Sheridan himself; he lost a horse under him in this battle, and doubtless was thunderstruck when the order came for him to be relieved. His accomplishments no one denied ; his abilities under certain contingencies would have been all sufficient. He simply did not possess that daring impetuosity, that splendid enthusiasm, that prompt, impatient, irresistible spirit which in other emergencies is indispensable. He was not a soldier to wring victory out of defeat, to seize upon an instant, to move without regard to flanks or reserves or even the enemy, to forget everything but the order to advance. Grant had found this out before, and supported Sheridan fully on this occasion.

The general-in-chief had three aides-de-camp with Sheridan this day, sending them in succession to communicate his views. Colonel Porter was instructed first to say that the movements of the main army would very much depend upon the result of Sheridan's operations; that Grant would have preferred to send him the Sixth corps, but it was at too great

distance to reach him in time, and the Fifth corps, being the nearest, had been dispatched instead. A little before noon Colonel Babcock arrived, with a verbal message from Grant to the effect that Sheridan was to have complete control of his own movement, that the responsibility would rest entirely with him; and that, if in his judgment, Warren should not prove equal to the task assigned him, Sheridan must not hesitate to relieve him and put another in command of the Fifth corps.

This message was the result of the experience of a year. Grant believed that disappointments and partial rebuffs had occurred again and again on both sides of the James, originating in Warren's peculiarities. In this view he had been confirmed by several of the events of the present campaign; and he was not willing to risk a repetition of the experience. The feelings of no man must be allowed to stand in the way of the interests of the country and the cause. Still, he was loath to mortify an able and loyal subordinate, who, doubtless, did his best, although his best was not enough. He hesitated some hours before sending this permission, which was, indeed, almost an invitation, to Sheridan. But when, on the morning of the 1st of April, he was fully aware of the inefficiency displayed in moving —disarranging all his plans, and disappointing all his expectations, and risking the success of the entire army—he gave the word.

It was Warren's misfortune not to succeed in inspiring his superiors with confidence in the heartiness of his support. He forgot that it was his duty to please them, not theirs to please him. He constantly criticised and changed, or sought to change,

his orders; and, like most critical natures, his was deficient in the force indispensable in the greatest exigencies. Brave enough personally, he utterly lacked audacity as a commander, and had no conception of rapidity in handling or moving troops. But audacity and rapidity are as essential to success in war as skill or vigilance. This battle was one of those tremendous occasions when both were required; when ordinary action is not enough; and Warren, devoting himself to details, placing himself at the less important positions on the field, unable to hold his troops in hand, or to perceive the necessity of intense, concentrated, instant action, failed at the moment when the genius of his commander became supreme. The success of the one is the explanation of the failure of the other.

CHAPTER XXXIII.

News of the battle of Five Forks—Grant orders assaults on Petersburg —Spirit of commanders—Lethargy of Lee—Wright carries rebel line— Parke carries outer line—Ord and Humphreys penetrate line in their front — Grant enters enemy's works — Enthusiasm of troops — Grant faces Meade's command eastward and envelops Petersburg—Rebel army falling back in great confusion—Fighting in front of Parke—Longstreet brought from north side of James—Capture of Fort Gregg—Sheridan's movements on left—Miles's battle at Sutherland station—Final success of Miles— Sheridan pursues the enemy to the Appomattox—Correspondence with Sherman—Grant's dispositions on night of April 2nd—Lee orders all troops to Amelia court-house—Object of *Lee—Evacuation of Petersburg—Entrance of national troops—Orders of Grant to intercept Lee—Grant's entry into Petersburg—Interview with Lincoln—Departure of Grant for Appomattox valley—Fall of Richmond—Conduct of Davis and Lee— Misery of inhabitants—Withdrawal of garrison—Firing of city—Night of April 2nd—Entrance of Weitzel—Richmond saved by national soldiers.

ON the night of the battle of Five Forks Grant was stilhat Dabney's saw-mill, expecting intelligence from Sheridan. Before him stretched in the darkness the forces of Ord and Meade, in front of the works which had withstood them so long. As far as the national lines extended, they still found themselves facing an enemy, and even when Grant had detached a portion of his command, Lee also divided his army. But this last act of the rebel chief had precipitated, and in reality assisted, the development of Grant's plans, and the national leader now only waited for news from the left, in order to attack the weakened front of his adversary. During the after-noon orders were issued to Humphreys, Wright, and Parke to assault at four A.M., and Ord also was held in readiness. The greatest issues hung upon the scales.

At 7.45 P. M., the general-in-chief sent word to the President: " Sheridan with his cavalry and the Fifth corps has evidently had a big fight this evening. The distance he is off is so great, however, that I shall not probably be able to report the result for an hour or two."

The rain was now over, and Grant sat outside of his tent, wrapped in the blue overcoat of a private soldier which he wore in this campaign. Two or three staff officers were with him, hovering around the camp fire in the wet and gloomy woods. Two had remained all day with Sheridan to bring the earliest reports. Suddenly the cheers of the troops were heard in the distance, as they gathered from an officer while he rode along the character of his news. Every one at head-quarters knew what it must be. Soon the aide-de-camp came up, and, before he dismounted, had told a part of his story. " The rebels didn't run," he said, " on any particular road." Five Forks was won, but the completeness of the success was still not known. Grant at once sent word to Meade : " Humphreys must push now, or everything will leave his front, and be concentrated against Sheridan." The instinct of battle was aroused, and he saw in an instant not only what the enemy should do, but what steps he himself must take in order to circumvent Lee.

Before long another officer arrived in great excitement, having ridden hard from the field.* He

* The bearer of the good news was Colonel Horace Porter, one of the most abstemious men in the army ; but he came up with so much 114

brought the full intelligence. Grant listened calmly to the report, only now and then interrupting to ask a question. When all was told, he rose, and without saying a word entered his tent, where a candle flickered on the table. He invited no one to join him, but wrote a dispatch in sight of the officers outside, and gave it to an orderly. Then, coming out to the fire again, he said, as calmly as if he were remarking, " it is a windy night,"—" I have ordered an immediate assault along the lines."

When it is remembered how often during the war these assaults had been made, and how often they were unsuccessful; in what light the country had come to regard attacks on fortified works; how possible repulse was even yet, and how disastrous repulse might be—with the army divided, and the cavalry and the Fifth corps miles away, the character and importance of the decision can be better appreciated. But Grant felt that the hour and the opportunity had arrived; he had that intuitive sympathy with his soldiers which all great commanders share; he knew that they must be inspired by Sheridan's victory as well as the rebels depressed; that this was the instant in which all things were possible ; and he ordered the assault.

The dispatch was to Meade, and in these words:

enthusiasm, clapping the general-in-chief on the back, and otherwise demonstrating his joy, that the officer who shared his tent rebuked him at night for indulging too freely in drink at this critical juncture. But Porter had tasted neither wine nor spirits that day. He was only drunk with victory.

His mate himself was not much calmer. He had been shot in the foot, and wore a steel boot on the wounded leg ; and when the order was given to mount and ride to the front, he laced up his boot on the unhurt limb before he discovered his blunder. Then Porter retaliated.

" Wright and Parke should both be directed to feel for a chance to get through to the enemy's line at once, and if they can get through, should push on to-night. All our batteries might be opened at once, without waiting for preparing assaulting columns. Let the corps commanders know the result on the left, and that it is still being pushed."

At the same time he sent word to the President, waiting anxiously in the adjutant-general's hut at City Point, for news from his armies: better news he got that night than ever before, in four long years; news to warm his patriotic heart at last, before it was chilled for ever. "I have just heard," said Grant, "from Sheridan. He has carried everything before him. . . . He has captured three brigades of infantry and a train of wagons, and is now pushing up his success. I have ordered everything else to advance and prevent a concentration of the enemy against Sheridan." This idea was constantly in his mind, and appeared in every dispatch—to prevent concentration against Sheridan.

To Ord also he said: " I have just heard from Sheridan. . . . Everything the enemy has will probably be pushed against him. Get your men up, and feel the enemy to see if he shows signs of giving way;" and, a little later, he telegraphed to Weitzel, north of the James: " I have directed Colonel Bowers to send you the report of Sheridan's success this afternoon. I have since ordered an attack to-night and pursuit. Communicate the result to your troops. Be ready also to push any wavering that may be shown in your front."

All was bustle and business now. The replies

from commanders were full of spirit. Ord declared that his troops would go into the enemy's lines " as a hot knife goes into melted butter," and Wright promised to " make the fur fly." " If the corps does half as well as I expect," he said, " we will have broken through the rebel lines in fifteen minutes from the word ' go.' " When this was reported to Grant, he said: "I like the way Wright talks. It argues success. I heartily approve." Wright, indeed, had been full of confidence ever since the beginning of the movement. He was ready to assault at any time, and inspired not only his subordinates but his superiors with his own belief in victory. Meade, too, felt the influence of the hour, and was even more prompt than Grant designed, for he sent out orders to attack without forming assaulting columns, and at 9.50 p. M. Grant telegraphed to him: " I did not mean that attack should be made without assaulting columns, but that batteries should open on receipt of orders. They can feel out with skirmishers and sharpshooters if the enemy is leaving, and attack in their own way." He knew that under the influence of success both troops and commanders could be trusted. The sanguine talk all day had assured him of this, even before the news from Sheridan arrived.

To Ord he said at this time: " General Wright speaks with great confidence of his ability to go through the enemy's lines. I think, as you have such difficult ground to go over, your reserves had better be pushed well over to the right, so that they can help him, or go in with you, as may be required."

The instructions to Meade were now made more

detailed: " I believe," said Grant, " with a bombardment beforehand, the enemy will abandon his works. If not pursued, Sheridan may find everything against him. Humphreys can push everything he has to his left, and if he finds the enemy breaking in his front, then push the single line left, directly to the front. If there is no break made by the enemy, then Miles's division can be pushed directly down the White Oak road. Parke and Wright can open with artillery and feel with skirmishers and sharpshooters, and if the enemy is giving way, push directly after him." Ord also was informed : " If it is impracticable for you to get through in your front, I do not want you to try it. But you can, in that case, draw out of your lines more men as a reserve, and hold them to throw in where some one else may penetrate. My opinion is you will have no enemy confronting you in the morning. You may find them leaving now. Understand, I do not wish you to fight your way over difficult barriers against defensive lines. I want you to see through if the enemy is leaving, and if so, follow him up."

Grant's great anxiety was that Lee should not escape before the assault was made, and precipitate himself on Sheridan. Before the news of the battle arrived, he had directed Meade to hold Miles's division, of the Second corps, in readiness to move to the left;* and at 9.30p. M., he said again: " I would fix twelve to-night for starting Miles's division down

* " Miles's division should be wheeled by the right immediately, so as to prevent reinforcing against Sheridan."— Grant to Meade, April 1, 5.45 p. M.

"Miles's division has been ordered to swing around to the White Oak road/'— Grant to Sheridan, April 1.

White Oak road to join Sheridan, if the enemy is not started by that time and the Second corps in pursuit. With Miles's division, and what he already has, I think Sheridan could hold all of Lee's army that could be got against him till we could get up." The corps commanders, however, reported that they could not be ready to assault before morning, and the order was finally made definite for four A. M. Parke and Wright were to attack positively, and Humphreys and Ord, if they found the enemy leaving, or if for any other cause an assault seemed feasible. Sheridan was now notified of the movement. "An attack," said Grant, "is ordered for four in the morning at three points on the Petersburg front; one by the Ninth corps, between the Appomattox and the Jerusalem plank road, one west of the Wei-don road, and the third between that and Hatcher's run. From your isolated position I can give you no specific directions, but leave you to act according to circumstances. I would like you, however, to get something done to the Southside road, even if you do not tear up a mile of it." During the night a messenger from Sheridan arrived, with further reports of the situation. He was quite prepared to receive an attack from Petersburg, but proposed himself to march by the White Oak road in the morning, against the right flank of Lee. The suggestion was approved by Grant, who still, however, was apprehensive that the enemy might desert his lines and fall upon Sheridan, before assistance could arrive, with the hope of driving him from his position, and opening a way for the retreat of the entire rebel army. To guard against this, not only was Miles's division sent to reinforce Sheridan and oc-

ULYSSES S. GRASTT.

cupy the White Oak road, by which Lee must move, but the furious bombardment begun before midnight was kept up till morning.

But Lee made no attempt whatever to escape, nor indeed to prepare for the assault which he must have seen was inevitable. On the contrary, he ordered Pickett to return towards Petersburg,* and left Longstreet with ten thousand men north of the James, f at the very moment when Grant was massing his forces to deal his heaviest blow. The bombardment presaged the coming storm, and Lee had received intelligence of the disaster at Five Forks. He still had in front of Grant, between the Appo-mattox and the Claiborne road, as many as forty .thousand effective men, J and a line of works as strong and as skilfully constructed as ever defended an army. The force before him was not more than sixty thousand in number, including the entire effective strength of Parke, Wright, Ord, and Humphreys, as they stood in line of battle. It would seem as if the gallant soldiers who had so long withstood the national armies might even yet have resisted an advance; or that the ingenuity and skill which had contrived so many manoeuvres might still have devised a plan by which those soldiers should have eluded their foe, and made one more effort to escape destruction.

* Pickett's Report.

t Lee's last return, February 20th, puts Longstreet's effective strength at 7,403, exclusive of Pickett. In emergencies the rebels habitually put their extra-duty men into battle, and these in Long-street's command were 2,100 in number on the 20th of February. Besides these, the local reserves in Richmond were sent to Longstreet on the 2nd of April. See Rebel War Clerk's Diary, Vol. ii, p. 465.

\'7b The numbers were 38,258, besides 4,207 on extra duty.

But Lee was apparently stunned, or bewildered, by the extent of his misfortunes or the prescience of further disaster. The right of his army had been wrenched violently from the centre, yet he allowed his left to remain separated by the James river from the bulk of his command, while he stood still to receive the blow which he knew was about to fall. He seems, indeed, to have lost his usual self-control, for, in his chagrin at the defeat of Pickett, he declared that he would place himself at the head of his troops when they next went into action, and he ordered his generals to put all stragglers in arrest, with plain reference to the conduct of the officers. But the inhabitants of Richmond had no warning of their danger, and there is no record that even the. rebel government was yet apprised of the calamity at Five Forks. Lee's whole conduct at this crisis was that of a man whose faculties were beginning to give way amid the wreck of his cause and the crash of his army tumbling into ruins around him.

On the morning of the 2nd of April, the assault was made by Wright and Parke; Ord and Humphreys at first waiting to ascertain the result on the right of the line.

Wright had assembled his troops at the point where, on the 25th of March, he had carried the rebel entrenched picket line, in front of his old left. This was within striking distance of the enemy's main entrenchments. The national line here turned to the south, so that the Sixth corps faced both north and west, and fronted towards the Boydton road. The command was formed in three divisions, the centre somewhat in advance, and the other two right and left in front respectively, in order to be ready to move promptly in either direction. Five batteries accompanied the assaulting column, and in addition twenty picked artillerymen, volunteers for the duty, who were supplied with tools for the purpose of turning any captured guns immediately upon the enemy. Pioneers were distributed in advance, to clear away obstructions, and the sharpshooters of the corps were disposed so as to render the most effectual service. Perfect silence was enjoined on the entire command until the moment of assault.

The ground in front, though clear of trees, was obstructed by marshes which partially covered the enemy's line, and immediately on the right was an inundation, rendering an approach in that direction entirely impracticable, while still further to the east were the strong works originally constructed for the defence of Petersburg. The fortifications to be assaulted consisted of a line of rifle-pits with deep ditches and high relief, covered at intervals of every few hundred yards by forts or batteries well supplied with artillery, and the whole preceded by three separate lines of abatis and fraise.

By some mischance or misapprehension the pickets in the vicinity of the forming columns began a fire while the troops were taking position, and thus brought a return fire, not only on themselves, but on the dense masses in their rear. This for a moment threatened to interfere with the plan of the attack, by precipitating an advance; but, although many casualties occurred, the officers succeeded in quieting the men, who remained without returning a shot or uttering a word to disclose their position to the enemy.

At four o'clock the unusual darkness rendered any connected movement still impracticable, but at 4.40 A. M. there was light enough for the men to see to step. Even then nothing was discernible beyond the distance of a few yards, but at that hour the columns moved. They broke at once over the rebel picket line, and made their way rapidly, under a heavy fire of artillery and a still more deadly one of musketry, towards the parapet. Abatis was cut away, and through the openings thus effected, and those left by the enemy for his own convenience of access to the front, the main defences were reached. Here the rebels made a gallant stand, but the struggle, though sharp, was brief, and in a few moments the works were carried, and Wright was in possession of the whole front of attack of his corps.

In the ardor of the movement it was quite impossible at once to check the advance of the troops, and parties from each division soon reached the Boydton road and the Southside railway, breaking up the rails and cutting the rebel telegraph wires. As promptly as possible, however, the lines were reformed and wheeled to the left; and then, with his left guiding on the rebel entrenchments, Wright moved down towards Hatcher's run. At first the enemy attempted resistance, but this was speedily overcome, and the entire rebel line from the point of attack to Hatcher's run, with all the artillery and a large number of prisoners, was soon in possession of the Sixth corps.

Parke's advance was made at the point where the Jerusalem plank road entered the rebel fortifications. During the night he had surprised and captured about half a mile of the rebel picket line, taking two hundred and fifty prisoners, but the movement disclosed the enemy's works well manned, the troops on the alert, and no apparent change in the force in front, either of artillery or infantry. In order not to precipitate the general assault, the captured picket line was abandoned. The musketry firing soon quieted down, and the concentration of the troops proceeded. Hartranf t was massed on the right of the Jerusalem road and Potter on the left, these two divisions forming the assaulting column. Storming parties, accompanied by pioneers provided with axes to clear away the abatis, preceded each division, and details of artillerymen to work any guns that might be captured were also in readiness.

Wilcox was to make a strong demonstration in his front, further to the right, to deceive the enemy as to the real point of attack, and at four o'clock he pushed out and captured a few of the rebel skirmishers, and even carried two hundred yards of the main line; but the enemy promptly concentrated upon him, and he was forced to retire. His movement, however, had the designed effect, and attracted the rebel attention away from the real point of assault.

At half-past four the signal for Parke's main attack was given, and the Ninth corps column moved swiftly and steadily forward. In a moment the rebel picket line was carried, the stormers and pioneers rushed on, and under a galling fire cut away openings in the abatis and chevaux-de-frise. The assaulting divisions followed close, and undeterred by a severe fire of cannon, mortar, and musketry from the now aroused main line, pressed gallantly on, capturing the rebel works in front, with twelve pieces of artillery and eight hundred prisoners. One

column swept to the right until the whole of what was called by the enemy Miller's salient was in Parke's possession. This part of the defences was heavily traversed and afforded a strong foothold, where the rebels fought from traverse to traverse with great tenacity. Parke, however, drove them back steadily for about a quarter of a mile, when, reinforced and aided by strong positions in the rear, they were able to check the national progress.

Parke now made a gallant attempt to carry the inner line. The captured guns were turned on the enemy, served at first by infantry volunteers, and afterwards by details of artillerymen from the batteries in the rear; but the rebels held their own. Potter at this point was severely wounded. It was now daylight, and no further attempt to advance was made, but attention was turned to securing what had been gained, and restoring the organization of the troops, unavoidably shattered in the heavy fighting and the advance in the dark over broken ground. The loss in officers had been very severe. The captured line was made tenable as speedily as possible, but the position was extremely exposed, the forts and batteries being open in the rear. Parke indeed had only carried an outer line, and, although it was of great strength, and the rebels had fought splendidly to retain it, they still possessed an interior and principal chain of works before Petersburg was reached. This inner line ran west for a short distance from the Jerusalem road, and then turned north to the Appomattox, inside of the works that Wright had carried, so that, after all the success of the morning, Petersburg was still in the possession of the enemy.

At 5.15 A. M., Wright reported his first success,

and Grant instantly sent word to Ord: " Wright has carried the enemy's line, and is pushing in. Now is the time to push your men to the right, leaving your line veiy thin, and go to his assistance." Next came the news of Parke's assault, and at six o'clock Humphreys also was ordered to advance. At 6.40, Grant sent his first dispatch to City Point, for the President: " Both Wright and Parke got through the enemy's line. The battle now rages furiously. Sheridan with his cavalry, the Fifth corps, and Miles's division of the Second corps I sent to him since one this morning, is now sweeping down from the west. All now looks highly favorable. Ord is engaged, but I have not yet heard the result on his front." Five minutes later, he said to Meade : " Wright can put in everything he has except the garrisons of the enclosed works. Ord is pushing by the shortest road to help Wright. I heard from Sheridan at 12.30 this morning." To Sheridan himself he said: " Wright and Parke attacked at daylight this morning, and carried the enemy's works in their front. Wright's troops, some of them, pushed through to the Boydton road, and cut the telegraph wire. Ord is now going in to reinforce Wright, and Humphreys is feeling for a soft place in the line south of Hatcher's run. I think nothing now is wanting but the approach of your force from the west to finish up the job on this side." It was time, however, to attend to the other end of the line, for Parke had reported the check to his advance, and at 7.10 A. M. Grant said to Meade : " There is more necessity for care on the part of Parke than of either of the other corps commanders. As I understand it, he is attacking the main line of works around Petersburg, whilst the others are only attack-

ing an outer line, which the enemy might give ,up without giving up Petersburg. Parke should either advance rapidly, or cover his men and hold all he gets." At the same time he cautioned Weitzel, north of the James: " The greatest vigilance is necessary on your part that the enemy do not cross the Ap-pomattox to overwhelm and drive back Parke." To the staff officer left in charge at City Point he said: " Instruct Benham to get the men at City Point out to the outer lines, and have them ready. While all our forces are going in, some enterprising rebels may possibly go through down there, in a fit of desperation, to do what damage they can." With all his aggressive audacity Grant never neglected the necessary precautions against similar traits in the enemy.

Meanwhile the two corps on the left of the Sixth had made their advance. The ground in front of Ord was difficult, and his troops at first did not succeed in penetrating the enemy's line; but, as the rebels weakened their force in his front in order to resist Wright and Parke, Ord also broke through the entrenchments. Humphreys too was doing well. At about half-past seven the entrenched picket line in his front was captured under musketry as well as artillery fire, and at eight o'clock Hays's division of the Second corps carried an important redoubt, with three guns and a large part of the garrison. Mott's division of the same corps was then pushed forward to the Boydton road, but found the rebels on that front had evacuated their line.

At 8.25 A. M., Grant thus summed up for the President the results that had been attained : " Wright has gone through the enemy's line, and now has a

regiment tearing up the track on the Southside railroad, west of Petersburg. Ord has gone in with Wright. I do not see how the portion of the rebel army north of where Wright broke through are to escape." While he wrote, a message arrived from the Twenty-fourth corps. Grant stopped to read it, and then continued: " Dispatch just received from Ord states some of his troops have just captured the enemy's works south of Hatcher's run, and are pushing on. This is bringing our troops rapidly to a focus with a portion of the rebels in the centre." Ten minutes later he announced the capture to Meade : " We have the forts next to Hatcher's run on both sides. I think there will be no difficulty in Humphreys marching forward now towards Petersburg, or towards the retreating foe." A little later he said to the officer in charge at City Point: " Notify Mulford to make no more deliveries of rebel prisoners whilst the battle is going on;" and in the same dispatch: " I have not yet heard from Sheridan, but I have an abiding faith that he is in the right place and at the right time."

Grant had remained at his head-quarters to receive reports until he learned that Ord as well as Wright had broken the lines, and then he rode out to direct the varying operations of his armies. It was now all one battle-field from Petersburg to beyond Five Forks. Everywhere the national columns had burst the rebel barriers, and were surging inward towards the railroad and the town that had been their goal for a year. The various corps were becoming confused as they converged, and it needed the chief to disentangle the lines. He soon approached the broken defences, and spurred his horse

over the works that had defied him so stubbornly. Just as he entered, he was met by a body of three thousand prisoners captured by Wright, marching to the rear. Next he came upon a division of the triumphant Sixth corps, moving with the haste of battle, but the cheers of the men as they passed told that they recognized who it was that had organized their victory. Grant galloped along, staying neither for prisoners nor cheers, receiving dispatches and instructing generals as he rode. The dead and the wounded showed that the works had not been too easily won.

Soon the news was brought that Ord had connected with Wright, and that Humphreys also had penetrated the lines. Grant at once decided to face the entire commands of Meade and Ord to the east and envelop Petersburg, moving rapidly against any further entrenchments that might be found. He rode himself to the right and soon came up with Meade. Directions for Parke to hold out were renewed ; Wright and Ord were to move along inside the captured works, and

Humphreys to come in on the left of Ord. Wright had halted at Hatcher's run to reform his lines, and one division of Ord's command now entered the works at the point carried by Wright, and passed along the front of the Sixth corps. Then together they retraced their steps, and advanced on the right and left of the Boydton road, towards Petersburg, Humphreys following with two divisions, leaving Miles still under the command of Sheridan.

The general-in-chief rode up on some high ground to watch the movement. The point was about a mile from the interior rebel line, and not three miles

from the heart of Petersburg. Here lie dismounted and sat on the ground near a farmer's house, and waited for reports. The rebel artillerists soon turned their guns against the group of officers and orderlies, and the place seemed hot for a while, even to men who were used to battle ; but just as the cannonading began, several officers arrived, and Grant remained to receive their intelligence, and write his orders in return. He was thus under fire for nearly a quarter of an hour, and his aides-de-camp, remembering the results that hung upon his life, ventured to suggest a change of position; but he sat unmoved, with his back to a tree, until the reports directed to this spot had all arrived. Then quietly, but rather maliciously, he remarked: "The enemy seems to have the range of this place. Suppose we ride away." A long breath, and a quick gallop, and the general-in-chief was out of danger.

At 10.45 A. M., he sent word again to the President: "Everything has been carried from the left of the Ninth corps. The Sixth corps alone captured more than three thousand prisoners. The Second and Twenty-fourth corps both captured forts, guns, and prisoners from the enemy, but I cannot yet tell the number. We are closing around the works of the city immediately enveloping Petersburg. All looks remarkably well. I have not yet heard from Sheridan."

The wrecks of the rebel army were now tumbling in from every direction towards Petersburg; cavalry, artillery, and infantry, all in rout and con-

k fusion. Gordon on the left was driven back by Parke; the centre under Hill had been pierced- and broken and almost destroyed by Wright; while Heth 115

and Wilcox, further to the west, were cut off by Humphreys and Ord. Pickett in the night had endeavored to gather up what he had saved from the ruin at Five Forks, and form a junction with the rebel right near Sutherland station, but, meeting the fugitives of Heth and Wilcox, who had thrown away their arms, he retraced his steps and hurried to cross the Appornattox at Exeter mills. Sheridan meantime was coming up by the White Oak road to shut off every avenue of escape, and complete the destruction of the enemy. It seemed for a while as if conquered and conquerors would enter Petersburg together, and whether Lee could retain any organization at all or the Appomattox be crossed, was a matter of doubt. The rebel chief had anticipated his defeat, and dressed himself that morning in full uniform, with his finest sword, declaring that if forced to surrender, he would fall in harness; and when it was announced that his works were carried, he simply said: " It has happened as I thought; the lines have been stretched until they broke." *

He fled with his escort from one position to another before the victorious columns, and once the advancing batteries were opened on a house where he had halted, and he was driven by their fire still nearer in towards Petersburg. At first but little effort seems to have been made to resist the national progress. Lee had been composed all through this terrible morning, but it was with the dull, apathetic composure of despair. It was necessary, however, to make some stand, or every man in the rebel army

* The statements in this chapter in regard to Lee's conduct and language are all taken from Pollard, McCabe, Cooke, or other rebel writers.

ULYSSES S. GRANT. 519

would be killed or captured then and there; and after a while he showed something of his ancient energy. Gordon was ordered, if possible, to force back Parke; Hill, Mahone, and Lee himself exerted themselves to stem the tide of flight and chase; the fragments of regiments were gathered up to man the yet uncaptured forts; and Longstreet was brought from the north side of the James. At forty minutes past ten, the rebel general sent the portentous news to Richmond: "I see no prospect," he said, " of doing more than holding our position here till night. I am not certain that I can do that."

Grant had early detected the movement of Long-street. At 10.45 A. M., he said to Weitzel: " One brigade of Mahone's division is here, and no doubt more will be here soon. Keep in a condition to assault when ordered, or when you may feel the right time has come." At 12.50 p. M., he telegraphed to the same commander: " Rebel troops are pouring over the Appomattox. Direct General Hartsuff to demonstrate against them on his front [at Bermuda Hundred], and, if there is a good showing, attack. The enemy will evidently leave your front very thin by night. I think I will direct you to assault by morning. Make your preparations accordingly."

Meanwhile, the rebels had made several attempts to regain the lines which had been wrested from them by Parke. These extended for a distance of about four hundred yards on each side of the Jerusalem road, and included several important forts and redans. The enemy had for several hours been busily planting guns to command the position,-and kept up an incessant sharpshooters' fire; but the

national reply had been so hot that every advance in line was at once repelled. At eleven o'clock, however, a heavy and determined assault was made, but was repulsed at every point with severe loss. Grant now ordered up two brigades from City Point to the support of Parke. The line was reversed, and the chevaux-de-frise transferred to the opposite front, while a cross line connected Parke's new right with the most advanced point of his original position. Every subsequent effort of the enemy in this direction was repelled. The desperate attempts to recapture this portion of the line were inspired by its proximity to Petersburg, which enabled Parke not only to command an important approach to the town, but with his artillery to threaten the bridge over the Appomattox, and the only possible exit of Lee.

At noon, the left wing under Sheridan was still unheard from, but the entire national centre and right were faced towards Petersburg, and approaching from south and west to envelop the town. Parke remained in the important position he had acquired; the Sixth and Twenty-fourth corps moved rapidly up to connect with the Ninth, and the two divisions of Humphreys were extending to the Appomattox on the north. The rebels, it has been seen, had constructed an interior line of works, running directly around the city, and outside of this was a series of enclosed and isolated forts, commanding the interval between the river and the line of fortifications carried at daybreak. What was left of the discomfited command of Lee had now been driven back upon this interior line. In the retreat several of the rebel batteries were dashingly handled, and inflicted considerable loss on the pursuing force, but with a sin-

gle exception they had all been thrust back, from point to point, inside the rebel lines. One battery, however, was captured, but not till its horses had been shot by the skirmishers of the Sixth corps.

Most of the outer works were speedily carried or abandoned, but two sister redoubts, Forts Gregg and Baldwin, offered stout resistance, and soon after midday the Twenty-fourth corps came up before them, They were the most salient and commanding works outside of Petersburg, and it was indispensable that they should be stormed. Accordingly, at one o'clock an assault on Fort Gregg was ordered. Three of Ord's brigades, under Turner and Foster, moved forward at once in close support, and a desperate struggle ensued. The garrison was composed of three hundred brave fellows, collected from various commands—artillery, infantry, and a body of mounted drivers called Walker's Mules, to whom muskets had been furnished, for the rebels habitually put even their teamsters into line of battle. These men had been driven from the picket line in the morning, and fled to Fort Gregg for shelter. Two rifled cannon constituted the armament. The rebels fought with splendid valor, and several times repulsed the assaulting party. At last the parapet was gained, but even then for half an hour a hand-to-hand conflict was maintained. Many of the garrison used their bayonets and clubbed muskets, and not until half-past two did the gallant remnant surrender. Two hundred and fifty officers and men were captured, and fifty-seven dead were found within the works. Several of Ord's regiments claimed the honor of first planting their colors on the parapet, but the real glory of this little battle indisputably belongs to the defend-

ers. It was the last fight made by rebel soldiers for their capital, and worthy of the old renown of the army of Northern Virginia.*

Fort Baldwin, the adjoining work, was at once evacuated, but the guns of Fort Gregg were turned on the retreating garrison, and the commander with sixty of his men surrendered.

The line of investment was now materially shortened, and the national troops closed in around Petersburg. The prolonged defence of Fort Gregg, however, had given Lee time to rally his disordered soldiers, and the arrival of Longstreet with Ms yet unbeaten command was a reinforcement that added spirit as well as strength to what was left of the routed army.

Meanwhile Sheridan had been busy on a more distant portion of the field. Miles reported to him at daybreak, and was ordered to move back towards Petersburg, and attack the enemy at the intersection of the White Oak and Claiborne roads. The rebels were found at this point, in force and in position, and Sheridan followed Miles immediately with two divisions of the Fifth corps. The enemy, however, withdrew from the junction, and Miles pursued with great zeal, pushing the fugitives across Hatcher's run, and following them up towards Sutherland station,

* The rebel writers, not satisfied with the legitimate glory won by the defenders of Fort Gregg, have magnified it into something marvellous. They declare that the garrison was only two hundred and fifty strong, and that these fought until only thirty were left alive. As the fort remained in the national possession, the rebels could not possibly have a knowledge of the number who surrendered. General Foster, who captured it, reported in April, 1865, before these fables were circulated, that two hundred and fifty were taken prisoner, officers and men, and fifty-seven dead were found inside.

ULYSSES S. GRANT.

on the Southside railroad. North of Hatcher's run, Sheridan came up with Miles, who had a fine and spirited division, and was anxious to attack, and Sheridan gave him leave. About this time Humphreys also arrived with the remainder of his corps, having made his breach in the lines, and moved up from the Boydton road. He now reassumed command of Miles, and Sheridan faced the Fifth corps by the rear, and returning* to Five Forks, marched out by the Ford road to Hatcher's run.

Grant, however, had intended to leave Sheridan in c<jp.mand of Miles, and indeed in full control of all the operations in this quarter of the field; and, supposing his views to have been carried out, it was at this juncture that he ordered Humphreys to be faced to the right and moved towards Petersburg. This left Miles unsupported by either Humphreys or Sheridan. Nevertheless, that gallant commander made his assault. But the rebel position was naturally strong as well as defended by breastworks and artillery, and Miles was compelled to retire. A second attack at half-past twelve met with no better fortune, although supported by a vigorous shelling from the artillery of the division. The position was important, for it covered the right of Lee's army; the rebels resisted vigorously, and Miles fell back to a crest about eight hundred yards from the

enemy's line.

News of the repulse was carried to Grant, now nearly five miles away, and for a while the general-in-chief was anxious about the fate of Miles. There was l*idently a movement to the west by the troops cut off from Lee, and these might concentrate.upon the isolated command and destroy it before they

retired. Humphreys was accordingly ordered to send another division to the support of Miles. He went himself with Hays's division, while Mott took position on the left of the line encircling Petersburg.

Sheridan meantime had sent Merritt westward to cross Hatcher's run, and break up the rebel cavalry, which had assembled in considerable force north of the stream; but the rebels would not stand to fight, and the national troopers pursued them in a northerly direction to the borders of the Appomat-tox river. Sheridan himself with the Fifth corps crossed Hatcher's run, and struck the Southside railroad, north of Five Forks; then, meeting with no opposition, he marched rapidly towards Sutherland, and came up in flank and rear of the enemy opposing Miles, just as Humphreys was returning on the right from Petersburg.

Miles, in the interval, had devised a plan not unlike the strategy of Sheridan at Five Forks, though on a smaller scale. He made a feint against the rebel right, pushing a strong skirmish line around that flank until he overlapped it and reached to the railroad; and, while the enemy's attention was thus diverted, at 2.45 p. M. he assaulted the opposite flank, sweeping rapidly down inside the breastworks, capturing nearly a thousand prisoners and' two pieces of artillery, and putting the remainder of the force to precipitate flight.

Sheridan overtook the rebels in their rout on the main road along the Appomattox river, and the cavalry and Crawford's division attacked them at nightfall; but the friendly darkness interposed, and the remnants of the force that had resisted Miles so stoutly threw away their arms and hid themselves

in the woods till morning. Miles had been ordered to pursue the enemy towards Petersburg, and advanced in that direction about two miles, when he met Humphreys with Hays's division coming up to his relief. He thereupon returned to Sutherland and went into bivouac.

The troops which he had encountered belonged to Heth and Wilcox's divisions, and possibly a few to Anderson's command. Pickett, we have seen, had endeavored to reach Sutherland during the day, having been ordered thither by Lee, but he found the road filled with unarmed fugitives from the battle, and concluded to cross the Appomattox without delay.

When Grant heard of the action at Sutherland, he declared to Meade : " Miles has made a big thing of it, and deserves the highest praise for the pertinacity with which he stuck to the enemy and wrung from him victory."

In the midst of the absorbing interest of the assaults on Petersburg, while directing the marches and counter-marches of his own converging columns, and planning to pursue and intercept the scattered forces of his routed adversary, Grant received dispatches from Sherman. At 4.30 p. M., a staff officer telegraphed from City Point: " A letter, of date 31st, from General Sherman is just received. He says the enemy is inactive in his front. He will move at the time stated to you. Thinks Lee will unite his and Johnston's army, and will not coop himself up in Kichmond. Would like to be informed if Sheridan swings off, that he may go out and meet him. Does not believe Sheridan can cross the Koanoke.for a month. Will send letter by mail." Grant replied

at once: " Send all my dispatches that have gone concerning operations to Sherman. . . . Have you stopped Mulford from delivering prisoners ? If he has any on hand for delivery, tell him to hold on to them." To Weitzel he now said: " You need not assault in the morning unless you have good reason for believing the enemy are leaving. We have a good thing of it now, and in a day or two I think I will be able to send you all the troops necessary."

At 4.40 P. M., the general-in-chief telegraphed to City Point: " We are now up, and have a continuous line of troops, and in a few hours will be entrenched from the Appomattox below Petersburg to the river above. ... The whole captures since the army started out gunning will not amount to less than twelve thousand men and probably fifty pieces of artillery. . . . All seems well with us, and everything quiet just now. I think the President might come out and pay us a visit to-morrow." To this Lincoln himself replied: " Allow me to tender to you, and all with you, the nation's grateful thanks for the additional and magnificent success. At your kind suggestion, I think I will meet you to-morrow." Grant thereupon telegraphed again: "If the President will come out on the nine A. M. train to Patrick station, I will send an escort to meet ,him. It would afford me much pleasure to meet the President in person at the station, but I know he will excuse me for not doing so when my services are so liable to be needed at any moment." At 8.40 p. M., he added to this : " I have just heard from Miles. He attacked what was left of Heth and Wilcox's divisions at Sutherland station, and routed them, capturing about a thousand prisoners. The enemy took the

road north to the Appomattox. As Sheridan was above them, I am in hopes but few of them will escape."

All west of the rebel centre had now been driven beyond the Appomattox by Sheridan, while all to the east was forced into Petersburg, from which there was no exit for Lee except by the country roads north of the river. The only question with Grant was, whether at once to assault the inner lines or wait for the rebels to move out from behind their works, and attack them in flight and undefended. The troops in front of Petersburg had been under arms for eighteen hours; they had assaulted the strongest lines known in modern war, swept down them several miles, and, returning, marched five miles east of the original point of attack ; they were too exhausted for another assault, unless it was absolutely necessary. Meade and others entitled to offer their opinions urged strongly that the whole army should be brought up to Petersburg, and the place assaulted in force; but Grant did not doubt that Lee had already determined upon flight, and a further assault of fortified works would only occasion unnecessaiy slaughter. He therefore decided to envelop the town on the southern side of the Appomattox, but to hold half his army in readiness for prompt pursuit. If the rebels should not withdraw, he meant, of course, to assault in the morning; but, if Lee evacuated the city in the night, the national troops in front of the town could take prompt possession of Petersburg, while Sheridan, and those disposed along the Appomattox, would be ready to intercept and pursue the flying columns. No assault was therefore ordered for the 2nd of April.

Sheridan had already been directed to cross the Appomattox west of Lee's army, with the Fifth corps and the cavalry. " You may cross where you please," said Grant. " The position and movements of the enemy will dictate your movements after you cross. All we want is to capture or beat the enemy." Humphreys also was held loose during the night, with orders to report to Sheridan. At 7.40 p. M., Grant said to Meade: " I would send Humphreys no orders further than to report to Sheridan, and return or cross the Appomattox as he wishes. . . . Sheridan thinks that all the rebel army that was outside the works immediately around the city are trying to make their escape that way. I think there is nothing in Petersburg except the remnant of Gordon's corps, and a few men brought from the north side to-day. I believe it will pay to commence a furious bombardment at five A. M. to be followed by an assault at six, only if there is good reason to believe the enemy is leaving. Unless Lee reaches the Danville road to-night, he will not be able to reach his army." At 9.45 p. M., he said, also to Meade: " Direct General Parke to use his siege artillery upon the railroad bridge to-night. If we can hit the bridge once, it will pay."

Grant was perfectly right in his intuitions. Lee was making all his preparations to evacuate Petersburg. He notified the authorities at Richmond of this at forty minutes past ten in the morning. " I see no prospect," he telegraphed, "of doing more than holding our position here till night. I am not certain that I can do that. If I can, I shall withdraw to-night north of the Appomattox, and if possible it will be better to withdraw the whole line to-night

from James river. The brigades on Hatcher's run are cut off from us; enemy have broken through our lines and intercepted between us and them, and there is no bridge over which they can cross the Appomattox this side of Goode or Bevil's, which are not very far from the Danville railroad. Our only chance, then, of concentrating our forces is to do so near Danville railroad, which I shall endeavor to do at once. I advise that all preparations be made for leaving Kichmond to-night. I will advise you later, according to circumstances."

At fifty-five minutes past four p. M., he said again: " I think the Danville road will be safe until to-mor-

row."Accordingly, during the afternoon Jefferson Davis and his chief confederates left the city, where for nearly four years they had defied the government to which they once had sworn allegiance. The exit of the rebel rule was as discreditable as its origin was dishonorable. The population of Richmond received no warning of the coming disaster. Not a rumor of the defeat at Five Forks had reached the rebel capital. On the contrary, it was announced and believed that a victory had been gained.* Davis was at church when Lee's telegram was handed to him. He read it, and left his prayers unfinished, while the clergyman dismissed his congregation at once, notifying them that the local forces were to assemble at three p. M., and afternoon service would not be held. The militia were hurried to the defences to relieve Longstreet's veterans, but still no public announcement of the ruin was made. Davis and his cabinet fled by a special train, leaving the

* Pollard's "Lost Cause."

population to take care of themselves. "It was after two p. M.," says the diary of a rebel war-clerk, " before the purpose to evacuate the city was announced, and the government had gone at eight."

At seven o'clock, Lee sent his last dispatch to the rebel Secretary of War, who alone of his government had remained at his post: " It is absolutely necessary," he said, " that we should abandon our position to-night, or run the risk of being cut off in the morning. I have given all the orders to officers on both sides of the river, and have taken every precaution that I can to make the movement successful. It will be a difficult operation, but I hope not impracticable. Please give all orders that you find necessary in and about Richmond. The troops will all be directed to Amelia court-house." *

When night fell on the 2d of April, Lee was still holding the semicircular line south of the Ap-pomattox which closely included Petersburg; while his extreme right, hard pressed by Sheridan, was fifteen miles west of the town. The forces from Richmond and the lines at Bermuda Hundred were already in motion to join him on the Appomattox; and Pickett and Bushrod Johnson were heading their scattered troops for Amelia court-house, crossing the river wherever they could find a bridge or a ford. Grant encompassed the city with his right wing, and his left extended parallel with the fragments of Lee'e command that had been left outside.

The whole object and aim of the rebel leader now was to effect a junction with Johnston, whose

* The three dispatches given in the text were the only reports made by Lee on the 2nd of April, and that dated seven o'clock was the last he sent to his government.

forces were massed at Smithfield, in North Carolina, half-way between Kaleigh and Goldsboro, and a little nearer than Sherman's troops to Petersburg. If Lee could possibly succeed in joining Johnston, he would still command a formidable army, and might hope even yet to give the national general serious trouble, or at least secure more favorable terms for the shattered Confederacy. The distance between the rebel armies was a hundred and fifty miles. To accomplish his purpose Lee must evade the columns of Grant, striking first for Burksville, at the junction of the Southside and Danville roads, fifty miles from Eichmond, and then move still further south towards Danville, to which point he might hope that Johnston would fall back in order to concentrate the two commands.

The Appomattox river, rising in the neighborhood of Lynchburg, and flowing east in a general course, ran directly across Lee's path, and as Grant had possession of the southern bank as far as Sutherland, the rebel general would be obliged to move on the opposite side for more than twenty miles; then, crossing at Goode or Bevil's bridge, he meant to strike for Amelia court-house on the Danville road, eighteen miles north of Burksville. At Amelia he expected to obtain supplies. Grant, of course, would divine his route and endeavor to follow or intercept his march; but Lee was no further from Burksville than the national army, and decidedly nearer to Amelia; * his troops would have the impetus of flight, and would start some hours in advance. By

* The rebel writers, with their habitual inaccuracy of military statement, declare that Grant had the interior line in these movements ; but a glance at the map is sufficient to disprove the assertion.

great exertions and expedition, the rebel chief still hoped to outmarch or outmanoeuvre his antagonist. He recovered from his first dejection of the morning, and later in the day gave orders for the concentration of all his forces for a night march.

But first he was present at the burial of a comrade. General A. P. Hill, one of the ablest of his corps commanders, had fallen in the assaults of the morning, and soon after dark Lee with his staff attended the hurried funeral. Then he rode out on the northern bank, and watched the movements of his retreating army, standing by the side of his horse, bridle in hand, at the junction of the roads to Richmond and Amelia. The rebel troops filed silently in the darkness past their chief out of the city they had defended so long. But there were no longer any lines to be held, any earthworks to be defended. The evacuation began at ten o'clock and was complete before three. Then Lee mounted his horse and followed his army. The forts on the James were blown up, and the bridges over the Ap-pomattox set on fire.

Desultory firing was kept up by Parke all night, and the batteries on his right opened at intervals upon the bridge, according to Grant's orders. As the evacuation was anticipated, the troops were instructed to use the greatest vigilance to detect any movement of the enemy, and at two A. M., Parke began feeling the rebel positions with skirmishers, but found the pickets still out. Before daylight, however, he reported that on two of his division fronts the rebel line, so far as developed, consisted only of skirmishers, and that a heavy explosion had occurred a little after three o'clock in the heart of Petersburg.

He pushed forward at once to ascertain whether the enemy had retired. Wright and Ord were notified of the report, and instructed also to push forward skirmishers to discover the condition of the enemy.

At four o'clock, Parke succeeded in penetrating the line in his front at all points almost simultaneously, capturing the few remaining pickets. Ely's brigade, of Wilcox's division, was the first to enter the town, near the Appomattox, and to Colonel Ely the formal surrender was made at 4.28 A. M. The Sixth corps also advanced, and the authorities must have been anxious to capitulate, for a second communication surrendering the town was forwarded by Wright to Meade. The flag of the Sixth Michigan sharpshooters was raised on the court-house, and guards were posted throughout the town. By the prompt efforts of officers and troops the main structure of the bridge was saved. Skirmishers were then pushed across the river, and numbers of stragglers were captured both in the city and outskirts.

At ten minutes past five Meade reported to Grant:" Colonel Ely is in possession of Petersburg;" and Grant instantly replied: " You will march immediately with your army up the Appomattox, taking the River road, leaving one division to hold Petersburg and the railroad." He followed this with a personal interview, and at six o'clock Meade issued his orders to the corps commanders. Mott's division of the Second corps was on the extreme left of the investing force, nearest the river, and Meade instructed Wright: " Send Mott up the River road to join Humphreys as soon as possible. Move with your whole corps at once, following Mott, and keeping control of him until he shall report to Humphreys."

To Parke, Meade said: " Leaving one division to guard Petersburg and the railroad, move with the rest of your command up the Cox road." At the same time Grant dispatched an officer to Sheridan, announcing the fall of the city, and ordering him to push to the Danville road with all speed, with Humphreys and Griffin, as well as the cavalry.

Before the troops were in motion, the general-in-chief telegraphed to City Point for the President: " Petersburg was evacuated last night. Pursuit will be made immediately." He had already said to Ord: " Efforts will be made to intercept the enemy, who are evidently pushing towards Danville. Push southwest with your command by the Cox road. The army of the Potomac will push up the River road."

Thus Grant's first orders were—not to follow Lee through Petersburg, but to intercept him, moving his whole command by the south side of the Appo-mattox towards the Danville railroad, while Lee was hastening on the northern bank to cross, as he had said, at Goode or Bevil's bridge. It was characteristic of the national general that he was not satisfied with pursuit. One division was left in Petersburg, and the army, without even entering the town it had besieged for nearly a year, was hurried westward to get in front of its retreating enemy.

To Weitzel, Grant now telegraphed : " I do not doubt but you will march into Richmond unopposed. Take possession of the city. Establish guards, and preserve order until I get there. Permit no man to leave town after you get possession. The army here will endeavor to cut off the retreat of the enemy."

At nine o'clock, the general-in-chief rode into

Petersburg to obtain what information he could in regard to the movements of Lee. The streets were nearly vacant, but here and there groups of women and children gazed curiously at the conqueror. The negroes came up closer, and a few gave cheers; but the entry into the captured town had none of the formalities of a triumph. Grant rode through the narrow streets, attended only by his staff, and alighted at the house of a citizen, where he sat in the porch, receiving intelligence and examining prisoners. Soon an officer from Sheridan arrived with reports. " Before receiving your dispatch," said Sheridan, " I had anticipated the evacuation of Petersburg, and had commenced moving west. My cavalry is nine miles beyond Namozine creek, and is pressing the enemy's trains. I shall push on to the Danville road as rapidly as possible." Grant replied, at 10.20 A. M. : " The troops got off from here early, marching by the River and Cox roads. It is understood that the enemy will make a stand at Amelia court-house, with the expectation of holding the road between Danville and Lynchburg. The first object of present movement will be to intercept Lee's army, and the second to secure Burksville. I have ordered the road to be put in order up to the latter place as soon as possible. I shall hold that place if Lee stops at Danville, and shall hold it anyhow, until his policy is indicated. Make your movements according to this programme."

Soon after this he received a dispatch from City Point, announcing that the President was coming up to Petersburg, and replied: " Say to the President that an officer and escort will attend him, but, as to myself, I start towards the Danville road with the

army. I want to cut off as much of Lee's army as possible."

Lincoln, however, arrived before Grant had left the town, and the two had a short interview in the rebel porch. The President, of course, was cheerful at the great success which had been achieved, but there was a dash of anxiety mingled with his satisfaction ; he foresaw the imminent civil complications that success involved. His great heart was full of charity, however, and he was planning already what merciful magnaminity he could show to those who had resisted and reviled himself and his government so long. Some of these plans he unfolded now to Grant.

There was no news yet of the capture of Richmond, and at 12.30 p. M. the general-in-chief telegraphed to Weitzel, showing the dispatch to the President: " How are you progressing ? "Will the enemy try to hold Richmond ? I have detained the division belonging to your corps, and will send it back if you think it will be needed. I am waiting here to hear from you. The troops moved up the Appomattox this morning." To Hartsuff, who was in command in front of Bermuda Hundred, he said : " What do you learn of the position of the enemy in your front ? If the enemy have moved out, try to connect pickets with the forces from Petersburg."

After remaining an hour and a half, the President returned to City Point, and Grant set out to join Ord's column, having yet received no message from Richmond. He had not ridden far, however, before a dispatch was handed him from Weitzel. It was in these words: " We took Richmond at 8.15 this morning. I captured many guns. Enemy left in great

haste. The city is on fire in two places. Am making every effort to put it out."

But the capture of the rebel capital had now become a comparatively unimportant circumstance. The all-absorbing object was the capture of the rebel army; and when the news that had been waited and wished for so long was communicated to the troops, it created no surprise, no especial exultation even. In the crowd of events and emotions that filled this day, it was only one great subject of rejoicing among many others. "Richmond is taken," was the word passed along the column. "Ah, is it?" the soldiers said; " well, we must make haste now to catch Lee."

It is difficult to conceive a more dastardly act or a more pitiable fate than supplemented and consummated the fall of Richmond. Here was a city of a hundred thousand inhabitants, which for nearly four years had been the capital of an armed rebellion; the centre and focus of the opposition to the government, now abandoned by its defenders and exposed alone to the punishment which its garrison should have remained to share; which had collected a surplus population, composed in large part of the adventurers and miscreants, the drunkards, and gamblers, and libertines, the characterless characters that congregate around a falling political conspiracy ; a city where every man had been engaged in treason, and was liable to its penalties, and every woman had abetted it; a city which had endured the privations of a siege, where provisions were scarce and dear, and money would now be annihilated; * a

* The so-called Confederate money of course became worthless wherever the national armies were in possession. It had been almost worthless for months in advance.

city crowded with a servile race who looked to the approach of the besiegers to set them free—and this place was left by the authorities and the army to await the entrance of its conqueror—without one soldier to keep order, or restrain pillage, or claim protection, or exchange military formalities with the captors. The so-called government fled in dismay and disgrace, and the conduct of the army was little better towards its capital in this emergency. Lee was as derelict as Davis, and equally with him deserved the execrations which the other received.* For Lee was general-in-chief, and knew of the flight of his superiors; he knew the destitution and desperation of the inhabitants; he was a soldier, and knew what horrors often come upon besieged cities when at last they fall. Yet he left not a company, not a squad, behind. He made no pretence of surrendering the forts or their armament, and therefore ran the risk of exasperating the victors; thus saving his military pride at the expense of his military honor. He did not attempt to protect the miserable wretches whom he abandoned, a prey to all the anguish of expectation and despair. His generals followed his example and his orders; f they withdrew after dark, and set fire to the warehouses in the most crowded part of the city as they fled; and

* I was sent to Richmond immediately after the close of this campaign, and found the inhabitants indignant at the conduct of Davis, and eager to learn of his capture. "Haven't they caught him yet ? " "What will they do with him ?" "Won't they hang him ? " were the constant inquiries of men and women whose sympathy had been entirely with the rebellion.

t "What I did was in obedience to positive orders that had been given to me. ... I did not exceed, but fell short of my instructions. "—Letter of General Ewell, written at Fort Monroe while he was a prisoner. 1865.

when night came on the rebellion went down under an accumulation of agony and dread such as the world has seldom seen.

When the news first spread that Richmond was to be evacuated, it was disbelieved. The citizens, we have seen, had been kept in utter ignorance of their danger, and even supposed a victory had been achieved. But the preparations at the Jefferson Davis house and in the government offices betrayed the truth. Wagons loaded with boxes and trunks were driven to the station of the Danville railroad, and the archives of the rebel government and the effects of the rebel president went off together as freight.

Next there came a street rumor of bloody fighting beyond Petersburg, on the Southside road, in which Pickett's division was said to have met with fearful loss. Nothing of this, however, was disclosed by the government, even to the clerks in the War Office; but the marching of veteran troops from the defences and the replacing of them hurriedly with militia indicated the emergency. At two p. M. it was known that the national army had certainly broken through Lee's lines and attained the Southside road.

Soon men in uniform were seen, some of them officers, hurrying away with their trunks; but they were not allowed to put them on the cars. The legislature of Virginia escaped by the canal, and, in less than an hour after the first appearance of wagons in the streets, the population of Richmond was involved in a panic. Every road leading north was crowded with vehicles, which commanded any price. Squads of local troops and reserves were marching

to and fro, but of no use. The negroes stood silent, wondering what would be their fate. Next, all horses were impressed. Then, committees were appointed by the city government to visit the liquor shops and destroy the spirits. Hundreds of casks were rolled out of doors and the heads knocked in. The streets ran with liquor, and women and boys— black and white—were seen filling their buckets from the gutters. The commissariat stores were also opened, and their contents thrown out to the excited throngs. Some of the shopkeepers offered clothes to the departing soldiers. The streets were filled with people hurrying to the different avenues of exit; porters, carrying huge loads, ran hither and thither; the banks were all open, and depositors were anxiously collecting their specie, directors as anxiously getting off their bullion. Millions of dollars of paper money were carried to the Capitol square, and buried there.

After nightfall Swell's command, the garrison of Richmond, was withdrawn, burning the three bridges across the James in its flight; and, worse still, an order was issued to fire the four principal tobacco warehouses. The magistrates protested, but, in the mad excitement of the hour, the protest was unheeded, and the torch was applied. These stores were near the centre of the city, side by side with important mills, and the flames soon seized the neighboring buildings, and involved a wide area of the richest portion of the town.

And now Pandemonium seemed let loose. The guards of the penitentiary fled from their posts, in imitation of their superiors, and numbers of the lawless and desperate villains incarcerated for crimes of

every grade and hue set fire to the workshops and made their escape, and donning garments wherever they could steal them, in exchange for their prison livery, roamed over the streets without let or hindrance. Richmond all night was ruled by the mob. The fumes of the whiskey in the gutters filled and impregnated the air. The crowd surged from street to street and store to store, breaking open and robbing houses and shops, and sometimes setting them on fire. No one opposed, for every one believed that the city would be sacked in the morning. The last train left for Danville after dark, and there was then no further egress.

Some of the soldiers had left the ranks when Ewell withdrew, and these now added to the confusion, and the shouts of the plunderers, the yells of the drunken, the cries of the timid, were heard on every side. The patrols could not be found; the militia had slipped by their officers ; and the mean-visaged crowds that in time of great public misfortune emerge from their dens were all abroad. The smoke and glare of the fire filled the streets; the flames reached to whole blocks of buildings, and before daylight one-third of Richmond was ablaze. The engine hose was cut.

At intervals came the terrible shocks caused by the explosion of the rams and gun-boats on the James, which were destroyed by order of Semmes, and the arsenal and laboratory, full of shells, were also fired.

The portion of the respectable population unable to get away remained in such of their houses as were not afire, collecting and secreting valuables, burying money and plate, or parting with those

friends who still hoped to join the fugitives; anxious even for the entrance of the national troops to put an end to the terrors of this awful night. One colonel in the rebel army made his way into Rich-mond after dark and was married, and then rejoined his command.

And thus amid acres of burning stores, and dwellings, and manufactories, and mills, and arsenals, and bridges, and vessels even; amid crowds of pillagers and fugitives, of slaves and soldiers, black and white; amid the crash of falling houses and exploding shells, under curtains of smoke that half obscured the blaze of the conflagration; amid rapine and riot and viler crimes—the city of Richmond fell*

Weitzel, meanwhile, had been on the alert all night, prepared to attack in the morning; but, about three A. M. on the 3rd, it became evident that the rebels were abandoning their lines. He immediately directed the troops to be wakened, and gave orders for a movement at daybreak, the pickets to advance at once and feel the enemy's position. Major General Devens,f commanding the Third division of the Twenty-fourth corps, was the first to report, at five o'clock, that his picket line had possession of the enemy's works. Upon this Weitzel sent two of his staff officers with a squadron of cavalry into Richmond, to preserve order until a larger force could arrive; while two divisions of infantry and all the

* Every incident and almost every word in this account of the condition of Richmond on the 2nd and 3rd of April is taken from rebel narratives. It has been my aim, throughout this entire history, to employ as far as possible the language of eye-witnesses or participants.

t Afterwards Attorney-General of the United States, under President Hayes.

cavalry advanced by different roads, with directions to halt at the outskirts for further orders.

The sun was an hour up, when suddenly there rose in the streets the cry of " Yankees ! Yankees !" and the mass of plunderers and rioters, cursing, screaming, trampling on each other, alarmed by an enemy not yet in sight, madly strove to extricate themselves and make an opening for the troops. Soon about forty men of the Fourth Massachusetts cavalry rode into the crowd, and, trotting straight to the public square, planted their guidons on the Capitol. Lieutenant de Peyster, of WeitzePs staff, a New York stripling, eighteen years of age, was the first to raise the national colors, and then, in the morning light of the 3rd of April, the flag of the United States once more floated over Richmond.

The command of Weitzel followed not far behind, a long blue line, with* gun-barrels gleaming, and bands playing " Hail Columbia," and " John Brown's soul goes marching on." One regiment was black.

The magistrates formally surrendered the city to Weitzel at the Capitol, which stands on a hill in the centre of the town, and overlooks the whole country for miles. The national commander at once set about restoring order and extinguishing the flames. Guards were established, plundering was stopped, the negroes were organized into a fire corps, and by night the force of the conflagration was subdued, the rioting was at an end, and the conquered city was rescued by the efforts of its captors from the evils which its own authorities had allowed and its own population had perpetrated.

CHAPTER XXXIV.

Flight of Lee from Petersburg—Expectation of joining Johnston—Grant moves to intercept Lee—Demoralization of enemy—Orders to Sherman— Parallel advance of Sheridan, Ord, and Meade—Sheridan intercepts Lee at Jetersville—Unselfishness of Meade—Army of Potomac moves by night without rations—Jefferson Davis at Burksville—Further instructions to Sherman—" Rebel armies only strategic points to strike at "—Meade arrives at Jetersville—Difference of opinion between Meade and Sheridan— Sheridan's dispatch to Grant—" I wish you were here yourself "—Grant's night ride to Jetersville—Grant reverses arrangements of Meade—Retreat of Lee from Jetersville—Strategical dispositions of Grant—Sufferings of enemy—Ord arrives at Burksville—Read's gallant fight at High bridge— Advance of army of Potomac—Urgency of Grant—Enemy encompassed on every side—Battle of Sailor's creek—Dispositions of Sheridan—Arrival of Sixth corps—Movements of Humphreys—Success of Sheridan's manoeuvres—Simultaneous attack of Wright and Merritt—Capture of Ewell's command—Flight of Lee to Farmville—Sheridan moves to Prince Edward—Advance of Ord to Farmville—Retreat of Lee across Appo-mattox—Humphreys crosses in pursuit—Fighting on northern bank—Complicated situation at Farmville—Arrival of Grant—Disentanglement of corps—Ord, Griffin, and Crook sent to Prince Edward—Grant demands surrender of Lee—Lee refuses to surrender—Advance of both wings of national command—Sheridan arrives at Appomattox—Intercepts Lee—Arrival of Ord and Griffin—Lee attempts to break through national lines—Fails—Rebel army completely surrounded—Lee offers to surrender —Interview at Appomattox—Terms granted to Lee—Rations sent to rebel army—Second interview at Appomattox—Gratitude of rebel officers— Grant returns to Washington—Army of Northern Virginia lays down its arms—Lee a prisoner in Richmond—Summary of campaign—Foresight of Grant—Contest between genius of two commanders—Designs of Lee— Combinations and energy of Grant—Annihilation of rebel army—Seventy-four thousand prisoners.

ON the morning of the 3rd of April, the scattered portions of Lee's command were all in flight by different roads in the valley of the Appomattox. The garrison of Richmond and the troops from Bermuda Hundred neck were crowding down from the north, and those that had held the inner lines of Petersburg were retreating westward, while the forces cut off by the battle of Five Forks and the subsequent assaults hastened, north or south of the river, as they could, to meet their chief at Amelia court-house, which he had appointed for a rendezvous. When these all should come together, Lee would still have more than fifty thousand soldiers, and he is said to have regained his spirits when daylight dawned, and he found himself, as he hoped, on the road to join Johnston's command. " I have got my army safely out of its breastworks," he said, " and, in order to follow me, my enemy must abandon his lines, and can derive no further benefit from his railroads or the James river."

Lee evidently supposed that Grant would attempt to follow the retreating army; and his own design must have been to fall in detail upon the national command, which would necessarily break up into corps and march over different roads. Turning with a concentrated force upon these divided columns, beating them back here and there, he might himself be able to avoid any formidable blow, and effect his junction with Johnston's army. Then, possibly, a long campaign, with the national forces far from a base and supplies, might still protract the war.

But Lee had yet no experience of the remorseless energy with which Grant pursued a routed enemy. He had not served at the West, and had, therefore, no recollection of the baifled plans, the intercepted supplies, the interrupted marches of the Vicksburg campaign; and no conception whatever of the battles which came fast upon flight, the rain of blows that accompanied demands for surrender, the .infantry that out-marched cavalry, the incessant attacks and manoeuvres and flanking movements with which his antagonist was wont to harass and overtake and destroy a flying foe.

Instead of moving, as Lee must have expected, if he made the remark attributed to him, behind and after the rebel army, Grant's idea from the first was to head and intercept his adversary. His plan was to move on the south side of the Appomattox and reach Burksville in advance of the enemy; and, instead of abandoning the railroads, Grant intended to put them in order as he marched. He knew already that the rebels must strike for Amelia courthouse, and they had hardly started when he directed Sheridan to cross their path. His dispatches and orders were full of these designs. On the 3rd of April, he said to Ord: " Efforts will be made to intercept the enemy, who are evidently pushing for Danville. Push south-west with your command." To Sheridan: " It is understood that the enemy will make a stand at Amelia court-house. . . . The first object of present movement will be to intercept Lee's army, the second to secure Burksville. I have ordered the railroad to be put in order up to the latter place." To Sherman: " It is my intention to take Burksville. The railroad from Petersburg can soon be put in order." To the President: " I want to cut off as much of the enemy as possible."

The columns moved according to orders, Sheridan in advance, on the River and Namozine roads, followed by Griffin, and then Meade with Humphreys and Wright; the Ninth corps stretching along behind, while Ord marched direct for Burksville, on the line of the Southside railroad. The Second corps had now been restored to Meade's command.

Soon after breaking camp Sheridan came upon proof of the demoralization of the enemy. He was on the road by which the rebels had retreated from Sutherland the night before, and Pickett and Heth and Wilcox, with the defeated cavalry, were fleeing before him. The rebel artillerists had thrown their ammunition into the woods and then set fire to the fences and trees among which the shells had fallen. Caissons and guns were lying in the road; small arms, knapsacks, and even clothing dotted the line of march; while the flankers and scouts were constantly bringing in prisoners from the farms and bypaths on either side.

There was some skirmishing in Merritt's front, but the opposition was easily brushed away, and it was not until Deep creek was reached that any serious fighting occurred. Here a strong body of infantry was encountered, but Merritt attacked with spirit, driving the enemy from the ford and pushing out vigorously on the opposite side. The Fifth corps followed rapidly and picked up many prisoners, as well as five pieces of abandoned cannon ; but there was no fighting this day except by the cavalry. By night Sheridan had captured thirteen hundred prisoners. The Fifth corps and the cavalry encamped at Deep creek, on the Namozine road; the Second corps was not far behind, at Winticomack church; and the Sixth and Ninth were in the neighborhood of Sutherland. Grant and Meade this night both slept at Sutherland.

The inhabitants along the road had now begun to understand that Lee was really overcome. They saw on every hand the evidence of rout and flight, and were suffering themselves. Their houses were

filled with wounded, their supplies were taken for the troops, and they were anxious for the end. The rebel soldiers, as they passed, declared that their cause was hopeless, and the women, stubborn to the last, who begged them to turn and face the Yankees once again, were laughed to scorn. The negroes everywhere were jubilant, grimacing and dancing with delight. " Where are the rebels ? " said Sheridan to a colored patriarch, leaning on a fence and doing uncouth homage with a tattered hat. " Siftin' souf, sah; siftin' souf," was the apt reply.*

As the only hope of the rebel commander now must be to unite with Johnston, Grant was of course extremely anxious in regard to the movements of Sherman, and this night sent him a long dispatch from Sutherland. After reciting the great events before Petersburg, he proceeded to direct the operations in North Carolina so as to combine them with his own; for Sherman's army, though a hundred and fifty miles away, was now more than ever only a wing of Grant's command. The battle-field reached from Richmond to Raleigh and Goldsboro.

" If Lee goes beyond Danville," said Grant, " you will have to take care of him with the force you have for a while. Should he do so, you will want to get on the railroad south of him, to hold it or destroy it, so that it will take him a long time to repair damages. Should Lee go to Lynchburg with his whole force, and I get Burksville, there will be no special use in your going any further into the interior of North Carolina. There is no contingency that I can see, except my failure to take Burksville, that will

* Newhall's " With Sheridan in Lee's Last Campaign."make it necessary for you to move on to the Roan-oke, as proposed when you were here."

He concluded with a soldier's panegyric of the forces under his own immediate command, inspired by what he had witnessed during the last few days. " This army," he said, " has now won a most decisive victory, and followed the enemy. This is all that it ever wanted to make it as good an army as ever fought a battle." No commander was ever more firmly convinced than Grant of the enhancement of spirit and strength and force that troops receive— not only from the excitement of victory, but from the sensation of following the enemy.

By daylight on the 4th, the cavalry was in motion again, Merritt moving towards the Appomattox, and following the force he had driven from Deep creek the day before, while Crook was ordered to strike the Danville road between Jetersville and Burksville, and then move up to Jetersville. This would throw him directly in front of Lee, who had now arrived at Amelia, where everything indicated that the rebels intended to concentrate. The Fifth corps also moved rapidly in the direction of Jetersville, about six miles south of Amelia court-house. Meade with the Second and Sixth corps followed on the Namozine road, south of the Appomattox. Grant this day marched with Ord's column on the Cox road, which follows the line of the Southside railroad. The roads were all bad, and the cavalry often cut into the infantry columns, which were instructed always to give it way.

At noon Sheridan sent a dispatch to Grant: " Merritt," he said, " reports that the force in.

his front have all crossed to the north side of the Ap-pomattox river. . . . Crook has, no doubt, reached the Danville road before this, and I am moving with the Fifth corps from Deep creek as rapidly as possible in the direction of Amelia court-house." Grant forwarded a copy of this to Meade, and directed him: " If you cannot find roads free from trains, let your troops pass them and press on, making as long a march to-day as possible." At the same time he instructed Meade to turn the Ninth corps into the Cox road, to guard the railway in the rear of Ord.

At 2.30 P. M., Meade replied : " The necessary orders have been sent to General Parke, who has now one division on the Cox road. ... I have also directed General Wright to push ahead with his command as far to-day as is consistent with its efficiency, and, if necessary, turning the Fifth corps and cavalry trains out of the road till he has passed." Meade, however, considered that there was no emergency calling for a night march. The Second corps arrived at Deep creek between seven and eight o'clock. The men were fatigued, having been marching, working, or standing for fourteen hours; they were out of rations, expecting to receive them during the night. Meade, therefore, directed Humphreys to go into bivouac.

During the day Grant got important news. Two railroad trains loaded with supplies were on the way from Danville for Lee's army, and had been run up the road to Farmville. He sent the information at once to Sheridan. " It was understood," he said, " that Lee was accompanying his troops, and that he was bound for Danville by way of Farmville. Unless you have information more positive of the
movements of the enemy, push on with all dispatch to Farmville, and try to intercept the enemy there."

But before receiving this dispatch Sheridan had come up with Lee. At five o'clock the head of the Fifth corps column arrived at Jetersville, after a march of sixteen miles. Here the national advance captured in the telegraph office a message from Lee, ordering two hundred thousand rations immediately from Danville, to feed his army—doubtless the supplies of which Grant had been informed. The dispatch had not yet gone over the wires, but Sheridan gave it to a scout to take to Burksville, and have it telegraphed from there, in the hope that the rations might be forwarded within the national lines. The scout succeeded in sending the message, but other news travelled quite as fast, and the rations went on to Farmville.

The dispatch, however, is evidence that Lee had at this time no expectation of meeting opposition on the Danville road. It has been seen that he expected to be followed, not intercepted, and hoped by interposing strong rear-guards to check any fierce pursuit; and his plans must have been sadly disarranged when he learned that the national forces, foot and horse, were entering Jetersville.

But here, in Sheridan's opinion, the rebel commander had one last chance to save his army. As yet only a small force confronted his advance. Mer-ritt and Mackenzie were miles away on the right, fighting the flank of the rebel command ; only Crook's cavalry and the head of the Fifth corps had arrived at Jetersville—together not ten thousand men; while Lee had more than forty thousand soldiers in and around Amelia. If he had promptly attacked and driven back Sheridan's inferior force, he might have pursued his way to Burksville junction, and gained that point before Ord arrived. From there the road was open to Danville and Johnston's army.

But at Amelia, Lee found himself entirely out of rations, and learned that Sheridan was in possession of the only road by which he could now obtain supplies.* His army had started with one day's rations from Petersburg, and thirty-six hours were past. The men were fatigued and hungry, and depressed by the influence of defeat; and the commander himself, disappointed and pursued, shared their depression. He ordered no attack nor advance, but entrenched himself, and sent out his troops in fragments in every direction to gather up what they could for food. The foraging parties had to go far, for the country was a wide tract of pine barren and straggling woods, and large numbers were taken prisoner by Merritt's 'cavalry. The grass had not yet begun to sprout, and the sufferings of the animals were keener even than those of the men. On the morning of the 4th of April, Lee sent off half of his artillery, to relieve the famished horses. The foragers brought little or nothing back. Some found a few ears of Indian corn, and the men who were fortunate were allowed two ears, uncooked, apiece; while others plucked the buds and twigs just swell-

* There is a story that Lee had ordered rations sent to Amelia, and that they went on by mistake to Richmond and were there destroyed. But I can find no authority for the statement. None of the accounts of eye-witnesses mention the arrival of the rations in Richmond. The supplies were probably those intercepted on their way from Burksville by the appearance of the national army.

ing in the early spring, and endeavored with these to assuage their hunger.

Meanwhile, discovering that Lee and his army were certainly at Amelia, Sheridan hurried up the Fifth corps, and ordered Griffin to entrench across the railroad until he could be reinforced. The isolated command went into position, throwing up breastworks as it arrived, and Sheridan at once sent information back to Grant that he had intercepted Lee. As Meade, however, was nearer than the gen-eral-in-chief, and time was of inestimable importance now, he dispatched an aide-de-camp also to the headquarters of the army of the Potomac, at Deep creek, where Humphreys had gone into camp—a long day's march from Jetersville. It was well into the night before the messenger arrived. Meade was unwell, and had taken to his soldier's bed, but he roused himself at the stirring news. His men were weary with their march, and with helping wagons out of the mire; they had no rations in their haversacks, and the supply trains were far in the rear. But the sick commander issued an order to march at three o'clock in the morning.

At 10.45 p. M., he sent word to Grant: " I have ordered Humphreys to move out at all hazards at three A. M. ; but if the rations can be issued to them prior to that, to march as soon as issued; or if the temper of the men on hearing the dispatch of General Sheridan communicated to them leads to the belief that they will march with spirit, then to push on at once as soon as they could be got under arms. . . . You may rest assured that every exertion will be made by myself and subordinate commanders to reach the point with the men in such condition that

they may be available for instant action. From all I can gather, Humphreys has nine or ten miles to march, and Wright from twenty-one to twenty-two."

Meade was full of fire on this occasion. Everything he said and did was in splendid soldierly spirit. " The troops will be put in motion," he said in his order, " regardless of every consideration but the one of ending the war. . . . The major-general commanding impresses on all, officers and men, the necessity of promptitude, and of undergoing the necessities and privations they are herein enjoined to. The major-general commanding feels he has but to recall to the army of the Potomac the glorious record of its repeated and gallant contests with the army of Northern Virginia, and when he assures the army that, in the opinion of so distinguished an officer as Major-General Sheridan, it only requires these sacrifices to bring this long and desperate contest to a triumphant issue, the men of his army will show that they are as willing to die of fatigue and of starvation as they have ever shown themselves ready to fall by the bullets of the enemy."

Meade himself was willing to make his own sacrifices. He was the senior of Sheridan in rank and service, but he sent him word: " The Second and Sixth corps shall be with you as soon as possible. In the meantime your wishes or suggestions as to any movement other than the simple one of overtaking you will be promptly acceded to by me, regardless of any other consideration than the vital one of destroying the army of Northern Virginia." This was the stuff of which commanders should be made.

Humphreys moved between one and two o'clock, and Wright at three in the morning, both corps without rations. Meanwhile Sheridan had recalled Merritt and Mackenzie from the right, and the head of Meade's command encountered the cavalry marching in the darkness. The double column crowded the road, and the infantry was delayed till Merritt's troopers had passed. At 4.30 A. M. on the 5th, Meade said to Sheridan: " If you wish the infantry to-day at Jetersville, you will have to send back and clear the road of cavalry. General Humphreys hopes to issue rations during the delay, but is ready to move as soon as the road is clear." It was indispensable, however, that the cavalry should have precedence, and Humphreys accordingly gave way, but took advantage of the enforced halt to issue rations to his command. Between seven and eight A. M. he moved again.

At night on the 4th, Grant was at Wilson's station, on the Southside road, with the army of the James, twenty-seven miles from Petersburg, and twenty-five from Burksville station— seventeen from the last camp. All day he had evidence of the spirit of his soldiers. Everywhere the national troops marched well, without stragglers, and cheered their chief whenever they caught sight of his little black pony, or the light blue overcoat he wore in this campaign. Everywhere he heard of stragglers and deserters from the rebel army. A railroad engineer, brought in this night, reported that Davis and his cabinet had passed through Burksville at three A. M. the day before, on their way south.

Before daylight on the 5th, Grant received Meade's dispatch of the night before, and replied at once, from his bivouac at Wilson's station :

" Your note of 10.45 last night and order for movement this morning is received. I do not see that greater efforts can be made than you are making to get up with the enemy. We want to reach the remnant of Lee's army wherever it may be found, by the shortest and most practicable route. That your order provides for, and has my veiy hearty approval. Ord will make a forced march with Gibbon's two divisions, and will come near reaching Burksville to-day."

Amid all the crowding interests and occupations of the pursuit the general-in-chief still kept Sherman in mind, and this morning sent him orders for his action under the new emergencies. He meant that the army in North Carolina should bear its part in all the shifting circumstances of the campaign. No force was to be wasted, no chance neglected, no effort unattempted, which could contribute to the complete result at which he was aiming. Success itself did not satisfy him, while that result in all its completeness was unattained.

" All indications now are," he said to Sherman, " that Lee will attempt to reach Danville with the remnant of his force. Sheridan, who was up with him last night, reports all that is left, horse, foot, and dragoons, at twenty thousand,* much demoralized. We hope to reduce this number one-half. I will push on to Burksville, and, if a stand is made at Danville, will in a few days go there. If you can possibly do so, push on from where you are, and let us see if we cannot finish the job with Lee and Johnston's armies. Whether it will be better

* This was an under-estimate. Lee surrendered 27,000 four days later, besides all he lost in battle in the meantime.

for you to strike for Goldsboro, or nearer to Danville, you will be better able to judge when you receive this. Rebel armies are now the only strategic points to strike at."

On the 5th of April, Grant still marched with the army of the James. Shortly after midday he arrived at Nottaway court-house, on the Southside road, only ten miles east of Burksville. At this point he halted for a few hours, to allow Ord's column to pass, and here he received a stirring dispatch from Sheridan: "The whole of Lee's army is at or near Amelia court-house, and on this side of it. General Davies, whom I sent out to Painesville on their right flank, has just captured six pieces of artillery and some wagons. We can capture the army of Northern Virginia if force enough can be thrown to this point, and then advance upon it. My cavalry was at Burksville yesterday, and six miles beyond, on the Danville road, last night. General Lee is at Amelia court-house in person. They are out of rations, or nearly so. They were advancing up the railroad towards Burksville yesterday, when we intercepted them at this point."

Thus Sheridan was accomplishing exactly what Grant had intended, sometimes before he received his orders. The instincts of the two commanders were identical. Sheridan perhaps possessed a more fiery energy than even Grant; he fairly blazed at times with the passion of war; but when the two were combined—Grant to conceive and concentrate and control, and Sheridan to execute and consummate and achieve—the result transcended not only the hopes of the nation, but the apprehensions of the enemy.

X

Meade now reported to Grant his position in the line of march. " Wright," he said, " reached this point by seven A. M., without having received his rations. I have directed three days' rations to be opened to him from the Fifth corps train, which is here. Wright will move on as soon as his rations are issued." Exertions such as these deserved and insured success. Meade continued: " Sheridan moving the cavalry would indicate the situation of affairs at Jetersville changed. I have sent forward to inquire, and if it is not necessary to go to Jetersville, I will move on the most direct road to Farmville." This would intercept the rebel army again, if Lee matched westward from Amelia, and Grant replied: "Your dispatch of 8.30 A. M. received. Your movements are right. Lee's wmy is the objective point, and to capture that is all we want. Ord has marched fifteen miles to-day to reach here, and is going on. He will probably reach Burksville to-night. My head-quarters will be with the advance."

The troops were now in superb condition and spirits, and marched with cheerful alacrity, though often without rations; but the hope of coming up with the enemy, they said themselves, was better than supplies. There was absolutely no straggling. As the infantry passed the spot where Grant and his staff were seated by the roadside, not knowing who composed the group of dismounted horsemen, more than once the soldiers cried: " Cavalry 'gin out ridin'. Cavalry 'gin out ridin'." And in reality the infantry marched as well and as far in this campaign as the horse.

Everything had been quiet at Jetersville during the night, and the troops that had reached there slept

undisturbed behind their hastily constructed breastworks. When the sun was well up and the enemy yet made no demonstration, Sheridan sent a brigade, under Davies, as far to the left as Paine's crossroads, five miles north-west of Jetersville, to ascertain if Lee was making any attempt to escape in that direction. Davies soon discovered that Sheridan's suspicions were correct. Lee was already moving a train of wagons toward Painesville, escorted by a considerable body of cavalry. Davies struck this force at the cross-roads, defeated the cavalry, burned a hundred and eighty wagons, and captured five pieces of artillery and several hundred prisoners. The rebels promptly sent out a force of infantry to attack and cut him off; but Smith and Gregg's brigades of Crook's division were at once dispatched to the support of Davies. A heavy fight ensued, and the rebel attempt was repelled.

By two o'clock Meade had arrived at Jetersville, in advance of the Second corps, which came up an hour later. Meade, however, was still unwell, and requested Sheridan to put the army of the Potomac in position as it arrived. Accordingly Sheridan put two divisions of Humphreys on the left of the Fifth corps, and one on the right, while Meade retired to a little house near by, where Sheridan had slept the night before. Merritt had also now come up, and was placed on the left of the infantry. The vigorous movement against Crook on the left led Sheridan to believe that Lee was attempting to escape in that direction, and he was anxious to attack at once with the force in hand—his cavalry and two corps of infantry ; but at this juncture Meade felt himself well enough to come out and assume command, and, much

to Sheridan's mortification, he decided not to attack until the arrival of the Sixth corps.

The country around Jetersville is open, and Griffin's line extended along a ridge which effectually commanded the wide valley that it overlooked. The ground occupied by the Second corps was not so favorable for defence, and in fact invited attack, for the land sloped upward in front of Humphreys, and the rebels could command the position of the corps. Meade feared that if he drew on battle now, Lee would fall on this exposed position of Humphreys, and he therefore decided to await the arrival of the Sixth corps, which would cover the right and prevent any movement of the enemy in that direction. But Sheridan wanted to tempt Lee to attack Humphreys, and when the rebels were all engaged, he meant to repeat his favorite manoeuvre and dash in upon them on the other flank with Griffin and Merritt's troops, now hidden behind the ridge. He moreover believed that if an attack were not made at once, Lee would escape in the night by the rebel right flank, and necessitate further pursuit. Meade, however, was the senior, and his opinion prevailed. Attack was delayed, and Merritt was transferred to the right of the army.

At this juncture Sheridan sent another dispatch to Grant, urging his immediate presence, and enclosing a captured letter which had just been brought to his head-quarters by a negro. The letter was from a rebel officer to his mother, and in these words: "Amelia court-house, April 5th. DEAR MAMMA, — Our army is ruined, I fear. We are all safe as yet. Byron left us sick. John Taylor is well; saw him yesterday. We are in line of battle this morning.

General Robert Lee is in the field near us. My trust is still in the justice of our cause and that of God. General Hill is killed. I saw Murray a few minutes since. Bernard Perry, he said, was taken prisoner, but may get out. I send this by a negro I see passing up the railroad to Mecklenburg. Love to all. Your devoted son, WM. B. TAYLOR, Colonel."

Meanwhile, Grant had advanced with the head of Ord's column, and by six o'clock he had arrived at a point half way between Nottaway court-house and Burksville. He gave the road to the troops, according to his custom, and was riding with his staff in a piece of woods, when a soldier in rebel uniform was brought up, just captured, who had asked to see the commanding general. One of Grant's staff recognized the man at once as a scout of Sheridan's, who had often brought messages before. He took from his mouth a piece of tobacco, in which was wrapped a small pellet of tinfoil. This, when opened, was found to contain a dispatch from Sheridan. It was in these words: " Jetersville, three P. M. I send you the enclosed letter, which will give you an idea of the condition of the enemy and their whereabouts. I sent General Davies' brigade this morning around on my left flank. He captured at Paine's cross-roads five pieces of artillery, about two hundred wagons, and eight or nine battle flags, and a number of prisoners. The Second army corps is now coming up. 1 wish you were here yourself. I feel confident of capturing the army of Northern Virginia, if we exert ourselves. I see no escape for Lee. I will put all my cavalry out on our left flank, except Mackenzie, who is on the right."

Grant was not long, after this appeal, in deciding

upon his course. Mounting a fresh horse on the road, without going into camp, he set out at once with four or five of his staff, and an escort of fourteen men, for Sheridan's head-quarters. First, however, he instructed Ord to push on to Burksville before halting for the night, and thus place a strong force in rear of Sheridan, and a second line in front of Lee. It was dark when he started for Jetersville, and the distance was twenty miles, for a long detour must be made to avoid the enemy. No one of the party but the scout had ever been over the ground before, which lay on the flank of the two armies. It was very possible that a considerable rebel force might be moving directly across their road.

Soon night came on, and the Ipng ride through the forest over a rough and muddy country was more dangerous still. Once or twice the officers with Grant became anxious about their guide. The scouts were always suspected men; they might perform the same office for the enemy they pretended to discharge for their friends. To bring the general-in-chief inside the rebel lines would secure an enormous reward ; and if this man was a rebel at heart, he had in his hands a prize beyond all count. He rode at the head of the little column, with one of the aides-de-camp by his side, who silently cocked a pistol, and all through that march was ready to fire, at the slightest symptom of treachery. They peered into the woods on either hand lest the forest should conceal a foe, and sometimes caught sight of rebel camp fires twinkling in the distance. But the scout was loyal, and at ten o'clock, after a four hours' ride, the party came upon Sheridan's outposts.

They were challenged of course by the pickets,

and had some difficulty in making themselves known. The men would hardly believe that the general-in-chief was riding at night, comparatively unattended, so near the rebel lines. It was still some distance from Sheridan's head-quarters, and the weary cavalrymen were bivouacked along the road. Grant and his party picked their way among them, if possible not to rouse the sleepers, and finally arrived at Sheridan's camp.

He found the cavalry commander more than anxious lest Lee should effect his escape. The Sixth corps had arrived at six o'clock, and was placed by Meade on the right of the army, but no arrangement had been made to advance before morning. Grant's first dispatch was to Ord: " In the absence of further orders," he said, " move west at eight A. M. tomorrow, and take position to watch the roads running south between Burksville and Farmville. I am strongly of opinion Lee will leave Amelia to-night to go south. He will be pursued at six A. M. from here, if he leaves. Otherwise, an advance will be made upon him where he is."

At 10.30 p. M., he said to Meade : "Your orders for to-morrow will hold good, in absence of others. It is my impression, however, that Lee will retreat during the night, and if so, we will pursue with vigor. I would go over to see you this evening, but it is late, and I have ridden a long distance to-day."

After further consideration, however, Grant could not be easy until he had seen Meade. The position of the army seemed to him to invite the escape of Lee. Meade's orders all contemplated a movement by the right flank, and his dispositions were entirely correct, looking to attack and pursuit in the morn-

ing; but Sheridan was convinced that Lee would not remain to be attacked, and Grant coincided entirely with Sheridan. The movement of the rebel wagon train to the left, the advance of Lee's infantry in the same direction, and the subsequent effort to cut off Davies, all betrayed the intention of the enemy; and Grant, as usual, determined to forestall the design. Accordingly, after midnight he visited Meade, whom he found in bed and still ailing.

Meade explained his views to Grant, but failed to convince him, and the general-in-chief took a pencil and wrote out instructions for the movement of the entire army, cavalry as well as infantry, reversing the plan of Meade, and directing the whole force to have coffee at four, and to move towards the left flank at daylight. He reminded Meade that the hour was late, and he had no time to lose. The enemy might already be on the march. Meade never failed in soldierly loyalty, and went to work at once to carry out Grant's instructions. Whether he approved of his orders or not, he always obeyed, and that not to the letter only, but with all the energy and skill and ability at his command.

At daylight the army of the, Potomac moved towards Amelia court-house, the Fifth corps along the Danville railroad, the Second corps about half a mile west of it, and the Sixth corps on the right or eastern side; the last two without regard to roads and across country. At the same time Sheridan with the cavalry was dispatched in the direction of Deatonsville, about five miles west of the railroad, and Ord was directed to cut the bridge over the Ap-pomattox at Farmville, where, if Grant's surmise was correct, the rebels would attempt to cross.

Mackenzie was returned to the army of the James. Before Meade's triple column had advanced three miles, the vanguard of each corps discovered that Lee had already withdrawn from Amelia. As Grant and Sheridan had anticipated, the rebels had moved in the night, and were endeavoring to pass around the national left, marching by the Deatonsville road, in the direction of Farniville. A column of rebel infantry with a wagon train could be distinctly seen not more than a mile and a half from the left of the Second corps.

Lee thus confessed his inability to make his way to Johnston by the road of his own selection, and could no longer hope to join him by any road whatever. The whole plan of the retreat had failed. The rebel columns now must head for Lynchburg, where there were still some few supplies, and from which point Lee perhaps had visions of scattering his forces in the mountains to keep up a partisan war. But Lynchburg is sixty miles from Amelia, and at Farmville the Appomattox must be re-crossed. Lee was marching now by a road parallel with Grant, only five miles distant, with his flank exposed to attack and his retreating column liable to be cut in pieces and destroyed in detail. With the hope of reaching Burksville must have vanished all hope of saving his army. Grant, he by this time knew, was not likely to slacken pursuit, or to leave any avenue of escape between the national columns. The Confederacy itself was utterly broken, its president a fugitive, its capital in ruins. All that military honor or loyalty to his cause demanded had been performed, and every life lost after this time was needlessly sacrificed by Lee. All the suffering

118

that his soldiers afterwards endured must be laid at his door.

What that suffering was eye-witnesses have described. Prom the moment when the men received the news of the evacuation of Kichmond and its partial destruction by fire, they became despondent. So many of them had their homes and families in that city, with what little property remained to them in the world, that they looked upon the loss of the rebel capital as the last hope of success destroyed. Desertions began at once, especially among the Virginia troops, who were nearest their homes and could reach them with little difficulty. But when the army arrived at Amelia and found no supplies, demoralization became disintegration. Many sank by the wayside exhausted, while others wandered from the line of march in search of a piece of bread only, to satisfy the cravings of actual starvation. For forty-eight hours the man or officer who had a handful of parched corn in his pocket was fortunate. The want of ordinary subsistence, the fighting by day and marching by night, became at last to many unendurable, and the bravest deserted and threw away their useless arms. Thousands, however, pressed on in sullen determination, obeying the orders of their commanders, and following blindly but resolutely the will of Lee.

On the morning of April 6th, Sailor's creek was reached, but Sheridan, the inevitable,* was in front with the cavalry, and three corps of the army of the Potomac were in flank and rear. The head of the retreating force was halted here in line of battle for

* " Sheridan, the inevitable, was in front of us."— Picket? s Men, p. 155.

several hours, while the artillery and wagon trains passed on to cross the Appomattox at Farmville.

But Grant had already directed Ord to cut the bridge at Farmville, a little town of less than a thousand inhabitants, about fifteen miles north-west of Burksville. The Southside railroad crosses the Appomattox twice in this immediate neighborhood, first at High bridge, five miles east of the town, and again directly in Farmville. The wagon road to Lynchburg also crosses the Appomattox in the town. The river was too deep to ford, and Farm ville therefore became the point aimed at by both armies.

Ord had arrived at Burksville late in the night of the 5th, and before daylight on the 6th he dispatched two small regiments of infantry and his own head-quarters' escort, under command of Colonel Washburne, with orders to push for High bridge as rapidly as the exhausted condition of men and horses would allow. Washburne was to make a reconnoissance, burn the bridge, if not found too well guarded, and return at once, using great caution during the entire expedition. After this force had started, Ord received word that Lee had broken away from Amelia, and was apparently moving direct for Burksville junction. The army of the James was immediately put in position to meet the enemy, but the rebel column turned off in the direction of Farmville.

Ord now became anxious lest his bridge-burning party should encounter the entire cavalry command of Lee. He had already sent General Theodore Eead, his chief of staff, to conduct the party, cautioning him to reconnoitre the country well before

approaching the bridge; and he now dispatched another officer to give warning to Read that Lee's whole army was in his rear, and that he could only return by pressing on, crossing the Appomattox, and making a circuit by way of Prince Edward courthouse. This second officer was driven back by rebel cavalry.

Read, however, came up with Washburne, led the cavalry into Farmville, examined the country, returned to the infantry, and was pushing for High bridge, when the cavalry of Lee's army overtook him within two miles of the river. Here about noon the gallant Read drew up his little band of eighty horse and five hundred infantry, rode along the front of his ranks, inspired the men with his own valor, and began the battle with an army in his front. Charge after charge was made by the chivalrous Washburne, who captured more rebels than he had men. But Read fell, mortally wounded, then Washburne, and at last not an officer of that cavalry party was left unwounded to lead the men; and not until then did they surrender. But the stubborn fight in his front led Lee to believe that a heavy force had struck the head of his column. He ordered a halt, and this whole portion of his army began entrenching; so that the rear-guard and wagon train were delayed in their march, and this gave time for Sheridan to come up with the flying column on the Deatonsville road.

As soon as the retreat of Lee from Amelia became a matter of certainty, the direction of the army of the Potomac was changed, and the whole command faced west instead of north. The Sixth corps, which had been on the right, was moved across the

rear of the army to the left; the Fifth corps marched to the extreme right, and the Second became the centre. This disposition afforded an admirable opportunity to attack the rebels in flank, and was made under the immediate direction of Grant. It was in conformity with his instructions of the night before, and carried out his idea of intercepting the flight of the enemy, whereas Meade's original orders had been calculated only for pursuit.

The country, however, was open, and the roads were numerous, and at first the rebels made good speed. They had started early in the night, and fear is a wonderful spur. Grant remained in Jeters-ville with Meade, overlooking the advance, and sending through him orders to, the corps commanders. To Humphreys he said: " The FiJth corps covers well your flank and rear, and Wright your left. You are therefore at liberty to push forward with your whole corps and to strike the enemy wherever you may find him. . . . Push on as rapidly as possible. . . . Sheridan will attack with three divisions. . . . Push on without fear of your flanks."

Humphreys never needed urging to advance against the enemy. He was one of the commanders after Grant's own heart, who attacked without orders, and " without fear of his flanks." He struck the rebel column almost at once, and Grant immediately sent word to Griffin, now making a detour on the right, so as to come in on the enemy's rear: " Humphreys has struck the enemy at Deatonsville. He reports the train and a column of infantry moving through Deatonsville. Another column is west of this one. Sheridan is moving on them. Wright moves south-west from here. General Ord moves

from Burksville at eight A. M. You will strike their column by pushing, and you will see from the position of the troops that it must go hard with the enemy." * Griffin accordingly moved around to the north and west, and pushed after the enemy with great vigor, forcing him to burn many of his wagons, and picking up hundreds of stragglers on the road.

At the same time Grant sent a dispatch to Ord, who bore an important part in all this programme. " The enemy," he said, " evacuated Amelia last night or this morning, and are now apparently moving south-west to get on the Farmville and Danville road. . . . You will move out to intercept them, if possible, taking roads according to the information you may get, recollecting that the capture of the enemy is what we want. . . . Get your provost-marshal or some one to ascertain if there is any movement from Danville this way."

Soon after midday the general-in-chief received a report from Sheridan. " My information is that the enemy are moving to our left with their trains and whole army. The trains and army were moving all last night, and are very short of provisions, and very tired indeed. I think now is the time to attack them with all your infantry. They are reported to have begged provisions from the people of the country and along the road as they passed. I am working around further to my left." This information was at once communicated to the infantry commanders through Meade: " Sheridan reports that the ad-

* These two dispatches to Humphreys and Griffin were in Meade's name, but really emanated from Grant. On such occasions Meade was careful to use as far as possible the very language of the general-in-chief.

vance of the enemy is checked. He urges an attack by all the infantry. The major general commanding sends this for your information, and feels sure that all will appreciate the necessity of rapid movement."

Grant was still at Jetersville, to be as near as possible to his various columns, and at five minutes past two, he notified Sheridan of the situation. "From this point," he said, "General Humphreys can be seen advancing over General Vaughn's farm. The enemy occupied that place two hours ago with artillery and infantry. Griffin is further to the right, and has been urged to push on. He is no doubt doing so. Wright is pushing out on the road you are on, and will go in with a vim any place you dictate. Ord has sent two regiments out to Farmville to destroy the bridge, and is entrenching the balance of his command at Burk's station. If your information makes it advisable for him to move out, notify him, and he will do so."

To this Sheridan replied from Flat creek: " The enemy's trains are moving on the pike through Dea-tonsville, in the direction of Burksville station. I am just getting ready to attack them. I have notified General Ord."

During the morning it had still been possible that the rebel chief might attempt to make a detour entirely around the national left, and head the remains of his command for Danville, in the hope of finally effecting a junction with Johnston's army; but, as the day waned, it became manifest that Lee had abandoned any such design, and was crowding all his force with desperate haste into the roads to Farmville. Grant accordingly turned his columns in the same direction, to close around the fugitives.

Wright had previously been instructed to continue the direct pursuit as long as it promised success; but at 4.20 P. M., he was ordered: " Unless you are in the immediate presence of the enemy, you will, on receipt of this, move by the nearest road to Farm-ville."* At the same time Grant said to Ord: " Send i Gibbon with his two divisions to Fannville to hold that crossing. The Sixth corps is also ordered. . . . Indications are that the enemy are almost in a rout. They are burning wagons, caissons, etc."

Having issued these instructions, the general-in-chief set out for Burksville, to direct in person the advance of Ord. He left the three columns of the army of the Potomac all in motion: Griffin nearest the Appomattox, and almost on the right of the enemy; Humphreys moving south on the Deatons-ville road, in the rebel rear; and the Sixth corps advancing to the support of Sheridan, against the left of Lee.

The condition of the rebel command was now one of appalling and unmitigated misery. The men were exhausted by incessant labors, by sleepless nights, by protracted marches, by defeat, by famine, and despair. Many were wounded, all were hopeless. They were burying their own artillery, and burning their own wagons, and time and again the horses and men lay on the ground together, ceasing to struggle, till they were roused by the shells of the enemy or their own exploding trains. But, surrounded by an indefatigable and adventurous foe, they escaped from one precarious position only to fall into another still more forlorn.

* This dispatch found Wright absolutely engaged, so that the movement it directed was not made.

As soon as the head of the wagon train appeared at Sailor's creek, the principal portion of Lee's command pushed on towards the Southside, here known as the Lynchburg, railroad. But Ord was found in force at Rice's station, entrenched, and effectually preventing any advance southward; while the gallant little band of Read and Washburne obstructed the flight nearer the Appomattox. The whole rebel column was halted, and before the opposition in front could be overcome, Sheridan discovered the wagon train on the Deatonsville road, escorted by heavy masses of infantry and cavalry. He at once ordered Crook to attack the flank of the train. But if Crook should find the defence too strong, Merritt was to pass to the left, and while Crook held fast and pressed the enemy, Merritt would attack at a point further on. Then Crook was to follow Mer-ritt's example, and so on, alternately, until one or the other should strike a weak point in the enemy's line.

Meanwhile, the Second corps had engaged the rebel rear nearer Deatonsville, and from a hill-top overlooking the country the enemy's skirmishers could be seen in the distance, falling back before Humphreys, halting occasionally to fire, and then retreating doggedly again. On Sheridan's left, Crook and Merritt were executing the manoeuvre he had directed, while in his front the rebel trains were in full view, not a thousand yards away, on high ground in the edge of a wood, with an open valley intervening. In the fields below the woods long lines of flanking troops were passing, with small parties of cavalry patrolling their front, to give warning of approaching danger.* It was important to detain this-force

* Newhall.

until Crook and Merritt could perform their task, and the Sixth corps, which Grant had ordered to support the cavalry, should arrive. Accordingly, Sheridan ordered Stagg's brigade to make a mounted charge against the rebel line, while Miller's battery of horse artillery, from a crest behind, fired over the heads of the cavalry and into the trains. Stagg made a gallant charge, leaving men and horses in front of the rebel works, for even at this juncture the enemy had thrown up breastworks, while the shells of the battery set fire to the wagons beyond. The demonstration completely accomplished its object, and prevented any large force of the enemy from moving against Merritt's cavalry.

At four o'clock, the head of the Sixth corps column came up, Seymour's division leading, and Sheridan at once ordered Wright to put Seymour into position, without waiting for the remainder of the corps. Wright promptly obeyed, and Seymour, advancing, carried the road at a point about two and a half miles south of Deatonsville. Humphreys, meanwhile, was following up the rear of the same force which Sheridan was attacking in flank, while on the left Merritt and Crook were endeavoring to strike the head of the column again. As soon as the road was in Wright's possession, Sheridan ordered him to wheel to the left and push Seymour after the enemy. The rebel resistance, however, was stubborn, and Wheaton's division, now coming up, took position on the left of the road, Seymour moving on the right, and both facing south. Wright and Sheridan rode between the columns.

Just behind the rebel position was a by-way running off westward at right angles with the Deatons-

ville road, and it was soon discovered that the enemy's line was broken, a part moving west in the direction of the Appomattox, and part still keeping the Dea-tonsville road. Humphreys was coming up at this moment, and Sheridan sent him word of this important news, requesting him to push on to the right, as he felt confident that together they could break up the enemy. Humphreys instantly deflected to the right in pursuit of the fragments which had broken off in the direction of the Appomattox, and was soon engaged in an independent encounter of his own; while the Sixth corps advanced on the Dea-tonsville road. Wright drove the enemy about two miles, through a thick jungle, until the battle reached Sailor's creek, a marshy and difficult stream, running westerly into the Appomattox. From the northern bank Sheridan could distinguish his own cavalry away to the left, on the high ground south, and the long line of smoke from the burning wagons.

Merritt had pushed on steadily in the overlapping movement, forded the creek a mile or two above the infantry, and swept around carefully to the opposite side of a ridge that rose in front of Wright; and a young cavalryman, named William Richardson, of Ouster's brigade, who had cleared the rebel troops in a charge beyond the crest, and come through their lines, now reported to Sheridan the position of Merritt's command. The cavalry was on the left flank of the road which Wright was following, behind the ridge, but approaching it rapidly. Ouster had the right, next to the ridge, Crook the centre, and Devin was on the left; Ouster not having broken off from the right in the overlapping movement when the point of attack was reached. All
PA
three were now ready to advance, and Sheridan sent them the word.

In the meantime the rebels in front of Wright had reformed their line on the opposite side of the creek, and thrown up breastworks at various points on the slope of the hill, as time permitted; but the two divisions of the Sixth corps crossed the creek, and charged the position under a terrible fire, Getty's division, which had now come up, remaining in reserve. The attack was splendidly made and worthy of the fame of the Sixth corps and its gallant commander. The position was almost carried. But at one point on the national right a rebel column, composed of the Marine brigade and other troops from the Richmond lines, made a counter-charge. The onset was astounding. These troops were really surrounded; two divisions of the Sixth corps were on their flanks, a fresh division and Wright's artillery in front, and Merritt's cavalry in their rear. Wright looked upon the entire command as prisoners, and had ordered the artillery to cease firing, out of humanity ; when this little force charged against the Sixth corps front and drove it across the creek. There was a moment of desperate hand-to-hand fighting, but the national troops moved up on every side; a tremendous storm of artillery from eighteen guns opened on the command, and there was nothing to do but yield. Some of the men floundered wildly back through the creek, and gave themselves up to the very brigades they had just driven across.

A moment later the two sections of the Sixth corps closed like gates upon the entire rebel force, while from the hillsides in the rear Merritt and Crook suddenly swept through the pine-trees like a

whirlwind. There was one bewildering moment in which the rebels fought on every hand, and then they threw down their arms and surrendered. Ewell, in command of the force, Kershaw, Custis Lee, Semmes, Corse, De Foe, Barton—all generals, hundreds of inferior officers, and seven thousand men, were prisoners. Fourteen guns fell into the hands of the cavalry, and the entire rear-guard of Lee's army was destroyed.

A few officers escaped on the backs of artillery horses, and some of the men broke their muskets before submitting. A part of the wagon train had gone on during the battle, but E well's command surrendered on the open field.

Getty's division was pushed on for a mile or two, in support of Devin's troopers, sent to beat up the country further on; but it was now long after dark, and the remainder of Sheridan's command, including the Sixth corps, went into bivouac south of Sailor's creek.

The rebel generals were taken to Sheridan's head-quarters, and the gray and the blue were clustered about the camp-fire in almost equal numbers. The prisoners shared the blankets as well as the suppers of their conquerors, but only an hour or two of sleep was allowed to either, for Sheridan started in pursuit of Lee before daylight, while the seven thousand captives were marched to Burksville junction.*

* On the 7th of April, Grant was moving in person between the commands, and I was left to receive dispatches in his absence. During the day the prisoners arrived at Burksville, and the general officers were brought to Grant's head-quarters. It was a sorry company of tired and hungry and dejected men. Ewell at once asked to be allowed to write a letter to Grant, in which he protested that he had

Humphreys meanwhile had pursued the force in his front to the mouth of the creek, a distance of fourteen miles, over every foot of which he kept up a running fight, wading streams and building bridges as he advanced. The country was broken, open fields alternating with forests, and dense undergrowth with swamp; at several points the enemy was partially entrenched; but the lines of battle followed the skirmishers so closely and rapidly as to astonish veteran soldiers. The last rebel stand in front of Humphreys was made at the creek, where a short but sharp contest gave him thirteen flags, three pieces of artillery, and several hundred prisoners. The whole result of the day to the Second corps was four guns, seventeen hundred prisoners, thirteen flags, and three hundred wagons.

The Fifth corps met this day no opposing force, save a small detachment of cavalry. It marched thirty-two miles, and captured three hundred stragglers, halting for the night at Ligonton.

An army was hardly ever so nearly surrounded in the open field as that of Lee on the night of the 6th of April. Ord held the flying rebels in front, Sheridan and Wright had struck them in flank and dismembered the column, while Humphreys and Griffin were on the right and rear. Their enemies encompassed them on every side. The only possible escape was by the roads nearest to the Ap-pomattox, in the direction of Farmville, and to this point Grant had already directed his columns.

only obeyed his orders in setting fire to the warehouses in Richmond. I gave them some whiskey, and they warmed themselves at the camp-fire, and then they were locked up in a house near by, under the orders of the provost marshal, Colonel Sharpe.

The success of the battle of Sailor's creek was largely due to the vigor and ability of Sheridan. After the combinations of the general-in-chief had produced the strategical situation, it was Sheridan's masterly tactics, his brilliant manoeuvring with the cavalry, his assault with the Sixth corps on the left of the rebel column; and, finally, his handling of both portions of his command in the presence of the enemy, bringing Wright and Merritt face to face, with the rebels between, which secured the result at which Grant was aiming—the destruction of almost a fourth of Lee's command. A result so complete was only to be achieved by the exercise of the highest qualities of military genius, whether in conception or performance.

It was late in the evening before Grant reached Burksville, where he found that Ord had moved to Rice's station, and entrenched in front of Lee. The general-in-chief at once reported the situation to the government: " The troops are pushing now," he said, " though it is after night, and they have had no rest for more than one week. The finest spirit prevails among the men, and I believe that in three days more Lee will not have an army of five thousand men to take out of Virginia, and no train or supplies." At the same time he continued his exhortations to Sherman: " We have Lee's army pressed hard, his men scattering, and going to their homes by thousands. He is endeavoring to reach Danville, where Davis and his cabinet have gone. I shall press the pursuit to the end. Push Johnston at the same time, and let us finish this job all at once."

This night he received an important dispatch from the President, who had gone to Richmond after the

fall of that place, and now recounted to Grant his conferences with the rebels, the partial sanction he had given to the assembling of the state legislature, and especially a promise that confiscations should be remitted to the people of any state which should promptly and in good faith withdraw its troops from resistance to the government. "I do not think it very probable," said Lincoln, " that anything will come of this, but I have thought best to notify you, so that, if you should see signs, you may understand them. From your recent dispatches it seems that you are pretty effectually withdrawing the Virginia troops from opposition to the government. Nothing I have done, or probably shall do, is to delay, hinder, or interfere with you in your work."

At midnight Grant received dispatches from Sheridan announcing his victory, and the first idea of the national chief was to intercept again the flight of Lee. If the rebels should not succeed in crossing the Ap-pomattox at Farmville, their only open road was by Prince Edward court-house, about ten miles northwest of Burksville, and five miles directly south of Farmville. At ten minutes past twelve, accordingly, Grant said to Meade: u Every moment now is important to us. Communicate this to General Griffin. Direct him to move out at once to our left, taking the most direct open road to Prince Edward court-house. Mackenzie's cavalry is already ordered there, and will be off from here at two A. M." To Ord he said: " Your troops are the nearest to Prince Edward unless the Fifth corps is between you and there. That corps was ordered to Prince Edward last night, and on the receipt of the news of our

captures at twelve P. M., the order was reiterated for them to push on without waiting for morning. Mackenzie is probably there now."

Sheridan's report from the battle had concluded with the words: " If the thing is pressed, I think that Lee will surrender." The general-in-chief forwarded a copy of the dispatch to Lincoln, who replied : " Let the thing be pressed."

Early on the morning of the Vth of April, Ord discovered that the rebels had broken away in the night from his front, and were making desperate speed for Farmville. His whole command was put in motion at once in three columns, and came up on the rebel flank and rear as Lee was entering the town, where seven railroad trains had just arrived, loaded with supplies for the rebel army. At this point the Lynchburg railroad passes to the southern side of the Appomattox, while the wagon road crosses to the northern bank, the roads coming together again at Appomattox court-house, twenty miles further west. Lee, hard pressed by Ord, was unable to hold Farmville long enough to unload the trains, and accordingly ordered them west by rail, while he marched himself by the wagon road on the northern bank, to strike the supplies at Appomattox court-house.

But Grant was at his heels. Sheridan had started from Sailor's creek before daylight, and soon discovering that the rebels had evaded the army of the James at Rice's station, he ordered Merritt to move with two divisions to Prince Edward, passing around by the left of Ord, while Crook continued the direct pursuit along the Appomattox, and arrived at Farmville nearly as soon as the army of the James. The Second corps also moved at half-past five, Barlow's division leading, and Humphreys soon came up with the rebel rear at High bridge, five miles east of Farmville, where also the wagon road and the railroad cross the Appomattox. The wagon bridge had just been fired, and the second span of the railroad bridge was burning. A redoubt on the southern bank was blown up by the rebels as Humphreys approached, and eight pieces of artillery were abandoned. The rebels, however, had drawn up a considerable force of infantry on the opposite side to oppose the passage, and redoubts had been erected to increase the strength of the position. It was important to save the wagon bridge, for the river was not fordable for infantry and hardly for cavalry. The rebel skirmishers attempted to hold the bridge until it could be consumed, but they were quickly driven from it, and the Second corps passed over, Barlow in advance. Humphreys at once ordered artillery in position to cover an attack, but the enemy moved off, abandoning ten more guns on the northern side. The railroad bridge, an elaborate structure, was saved with the loss of four spans.

The rebels retreated in two columns, one moving along the river side towards Farmville, but the main body marching in a north-westerly direction. Humphreys followed the larger force with two divisions, and sent Barlow on the left to Farmville. Artillery could not accompany Barlow, for he marched along the railroad. Farmville was found in possession of a strong rebel force, burning the bridges and covering their wagon train. Barlow, however, attacked at once, and the enemy abandoned the town, burning a hundred and thirty wagons, and then falling rapid-ly back upon the main rebel force. But the bridges had been destroyed. Lee was now entrenched in a strong position on the crest of a hill, crowned with entrenchments and batteries, at the intersection of the Farmville and High bridge roads, about five miles north of Farmville. He was evidently making a stand to cover the withdrawal of his trains.

As soon as Humphreys ascertained that he was in front of all that was left of the rebel army, he promptly ordered Barlow up from Farmville, but still thought Lee's position too strong to attack single-handed. He therefore sent back to Meade, now at High bridge, and asked that an advance might be made from Farmville, in support of the Second corps. But the army of the Potomac had passed entirely beyond High bridge on the southern side, and the bridges at Farmville were destroyed. Immediate reinforcement was therefore impracticable. The situation of Humphreys now became precarious. He was alone, north of the river, in front of a superior and desperate force, while the various national columns on the opposite side, were either heading for Prince Edward, in an entirely different direction, or else effectually prevented from crossing to his relief at Farmville.

The Sixth corps had started early in the morning, following the enemy on the Farmville road; but at Rice's station, Wright found that the army of the James had already passed, and was, of course, in his advance. His march was now greatly impeded by the movements of both Ord and Crook in his front. Nevertheless, he advanced to the vicinity of Farmville, and massed his corps on the high ground overlooking the town. Meanwhile, the Fifth corps had passed by the rear of both Humphreys and Wright, and was now marching for Prince Edward, according to Grant's orders of the night before.

At this juncture, when Humphreys was unsupported north of the river, Ord, Crook, and Wright entangled on the southern bank, with the bridges destroyed, and no one to direct the corps commanders —for Sheridan had moved forward on the road to Prince Edward, while Meade was still at the rear at High bridge—Grant arrived at Farinville, riding up from Burksville junction.

He at once ordered Crook to ford the river and proceed to the support of Humphreys, and the cavalry waded belly-deep across the Appomattox. Next, a re-assuring message was sent to Humphreys: " Your note of 1.20 p. m. to Major General Meade is just seen. Mott's division* of your corps and Crook's cavalry are both across the river at this point. The Sixth and Twenty-fourth corps are here. The enemy cannot cross at Farmville." The army of the James was then ordered out of the way, to follow Sheridan on the road to Prince Edward, and Wright was directed to build a foot-bridge for his infantry, and to bring up pontoons for the artillery and the trains. These orders were all obeyed, and before dark Wright's column was filing across the Appomattox, Crook was fighting on the northern bank, and Ord far on the road to Prince Edward.

Meanwhile, Humphreys had been waiting the arrival of Barlow and the Sixth corps; but heavy firing was heard in the direction of Farmville, which he supposed to proceed from the guns of Wright. He

* It was in reality Barlow's division, and not Mott's, which was north of the river at Farmville.

therefore extended his own command to envelop the enemy's left, and made an advance with Miles's division, but was repulsed with considerable loss. Barlow, however, soon came up, but it was dark before he could take position, and no further attack was made by the Second corps.

The firing Humphreys had heard was from a battle of the cavalry. Crook had found great difficulty in fording the river, and when he attacked the enemy's trains on the northern bank, he encountered a large infantry force. A sharp fight ensued, in which Gregg was captured and the head of Crook's division was repelled.

Thus, two separate attacks had on this day been successfully resisted by the retreating but gallant forces of Lee. Both these affairs, it is true, were temporary defences, made to allow the artillery and ammunition trains to be withdrawn, but they demonstrated the lingering quality of the troops, which, though driven and crowded so far and so fast, could still be induced to turn and hold off for an hour or more their triumphant and advancing enemy.

Nevertheless, the converging and crossing columns of Grant were on every road, and the toils were drawn constantly closer around the fugitive army. At night the rebels had been chased for miles along the banks of the Appomattox, and forced to cross the river in such haste that they could only partially burn their bridges, and left eighteen cannon behind. The army of the Potomac had pursued with tremendous vigor, the infantry crossing at one bridge which had already been fired, and building another, and the cavalry wading ;• the vanguard of both Humphreys and Crook had come

up with the enemy north of the river, while on the southern side Sheridan, followed by Griffin and Ord, was stretching out rapidly, once more to head the flying column of Lee and cut off his hoped-for supplies.

From Farrnville, Grant said to Sheridan: " The Second corps and Crook's cavalry are north of the river at this place. ... I think on the whole you had better throw your cavalry up the river towards Chickentown, to watch the different crossings. The Twenty-fourth corps will move up the south bank of the river. . . . You may be able to get in the rear of the enemy, possibly. It is reported among the citizens here that Lynchburg was evacuated last night. I do not doubt but Stoneman is there."

Sheridan arrived at Prince Edward at three o'clock, and finding Mackenzie already on the ground with his little division, he ordered him to make a reconnoissance as far as Prospect station, on the Lynchburg railroad, and ascertain if the enemy was moving past that point.

Meanwhile he learned that Lee had crossed to the north side of the Appomat-tox. Merritt was, therefore, pushed forward on the southern side to Buffalo creek, while Crook was ordered to recross the Appoinattox and rejoin Sheridan at Prospect station, in advance of Ord. At 6.45 p. M., Sheridan reported his movements to Grant: " I am following," he said, " with the First and Third cavalry divisions, and will reach the vicinity of Prospect station to-night, if I do not go to Chickentown."

Still later he sent further and important news to the general-in-chief, from Prospect station. "I am moving the cavalry column on Appomattox depot. There are eight trains of cars at that point, to sup-

ply Lee's army. Everything is being run out of Lynchburg towards Danville. Our troops are reported at Liberty. This must be Stoneman."

When Crook received his orders to rejoin Sheridan, he was very unwilling to obey, and went in person to Grant to complain. His troops, he said, were tired and worn; they had marched all day, forded the river, and fought a battle, in which they had been repelled. Not a thousand men were fit to move. But Grant was peremptory ; the emergency was immediate; Sheridan had asked, and Crook was obliged to conform. Accordingly, the cavalry crossed the stream again in the night, and set out to rejoin Sheridan.

At the same time Grant sent directions to Ord to hasten on the heels of Sheridan, picking up Griffin's corps at Prince Edward on the way, and with both corps to attack the head and front of Lee.

To Sheridan himself he said : " The Second and Sixth corps will press the enemy to-morrow on the north side of the river, the Sixth corps keeping next to the river. The Fifth and Twenty-fourth corps will push up by Prospect station, and will be ready to turn upon the enemy at any time. I will move my head-quarters up by the south bank in the morning." At 9.30 p. M., he instructed Meade to the same effect, and added: " The enemy cannot go to Lynchburg, possibly. I think there is no doubt but that Stoneman entered that city this morning. I will move my head-quarters up with the troops in the morning, probably to Prospect station."

Stoneman had indeed started, in the last days of March, from East Tennessee, in obedience to the orders of Grant, and was at this time moving against

the railroad west of Lynchburg. He had not yet entered the town, but was completing the contracting circle, and threatening the last possible avenue of exit left to Lee.

Nearly all this night the Sixth corps was passing through Farmville, and the little town was crowded with an unfamiliar company, cavalry, artillery, and infantry; rebel prisoners, wagon trains, ambulances filled with wounded, officers and men looking for quarters—all the impedimenta of an army. Camp fires were burning in the streets and over all the country outside, and the frightened inhabitants peered from their windows at the regulated turmoil of war.

Grant had taken possession of the Farmville hotel, a homely country inn, where Lee had slept the night before, and there received reports from Sheridan and Ord and Meade, and issued orders not only to his principal commanders, but to their subordinates ; for in the complicated dispositions of this day he was at the focus, while the army chiefs were far away: Sheridan at Prospect station, Ord at Prince Edward, and Meade at Rice's station. He approved of Sheridan's advance and forwarded him support, he encouraged Humphreys, and stimulated Crook; he sent information to Meade, and directions to Wright and Griffin and Ord.

During the evening he came out in the porch and watched the Sixth corps column marching by. The night was dark, but the camp fires threw their gleams across his face, and the soldiers recognized the chief whom a week before they had cheered inside the rebel lines at Petersburg. Their shouts rang out again, for every man felt that he had led them to such a victory as had seldom been won in any war; that their marches and labors were now nearly ended, and the object of them all attained. Grant stood till the last battalion had passed, and then went in and wrote a letter to Lee.

It was in these words : " FAEMVILLE, April 7th, 1865. General: The results of the last week must convince you of the hopelessness of further resistance on the part of the army of Northern Virginia in this struggle. I feel that it is so, and regard it as my duty to shift from myself the responsibility of any further effusion of blood, by asking of you the surrender of that portion of the Confederate States' army known as the army of Northern Virginia.— U. S. GEANT, Lieutenant-General."

At this juncture Lee's own officers had proposed to him to surrender. The condition of his soldiers, baffled, beaten, followed, famished, wounded, footsore, despairing, was such that nothing but destruction could be looked for. For two days no return of troops had been made. The disintegration of the scattered brigades was such that all attempt to number them was vain. Lee had himself no idea of the strength of his command. The officers were involved in the demoralization of the men; they made no effort to prevent straggling, and shut their eyes on the hourly reduction of their force, riding, dogged and indifferent, in advance of their commands. Only when the national columns caught up and attacked the rear did some of the old spirit seem to re-animate these jaded veterans. Whenever they were summoned to resist, they faced boldly around, and then, like wounded beasts, they struck out terrible blows. The fighting at Sailor's creek was as desper-

ate for a while as in any battle of the war; and the repulse of Miles on the 7th, the capture of a portion of Crook's cavalry with Gregg himself at their head, showed like the expiring flashes of a nearly burnt out fire.

The high commanders of Lee saw that the suffering was in vain, that no effort of gallantry or despair could now avail, and several of them approached him with the recommendation to yield. But he was yet unwilling. " I have too many brave men," he said; " the time is not yet come for surrender." Nevertheless, he answered Grant's note, on the night of the 7th, in ,these words: " General, I have received your note of this day. Though not entirely of the opinion you express of the hopelessness of further resistance on the part of the army of Northern Virginia, I reciprocate your desire to avoid useless effusion of blood, and therefore, before considering your proposition, ask the terms you will offer on condition of its surrender."

This note was handed to Grant early on the morning of the 8th, while he was still at Farmville, and he immediately replied: " Your note of last evening in reply to mine of same date, asking the conditions on which I will accept the surrender of the army of Northern Virginia, is just received. In reply I would say that peace being my great desire, there is but one condition I would insist upon, namely : that the men and officers surrendered shall be disqualified for taking up arms again against the government of the United States until properly exchanged. I will meet you, or designate officers to meet any officers you may name for the same purpose, at any point agreeable to you, for the purpose of arranging def-

initely the terms upon which the surrender of the army of Northern Virginia will be received."

He made no delay, however, in the pursuit. Meade was ordered to follow north of the river, while Sheridan with all the cavalry pushed, on the opposite side, for Appomattox, followed by the army of the James and the Fifth corps. To Sheridan, Grant said: " I think Lee will surrender to-day. I addressed him on the subject last evening, and received a reply this morning, asking me the terms I wanted. We will push him until terms are agreed upon." This day also he sent a dispatch to Stanton in these words: " The enemy so far have been pushed from the road towards Danville. I feel very confident of receiving the surrender of Lee and what remains of his army by to-morrow."

During the night the enemy abandoned his position in front of the Second corps, and at five A. M. on the 8th, Humphreys resumed the pursuit on the Lynchburg stage road, Wright following on a parallel road. No halt was made by the Second corps till sunset, and then after two hours' rest, the march was renewed. But the rebels fled fast, and at midnight there seemed no prospect of overtaking them in the darkness. The head of the column was therefore halted again. The men were exhausted by fatigue and want of food, and the rear of the column did not get up till morning; while the supply train of two days' rations was still later. But as soon as the rations could be issued the Second corps moved forward again; and at eleven o'clock on the 9th, Humphreys came up with the rebel skirmishers about three miles from Appomattox court-house. The Sixth corps marched on the 8th to New Store,

seventeen miles, and on the 9th, Wright followed Humphreys to the vicinity of Appomattox, where both commanders were halted by a flag of truce from Lee.

From Buffalo river, where he camped, Sheridan, early on the 8th, sent a dispatch to Grant, with information derived from Merritt, who was in the advance : " If this is correct," he said, " the enemy must have taken the Pine road north of the Appomattox. I will move on Appomattox court-house. Should we not intercept the enemy, and he be forced into Lynchburg, his surrender is then beyond question."

The troopers were in the saddle as soon as the sun was up, and Merritt led off, Ouster in the advance, followed by Devin. At Prospect station the command was joined by Crook, who now brought up the rear. Soon after the march began, Sheridan's scouts reported four trains of cars at Appomattox station, five miles south of the court-house, loaded with supplies for Lee. These were doubtless the same supplies that had been chased from Burksville to Farmville, and from Farmville to Appomattox ; for days they were almost in sight but never in reach of the famished enemy. Merritt and Crook were promptly notified, and the entire command pushed briskly on for twenty-eight miles, halting only once for rest and water.

It was a day of uneventful marching; hardly a human being was encountered on the way. The country was enchanting; the peach orchards were blossoming in the southern spring, the fields had been peacefully ploughed for the coming crops, the buds were beginning to swell, and a touch of verdure was perceptible on the trees and along the hillsides.

The atmosphere was balmy and odorous ; the hamlets were unburnt, the farm-houses inhabited, the farms all tilled. In this distant valley of the Appo-mattox those who had plunged their country into war had hitherto escaped the punishment of treason and rebellion. But this placid neighborhood was destined to witness the hurried flight of routed legions and the impetuous march of the conqueror; and remote and unfamiliar until this day—to be associated in all time with one of the most memorable events in American history.

When Ouster arrived at Appomattox it was nearly dark, and he skillfully threw a force in rear of the station, and captured four heavily loaded trains —engines, cars, and supplies. But they were hardly in his hands when a rebel force of infantry and artillery appeared. One of the trains was burned, but Ouster hastily manned the other three and sent them off towards Farmville. Then, without halting, he pushed the enemy in the direction of the court-house, capturing twenty-five pieces of artillery, a hospital train, and a large number of prisoners, the advance of a heavy column, coming up on the Farmville road for supplies, and with no idea of meeting an enemy.

Sheridan now rapidly brought up Devin, who went into position on the right of Ouster. The fighting continued till after dark, and the enemy was driven to the court-house. A reconnoissance was then sent across the river, and Lee's entire command was discovered moving up on the Farmville road. Sheridan had headed the rebel army. At this great news, although he had only cavalry to oppose to all that was left of Lee's command, Sheridan held fast to what he had gained, and at 9.20 P. M. sent infor-

mation back to Grant. " If General Gibbon and the Fifth corps can get up to-night," he said, " we will perhaps finish the job in the morning. I do not think Lee means to surrender until compelled to do so." He also sent word to Ord and Gibbon and Griffin that if they pressed on there would be no possibility of escape for Lee.

Early on the 8th, Grant had set out from Farm-ville to join Sheridan's advance. But he had been absent from his own head-quarters several days, sleeping in rebel houses, and messing with any general officers whom he passed. Worn out with mental anxiety and physical fatigue, loss of sleep and the weight of responsibility, he became very unwell, and was obliged to halt at a farm-house on the road, where he spent most of the day.

About midnight, while unable to sleep from pain, he received the following communication from Lee. " April 8th : I received at a late hour your note of today. In mine of yesterday, I did not intend to propose the surrender of the army of Northern Virginia, but to ask the terms of your proposition. To be frank, I do not think the emergency has arisen to call for the surrender of this army ; but as the restoration of peace should be the sole object of all, I desired to know whether your proposals would lead to that end. I cannot therefore meet you with a view to surrender the army of Northern Virginia; but, as far as your proposal may affect the Confederate States forces under my command, I should be pleased to meet you at ten A. M. to-morrow, on the old stage road to Richmond, between the picket lines of the two armies."

This disingenuous letter was hardly worthy of

so great a commander. Lee had undoubtedly the day before given Grant to suppose that he was willing to make terms of surrender. He said nothing then about the restoration of peace. But this was when he was entangled in crossing the Appornattox; his wagons were ablaze, and his rear-guard was fighting for existence, with Crook and the Second corps. When he wrote his second letter, he was far away from Meade on the Lynchburg. road, and ignorant that Sheridan was across his path. He thought himself sure of supplies at Appomattox, and refused to meet the national general with a view to surrender his army. Much may be forgiven to a man in his condition, and the hope of escape, of avoiding the humiliation of absolute surrender, is his apology; but the apology is required.

Grant was more direct. He knew what he was aiming at, and was not to be enticed or entrapped into negotiations for peace. What he wanted, and meant to have, was the destruction of the army of his antagonist. Brushing away the cobwebs of artifice, he sent the following answer to Lee on the morning of the 9th of April: "Your note of yesterday is received. I have no authority to treat on the subject of peace. The meeting proposed for ten A. M. to-day could lead to no good. I will state, however, General, that I am equally desirous for peace with yourself, and the whole North entertains the same feeling. The terms upon wliich peace can be had are well understood. By the South laying down their arms they will hasten that most desirable event, save thousands of human lives, and hundreds of millions of property not yet destroyed. Seriously hoping that all our difficulties may be settled without the loss of

another life, I subscribe myself, etc., U. S. Grant, Lieutenant-General."

He then set out to join Sheridan's column, and to hasten the emergency which, in Lee's opinion, would call for the surrender of the rebel army.

Ord marched his men from daylight on the 8th until daylight on the 9th of April, halting only three hours on the road—a terrible march; but the men understood that they were conquering their enemy as effectually by marching as by fighting, and did not murmur. Griffin did as well as Ord. His troops marched twenty-nine miles, and bivouacked at two A. M. on the 9th; then moved again at four, and reached Sheridan's position at six, just as Lee was approaching in heavy force to batter his way through the cavalry.

Ord was the senior in rank on the field, and therefore in command of the infantry. He held a short consultation with Sheridan, after which the cavalry leader proceeded to the front, while Ord deployed his two corps across the head of the valley where Lee must pass. The army of the Potomac was close in the rebel rear on the north and east, and Sheridan, apparently with cavalry only, in front. Sheridan directed the cavalry, which was all dismounted, to fall back gradually, resisting the enemy, so as to give time for Ord to form his lines and march to the attack; and when this was done, the troopers were to move off to the right flank and mount.

Crook was soon hotly engaged. He ran his guns to the front and held his ground, in spite of a heavy onset of the enemy, for the rebels must make their way through now, or all was lost. Lee's force was

infantry, and greatly outnumbered Sheridan, and the cavalry leader soon sent back, urging Ord to hasten forward; at the same time he directed Crook to fall back slowly, and sacrifice no more men in trying to check this heavy force. Gibbon, Griffin, and a division of colored troops were ensconced in the woods, waiting for orders to advance. It looked as if Sheridan was deserting the field, and meant to allow the rebel army to pass. Lee's men gave once more the battle-yell, and quickened their pace, and doubled their fire, when suddenly, the cavalry having all retired, the infantiy line emerged from the woods, and —the Kebellion was over.

The rebels neglected to fire, and their line rolled back, wavering and staggering, with the certainty that they were doomed. The three commands of infantry all advanced at the double-quick step, covering the valley and all the adjacent hillsides, while Sheridan moved briskly around to the enemy's left, and was about to charge on the confused mass, when Lee sent forward a white flag with a request for a cessation of hostilities.

Sheridan rode over to Appomattox court-house, and there met Generals Gordon and Wilcox of the rebel army, who informed him that negotiations for a surrender were pending between Grant and Lee. Sheridan, however, declared that, if this were so, the attack upon his lines with a view to escape should not have been made, and he must have some assurance that a surrender was intended. This Gordon personally gave, and an agreement was made to meet again in half an hour. At the specified time a second interview was had, Ord and Longstreet -now accompanying Sheridan and Gordon; and Longstreet 120 repeated the assurance that Lee intended to surrender, and was only awaiting the arrival of Grant. Hostilities then ceased until the general-in-chief rode up.

Sheridan had been right in denouncing the conduct of Lee. The rebel chief, in his latest letter to Grant, on the 8th, had peremptorily declined all propositions for surrender, and in accordance with this announcement, on the morning of the 9th he attempted to break through the national lines ; but as soon as he discovered the presence of infantry as well as cavalry in his front, he informed Sheridan that he was negotiating for a surrender. But no communication to that effect had yet been made to Grant. Either the rebel statement was untrue, or Lee allowed his advance to attack the national forces after dispatching a letter indicating his willingness to yield. In either event, the last act of war of the rebellion was a subterfuge.

The fact is, that when Lee perceived his inability to force a passage through Sheridan's lines, he was conscious that, unless he quickly submitted to whatever terms Grant chose to impose, he and every man in his army would be annihilated. With Sheridan, Ord, and Griffin in front, and Meade with Humphreys and Wright in rear, there was no possible avenue of escape.

One solitary rough country road over the hills was indeed still open to Lynchburg, and by this route one of Lee's nephews, General Fitz-Hugh Lee, even now led a few hundred cavalrymen, in opposition, it is said, to the wish of his uncle, and in direct violation of all military obligations either to his own chief or to his enemy. But it was impossible for Lee to save his army by this road; and all

that was left of the host that had so long defended Richmond was in reality enclosed by the lines of the conqueror. Lee therefore undoubtedly intended to yield when he declared to Sheridan that he had already done so. But if he had sent to Grant, he had no right to fight Sheridan; and if he had not sent, he had no right to say that he was negotiating.

The dispatch that he wrote to Grant on the 9th was in these words: " I received your note of this morning on the picket line, whither I had come to meet you, and ascertain definitely what terms were embraced in your proposal of yesterday with reference to the surrender of this army." Even this was not ingenuous, for Grant's terms had been explicitly stated; and Lee evidently understood them, for he continued: " I now ask an interview, in accordance with the offer contained in your letter of yesterday, for that purpose." This was definite enough, and doubtless hard enough to say; and a brave man struggling against misfortune and humiliation should receive the generous consideration, especially of victorious enemies. Nevertheless, there is a noble, manly way of confessing defeat, and Lee's method of submitting to the inevitable was neither frank nor altogether honorable.

Grant had started for Sheridan's front at an early hour, and Lee's communication was sent by the way of Meade's command. It therefore did not reach the general-in-chief until nearly mid-day. He immediately replied : " Your note of this date is but this moment (11.50 A. M.) received, in consequence of my having passed from the Richmond and Lynch-burg roads to the Farmville and Lynchburg road. I am at this writing about four miles west of Walk-

er's church, and will push forward to the front for the purpose of meeting you. Notice sent to me on this road where you wish the interview to take place will meet me." This note was carried forward through Sheridan's lines by Colonel Babcock, of Grant's staff, who passed the enemy's pickets and was conducted to Lee.

The great rebel was sitting by the roadside under an apple-tree, surrounded by his officers; but he immediately mounted and rode forward to select the place for an interview, in accordance with the suggestion of Grant. First, however, he desired to send a message to Meade. He had been so anxious to avoid any further fighting, that he had requested of Meade, as well as Sheridan, a cessation of hostilities ; and Meade, as well as Sheridan, at first declined to receive the proposition, declaring that he had no authority, but finally agreed to a truce until two p. M., by which time it was supposed the generals-in-chief would have met. Lee informed Babcock of this arrangement, and requested that word might be sent to Meade, and the truce extended. Babcock accordingly wrote a line to Meade, notifying him of the circumstances, and requesting him to maintain the truce until positive orders from Grant could be received.

But the hours were passing, and the distance to Meade's head-quarters, around the national front, was nearly twelve .miles, while through the rebel army it was"not more than two miles; and, in his anxiety lest the fighting should recommence, Lee now volunteered to send an officer through his own lines with the message to Meade. Babcock's note was accordingly transmitted in this way by General

Forsyth, of Sheridan's staff, escorted by a rebel officer.

Lee then rode on to the village of Appomattox, and selected the house of a farmer named McLean for the interview with Grant. Information was at once sent back to Sheridan's head-quarters, not half a mile away, where the cavalry leader was impatiently awaiting the arrival of his chief. Firing of course had ceased, and Sheridan was at the very front with a handful of officers. Aware that Grant now held the remainder of the army of Northern Virginia in his grasp, and indignant that Lee should have continued to fight after he had proposed to surrender, the national trooper was inclined to consider the rebel overture a ruse—invented only to gain time to escape. He was pacing up and down in a little farm-yard, like a panther in a cage,* when the general-in-chief arrived, and assured him of the truth—that Lee, finding himself circumvented and surrounded, had indeed expressed a willingness to surrender.

A few words from Sheridan explained the situation in his front, and made Grant aware how completely the rebel leader and the fragments of the rebel army were at his mercy. With the army of the Potomac on the north and east, and Sheridan and Ord on the south and west, the circle was complete, and the enemy that had withstood, and repelled, and averted, and avoided Grant so long was

* I had been on some duty that separated me from the staff, and chanced to ride up to Sheridan's head-quarters in advance of the general-in-chief. "What do you think? What do you know?" he asked. "Is it a trick? Is he negotiating with Grant? I've got 'em," he continued, "I've got'em, like that!' 1 ' 1 and he doubled up his fist and clinched it, as if to hold them fast.

absolutely in his power. He proceeded at once to the interview.

The two armies carne together in a long valley at the foot of a ridge, and Appomattox was on a knoll between the lines, which could be seen for miles. The McLean house stood a little apart—a plain building with a verandah in front. Grant was met by Lee at the threshold. There was a narrow hall and a naked little parlor, containing a table and two or three chairs. Into this the generals entered, each at first accompanied only by a single aide-de-camp, but as many as twenty national officers shortly followed, among whom were Sheridan, Ord, and the members of Grant's own staff. No rebel entered the room but Lee and Colonel Marshall, who acted as his secretary.

The two chiefs shook hands, and Lee at once began a conversation, for he appeared more unembarrassed than his victor. He, as well as his aide-de-camp, was elaborately dressed. Lee wore embroidered gauntlets and a burnished sword, the gift, it was said, of the state of Virginia, while the uniforms of Grant and those who accompanied him were soiled and worn; some had slept in their boots for days, and Grant, when he started for Farmville two days before, had been riding around in camp without a sword. He had not since visited his own head-quarters, and was therefore at this moment without side-arms. The contrast was singular, and Colonel Marshall was asked how it came about that his chief and he were so fine, while the national officers had been unable to keep themselves free from the stains of battle and the road. He replied that Sheridan had come upon them suddenly a day or two before, and they were obliged to sacrifice their head-quarters' train; and as they could save but one suit of clothes, each hurriedly selected the best that he had, and so it was that at this juncture Lee and his aide-de-camp were better dressed than the men who had pursued them.

Lee was tall, large in form, fine in person, handsome in feature, grave and dignified in bearing; if anything, a little too formal. There was a suggestion of effort in his deportment; something that showed he was determined to die gracefully; a hint of Caesar mufiling himself in his mantle. But apart from this there was nothing to criticise.

Grant as usual was simple and composed, but with none of the grand air about him. No elation was visible in his manner or appearance. His voice was as calm as ever, and his eye betrayed no emotion. He spoke and acted as plainly as if he were transacting an ordinary matter of business. No one would have suspected that he was about to receive the surrender of an army, or that one of the most terrible wars of modern times had been brought to a triumphant close by the quiet man without a sword who was conversing calmly, but rather grimly, with the elaborate gentleman in grey and gold.

The conversation at first related to the meeting of the two soldiers in earlier years in Mexico, when Grant had been a subaltern and Lee a staff officer of Scott. The rebel general, however, soon adverted to the object of the interview. " I asked to see you, General Grant," he said, "to ascertain upon what terms you would receive the surrender of my army." Grant replied that the officers and men must become prisoners of war, giving up of course all munitions, weapons, and supplies, but that a parole would

be accepted, binding them to go to their homes and remain there until exchanged, or released by proper authority. Lee said that he had expected some such terms as these, and made some other remark not exactly relevant. Whereupon Grant inquired: "Do I understand, General Lee, that you accept these terms ?" " Yes," said Lee; " and if you will put them into writing, I will sign them."

Grant then sat down at the little table and wrote the following letter:

" APPOMATTOX COURT-HOUSE, VIRGINIA, April 9, 1865.

" GENERAL : In accordance with the substance of my letter to you of the 8th instant, I propose to receive the surrender of the army of Northern Virginia on the following terms, to wit: Rolls of all the officers and men to be made in duplicate, one copy to be given to an officer to be designated by me, the other to be retained by such officer or officers as you may designate. The officers to give their individual paroles not to take up arms against the government of the United States until properly exchanged ; and each company or regimental commander to sign a like parole for the men of their commands. The arms, artillery, and public property to be parked and stacked, and turned over to the officers appointed by me to receive them. This will not embrace the side-arms of the officers nor their private horses or baggage. This done, each officer and man will be allowed to return to his home, not to be disturbed by United States authority so long as they observe their paroles and the laws in force where they may reside.

"U. S. GRANT, Lieutenant-General.

11 General R. E. LEE."

While Grant was writing he chanced to look up at Lee, who sat nearly opposite, and at that moment noticed the glitter of his sword. The sight suggested an alteration in the terms, and he inserted the provision that officers should be allowed to retain their side-arms, horses, and personal property. Lee had accepted Grant's conditions without this stipulation, and doubtless expected to surrender his sword. But this humiliation he and his gallant officers were spared. When the terms were written out, Grant handed the paper to his great antagonist, who put on his spectacles to read them. He was evidently touched by their general clemency, and especially by the interpolation which saved so much to the feelings of a soldier. He said at once that the conditions were magnanimous, and would have a very good effect upon his army.

He next attempted to gain a little more. The horses of his cavalry and artillery, he said, were the property of the soldiers. Could these men be permitted to retain their animals ? Grant said the terms would not allow this. Lee took the paper again, and, glancing over it, said: " No. You are right. The terms do not allow it." Whereupon Grant replied: " I believe the war is now over, and that the surrender of this army will be followed soon by that of all the others; I know that the men, and indeed the whole South, are impoverished. I will not change the terms of the surrender, General Lee, but I will instruct my officers who receive the paroles to allow the cavalry and artillery men to retain their horses and take them home to work their little farms." Lee again expressed his acknowledgments, and said this kindness would have the best possible effect.

He then wrote out his letter of surrender in these words:

" HEAD-QUARTERS, ARMY OF NORTHERN VIRGINIA,

"Aprils, 1865.

" GENERAL : I received your letter of this date containing the terms of the surrender of the army of Northern Virginia, as proposed by you. As they are substantially the same as those expressed in your letter of the 8th instant, they are accepted. I will proceed to designate the proper officers to carry the stipulations into effect.

"K. E. LEE, General.

Lieutenant-General U. S. GRANT."

While the conditions were being copied the various national officers were presented to Lee. He was collected and courteous, bowed to each, but offered none his hand. One—General Seth Williams —who had served closely with him in the old army, attempted to revive old memories, but Lee repelled the advances coldly. He was in no mood to remember ancient friendships, or to recall pleasantly his service in the army of which he was now a prisoner, or under that flag which he had betrayed.

He had, however, another request to make. His men were starving; they had lived, he said, on two ears of corn a day for several days. Would Grant supply them with food ? There was a train of cars at Lynchburg loaded with rations, which had come from Danville for his army. Would Grant allow these to be distributed among the prisoners ? Grant, however, informed him that this train had been captured the day before by Sheridan. Thus, at the moment of his surrender, Lee was absolutely dependent for supplies upon his conqueror. Grant

of course acquiesced in the request, and asked how many rations Lee required. But the rebel general declared that he could not answer the question. He had no idea of his own strength. No return of a brigade had been made for several days.* Besides those lost in battle, killed, captured, or wounded, and left on the roadside, the men had been deserting and straggling by thousands. He could not tell what number he had left. All his public and private papers had been destroyed, to prevent their falling into the national hands. Grant finally inquired if twenty-five thousand rations would suffice; and Lee replied he thought that number would be enough. Twenty-five thousand, therefore, was Lee's estimate at Appomattox of the number he surrendered. Grant turned to the officer of the commissariat on his staff, and directed him to issue twenty-five thousand rations that night to the army of Northern Virginia. The order was obeyed, and before the rebels gave up their arms they were fed by their enemies.

Lee also requested Grant to notify Meade of the surrender, so that no lives might be needlessly lost on that front; and, on account of the distance to Meade's head-quarters, two national officers w^ere again dispatched with a rebel escort through the lines of the army of Northern Virginia, this time carrying the news of the surrender of that army.

The formal papers were now signed; a few more words were exchanged by the men who had opposed

* In spite of this assertion of his chief, Colonel Taylor, Lee's adjutant-general, has dedicated his work, "Four Years with General Lee," to the "8,000 veterans (the surviving heroes of the army of Northern Virginia) who in line of battle, on the 9th day of April, 1865, were reported present for duty." There was no report of the army of Northern Virginia made on the 9th of April, 1865.

each other so long; they again shook hands, and Lee went to the porch. The national officers followed and saluted him; and the military leader of the rebellion mounted his horse and rode off to his army, he and his soldiers prisoners of war.

As the great rebel entered his own lines the men rushed up in crowds to their chief, breaking ranks, and struggling to touch his hand. Tears streamed down his cheeks as he said: "

Men, we have fought through the war together. I have done the best I could for you." They raised a few broken cheers for the leader whom they had followed in so many a fierce battle and arduous march; and the career of the army of Northern Virginia was ended.

Grant also returned at once to his head-quarters' camp, now pitched almost at the front of Sheridan's command. As he approached the national lines the news had gone before him, and the firing of salutes began; but he sent at once to stop them. "The war is over," he said; "the rebels are our countrymen again, and the best sign of rejoicing after the victory will be to abstain from all demonstrations in the field." But he had not yet reported the capitulation to the government, and dismounting by the road-side, he sat on a stone and called for paper and pencil. An aide-de-camp offered his order-book, and at 4.30 p. M. on Sunday, the 9th of April, he announced the end of the rebellion in these words:

"Hon. E. M. STANTON, Secretary of War, Washington : " General Lee surrendered the army of Northern

Virginia this afternoon on terms proposed by my-

self. The accompanying additional correspondence will show the conditions fully.

" U. S. GKANT, Lieutenant-General?'

At his head-quarters he remained as calm as ever, but talked freely of the importance of the event and of its consequences. He declared that this was the end of the war; that all the other rebel armies would quickly yield: there might be guerillas, or partisan fighting here and there, but no great battle or campaign could now occur; and he announced his intention of returning to Washington on the morrow, to direct the disbanding of the armies. His officers were disappointed at this determination, for they had hoped to see something of the army they had contended with so long; and those who were intimate enough suggested that he should remain at Appomattox at least a day. But the expenses of the war amounted to four millions of dollars a day, and it was important to save this cost to the country. Grant was indifferent to the spectacle of his triumphs, and only anxious to secure their reality and result. One of the most important results would be the diminution of this immense outlay.

It was ascertained, however, that the Petersburg and Lynchburg railroad could be put in condition from a point a few miles off by noon of the following day, and as no time would be gained by starting sooner, the general-in-chief consented to visit the rebel lines. Accordingly, at about nine o'clock on the morning of April 10th, he rode out with his staff, accompanied also by Sheridan, Ord, Griffin, and several of their officers, a small cavalry, escort attending. The party proceeded to the mound in

the valley between the two armies, but when they arrived at the rebel pickets it was discovered that no directions had yet been given to admit national officers. A messenger, however, was promptly sent to Lee's head-quarters for orders, and when the great prisoner learned that Grant was at the picket line, he at once mounted his horse and with a single orderly came out to meet him.

Grant waited for him on the hillock, and then, sitting on their horses, in sight of the two armies, whose lines could be seen stretching away under the bright spring sun for miles, the two generals conversed for more than an hour. The officers and men who had accompanied Grant fell back a rod or two, to be out of hearing, and formed a semicircle behind him of fifty men or more; with Lee was his single orderly. An orchard of peach-trees was in full blossom on one side of the knoll. The sky was blue and without a cloud. The armies which had fought each other so bitterly were closer than often before, but no longer in angry contact; and from the mound one could see national and rebel cannon never again to open on each other.

The two great opponents found much to say. Both were convinced, Lee as firmly as

Grant, that the war was over; and Lee expressed his satisfaction at the result. Slavery, he said, was dead. The South was prepared to acquiesce in this as one of the consequences of national victory. The end had been long foreseen. The utter exhaustion of resources, the annihilation of armies, which had been , steadily going on for a year, could have but one termination. Johnston, he said, would certainly follow his example, and surrender to Sherman; and

the sooner the rebel armies were all surrendered, the better, now. Nothing could be accomplished by further resistance.

When Grant discovered that Lee entertained these opinions, he urged him to address the rebel government and people, and use his great influence to hasten the result which he admitted was not only inevitable, but, under the circumstances, desirable. But this step Lee was not inclined to take. He said that he was now a prisoner, and felt a delicacy about advising others to put themselves in his position. But he had no doubt they would speedily arrive at the same conclusion without his urging.

The conversation was protracted, and the restless Sheridan, not used to waiting, at last rode up and asked permission to cross the lines and visit some of his old comrades in the rebel army. Leave of course was given, and with Sheridan went Generals Ingalls and Seth Williams, both men of the old army, with as many personal friends among the rebel officers as under the national flag. They soon found acquaintances, and, when the interview between Grant and Lee was over, the three returned, bringing with them nearly every officer of high rank in the rebel army, to pay their respects to Grant and thank him for the terms he had accorded them the day before. Lee now bade good-morning, and returned to his own head-quarters, while the national chief and those with him repaired to the farm-house hard by, where the capitulation had been signed.

Hither also came Longstreet, Gordon, Heth, Wil-cox, Pickett, and other rebel officers of fame, splendid soldiers, who had given their enemies much- trouble; and Sheridan, Ord, Griffin, and the men on

Grant's staff, met them cordially. First, of course, the rebels were presented to Grant, who greeted them with kindness. Most of them he knew personally. Longstreet had been at his wedding; Cadmus Wilcox was his groomsman; Heth was a subaltern with him in the Mexican war. Others he had served with in garrison or on the Pacific coast. They all expressed their appreciation of his magnanimity. To be allowed not only their lives and liberty, but their swords, had touched them deeply. One said to him in my hearing: " General, we have come to congratulate you on having wound us up." " I hope," replied Grant, " it will be for the good of us all."

Then the other national officers took their turn, shaking hands cordially with men whom they had met in many a battle, or with whom they had earlier shared tent or blanket on the Indian trail or the Mexican frontier; with classmates of West Point and sworn friends of boyhood. Some shed tears as they hugged each other after years of separation and strife. Countrymen all they felt themselves now, and not a few of the rebels declared they were glad that the war had ended in the triumph of the nation.

Their humility indeed was marked. They felt and said that they had staked all and lost. They inquired if they would be permitted to leave the country, for none dreamed that they would ever regain their property. They spoke of estates which once they owned, forfeit now by the laws of war and of nations; for they did not scruple to admit that they were defeated rebels. The absurd idea of their ever again enjoying political rights did not occur to one of them. They would have thought it

cruel mockery to mention such a possibility. They were thankful not to be tried and executed for treason, like other men who attempt to subvert a government and fail; grateful that they were not condemned to languish in long captivity, but might return at once to their unfamiliar homes.

And not one word of reproach was uttered by those who had been their enemies. No exultation was manifest, only joy and good feeling that the war between brethren was over; that, though worn, and famished, and suffering, the prodigal, even if forced, had yet returned.

We sat for an hour or more on the steps of the porch, or in the verandah, and at noon Grant mounted his horse and set out for Washington, not having entered the rebel lines.

On the 12th of April, the army of Northern Virginia was formed by divisions for the last time. Lee had already given his personal parole, and was not present. But commissioners had been appointed on each side, under whose direction the troops marched to a spot in the neighborhood of Appomattox courthouse. The national column halted on a distant hill, where a white flag was waving. No guns were in position, no bands played; no cheers taunted the unfortunate. In profound silence the Southerners dressed their lines, fixed bayonets, stacked arms, and deposited their accoutrements. Then slowly furling their flags, they laid them down; and many a veteran stooped to kiss the stained and tattered colors, under which he might fight no more. All day the

ceremony went on, the disarmed men streaming provost marshal's tent for their paroles. Then

ththstarted for their homes. 121

Hardly a man possessed a particle of money, and some had a thousand miles to travel in a country where railroads had been annihilated. They were allowed to wear their uniforms, but without insignia, and to pass free over all government transports and railroads.

Lee rode from Appomattox court-house to Richmond, which he entered on the 12th, while his army was laying down its arms. A few of the inhabitants gathered around him on the way to his house, but he discouraged any demonstration, and no disturbance occurred. The population had been fed by the national authorities since the capture of the town; and the officer who had charge of this duty, aware that Lee must be entirely destitute, sent at once to ask if he would like supplies. Lee expressed his thanks and said that he had no other resource, and unless this assistance had been extended, he did not know where he should have found a meal. There was only one way in which the provisions could be distributed. A law of Congress provided for such emergencies, allowing what was called the " destitute ration" to be supplied to negroes and others in captured towns. A printed form was issued, and the name of the recipient must be written on the paper before the ration could be drawn. A ticket for a " destitute ration " was accordingly made out for General Robert E. Lee.*

* I have already stated that I was sent to Richmond by General Grant after the close of the Appomattox campaign ; and it fell to me to make the inquiry, mentioned in the text, of General Lee, and to write his name on the order for the supply.

Subsequently I had an important interview with the rebel chief. He made a verbal request of General Grant, through me, that the soldiers captured at Sailor's creek, among whom was his own son, General

When Grant broke camp at City Point on the 29th of March, his chief commissary of subsistence inquired what number of supplies should be carried for the troops, and the general-in-chief replied: " Twelve days' rations." The surrender of Lee occurred on the twelfth day.

This was not the only part of his scheme which had been foreshadowed before its accomplishment. The instructions to Sheridan and the dispatches to Sherman during the last days of March laid down almost the exact plan which was followed to the end. On the 16th of March, it will be remembered, Grant said to Sherman : " I shall be prepared to pitch into Lee, if he attempts to evacuate the place." On the 21st, he said to Sheridan : " There is now such a possibility, if not probability, of Lee and Johnston attempting to unite, that I feel extremely desirous not only of cutting the lines of communication between them, but of having a large and properly commanded cavalry force ready to act, in case such an

Custis Lee, should be placed on the same footing as those who surrendered at Appomattox—that is to say, released on parole ; but this was not immediately acceded to.

During the conversation, Lee spoke of his acquiescence in the result of the war, and declared he had thought at the beginning we were better off as one nation than as two, and, he added, " I think so now." I could not resist asking how then he came to serve against the government, and he replied that it was President Lincoln's proclamation calling for troops to coerce the South which decided him to act with his section.

He spoke very bitterly of the course of England and France during the war, and said that the South had as much cause to resent it as the North ; that England especially had acted from no regard to either portion of the Union, but from a jealousy of the united nation, and a desire to see it fall to pieces. England, he said, had led the Southerners to believe she would assist them, and then deserted them when they most needed aid.

attempt is made." On the 22nd, he wrote to Sherman : " Sheridan's instructions will be to strike the South side road as near Petersburg as he can, and destroy it so that it can not be repaired for three or four days, and push on to the Danville road as near to the Appomattox as he can get." This is precisely what Sheridan did, about two weeks later, only in the presence, and in spite of all of Lee's army.

"When this movement commences," continued Grant, " I shall move out by my left with all the force I can, holding present entrenched lines. ... I shall go along myself, and will take advantage of anything that turns up. If Lee detaches, I will attack, or if he comes out of his lines, I will endeavor to repulse him, and follow it up to the best advantage" It would be difficult to find words to describe more exactly the operations which actually occurred than these written in advance. The same general ideas, pervaded by the same spirit, were communicated to Sherman in person, when he visited City Point on the 28th; were explained to Lincoln, and again included in the final instructions to Meade and Sheridan and Ord. In all there was the same definiteness of outline and aim which always characterized Grant's strategy, and the same distinct intention to take advantage of emergencies as yet unforeseen.

When the campaign began, everything proceeded regularly towards the designed consummation. The very difficulties and delays of the first three days facilitated the development of the plan. The dangers to which Lee was subjected by the threatening movement to the left compelled him to make some desperate effort, or to lose all; and the effort was what Grant had foreseen. Lee detached an impor-

tant part of his army, and thus presented the opportunity already provided for. Grant attacked in return, with his fiery subordinate, and the defeat of Pickett was instantly followed by the assaults on Petersburg. Not a moment was left the rebel chief to recover from the effect of the disaster at Five Forks, either to bring back Pickett, or himself to move in prompt endeavor to escape; but while Lee was still stunned and bewildered by the immensity of his misfortune and his peril, the terrible blow descended like the thunderbolt of a god. Richmond, Petersburg, cities, fortifications, populations, Presidents, armies, armaments—all went down in one tremendous crash, as if the world itself was at an end.

Even then Grant did not wait a moment. He did not even move his army eastward to occupy or capture Petersburg; he was certain it would fall without a final effort, and before the town was in his hands, his forces were stretching out westward, to intercept the flying defenders, who themselves had not yet escaped from the lines which had protected them so long. Sheridan and Humphreys and Griffin were held loose on the night of April 2nd, in the certainty that Lee would evacuate Petersburg before morning.

For when once the citadel of the rebellion was gone, when the rebels were driven from cover, Grant knew well what the next and only object of Lee must be. He must attempt to unite with Johnston's army. Should this be accomplished, the war might very possibly last yet another year. The two great rebel forces combined might retire into the interior, and in some way find supplies; and though' they probably could not damage the national armies seri-

ously, they miglit occasion infinite trouble and cost before they could be subdued.

This was the spur and incitement of Grant's terrible energy. It was not the mere pursuit of a routed foe, but the accomplishment of a great strategical and political object that he was aiming at, and there were plenty of difficulties in his path. Lee had the shorter road and fewer impediments. He had the wonderful impetus of flight, with the chance of safety and something like success before him as his prize. He, besides, was moving towards supplies, while Grant must leave his base, and rebuild a railroad in order to provision his army. There was every military chance, when Lee fled from Petersburg, that he would succeed in eluding his pursuer.* Accordingly he ordered supplies from Danville to meet him, and by daylight on the 3rd of April his advance was sixteen miles on the road to Amelia.

And now came a contest between the wits and genius of the two commanders. For the first time they were pitted against each other, absolutely outside of works, and in the open field. Lee no longer had elaborate fortifications to protect his army, but only the breastworks that he threw up along the road, in the intervals of flight. Grant, on the other hand, could with difficulty concentrate his superior numbers while in motion, and they were therefore at times an absolute encumbrance, crowding the roads in each other's way, and exposed, if separated, to a sudden blow from the enemy. Lee had only a single

* " The intention was to take the direction of Danville, and turn to our advantage the good line for resistance offered by the Dan and Staunton rivers. The activity of the Federal cavalry and the want of supplies compelled a different course."— Four Tears with General Lee.

object now—to elude the columns of his adversary, and effect his junction with Johnston. If he succeeded in this, Grant was baffled and beaten, despite the evacuation of Richmond and Petersburg, and the rebellion was not over. So Jefferson Davis thought, and issued a proclamation from Danville on the 5th of April, announcing to the people of the South that their cause was still not lost.

But neither Lee nor Davis even yet understood the man with whom they were dealing. For now began the unintermitted succession of manoeuvres and marches and battles and blows which, unintermitted, could have but one end. While Lee was making for the Appomattox and attempting to cross the river and collect his scattered troops at Amelia, Grant pushed rapidly forward for the same point, on the opposite side. He was aware of Lee's intention almost as soon as it was formed, and long before night on the 3rd of April, his columns were all in motion for the Danville road, to intercept his adversary. On the 4th, the flight was continued on the northern bank, and the parallel movement on the opposite side, Sheridan stretching ahead in the race, and gaining step by step on the advance of the enemy. This day Lee arrived at Amelia, and Sheridan came up, not only with his cavalry, but with the head of Griffin's corps, to Jetersville, having thus absolutely outmarched the rebel army. At this point the supplies that Lee had ordered were intercepted, on their way from Danville, and the rebel chief was obliged to wait a day and gather food and forage from the inhabitants.

And now the energy of the chief of the advance was not more conspicuous nor commendable than the

efforts of Meade and his subordinates. All night the army of the Potomac marched, though it had been allowed no rest for five full days and nearly as many nights; marched without food, as its commander said, " as ready to die from fatigue and starvation as from the bullets of the enemy." Ord, meanwhile, pushed on nearly as hard; for Grant constantly used the army of the James to cut off and prevent any possible flight or escape of Lee by a detour in the direction of Danville. He was at this time striking hard with one wing of his command, and extending the other to retain the rebels in a position where they could be struck. In this way Ord did as good service as Meade.

At Jetersville, on the 5th, the army of the Potomac and the cavalry were in front of Lee; the rebels were intercepted; the national forces were thrown directly across the road to Johnston's army. And here, if Meade had possessed the highest genius for generalship, he would have attacked and destroyed the remainder of the rebel command. Jetersville, instead of Appomattox, would have seen the termination of the war. Lee must inevitably have been crushed, and nothing but the fragments of his army could have escaped. It is not possible that any organized rebel force could have resisted or remained, after an onset of the national troops at Jetersville.

But, though Lee himself had also neglected to use his chance, and push through Sheridan's little advance while the rebels were superior; failing, as he always did, in bold aggressive action; he nevertheless was always admirable in flight and evasion ; he had a positive genius for eluding his enemy ; and,

finding that Meade made no attack, the rebel general, in the night, with admirable secrecy and skill, did exactly what Sheridan had foretold, and what Grant, as soon as he arrived on the spot and understood the situation, concurred in anticipating—he moved again by his right flank; and before Grant had time to reverse the arrangements of Meade, the army of Northern Virginia was once more on the march.

Not, however, to escape unhurt or entire. Instantly changing the direction of his columns, Grant again disposed them, not only to pursue, but again to intercept his adversary. Then came the exciting race, and all the movements by which Ord held Lee in front long enough for Sheridan to attack in flank with Wright and the cavalry, and Humphreys to come up with the rear—as complete a strategical success as was ever achieved. The whole rebel rearguard was annihilated. Generals, soldiers, arms, and ammunition were the prize.

But even now a portion of the enemy had escaped, and with marvellous resolution and endurance was pressing on. No grander exhibition of fortitude has ever been made than on this march. The chance of reaching Johnston was quite gone. Lee himself could not have hoped to save any force that could ever resist an army again. His officers and men understood the situation as well as he. But the subordinates were steadfast and loyal to their leader, and the chief was stubborn to the last.

During the night of the 6th, the rebels again evaded the army of the James. On the 7th, the Appomattox was crossed, over burning bridges" and amid exploding forts. The wagons were ablaze and

the guns were abandoned; but the rebels pressed on, and beyond Farmville they turned once more with indomitable courage to hold off their energetic foe. But the pursuit was as terrible and uninter-mitted as the flight; the columns were all advancing, though generals were captured and divisions repelled ; the cavalry crossed and re-crossed the Ap-pomattox; solitary corps were endangered; others were obstructed; others marching across each other's path, and the troops entangled on the unfamiliar roads. But the chief was never more a chief than on this day; bringing order out of chaos, directing all his commanders, perfecting and developing his original strategy all the time; and at night, after all the confused events of the day—the army of the Potomac was north of the Appomattox, close up against the rebel entrenchments, while the cavalry and the left wing were still stretching out westward to head the wearied columns of the foe.

That night once more the rebels evacuated their works, this time in front of Meade, and when morning dawned were far on their way, as they fondly thought, to Lynchburg; and Lee defiantly informed his pursuer that the emergency for surrender had not arrived. But he reckoned without his host. He was stretching, with the terrific haste that precedes despair, to Appomattox, for supplies. He need hardly have hastened to that spot, destined to be so fatal to himself and his cause. Grant's legions were making more haste than he. The marvellous marching, not only of Sheridan, but of the men of the Fifth and Twenty-fourth corps, was doing as much as a battle to bring the rebellion to a close. Twenty-eight, thirty-two, thirty-five miles a day, in

succession, these infantry soldiers marched; all day and all night. From daylight till daylight again, after more than a week of labor and fatigues almost unexampled, they pushed on, to intercept their ancient adversary, while the remainder of the army of the Potomac was at his heels.

Finally, Lee, still defiant, and refusing to treat with any view of surrender, came up to his goal, but found the national cavalry had reached the point before him, and that the supplies were gone. Still he determined to push his way through, and with no suspicion that men on foot could have marched from Rice's station to his front in thirty hours, he made his last charge, and discovered a force of infantry greater than his own before him, besides cavalry—while two corps of the army of the Potomac were close in rear. He had run straight into the national lines. He was enclosed, walled in, on every side, with imminent, instant destruction impending over him. He instantly offered to submit to Grant, and in the agony of alarm lest the blow should fall, he applied to Meade and Sheridan also for a cessation of hostilities. Thus in three directions at once he was appealing to be allowed to yield. At the same moment he had messengers out to Sheridan, Meade, and Grant. The emergency whose existence he had denied had arrived. He was out-marched, and out-fought, out-witted, out-generalled; defeated in every possible way. He and his army, every man surrendered. He and his army, every man was fed by the conqueror.

Twenty-seven thousand five hundred and- sixteen officers and men were paroled at Appornattox

court-house.* In addition to these, forty-six thousand four hundred and ninety-five rebels were captured by the armies of the Potomac and the James and the cavalry, between the 29th day of March and the 9th of April, 1865; making a total of seventy-four thousand and eleven prisoners, in this campaign. The wounded were probably all paroled, but it is hardly possible that fewer than five thousand were killed.

The losses in the national army during the same period were ten thousand and sixty-six; of these, two thousand were killed, six thousand five hundred wounded, and twenty-five hundred were reported missing.f

* Every rebel who has written about Appomattox declares that only 8,000 of those who surrendered bore arms—a statement which would not be creditable to them, if true. But as every rebel who was at Appomattox was himself a prisoner, the assertion is worthless. The fact is, that 22,633 small arms were surrendered ; and Lee did not carry many extra muskets around in wagons during the retreat from Petersburg.

t See Appendix for returns of the national and rebel losses in this campaign, from the adjutant-general's office.

CHAPTER XXXV.

Grant returns to Washington—Reduction of expenses of government—Rejoicing of country—Assassination of Lincoln—Negotiations between Sherman and Johnston—Manoeuvres of rebels—Sherman's terms—Disapproved by government—Grant in North Carolina—Second arrangement between Sherman and Johnston—Approved by Grant—Excitement of country—Grant's friendship for Sherman—Movements of Stoneman—Operations of Canby—Evacuation of Mobile—Operations of cavalry—Surrender of all the rebel armies—Capture of Jefferson Davis—Collapse of the revolt—-Sagacity of Grant—Gratitude of rebels—Acclamations of country—Review of Grant's career—Educated by earlier events for chief command—His view of situation—Comprehensiveness of plan—Character and result of Wilderness campaign—Desperation of rebels—Development of general plan—Consummation—Completeness of combinations—Victory not the result of brute force—Faithful support of government—Executive greatness of Sherman and Sheridan—Characteristics of Meade, Thomas, and Lee —Further traits of Lee—Fitting representative of the rebellion—Characteristics of national and rebel soldiers—Necessity of transcendent efforts —Characteristics of a commander-in-chief in civil war—Nations never saved without a leader—Grant protects Lee from trial for treason.

THE surrender at Appomattox court-house ended the war. The interview with Lee occurred on the 9th of April, and on the 13th Grant arrived at "Washington, and at once set about reducing the military expenses of the government. He spent the day with the President and the Secretary of War, and at night the following announcement was made to the country:

"WAR DEPARTMENT, WASHINGTON, "AprUlZtb, 6 P. M.

"The Department, after mature consideration and consultation with the Lieutenant-General upon the results of the recent campaign, has come to. the following determinations, which will be carried into

effect by appropriate orders to be immediately issued.

"First, to stop all drafting and recruiting in the loyal states.

" Second, to curtail purchases for arms, ammunition, quartermaster, and commissary supplies, and reduce the military establishment in its several branches.

" Third, to reduce the number of general and staff officers to the actual necessities of the service.

" Fourth, to remove all military restrictions upon trade and commerce, so far as may be consistent with the public safety."

These important reductions proclaimed the overthrow of the rebellion and the restoration of peace; and enthusiastic rejoicings at once broke out all over the land. In Washington an illumination of all the public and many of the private buildings took place, and on the 14th of April, it was announced in the newspapers that the general-in-chief would accompany the President in the evening to the theatre. But Grant had not seen his children for several months, and, declining the invitation of the President, he started for Burlington, in New Jersey, where his children were at school. That night the President was assassinated—shot by an actor, one of a band of conspirators who, it was afterwards proved, intended also to take the life of Grant. The Secretary of State was wounded in his bed, and doubtless the designs included attacks upon the Vice-Presi-dent and the Secretary of War, which, however, were not carried into effect. Stanton at once telegraphed to the general-in-chief, who returned the same night to Washington.

The President lingered a few hours, and expired on the morning of the 15th, at the moment of the triumph of that cause of which he had been the devoted servant as well as the indefatigable and beloved leader, and of which he now became the most exalted and lamented martyr. His successor, Andrew Johnson, was inaugurated on the same day.

These astounding events imposed unforeseen and important duties on all connected with the government, and Grant, of course, remained at the capital.

Meanwhile, the expected sequel to the surrender of Lee had come to pass. On the 10th of April, in obedience to Grant's orders to " push on and finish the job with Lee and Johnston's armies," Sherman advanced against Smithfield, and Johnston at once retreated rapidly through Raleigh, which place Sherman entered on the 13th. On the 14th, he received a message from Johnston, dictated by Jefferson Davis, who was living in a box car on the railroad, at Greensboro, the inhabitants refusing him any other shelter.

The rebels had learned the surrender of Lee, and their communication was to inquire whether Sherman was " willing to make a temporary suspension of active operations, and to communicate to Lieutenant-General Grant, commanding the armies of the United States, the request that he would take like action in regard to other armies—the object being to permit the civil authorities to enter into the needful arrangements to terminate the existing war."

Sherman replied on the same day that he was fully empowered to arrange any terms for the suspension of further hostilities between his own army and that of Johnston, and was willing to confer to

that end. He undertook to abide by the same terms and conditions as were allowed by Grant to Lee at Appomattox, and, furthermore, to obtain from Grant an order to suspend the movements of any troops from the direction of Virginia. He also offered to order Stoneman, now in front of Johnston's army, to suspend any devastation or destruction contemplated by him.

No reply to this was received until the 16th, when Johnston agreed to meet Sherman on the following day at a point midway between the two armies. Just before starting for the interview, Sherman received a telegram announcing the assassination of Lincoln, and, as soon as the two commanders were alone, he showed the dispatch to Johnston, who did not attempt to conceal his distress, but declared that the event would prove the greatest possible calamity to the Confederacy.

The discussion of the object of the interview then began. Sherman at once declined to receive any propositions addressed to the government of the United States by those claiming to be civil authorities of a Southern Confederacy; whereupon Johnston proposed that the two generals should themselves arrange the terms of a permanent peace; and the conditions which might be allowed to the rebellious states on their submission to the government were discussed. The terms were not entirely agreed upon, as Sherman desired to be certain of Johnston's authority to speak for " all the Confederate armies." The conference was therefore suspended until the following day, to give opportunity for Johnston to obtain this authority.

Immediately after the close of the interview

Johnston telegraphed to Breckenridge, who had proceeded as far as Charlotte, with the fugitive govern-ment. Breckenridge came promptly at the summons, together with Reagan, the Postmaster-General of the rebel cabinet. A memorandum was then drawn up of the terms which Davis and his advisers considered desirable, and, on the 18th, Johnston and Breckenridge repaired together to the place of rendezvous. Sherman, however, objected to the presence of a member of the Richmond cabinet, whereupon Johnston proposed that Breckenridge should be admitted to the interview in his capacity of major-general in the rebel army. To this Sherman consented, and the terms written out by Reagan were presented by Breckenridge and Johnston. Sherman, however, preferred to write his own, which were substantially the same as those proposed by the rebels.*

An armistice was to be established maintaining the status quo, not to be terminated without forty-eight hours 7 notice by either commander. All the rebel armies in existence were to be disbanded and conducted to their state capitals, there to deposit their arms and public property;

the arms to be subject to the further action of Congress, and in the mean time to be used solely to maintain peace and order within the borders of the states respectively. The state governments were to be recognized upon their officers and legislatures taking the oath of allegiance to the national government; the United

* "His paper differed from mine only in being fuller."— Johnston's Military Narrative, p. 405.

"General Johnston's account of our interview in his 'Narrative,' (page 402 et seq.\'7d is quite accurate and correct."— Sherman's Memoirs, vol. ii., p. 350.

122

States' courts were to be re-established; the people of all the states to be guaranteed their political rights and franchises, as well as their rights of person and property, and not to be disturbed by reason of the war, so long as they abstained from acts of armed hostility and obeyed the laws. In fine, peace and a general amnesty were to be declared, on condition of the disbandment of the rebel armies, the distribution of arms, and the resumption of peaceful pursuits by the officers and men of those armies.

This memorandum covered a great deal of ground. It included "all the Confederate armies in existence "; it defined the future status of the states and populations in rebellion; and conceded every point that the rebels could possibly claim or hope to carry, except the single one of the supremacy of the government. It said nothing, however, about the abolition of slavery, the right of secession, the punishment of past treason, or security against future rebellion.

The concluding paragraph was in these words: " Not being fully empowered by our respective principals to fulfill these terms, we individually and officially pledge ourselves to promptly obtain the necessary authority, and to carry out the above programme."

The next day Sherman published an order to his troops, beginning: "The general commanding announces to the army a suspension of hostilities, and an agreement with General Johnston and high officials, which, when formally ratified, will make peace from the Potomac to the Rio Grande."

A. messenger was instantly sent to convey these terms to Washington, under cover to Grant. The

dispatches were received by the general-in-chief on the night of April 21st. He at once perceived that the terms were such as could not possibly be approved, and accordingly wrote the following note to the Secretary of War: " I have received and just completed reading the dispatches brought by the special messenger from General Sherman. They are of such importance that I think immediate action should be taken on them, and that it should be done by the President in council with the whole cabinet. I would respectfully suggest whether the President should not be notified, and all the cabinet, and the meeting take place to-night."

The cabinet meeting was called before midnight. The President and his ministers were unanimous in condemning the propositions of Sherman. Indeed, their language was so vehement that Grant, while agreeing fully with them that the terms were inadmissible, yet felt it his duty to his friend and subordinate to defend him against the imputations that were freely made. The President was especially indignant at Sherman's course, and the sympathy with rebels which it was thought to betray; w^hile Stan-ton did not hesitate to call it treason. But Grant at once declared that the services Sherman had rendered the country during now four years entitled him to the most lenient judgment, and proved that, whatever might be thought of his opinions, his motives should be unquestioned.

Nevertheless, the general-in-chief was instructed to give notice to Sherman of the President's disapproval of the memorandum, and to direct him to resume hostilities at the earliest possible moment. The instructions of Lincoln to Grant on the 3rd of

March, communicated by Stanton, were to be observed by Sherman,* and Grant was ordered to proceed immediately to Sherman's head-quarters and direct in person operations against the enemy. Instructions were also sent in various directions to Sherman's subordinates to disregard his orders.

Grant started before daybreak on the 22nd, and from Fort Monroe, at 3.30 p. M. the same day, he telegraphed to Halleck, who had been placed in command at Richmond: " The truce entered into by Sherman will be ended as soon as I can reach Raleigh. Move Sheridan with his cavalry toward Greensboro, North Carolina, as soon as possible. I think it will be well to send one corps of infantry also, the whole under Sheridan." Arriving at Raleigh on the 24th, he informed Sherman as delicately as possible of the disapproval of his memorandum, and directed him to impose upon Johnston the same terms which had already been laid down to Lee. Sherman was thoroughly subordinate, and at once notified • Johnston that their arrangement had not been ratified. " I have replies from Washington," he said, "to my communication of April 18th. I am instructed to limit my operations to your immediate command, and not to attempt civil negotiations. I therefore demand the surrender of your army on the same terms as were given to General Lee at Appomattox, April 9th instant, purely and simply." In another

* "The President directs me to say that he wishes you to have no conference with General Lee, unless it be for the capitulation of Lee's army, or on solely minor and purely military matters. He instructs me to say that you are not to decide, discuss, or confer upon any political question ; such questions the President holds in his own hands, and will submit them to no military conferences or conventions." — Stanton to Grant, March 3d. See page 401.

dispatch sent at the same time, lie gave notice of the termination of the armistice in forty-eight hours. Both these papers were of course submitted to Grant and received his approval before they were forwarded.

Johnston immediately communicated the substance of Sherman's dispatches to Davis, and asked for further instructions. The next morning, April 25th, he was directed to disband the rebel infantry, and bring off his cavalry and all soldiers who could be mounted, with a few light field pieces. He, however, decided to disobey these — the last instructions he received from the rebel government. They were intended, he said, to secure the safety of certain high civil officers, but neglected that of the Southern people and army. He declared that it would be a great crime to prolong the war; while to send a cavalry ^escort to Davis too heavy for flight, but not strong enough to force a way for him, would spread ruin over the South by leading the great in. vading armies in pursuit. He, therefore, proposed to Sherman another armistice and conference, suggesting as a basis the clause in the recent convention relating to the army; and reported his action to what had been called the Confederate government. Thus the last blow to the rebel President was dealt by his bitter and personal enemy; and the chagrin of the general who was relieved by Hood was avenged by the anguish of the fallen chief, deserted and disobeyed by the subordinate whom he had wronged.

On the 26th, another interview occurred between Johnston and Sherman, at which no member of the rebel cabinet attended, and terms were agreed upon

similar to those arranged between Grant and Lee. All acts of war on the part of Johnston's army were to cease at once; all arms and public property to be delivered to an ordnance officer of the United States, at Greensboro ; the officers and men to give their individual obligations not to take up arms against the United States until properly released from this parole ; and then to be permitted to return to their homes, not to be disturbed by national authorities so long as they observed their obligations and the laws.

This, it will be seen, was a purely military convention, and referred only to the surrender of Johnston's command. The great civil questions of amnesty, the courts, the state governments, and of political and personal rights and franchises were remitted to the civil authorities. Thirty-one thousand two hundred and forty-three men of Johnston's army were paroled.*

During these negotiations Grant kept himself carefully in the background. He was not present at any interview with Johnston, remaining at Raleigh while Sherman went out to the front, and his name did not appear on any of the papers, except when he wrote, after the signatures of Sherman and John-ston~ " Approved, U. S. Grant." Even this the rebel commander was not aware of, and Grant went

* Yet General Johnston, one of the most honorable of the rebel commanders, does not hesitate, in his "Military Narrative," p. 398, to designate the entire remaining rebel command as "an army of about 20,000 infantry and artillery and 5,000 mounted troops," and to contrast this with what he calls " Grant's, of 180,000 men ; Sherman's, of 110,000 at least; Canby's, 60,000—odds of seventeen or eighteen to one."

Over 70,000 rebels were surrendered by Johnston and Richard Taylor alone.

ULYSSES S. GKA1ST.

635

back to Washington without allowing his presence to be known to the enemy. He had assumed no command, received no surrender, and manifested, as he felt, no diminution in his respect and regard for Sherman.

Before reaching the capital, however, he found that the Secretary of War had published a remarkable document, denouncing Sherman, and that an intense excitement prevailed among the loyal people at the North. But Grant made it his especial duty to vindicate his great lieutenant, throwing around his friend the shield of his own reputation, and assuring every one that Sherman's loyalty was as unquestionable as his own. The indignation of the country, however, was at first extreme, and nothing but Grant's own popularity, and the persistency with which he defended Sherman, saved that illustrious soldier from insult, and possibly degradation. Before long, however, the feeling changed, and Sherman resumed his natural and appropriate place in the estimation and affection of the people whom he had so nobly served.

The country and posterity will doubtless always hold that Sherman erred in judgment at this crisis. But it was from the generous impulse of a soldier, who sees his enemy defeated and in his power, and would blush to strike a fallen foe. He doubtless also felt a noble ambition to avert any further misery from the land that had suffered so much, and to restore at once to a united country the long-absent benefits of peace. He had the knowledge of Grant's clemency at Appomattox, and was aware of the charity which had animated Lincoln's great heart. Everything conspired to make him accede too readily

to the specious propositions by means of which the wily Confederates sought still to secure all that they had lost by war. The frank and outspoken soldier was no match in diplomatic arts for those who had conspired to betray their country and piloted the sinking cause of the rebellion through desperate and stormy years. He did not perceive the object of the skilful machinations which first suggested the presence of a cabinet officer, and then secured amnesty for the rebel government. He was looking so intently to the respite from war that the precautions of politicians and statesmen were neglected. But the mistake outside of his profession left no blot on his career as a soldier or his reputation as a patriot, and never for one moment disturbed his relations with his chief and friend.*

While these important events were occurring in North Carolina and Virginia, the remaining combinations of the general-in-chief had proceeded to their designed development.

The forces of Stone-

* I chanced to bear to General Grant in North Carolina the news of the publication of Secretary Stanton's famous memorandum, and I never saw the general-in-chief so much moved as on this occasion. He had hoped that the original excitement displayed at the cabinet meeting would be concealed from the country, and when he discovered the contrary his indignation was extreme. He declared it was "infamous " that a man who had done such service as Sherman should be subjected to imputations like these.

Sherman's own resentment was intense, and Grant strove hard to appease it, and to bring about amicable relations between two men so signally important to their country as the great War Minister and the soldier of Atlanta and the March. But it was long before the sense of injustice which Sherman felt could be allayed.

Some very interesting letters on this subject, which I am allowed to publish, will be found in the Appendix, together with all the official documents necessary to the history of the episode.

The rebel account will be found in full in Johnston's " Military Narrative."

man and Canby moved on the 20th, and those of Wilson on the 22nd of March. No formidable army opposed either of these commanders, for their expeditions were directed towards the interior of the region which had been stripped bare on account of the exigencies in front of Johnston and Lee.

Stoneman marched from East Tennessee, at first into North Carolina, but soon turned northward, and struck the Tennessee and Virginia railroad at various points, destroying the bridges and pushing on to within four miles of Lynchburg, so that all retreat of Lee in that direction was cut off. Then returning to North Carolina in the rear of Johnston, he captured large amounts of scattered stores, fourteen guns, and several thousand prisoners, but was checked by the news of the surrender of both the great rebel armies.

On the 27th of March, Canby's force arrived before Mobile; it was in three divisions, commanded by A. J. Smith, Gordon Granger, and Steele. Smith and Granger were ordered to attack Spanish Fort, on the eastern side of Mobile bay, while Steele invested Blakely, above the town. Both these places were taken on the 9th of April, Blakely by assault, and after severe and gallant fighting on both sides; and on the 11th, Mobile was evacuated. In these operations two hundred guns were captured, and four thousand prisoners; but the bulk of the garrison, nine thousand in number, escaped.

Wilson's command, consisting of twelve thousand five hundred mounted men, marched south from the Tennessee river into the heart of Alabama. Forrest was in front with a motley force, made up of conscripts and local militia: old men and boys,

clergymen, physicians, editors, judges—the people usually left behind in time of war. To these the rebel commander added two or three thousand cavalry-men, and altogether his numbers amounted to seven thousand. On the 1st of April, Wilson encountered this enemy at Ebenezer Church, and drove him across the Cahawba river in confusion. On the 2nd, he attacked and captured the fortified city of Selma, took thirty-two guns and three thousand prisoners, and destroyed the arsenal, armory, machine-shops, and a vast quantity of stores. On the 4th, he captured and destroyed Tuscaloosa. On the 10th, he crossed the Alabama river, and, on the 14th, occupied Montgomery, which the enemy had abandoned. Here he divided his force, sending one portion upon West Point, and the other against Columbus, in Georgia. Both these places were assaulted and captured on the 16th of April, the latter by a gallant night attack, in which Generals Upton and Winslow particularly distinguished themselves. This was the last battle of the war.

On the 21st, Macon was surrendered, with sixty field guns, twelve thousand militia-men, and five generals, including Howell Cobb, who had been a member of Buchanan's cabinet, and afterwards rebel governor of Georgia. At Macon, the cavalry career was checked by news of the armistice between Johnston and Sherman, which included Wilson's command. In twenty-eight days the cavalry had marched five hundred and twenty-five miles, and captured five fortified cities, six thousand two hundred prisoners, two hundred and eighty pieces of artillery, ninety-nine thousand stand of small arms, and whatever else of military advantage was left in the state of

Alabama. The country was simply overrun. There was nobody to defend it, and no defense worthy of the name.

In fact, the history of the war after the 9th of April is nothing but an enumeration of successive surrenders. On the 14th of April, Johnston made his first overtures to Sherman; on the 21st, Cobb yielded Macon; on the 4th of May, Richard Taylor surrendered all the rebel forces east of the Mississippi. On the 11th of May, Jefferson Davis, disguised as a woman and in flight, was captured at Irwinsville, Georgia; and on the 26th of the same month, Kirby Smith surrendered his entire command west of the Mississippi river. On that day the last organized rebel force disappeared from the territory of the United States. Every man who had borne arms against the government was a prisoner. One hundred and seventy-four thousand two hundred and twenty-three rebel soldiers were paroled.

This speedy and absolute collapse of the revolt was one of the most remarkable incidents of the war. Not a gun was fired in anger after the surrender of Lee was known. Not a soldier held out; not a guerilla remained in arms. None retreated to a mountain fastness; none refused to give a parole, or even an oath of allegiance to the national authority. Great part of this acquiescence was doubtless due to the terms that had been accorded by Grant. Aware as he was of the exhausted condition of the rebels, that they could hope for no after-success, and yet might prolong the war indefinitely in the interior— holding out in detachments here and there all-over the country, coming together again as fast as they

were separated, renewing the fight after they seemed subdued—he determined to grant them such terms that there should be neither object nor excuse for further resistance.

The wisdom of his course was proved by the haste which the rebels made to yield everything they had fought for. They were ready not only to give up their arms, but literally to implore forgiveness of the government. They acquiesced in the abolition of slavery. They abandoned the heresy of secession, and waited to learn what else their conquerors would dictate. They dreamed not of political power. They only asked to be let live quietly under the flag they had outraged, and attempt in some degree to rebuild their shattered fortunes. The greatest general of the rebellion asked for pardon.

All proclaimed especially their admiration of Grant's generosity. Lee refused to present his petition for amnesty until he had ascertained in advance that Grant would recommend it. The wife of Jefferson Davis applied to him for the remission of a part of the punishment of her husband; and throughout the entire South his praises were on the lips of his conquered enemies.

While this was the feeling at the South, the North awarded him a unanimity of praise and affection such as no other American had ever received. Houses were presented to him in Philadelphia, Washington, and Galena ; military rank was created for him by Congress; cities were illuminated because he visited them; congregations and audiences rose in his honor; men of every grade and shade of political, religious, and social opinion or position united in these acclamations.

ULYSSES S. GRANT.

641

Amid them all lie preserved the same quiet demeanor, the same simplicity of speech, the same unobtrusive modesty for which he had hitherto been known ; and, while he accepted and appreciated the plaudits of the nation, he made haste to escape from the parade and the celebration to the society of his intimates or the retirement of his home.

When the war was over, Grant had fought and beaten every important rebel soldier in turn : Buck-ner at Donelson, Beauregard at Shiloh, Pemberton and Johnston at Vicksburg, Bragg at Chattanooga, Lee in Virginia, and all of them altogether in the last year of the rebellion. From Belmont, the initial battle of his career, he had never been driven from the field, and had never receded a step in any of his campaigns, except at Holly Springs, and then the rebels were in retreat before him, and Grant, unable to follow fast enough to overtake them, withdrew, only to advance on another line.

He went on st.eadily from the start, gaining in reputation and skill, acquiring experience, developing his powers, but manifesting at the beginning many of the traits which were always conspicuous in his generalship. At Belmont, there was the same steadfastness under difficulties, the same sufficiency of resource, the same invention in unexpected emergencies which were afterwards so often displayed; at Donelson, the same daring which attacked superior numbers, and the fortitude undismayed at temporary reverse, as well as the quick intuition which detected the intention of the enemy from apparently insignificant circumstances, like the three days' rations in the haversacks; and, above all, the perception that the crisis had come when both armies were

nearly exhausted, and whichever first attacked would win ; and then he declared: " The rebels will have to be very quick, if they beat me." At Shiloh, there was the same indomitable perseverance and confidence which made him say to Buell at the darkest moment of the fight, when that commander inquired, " What preparations have you made for retreating ?" " I haven't despaired of whipping them yet; " and inspired the orders to Sherman to advance on the morrow, before Buell had arrived. At Vicksburg, he displayed again the untiring persistency, the willingness to try all schemes until the right one was found; then the bold conception of running the batteries and separating his army from its base, plunging into the interior between two hostile forces, contrary to all the rules of the schools and the urgent counsel of his ablest subordinates; and finally the celerity, the audacity, the strategical manoeuvres, the marches, the counter-marches, the five successful battles of the great campaign—except the Appomattox week, the most brilliant episode of the war. At Chattanooga, there came the larger responsibilities, the wider sphere, the varied combinations of the three armies, culminating in the elaborate tactical plans and evolutions of Lookout mountain and Missionary ridge — a meet preparation for the still grander duties he was to assume and the more comprehensive strategy he was to unfold as general-in-chief of the whole.

His entire career was indeed up to this point a prelude and preface for what was to follow. Events were educating him for the position he was destined to occupy. He learned the peculiar characteristics of American war. He found out that

many of the rules applicable in European contests would fail him here. He discovered, years before the Germans, the necessity of open order fighting; his troops became proficient in field fortifications; his cavalry was used to the system, afterwards so successfully employed by the Uhlans, of mounted infantry; he limited the use of artillery; he perceived that the day for cavalry charges was nearly past. He also invented the long campaigns without a base, which astonished the enemy and the world. But above all, he understood that he was engaged in a people's war, and that the people as well as the armies of the South must be conquered, before the war could end. Slaves, supplies, crops, stock, as well as arms and ammunition—everything that was necessary in order to carry on the war, was a weapon in the hands of the enemy; and of every weapon the enemy must be deprived.

This was a view of the situation which Grant's predecessors in chief command had failed to grasp. Most of the national generals in every theatre, prior to him, had attempted to carry on their operations as if they were fighting on foreign fields. They sought to out-manoeuvre armies, to capture posts, to win by strategy pure and simple. But this method was not sufficient in a civil war. The passions were too intense, the stake was too great, the alternatives were too tremendous. It was not victory that either side was playing for, but existence. If the rebels won, they destroyed a nation; if the government succeeded, it annihilated a rebellion. It was not enough at this emergency to fight as men fight when their object is merely to outwit or even outnumber the enemy. This enemy did not yield because he was

outwitted or outnumbered. It was indispensable to annihilate armies and resources; to place every rebel force where it had no alternative but destruction or submission, and every store or supply of arms or munitions or food or clothes where it could be reached by no rebel army.

Grant's greatness consisted in his perception of this condition of affairs, and his adaptation of all his means to meeting it. When he became general-in-chief he at once conceived this idea, and understood the terrible nature of the task he must assume. He made all his plans and combinations with this in view. The scope of those plans included the entire republic. The army of the Potomac at the East and Sherman's forces at the West constituted the two great motive powers; but in Virginia, Butler on the James and Sigel in the Valley were to assist Meade on the Rapidan, while at the West, Banks was to meet Sherman, both marching towards Mobile. All were combined and directed with a common purpose and a central aim.

These combinations were sometimes interrupted or thwarted in their development. Grant and Sherman each met many obstacles before either sat down in front of the strategical objective point of his army; Butler and Sigel both failed in their cooperation in Virginia, while Banks failed to co-operate at all before Mobile. Grant himself entered upon an encounter as terrible as that of Christian with Apollyon in the Valley of the Shadow of Death. The struggle was prolonged and bitter, and the national commander received as well as inflicted appalling loss; but he persisted in his advance amid carnage and assaults with that awful

composure and confidence which to many natures is not only inscrutable but absolutely repelling, but which, nevertheless, was the especial quality which enabled him to succeed. He pushed his army through such a month of ceaseless and seemingly resultless battle as the world has hardly ever seen ; dealing, however, as he knew, the blows from which his antagonist would never recover. In the Wilderness the rebellion received its death stroke. It lingered months afterwards, and all the skill and strength of the nation and its soldiers were required to push the blade to the heart, but the iron entered in May, 1864. But for just this terrific strife, just this persistent attack, just this bloody wage, the result would have been deferred or different.

But the rebels felt that this commander could neither be deterred nor avoided; that no skill nor fortitude could elude or withstand the man who wielded such weapons with such unintermitting power. They lost not only force, but heart, in the Wilderness campaign.

When the month of war was over and the smoke had cleared away, the nation failed to perceive the actual result, and the government, though determined, was not sanguine. The enemy, too, was still desperate. The rebels, indeed, always hated more bitterly and more passionately than their opponents. As they wished to separate forever, they cared neither to spare nor propitiate those with whom they fought; while the national forces, desiring to bring about the old Union, always spared their adversary when he was down, and constantly strove to propitiate even while injuring; did not regard a rebel as a personal foe, but a misguided country-

123

man; were earnest and determined, but never so frantic as the Southerners. Then, too, they were never so hard pushed; their territory was not invaded, their homes were not burned, their fields were not devastated, their families not impoverished. But the rebels had staked all, and could lose no more than all. They could take every risk, throw away every restraint, incur every danger.

This superior desperation of the enemy was an enhancement of Grant's difficulties, and from June to January another phase of the war went on. Although he had fought it out on the same line, he still had not won. He had reached the position he set out for in May, but had not yet cut the great southern roads leading into Richmond. He had shaken the whole fabric of the rebellion, and shattered, if he had not overthrown, its most powerful armies; but it was necessary to renew his combinations and adapt them to the shifting necessities. There was no change in the general plan or aim. Lee and Johnston's armies were still the principal object of his campaigns, and he still sought to compress and contract and drive to a single focus all the other and subsidiary forces of the rebels; still to destroy their resources, and exhaust their supplies, and annihilate their armies. But the method now was to hold Lee in Richmond, and to sweep all the other rebel forces towards the same point with his wide, encompassing command.

In September, Sherman captured Atlanta, but he still had the army of Hood to contend with; and although he had won a victory, as yet reaped none of its results. On the contrary, by the advance of Hood he was speedily placed in a more precarious

position than before Atlanta fell. But his brilliant strategical genius, just fitted to cope with such emergencies, enabled the great manceuvrer to extricate himself from his difficulties and to reverse the situation, himself threatening rebel lines and attacking rebel rears.

About this time occurred the presumptuous movement of Early, who, however, was speedily repelled from Washington; and then the great fighter sent to the Valley dealt him blow after blow. These two northward advances of Hood and Early gave an appearance of boldness to the rebel strategy, and were calculated to impose on unwary or impatient opponents. Hood and Early both conceived audacious plans, but failed utterly in their accomplishment. They were typical of the whole genius and character of the rebel policy; bold at the outset, dazzling in immediate effect, formidable at first to an adversary; but, when opposed by soldiers like Sherman and Sheridan and Grant, their strength was wasted, their struggles vain, their endurance failed.

Next came Sherman's march and Thomas's defence; then the two attacks on Wilmington; and at last the consummation began to dawn. Out of the chaos men saw streaks of light here and there; and finally, in all quarters the firmament was clear. The great congeries of campaigns and combinations was visible to the dullest comprehension, like the sun above the horizon. Sherman strode across the continent and then marched northward, driving Johnston ; Thomas destroyed or scattered Hood; Sheridan had beaten and battered Early's army, literally, into pieces. Only the command in front of Richmond was left. This had been so securely held by

Grant that Lee had not dared to dispatch any force to the aid of his endangered subordinates. He remained, as he doubtless felt, only to be the last destroyed.

The rebel chief, it is claimed, desired to leave Kichmond during the last few months of the war, but was restrained from this course by the civil authorities, his superiors. These were mere political managers, unable to cope with emergencies that required superlative courage; full of chicanery and subtlety, and the weaker arts of weaker men, but lacking those grand qualities which alone succeed in times of war and revolution. They were afraid, at this juncture, to take the chance of flight, and, like all timid people, suffered more than if they had been brave; submitting to the horrors of assault and the possibilities of capture rather than leave what seemed defenses, but at last were only snares. If Lee perceived this situation, he had not the force to impress it on his coadjutors, and therefore lacked the greatness essential in his position at such a crisis.

When finally all things were ready and the great blow was struck, it was seen how complete had been the preparations and combinations which had preceded the end; how absolute the execution of the scheme devised a year before. Lee surrendered because he had nothing else to do. He could not run away. Johnston and Maury and Richard Taylor and Kirby Smith surrendered for exactly the same reason. The various victories were not hap-hazard; it was not that each man chanced to come out right. All the arrangements were made in advance. Army after army came up to surrender, like the pieces in chess in a complicated game, when the beaten play-er has only one move for each, and that to give it away. Nor was it only because of Appomattox, or because they had lost heart, that the lesser rebels yielded. Johnston was absolutely surrounded, for Stoneman and Thomas and Wilson were in his rear, while Sherman was in front, and Meade and Sheridan were approaching from the North. The troops that escaped from Mobile were between Canby and the cavalry, and if they had tried could have done no better than their fellows. The rebellion was conquered at all points at the same time. It had no armies except in front of greater ones. It had no supplies except separated from its armies. It had no arsenals, no armories, no railroads left; yet it surrendered a thousand cannon and a hundred and seventy thousand soldiers.

This was not the result of brute force. This was not mere outnumbering or overwhelming. It was the disposition of the national armies, between, around, and among the rebel forces, as well as the incessant blows dealt by those armies, which made it impossible, after Appomattox, for any organized rebel force to make a move in any direction that did not entail upon itself absolute and immediate destruction.

These splendid successes of the general-in-chief, however, could never have been accomplished without the faithful support of the government and the executive ability of subordinate commanders, as well as the peculiar quality of the national soldiers. Not even the appreciation of the situation, the conception of the plan, nor the power to work out the combinations, nor all these altogether would have sufficed. Grant was indeed peculiarly and fortunately placed.

He stood between Lincoln and Stanton, the two great men in civil life whom the epoch produced, on one hand, and Sherman and Sheridan, with their eminent executive military genius, on the other. He participated in the authority and the power of the government; he was of its councils and in its confidence ; he had to assume responsibilities co-extensive with its own; he was in some of his relations almost a civil officer, and at the same time he shared the executive quality and duties of his great subordinates.

He had, indeed, magnificent men on both sides to deal with: Lincoln, with his exceptional fitness for his place, his political sagacity, his intuitive sympathy with the people, his purity of patriotism, his devotion to the cause; and Stanton, with his energy and directness and earnestness and administrative force; both, too, strong in the confidence of the nation which they served; while no general-in-chief was ever supported by two greater lieutenants than the strategist whose boldness of imagination and infinite resource equaled any ever displayed in war, and that marvelous tactical fighter whose intuitions and judgments in battle were like passions incarnate in arms or arms inspired by intellect.

Grant required a degree of all these traits which his great allies possessed. He did not lack the energy of Stanton nor the sympathy of Lincoln with the people; his strategy was not inferior to that of Sherman, and he proved himself equal to Sheridan in that power of audacious and skillful combination in the presence of the enemy which, above and beyond every other trait, is what is highest and most essential in a general.

There were other soldiers, however, besides the chief and his two greatest subordinates, whose ability was conspicuous and whose aid was important. Meade and Thomas, especially, were excellent commanders ; men of the calibre and with many of the characteristics of Lee; soldiers according to rule, and able to do elaborate and efficient service. Any one of the three was admirable in defensive situations. Meade at Gettysburg, Thomas at Chickamauga, Lee in the Wilderness, achieved a splendid fame; but no one of the three possessed in a high degree the talent of the initiative—of forcing the enemy to do his will. No one of the three dared at critical moments to take a terrible aggressive responsibility. Neither would have persisted as Grant did at the Wilderness. Neither would have ventured as Grant did at Vicksburg. Neither would have combined strategical dispositions as Grant did during the last year of the. war, or was capable of the accelerated and at the same time elaborate energy which inspired and accomplished the final assaults on Petersburg and the evolutions of the subsequent pursuit, the movements which brought about the battle of Sailors' creek and extricated the troops at Farmville and compelled the concentration which culminated at Appornattox court-house. No one of the three ever rose to the conception that superlative courage in war is an economy of life in the end.

Lee, indeed, always lacked sustained audacity. He never, at least after Grant commanded in his front, succeeded in anything that required that trait. He thought more boldly than he acted. He was driven back in the Wilderness when he attacked in force; and in the policy which he so often essayed

before Petersburg, when lie sought to overwhelm Grant's left in the extending movements, he invariably failed. All that he ever accomplished in these operations was to annoy, and disturb, and injure his antagonist. He never defeated Grant's aim; he never drove him from a position; he never compelled him to withdraw.

Full, however, of the devices of a wily strategy, the rebel chief was often able to elude a force which he could not withstand; he fled with eminent success ; and as a purely defensive fighter was probably never surpassed. The national soldiers had a saying that Lee knew how to feed a fight; he discovered the point where troops were most needed, and there he threw them constantly and continuously. No one would probably have held off the national armies longer than he, and it is doubtful whether an offensive defence would have succeeded better against Grant.

Elaborate, specious, elusive, not free from the besetting sin of the South—a tendency to duplicity —but stubborn, valiant, and arrogant, Lee was on the whole a fitting representative of a cause which, originating in treason, based on the enslavement of a race, and deriving its only chance of success from men who had been false to their military oaths, was, < in reality, a rebellion against the rights of man, and a defiance of the instinct and judgment of the civilized world. He fought with the splendid energy of that arch rebel who was expelled from heaven, and his downfall was as absolute.

To overthrow him and his desperate supporters, Grant needed more help than he could get even from the government and his generals. He needed soldiers with many of his own traits. And as any man

of surpassing success probably represents and typifies his time, it is not surprising that some of the same qualities which distinguished him as a commander can be detected in the men whom he commanded. The national soldiers were not, as a rule, so brilliant as the rebels in a charge, and no better behind works, but they were more persistent in attack, and better able to perform evolutions under fire. They were not so apt to lose head in battle, and recovered sooner from the effects of disaster. The enemy oftener succeeded by surprise, but seldom reaped the full result of a victory; and rarely won except by a first, impulsive, and unexpected onset. In this the Southerners were like the negroes. But, when it came to sustained, renewed, deliberate assault, it was the national soldiers who bore away the prize.

But, after all, it is only by transcendent effort that transcendent success is ever attained. Excellent people, good soldiers, brave men, careful generals, are not enough in offensive war with determined foes. The troops who do what can neither be expected nor required are the ones who are victorious. The men who, tired, and worn, and hungry, and exhausted, yet push into battle, are those who win. They who persist against odds, against obstacles, against hope, who proceed or hold out unreasonably, are the conquerors.

And for chiefs—there are only two or three in a generation. It is no disparagement of a man that he has not genius. We cannot expect every one to be the exception. There were many admirable tacticians, and strategists, and engineers, as well as loyal subordinates and faithful, heroic patriots in the

national army; there could be in the nature of things only two or three supereminent commanders. Only one could be at the top.

In such an one there should be found, above all things, a comprehensive grasp of the situation, of the relations of the various points and events of the field to each other, and to the general purpose; a faculty of retaining the head under unexpected circumstances; not only of planning in advance, but of originating new combinations when the old ones are interrupted; and, as much as anything, a judgment and impulse combined, both audacious yet neither incautious; a decision in acting on this judgment and impulse instantaneously, without waiting to balance chances; and, thereafter, neither doubt nor delay, but only belief and persistence to the end.

Such an one, if simple, honest, unambitious, and magnanimous, might aptly represent the best results of a republic, and worthily command its armies even in those crises when nations are never saved without a leader.

Early in June, 1865, steps were taken with the sanction of the government to procure the indictment of Lee and others for the crime of treason. The former rebel chief at once appealed to Grant, who went in person to the President, and protested verbally and in writing against the measure. Johnson, however, was obstinate, and Grant finally declared that he would resign his commission in the army if the paroles which he had granted should be violated. This determination was conclusive. The proceedings were abandoned, and the communication of this decision was the last official act in the intercourse of Lee and Grant.

APPENDIX TO CHAPTER XXV.

SHERIDAN'S STRENGTH IN THE CAMPAIGN IN THE VALLEY OP VIRGINIA, 1864.

GENERAL SHERIDAN TO ADJUTANT-GENERAL OF THE ARMY.

HEAD-QUABTERB, MIDDLE MILITARY DIVISION, I September 13,1864. j

GENERAL: I have the honor to forward as complete a field return as is possible at the present time. The most strenuous exertions are being made by me to obtain a full return, but the difficulty in obtaining such from the commanding officer, Department of West Virginia, because of his command covering so great an extent of country, has so far prevented.

The enclosed return does not include the cavalry under Averill, about 2,500, or the troops of the Department of Washington, Susque-hanna, or Middle.

I simply forward it you as a statement showing the number of men for duty south of the Potomac. Hoping soon to furnish complete all reports required,

Very respectfully, your obedient servant,

P. H. SHEPJDAN, Major-General. Brigadier-General L. THOMAS,

Adjutant-General, United States Army.

FIELD RETURN OF TROOPS IN THE FIELD BELONGING TO THE MIDDLE

MILITARY DIVISION, SEPTEMBER 10, 1864.

PRESENT FOR DUTY.

APPENDIX.

This return is the only one made by Sheridan to the Adjutant-General prior to the battle of Winchester; and, as it was accompanied by a statement of its incompleteness, I applied to his head-quarters for a return of his effective strength, but, owing to the loss of all his papers in the Chicago fire, I was unable to obtain either the numbers or organizations detached from his army south of the Potomac. It was stated, however, that the garrisons of Harper's Ferry, Charleston, Martinsburg, and other points, together with escorts to trains, were of sufficient size to reduce the force in the field to the numbers given in Sheridan's report to Grant, which were taken at the time from the official returns of effective or fighting strength present for duty. But as these returns were never sent to Washington, and were destroyed as above stated, it was impossible to furnish copies of them.

At Grant's head-quarters it was always understood that Sheridan's effective force in the Valley campaign was about thirty thousand men. — AUTHOB.

APPENDIX TO CHAPTER XXVII.

GENERAL EAELY TO GENERAL LEE.

POKT REPUBLIC, September 25, 1864.

GENERAL: I had determined to write you a full account of recent events, but I am too much occupied to do so. In the fight at Winchester I drove back the enemy's infantry and would have defeated that, but his cavalry broke mine on the left flank, the latter making no stand, and I had to take a division to stop the progress of the former and save my trains, and during the fighting in the rear the enemy again advanced and my troops fell back, thinking they were flanked. The enemy's immense superiority in cavalry and the inefficiency of the greater part of mine has been the cause of all my disasters. In the affair at Fisher's Hill the cavalry gave way, but it was flanked. This would have been remedied if the troops had remained steady, but a panic seized them at the idea of being flanked, and, without being defeated, they broke, many of them fleeing shamefully. The artillery was not captured by the enemy, but abandoned by the infantry. My troops are very much shattered, the men very much exhausted, and many of them without shoes. When Kershaw arrives I shall do the best I can, and hope I may be able to check the enemy, but I cannot but be apprehensive of the result. I am informed that all the reserves have been called from the Valley. I think Sheridan means to try Hunter's campaign again, and his superiority in cavalry gives him immense advantage. If you could possibly spare Hampton's division, it might be sent here at once.

I deeply regret the present state of things, and I assure you everything in my power has been done to avert it. The enemy's force is very much larger than mine, being three or four to one. Respectfully,

J. A. EARLY, Lieutenant-General.

GENERAL LEE TO GENERAL EARLY.— (CONFIDENTIAL.)

HEAD-QUAKTERS, PETKBSBURG, September 27, 1864.

GENERAL : Your letter of the 25th is received. I very much regret the reverses that have occurred to the army in the valley, but trust they can be remedied. The arrival of Kershaw will add greatly to your strength, and I have such confidence in the men and officers that I am sure all will unite in the defense of the country. It will require that every one should exert all his energies and strength to meet the emergency. One victory will put all things right. You must do all in your power to invigorate your army. Get back all absentees. Manoeuvre so, if you can, as to keep the enemy in check until you can strike him with all your strength. ^ As far as I can judge at this distance, you have operated more with divisions than with your concentrated strength. Circumstances may have rendered it necessary, but such a course is to be avoided if possible. It will require the greatest watchfulness, the greatest promptness, and the most untiring energy on your part to arrest the progress of the enemy in his present tide of success. All the reserves in the valley have been ordered to you. Breckenridge will join you or co-operate, as circumstances will permit, with all his force. Rosser left this morning for Burksville (intersection of Danville and Southside railroads), where he will shape his course as you direct. I have given you all I can. You must use the resources you have so as to gain success. The enemy must be defeated, and I rely upon you to do it. I will endeavor to have shoes, arms, and ammunition supplied you. Set all your officers to work bravely and hopefully, and all will go well. As regards the western cavalry, I think for the present the best thing you can do is to separate it. Perhaps there is a lack of confidence between officers and men. If you will attach one brigade to Rosser, making him a division, and one to Fitz Lee's division, under Wickham, Lomax will be able, I hope, to bring out the rest. The men are all good, and only require instruction and discipline. The enemy's force cannot be so greatly superior to yours. His effective infantry I do not think exceeds 12,000 men. We are obliged to fight against great odds. A kind Providence will yet overrule everything for our good. If Colonel Carter's wound incapacitates him for duty, you must select a good chief of artillery for the present. "Wishing you every prosperity and success, I arn very truly yours,

    R. E. LEE, General. General J. A. EARLY, commanding Valley.

    (Official Copy\'7d C. MARSHALL, Aide-de-camp.

    GENERAL EARLY TO GENEKAL LEE.

    NEW MARKET, October 9, 1864.

    GENERAL: Bosser, in command of his own brigade and the two brigades of Fitz Lee's division, and Lomax with two brigades of his own cavalry, were ordered to pursue the enemy, to harass him and ascertain his purposes, while I remained here so as to be ready to move east of the Kidge if necessary; and I am sorry to inform you that the enemy, having concentrated his whole cavalry in his rear, attacked them and drove them back this morning from near Fisher's Hill, capturing nine pieces of artillery and eight or ten wagons. Their loss in men is, I understand, slight. I have not heard definitely from Rosser, but he is, I understand, falling back in good order, having rallied his command, which is on what is called Back road, which is west of the pike; but Lomax's command, which was on the pike, came back to this place in confusion. This is very distressing to me, and God knows I have done all in my power to avert the disasters which have befallen this command; but the fact is that the enemy's cavalry is so much superior to ours, both in numbers and equipment, and the country is so favorable to the operations of cavalry, that it is impossible for ours to compete with his. Lomax's cavalry is armed entirely with rifles, and has no sabres, and the consequence is that they can not fight on horseback, and, in this open country, they cannot successfully fight on foot against large bodies of cavalry; besides, the command is and has been demoralized all the time. It would be better if they could all be put into the infantry; but, if that were tried, I am afraid they would all run off.

    Sheridan's infantry moved off from Fisher's Hill this morning, and I am satisfied that he does not intend moving this way again, as he burned all the bridges in his rear as he went down, and the question now is what he intends doing—whether he will move across the Ridge, send a part of his force to Grant, or content himself with protecting the Baltimore and Ohio railroad. If he moves across the Ridge, I will move directly across from this place to meet him, and I think I can defeat his infantry and thwart his movements on the east of the mountains. But what shall I do if he sends reinforcements to Grant, or remains in the lower Valley ? He has laid waste nearly all of Rocking-ham and Shenandoah, and I will have to rely on Augusta for my supplies, and they are not abundant there. Sheridan's purpose, under Grant's orders, has been to render the Valley untenable by our troops

by destroying the supplies. My infantry is now in good heart and condition, and I have sent a special messenger to you to get your views. Without Kershaw, I would have about six thousand muskets. Very respectfully,

J. A. EAKLY, Lieutenant-General. General R. E. LEE, commanding Army Northern Virginia.

GENERAL EARLY TO GENERAL LEE.

GALLEY DISTKIC October 9,1864.

HEAD-QUABTEBS, VALLEY DISTRICT (NEW MABKET),)

General R. E. LEE :

GENEBAL : In advance of a detailed report, I have determined to give you an informal account of the recent disasters to my command, which I have not had leisure to do before.

On the 17th of September, I moved two divisions—Rhodes's and Gordon's—from Stevenson's depot, where they, together with Breck-enridge's division, were encamped (Ramseur's being at Winchester, to cover the road from Berryville), to Bunker Hill; and, on the 18th, I moved Gordon's division, with a part of Lomax's cavalry, to Martins-burg, to thwart efforts that were reported to be making to repair the Baltimore and Ohio railroad. This expedition was successful, and the bridge over Back creek was burned by a brigade of cavalry sent there. On the evening of the 18th, Rhodes was moved back to Stevenson's depot, and Gordon to Bunker Hill, with orders to start at daylight to return to his camp at Stevenson's depot, which place he reached at a very early hour next morning. About the time of Gordon's arrival on that morning, firing was heard in Ramseur's front; and now a report reached me that the enemy's cavalry had appeared on the Berryville road. I ordered Rhodes, Gordon, and Breckenridge to have their divisions under arms ready to go to Ramseur's assistance, and rode to his position to ascertain the extent and character of the demonstration. On getting there, I found Ramseur's division in line of battle, and the enemy evidently advancing with his whole force. The other divisions were immediately ordered up, and the trains all put in motion for their security. Rhodes and Gordon arrived just before the enemy commenced advancing a heavy fire in Ramseur's left for the purpose of overwhelming him; and, when their columns commenced advancing on Ramseur, I attacked them with Rhodes and Gordon's divisions, and drove them back with great slaughter, the artillery doing most splendid service, Braxton's battalion driving back, with canister, a

heavy force, before which Even's brigade of Gordon's division, which was on the left, had given way. This brigade was now rallied, and, Battle's brigade coming to its assistance, the enemy was pushed back a considerable distance, and we were successful. Breckenridge's division did not arrive for some time, because General Breckenridge had moved it out, after my orders to him, to drive back some of the enemy's cavalry which was crossing the Opequan, and I sent for him again, and he came up in the afternoon before the enemy had made any further attack; but, as he reported the enemy's cavalry advancing on the road from Charlestown and Stevenson's depot, I ordered one of his brigades to the left on that road, and directed General Fitz Lee to take charge of all the cavalry on that flank (my left), and check the enemy's cavalry, and moved the other two brigades of Breckenridge's division towards the right, where our forces were weakest and the enemy was making demonstrations in force. Breckenridge was scarcely in position before our cavalry on the left was discovered coming back in great confusion, followed by the enemy's, and Breckenridge's force was ordered to the left to repel this cavalry force which had gotten in rear of my left; and this, with the assistance of the artillery, he succeeded in doing. But, as soon as the firing was heard in rear of our left flank, the infantry commenced falling back along the whole line, and it was very difficult to stop them. I succeeded, however, in stopping enough of them in the old rifle-pits constructed by General Johnston to arrest the progress of the enemy's infantry, which commenced advancing again when the confusion in our ranks was discovered, and would have still won the day if our cavalry would have stopped the enemy's; but so overwhelming was the battle, and so demoralized was a larger part of ours, that no assistance was received from it. The enemy's cavalry again charged around my left flank, and the men began to give way again, so that it was necessary for me to retire through the town. Line of battle was formed on the north side of the town, the command reorganized, and we then turned back deliberately to Newtown and the next day to Fisher.

We lost three pieces of artillery, two of which had been left with the cavalry on the left, and the other was lost because the horses were killed and it could not be brought off. In this fight I had already defeated the enemy's infantry, and could have continued to do so, but the enemy's very great superiority in cavalry and the comparative inefficiency of ours turned the scales against us. In this battle the loss in the infantry and artillery was: killed, 226; wounded, 1,567; rniss-124

ing, 1,818—total, 3,611. There is no full report of the cavalry, but the total loss in killed and wounded from September 1st to 1st October is: killed, 60; wounded, 288—total, 348 ; but many were captured, though a good many are missing as stragglers, and a number of them reported missing in the infantry were not captured, but are stragglers and skulkers. Breckenridge's division lost six colors, and Rhodes's division captured two. Rhodes's division made a very gallant charge, and ho was killed conducting it. I fell back to Fisher's Hill, as it was the only place where a stand could be made, and I was compelled to detach Fitz Lee's cavalry to the Luray valley to hold the enemy's cavalry in check should it advance up that valley. The enemy's loss at Winchester was very heavy. Dr. McGuire has received a letter from a member of his family, who states that 5,800 of the enemy's wounded were brought to the hospital at Winchester, and that the total wounded was between 6,000 and 7,000; and a gentleman who passed over the field says that the number of killed was very large. Sheridan's medical director informed one of our surgeons, left at Woodstock, that the number of wounded in hospital at Winchester was the same as stated in the letter to Dr. McGuire, and I am satisfied from what I saw that the enemy's loss was very heavy.

The enemy's infantry force was nearly, if not quite, three times as large as mine, and his cavalry was very much superior both in numbers and equipment. This I have learned from intelligent persons who have seen the whole of both forces.

I posted my troops in line at Fisher's Hill with the hope of arresting Sheridan's progress; but my line was very thin, and having discovered that the position could be flanked, as is the case with every position in the Valley, I had determined to fall back on the night of the 22nd ; but, late that evening, a heavy force was moved under cover of the woods on the left, and drove back the cavalry there posted and got in the rear of my left flank; and, when I tried to remedy this, the infantry got into a panic and gave way in confusion, and I found it impossible to rally it. The artillery behaved splendidly, both on this occasion and at Winchester. I had to order the guns to be withdrawn; but the difficulties of the ground were such that 12 guns were lost, because they could not be gotten off. The loss in the infantry and artillery was 30 killed, 210 wounded, and 995 missing—total, 1,235. I have been able to get no report of the loss in the cavalry, but it was slight. Yery many of the missing in the infantry took to the mountains ; a number of them have since come in, and others are still out.

The enemy did not capture more than 400 or 500; but, I am sorry to say, many men threw away their arms.

The night favored our retreat, and by next morning the commands were pretty well organized. At Mount Jackson next day I halted, and drove back a force of cavalry which was pursuing, and then moved to Rode's Hill, where I halted until the enemy's infantry came up next day and was trying to flank me, when I moved off in line of battle for eight miles, occasionally halting to check the enemy. This continued till nearly sundown, when I got a position at which I checked the enemy's further progress for that day, and then moved under cover of night towards Port Republic to unite with Kershaw.

After doing this, I drove a division of cavalry from my front at Port Republic, and then moved to Waynesboro, where two divisions under Torbert were destroying the bridge, and drove them away; and, after remaining there one day, I moved to the vicinity of Mount Crawford, where I awaited the arrival of Rosser's brigade to take the offensive ; but, before it arrived, the enemy was discovered to be falling back on the morning of the 6th. I immediately commenced following the enemy, and arrived here on the 7th, and have been waiting to ascertain whether Sheridan intends crossing the Blue Ridge before moving further. Respectfully,

J. A. EARLY, Lieutenant-General. Official.

SAM. W. MELTON,

Lieutenant-Colonel and Assistant Adjutant-General.

GENEEAL EAKLT TO GENERAL LEE.

NEW MABKET, October 20,1864.

General R. E. LEE,

commanding Army of Northern Virginia:

GENERAL : The telegraph has already informed you of the disaster of the 19th. I now write to give you a fuller account of the matter.

Having received information that the enemy was continuing to repair the Manassas road, and that he had moved back from Fisher's Hill, I moved on the 12th towards Strasburg, for the purpose of endeavoring to thwart his purposes if he should contemplate moving across the Ridge, or sending troops to Grant. On the 13th I made a reconnoissance in force beyond Strasburg, and found the enemy on the north bank of Cedar creek, and on both sides of the pike; this was too strong a position to attack in front; I therefore encamped my

APPENDIX.

force at Fisher's Hill, and waited to see whether the enemj would move; bat he commenced fortifying. On the night of the 16th, Rosser, with two brigades of cavalry and a brigade of infantry mounted behind his men, -was sent around the left to surprise what was reported by his scouts to be the camp of a division of cavalry ; he found, however, that the camp had been moved, and he only found a picket, which he captured. As I could not remain at Fisher's Hill, for want of forage, I then determined to try and get round one of the enemy's flanks, and surprise him in camp. After ascertaining the location of the enemy's camps, from observations from a signal station on Massa-wattan mountain, I determined to move around the left flank of the enemy. I selected this flank from information furnished by General Gordon and Captain Hotchkiss, who had gone to the signal station, and because the greater part of the enemy's cavalry was on his right, and Kosser's attempt had caused that flank to be closely picketed. To get around the enemy's left was a very difficult undertaking, however, as the river had to be crossed twice, and between the mountain and river, where the troops had to pass to the lower ford, there was only a rugged pathway; I thought, however, the chances of success would be greater, from the fact that the enemy would not expect a move in that direction, on account of the difficulties attending it, and the great strength of their position on that flank.

The movement was, accordingly, begun on the night of the 18th, just after dark, Gordon's, Ramseur's, and Pegram's divisions being sent across the river and around the foot of the mountain, all under the command of General Gordon, and late at night I moved with Ker-shaw's division through Strasburg, towards a ford on Cedar creek, just above its mouth, and Wharton was moved on the pike, towards the enemy's front, on which road the artillery was also moved. The arrangement was for Gordon to come around in the rear, for Kershaw to attack the left flank, and for Wharton to advance in front, supporting the artillery, which was to open on the enemy when he should turn on Gordon or Kershaw, and the attack was to begin at 5 A. M. on the 19th. Rosser was sent to the left to occupy the enemy's cavalry, and Lomax, who had been sent down the Luray valley, was ordered to pass Front Royal, cross the river, and move across towards the Valley pike. Punctually at 5, Kershaw reached the enemy's left work, attacked and carried it without the least difficulty, and very shortly afterwards Gordon attacked in the rear, and they swept everything before them, routing the Eighth and Nineteenth corps completely, getting

APPENDIX.

possession of their camp, and capturing eighteen pieces of artillery and about 1,300 prisoners; they moved across the pike towards the camp of the Sixth corps, and Wharton was crossed over, the artillery following him ; hut the Sixth corps, which was on the enemy's extreme right of his infantry, was not surprised in camp, because Rosser had commenced the attack on that flank about the same time as the attack on the other, and the firing on the left gave that corps sufficient time to form and move out of camp, and it was found posted on a ridge on the west of the pike and parallel to it, and this corps offered considerable resistance. The artillery was brought up and opened on it, when it fell back to the north of Middletown, and made a stand on a commanding ridge running across the pike. In the meantime, the enemy's cavalry was threatening our right flank and rear, and, the country being perfectly open, and having on that flank only Lomax's old brigade, numbering about 300 men, it became necessary to make dispositions to prevent a cavalry charge, and a portion of the troops were moved to the right for that purpose, and word was sent to Gordon, who had got on the left with his division, and Kershaw, who were then also to swing around and advance with their divisions; but they stated in reply that a heavy force of cavalry had got in their front, and that their ranks were so depleted (by the number of men who had stopped in the camps to plunder) that they could not advance them. Rosser also sent word that, when he attacked the cavalry, he encountered a part of the Sixth corps supporting it, and that it was too strong for him, and that he would have to fall back. I sent word to him to get some position that he could hold, and, the cavalry in front of Kershaw and Gordon having moved towards Rosser, they were moved forward, and a line was formed north of Middletown, facing the enemy. The cavalry on the right made several efforts to charge that flank, but was driven back. So many of our men had stopped in the camp to plunder (in which I am sorry to say that officers participated), the country was so open, and the enemy's cavalry so strong, that I did not deem it prudent to press further, especially as Lomax had not come up. I determined, therefore, to content myself with trying to hold the advantages I had gained, until all my troops had come up, and the captured property was secured. If I had had but one division of fresh troops. I could have made the victory complete and beyond all danger of a reverse. We continued to hold our position until late in the afternoon, when the enemy commenced advancing, and was driven back on the right centre by Ramseur; but Gordon's division on the left subse-

quently gave way, and Kershaw's and Ramseur's did so also, -when they found Gordon's giving way, not because there was any pressure on them, but from an insane idea of being flanked; some of them, however, were rallied, and, with the help of the artillery, the army was checked for some time; but a great number of men could not be stopped, but continued to go to the rear. The enemy again made a demonstration, and General Ramseur, who was acting with great gallantry, was wounded, and the left again gave way, and then the whole command was falling back in such a panic that I had to order Pe-gram's and Wharton's commands, which were very small and on the right, to fall back, and most of them took the panic also. I found it impossible to rally the troops; they would not listen to entreaties, threats, or appeals of any kind. A terror of the enemy's cavalry had siezed them, and there was no holding them back; they left the field in the greatest confusion. All the captured artillery had been carried across Cedar creek, and a large number of captured wagons and ambulances, and we succeeded in crossing our own artillery over, and everything would have been saved if we could have rallied 500 men; but the panic was so great that nothing could be done. A small body of the enemy's cavalry dashed across Cedar creek above the bridge, and got into the train and artillery, running back on the pike, and passed through our men to this side of Strasburg, tore up a bridge, and thus succeeded in capturing the greatest part of the artillery and a number of ordnance and medical wagons and ambulances. The men scattered on the sides, and the rout was as thorough and disgraceful as ever happened to our army. After the utter failure of all my attempts to rally the men, I went to Fisher's Hill with the hope of rallying the troops there, and forming them in the trenches; but, when they reached that position, the only organized body of men left was the prisoners, 1,300 in number, and the provost guard in charge of them; and I believe that the appearance of these prisoners, moving back in a body, alone arrested the progress of the enemy's cavalry, as it was too dark for them to discover what they were. Many of the men stopped at Fisher's Hill, and went to their old camps, but no organization of them could be effected, and nothing saved us but the inability of the enemy to follow with his infantry, and his expectation that we would make a stand there. The state of things was distressing and mortifying beyond measure; we had within our grasp a great and glorious victory, and lost it by the uncontrollable propensity of our men for plunder, in the first place, and the subsequent panic among

those who had kept their places, which was without sufficient cause, for I believe that the enemy had only made the movement against us as a demonstration, hoping to protect his stores, etc., at "Winchester, and that the rout of our troops was a surprise to him. I had endeavored to guard against the dangers of stopping to plunder in the camps by cautioning the division commanders, and ordering them to caution their subordinates and take the most rigid measures to prevent it, and I endeavored to arrest the evil while in progress without avail. The truth is, we have very few field or company officers worth anything, almost all our good officers of that kind having been killed, wounded, or captured, and it is impossible to preserve discipline without good field and company officers.

I send you a map of the battle-field with the surrounding country. You will see marked out on it the different routes of the several columns. The plan was a bold one and was vigorously pursued by the division commanders, and it was successful, but the victory already gained was lost by the subsequent bad conduct of the troops. The artillery throughout, from first to last, in this as well as in all the actions I have had, behaved nobly, both officers and men, and not a piece of artillery has been lost by any fault of theirs. I attribute this good conduct on their part to the vast superiority of the officers. Colonel Carter and all his battalion commanders richly deserve promotion. They not only fought their guns gallantly and efficiently, but they made the most strenuous efforts to rally the infantry. It is mortifying to me, General, to have to make these explanations of my reverses; they are due to no want of effort on my part, though it may be that I have not the capacity or judgment to prevent them. I have labored faithfully to gain success, and I have not failed to expose my person and to set an example to my men. I know that I shall have to endure censure from those who do not understand my position and difficulties, but I am still willing to make renewed efforts. If you think, however, that the interests of the service would be promoted by a change of commanders, I beg you will have no hesitation in making the change. The interests of the service are far beyond any personal considerations, and if they require it I am willing to surrender my command into other hands. Though this affair has resulted so disastrously to my command, yet I think it is not entirely without compensating benefits. The Sixth corps had already begun to move off to Grant, and my movement brought it back, and Sheridan's forces are now so shattered that he will not be able to send Grant any efficient aid for some time. I

APPENDIX.

think he will be afraid to trust the Eighth and Nineteenth corps. The enemy's loss in killed and wounded was very heavy, and we took 1,300 prisoners, making, with some taken by Rosser, and others taken on the day of reconnoissance, over 1,500.

My loss in killed and wounded was not more than 700 or 800 men, and I think very few prisoners were lost. A number of my men are still out, but they are coming in. Except for the. loss of my artillery, the enemy has far the worst of it. "We secured some of the captured artillery, and our net loss is twenty-three pieces. I still have twenty pieces, besides the horse artillery.

The enemy is not pursuing, and I will remain here and organize my

troops.

Respectfully,

J. A. EARLY. Official.

JOHN BLAIE HOGE, Major and Acting Adjutant-General.

APPENDIX TO CHAPTER XXVIII.

GENERAL HALLECK TO GENERAL GRANT.

WASHINGTON, D. C., October 2, 1864.

Lieutenant- General GEANT, City Point:

GENERAL : Some time since General Sherman asked ray opinion in regard to his operations after the capture of Atlanta. While free to give advice to the best of my ability, I felt it my duty to refer him to you for instructions, not being advised of your views on that subject. I presume, from his dispatches, that you have corresponded upon the subject, and perhaps his plan of future operations has already been decided upon.

At one time he seemed most decidedly of opinion that he ought to operate by Montgomery and Selma, and connect himself with Canby and Farragut on the Alabama river, thus severing the northern part of Georgia and Alabama, and almost Mississippi, from the rebel confederacy. This view was taken in his letters to General Canby, copies of which were sent to the Adjutant-General's office, and in his opinion I fully concurred, and so wrote both to him and Canby, directing them, however, to make no important movements until they received your instructions.

I judge, from a dispatch just received from General Sherman, that he is now proposing to move eastwardly towards Augusta or Millen, expecting to connect with the coast by the Savannah river. Whether this is simply a suggestion or change of opinion on his part, or the result of his consultation with you or of your orders to him, I have no means of knowing; all I wish to say or hear upon the subject is, that if any definite plans have been adopted, it is desirable that the Secretary of War or myself should be informed of that plan as early as possible. Large requisitions have been received within the last day or two from General Canby's staff-officers for water transportation, and quartermaster, commissary, and medical stores, to be sent to Mobile and Pensacola, for an army of thirty or forty thousand men. Indeed, in the single article of forage more is asked for than can pos-

sibly be furnished in the northern and eastern states, and more than all the available sea-going vessels in northern ports could float. On receiving the requisitions I directed General Meigs to take active measures to fill them, so far as possible, but to make no shipments till further orders.

Now, if General Sherman is going east to connect with the coast by the Savannah river, these stores should not be shipped to Mobile or Pensacola, but to Hilton Head, and transportation be sent to New Orleans to move all available troops to that point. Moreover, operations at Mobile should, in that case, be limited to mere demonstrations, and that only so long as they may serve to deceive the enemy. It is exceedingly important that some definite conclusion should be arrived at as early as possible, for the expenses of the water transportation, and especially of the demurrage of large fleets, are enormous.

Perhaps it may be desirable that I should give my reasons in brief for concurring with General Sherman in his first proposed plan of operations.

In the first place, that line of connection with the coast is the shortest and most direct.

2nd. By cutting off a smaller slice of rebel territory it is not so directly exposed, and leaves a smaller force to attack in rear.

3rd. It does not leave Tennessee and Kentucky so open to rebel raids.

4th. The Alabama river is more navigable for our gunboats than the Savannah.

5th. The line is more defensible for General Canby's troops than the other.

6th. Montgomery, Selma, and Mobile are, in a military point of view, more important than Augusta, Millen, and Savannah.

7th. Mobile can be more easily captured than Savannah.

8th. This line will bring within our control a more valuable and important section of country than that by the Savannah.

There is a section of country, from fifty to one hundred and fifty miles wide, extending from Selma west to Meridian, and thence north on both sides of the Tombigbee to Columbus, Aberdeen, and Okalona, more rich in agricultural products than any equal extent of country in the Confederacy. Slave labor has been but very little disturbed in this section, and the large crops of this year are being collected at Demopolis, Selma, Montgomery, and other points for the use of the rebel army. By moving on that line they will be converted to our

use or be destroyed; by moving on Augusta they will be left for the use of Hood's forces.

I do not write this for the purpose of influencing your adoption of a particular plan of campaign, or of changing your decision, if you have adopted any plan, but simply to urge on you an early decision, if you have not already made one. It is proper, however, to remark that I have taken every possible means to obtain correct information on the subject, and present these conclusions only after thorough examination and the most mature consideration.

Very respectfully, your obedient servant,

H. W. H ALLEGE, Major-General, Chief of Staff.

REBEL EFFORTS IN LOYAL STATES.

GENERAL TOWNSEND TO GENERAL FRY.— (TELEGRAM.)

ALBANY, NEW YOBK, October 12,1S64.

Brigadier- General FRY, Provost-Marshal- General:

I am just informed that an effort is to be made to-day to capture the steamer Michigan, and release the prisoners on Johnson's Island, by a party that is to rendezvous at Port Keeler, said to be 2,000 strong.

I have sent the persons bringing me the information directly to Major-General Dix, and also telegraphed him.

F. TOWNSEND, Assistant Provost-Marshal-General

GENERAL ORDER OF GENERAL DIX.

PARTMETfT OF TUB

October 26, 1864.

HEAD-QUARTERS, DEPARTMENT OF TUB EAST, NEW YORK CITY,)

General Orders.

Satisfactory information has been received by the major-general commanding that rebel agents in Canada design to send into the United States and colonize at different points large numbers of refugees, deserters, and enemies of the government, with a view to vote at the approaching presidential election, and it is not unlikely, when this service to the rebel cause has been performed, that they may be organized for the purpose of shooting down peaceable* citizens and plundering private property, as in recent predatory incursions on the Detroit river and at St. Albans.

Against these meditated outrages on the purity of the-elective franchise and these nefarious acts of robbery, incendiarism, and mur-

der, it is the determination of the major-general commanding to guard by every possible precaution, and to visit on the perpetrators, if they shall be detected, the most signal and summary punishment.

All the classes of persons enumerated, whether citizens of the insurgent states who have been in the rebel service engaged in acts of hostility to the government, deserters from the military service of the United States, or men drafted or subject to draft who have fled to evade their duty to their country, are liable to punishment for their crimes they have already committed, and no effort will be spared to arrest them.

For this purpose, all provost-marshals and their deputies within this department are commanded to exercise all possible vigilance, and to adopt such measures as may be necessary to detect persons coming into the United States for the purpose of voting, or of committing depredations on private property, and to prevent their escape; and it is earnestly recommended to the electors of the states in this department to take within their respective election districts such measures as may be required for their own security, and to aid the military authorities in frustrating the designs of rebel agents and emissaries, or in bringing the perpetrators to punishment.

Should any of these malefactors succeed in perpetrating their crimes, effective measures will be taken to prevent their return to Canada; and for this purpose special direction will be given, and suitable guards for the frontiers will be provided, before the day of election.

As a further precaution, all persons from the insurgent states, now within this department, or who may come within it on or before the 3d of November, proximo, are hereby required to report themselves for registry on or before that day, and all such persons coming within the department after that day will report immediately on their arrival.

Those who fail to comply with this requirement will be regarded as spies or emissaries of the insurgent authorities at Richmond, and will be treated accordingly.

The registry in this city will be at the head-quarters of Major-General John J. Peck, second in command in the department, at No. 37 Bleecker street, and in all other places out of this city at the office of the nearest provost-marshal. The registry will contain a complete description of the persons reporting, and also their places of residence, which must not be changed without notice at the place of registry. By command of

Major-General JOHN A. DIX.

CAPTAIN ROGERS TO GENERAL FRY.— (TELEGRAM.)

BUFFALO, NEW YOEK, October 30,1864.

Brigadier- General J. B. FEY, Frowst-Marshal- General :

The following telegram has just been received by me, dated " Toronto, O. W., October 30, 1864. To Provost-Marshal, Buffalo: I have received information this afternoon, from a source which I think is entitled to confidence, that a party of Southern rebels and sympathizers left here yesterday to be joined by others at different points, in all about one hundred, with the intention of going to Buffalo or Detroit, or both places, for the purpose of burning and committing other depredations; and I think it is not uulikely they may begin operations to-night. They were provided with arms, combustible materials, etc., necessary for their intended operations. I judge it is their intention to cross the river in small boats. They also talked of Suspension Bridge and Niagara Falls. Their preparations have been going on for some time, and, if my information is correct, are very complete. Their arms have been brought in from the "West, and they are leagued with parties in that direction. Two of those who left Toronto have commissions from the rebel government.

"R. J. KIMBALL, United States Consular Agent.' 1 ' 1

The military of the city are now assembling, and proper preparations will be made to secure the safety of the city to-night.

WILLIAM F. ROGERS, Captain P. Jf., 80th District.

MR. WHEELER TO SECRETARY 8TANTON.— (TELEGBAM.)

MALONE, October 81, 1864.

Hon. E. M. STANTON :

We have a village of over three thousand inhabitants, ten miles from the Canada line; principal shops of Ogdensburg road here; we will take care of ourselves, if you will give us arms and ammunition. The fire-arms under the control of the provost-marshal here are worthless. Will you give him arms for our use? Refer to Major McKeever, in your department, Governor Morton, or Treasurer Spinner.

Respectfully,

W. H. WHEELER.

ME. JACKSON TO SECRETARY 6EWARD.-(TELEGBAM.;

HALIFAX, N. S.. November 1,1864.

Hon. W. H. SEWARD, Secretary of State:

It is secretly asserted by secessionists here, that plans have been formed and will be carried into execution by rebels and their allies, for setting fire to the principal cities in the Northern states on the day of the presidential election.

M. M. JACKSON, United States Consul.

GENERAL DIX TO SECRETARY ST ANTON.— (TELEGB AM.)

NEW YORK, November 4,1864.

Eon. E. M. STANTOX, Secretary of War :

When I saw you a fortnight ago to-morrow, you told me you would ask General Grant to send me five thousand troops, of which I informed you I wished to place three thousand on the frontier, not only in reference to threatened attack, but to secure the efficient execution of the order in regard to colonizing from Canada for the election; and that I would retain two thousand in New York. If I cannot divide the force under General Butler, two of the chief objects in view will be defeated.

I will give General Butler, as is due to his rank, the choice of remaining here or of taking command of the two northern districts of New York and state of Vermont, including Albany, Buffalo and St. Albans. If his force must not be divided, I will send into those districts the troops garrisoning forts in this harbor, although they are altogether inadequate to the object in view.

JOHN A. DIX, Major-General.

COLONEL SWEET TO GENERAL HOFFMAN.-(TELEGRAM.)

CHICAGO, ILLINOIS, November 7,1864.

Brigadier- General W. HOFFMAN :

Have made during the night the following arrests of rebel officers, escaped prisoners of war, and citizens in connection with them: Colonel G. St. Leger Greenfell, Morgan's adjutant-general, in company with J. F. Shanks, an escaped prisoner of war, at Richmond House; J. F. Shanks; Colonel Vincent Marmaduke, brother of General Marmaduke; Brigadier-General Charles Wallace, of the Sons of Liberty; Captain

APPENDIX.

675

Cantrill, of Morgan's command; Charles Traverse, Butternut. Can-trill and Traverse arrested in Walsh's house, in which was found two cart-loads large-sized revolvers, loaded and capped; two hundred stand of muskets, and ammunition. Also seized two boxes guns concealed in a room in the city; also arrested Judge Buck Morris, treasurer of the "Sons of Liberty," having complete proof of his assisting Shanks to escape, and plotting to release prisoners at this camp. Most of these rebel officers were in the city on the same errand in August last, their plan being to raise an insurrection and release prisoners of war at this camp. There are many strangers and suspicious persons in the city, believed to be guerillas and rebel soldiers. The plan was to attack the camp on election. All prisoners arrested are in camp. Captain Nelson and A. 0. Coventry, of the police, rendered

very efficient service.

J. B. SWEET, Colonel Commanding Post.

MR. WHITE TO SECRETARY STANTON.— (TELEGRAM.)

CHICAGO, November 7,1864.

Hon. E. M. STANTON, Secretary of War:

Colonel Sweet, by his energetic and decisive measures last night, has undoubtedly saved Camp Douglas from being opened, and the city from conflagration. I respectfully suggest that you send him a word of

commendation.

HORACE WHITE.

STATEMENT SHOWING THE STRENGTH OF THE ARMY UNDER THE IMMEDIATE COMMAND OF MAJOR-GENERAL GEORGE H. THOMAS ON THE 318T OF OCTOBER, 20rn AND 80TH OF NOVEMBER, AND lOra OF DECEMBER, -1864, AS REPORTED BY THE RETURNS ON FILE IN THE OFFICE OF THE ADJUTANT-GENERAL.

OCTOBER 81, 1864.

APPENDIX.

NOVEMBER 20, 1864.

NOVEMBER 30, 1864.

* A. J. Smith's Divisions.

DECEMBER 10, 1864.

* A. J. Smith's Divisions.

The battle of Franklin was fought November 30, 1864, and the battle of Nashville December 15 and 16, 1864.

The total number of officers and men for battle, October 81, 1864, was 53,415

" " " " " November 20, 1864, was 59,5'34

" " " " " " " November 30,1864, u 71,452
" " " " " " " •' " December 10,1864, " 70,272

THE STRENGTH OF GENERAL HOOD'S AKMY, AS PER RETURNS ON FILE IN THE ARCHIVE OFFICE, ON THE CTH OF NOVEMBER AND IOTH OF DECEMBER, 1864:

NOVEMBER GTH.

Effective total present 30,600

Total present 40,740

Aggregate present 45,719

Total present and absent 38,793

Aggregate present and absent 96,867

DECEMBER lOin.

Effective total present 23.058

Total present 83,393

Aggregate present 34,439

Total present and absent 80,125

Aggregate present and absent 86,955

Covering the period in question, there are no returns of the Confederate army of Tennessee in possession of the Archive Office, except those enumerated above.

E. D. TOWNSEND, Adjutant-General.

ADJUTANT-GENERAL'S OFFICE, WASHINGTON, April 28, 1879. 125

APPENDIX TO CHAPTER XXX.

EAEL BUSSELL TO ME. MASON.— (EXTRACT.)

FOBEIGN OFFICE, August 2,1862.

You state that the Confederacy has a population of twelve millions; that it has proved itself for eighteen months capable of successful defence against every attempt to subdue or destroy it; that in the judgment of the intelligence of all Europe the separation is final; and that under no possible circumstances can the late Federal Union be restored.

On the other hand, the Secretary of State of the United States has affirmed, in an official dispatch, that a large portion of the once disaffected population has been restored to the Union, and now evinces its loyalty and firm adherence to the government; that the white population now in insurrection is under five millions, and the Southern Confederacy owes its main strength to hope of assistance from Europe.

In the face of the fluctuating events of the war, the alternations of victory and defeat, the capture of New Orleans, the advance of the Federals to Corinth, to Memphis, and the banks of the Mississippi as far as Vicksburg, contrasted, on the other hand, with the failure of the attack on Charleston and the retreat from before Richmond; placed, too, between allegations so contradictory on the part of the contending powers, her Majesty's government are still determined to wait.

In order to be entitled to a place among the independent nations of the earth, a state ought to have not only strength and resources for a time, but afford promise of stability and permanence. Should the Confederate States of America win that place among nations, it might l>e right for other nations justly to acknowledge an independence achieved ly victory and maintained ly a successful resistance to all attempts to overthrow it. That time, however, has not, in the judgment of her Majesty's government, yet arrived.

Her Majesty's government, therefore, can only hope that a peaceful termination of the present bloody and destructive contest may not be distant. I am, etc.,

LORD RUSSELL TO MASON, SLIDELL, AND MANN.

FOREIGN OFFICE, February 13, 1865.

GENTLEMEN : Some time ago I had the honor to inform you, in answer to a statement which you sent me, that her Majesty remained neutral in the deplorable contest now carried on in North America, and that her Majesty intended to persist in that course.

It is now my duty to request you to bring to the notice of the authorities under whom you act, with a view to their serious consideration thereof, the just complaints which her Majesty's government have to make of the conduct of the so-called Confederate government. The facts upon which these complaints are founded tend to show that her Majesty's neutrality is not respected by the agents of that government, and that undue and reprehensible attempts have been made by them to involve her Majesty in a war in which her Majesty had declared her intention not to take part.

In the first place, I am sorry to observe that the unwarrantable practice of building ships in this country, to be used as vessels of war against a state with which her Majesty is at peace, still continues. Her Majesty's government had hoped that this attempt to make the territorial waters of Great Britain the place of preparation for warlike armaments against the United States, might be put an end to by prosecutions and by seizure of the vessels built in pursuance of contracts made with the Confederate agents. But facts which are, unhappily, too notorious, and correspondence which has been put into the hands of her Majesty's government by the minister of the government of the United States, show that resort is had to evasion and subtlety in order to escape the penalties of the law ; that a vessel is bought in one place, that her armament is prepared in another, and that both are sent to some distant port beyond her Majesty's jurisdiction, and that thus an armed steamship is fitted out to cruise against the commerce of a power in amity with her Majesty. A crew composed partly of British subjects is procured separately; wages are paid to them for an unknown service. They are dispatched, perhaps to the coast of France, and there or elsewhere are engaged to serve in a Confederate man-of-war.

Now, it is very possible that by such shifts and stratagems the penalties of the existing law of this country, nay, of any law that could be enacted, may be evaded; but the offence thus offered to her Majesty's authority and dignity by the de facto rulers of the Confederate States, whom her Majesty acknowledges as belligerents, and whose agents in the United Kingdom enjoy the benefit of our hospitality in quiet security, remains the same. It is a proceeding totally unjustifiable, and manifestly offensive to the British crown.

Secondly, the Confederate organs have published, and her Majesty's government have been placed in possession of it, a memorandum of instructions for the cruisers of the so-called Confederate States, which would, if adopted, set aside some of the most settled principles of international law, and break down rules which her Majesty's government have lawfully established for the purpose of maintaining her Majesty's neutrality. It may, indeed, be said that this memorandum of instructions, though published in a Confederate newspaper, has never as yet been put in force, and that it may be considered as a dead letter; but this cannot be affirmed with regard to the document which forms the next ground of complaint.

Thirdly, the President of the so-called Confederate States has put forth a proclamation acknowledging and claiming as a belligerent operation, in behalf of the Confederate States, the act of Bennett G. Bur-ley in attempting, in 1864, to capture the steamer Michigan, with a view to release numerous Confederate prisoners detained in captivity in Johnson's Island, on Lake Erie.

Independently of this proclamation, the facts connected with the attack on two other American steamers, the Philo Parsons and Island Queen, on Lake Erie, and the recent raid at St. Albans, in the state of Vermont, which Lieutenant Young, holding, as he affirms, a commission in the Confederate States army, declares to be an act of war, and therefore not to involve the guilt of robbery and murder, show a gross disregard of her Majesty's character as a neutral power, and a desire to involve her Majesty in hostilities with a coterminous power with which Great Britain is at peace.

You may, gentlemen, have the means of contesting the accuracy of the information on which my foregoing statements have been founded; and I should be glad to find that her Majesty's government have been misinformed, although I have no reason to think that such has been the case. If, on the contrary, the information which her Majesty's government have received with regard to these matters can-

not be gainsaid, I trust that you will feel yourselves authorized to promise, on behalf of the Confederate government, that practices so offensive and unwarrantable shall cease, and shall be entirely abandoned for the future. I shall, therefore, await anxiously your reply, after referring to the authorities of the Confederate States.

I am, etc.,

EUSSELL.

J. M. MASON, Esq., J. SLIDELL, Esq., J. MANN> Esq.

SECRETARY OF STATE SEWAED TO HON. CHAELES F. ADAMS, UNITED STATES MINISTER TO ENGLAND.-(Ex T BACT.)

DEPARTMENT OF STATE, WASHINGTON, (March 9, 1865. f

In accordance with Earl Russell's suggestion, the Secretary of War has, by direction of the President, transmitted to Lieutenant-General Grant the British official copy of Earl Russell's letter to John Slidell, James M. Mason, and Dudley Mann, with a direction to deliver it by flag of truce to General Lee, the general in command of the insurgent forces. I give you a copy of my note written on that occasion to the Secretary of War, and so soon as we shall have received a report from the Lieutenant-General of his proceedings in the matter, I will communicate the result to you for the information of Earl Russell.

SECEETAEY OF STATE SEWAED TO SECEETAEY OF WAR STANTON.

DEPARTMENT OF STATE. WASHINGTON, j March 8, 1S65. j

SIR : The enclosed paper has been received at this department from Earl Russell, her Britannic Majesty's principal Secretary of State for Foreign Affairs, with a request that facilities might be afforded for its passage through the military lines of the United States forces. I have to request that the paper be sent forward to the Lieutenant-General, with directions to cause the same to be conveyed to General Lee by flag of truce. I have further to request to be informed of the Lieutenant-General's proceedings in the premises.

I have the honor to be, sir, your obedient servant,

WILLIAM H. SEWARD. Hon. E. M. STANTON, Secretary of War.

GENERAL GRANT TO GENERAL LEE.

HEAD-QUARTERS, ABMIES OP THE UNITED STATES, J March 13,1866. f

GENERAL: Enclosed with this, I send you a copy of a communication from Earl Russell, Secretary of State for Foreign Affairs, England, to Messrs. Mason, Slidell, and Mann. The accompanying copy of a note from the Hon. W. H. Seward, Secretary of State, to the Secretary of War, explains the reason for sending it to you.

Very respectfully, your ohedient servant,

U. S. GRANT, Lieutenant-General. General R. E. LEE, commanding Confederate States Armies.

GENERAL LEE TO GENERAL GRANT.

HEAD-QUARTEES, C. 8. ABMIES,) March 23, 1865. f

GENERAL : In pursuance of instructions from the government of the Confederate States, transmitted to me through the Secretary of War, the documents recently forwarded by you are respectfully returned.

I am directed to say "that the government of the Confederate States cannot recognize as authentic a paper which is neither an original nor attested as a copy; nor could they under any circumstances consent to hold intercourse with a neutral nation through the medium of open dispatches sent through hostile lines, after being read and approved by the enemies of the Confederacy."

I have the honor to be, very respectfully,

Your obedient servant,

R. E. LEE, General Lieutenant-General U. S. GRANT,

commanding United States Armies.

APPENDIX TO CHAPTER XXXII.

LIEUTENANT-GENERAL GEANT TO MAJOB-GENERALS MEADE, OED, AND 8HEEIDAN.

CITY POINT, VIRGINIA, March 24, 1865.

GENERAL: On the 29th instant the armies operating against Kich-mond will be moved by our left, for the double purpose of turning the enemy out of his present position around Petersburg, and to ensure the success of the cavalry under General Sheridan, which will start at the same time, in its efforts to reach and destroy the Southside and Danville railroads. Two corps of the army of the Potomac will be moved first, in two columns, taking the two roads crossing Hatcher's run nearest where the present line held by us strikes that stream, both moving towards Dinwiddie court-house.

The cavalry, under General Sheridan, joined by the division now under General Davies, will move at the same time, by the Weldon road and the Jerusalem plank-road, turning west from the latter before crossing the Nottoway, and west with the whole column before reaching Stony creek. General Sheridan will then move independently under other instructions, which will be given him. All dismounted cavalry belonging to the army of the Potomac, and the dismounted cavalry from the Middle Military Division not required for guarding property belonging to their arm of service, will report to Brigadier-General Benham, to be added to the defences of City Point. Major-General Parke will be left in command of all the army left for holding the lines about Petersburg and City Point, subject, of course, to orders from the commander of the army of the Potomac. The Ninth army corps will be left intact to hold the present line of works, so long as the whole line now occu-

pied by us is held. If, however, the troops to the left of the Ninth corps are withdrawn, then the left of the corps may he thrown back so as to occupy the position held by the array prior to the capture of the Weldon road. All troops to the left of the Ninth corps will be held in readiness to move at the shortest notice by such route as is designated when the order is given.

General Ord will detach three divisions, two white, and one colored, or so much of them as he can, and hold his present lines, and march, for the present, left of the army of the Potomac. In the absence of further orders, or until further orders are given, the white divisions will follow the left column of the army of the Potomac, and the colored division the right column. During the movement, Major-General "Weitzel will be left in command of all the forces remaining behind from the army of the James.

The movement of troops from the army of the James will commence on the night of the 27th instant. General Ord will leave behind the minimum number of cavalry necessary for picket duty in the absence of the main army. A cavalry expedition from General Ord's command will also be started from Suffolk, to leave there on Saturday, the 1st of April, under Colonel Sumner, for the purpose of cutting the railroad about Hicksford. This, if accomplished, will have to be a surprise, and therefore from three to five hundred men will be sufficient. They should, however, be supported by all the infantry that can be spared from Norfolk and Portsmouth, as far out as to where the cavalry crosses the Blackwater. The crossing should probably be at Uniten. Should Colonel Sumner succeed in reaching the Weldon road, he will be instructed to do all the damage possible to the triangle of roads between Hicksford, Weldon, and Gaston. The railroad bridge at Weldon 'being fitted up for the passage of carriages, it might be practicable to destroy any accumulation of supplies the enemy may have collected south of the Roanoke. All the troops will move with four days' rations in haversacks, and eight days' in wagons. To avoid as much hauling as possible, and to give the army of the James the same number of days' supplies with the army of the Potomac, General Ord will direct his commissary and quartermaster to have sufficient supplies delivered at the terminus of the road to fill up in passing. Sixty rounds of ammunition per man will be taken in wagons, and as much grain as the transportation on hand will carry, after taking the specified amount of other supplies. The densely wooded country in which the army has to operate making the use of much artillery im-

APPENDIX.

practicable, the amount taken with the array will be reduced to six or eight guns to each division, at the option of the army commanders.

All necessary preparations for carrying these directions into operation may be commenced at once. The reserves of the Ninth corps should be massed as much as possible. Whilst I would not now order an unconditional attack on the enemy's line by them, they should be ready, and should make the attack, if the enemy weakens his line in their front, without waiting for orders. In case they carry the line, then the whole of the Ninth corps could follow up so as to join or co-operate with the balance of the army. To prepare for this, the Ninth corps will have rations issued to them the same as to the balance of the army. General Weitzel will keep vigilant watch upon his front, and if found at all practicable to break through at any point, he will do so. A success north of the James should be followed up with great promptness. An attack will not be feasible unless it is found that the enemy has detached largely. In that case, it may be regarded as evident that the enemy are relying upon their local reserves, principally, for the defence of Richmond. Preparations may be made for abandoning all the line north of the James, except enclosed works; only to be abandoned, however, after a break is made in the lines of the enemy.

By these instructions, a large part of the armies operating against Richmond is left behind. The enemy, knowing this, may, as an only chance, strip their lines to the merest skeleton, in the hope of advantage not being taken of it, whilst they hurl everything against the moving column, and return. It cannot be impressed too strongly upon commanders of troops left in the trenches, not to allow this to occur without taking advantage of it. The very fact of the enemy coming out to attack, if he does so, might be regarded as conclusive evidence of such a weakening of his lines. I would have it particularly enjoined upon corps commanders, that in case of an attack from the enemy, those not attacked are not to wait for orders from the commanding officer of the army to which they belong, but that they will move promptly, and notify the commander of their action. I wish, also, to enjoin the same action on the part of division commanders, when other parts of their corps are engaged. In like manner, I would urge the importance of following up a repulse of the enemy.

U. S. GRANT, Lieutenant-General. Major- Generals MEADE, ORD, and SHERIDAN.
APPENDIX.
GENERAL SHERIDAN TO GENERAL GRANT.

HEAD-QUARTERS, CAVALRY, DINWIDDIE COURT-HOTTSE, \'7b March 81, 1865.

Lieutenant-General U. S. GEANT, commanding Armies United States:

GENEBAL : The enemy attacked me about ten o'clock A. M. to-day on the road coming in from the west of Dinwiddie court-house. This attack was very handsomely repulsed by General Smith's brigade of Crook's division, aDd the enemy was driven across Chamberlain's creek. Shortly afterwards the enemy's infantry attacked on the same creek in heavy force, and drove in General Davies' brigade, and, advancing rapidly, gained the forks of the road at J. Boisseau's. This forced Devin—who was in advance—and Davies to cross the Boydton road. General Gregg's brigade and General Gibbes's brigade, which were towards Dinwiddie, then attacked the enemy in rear very handsomely: this stopped his march towards the left of our infantry, and finally caused him to turn towards Dinwiddie and attack us in heavy force. The enemy then again attacked at Chamberlain's creek and forced General Smith's position. At this time Capehart's and Pennington's brigades of Ouster's division came up, and a very handsome fight occurred.

The enemy have gained some ground; but we still hold in front of Dinwiddie court-house, and Davies and Devin are coming down the Boydton plank-road to join us.

The opposing force was Pickett's division, Wise's independent brigade, and Fitz Lee's, Rosser's, and W. H. F. Lee's cavalry commands.

The men have behaved splendidly. Our loss in killed and wounded will probably number four hundred and fifty men; very few men were lost as prisoners. We have of the enemy a number of prisoners.

This force is too strong for us. I will hold on to Dinwiddie courthouse until I am compelled to leave. We have also some prisoners from Johnson's division. Our fighting to-day was all dismounted.

P. H. SHERIDAN, Major-General.

OFFICIAL STATEMENT OF THE EFFECTIVE FORCE OF THE CAVALRY UNDER THE COMMAND OF MAJOR-GENERAL SHERIDAN IN THE OPERATIONS OF DINWIDDIE COURT-HOUSE, VIRGINIA, MARCH 31, 1865, AND FIVE FORKS, VIRGINIA, APRIL 1, 1865.

March 27, 1865.—General Merritt's command, Devin's First and Ouster's Third cavalry divisions 5,700

General Crook's command, Second cavalry division 3,300

March 31,1865.—Total effective force 9,000

[Authority : General Sheridan's official report, based on returns of effective force as reported by the commanding officers named.]

APPENDIX.

691

Deduct losses at Dinwiddie court-house, March 31,1865 450

[Authority: General Sheridan's report.]

April 1,1865.—Effective cavalry force prior to Mackenzie's arrival 8,5.; 0

" Strength of Mackenzie's cavalry brigade, army of the James [Mackenzie's report] 1,682

April 1, 1865.—Total effective force of all the cavalry 10,232*

Crook's strength, March 31st (morning) 8,300

Crook's loss at Dinwiddie court-house, say 250

Crook's strength April 1,1865 (morning).

8,050

From total effective April 1,1865 = 10,232

Take Crook's strength " " 8,050

Total cavalry [Merritt's and Mackenzie's] engaged at Five Forks. 7,182

HEAD-QUARTERS, MILITARY DIVISION OF THE MISSOURI,) CHICAGO, ILLINOIS, November 26,1880. f

I certify that the numbers given as the strength of the commands in the above statement—except the estimated loss of Crook's command at Dinwiddie court-house—are all taken from official reports now on file at these head-quarters.

GEORGE A. FORSYTH,

Lieutenant- Colonel, Aide-de- Camp.

* This includes Crook's command, no portion of which was engaged at Five Forks, that entire command being south of Dinwiddie court-house and Stony creek, about four miles from the battle-field.

With reference to this statement I refer the reader to my remarks in Appendix to Chapter XXV. I have no doubt that all the deductions claimed could be legitimately made; but I have adopted the rule of accepting the official returns of effective strength made to an adjutant-general, whether by rebel or national officers, and am obliged to abide by it in this instance, as in all others. It will not be found to act unfairly, as I decline to depreciate the numbers reported by the enemy as well as those of the national forces.— AUTHOR.

APPENDIX TO CHAPTER XXXIV.

LOSSES IN REBEL AND NATIONAL ARMIES IN APPOMATTOX CAMPAIGN.

GENERAL BEECK TO AUTHOR.

WAB DEPARTMENT, ADJUTANT-GENERAL'S OFFICE,) WASHINGTON, July 13, 1868. f

Brevet Brigadier-General ADAM BADEATJ, A. D. C.,

Head-quarters, Armies of the United States:

GENERAL : In reply to your communication of the 10th instant, I have to furnish you with the following information from the Kecords of Prisoners of War filed in this office:

The number of rebel prisoners captured in the lattles of the army of the Potomac, army of the James, and cavalry command of General Sheridan, between the 29th day of March, 1865, and the 9th day of April, 1865, inclusive, amount to 46,495.

The number of rebel prisoners paroled at Appomattox court-house, Virginia, April 9, 1865, amount to 27,416.

The number of rebel prisoners paroled at Eichmond, Virginia, during the month of April, 1865, amount to 1,610.

I am, General, very respectfully, your obedient servant, SAMUEL BKEOK,

Assistant Adjutant-General.

APPENDIX.

693

LOSSES IN THE ARMY OP THE POTOMAC FROM MARCH 29 TO APRIL 9, 1865, COMPILED FROM THE RECORDS OF THE ADJUTANT-GENERAL'S OFFICE.

SOUBCES OF INFORMATION. * Nothing in reports or returns.

t Report of Major-General P. H. Sheridan (returns fail to show losses). $ Report of Major-General A. A. Humphreys, commanding. § Returns.

II Report of Major-General John G. Parke, commanding. t Report of Major George Ayer, Chief of Artillery. ** Report of Brigadier-General H. L. Abbott, commanding. tt Report of Major-General John Gibbon, commanding. & Report of Major-General G. "Weitzel, commanding.

APPENDIX TO CHAPTER XXXV.

CORRESPONDENCE RELATIVE TO SURRENDER OF GENERAL JOHNSTON, APRIL, 1864.

GENERAL JOHNSTON TO GENERAL SHERMAN.— (DICTATED BY JEFFERSON DAVIS.)

HEAD-QUARTERS, IN THE FIELD, April 14,1864.

Major-General SHEEMAN, commanding United States Forces:

The results of the recent campaign in Virginia have changed the relative military condition of the belligerents. I am, therefore, induced to address you in this form the enquiry whether, to stop the further effusion of blood and devastation of property, you are willing to make a temporary suspension of active operations, and to communicate to Lieutenant-General Grant, commanding the armies of the United States, the request that he will take like action in regard to other armies, the object being to permit the civil authorities to enter into the needful arrangements to terminate the existing war.

I have the honor to be, very respectfully, your obedient servant,

J. E. JOHNSTON, General

GENERAL SHERMAN TO GENERAL JOHNSTON.

HEAD-QTTAETEES. MILITARY DIVISION OF THE MISSISSIPPI, IN THE FIELD,) RALEIGH, NOBTH CABOLINA, April 14, 1865.

General J. E. JOHNSTON, commanding Confederate Army:

GENEEAL : I have this moment received your communication of this date. I am fully empowered to arrange with you any terms for the suspension of further hostilities between the armies commanded by you and those commanded by myself, and will be willing to confer with you to that end. I will limit the advance of my main column, to-morrow, to Morrisville, and the cavalry to the university, and expect that you will also maintain the present position of your forces until each has notice of a failure to agree.

That a basis of action may be had, I undertake to abide by the same terms and conditions as were made by Generals Grant and Lee at Ap-pomattox court-house, on the 9th instant, relative to our two armies; and furthermore, to obtain from General Grant an order to suspend the movements of any troops from the direction of Virginia. General Stoneman is under my command, and my order will suspend any devastation or destruction contemplated by him. I will add that I really desire to save the people of North Carolina the damage they would sustain by the march of this army through the central or western parts of the state.

I am, with respect, your obedient servant,

W. T. SHERMAN, Major-General.

GENERAL SHERMAN TO GENERAL GRANT.

HEAD-QUABTEKS, MILITARY DIVISION OF THE MISSISSIPPI, IN THE FIELU, I RALEIGH, NOBTH CAEOLINA, April 18, 1865.

Lieutenant- General U. S. GRANT,

or Major- General HALLECK, Washington, D. C.:

GENERAL : I enclose herewith a copy of an agreement made this day between General Joseph E. Johnston and myself, which, if approved by the President of the United States, will produce peace from the Potomac to the Rio Grande. Mr. Breckenridge was present at our conference, in the capacity of major-general, and satisfied me of the ability of General Johnston to carry out to their full extent the terms of this agreement; and if you will get the President to simply endorse the copy, and commission ine to carry out the terms, I will follow them to the conclusion.

You will observe that it is an absolute submission of the enemy to the lawful authority of the United States, and disperses his armies absolutely ; and the point to which I attach most importance is that the dispersion and disbandment of these armies is done in such a manner as to prevent their breaking up into guerilla bands. On the other hand, we can retain just as much of an army as we please. I agreed . to the mode and manner of the surrender of arms set forth, as it gives the states the means of suppressing guerillas, which we could not expect them to do if we stripped them of all arms.

Both Generals Johnston and Breckenridge admitted that slavery was dead, and I could not insist on embracing it in such a paper, because it can be made with the states in detail. I know that, all the men of substance South sincerely want peace, and I do not believe

APPENDIX.

they will resort to war again during this century. I have no doubt tnat they will in future be perfectly subordinate to the laws of the United States. The moment my action in this matter is approved, I can spare five corps, and will ask for orders to leave General Schofield here with the Tenth corps, and to march myself with the Fourteenth, Fifteenth, Seventeenth, Twentieth, and Twenty-third corps via Burkes-ville and Gordonsville to Frederick or Hagerstown, Maryland, there to be paid and mustered out.

The question of finance is now the chief one, and every soldier and officer not needed should be got home at work. I would like to be able to begin the march north by May 1st.

I urge, on the part of the President, speedy action, as it is important to get the Confederate armies to their homes as well as our own. I am, with great respect, your obedient servant,

W. T. SHERMAN", Major-General commanding.

MEMORANDUM, OR BASIS OF AGREEMENT, MADE THIS 18TH DAY OF APRIL, A. 0 1865, NEAR DURHAM'S STATION, IN THE STATE OF NORTH CAROLINA, BY AND BETWEEN GENERAL JOSEPH E. JOHNSTON, COMMANDING THE CONFEDERATE ARMY, AND MAJOR-GENERAL WILLIAM T. SHERMAN, COMMANDING THE ARMY OF THE UNITED STATES IN NORTH CAROLINA, BOTH PRESENT:

1. The contending armies now in the field to maintain the statu quo until notice is given by the commanding general of any one to its opponent, and reasonable time, say forty-eight hours, allowed.

2. The Confederate armies now in existence to be disbanded and conducted to their several state capitals, there to deposit their arms and public property in the state arsenal; and each officer and man to execute and file an agreement to cease from acts of war, and to abide the action of the state and federal authority; the number of arms and munitions of war to be reported to the chief of ordnance at "Washington city, subject to the future action of the Congress of the United States, and, in the meantime, to be used solely to maintain peace and order within the borders of the states respectively.

3. The recognition, by the Executive of the United States, of the several state governments, on their officers and legislatures taking the oaths prescribed by the constitution of the United States, and, where conflicting state governments have resulted from the war, the legitimacy of all shall be submitted to the Supreme Court of the United States.

states, with powers as defined by the Constitution of the United States and of the states respectively.

5. The people and inhabitants of all the states to be guaranteed, so far as the Executive can, their political rights and franchises, as well as their rights of person and property, as defined by the Constitution of the United States and of the states respectively.

6. The executive authority of the government of the United States not to disturb any of the people by reason of the late war, so long as they live in peace and quiet, and obey the laws in existence at the place of their residence.

7. In general terms, the war to cease; a general amnesty, so far as the Executive of the United States can command, on condition of the disbandment of the Confederate armies, the distribution of the arms, and the resumption of peaceful pursuits by the officers and men hitherto composing said armies.

Not being fully empowered by our respective principals to fulfil these terms, we individually and officially pledge ourselves to promptly obtain the necessary authority, and to carry out the above
programme.
W. T. SHERMAN, Major-General,
Commanding Army of the United States in North Carolina.
J. E. JOHNSTON, General, Commanding Confederate States Army in North Carolina.
WAR DEPARTMENT, WASHINGTON CITY, April 21, 1865.
Lieutenant- General GEANT :
GENEBAL : The memorandum or basis agreed upon between General Sherman and General Johnston having been submitted to the President, they are disapproved. You will give notice of the disapproval to General Sherman, and direct him to resume hostilities at the earliest moment.

The instructions given to you by the late President, Abraham Lincoln, on the 3rd of March, by my telegraph of that date, addressed to you, express substantially the views of President Andrew Johnson, and will be observed by General Sherman. A copy is herewith appended.

The President desires that you proceed immediately to the headquarters of Major-General Sherman, and direct operations against the enemy. Yours truly,
EDWIN M. STANTON, Secretary of War.
GENERAL GRANT TO GENERAL SHERMAN.
HEAD-QUARTERS, ARMIES OP THE UNITED STATES,)
WASHINGTON, D. C., April 21, 1865. f
Major-General W. T. SHERMAN,
commanding Military Division of the Mississippi:
GENERAL: The basis of agreement entered into between yourself and General J. E. Johnston, for the disbandment of the Southern army, and the extension of the authority of the general government over all the territory belonging to it, is received.

I read it carefully myself before submitting it to the President and Secretary of War, and felt satisfied that it could not possibly be approved. My reason for these views I will give you at another time, in a more extended letter.

Your agreement touches upon questions of such vital importance that, as soon as read, I addressed a note to the Secretary of War, notifying him of their receipt, and the importance of immediate action by the President; and suggested, in view of their importance, that the entire cabinet be called together, that all might give an expression of their opinions upon the matter. The result was a disapproval by the President of the basis laid down; a disapproval of the negotiations altogether—except for the surrender of the army commanded by General Johnston, and directions to me to notify you of this decision. I cannot do so better than by sending you the enclosed copy of a dispatch (penned by the late President, though signed by the Secretary of War) in answer to me, on sending a letter received from General Lee, proposing to meet me for the purpose of submitting the question of peace to a convention of officers.

Please notify General Johnston immediately on receipt of this, and resume hostilities against his army at the earliest moment you can, acting in good faith.

Very respectfully, your obedient servant,

U. S. GRANT, Lieutenant-General.

FIRST BULLETIN.

WAR DEPARTMENT, WASHINGTON, April 22,1865.

Yesterday evening a bearer of dispatches arrived from General Sherman. An agreement for the suspension of hostilities, and a memorandum of what is called a basis for peace, had been entered into on the 18th inst, by General Sherman, with the rebel General Johnston. Brigadier-General Breckenridge was present at the conference.

APPENDIX.

699

A cabinet meeting was held at eight o'clock in the evening, at which the action of General Sherman was disapproved by the President, by the Secretary of War, by General Grant, and by every member of the cabinet. General Sherman was ordered to resume hostilities immediately, and was directed that the instructions given by the late President, in the following telegram which was penned by Mr. Lincoln himself at the Capitol, on the night of the 3rd of March, were approved by President Andrew Johnson, and were reiterated to govern the action of military commanders.

On the night of the 3rd of March, while President Lincoln and his cabinet were at the Capitol, a telegram from General Grant was brought to the Secretary of War, informing him that General Lee had requested an interview or conference, to make an arrangement for terms of peace. The letter of General Lee was published in a letter to Davis and to the rebel congress. General Grant's telegram was submitted to Mr. Lincoln, who, after pondering a few minutes, took up his pen and wrote with his own hand the following reply, which he submitted to the Secretary of State and the Secretary of War. It was then dated, addressed, and signed by the Secretary of War, and telegraphed to General Grant:

" WASHINGTON, March 8,1865,12 p. M. " Lieutenant-General GRANT :

" The President directs me to say to you that he wishes you to have no conference with General Lee, unless it be for the .capitulation of General Lee's army, or on some minor or purely military matter. He instructs me to say that you are not to decide, discuss, or confer upon any political questions. Such questions the President holds in his own hands, and will submit them to no military conferences or conventions.

" Meantime, you are to press to the utmost your military advantages.

"EDWIN M. STANTON,

" Secretary of War."

The orders of General Sherman to General Stoneman to withdraw from Salisbury and join him will probably open the way for Davis to escape to Mexico or Europe with his plunder, which is reported to be very large, including not only the plunder of the Richmond banks, but previous accumulations.

A dispatch received by this department from Richmond says: " It is stated here, by respectable parties, that the amount of specie taken

south by Jeff Davis and his partisans is very large, including not only the plunder of the Kichmond banks, but previous accumulations. They hope, it is said, to make terms with General Sherman, or some other commander, by which they will be permitted, with their effects, including this gold plunder, to go to Mexico or Europe. Johnston's negotiations look to this end."

After the cabinet meeting last night, General Grant started for North Carolina, to direct operations against Johnston's army.

EDWIN M. STANTON,
"Secretary of War.

At the same time with the publication of the above, the following reasons for the rejection of Sherman's memorandum were set forth, unofficially, but by authority:

1st. It was an exercise of authority not vested in General Sherman, and, on its face, shows that both he and Johnston knew that General Sherman had no authority to enter into any such arrangements.

2nd. It was a practical acknowledgment of the rebel government.

3rd. It undertook to re-establish rebel state governments, that had been overthrown at the sacrifice of many thousand loyal lives and immense treasure, and placed arms and munitions of war in the hands of rebels at their respective capitals, which might be used, as soon as the armies of the United States were disbanded, and used to conquer and subdue loyal states.

4th. By the restoration of rebel authority in these respective states, they would be enabled to re-establish slavery.

5th. It might furnish a ground of responsibility on the part of the Federal government to pay the rebel debt; and certainly subjects loyal citizens of rebel states to debts contracted by rebels in the name of the state.

6th. It puts in dispute the existence of loyal state governments, and the new state of West Virginia, which had been recognized by every department of the United States government.

7th. It practically abolished confiscation laws, and released rebels of every degree, who had slaughtered our people, from all pains and penalties for their crimes.

8th. It gave terms that had been deliberately, repeatedly, and solemnly rejected by President Lincoln, and better terms than the rebels had ever asked in their most prosperous condition.

9th. It formed no basis of true and lasting peace, but relieved rebels from the presence of our victorious armies, and left them in a condition to renew their efforts to overthrow the United States government and subdue the loyal states, whenever their strength was recruited, and any opportunity should offer.

GENERAL SHERMAN TO GENERAL GRANT.

HEAD-QUARTERS, MILITARY DIVISION OF THE MISSISSIPPI, IN THE FIELD, | RALEIGH, NORTH CAROLINA, April 25, 1865. j

Lieutenant-General U. S. GRANT, present:

GENERAL: I had the honor to receive your letter of April 21st, with enclosures yesterday, and was well pleased that you came along, as you must have observed that I held the military control so as to adapt it to any phase the case might assume.

It is but just I should record the fact, that I made my terms with General Johnston under the influence of the liberal terms you extended to the army of General Lee, at Appomattox court-house, on the 9th, and the seeming policy of our government, as evinced by the call of the Virginia legislature and governor back to Richmond, under yours and President Lincoln's very eyes.

It now appears this last act was done without any consultation with you or any knowledge of Mr. Lincoln, but rather in opposition to a previous policy, well considered.

I have not the least desire to interfere in the civil policy of our government, but would shun it as something not to my liking; but occasions do arise when a prompt seizure of results is forced on military commanders not in immediate communication with the proper authority. It is probable that the terms signed by General Johnston and myself were not clear enough on the point, well understood be- -tween us, that our negotiations did not apply to any parties outside the officers and men of the Confederate armies, which could easily have been remedied.

No surrender of any army not actually at the mercy of an antagonist was ever made without "terms," and these always define the military status of the surrendered. Thus you stipulated that the officers and men of Lee's army should not be molested at their homes so long as they obeyed the laws at the place of their residence.

I do not wish to discuss these points involved in our recognition of the state governments in actual existence, but will merely state my conclusions, to await the solution of the future.

Such action on our part in no manner recognizes for a moment the so-called Confederate government, or makes us liable for its debts or acts.

The laws and acts done by the several states during the period are void, because done without the oath prescribed by our Constitution of the United States, which is a'"condition precedent."

We have a right to use any sort of machinery to produce military results • and it is the commonest thing for military commanders to use the civil governments in actual existence as a means to an end. I do believe we could and can use the present state governments lawfully, constitutionally, and as the very best possible means to produce the object desired, viz., entire and complete submission to the lawful authority of the United States.

As to punishment for past crimes, that is for the judiciary, and can in no manner of way be disturbed by our acts; and, so far as I can, I will use my influence that rebels shall suffer all the personal punishment prescribed by the law, as also the civil liabilities arising from their past acts.

What we now want is the new form of law by which common men may regain the positions of industry, so long disturbed by the war.

I now apprehend that the rebel armies will disperse, and, instead of dealing with six or seven states, we will have to deal with numberless bands of desperadoes, headed by such men as Mosby, Forrest, Red Jackson, and others, who know not and care not for danger and its consequences.

I am, with great respect, your obedient servant, W. T. SHERMAN,

Major- General commanding.

GENERAL SHEKMAN TO SECEETAEY STANTON.

HEAD-QUABTKBS, MILITARY DIVISION OF THE MISSISSIPPI, IN THE FIELD, | KALEIGH, NOKTH CAEOLINA, April 25,1865. f

Eon. E. M. STANTON, Secretary of Far, Washington :

DEAR SIR : I have been furnished a copy of your letter of April 21st to General Grant, signifying your disapproval of the terms on which General Johnston proposed to disarm and disperse the insurgents, on condition of amnesty, etc. I admit my folly in embracing in a military convention any civil matters; but, unfortunately, such is the nature of our situation that they seem inextricably united, and I understood from you, at Savannah, that the financial state of the country demanded military success, and would warrant a little bending to policy.

When I had my conference with General Johnston, I had the public examples before me of General Grant's terms to Lee's army, and General Weitzel's invitation to the Virginia legislature to assemble at Richmond.

I still believe the general government of the United States has made a mistake; but that is none of my business—mine is a different task; and I had flattered myself that, by four years of patient, unremitting, and successful labor, I deserved no reminder such as is contained in the last paragraph of your letter to General Grant. You may assure the President that I heed his suggestion. I am, truly, etc.,

W. T. SHERMAN,

Major-General commanding.

TERMS OF A MILITARY CONVENTION, ENTERED INTO THIS 26rn DAT OF APRIL, 1865, AT BENNETT'S HOUSE, NEAR DURHAM'S STATION, NORTH CAROLINA, BETWEEN GENERAL JOSEPH E. JOHNSTON, COMMANDING THE CONFEDERATE ARMY, AND MAJOR-GENERAL W. T. SHERMAN, COMMANDING THE UNITED STATES ARMY, IN NORTH CAROLINA.

1. All acts of war on the part of the troops under General Johnston's command shall cease.

2. All arms and public property to be deposited at Greensboro' and delivered to an ordnance officer of the United States army.

8. Eolls of all the officers and men to be made in duplicate; one copy to be retained by the commander of the troops, and the other to be given to an officer to be designated by General Sherman. Each officer and man to give his individual obligation in writing not to take up arms against the government of the United States, until properly released from this obligation.

4. The side-arms of officers, and their private horses and baggage, to be retained by them.

5. This being done, all the officers and men will be permitted to return to their homes, not to be disturbed by the United States authorities so long as they observe their obligation and the laws in force where they may reside.

W. T. SHERMAN, Major-General, Commanding United States Forces in North Carolina.

J. E. JOHNSTON, General, Commanding Confederate States Forces in North Carolina.

APPROVED. —U. S. GKANT, Lieutenant-General.

SECOND BULLETIN.

WAR DEPARTMENT, WASHINGTON,) April 27, 9.30 A. M. f

To Major-General Dix:

The department has received the following dispatch from Major-General Halleck, commanding the Military Division of the James. Generals Canby and Thomas were instructed some days ago that Sherman's arrangements with Johnston were disapproved by the President, and they were ordered to disregard it, and push the enemy in every

direction.

E. M. STANTON, Secretary of War.

GENERAL HALLECK TO SECRETARY STANTON.

"RICHMOND, VIRGINIA, April 26, 9.80 p. M. "Hon. E. M. STANTON, Secretary of War:

" Generals Meade, Sheridan, and Wright are acting under orders to pay no regard to any truce or orders of General Sherman respecting hostilities, on the ground that Sherman's agreement could bind his command only, and no other.

" They are directed to push forward, regardless of orders from any one, except from General Grant, and cut off Johnston's retreat.

" Beauregard has telegraphed to Danville that a new arrangement has been made with Sherman, and that the advance 6f the Sixth corps was to be suspended until further orders.

" I have telegraphe^, back to obey no orders of Sherman, but to push forward as rapidly as possible.

"The bankers here have information to-day that Jeff Davis's specie is moving south from Goldsboro', in wagons, as fast as possible.

" I suggest that orders be telegraphed, through General Thomas, that Wilson obey no orders from Sherman, and notifying him and Canby, and all commanders on the Mississippi, to take measures to intercept the rebel chiefs and their plunder.

"The specie taken with them is estimated here at from six to thirteen million dollars.

" H. W. HALLECK, Major-General commanding.' 1 ' 1

GENERAL SHERMAN TO GENERAL GRANT.

HEAD-QUARTERS, MILITARY DIVISION OF THE MISSISSIPPI, ix THE FIELD, |
RALEIGH, NORTH CAROLINA, April 28, 1865. >

Lieutenant-General U. S. GRANT, General-in-Chief, Washington, D. C. :

GENERAL: Since you left me yesterday, I have seen the " New York

Times" of the 24th, containing a budget of military news, authenti-

cated by the signature of the Secretary of War, Hon. E. M. Stanton, which is grouped in such a way as to give the public very erroneous impressions. It embraces a copy of the basis of agreement between myself and General Johnston, of April 18th, with comments, which it will be time enough to discuss two or three years hence, after the government has experimented a little more in the machinery by which power reaches the scattered people of the vast country known as the "South." In the meantime, however, I did think that my rank (if not past services) entitled me at least to trust that the Secretary of War would keep secret what was communicated for the use of none but the cabinet, until further enquiry could be made, instead of giving publicity to it along with documents which I never saw, and drawing therefrom inferences wide of the truth. I never saw or had furnished me a copy of President Lincoln's dispatch to you of the 3rd of March, nor did Mr. Stanton or any human being ever convey to me its substance, or anything like it. On the contrary, I had seen General Weitzel's invitation to the Virginia legislature, made in Mr. Lincoln's very presence, and failed to discover any other official hint of a plan of reconstruction, or any ideas calculated to allay the fears of the people of the South, after the destruction of their armies and civil authorities would leave them without any government whatever.

We should not drive a people into anarchy, and it is simply impossible for our military power to reach all the masses of their unhappy country.

I confess I did not desire to drive General Johnston's army into bands of armed men, going about without purpose, and capable only of infinite mischief. But you saw, on your arrival here, that I had my army so disposed that his escape was only possible in a disorganized shape; and as you did not choose to " direct military operations in this quarter," I inferred that you were satisfied with the military situation; at all events, the instant I learned what was proper enough, the disapproval of the President, I acted in such a manner as to compel the surrender of General Johnston's whole army on the same terms which you had prescribed to General Lee's army, when you had it surrounded, and in your absolute power.

Mr. Stanton, in stating that my orders to General Stoneman were likely to result in the escape of " Mr. Davis to Mexico or Europe," is in deep error. General Stoneman was not at " Salisbury," but had gone back to " Statesville." Davis was between us, and therefore Stone-

man was beyond him. By turning toward me he was approaching Davis, and, had he joined me as ordered, I would have had a mounted force greatly needed for Davis's capture, and for other purposes. Even now I don't know that Mr. Stanton wants Davis caught, and as my official papers, deemed sacred, are hastily published to the world, it will be imprudent for me to state what has been done in that regard.

As the editor of the " Times " has (it may be) logically and fairly drawn from this singular document the conclusion that I am insubordinate, I can only deny the intention.

I have never in my life questioned or disobeyed an order, though many and many a time have I risked my life, health, and reputation in obeying orders, or even hints, to execute plans and purposes, not to my liking. It is not fair to hold from me the plans and policy of government (if any there be), and expect me to guess at them; for facts and events appear quite different from different standpoints. For four years I have been in camp dealing with soldiers, and I can assure you that the conclusion at which the cabinet arrived with such singular unanimity differs from mine. I conferred freely with the best officers in this army as to the points involved in this controversy, and, strange to say, they were singularly unanimous in the other conclusion. They will learn with pain and amazement that I am deemed insubordinate, and wanting in common-sense; that I, who for four years have labored day and night, winter and summer; who have brought an army of seventy thousand men in magnificent condition across a country hitherto deemed impassable, and placed it just where it was wanted, on the day appointed, have brought discredit on our government! I do not wish to boast of this, but I do say that it entitled me to the courtesy of being consulted before publishing to the world a proposition rightfully submitted to higher authority for adjudication, and then accompanied by statements which invited the dogs of the press to be let loose upon me. It is true that non-combatants, men who sleep in comfort and security while we watch on the distant lines, are better able to judge than we poor soldiers, who rarely see a newspaper, hardly hear from our families, or stop long enough to draw our pay. I envy not the task of "reconstruction," and am delighted that the Secretary of War has relieved me of it.

As you did not undertake to assume the management of the affairs of this army, I infer that, on personal inspection, your mind arrived at a different conclusion from that of .the Secretary of War. I will therefore go on to execute your orders to the conclusion, and, when done, will with intense satisfaction leave to the civil authorities the execution of the task of which they seem so jealous. But, as an honest man and a soldier, I invite them to go back to Nashville, for they will see some things and hear some things that may disturb their philosophy. "With sincere respect,

W. T. SHERMAN,

Major- General commanding.

P. S. As Mr. Stanton's most singular paper has been published, I demand that this also be made public, though I am in no manner responsible to the press, but to the law and my proper superiors.

W. T. S., Major-General.

CERTAIN PRIVATE LETTERS OF GENERAL SHERMAN.

The letters of General Sherman of May 10 and 28, 1865, given below, were opened by me in my capacity of Military Secretary, and after General Grant had read them, he directed me to seal them up, and allow them to be seen by no human being without his orders. They remained sealed until 1877, when, with General Grant's sanction, I applied to General Sherman for permission to use them in this work, and received the following reply:

GENERAL SHERMAN TO AUTHOR.

HEAD-QUARTERS, ARMY OP THE UNITED STATES, (WASHINGTON, D. C., March 16.1877. f

General BADEATJ, London, England:

DEAR BADEAU : Yours of February 28th is received; but I think you intended to enclose a copy of a letter from me to General Grant of May 10, 1864. ... I kept no copy; indeed I wrote hundreds of letters familiarly and privately, just as I do this, without thinking of their ever turning up. The one of May 28, 1864, was official, and is copied in my letter-book.

Now I freely concede to you the right to use anything I ever wrote, private or public, to give the world a picture of the feelings, even passions, of the time. I did contend then, it may be savagely and unwisely, that no man in authority could be justified in stamping the act of a general at the head of an army in the field in the manner that Stanton did me. I give to Stanton every possible credit for his patriotism, for his talents—yea, genius; but he sometimes forgot that other men had strong natures and feelings that could be wounded to the quick. I then thought him malicious, desirous to ruin me because I was one of the successful, likely to stand in his way politically. But now, with all the lights before me, I am convinced that he was stampeded by Mr. Lincoln's assassination, and that his usually good judgment was swerved by that cause. I am glad you were a personal witness to General Grant's exhibition of feeling on seeing Stan-ton's published orders, which he characterized as "infamous."

At this moment I received your second letter of March 1, with the copies. I have endorsed each fully and frankly, and you are at full liberty to treat them according to your judgment.

I propose now to be a peacemaker, and do not want to re-create any of the old feeling; but no picture is perfect without an atmosphere, and the atmosphere is the feeling of the moment—afterwards comes out the sunshine, dissipating the clouds and mists that give beauty and variety to the picture.

To paint the war, you must recognize the truth. In 1864, if we saw horsemen in our road, we unlimbered a battery and fired case-shot without stopping to inquire who they were. Now the case is entirely different. To describe that war, you must re-create the feelings and ideas of the day, which were as much a part of the war as the dead and wounded which encumbered the ground after the battle. . . .

As ever, your friend,

W. T. SHERMAN.

GENERAL SHERMAN TO GENERAL GRANT.

HEAD-QUABTEBS, MILITABY DIVISION OF THE MISSISSIPPI, IN THE FIELD, ? CAMP OPPOSITE RICHMOND, May 10,1865.

Lieutenant-General. S. GKANT, Washington, D. C.:

DEAB GENERAL : I march to-morrow at the head of my army through Richmond for Alexandria, in pursuance of the orders this day received by telegraph from you. I have received no other telegram or letter from you since you left me at Raleigh. I send by General Howard, who goes to Washington in pursuance of a telegram dated 7th instant, received only to-day, my official report of events from my last official report up to this date.

I do think a great outrage has been enacted against me by Mr. Stan-ton and General Halleck. I care naught for public opinion; that will regulate itself; but to maintain my own self-respect, and to command men, I must resent a public insult.

APPENDIX.

On arriving at Old Point, I met a dispatch from General Halleck, inviting me to his house in Richmond. I declined most positively, and assigned as a reason the insult to me in his telegram to Secretary Stauton of April 26th. I came here via Petersburg, and have gone under canvas. Halleck had arranged to review my army in passing through Richmond. I forbade it. Yesterday I received a letter, of which a copy is enclosed. I answered that I could not reconcile its friendly substance with the public insult contained in his dispatch, and notified him that I should march through Richmond, and asked him to keep out of sight, lest he should be insulted by the men. My officers and men feel his insult as keenly as I do. I was in hopes to have something from you before I got here to guide me, and telegraphed you with that view from Morehead city, but I have not received a word from you, and have acted thus far on my own responsibility. I will treat Mr.

Stanton with like scorn and contempt unless you have reasons otherwise; for I regard my military career as ended, save and except so far as necessary to put my army into your hands. Mr. Stanton can give me no orders of himself. He may, in the name of the President, and those shall be obeyed to the letter, but I deny his right to command an army. Your orders and wishes shall be to me the law, but I ask you to vindicate my name from the insult conveyed in Mr. Stanton's dispatch to General Dix of April 27tb, published in all the newspapers of the land. If you do not, I will. No man shall insult me with impunity as long as I am an officer of the army. Subordination to authority is one thing —submission to insult is another. No amount of retraction or pusillanimous excusing will do. Mr. Stanton must publicly confess himself a common libeller, or— But I won't threaten. I will not enter Washington except on your or the President's emphatic orders ; but T do wish to remain with my army till it ceases to exist, or till it is broken up and scattered to other duty. Then I wish to go for a time to my family, and make arrangements for the future. Your private and official wishes, when conveyed to me, shall be sacred, but there can be no relations between Mr. Stanton and me. He seeks your life and reputation as well as mine. Beware! But you are cool, and have been most skilful in managing such kind of people, and I have faith that you will have penetrated his designs. He wants the vast patronage of the military governorships of the South, and the votes of the negroes, now loyal citizens, for political capital, and whoever stands in his way must die. Keep above such influences, or you no

APPENDIX.

will also be a victim. See in my case how soon all past services are ignored or forgotten.

Excuse this letter. Burn it, but heed my friendly counsel. The lust for power in political minds is the strongest passion of life, and impels ambitious men (Richard III.) to deeds of infamy.

Ever your friend,

W. T. SHERMAN.

Endorsement by General SHERMAN on above.

March 16,1876.

I recall from the within letter the feelings of bitterness that filled my soul at that dread epoch of time. The letter must have been written hastily and in absolute confidence—a confidence in General Grant that I then felt and still feel. Because I sent to Washington terms that recognized the war as over, and promising the subjugated enemy a treatment that would have been the extreme of generosity and wisdom, I was denounced by the Secretary of War as a traitor, and my own soldiers commanded to disobey my orders; and this denunciation was spread broadcast over the world.

Now, after twelve long eventful years of political acrimony, we find ourselves compelled to return to the same point of history, or else permit the enemy of that day to become the absolute masters of the country.

To-day I might act with more silence, with more caution and prudence, because I am twelve years older. But these things did occur, these feelings were felt, and inspired acts which go to make up history; and the question now is not, was I right or wrong? but, did it happen? and is the record of it worth anything as an historic example ?

W. T. SHERMAN,

General.

GENERAL SHERMAN TO GENERAL GRANT.

HEAD-QUARTERS, MILITARY DIVISION OP THE MISSISSIPPI, J WASHINGTON, D. C., May 28,1866.)

Lieutenant- General U. S. GRANT,

Commander-in-Chief, Washington, D. C.:

DEAR GENERAL : As I am to-day making my arrangements to go West, preparatory to resuming my proper duties, I think it proper to

state a few points on which there is misapprehension in the minds of strangers.

I am not a politician, never voted but once in my life, and never read a political platform. If spared, I never will read a political platform, or hold any civil office whatsoever. I venerate the Constitution of the United States, think it as near perfection as possible, and recent events have demonstrated that it vests the general government with all the power necessary for self-vindication, and for the protection to life and property of the inhabitants. To accuse me of giving aid and comfort to copperheads is an insult. I do not believe in the sincerity of any able-bodied man who has not fought in this war, much less in the copperheads who opposed the war itself, or threw obstacles in the way of its successful prosecution.

My opinions on all matters are very strong; but if I am possessed properly of the views and orders of my superiors, I make them my study, and conform my conduct to them as if they were my own. The President has only to tell me what he wants done, and I will do it.

I was hurt, outraged, and insulted at Mr. Stanton's public arraignment of my motives and actions, at his endorsing General Halleck's insulting and offensive dispatch, and his studied silence, when the press accused me of all sorts of base motives, even of selling myself to Jeff. Davis for gold, of sheltering criminals, and entertaining ambitious views at the expense of my country. I respect his office, but cannot him personally, till he undoes the injustice of the past. I think I have soldierly instincts and feelings ; but if this action of mine at all incommodes the President or endangers public harmony, all you have to do is to say so, and leave me time to seek civil employment, and I will make room for some one else. I will serve the President of the United States not only with fidelity but with zeal. The government of the United States and its constituted authorities must be sustained and perpetuated, not for our good alone, but for that of coming generations.I would like Mr. Johnson to read this letter, and to believe me that the newspaper gossip of my having presidential aspirations is absurd and offensive to me, and I would check it if I knew how. As ever, your ardent friend and servant,

W. T. SHERMAN,
Major-General.
APPENDIX.
Endorsement ly General SHERMAN on above.
March 16,1877.

This letter also was private, and not copied into my usual letter-book. I had forgotten it, but to-day it expresses my feelings and opinion, and must have been penned hastily, but as the result of long conviction.

I think my life up to this minute has been consistent therewith. Now it sounds somewhat absurd, but at that day I was accused of everything bad, because I had consented to submit to the President and his cabinet for their consideration certain general propositions looking to reconstruction after a great civil war. I hereby authorize General Badeau to make whatever use he pleases of it in his biography of General Grant, to whom I then looked as my superior officer, and as the personal embodiment of the results of the war. I was as loyal to him as man could be, and I take pride in the belief that he wanted just such following; and had he, when President, confided in men whose attachment had been tried in the days of adversity and battle, I believe his civil administration would have been, if not more successful, at least more comfortable. In any event and always, I shall hope for his ultimate reward in the consciousness of deeds well done.

W. T. SHERMAN, General.
GENEKAL TOWNSEND TO GENERAL EAWLINS.

WAR DEPARTMENT, ADJUTANT-GENERAL'S OFFICE,) WASHINGTON, May 19,1868. J"

Brevet Major-General JOHN A. RAWLINS,

Chief of Staff, Armies of the United States :

GENERAL : In compliance with your request of the 22d ult., I have to transmit herewith statements from the regimental records on file in this office, showing the losses sustained by the army of the Potomac in killed, wounded, and missing, from May 5,1864, to April 9, 1865; also statements from the regimental records on file, showing the losses sustained by the army of the James, in killed, wounded, and missing, from May 5, 1864, to April 9, 1865; together with the recapitulation, showing a total of losses sustained by both armies during the period above named.

Very respectfully, your obedient servant, E. D. TOWNSEND,

Assistant Adjutant-General.

APPENDIX.

STATEMENT OF CANNON AND SMALL-ARMS SURRENDERED TO THE UNITED STATES FROM APRIL 8 TO DECEMBER 30, 1865.

The records of the Ordnance Office do not show from what general the surrendered arms, etc., were received, except in the case of Johnston's army to General Sherman. ORDNANCE OFFICE, WAR DEPARTMENT, December 80,18SO.

EXTRACT FROM A MEMORANDUM COPT OF A CONSOLIDATED REPORT OF EXCHANGED AND PAROLED PRISONERS OF WAR DURING THE REBELLION, MADE BY THE COMMISSARY GENERAL OF PRISONERS TO THE SECRETARY OF WAR, DECEMBER 6, 1865.

PAROLED ARMIES, " REBEL."

Army of Northern Virginia, commanded by General R. E. Lee * 27,805

Army of Tennessee, and others, commanded by General J. E. Johnston 31,243

General Jeff. Thompson's Army of Missouri 7,978

Miscellaneous Paroles, Department of Virginia * 9,072

Paroled at Cumberland, Maryland, and other stations 9,877

Paroled by General McCook, in Alabama and Florida 6,428

Army of the Departm en t of Alabama, Lieutenant-General R. Taylor 42.293

Army of the Trans-Mississippi Department, General E. K. Smith 17,686

Paroled in the Department of Washington 3,390

Paroled in Virginia, Tennessee, Georgia, Alabama, Louisiana, and Texas 13,922

Surrendered at Nashville and Chattanooga, Tenn 5,029

Total

ADJUTANT-GENERAL'S OFFICE, January 3,1831.

174,223

GENERAL BRECK TO AUTHOR.

WAB DEPARTMENT, ADJUTANT-GENERAL'S OFFICE, \ WASHINGTON, July 29,1S68. J

Brevet Brigadier-General ADAM BADEATJ,

Head-quarters, Armies of the United States, A. D. C.

Washington, D. C.:

GENERAL: In reply to your communication, of the 24th instant, I have to furnish you the following information, from the "Records of Prisoners of War," filed in this office:

APPENDIX.

715

The number of rebel prisoners captured by the United States forces in the War of the Rebellion, subsequent to March 17, 1864, amount to 92,405.

The number of rebel prisoners surrendered to the United States forces, subsequent to March 17, 1864, amount to 176,384, making a total of captures and surrenders for that period of 268,789. I am, very respectfully, your obedient servant, SAMUEL BRECK,

Assistant Adjutant- General.

MEMORANDA RELATIVE TO GENERAL LEE'S APPLICATION FOR PARDON AND PROPOSED TRIAL FOR TREASON, WITH GENERAL GRANT'S ENDORSEMENTS. FROM "RECORDS OF HEAD-QUARTERS, ARMIES OF UNITED STATES."

BRIEF.

RICHMOND, VIRGINIA, June 13,1S65.

LEE, General R. E.

Application for benefits and full restoration of rights and privileges extended to those included in Amnesty Proclamation of the President, of May 29, 1865.

Endorsement on the Foregoing ly Lieutenant-General U. 8. Grant :

HEAD-QUARTERS, ARMIES OF THE UNITED STATES, June 16,1865.

Respectfully forwarded through Secretary of War to the President, with earnest recommendation that the application of General Robert E. Lee, for amnesty and pardon, may be granted him. The oath of allegiance required by recent order of the President to accompany application does not accompany this, for the reason, as I am informed by General Ord, the order requiring it had not reached Richmond when this was forwarded.

U. S. GRANT, Lieutenant-General.

BRIEF.

RICHMOND, VIRGINIA, June 13,1865.

LEE, General R. E.,

States, that being about to be indicted with others, for crime of treason, by grand jury at Norfolk, Virginia, says that he is ready to meet any charges that may be preferred against him.

Had supposed his surrender protected him. Desires to comply with provisions of the President's proclamation. Encloses application, etc.

APPENDIX.

Endorsement on the Foregoing ly Lieutenant- General U. S. Grant:

HEAD-QFABTEBS, ABMIES OF THE UNITED STATES, June 16,1865. In my opinion the officers and men paroled at Appomattox court-house, and since, upon the same terms given to Lee, cannot be tried for treason so long as they observe the terms of their parole. This is my understanding. Good faith, as well as true policy, dictates that we should observe the conditions of that convention. Bad faith on the part of the government, or a construction of that convention subjecting officers to trial for treason, would produce a feeling of insecurity in the minds of all the paroled officers and men. If so disposed, they might even regard such an infraction of terms by the government as an entire release from all obligations on their part. I will state further, that the terms granted by me met with the hearty approval of the President at the time, and of the country generally. The action of Judge Underwood, in Norfolk, has already had an injurious effect, and I would ask that he be ordered to quash all indictments found against paroled prisoners of war, and to desist from further prosecution of them.

U. S. GRANT, Lieutenant-General.

The names of national officers are in SMALL CAPITALS ; those of rebels, in it

ABERCROMBIE, GENERAL J. J., attacked at White House, ii.. 391.

national army and dictate

INDEX.

INDEX.

broken in Wilderness campaign, 319; reinforcements and total numbers in Wilderness campaign, 326; losses in Wilderness campaign, 329; first assaults on Petersburg, 360-380 ; Weldon road, 514-532; Peeble's farm, iii.. 74-78; Hatcher's run, 115-128 ; disaffection and desertion in, 352; strength, March, 1865, 439 ; at Fort Steadman, 445-450; final defence of Petersburg, 500-529; flight to Appomattox, 544-597 ; demoralization after fall of Richmond, 566, 589; sufferings of, 552, 566, 572; high officers in, propose to Lee to surrender ; 590 ; fed by Grant, 607; lays down its arms, 613.

Ohio, Buell in command of department of, i., 23.

ORD, GENERAL E. 0. C., in pursuit of rebels at Hatchie river, i., 118; succeeds McClernand before Vicksburg, 363; in command of Eighteenth corps, ii., 465; captures Fort Harrison, iii., 71; wounded, 71; succeeds Butler in command of army of the James, 329; before Petersburg, 452,501; final assault on Petersburg, 501-516; parallel advance to Appomattox with Sheridan and Meade, 546, 556, 558, 578, 584; at Rice's station, 573; at Appomattox, 598; at surrender of Lee, 602.

Ossabaw sound opened by Sherman, iii., 263 ; Sherman's arrival at, 297.

OSTERHAUS, GENERAL P. J., battle of Champion's hill, i., 262; assault on Vicksburg, 320 ; battle of Lookout mountain, 499.

Paducah, seizure of, i., 11.

PALMER, GENERAL I., movement against Weldon railroad, iii., 226 ; movement to hinder reinforcement of Wilmington, 228, 235.

Pamunkey river, crossing of, ii., 263-268; topography of surrounding country, 267.

PARKE, GENERAL J. G., at siege of Vicksburg, i., 358; in East Tennessee, 545 ;"in command of Ninth corps, ii., 489; at Poplar Spring church and

Shenandoah Valley, iii., 19-38 ; battle of Winchester, 29,30; pursuit of Early's army, 31; battle of Fisher's hill, 31-33; effect of successes of, at North, 34; retrograde movement. 85; summoned to Washington, 89; battle of Cedar creek, 95-99 ; eleven weeks' work, 102-105 ; cutting Virginia Central railroad by, 229-246; movement from Shenandoah Valley to Richmond, 382, 442; at Dinwiddie court-house, 453; movement against Five Forks, 457; battle of Dinwiddie, 471-176; battle of Five Forks, 489-494; relieves Warren from command, 494: at Jetersville, 551-561-565; at battle of Sailor's creek, 566-577; at Appomattox, 591, 611.

SHERMAN, GENERAL W. T., relations with Grant, i., 57, 183, 454, 572; ii., 17, 22-24, 551; iii., 161, 162, 362, 363, 436, 631, 635, 649, 650 ; in command of division, i., 69; battle of Shiloh, 71-91; at Memphis, 109,128; Yazoo river expedition, 132-138,143-148; Arkansas Post, 148,149 ; Steele's bayou, 174-178; opposes Grant's movement south of Vicksburg, 183-185: demonstration against Haine's bluff, 201; Vicksburg campaign, 227-280 ; assault on Vicksburg, 302-326 ; siege of Vicksburg, 331-385; denounces McClernand, 362; ordered to march against Johnston, 385; movement against Jackson, 393-397 ; brigadier-general in regular army, 402; ordered to West Tennessee, 420; march of four hundred miles, 463;

INDEX.

movement to Chattanooga, 469; battle of Chattanooga, 476-505; movements after battle of Chattanooga, 516; movement to Knoxville of, 533, 543, 547; Meridian expedition, 552-560; letter to Grant on lieutenant-generalcy, 573 • in command of Military Division of the Mississippi, ii., 17 ; contrasted with Grant, 19-24; anxiety of, in regard to supplies, 50; operations against Forrest, 54; relations to Eed river campaign, 68, 70-76; his part in the general plan of 1864, 34, 36, 89, 100, 150, 195, 224, 336, 346, 400, 456, 459 ; encouraged and supported by Grant, 503 ; Atlanta campaign, 508-553; moves from Chattamooga, 533; captures Eesaca, 535; drives Johnston across the Oostenaula and Etowa rivers, 535; captures Cassville and Kingston, 535; battle of New Hope church, 536 ; assaults Kenesaw mountain. 538 ; enters Marietta, 538 ; crosses Cnattahoochee river, 539; in front of Atlanta. 543; repulse of Hood, 544; besieges Atlanta, 542-546 ; situation in Georgia, iii., 41-43; discussion of new campaign with Grant, 43, 45, 48, 53, 54, 59, 61, 62, 153-162; retrograde movement towards Tennessee, 50-59,151,152; relations with Thomas, 153, 155 ; return to Atlanta, 164-166, 173, 174; march to the sea, 282-300 ; invests Savannah, 295, 305; carries Fort McAllister, 296; thirty-one days' march, 297 ; public appreciation of, 299-301; Grant's congratulations to, 301-304; evacuation of Savannah, 306 ; proposal of a lieutenant-generalcy lor, 362; operations northward from Savannah, 373; at Columbia, Cheraw, and Fayetteville, 410-425; at Winnsboro, 424: battle of Bentonsville, 429-432 ; visits City Point, 436; advance against Smith-field, 627 j enters Kaleigh, 627; conference with Johnston, 627, 628; suspends hostilities, 630; terms disapproved by government, 631; President Johnson's action towards, 631; denounced by Stanton, 635; protected by Grant, 635; error in judgment of, 635; Grant's indignation at Stan-ton's treatment of, 636 ; final conference with Johnston, 633.

Shiloh, battle of, i., 72-95; determination of troops on both sides, 95; false reports at the West of, 100.

SIGEL, GENERAL FRANZ, in Valley of Virginia, ii., 416 ; beaten by Brecken-ridge, 417; superseded by Hunter, 417 ; evacuates Martinsburg, 432; removal from command, 436.

Signals, in use by both armies, the same code of, ii., 222.

Slavery, cause of the rebellion, i., 2.

Slaves, rebel proposal to arm ? iii., 352; rebel apprehension regarding, 354 ; conduct of, during the war, 355; arming the, 356.

SLOCUM, GENERAL H. W., takes possession of Atlanta, ii., 546 ; in command of

THE END.

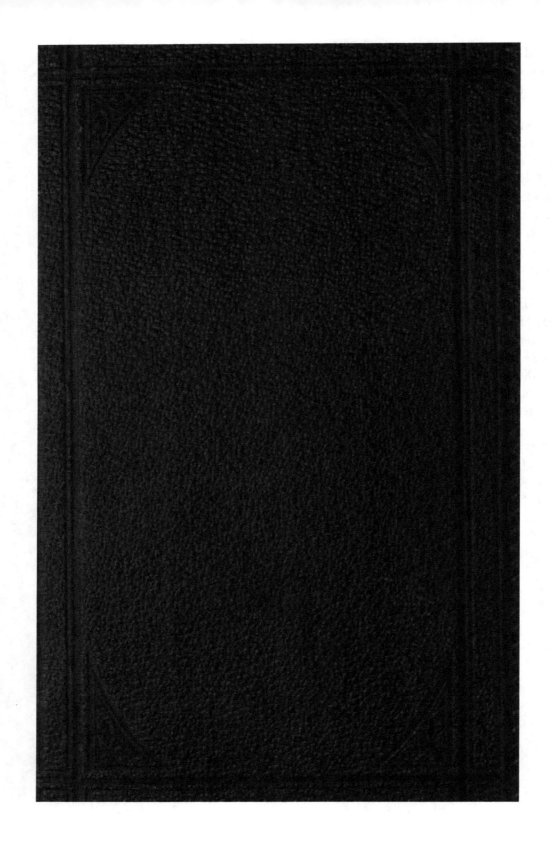